THE MIGRANT

a novel by
Nicholas Sheridan Stanton

authorHOUSE™

1663 LIBERTY DRIVE, SUITE 200
BLOOMINGTON, INDIANA 47403
(800) 839-8640
WWW.AUTHORHOUSE.COM

First published by AuthorHouse 12/21/05

ISBN: 1-4259-0812-8 (sc)
ISBN: 1-4259-0811-X (dj)

Library of Congress Control Number: 2005911246

Printed in the United States of America
Bloomington, Indiana

This book is printed on acid-free paper.

For my family:

Mom & Dad, Tina, Candice, Sean, Chuck, Richard, Robert, and Glenn

(...Love is patient, love is kind...It always protects, always trusts, always hopes, always perseveres. Love never fails ...1 Corinthians 13:4-8)

There are those in my life who show me every day exactly what this passage is all about. Because of them, the words come easily...

Brenda, my muse, and my friend, thank you for seeing in me what I could not see for myself. *Thanks for the perfect ending.*

The "Boys," Kenny, Paulie, Sparky, Jay, Cullen, Ernie, Bob, Coop, Doc, Lonny, Sean, and Steve...you guys keep me grounded with all the chops, slams, chuckles, and belly laughs. You guys made this fun.

Rose, thanks for your humble opinions, and for putting up with all of our nonsense.

Roman, thanks *"top bunk"* for helping me with my Spanglish.

Hap, thanks for *"Tuesday's with Morrie."* Thanks for all of your encouragement, your love, and the wonderful gift of your poetry.

Prologue

("Delight yourself in the Lord; And He will give you the desires of your heart."...Psalm 37:4)

Groveland, California, 2003

This summer I will celebrate my fifty-fourth birthday, not old, not really, but feels like old at times. As I sit on this porch, rocking in this comfy chair that my wonderful wife gave to me for last year's birthday, and listen to the roar of the rushing river below, I find myself in a reflective mood today, and feeling rather chatty. So yeah, maybe I'll take advantage of this lazy Sunday afternoon and share with you a story. Maybe this would be a good time to tell you about how I got to here from there. Maybe this would be a good time to retrace the steps I took along life's narrow path to the happiness that I never knew existed, much less ever hoped to realize. So, let's see, where should I start?

The nineteen sixties was a decade when we were encouraged to believe anything was possible. When we were challenged as a nation to *"ask NOT what your country can do for you, ask what YOU can do for your country."* When we were told to reach for the moon, literally. It seemed like forward was the direction everyone and every group was moving in. At least the decade started that way. Then, one by one the leaders of most of the movements for change and social evolution disappeared. More accurately, we killed them, or jailed them, or ignored them. The Kennedy's, Dr. King, Malcolm X, Eldridge Cleaver, Cesar Chavez, Eugene McCarthy, and a dozen or so others. The sixties ended with the country at war on two fronts, overseas with the communists, and at home with each other. Young and old alike became jaded and escaped into self-pity and self-indulgence, and voila the seventies were born.

The nineteen seventies were the decade of discovery. The nation discovered that we were not invulnerable. We learned that in order to rebound we had to hit bottom. We lost a war, a President, scads of business and industry, and our innocence. The one thing that we didn't lose was our stubborn need to preserve our dignity. No plan was too risky, no change too drastic, no leadership too corrupt, as long as we came out ahead.

And with that resolve we marched into the eighties, the decade of rebirth. With a strong new President and a *tough as nails* attitude, the nation gave notice to the world that we were out to kick ass and take names. But at what cost, true family values, basic ethics, or the soul of a nation?

These were the times in which I came of age. And although they were decades of amazing events and historic changes, it would be the heart of one young woman, a mere child, that would inspire so many of us, and restore hope to a shallow people. As I tell this story you may find yourself thinking, *I know of this girl, I've heard this somewhere.* Perhaps you did, after all, it is said that the God of all people is omnipresent. And if that is so and you happen to believe, even just a little bit, then maybe you did, maybe we all did...

PART ONE

1960-1968

Life, the first gift...then what?

One

(…"daughter, take courage; your faith had made you well"…Matthew 18:22)

Mendota, California, June 1960

The child played with a butterfly as she lay in the yellow green grass, next to the field where her parents were working. It was early summer and all the schools had just let out for the long vacation. Not that it mattered much to her; she was only five years old after all. The butterfly stood nearly motionless on her forearm, its green blue wings moving up and down slowly, as if steadying itself. She squinted in the bright sunlight as she looked up to catch a glimpse of her mother in the cantaloupe field a few yards away. She smiled broadly revealing neat rows of perfect little baby teeth as she made eye contact with *mama*. Her mother shielded her eyes from the sun as she stood and straightened up, arching her sore back, her free arm behind her, low on her hip. She waved high and slowly to her daughter and called out to her husband a couple of rows over.

"*Victor, mira la nina!*" Her husband waved from over his shoulder without looking up from his work. Maria Lopez shook her head tiredly, and waved again to her daughter as she squatted back down to continue her labors.

"*Panson,*" she muttered.

"She'll be grown and waving to her own children before he knows it!" she said to herself, settling onto her knees and leaning back onto her heels.

1

Maria chopped at another stem and placed a good-sized melon into her rucksack, inching forward to swipe at the next one. The little girl stood up and waved her arm, gently setting the butterfly free to sail away on the breeze. It was beginning to get hot out as the sun rose high in the sky. The warm wind felt good on her face and she twirled round and round in the open field. When she got too dizzy to stand, she fell to the ground squealing with laughter. Streaks of bright white sunlight ran across the clear blue sky as if they were chasing one another around the heavens, and she raised her hands to shade her eyes.

Then suddenly something broke her concentration, and she rose up to her elbows, tilted her head and listened intently. She could barely make out the faint cry over the chattering of the crows gathered on the power lines along Third Ave. Nevertheless, there it was again, getting a little louder with each passing moment. Then it was clear, a wailing infant. She listened to the shrill cries followed by brief seconds of silence as the baby caught its breath. The poor thing was probably hungry or wet and needed changing. It took a little while for the parents to notice the cries for attention. Soon the little girl could see a young woman running from the field in the direction of the urgent cries, the mother perhaps. Some older children were trying to quiet the baby, singing songs, and making funny faces, it was all just game to them. The little girl stood up as the young mother passed her on a dead run, her long ponytail flying parallel to the ground behind her with the speed at which she was moving. Instinctively she started to chase after her, but stopped after only a few strides. Mama had warned her not to wander out of eyesight, and she knew better than to disobey. She did not want to receive a swat or two from her mother's sandal.

She watched as the young mother disappeared past the irrigation ditch then walked back to where she had caught the butterfly. She looked around, searching again for her own mother working in the field yonder. When she spotted her, she sat back down and began to play with a roly-poly bug, poking at it with her finger making it curl up into a ball. She studied the bug intensely, marveling at its defensive mechanism. Suddenly, a shrill scream came from beyond the ditch.

"AYIEEEE, Madre Dios!"

Everyone within earshot had heard the panicked cry, and everyone understood it to mean the worst kind of trouble. Heads began to pop up from all over the cantaloupe field. Some of the men had already dropped their tools and started running toward the commotion. The little girl felt her eyes moisten as the drama and confusion of the moment overwhelmed her. She again looked quickly for her mother and wiped away a tear with the palm of her little hand when she saw her walking quickly toward her.

"Mija, bente akee!" her mother said to her calmly.

The little girl ran to her and lost herself in her mother's embrace. It was warm there and she was safe, but she could still hear the wailing in the distance. She peeked out from behind her mother's long black hair and saw that a small crowd had gathered atop the steep embankment of the irrigation ditch. The men held their hats in their hands, and the women crossed themselves, some of them crying softly. The crowd parted slowly, making room for a young woman to pass between them, a small bundle, a motionless child wrapped in a Navajo receiving blanket held close to her breast. The young woman was sobbing deeply and the little girl recognized her as the one who had raced past her towards the crying baby. A small group of children followed behind her, and as they passed through the crowd, one by one, their own parents scooped each of them up. Maria held her daughter a little tighter as the young woman approached them. As she passed by them, the little girl could feel the intensity of the young woman's pain, something that was well beyond her years to understand. She felt compelled to go to her, to throw her little arms around her, as if she could stop the hurting. She squirmed in her mother's arms trying to get down, but Maria would not release her.

"Quiet mija, be still, that woman has lost her child," her mother said to her, her voice stern from fright and not anger.

The young woman reached the dirt access road and walked past the flatbed tractor-trailer that held the stacks of melon crates. A man stood waiting, his face wet with tears, his strong-callused hands in tight fists as he held his Stetson hat in front of him. He embraced his wife and child tightly when they reached him, the small bundle disappearing between the young couple. They cried together for a long time, the presence of death creating a deafening silence. Several people, family and friends, surrounded them in a close circle of love and support. The little girl squirmed again in her mother's arms.

"Alright LaTina, hold my hand and we will go to your father," her mother said tiredly.

The two of them walked slowly, side by side towards the small crowd of mourners. A large man, his shirt soaked with sweat had come up to the young couple, and joined in their silent vigil. He may have been a relative, a grandfather or an uncle. Maria seemed to remember him as the grandfather of the young woman. He held a rosary made of wood in his left hand and stroked the young mother's long dark hair with his right hand, as her head rested on his barrel chest.

Tina and her mother were now standing with her father. Victor knelt down beside his daughter and put his arm around her.

"Why is she crying Poppi?" little Tina asked, whispering in her father's ear.

"Her baby has died *mija*," Victor answered, pulling her closer to him.

"Why?" Tina asked.

"If you ask me why this thing has happened *mija*, I cannot say for sure," her father whispered.

"The Lord, he works in his way, and we must not question his will," he added.

"Why?"

"I don't know *mija*. You'll have to ask God that yourself, maybe he'll answer you," Victor replied, sighing deeply.

"Her child is with God now. It is better I think, better than sweating for nothing in these *damn fields,*" he added quickly, his tone bitter.

The words were beyond her understanding. Her father was really talking to himself of course. The bitterness in his voice masked his guilty conscience, ashamed of his joy and relief, grateful that his own child had been spared. This was likely a common sentiment at this moment. Victor looked up at his wife and stood to embrace her, to ease the sorrow, to take away the sad and helpless look on her face. As her parents comforted each other, Tina began to walk forward, towards the grieving couple and the big scary Grandfather. Oddly, the closer she came to them, the more joy she began to feel in her own heart. By the time she was close enough to hear them weeping their words of encouragement to each other, the little girl was feeling near elation herself. Just as she had at her early birthday party, only a few days before, when she was taking her turn at swatting the piñata stuffed with candies and cakes.

The big man noticed her first and looked down on her smiling face. He sniffled loudly and wiped his tear stained face with his shirtsleeve. The young parents looked down on her now as well, and she looked up at each of them, smiling at them in turn, as they made eye contact individually. Tina stepped closer and touched the dirty apron hanging from the mother's waist. She tugged at it lightly and the woman looked curiously at her husband. She looked back down at Tina, and knelt beside her, reached out and gently stroked the little girl's hair. Although grief stricken, and in spite of the tremendous pain she was feeling, she could not keep herself from smiling back at the little girl.

"Que pa so mijita?" the young mother said gently. Tina did not reply she just continued to smile, her amber colored eyes sparkling in the bright sunlight.

The young mother looked back up at her husband and then at her Grandfather, a perplexed look on her face, embarrassed by her nervous laughter. Before anyone could think of something appropriate to say, the little girl reached over and turned down the blanket revealing the face of the dead child. The baby was cold and blue, his little eyes closed but still wet with tears. The mother looked back quickly, just in time to see the little girl lean in and kiss her baby's face. Tina looked up at the baby's mother, smiled at her, and then reached up and touched her cheek with her tiny hand. The young woman pulled away instinctively, startled by the girls sudden appearance, and then stared back at the child. The sun shined brightly behind the small girl, her little body outlined in sunlight, making her appear more like a shadow than a person. As she started to speak, the woman felt a stirring in her arms, then there was a sharp pain in her right breast as her teething child tried to nurse. Gasping, she fell back onto her bottom and wriggled backward a couple feet in the dirt, frightened out of her wits. Holding her baby like a basketball in outstretched arms, she looked to her husband for an explanation, for help. This simply *could not* be happening, it just couldn't, her baby was stone dead just a moment ago! The small circle of people that had surrounded them retreated a yard or two. Several of them, male and female, were now on their knees crossing themselves and *'panic praying'* the rosary.

"Hail Mary full of grace, blessed are thou among women, blessed is the fruit of thy womb Jesus. Holy Mary, mother of God…"

A hot breeze gusted, blowing dirt from the road every which way, people covered their faces with multi colored bandanas and pulled their hats low over their eyes. The young couple sat together on the ground in awe of this *happening*, laughing and crying at the same time. Their child was wailing loudly know, a hungry cry, he wanted to eat and his mother offered her breast happily.

"Nina," the young mother called to Tina, her face a flush with fear and confusion.

"Nina, gracias mija, muchas gracias la Senor, muchas gracias!" she said, as she began to sob uncontrollably.

The girl continued to smile broadly, a broad, beaming smile branded on her little face. She was almost trancelike in her posture, and it made her appear more like a doll than a real child. Several people began to gather around her, talking amongst themselves. They searched for signs of some kind, for anything that could explain what they had just witnessed. The Grandfather walked toward Tina, and she stood still and unafraid. He stopped in front of her, and then fell to his knees, his face buried in his large hands, weeping softly. Tina came forward and took hold of a finger on each of his big hands, tugging on them gently. He looked up sheepishly, a large smile breaking across his tear stained face. He pulled the child close to him and hugged her gently, she disappeared behind his strong arms, only her tiny hands were visible, her little fingers patting his big shoulders while he wept.

In the crowd of people, a small man with a handlebar moustache stumbled forward as a woman pushed her way into the center of all the commotion. It was Maria, frantically looking for her daughter.

"Tina!" she called out loudly.

Maria stopped abruptly when she saw her daughter peek out from behind the big man kneeling on the ground. She ran towards them, sliding the last couple of feet on her knees in the dirt as she dropped to scoop up her daughter into her arms.

"I told you never to wander from me like that, didn't I?"

"Do I have to get my shoe little one?"

"No mama, lo ciento, por favor, lo ciento," said Tina, suddenly out of her trance and back to reality.

"You scared me *mija*, you scared me, *yo mi vida, no?*" Her mother said softly, hugging and kissing her child.

"Si mama, *si."*

The big man, stood up finally, steadying himself, his left hand on his right knee as he rose. He walked over to Maria and Victor as they stood near the crowd of people, the two of them each held one of Tina's little hands. The old gentleman stopped in front of them, and put a large hand on the shoulders of her parents. He turned slowly and pointed to the young couple sitting with their baby, family and friends surrounding them. He turned back to face Tina and her parents, then he reached down and touched the little girl's cheek with the back of his right index finger. Looking back up at her parents, he leaned in and whispered something into Victor's ear. Then the old Grandfather kissed Maria lightly on her forehead, turned, and walked away slowly. He walked past the young couple without stopping, and returned to the cantaloupe field, back to work. Soon others followed his lead and walked slowly back into the field as well.

The commotion was officially over, and there was still a full day's work to do. In a few minutes, only the young couple and their baby remained with Tina and her parents on the quiet dirt road. The young father stood and helped his wife and child up. He turned, looked over at Tina and tipped his hat. His wife waved and then crossed herself as they turned and walked toward the field to join everyone else. Maria turned her head toward her husband, wrinkled her nose and squinted in the sunlight shining from over his shoulder.

"What did the old man say to you anyways?" Victor did not answer; he looked down at his daughter instead. Maria socked him in the arm and asked again.

"What did the old man say to you, *Panson?"* Victor looked over at his wife.

"He said that he met the Lord today."

"The old man said that the Lord spoke to him through the eyes of a child."

Victor knelt down beside his little girl and turned her to face him. He looked deeply into her eyes searching for sign of what the old man had seen. Tina began to giggle at the queer look on her father's face, and she reached out and pinched his nose. She squealed, ran back a couple of steps, turned and showed her dad her tiny left hand. She held her thumb between her index and middle finger, waving her hand back and forth.

"Got your nose," she squealed, *"Got your nose!"*

Victor made a loud snarffling sound and chuckled himself. Maria looked at both of them like they were from Mars and began to giggle as well. The excitement over, the three of them followed the others back to the field, there was still much work to do after all. He shaded his eyes with the brim of his hat and looked high up into the clear blue, mid-morning sky.

"MAN, it's going to be a hot one today," he said aloud.

Victor and his wife went back to work, chopping stems and picking melons. Maria looked back over her shoulder to catch sight of her daughter as she played in the grass nearby. She smiled to herself, reciting a silent prayer as she freed another melon from its vine and placed it in her burlap sack. She watched her daughter sit idly in the field, concentrating intensely on something that Maria could not see from where she worked. The events of the morning already forgotten, LaTina had her eye on a grasshopper that needed catching!

Two

("time is on my side, yes it is"…Rolling Stones)

<u>*Albany, New York, September 1964*</u>

The country was just climbing out of its blue funk since the death of President Kennedy. The British had invaded the airwaves and the race to space was on! But like most teenagers, I was only thinking of myself for now. Nervous about the coming semester, *Ethan Kelly's first year in High School*, I worried about all the little things. About not fitting in, about my ears being too big, about my hair being too short, about gym and the communal showers, YIKES! The summer seemed to drag on endlessly even though my folks had done their best to fill it up with the usual family activities and outings. There was the *"Flag Day"* barbecue in June at Uncle Liam's farm in Lancaster County. This was always a big gathering, but hard to fit in among the Amish and the Mennonites and their odd customs and traditions. It was awkward enough being Irish Catholic, but those frocks, oh my gosh, surely they know that it was the sixties now, had they never heard of the Beatles? Then of course, there was the big Fourth of July gala that Mother organized each year. Everyone always managed to have a great time at those, it was my favorite of the annual shindigs.

This year's bash was a particularly memorable event, as it would go into my journal as the year I kissed my first girl. Truth be told, kissing wasn't the only *first experience* I had that day. Turns out, that on this particular afternoon of carnal exploration, my neighbor Sandy Pulchoski, an early bloomer, would prove to be quite an enthusiastic tour guide, well beyond my wildest imaginings. Ahh, the advantages of having a college age sister who still lived at home. Suffice to say that I learned some new terminology with regard to female undergarments, specifically the subtle difference of hooks versus snaps. By the way, for you curious nubies out there, if you can snap your fingers, you have a running start at *'second base'*. I also learned that caressing is good and inspires enthusiastic participation, while pinching is bad and results in a loud *'HEY'* followed by a sock in the beezer! A useful discovery and surprising bonus, was that Sandy's retainer could be removed for emergencies, *my, my, my.*

Finally, the annual trip to summer camp in early August up at Lake George came and went without much fanfare. Not that I didn't enjoy the swimming and hiking and baseball (always loved the baseball), as well as the horsing around with all my pals, Mikey, Kenny, Paul, Sparky, and J. Cullen Wainwright Hollenbeck IV (nerd), that stuff was always cool. And although this should have been Nirvana for any normal fourteen-year old boy, for me, well, somehow I just knew that I was about to enter a new and wonderful world. I had no idea how prophetic that feeling would turn out to be.

Fate happened to be riding along with me as we made our way back home, traveling Rt. 9 and then Interstate 87 through the beautiful blue Adirondack Mountains on that old white jalopy of a school bus from O'Sullivan's camp. Life up and slapped me good and hard the minute I waved off the driver and started up the walkway to the house. My kid sister Shannon ran up to me crying, dragging my teddy bear *'Buster'* by his ragged little arm. She always slept with it whenever I was away from home. With mother and Dad both working at the dry cleaners they owned 14 hours a day, I was responsible for taking care of her needs. Shannon was a doll, pretty and precocious, only 5 years old and so excited about starting Kindergarten this year.

"Peepers," she cried as she leaped into my arms, nearly knocking me over and making me drop my duffel bag. My family has always called me peepers because of my blue eyes. The rest of the family being dark haired and brown eyed. Dad liked to tease Mom about me looking more like the milkman then himself.

"*Peepers,* mommy is crying and daddy is *berry thick.*"

Shannon had a slight lisp and even though the mood was dark I could not help smiling, she was just too cute. We went inside together and mother met us in the foyer, and five minutes later, I was up to date with all the bad news. This would be a pivotal time in my life, it would be the year my father, Edward Lee Kelly, would be diagnosed with the cancer. This would be the year that I would learn about great loss, and sacrifice, about love and hate, and about the path, my life would follow. These lessons, that usually take years to manifest themselves, would unfortunately hit me one after the other with a machine gun like cadence. The long summer spent anticipating the shiny start of a new chapter in my life, in a new school, in a new era, suddenly dimmed with the realization that it was no longer all about me.

My mother kissed me on the forehead, then wet her thumb and removed the smudge that her lipstick left behind. She picked up my sister and started walking towards the kitchen. I knew that she would get her a glass of milk and an oatmeal cookie or two to help soften the blow as she explained what all of this really meant to us.

"Come on Peepers, *Mommy wait for Ethan!*" Shannon pleaded.

"I'll be there in a minute Squirt," I said to her.

Mom waived and smiled weakly then continued on to the kitchen with Shannon. I stood alone in the foyer for a moment longer. The house seemed quieter than usual, and I was feeling kind of silly standing there all by myself. I wondered if Dad was home, but thought not, because I didn't hear the TV or his whistling. Dad always whistled to himself whenever he was working or puttering around the house. Usually it was "When Irish Eyes are Smiling" or *'With a little Bit of Luck'* from *'My Fair Lady'*. No matter what he chose mother would wince and wrinkle her nose shouting "Darn it Eddy, must you torture everyone with that confounded noise!" And, given the time of year, nine times out of ten there would be a Yankee game playing in the background. Dad loved the Yanks, loved the *'Yankee Clipper'* and *'Mantle'* and laughed out loud at *'Yogi'*. Truth be told, he loved the *'Splendid Splinter'* (Ted Williams) as well. However, because he was a Red Sock, my Father had to hate him officially! Today there was none of the normal, comforting sounds that made this house a home.

I walked through the living room past the Colonial furniture rich with all the deep polished maple wood color, reflecting the sunlight as it shone through the bay window. The television was not on and the room was empty except for an open book, upside down resting on Dad's big armchair. His reading glasses were on the table next to the chair, along with his pipe rack. The odd thing about these items was that Dad would always remove his glasses whenever anyone entered the room, still suffering from the sin of pride. And, as for the pipes, well, he didn't smoke. He just liked the way they looked in the fancy sculpted rack.

"I can look grand without actually taking up the nasty habit," he would say.

"Besides Sonny, this way your Mother will kiss me more often," he would tease.

"That's good advise boy, you'll thank me for that one later in life" he'd chuckle to himself.

He always poked me in the stomach with his finger whenever he told me that, and I would blush and squeal *"Ahhh, Da!"* I loved my Father, and although he was stern and proper, and shy about showing too much affection for fear of appearing weak and easy, in these little exchanges he always showed me that he loved me back. At least that's how I always looked at it.

I walked into the hall and went towards my parent's room. The door was ajar and I could hear no noise as I placed my ear near it. I tapped lightly on the door and called out.

"Are you in there Da?" No answer, I knocked a little harder.

"Da, are you in there sir?" Still no sound, so I went inside to take a look around, and see what I could see. The room was empty. The four-poster bed was made up neatly, hospital corners and all, with nary a wrinkle on the pastel colored comforter. My mother was a stickler for neatness, so I was accustomed to the museum like appearance of the room. Everything in its place, not even a stray hair in the brush on her dressing bureau. Dad's suit was already laid out on the dressing rack for Monday morning. His Oxford wingtips neatly placed underneath with a fresh pair of argyle socks across the shoes. Even the laces had been tucked neatly under the tongue, and not left to hang sloppily over the side like some commoner's. As I said, my mother was a stickler. Years later I would discover in school that there was a term for this behavior, but I could never use that word in her presence lest I treasured the taste of Lifebouy!

Satisfying myself that he was not anywhere nearby, I headed for my room to unpack my duffel bag. Then it occurred to me, whenever my father was struggling with something, he always went into the backyard and lay down in the grass. He claimed that sunlight could cure anything mental or physical. I had tried this myself on several occasions, and darned if he wasn't right. Tossing my duffel onto my bed, I raced for the sliding glass door in the dining room making for the yard.

"ETHAN ANDREW KELLY, you get back here this instant and close this door. Is it millionaires you think we are?" my mother hollered.

I quickly peeked past the hedges to see if my hunch was right, and it was, there was my father lying smack in the middle of the lawn, flat on his back, his hands folded behind his head. Wearing his usual weekend uniform of blue jeans, white tee shirt and "smiley" sneakers, the one's with the blue smile swooshed across the toe like a big grin, Dad looked peaceful enough. I mean, he didn't look any different, but my intuition was telling me that things were not as right as they seemed. I ran back to the house, peeked inside and winked at Shannon, who was coloring at the table, eating an

11

oatmeal cookie. Then I carefully closed the sliding glass door and returned to my hunt for Dad.

Walking slowly towards where my father was resting I stopped for a minute at the edge of the lawn next to the driveway. I looked over at the garage and noticed that the car hadn't been parked all the way inside. If I were playing basketball, I would not be able to finish a lay-up as the rear bumper was directly under the hoop. I made a mental note to ask Dad if I could finish parking the car, I was a teenager after all! Turning my attention back to my father, I noticed that he was sitting up now, his arms hugging his knees, and he was looking my way. He squinted in the bright sunlight and motioned for me to come over to him. All of the sudden there was a lump in my throat and I could feel tears welling up in my eyes. SHOOT, I didn't want him to see acting like a baby. I pretended to sneeze and used the opportunity to rub my eyes dry and wipe my face with my shirtsleeve. Dad was smiling as I walked up to him, and he held up his left hand toward me.

"Help your old man up Sonny," he said.

I took hold of his hand and he pulled himself up, making that sound that all Dads make when they get up from so far down.

"Ah, you're a good boy Ethan, a good boy son" he said rubbing his lower back with both hands.

"How was camp, did you have a grand time?"

"It was fine sir, I did sir."

"Well, that's good, a boy your age should have all kinds of fun in the summertime" he said smiling.

"Yes sir, thank you sir," I said uneasily.

"That's enough of the sirs' son. Let's just be Dad and Ethan the rest of the day, OK?" he asked mussing my hair.

"Sure Da, that'll be swell," I said smiling back for real.

"Your mother, she talk to you did she?"

"Yes Da, she did," I replied, feeling the lump coming back in my throat, I swallowed hard.

"Yeah, I guess she would at that," he said frowning slightly.

"Ethan! Why run over to the garage and fetch the mitts and a baseball. Let's have us a catch, just you and me," he said gesturing over his shoulder with his thumb.

"Sure Da, I'll be back in a jiffy!" I said, and started jogging toward the garage.

"We can chat while we toss the baseball son, there are things I need to share with you," Dad said as I ran past him. The words hit me like arrows in the back, and I tripped over my own feet, falling down clumsily. I skidded along the concrete on my knees, tearing a small hole in my jeans, and leaving a decent sized strawberry on my right leg.

"I'm OK Da, didn't hurt," I yelled back at my father as I jumped up and ran into the garage.

While I composed myself, I searched for the gloves and the baseball, finding them finally at the bottom of an old, rusty wheel barrel, under a bag of grass seed. I stuffed the gloves under my arm and palmed the ball, then trotted back out to stand with my Dad. He took his glove, and put it on while I ran across the yard and stood near the back fence. Dad tossed the ball to me, high and outside, but still with the usual *zip* on it. At least he seemed like his old self. I could see my mother in the kitchen window, she was watching us, and I noticed that she crying. Dad looked back over his shoulder at the house, and Mother quickly looked down at the sink, so he didn't notice her tears. It was at this moment when I realized just how tough all of this was going to be, on everyone.

We tossed the baseball back and forth while Dad retold the story of the day he was at Yankee Stadium and Mickey Mantle hit one out of the park! After a few other such stories he laid out to me the whole situation of his illness, at least as he understood it. The words were kind but the message was harsh and uncomfortably certain. As he talked to me, he kept reassuring me that it was still his belief that God was just. With the sound of conviction in his voice, and true passion in his eyes, he tried to pass on his deep faith. With each passing moment the distance between us closed, until we no longer needed to toss the ball, we just kept handing it back and forth. When he was through, when the words were all out, he set his glove on the grass in front of him. He spread his arms wide and invited me in for a hug. That opened the flood gates, I could hold it in no longer. I wasn't ready to be a man just yet. I ran to my father and he picked me up like I was a six-year-old, hugging the stuffing right out of me with his powerful arms. I wrapped my skinny legs around him like I did when I was a small boy, and cried on his shoulder quietly, trying not to sob. He held me for a long time and when he set me down he said, "Well, we've got that out our system now. And we've a man's job ahead of us Ethan. Let's see if we can tackle this like Kelly's, are you game son?" I looked up at him, his eyes were dry, but they were still red. He was smiling at me again and he held out his hand for me to take as a grown-up would.

"Yeah Da, like Kelly's, I can do that" and I took his hand and squeezed it as hard as I could, a real man's handshake, like I had seen he and his brothers exchange at every family gathering.

"OK, OK, enough dawdling you two, are you going to lollygag out there all day?" my mother yelled from the house.

"Shake a leg now, my supper's turning to ice before my very eyes!"

"We'll be in straight away Maggie, don't get your knickers in a twist my sweet," Dad said laughing. He picked up his glove and tossed it to me.

"Put this back where you found it and then come in and wash up boy" he said running towards the house, chasing after my mother as she giggled like a schoolgirl. I smiled big through my tears, watching my father scoop up Shannon and then chase my mother around the table. I already missed him, but there wasn't any time for that, it was time for me to grow up.

Three

("Blessed are the pure in heart, for they shall see God..." Matthew 5, the beatitudes)

Albany, New York, December 1966

My father died quietly early on Saturday morning while we were sleeping. It was only a couple of weeks before Christmas, old man winter had just brought us a good snowfall, and Shannon was beside herself with anticipation. My little sister awakened me on that day. She was standing next to my bed brushing out the tangles from her long auburn hair.

"Are you awake *now?*" she asked sternly. I managed to mumble something inaudible, and she swatted me with her brush.

"ETHAN, you have to get up, *something's the matter with Daddy!*" she said, stamping her feet for effect. That was all the push that I needed, and I jumped up out of bed.

Shannon then jumped up into my bed to take my place, after first retrieving Buster from under my bed. I made a mental note that maybe it was time to give that teddy bear to her anyway. This was a drill I had become accustomed to, especially these last few months. It had been a little more than three years since we found out about Da's cancer. To be honest, the first year did not bring all of the ghastly changes I had prepared myself for. In fact, we were beginning to believe that maybe we had dodged a bullet, but the luck of the Irish caught up with us, and what had been brewing inside

15

my father began to boil over. In no time at all, the man that had always been larger than life to me wilted like a cut flower, right before my eyes. And, like cut flowers, no matter how carefully that you tended to them, their days were numbered.

I walked into my parent's room through the open door. Mother was sitting at her dressing table brushing her hair (which was beginning to show streaks of gray), slowly and methodically. I stopped just inside the doorway and looked over to their bed. Dad was laying on his back, his head and shoulders elevated slightly by two pillows. I glanced back over at my Mother and saw that she was watching me in the mirror. She had had put her brush down and was fidgeting with her crucifix while she looked at my face. In her eyes, I could see a question hanging on the moment. As strong and stoic as my Mother always tried to be, in truth she was just a softie, a small town girl who had been transplanted to this country by her ambitious beau. I could sense her uneasiness and knew that she was holding back her urge to cry, trying to retain some semblance of strength for me and for Shannon. I looked back at my Father and moved the last few steps to his bedside. His features were familiar, but I knew immediately that he was gone.

"Ah, Da," I said softly, a weak smile breaking across my face.

I knelt beside their bed and took his hand from atop his chest. It wasn't really cold, but it wasn't actually warm either. I pulled it up to my face and rubbed my cheek back and forth, letting the hair on the back of his hand tickle me slightly. The sensation made me think for a second that he might still be here after all. A tear dropped from my eye onto my forearm, and I returned my father's hand to his still chest. Composing myself, I got up on my feet and went over to Mother. She watched me approach her in the mirror. When I reached her, I put my hands on her shoulders and she placed her hands on mine.

"It was only a couple of hours ago Ethan" she said softly.

"I woke around 3am when I didn't feel him next to me."

"I never have been able to sleep well without his arm around me. He always said he was my *dream sentry*, imagine that, my *dream sentry*," she sighed.

My mother had already shared more in these last moments than she ever had before about their personal life. I couldn't think of any words to say to her, even though I desperately wanted to comfort her somehow, I just felt helpless. She turned in her chair and took my hands in hers. She looked directly into my eyes, so deeply that I could not look away. She pulled my hands to her lips and kissed them tenderly.

"Ethan, *son*, your Da loved you so very much" she said in a broken whisper.

"I know that at times he was cross sounding, and that maybe he pushed you harder then was necessary. But he always loved his babies" she said with a stronger voice, emphasizing her point by squeezing my hands tightly. There was a minute of silence, and then she spoke again.

"This will be hardest on Shannon, she'll be needing us both to be strong, to be there for her. To be as normal as possible in all the chaos that will be surrounding this house in the coming days. I'll be needing your help Ethan, can you do this for me boy?" she asked, her eyes glistening again.

"Yeah Mom, you know that I will, I swear," I said with conviction. She smiled now, and wiped her tears away with my hands.

"OK then son, for your Da, remember we're Kelly's, *no tears, no fears*," she said, smiling through her contradicting tone. My mother got up, and retied her gown. She hugged me and tussled my hair.

"*Ugh*, what a frightful mess you have on top your head boy! You better be fixing that pretty soon," she said wrinkling her nose and sounding like herself again.

"You go make some breakfast for you and your sister, I'll be along soon."

"We'll tell her together Ethan, OK," she said as she walked past me to her bed.

"All right maam, OK," I replied, wiping my own eyes dry. I walked towards the door and then looked back. Mom had crawled back into bed and pulled Da's arm around her like a blanket. She allowed herself to let go and as I closed the door behind me I swear I could hear her whistling softly to herself, '*When Irish Eyes are Smiling*'.

The next few days were busy, busy beyond belief. All of the arrangements, the telegrams, the phone calls, and the visitors (all bearing food), produced the chaos that Mom had spoke of on that morning. Uncle Liam and Aunt Jo (Josephine) had come in on Sunday to help Mother with everything that needed doing. Together they handled nearly everything without major incident. Although, there had been a slight commotion when Uncle Liam took on the Great State of New York. It was over the planning of my Father's viewing/wake in our living room versus the funeral home. In the end, my Uncle capitulated but not before he accused the Governor of the State of planning to steal the pennies from his dead brother's eyes! To say the least my family was colorful, to say the most we were certifiable!

I had to take Shannon into town for ice cream and new shoes so she would not be there when the mortuary came by to pick up Dad's body. Mother was settling into her *"take charge"* personality, keeping everything and everyone at bay. However, whenever we caught each other's eye she gave me the look that reminded me how fragile the ground was beneath her feet. I did my best to keep the mood light by telling as many of Da's silliest stories as I could remember.

By Monday, the oldest of my Father's brothers arrived to lend a hand. Uncle Chuck (Edward Charles really) and Aunt Debbie (Deborah Ann) had come all the way from California. He was Da's favorite, because he could make us all laugh until our stomachs hurt. And, on occasion, he would unleash his comedic timing on an unsuspecting Uncle Liam and cause him to spew beer from his nose, always a crowd pleaser! Uncles Glenn, Richard and Robert came in on Tuesday from the city. These were the three youngest, still out trying to make their fortune, and still unattached as far as we knew. Each day more and more family arrived, some squeezing into our house, but most billeted at the Holiday Inn near the expressway.

The Mass had been scheduled for Friday morning at St. Kate's (Katherine), with a viewing and a reading set for the night before at the funeral home. The wake, minus the guest of honor thanks to the Governor of New York State, would be here at the house after the burial service at the Church's cemetery. My Mother had planned the entire event herself, every detail, and had chosen the most moving music for the march from the Church to the grave. Since I was too small to help carry the casket, Mother had decided that I would walk ahead, leading the way. Mother and Shannon would follow behind Dad and his pallbearers, and everyone else would trail behind them. My Uncles and a close friend of Dad's would have the honor of carrying him to his rest. My Dad's friend looked a little surprised when he learned the details of the processional, discovering that he would be required to wear the traditional Irish kilt and frock coat as a pallbearer. Mother whispered to him discretely as he listened, warning him not to refer to the kilt as dress lest there be a need to carry two bodies that day!

By Wednesday, I was quite tired of the smell of ham, cabbage and boiled potatoes. I longed for a plate of spaghetti and meatballs or some macaroni and cheese, or better still a chilidog from Nathan's in Atlantic City! Just when I thought that the only answer would be a hunger strike, Uncle Chuck came to the rescue. He showed up at the door with bags and bags of cheeseburgers and fries, and a box full of chocolate milkshakes from some new hamburger place called McDonald's. And, just before bedtime, Uncle Chuck came through again when the house erupted in laughter during the retelling of my Father's flatulent episode during his christening back in Ireland. Uncle Liam lost control and spewed beer from his nose when Uncle Chuck did his impression of the bubbles surfacing from the Holy Water in the presence of His Eminence. I could hear my Mother laughing loudest of all, and I took this smile to my room with me and had the first restful sleep in days.

We spent most of Thursday preparing for the viewing and reading scheduled for later in the day at the funeral home. Uncle Liam was planning to recite, 'Johnny we hardly knew ye,' and Mom had a poem by Emily Dickinson that she wanted to share. I had struggled all week with what to share myself and finally settled on my Father's favorite Psalm (23), the one that began, '...The Lord is my Shepard, I shall not want...' I knew it was short, but I wasn't certain I could get up in front of God and family without breaking down, so short was good, very good. As it turned out however, it was at the viewing and the reading service where most of the tears are shed at a typical Irish ceremony. So nobody really noticed me blathering through half of King David's beautiful Psalm. The Mass and burial are usually where everyone wears a stone face and walks through the ceremony with the dignity of royalty. The wake afterward is where all the emotions come out, but then that's because most of the people are good and pissed by the time all of the toasting, remembering, and story telling is done.

I woke up early before everyone else on Friday morning. Today we would lay my Father to rest. I rubbed the sleep from my eyes and swung my legs out from under the covers. Uncle Robert was sleeping soundly and snoring softly on the rollaway bed in the corner of my room. I almost yelled out when my bare feet touched the icy cold wood floor. My Uncle liked to sleep with the window open and December in Albany can get pretty darn frigid! I threw on some clothes and warm socks, grabbed my sneakers and tipped toed out the door. The house was full of sleeping relatives, and I was glad because they kept Mom busy and her mind occupied. Passing through the living room and into the kitchen, I opened the fridge and took a long drink from the milk bottle. I looked around guiltily; wiping my mouth on my sleeve, making sure my Mother was standing behind me, *SAFE!* Feeling pretty sure of myself, I took another long drink and replaced the cap on the bottle, putting it back into the refrigerator and closing the door silently.

I took a peek out into the back yard and gazed at the spot where Dad used to lay in the grass. This morning it was covered with fresh snow, and I smiled to myself, suddenly having a great idea. Making my way around the sleeping bags and cots, I went into the dining room and opened the sliding glass door. It was freezing outside, and I was instantly chilled to the bone. I closed the door quickly after I went out into the yard, my breath creating a cloud around me as it met the cold air. I stamped my feet hard on the ground a couple of time to jump-start my circulation and then ran over to Da's spot in the lawn. Hoping I could do this thing without getting frostbite, I looked up into the clear morning sky, and I could see all the way to heaven I thought. Then smiling broadly I shouted at the top of my lungs, **"Can you hear me Da?"**

"Look, tis for you sir," I hollered, dropping flat on my back and waiving my arms and legs in jumping jack like movements, making the grandest snow angel ever. This was brilliant I thought to myself! Sure as there is a God in Heaven, my Father and Jesus himself must be dancing a jig right now, arm in arm right, marveling at this grand sight. And my Father would be saying to him.

"Will you look at that Jesus, didn't I tell you my son was a pistol"

"ETHAN, are you daft boy, *Jesus, Mary, and Joseph*!" Uncle Liam hollered from the open sliding glass door, standing there in his boxers and undershirt.

"Get your tail in here before you catch your death!" he shouted again, motioning me over to him with his skinny accountant's arm. Winking at the sky, I waived to my Uncle and said I would be right along. I jumped up to do what I was told, shaking off the cold snow and jogging toward the door. On the way I thought, "You know, it just *may* be possible to freeze one's butt off," it sure felt that way at the moment!

After a truly grand breakfast of eggs and sausages, fried potatoes, and some juice and cocoa,I found myself back in my room trying to figure out how to wear this stupid kilt. I had seen my Da wear them on occasion, but never really thought much about them beyond how nerdy they seemed, and hoping that I would never have the occasion to wear such a thing. I was mostly worried that my knickers would be hanging out for all to see, I mean we would be out in public after all. Uncle Robert was already dressed and fixing the wool cap on his head, studying his look in the mirror. He saw me holding the kilt in front of me with one hand and my clean underpants in the other.

"Don't worry Ethan, you'll not be turning cartwheels at Mass, no one will see son, no one will see" I must have had a funny look on my face because he laughed out loud. He walked by me and messed up my hair.

"You'll figure it out boy!" he laughed as he went by me towards the kitchen for some coffee.

I stood there a minute longer before the light came on. I blushed a little and then smiled to myself, it all made perfect sense if you thought about it in a practical way. So, I went about getting dressed in the heavy woolen kilt, the white dress shirt and the short black frock coat. I sat on the bed and pulled on the long, heavy and colorful wool stockings, and adjusted the orange tassels that fell from the spats. I finished lacing my shoes and then went out into the hall looking for someone to help me with my tie. Mother caught sight of me as she came out of her room, and she quickly put her hand to her mouth, stifling a gasp. Her eyes became wet with tears and she stamped her foot.

"Darn it Ethan Andrew, you look just like your Father!" She walked over to me and smudged my forehead with a kiss. Then she wet a face towel that she was holding with saliva and wiped away the mark. I gave her the tie and she fixed it for me just as she had for Dad so many times in the past.

"Well now, that should do it, are you ready?" she asked, taking the same towel and dabbing her eyes.

"Yes maam, I am maam" I answered.

We walked into the living room and everyone was either standing or sitting, all of them waiting for the word to start off to the Church. My sister Shannon was sitting on Uncle Glenn's lap, uncharacteristically silent with so many available people to pester. She was dressed in her Sunday school clothes, complete with a black scarf and little black handbag. She also had Buster with her, and I looked back at Mother and she nodded approvingly. I was glad, I would be busy at the service and would not be able to sit with her and keep her quiet.

"Shall we all make our way now?" Mother said to one and all, as she pulled the black veil across her face. With that being said everyone started for the door and out to the waiting cars.

The Mass was long as usual and hard on the knees with all the praying and genuflecting. I was sitting with the pallbearers, my Uncles and Dad's friend, in the first row on the left side of the Church. The knee rest on our row squeaked every time we knelt and rose, and I was certain that Father McKenzie would be frowning at me whenever I looked up, he was. I looked across the aisle and made eye contact with Shannon who was sitting with Mother and all of my Aunts and cousins. She stuck out her tongue and wrinkled her nose, so all was well with her anyway. I knew we were nearing the end when the good Father walked around Dad's casket sprinkling it with Holy Water. When he finished his laps, Father McKenzie walked back up the steps to the altar, and turned to face the congregation. He raised his outstretched hands slowly, palms up and invited us all to stand. From the balcony high above the altar, a 'bodhran' sort of a tiny kettledrum began a slow steady beat, soft and light. Then a lone violin began to play a slow, soft, melodic tune, the drummer keeping time softly in the background. Uncle Liam tapped me on the shoulder lightly and pointed to the aisle way, indicating that I was to take my place at the foot of Da's casket. Butterflies began to fly around in my stomach, and I fought the urge to retch. I walked calmly into the aisle, catching my Mother's eyes as I did so. She smiled at me and all of my strength returned.

The violin continued with its beautiful melody and now a lone fife, whistling the same melodic tune in unison, the drummer still keeping time but just a little louder now, joined it. The pallbearers filed out behind me and took their places on either side of the bier. They all looked so grand in their kilts and frocks, standing around the coffin draped by the flag of Dad's homeland. Everyone was watching us, and I suddenly realized just how many people were here today, I could feel those darn butterflies again. The music became louder still, as a few more instruments joined the others playing the same sweet melody. The fifes, penny whistles, and piccolos were haunting as they enhanced the sweetness of the strings, there were two drummers now and the music was becoming a march. I looked back in time to see Da's brothers and his good friend lift up his casket, and place it onto their shoulders. Each of them then folded their white-gloved hands in front of their bodies and Uncle Liam nodded at me to begin the slow march up the aisle leading the way to the waiting hearse. I turned and looked at all of the people, swallowed the lump in my throat and started the *one step, pause, next step, pause* march, keeping in time with the music that was filling the Church. With every step the music seemed to get louder, fuller, and richer. I was there and I was not there, it felt more like a dream than real life. I looked ahead at the stained glass in the front of the Church, and the sunlight made all of the colored figures come to life. As we passed row after row, I felt everyone's stare, and I thought I might pass out right then and there. When out of the corner of my eye, I caught sight of my mates, all them dressed in their Sunday best, and none of them laughing at me, or pointing and making faces. Kenny reached out and touched me on the arm reassuringly as I passed, and that steadied me enough to finish.

The pallbearers loaded Da into the hearse, and we all followed in a slow walk to the cemetery. Shannon and I stood on either side of our Mother, each holding a hand. She wore black gloves and I remember thinking, well, it's cold out today. The snowplows had cleared a path from the drive to the gravesite, and mercifully, the weather was supportive. After the pallbearers set the casket next to the hole in the earth, Father McKenzie continued with the graveside service.

It was short and sweet, and my Mother accepted the folded Irish flag as well as the American flag for Da's service in Korea. Shannon touched his casket with her little gloved hand and then blew him a kiss skyward. Each of my Uncles took their turn saying their goodbyes, and then all five of them knelt beside the grave, held hands and prayed the rosary together, my Uncle Richard's voice cracking slightly. Finally, it was my turn to say farewell, and I walked over to him and placed both hands on the coffin. I leaned forward, kissed the shiny lacquered wood, and could not resist the temptation to knock lightly on the top, just in case. Then from the inside pocket of my frock coat I pulled out three cards. I held them close to me and then whispered something that only my Father could hear. When I finished whispering my secret message, I placed them all on top of the coffin in this order, *DiMaggio, Mantle, and Berra*. I could let go now; I knew he wouldn't be alone. I walked back towards my family, whistling softly to myself, I knew I would not be alone either.

Four

("The rich and the poor have this in common: the Lord is the maker of them all…" Proverbs 21:2)

Firebaugh, California, December 1966

Maria Lopez stood at the counter in her small kitchen, transforming little balls of dough into thin tortillas. As she finished rolling and stretching each one, she flipped them onto the hot iron griddle radiating on top of the brand new *'Kitchenaire'* stove to her right. The appliance had been an early Christmas gift from her husband Victor. It was something she had been secretly hoping for, ever since they arrived here two years ago. That was when Victor had taken a new job as the harvest foreman on Senor Donnelly's citrus ranch. Arthur Donnelly II was a bearish, gruff old man, but generous and fair to a fault if you asked anyone who had spent more than five minutes around him. And in 1964, while Maria was pregnant with her second child, he changed their lives with the offer of this job. It provided them a new start in life, one with luxuries she never dreamed she would have. Things like a yard for the children to play in, a room for them to share, and running water in the house, praise God no more carrying water from a smelly old well! So in the light of their windfall, getting up early to start a fire in the wood-burning stove was a small burden, not worthy of audible complaint, especially for a good Christian woman. But still, to have heat at the turn of a knob, now that would be living! And so, since she believed in her heart that all prayers are answered sooner or later, here it was! Right after the spring harvest ended and work became scarce, Victor received a phone call from his brother Raymond in Fresno offering him a spot on his loading team for the summer. Of course they jumped at the chance to earn some extra money for the kids and themselves.

And earn he did, making a tidy sum *'boosting'* on the lettuce and melon circuit from Fresno to Yuma. Keeping in character, he saved every dime for his family, sleeping in his truck and spending only what he needed for gas and food. *'Boosting'* was a term for a day laborer who substituted for actual employees who might be sick or who wanted some time off without losing their jobs. The *"boosting"* laborers would then receive daily payouts in cash, no questions asked. In these situations, the *Feds* tended to look the other way to keep commerce moving. This hard working band of nomads would follow the freight trains as they stopped at each of the packinghouses on all the major farms from Central California to the Arizona border.

Sure, it was harder work than cutting, raking, and bailing hay and Sudan grass, which is what he would normally do between harvests, but the pay was much better, and they're family was still growing. The days would be long and hard, usually sixteen hours of back breaking lifting and stacking; all of it in and around an endless procession of superheated railroad cars. These were the kind of conditions that quickly weeded out the arrogant and unprepared. You know the types, the guys that dressed as if they were cutting Daddy's lawn on the weekend. The *mensas* would show up wearing shorts and tank tops, and you just knew that these guys wouldn't last a week. Hell, most wouldn't finish the day. Only the experienced and motivated lasted the whole summer, but the work could make a young man old way before his time. On top of all that, this kind of work took him away from home for three months at a time. And that was hard on the children, and on her as well, she missed keeping her cold feet warm next to him a night. But this was their world, and these opportunities were a Godsend. There were no eight to five, shirt and tie type jobs for those lacking a SSN or the right colored papers. Victor would say, *"The Lord does his part and we do ours,"* removing his hat and folding his hands in prayer fashion, just a hint of sarcasm in his voice, rolling his big brown eyes to the heavens.

"He provides the work, we bring the sweat," he would finish, winking at whoever was nearby, taking a long drink from an ever-present can of beer. And, while he would have loved to give his wife something extravagant and sparkly, he knew how hard she labored, so he brought to her something that would make life a little easier. Now, every time she looked at the beautiful white stove and oven she would smile to herself. Her husband may be a man of few words, but his actions could fill a library, she thought to herself, smiling and humming *'Monday, Monday'* by the *'Mamma's and the Papa's'*

"AIYE!" she yelped, burning her finger while turning a tortilla.

"That *panson* had better eat dozen of these before he rushes to work," she muttered to herself as she sucked on her reddening thumb.

"Tina, breakfast is ready, go get your father, he's outside by the truck," Maria said to her daughter who had just walked into the kitchen.

"Si Mama," she answered singingly, going out the screen door still brushing her hair.

She hopped down the wooden steps to the soft dirt and turned toward the garage. She could see her Father's legs jutting out from under the pick-up where he was busy giving the zyrc fittings a quick lube with the grease gun. Caring for the equipment was just one of the endless lists of chores on a working ranch or farm. Tina walked over to where he was working and sat down on his boots.

"What the...OUCH!" Victor hollered, bumping his head on the driveshaft, startled by the sudden appearance of his daughter.

"Papa, mira comida, OK," Tina said cheerfully, nonplussed by her Father's little accident.

She stood up, her head down, her long hair hanging in her face while she combed out the tangles from underneath.

"PAPA, come *ON!"*

"Yeah, yeah, I'll be right there *mija,"* he replied still rubbing the sting off his forehead. She swatted his boot with her brush, stamped her foot for effect then placed both hands on her tiny hips, and shot him the *'look'* as she ran back towards the house.

It was shaping up to be a usual California Christmas weather wise, not a cloud in the sky, seventy-two degrees and just a whisper of a breeze. Tina could hear her little brother fussing as she got to the backdoor. Her mother was sitting at the kitchen table trying to feed Gilbert some scrambled egg and frijoles, but he wasn't exactly cooperating. He kept turning his head as the spoon came close and had more food in his hair and his ears than he did in his mouth.

"Hold still gordito, do you want Papa to see you fussing and crying?" Maria said with a sigh, puffing her cheeks and blowing her hair away from her face.

Gilbert just squirmed all the more in his highchair, and started to put some real feeling into his wailing. The door swung open forcefully, slamming into the side of the house with a loud BANG!

"WHO IS MURDERING MY SON?" Victor said with a gasp, clutching his chest and winking at his wife.

"*Madre Dios*, my son, your mother has scared the beans right out of you!"

"And what is this yellow stuff, *brains* maybe?" Victor picked a clump of scrambled egg off Gilbert's head and popped it into his mouth.

"*Hey*, these *brains* are good, maybe I should try some *chicken* too, no?" And he quickly dropped to his knees grabbing his son's chubby little arm and started gnawing on it, grunting like a feeding sow. Gilbert started to squeal with laughter, as he was familiar with this little game that his Father liked to play. Maria walked over to the two of them and snapped a wet dishtowel at her husband.

"*Qiayate Panson*, this child's a mess, and all my hard work is getting cold!"

"Eat your breakfast while I clean him up," Maria said giggling, wiping the beans from her son's face.

"OK, OK, we surrender General," her husband said, bowing deeply, waiving his hat in a mock salute.

He playfully slapped his wife on her bottom as he passed her, making his way to the kitchen table. Maria yelped, "*Behave*, there was time for that this morning, remember?" she smiled and then blushed when she noticed her daughter was watching them. Tina just grinned at her, showing off her missing front teeth, waiving at her Father as he came near her chair. He sat beside her and helped himself to some eggs, beans, and a couple of the warm tortillas from under the covered plate. The steam rose from under the towel and the aroma of fresh tortillas filled the room. Victor tore off a section of a folded tortilla and scooped up a healthy bit of the tasty dish, eating sumptuously.

"*Victor*, slow down, and use your fork!" she pleaded.

"*Por favor*, can you at least try to help me teach these children some manners!"

Her husband picked up a napkin, wiped his fingers clean and capitulated. Picking up his fork, he held it daintily in his right-hand, pinky finger extended, and continued feeding himself. Maria shook her head in frustration and returned to cleaning up her son. Just another everyday at the Lopez casa, she was happy, the children were happy, and he was *loco!*

By 9am, the morning rush had ended and a rare silence hung over the household. Victor had driven off to start the *'wets'* on opening the turnouts in the orange groves. They would be getting water from the County share wells later this morning for irrigation, so the family would not be seeing him again until late in the day. Maria was busy bathing and dressing Gilbert, looking forward to a little time to herself, once she handed him off to his sister to baby-sit of course. And, Tina was taking advantage of the lull in the daily routine, lying quietly on her bed watching the sunlight streak through the window curtains. The patterns on the white lace produced beams of light in various shapes, going every which way. You could see the dust particles hang on each beam, giving the illusion that they were in motion. She lay on her side, her knees pulled to her waist, dangling a foot over the edge of the bed. She twirled her foot around and around until her sandal dropped, making her smile for some reason. A game she must have been playing perhaps, who knows what a child is really thinking anyway?

Tina's peace and quiet was abruptly interrupted when her mother walked into the room carrying her brother. It's funny how all women have that natural instinct about toting children around. Men just don't get it, they all look like they are carrying a football or taking out the trash. But women, all women, even little girls, pick up children the same way. In one smooth motion they scoop them up swinging out their hip and settling the child in that "sweet spot" where the kids weight is totally supported and the stress on the woman's back is minimal. And the kids love it, sorta like riding a hobbyhorse really.

"*Mija*, look after your brother while I start the laundry. You can help me hang the clothes on the line later, and then we can make a nice lunch together.

"OK Mama, OK"

Her mother set Gilbert on the floor and then left the room. Tina watched him sit there for a minute, looking around the room for something to pounce on. Fixing his eyes on her bookcase, he tipped himself over in the general direction of his target, and started crawling to beat all get out. He was really able to walk now, but he was a lazy child and preferred to crawl than to exert the extra effort to stand. Tina jumped up from her bed to head him off before he reached her books. A six-year-old typically doesn't have too many treasures, but her books, especially the Dr. Seuss books, were her gems. She loved when her father read to her whenever he had some free time. *'Hop on*

Pop' was her favorite, Papa's too. He sometimes asked to borrow it after he finished the story.

"I think your mother needs to hear this story again," he would say as he turned out the light. Then Tina would hear her mother laughing heartily in the kitchen.

"Aiye panson, you're impossible!"

"If you want to please me so much pick up a towel and start drying," she would say just before the giggling started. Frustrated but not angry, her brother diverted his attention to the stuffed tiger in the corner, and settled on wrestling with that for the moment. Tina picked up an old deck of cards and sat on the floor next to him. She flashed the cards to him one at a time trying to coax him into repeating her words.

"*Jack*, say *Jack* gordito"

Gilbert just sat there, the tiger's tail in his mouth. The most she could get him to do was grunt, it would do for now, he was smiling at least. The telephone rang loudly in the hall. It was mounted high on the wall to keep it out of the reach of curious rug racers. Maria picked it up on the third ring, running in from the service porch off the kitchen.

"*Bueno*" she said into the handset.

Curious, Tina walked towards the hall stopping to lean against the doorjamb. She reached up and fiddled with the long black cord, swinging it back and forth between the wall and her mother's leg. Gilbert appeared at her feet and pulled himself up by her pant leg, standing next to her. She leaned over to pick him up, but he was too heavy to hold for very long. So she sat down on the floor with him in her lap. She listened as he mumbled something unrecognizable into her right ear while trying to hear her mother's conversation with the left one.

"*Si*, I know, *I know*" Her mother's tone was sympathetic and she was nodding her head in agreement with whatever the caller was saying. Tina wondered what they were talking about, but she knew it wasn't good by the look on Mama's face.

"*Si, bueno*, we will be here, see you when you get here, I'll make coffee," she said and then replaced the handset to the phone cradle. Maria chewed on her thumbnail, a habit from childhood, one she exercised every time she was uneasy about something. She looked down at her children and then knelt beside her daughter.

"Little one, you know your friend Hector from school?" Tina nodded and smiled, "yes," she said cheerfully.

"That was his sister Rosa on the telephone, you remember her don't you?"

"Yes," she said still smiling.

"Honey, Hector's sister is going to have a baby soon," Maria said, searching her daughter's face for a sign that she understood.

"*Si* mama, I know" she replied, watching their tabby, *El Guappo* jump onto the windowsill.

"*Mija* can you help her, the way you helped the others?" she asked, pausing for a reply.

Maria was not comfortable dealing with these things. She prayed to God each day to take back this gift he had given to her little girl. She did not want this for her, for any of them. In her heart, she knew it was a call to serve, but in the same heart, she knew that it was too much to ask of one so small. It seemed too much to ask of anyone, and she was terrified of the potential consequences. Given their illegal residence status, Maria always worried about deportation, forced to leave behind what they had worked so hard for. To be sent back into abject poverty, to the country she was born to. Those in their situation knew better than to call too much attention to themselves lest the wrong people took notice.

Ever since that day in the field, when Tina laid her hands on the dead baby, their lives ceased to be normal. Each day someone new appeared at the door, searching for a miracle. They came at all hours, each with a need more pitiful or heartbreaking than the one before. After a couple of months of constant appeals, the strain on her family became too much to bear. Victor quit his job and moved them all to Fresno to stay with his brother and his family. They all shared a home in town, eleven people in four rooms and no bath. What work he could find was hard and seasonal, and he earned what he could as a laborer at various construction sites. Living in the city brought new hazards. In particular, the constant threat of INS raids and the stigma of being necessary but unaccepted, unwanted. But, even with the hardships, at least there was peace again in their lives.

They were far enough away from the past that they could live freely, without intrusion, left blissfully alone. Now the new job, the newfound success had brought them back into contact with the past. She had hoped that enough time had passed, that people would have forgotten about them, and that they could return to hide in plain sight. However, it was not to be, and days after they arrived in their new home, the *pilgrims* came with their sad stories. Unable to deny her daughter's destiny any longer, Maria made a pact with God. If he would protect Tina from the wolves, she would turn no one away, they would give of themselves, joyfully and completely.

"*Nina*, did you hear me?"

"*LaTina*, answer your mother" she said sternly, lifting Tina's chin with her index finger.

"Yes Mama, I heard you. Can I have some Kool-Aid?" she asked, moving her brother from her lap to the floor, he was falling asleep anyway.

"If your father left any you can, go into the kitchen while I put your brother in his bed"

They got up simultaneously and went in opposite directions. Tina went right to the fridge and pulled out the plastic container of *'Goofy' Grape'* Kool-Aid. Setting it on the kitchen table, she dragged a chair over to the counter and climbed up to reach the cabinet where the glasses were stored. She picked out her favorite jelly jar glass, the one with *Barney and Betty Rubble* on it. While she was carefully pouring her drink, there was a loud knock at the screen door. Startled she spilled a little on the Formica tabletop.

"*OOPSY,*" she said, looking over her shoulder to see if anyone had seen. Tina grabbed a handful of napkins from the holder on the table and mopped up the spill while she leaned forward and slurped her drink reducing the volume to a manageable level. She heard the screen door rattle again with another loud rap.

"Maria, *ola Maria,*" a woman said from the back porch.

"*Una momento por favor,* I'll be right there Rosa," Tina's mother called from the back bedroom. The door opened and Hector's sister walked into the kitchen.

"*Ola nina,* you are my brother's little friend, no?" Rosa asked as she approached the table cautiously.

"Yes," Tina replied her Kool-Aid in one hand and holding onto the back of a chair with the other.

She was standing on one foot while she kicked the other back and forth nervously like she needed to tinkle or something. She watched the woman waddle slowly to the table and pull out a chair. Rosa looked at the chair with a sad face and sighed, "*Oh my goodness,* these things seem lower and lower the fatter I get," she said to herself. Taking in and letting out a deep breath, she tugged on the chair again to allow herself maximum clearance. She steadied herself, one hand on the table, one hand on the chair as she sat down. It was more of a controlled crash really, but by the look of relief on her face, you could tell she was pleased with the landing.

31

"So little one, you're the angel everyone whispers about," she said reaching behind her and rubbing her sore back.

Tina did not reply she just stood there swinging her foot and holding her glass up to her mouth, not really drinking, just standing by. The woman made her uneasy, and she could see that she was anxious about something. Likewise, Rosa did not like the way the little girl stared at her, but she was afraid to say anything, to upset her in any way. If what they said about her was true, she needed her more than anything right now. Rosa Hernandez very was young, but she instinctively knew something was wrong, her baby had not moved in days, and then there was the spotting during the past few days as well. But there was no money for visits to the doctor, or time to visit the clinic, not that she wanted to go there again anyway. It was an earlier visit to that place that put her in this condition after all. That baby-faced, gringo doctor, pretending to be so helpful, so pious, she thought. He was just helping himself to what he really wanted from all the pretty young women and girls. His victims were the most vulnerable, those who could not hope for protection from the authorities, or from a community that refused to recognize or even acknowledge their existence. She wished she had the courage to tell her mother and father the truth, but she needed to protect her family. Who would the police believe anyway, a couple of *'wetback'* pickers or a respected member of the Anglo community, there could be no justice, not for them. It was just as easy to make up a story about a pretend boyfriend to appease her angry family, than to risk their very livelihood on the truth. Now this, what could she do, she was more frightened of disappointing her parents than she was of meeting this little girl, angel or devil, she wasn't sure which it would be yet.

"*Rosa, Rosa*, are you comfortable *mija?*" asked Maria as she jogged into the room carrying Gilbert on her hip. She glanced quickly in Tina's direction and then set her son down on the kitchen floor, handing him a cookie from the jar on the counter and then taking a seat between her daughter and her visitor.

"I am OK Senora Lopez, *I mean I think I'm OK?*" she replied not very convincingly. She fidgeted in her seat a little trying to get comfortable. That was when Maria noticed the small dark stain on the young woman's sweatpants. She had been hoping that this would just be a false alarm. That the poor girl was only upset and wanted to talk to someone older, to say things to her that perhaps she was unable say to her own mother. That wasn't going to be the case, she realized that now, as the bloodstain darkened and grew larger. She wished Victor were here right now, to take charge, he was so much better under pressure, especially when it would involve their child and the power.

"*OH MY GOD!*" Rosa shrieked as she became aware of her worsening situation.

She tried to stand but she was sitting awkwardly, and there was blood on the linoleum floor now. Each time she tried to stand her sneakers would squeak as she lost traction in the warm sticky spill spreading on the floor. Maria ran behind her and lifted Rosa from under her arms, kicking the chair across the room as she did so. Together they got to the floor and Maria laid the terrified girl onto her back.

"**Quiet Rosa**, *be quiet and very still mijita!*" she snapped at her out of fright, not anger.

She went to the sink and splashed her face with cold water then soaked a washcloth. She dabbed her face dry and then went to Rosa and placed the cool towel on her forehead. The frightened girl was instinctively taking small quick breaths trying to calm herself. Her eyes showed that she was responding to Maria's calm handling of the situation. This was good news because Maria was really on the brink of hysteria herself, but when she saw the weak smile on Rosa's face silently saying to her '*I trust you,*' she found herself back in control.

"Be still little mother, I think that your baby wants to be born now, one way or the other," (meaning live or dead). Rosa was sweating even with the cold washcloth on her head. She continued to smile weakly and to breathe in quick little gasps.

"Please Senora, *please*, this kid feels like a stone, my belly is cold like a tomb, feel it, *TOUCH IT!*"

Maria placed her hand under the young girl's blouse and felt her stretched skin. She pressed slightly and thought she could feel a foot or something, but the girl was right, her skin was cold to the touch, even with all of that warm blood running through her, she was freezing. Uncharacteristically, she formulated a plan quickly. The baby needed to be delivered soon, or the young mother might die as well. She got up, quickly, rummaging through the utensil drawer and found the sharpest knife she owned. Running back to Rosa she dropped to her knees and lifted the front of her sweatpants, swung the sharp knife in a short downward arc, and sliced them open to the crotch, exposing her sex. She was surprised to see that Rosa's water had not yet broken, and that her vagina was not the slightest bit swollen or discolored in preparation for giving birth. She may not have been a mid-wife, but she had delivered two children of her own and she felt as though she knew what was normal, what to expect. At that, exact moment there was a loud scream and the sound of breaking glass just behind her.

"WHAT ON GOD'S GREEN EARTH IS GOING ON HERE!" screeched the woman who had just entered the house. Senora Donnelly was standing just inside the kitchen having come in through the open front door. She must have witnessed Maria hacking open the bleeding young woman's pants and then dropped the cake she had brought over for the family. Lord knows what was running through her mind just then, but Alma Donnelly was no shrinking violet, and it didn't take Maria many words to explain the situation.

"All right dear, it's all right, I'll call for help, you stay with the girl," she said calmly. Alma knelt beside Rosa and pushed her wet hair away from her face. She smiled at her reassuringly.

"You're going to be fine baby girl, you're going to be just fine, I promise."

She was so convincing, that Maria even believed it herself for a second, but she couldn't wait for help, the nearest hospital was twenty miles away. She leaned forward and whispered to Rosa that she was going to have to touch her and see if she was close to delivering. Rosa nodded and continued breathing in short quick breaths. Maria went to the sink and washed her hands as clean as she could and then returned to Rosa, her hands still dripping from the scrubbing. She smiled weakly at Rosa and then reached down to inspect her body to see if her cervix was dilating. Maria was trying to remember everything that the doctors had done to her when she was giving birth, so that she could repeat the process as best she could. Rosa's voice squeaked slightly as Maria entered her, and she stared at the ceiling wincing occasionally until Maria finished her amateur exam.

"Oh my goodness Rosa, I don't know, *I don't know*, you don't feel ready, you're still too tight, the opening is too small," Maria said quietly, a worried look on her face.

Where was all this blood coming from if not the placenta in the preamble to birth? Suddenly she got it, *the baby,* the baby was bleeding out somehow, it was why Rosa's body was so cold, there wasn't any need for her heart to pump blood to a dead child. She looked to Rosa, her eyes glistening, a weak smile turning to a trembling chin. Before she could get the words out, a hand appeared suddenly on her shoulder, startling her. It was Tina, she had forgotten that she was there. She had been standing by watching the whole thing, never saying a word, never making a sound. Maria reached for her and Tina eased into her mother's arms. Her daughter whispered into her ear, "I can help now mama." Her head still resting on her Maria's shoulder, Tina twirled her mother's hair in her tiny fingers, waiting for her to release her.

"How is our patient?" asked Alma walking back into the room.

"An ambulance is on the way, won't be long now," she continued.

Maria didn't answer right away. She just hugged her daughter tightly and then let her go. It would all be out in the open now she thought to herself. Senora Donnelly was about to witness something that she would not believe much less understand. Nobody outside of this close-knit community would be able to keep this a secret, not for long anyway. Many more pilgrims would come, then the curious, and finally the police, they always came in the end. But now was not the time to be selfish, she had made her pact with God, she had done her part, she would have faith, and she would trust that he would to do his as well.

"*It's dead,*" Rosa said sobbing quietly. "My baby's dead," she recited to herself over and over. Maria reached down and stroked the girl's hair wiping the tears from her cheek.

"Please little one, *por favor*, bring her back, *bring my baby back*," Rosa said weakly to Tina who was peering at her from her mother's side.

"What is she talking about Maria?" Alma asked as Tina knelt beside Rosa, taking her hand.

"*Maria, what is going on here,*" Alma demanded. Maria rose to her feet and walked over to Senora Donnelly. She cupped her face in her hands and looked deeply into her eyes. Alma Donnelly raised her hands and placed them over Maria's, holding her gaze and then asked again, in a hushed voice, "What's happening?"

"The Lord's work Senora, the Lord's work," Maria answered without looking back at Tina and Rosa.

Alma Donnelly leaned to her right, her face still in Maria's hands, and watched as the little girl lay beside Rosa. Her knees were bent, her body still exposed on the cold kitchen floor. Tina put her arm onto Rosa's swollen stomach and scootched as close to her as she could. Her little face was near Rosa's breast and she began to hum to herself a tune that she had made up, nothing that anyone would recognize really. She rubbed her little hand back and forth across Rosa's belly as if she was scratching an itch. Senora Donnelly watched intently, unable to speak, not even trying to pull away from Maria's grasp. Tina rubbed and rubbed, still humming her tune, when all of a sudden she began to tremble as if chilled to the bone. She clutched at Rosa's blouse and buried her face in the space between Rosa's arm and chest. The young *mother* gasped as a ripple of movement made its way across her belly. *THE*

BABY had rolled, and she felt a familiar kicking. She had convinced herself only moments ago, that she never feel that again. Mrs. Donnelly pushed away from Maria's hold and shrieked.

"*Jesus H. Christ*, this girl is giving birth, *RIGHT NOW!*"

She ran to Rosa and knelt between her legs, arriving just as her water broke. The warm liquid spread quickly across the floor, mixing with the blood, making an eerie pink mosaic of the speckled linoleum. Rosa began to scream as the contractions came, one after the other, she was already in transition. Maria snapped out of her trance and rushed to help with the birth, grabbing a towel from the laundry basket near the back door. A moment after she knelt beside Senora Donnelly the baby came, cold and blue. Alma, held the tiny girl in her hands, she was so small and definitely not breathing. The women looked at one another and then yelped as the afterbirth came shooting out immediately following the baby.

Maria picked up the knife she had used to cut open Rosa's sweatpants and cut the umbilical cord. Alma reached her pinky finger into the newborn's mouth and fished out a wad of mucus. Then placing her mouth over the baby's mouth she blew in a quick, hard puff of air causing the baby's cheeks to swell and mucus to shoot out of its nostrils. A split second later Rosa's newborn daughter let out a loud cry, wailing long and hard. Maria wrapped the child tightly in the warm towel as the two women began to laugh uncontrollably, hugging one another while the baby cried and cried between them. Looking over to Rosa, they were alarmed to see that she was unconscious, but then were relieved when they saw that she was still breathing, her chest rising and falling rhythmically. She was OK, just exhausted, too weak to enjoy the moment.

Outside the long singsong siren of an approaching ambulance could be heard, growing louder as it drew nearer to the house. Alma Donnelly got up, ran to the bedroom, and fetched a blanket off of Maria's bed. She modestly covered Rosa's exposed little body and stared down at Tina sleeping peacefully at her side. Senora Donnelly tucked the blanket under the chin of Rosa, making sure Tina was covered as well. She leaned down and kissed each of them and then joined Maria at the sink where she was cleaning the newborn with a warm washcloth. Alma put her arm around Maria and lay her head on her shoulder.

"So, they're true, all the stories that they tell around the valley, they're true," she said in a whisper.

"Yes Alma, *si Senora*, its all true, all of it."

Mrs. Donnelly turned and looked back at the pair of girls sleeping peacefully on the floor, the one not all that much older than the other. She wiped a tear as it fell from her eye and turned back to see Maria leaning against the counter, the newborn quiet in her arms, the two women smiled at one another from across the room. Tina's little brother, Gilbert, interrupted the brief moment of silence as he toddled into the kitchen, a binky in one hand and a jelly stained teddy bear in the other. Senora Donnelly scooped him up, and swung him into that *'sweet spot'* on her hip and flashed a smile at Maria.

"Everyone else seems to have a child to hold, I don't want to feel left out," she said smiling.

Maria laughed and nodded her head approvingly.

"We did OK, didn't we Alma," she said with a sigh. Alma nodded back and set Gilbert on the counter handing him a cookie from the jar. She looked out the kitchen window, the ambulance had just pulled up to the house, a cloud of dirt swirling all around it as it came to a stop.

"Maria, this stays between us, you can count on me," she said still looking out the window.

"Gracias Senora, *thank you.*"

The ambulance attendants rushed in through the back door and went straight to work. Maria thought about what she might say to Victor when he asked how her day was. She smiled to herself and kissed the newborn. I hope your mother names you Elena, I've always liked that name, beautiful and strong, it suits you little one, it suits you. She handed the baby to one attendant and took her own daughter from the other. Tina was fast asleep, her long hair hanging over Maria's arm as she held her.

"Do you know how special you are?" she whispered, kissing her daughter softly.

"But will become of you *mija*, what's to become of you now?"

Five

*("...And the first one now, will later be last, for the
times, they are a changing"...Bob Dylan, 1964)*

Boston, Massachusetts, April 1968
Holy Cross University, First Year

The rain had been falling steadily for hours and frankly, I was getting a little tired of it. The heavy, fat drops were hitting the roof so hard that the television reception was turning to snow while the antenna took a serious pounding. There was so much water running through the streets now, I half expected to see Noah himself sail by on a reunion tour. It had been raining for two days straight and some of us had started adding prayers for spring at morning Vespers. I was looking forward to this little break from school, and continued packing while I just listened to an episode of *'I Love Lucy'* on the TV.

"Lucy, you have some splainin to do!" Ricky said in the background.

"WAAAAAAAA!"

You have to love that show, and Fred Mertz must have been modeled after my Uncle Liam, they're peas in a pod those two I swear! I smiled to myself with that thought and tossed a handful of bundled socks into the suitcase. Closing the top and fixing the latches, I set the luggage on the floor near the door. Fairly light traveling I thought, one suitcase and a duffel bag

38

full of laundry and darning to take home to mother, she will be so pleased to know how much I still need her. Well, that's what I'm counting on anyway, never did master a needle and thread. Like, as not she'll swat me on the shoulder after she kisses me hello and lovingly complain about my taking advantage of her good Christian nature.

"So boy, this is how you reward your poor mother! A heap of shirts, pants and stinky socks soiled by your nasty little feet?" she'll say.

And then I'll catch her talking to herself as she sorts through my clothes, asking where did this or that come from. And tearing up when she would come across an item she remembered giving me, or a shirt that used to belong to Da. My mother missed him so much, and when I went away to school it was like losing him all over again. The first year he was gone was hard for her, but she seemed to past the worst of the grieving now, I could hear it in her voice each time I called home to check in. The door opened and my roommate, the infamous *Sean Michael Andrews* burst in shaking the cold rain off him like a wet hound. Managing to soak everything in the process, easily done given the size of the tiny dorm room, he pulled back the hood of his Mac and flashed his big toothy smile, announcing his arrival.

"Well, I see we're off to visit mommy and '*lil sis*'," he said with his usual sardonic flair.

"Yeah, I am at that, and thanks for the second shower ya heathen brute!"

"Not at all, don't mention it," he said waiving his hand in the air like a drunken thespian, removing his coat.

Sean and I had been assigned this room together from day one at the seminary. We became fast friends with a definite '*Ying & Yang*' relationship. I was the Felix to his Oscar in this '*Odd Couple*' pairing. The headmaster must have a sense of humor when it comes to billeting the student body, because you could see these sorts of like arrangements all around the dorm. Pairing boys from polar opposite backgrounds with one another. I believe it was his intention for us to learn from each other as we went about learning our lessons. So that we would see how the same messages could be heard by one and all simultaneously, and then interpreted so very differently given each individual perspective. It would give us an opportunity to practice the virtue of patience with one another, often times on a daily basis where Sean and I were concerned.

I gave his coat that was on the floor right where he dropped it, a boot as I made my way to the door.

"*Jesus Sean*, the coat rack is right on the door, how hard can it be ya lazy lout," I scolded him, picking up the coat and hanging it on the back of the door.

"Ah, well now, you'll burn for that one young Master Ethan, you'll burn for sure!"

"That'll be five '*Our Father's*' and ten '*Hail Mary's*' for your penance, now be gone with ya," he mockingly scolded me, gesturing towards the door as he flopped onto his bed.

"You're a piece of work Sean, a real piece of work," I laughed picking up my stuff to leave.

"Last chance, come to Albany with me, you shouldn't stay here all week alone," I said. Sean lay there with his hands folded behind his head staring back at me, his hair still dripping wet, a long strand of blond hair hanging in his eyes. He reached over and tapped the stack of books on his nightstand.

"I won't be alone Ethan, I've got Plato, Ivanhoe, and Mr. Robinson Crusoe sitting right here," he said nonchalantly.

"And if they don't fill my days, well, there is always the good book to be read, at the local boozer with a pint or two of Sir Arthur's Guinness' fine stout of course!" he snickered, waiving me off.

"Off ya go now my favorite little neatnik, off to hearth and home!"

"OK, OK, I'm outta here man, see ya in a week."

"*Try not to drown on the way to the train station,*" he shouted from behind the closed door. I raised the hood of my coat and walked out into the deluge. There wasn't enough money for a cab ride and the buses were going to be too crowded to carry on all my stuff. So I slung the duffel bag with all the laundry over my shoulder, held the suitcase good and tight by the leather handle, and started the 10-block walk to catch the 11:00 o'clock train to Albany.

I arrived at the station by 10:40 and just made the train as they were announcing last call. Making my way up the narrow aisle I settled in at a window spot, removing my coat and stuffing it under the seat. I wiped my face dry with my left hand and then ran both hands through my wet hair, pulling it back away from my face. "*Man,*" I thought to myself, "*I wish I would have gotten a haircut before this trip.*"

"*Ma'am will box my ears for sure,*" I said out loud, not realizing it.

"Excuse me," a soft voice said from across the aisle. I turned to answer and found myself looking into the eyes of prettiest girl I had ever seen up close. I'm not sure what I said initially, but it was obviously unrecognizable as English.

"I beg your pardon, I didn't understand," she said sweetly. Composing myself, I finally replied weakly.

"Um, forgive me, I ah, hope I didn't disturb you." I smiled at her, I think, and tried to look more comfortable than I was. I couldn't understand why I was so flummoxed, I had seen my share of pretty girls, this was just too weird?

"No, you didn't disturb me, I just thought you were saying something to me," she said looking at me with beautiful, brown, almond shaped eyes. I swallowed and replied, "Uh Huh."

"*Smooth Ethan,*" I said under my breath.

"Pardon?"

"Oh, nothing, um, my name is Ethan, Ethan Kelly," I managed and reached across the aisle to shake her hand. She took my hand lightly and allowed me to gently make her acquaintance.

"I'm Brenda," she said smiling, and I smiled back, sort of, what was my problem!

"Are you going home for the break as well," I asked?

"Yes, but I'm only passing through Albany to see my favorite Aunt, my family lives on Long Island." *Posh* I thought to myself, and then replied.

"Nice, where are you going to school in Boston?"

"I am in my senior year at Harvard, what about you?"

"I am at Holy Cross preparing for the Seminary," I said, quickly adding, "Harvard, *wow*, what are you studying, law?"

"No, I am a business and finance major, my Father is hoping that I will follow him into the family business after I graduate."

"*That's grand,*" I said smiling more confidently now, still warm under the collar, but no longer sweating, thank God!

This girl would be out of my league even if I weren't going into the priesthood. And in spite of the negative analysis of my chances, I uncharacteristically pursued a lengthy chat with her. We spent the next couple of hours talking about everything, school, family, movies, books, dreams, just anything and everything really, getting along famously. I couldn't explain it, but I never felt more comfortable with anyone, ever. It was if we had already known each other for years and years, I was actually disappointed when the conductor announced that we were nearing the Albany station.

"ALBANY, New York, next stop," he said walking down the aisle, winking at me as he passed.

"Oh, I guess we're here, *my goodness*, where did the time go," I said reaching for my coat under the seat. I looked out the window for the first time since we left Boston, we were on the outskirts of town, and I could see the expressway in the distance. At least it wasn't raining, but the sky was dark and it looked like the storm would be following me from school to home. I looked back at my traveling companion. She was combing her long dark hair. I caught a scent of lilac as she raised her arms and pulled her hair back into a ponytail, she looked over at me and smiled.

"It was very nice talking with you Ethan, have fun with your visit home, and good luck with school"

"You're the first novice priest I have ever met," she said and reached across to shake my hand again.

"Uh, yeah, I had a great time talking to you as well," I said shaking her hand, trying not to notice how wonderful her touch felt.

The train rolled slowly to a stop and she gathered her things, then walked up the aisle, turning to smile and waive to me as she neared the exit. I waived back mouthing a goodbye that she didn't see, and then she was gone. I was suddenly a little sad and tried to catch a glimpse of her through the window as she left the train, but was nudged back into reality as a large man bumped into me as he passed towards the same exit. Sighing, I picked up my coat and made my way into the aisle, heading for the baggage compartment to retrieve my stuff. My mother would be out there somewhere, waiting impatiently for me to appear for the group hug with her and Shannon. Slinging my coat over my shoulder I whistled my way toward the exit.

Shannon saw me first and yelled out as she ran to meet me, "PEEPERS, *PEEPERS*, over here," she squealed. I caught her in mid air as she jumped up into my arms like always, causing me to drop everything in the process. She had grown some while I was away, and managed to knock me back a step or two upon impact.

"Hello girl, how's my favorite pound pup," I teased her, it was one of many nicknames I had for her. This one was her favorite though, whenever she was sad I would sit her on my lap and tell her to close her eyes. Then while I wiped away her tears I would tell her to picture herself on the grass in the yard where Da would lay, and imagine that she had a half dozen puppies crawling all over her licking her face and nipping at her legs. Then I would make little yelping sounds and pinch her arms and face and she would giggle hysterically and *voila* no more tears! If you think about it, who could be sad around a bunch of cute puppy dogs anyways? It would be like trying to sing a sad song with a banjo, not possible!

"ETHAN," my mother called from behind the gate, waiving to us.

I set Shannon down and picked up my bags, then held her hand as we walked over to our mother.

"Hi Mom," I said bending down a little to accept her kiss and let her hug me and tussle my hair. Ah, here it came, "Ethan Kelly, look at this mop on your head, have you no shame boy?"

"We'll be visiting Ernie's while you're in town and have him fix you up like a proper gentleman we will," she said taking Shannon's hand and steering us towards the parking lot. I smiled and nodded, there would be no arguing with her that was for sure. Besides I always liked getting my haircut at Ernie's, he told the funniest stories and had the most infectious laugh, he cracked himself up! I scanned the parking lot to see if I could see Brenda somewhere, but no such luck. I smiled to myself, *"the people you meet in life, you just never know,"* I murmured.

"What son," my mother asked.

"Nothing Mom, *nothing*, there's the car," I pointed.

We tossed my bags in the trunk of Da's prized Chevy Camaro, ah he loved this car. It seemed a little sporty for Mom, but she would never trade it. She said she could still fell him in the upholstery, and that sometimes she would talk to him as if he were in the seat next to her. She said she would get some looks from people while she was driving, but it was none of their affair so she would just waive and drive on! Mom threw me the keys and said, "You drive, you're all grown up now aren't you?"

"Thanks," I said and jumped at the chance to drive again. I didn't get many chances to do this at Holy Cross, and I missed the High School days driving around town with Kenny and Paulie, the *three amigos* as Mom referred to us. I wondered if they would be home for the break as well. I knew that Paulie had joined the Navy, but Mom had said he was in town on leave from Norfolk, and Kenny was supposed to be home for the break from Pitt. I hoped we would get some time to catch up, I missed those guys a lot.

"Mom, can we stop at the Dairy Queen on the way home," Shannon pleaded bouncing up and down in her seat, her hands in front of her as if praying.

"Yeah Mom, *can we, can we*," I mockingly pleaded as well, trying to help my sister's cause.

"Enough you two, alright but just a cone, I have a fine supper waiting and I'll not have you spoil your appetite with junk!" I started the car, and the engine roared to life, *"Ah Da, you were a master with a wrench,"* I thought to myself. We drove out of the lot onto the beltway heading for a little soft ice cream and some giggles while we brought one another up to speed on all the family news.Shannon and mother talked non-stop all the way home afterward and it was music to my ears. I pulled into the driveway and shut off the engine.

"We're here," I said.

"That we are sonny, it's nice to have you home Ethan," Mom said, leaning across the seat and kissing my cheek, wiping away the lipstick in one motion. Shannon wrestled me for a bag to carry and we all went into the house. It's queer how sites, sounds and smells can bring on such vivid memories. And as I walked into the living room I swear I could hear my father whistling somewhere? My mother grabbed my duffel and headed for the utility room.

"Do they have no soap and water at that fancy school of yours," she asked playfully?

"So, this is how you reward your poor mother for giving birth and the long years of service," she said mockingly without looking back. But I knew she was smiling, she couldn't fool me, she loved being a mother, every bit of it!

"Shannon, you go and wash that ice cream face of yours this instant, and Ethan you get settled son, supper will be ready in a little bit," she called from the back of the house.

Shannon swatted my leg as she ran past me heading for the bathroom. I walked to my room and set my suitcase on the bed. I looked around, neat and clean, everything in its place and all the linen had that freshly washed smell. Nobody came close to equaling my mother when it came to keeping a tidy home. The passage that reads *'cleanliness is next to godliness'* should have her picture embossed next to it! After unpacking and placing all of my things in their proper places (there would be an inspection, you could count on that), I took off my shoes and walked back into the living room in my stocking feet. I stood in the center of the room and looked around for a moment, drinking in the familiar vibrations. Then I walked over to my Da's chair and sat down, putting my feet up on the ottoman. I wriggled in the chair a little until I found just the right position and then leaned my head back into the soft cushion. I looked at the acoustic spray on the ceiling for a minute, trying to identify shapes in the shadows. I imagined I saw a spaceship and a tiger as my eyes scanned from left to right.

The stereo came on and I could hear Johnny Mathis singing Misty in the background. My mother loved that album, and always played it for company. I closed my eyes and listened to the song, remembering bits of the conversation I had with the girl on the train. Smiling to myself, I opened my eyes and rolled my head slowly to the right. My Dad's pipes were still on the table in their stand. I selected one and picked it up and looked it over. I put it close to my nose and sniffed slightly, but there was no aroma of sweet tobacco, my Dad never did take up smoking. I placed the pipe in my mouth and practiced holding it properly or at least as I had seen professors at school hold theirs. You know, it did make me feel sophisticated somewhat, maybe I would try this sometime. I was certain that Sean had tried at least this much, so I made a mental note to pick his brain a little when I got back.

"ETHAN, SHANNON, suppers ready you two, shake a leg!"

Shannon ran past me towards the kitchen, making sure to mess up my hair as she passed behind me. I stood up and re-combed my hair with my fingers and walked after her. It was good to be home, it's always good to come home I thought.

"*Let's go eat Da*," I said to his still warm spirit, elevating my walk to a jog.

Six

("...round, round, get around I get around,"...The Beach Boys)

Albany, New York, April 1968
Spring Break

Springtime in upstate New York is glorious. There are so many vivid and vibrant colors around you that your eyes almost seemed assaulted. And when the sun was at its highest point in the sky the world around you was lousy with the abundance of life. There were so many bees buzzing, birds singing, dogs barking, cats mewing, and kids squawking, that if you hummed the right tune you'd have created a symphony comparable to anything Mozart ever composed. I sat at the breakfast table in the kitchen and looked out at all of this beauty, sipping on my coffee. Yes, I had become a coffee drinker since going away to university. And I really *tried* to drink it like a man, *black and strong*. But there was just enough sissy in me to enjoy the luxury of some sweet cream and sugar. I was sure that Da would forgive me the indulgence and only squirm in his grave a little. But I made a mental note to avoid drinking coffee around Uncle Chuck, lest I be referred to ever more as a *"wee girl."* I didn't think I could live with all of the jibes like, "would you be passing me the salt there Shirley," or the worst pun ever, "don't be getting your panties in a bunch Princess!"

"DEAR GOD NOT THAT," I thought out loud, shuddering and shaking myself out of that unpleasant vision.

"Good morning Ethan, did you sleep well boy," my mother asked as she walked into the kitchen?

"Yeah mom, just fine" My mother set out a bowl and spoon for my sister's breakfast. It would be the usual, porridge with butter and brown sugar, toast and jam, milk and OJ.

"Ethan, will you get the milk from the fridge for me please?"

"You bet," I answered, and got up to do as I was asked. Setting the milk bottle on the table I stuck my tongue out at my sister as she walked sleepily into the room.

"Morning squirt," I said cheerfully.

"Moooorrrnnning," she said through a yawn, raising both arms high, her little fists clenched. A real *'BIG GIRL STRETCH'* for one so small. I sat back down next to my sister and shot her a quick wink.

"Would you like a refill *MR. KELLY,*" mother teased, a hand on her hip, while she waived the coffeepot back and forth above me.

"Sure Mom, and the porridge smells grand as well"

"Nice to have my cooking noticed again," she quipped.

"This one here just plays with her meals, I have to wrestle each morsel into her mouth!"

"Nuh Uh!" Shannon grunted, opening her mouth wide to show us the gross evidence of her healthy appetite this fine morning.

"SHANNON ELIZABETH KELLY," mother hollered!

"Is that the face you want our Lord to freeze on your insolent gob for the rest of this day?"

My sister quickly closed her mouth and swallowed, covering her face with her hands to keep any flack from escaping her lips. Choking, she reached for her glass of milk in a slight panic, trying to help herself avoid retching. It was almost an Uncle Chuck *'through the nose episode',* but only almost, DARN IT! I reached over and patted her on the back until she recovered, and there were a couple of tears at the corners of her eyes from the strain.

"Tanks Ethan, *my hero,"* she said sweetly, batting her eyes at me!

"Not at all dear, *not at all,"* I replied in my *'most proper'* gent tone. I looked over to mother who was leaning back against the kitchen counter, sipping her tea and smiling at her brood from over the rim of her cup. She winked at the two of us.

"OK children, let's get on with this meal without further incident, shall we?" She brought over my bowl of porridge and placed a pat of butter on top.

"There you go sonny, that should stick to your middle for awhile!"

"Thanks Mom, looks good."

"So, you're off on your annual pilgrimage to Cooperstown today are you boy," she asked?

"Yes ma'am, if that's OK with you of course"

"Not a worry Ethan, so long as you and those hooligan friends of yours are careful, **and** back by suppertime tomorrow night," she said.

"Your Uncle Liam and Aunt Deb will be here for Sunday supper," she added.

"Ah, I completely forgot, Mom can I ------?" She cut me off with a raised hand and a quick turn of her head.

"NO, Ethan, your family has not seen you for months," she said sternly!

"Do you think that poor man will live forever?" Actually, I was pretty sure that the old codger would out live us all! He was too mean and ornery for Heaven or Hell. "Sorry Mom, of course you're right, we'll be back on time, don't worry," I said reassuringly. Shannon got up from her seat, wiping her mouth with the back of her hand.

"May I be excused please?"

"Ah, Shannon, you've the manners of a street urchin," Mother sad sadly.

"*Yes,* you're excused child, now go wash up and make your bed before you go out into the neighborhood," Mom continued, watching her daughter sprint out of the room. Actually, Shannon was already out of earshot once Mother had said '*yes*' so it wasn't likely that she heard any of the chore assignments.

"Ah, that *chiseller* has no patience at all," Mom said tiredly. "She can hardly stay still long enough for a decent *chinwag!*"

"She is almost as precocious as *you were as a cub* sonny," she said giggling softly.

"*MY PROGENEY,* Lord above," Mother said, raising her teacup to Heaven and shaking her head slowly.

There was a slight screech from the driveway outside. Sounded like Paulie had arrived a tad early to pick me up for the two-hour drive to the hallowed ground of '*Baseball's Hall of Fame*'. Kenny, Paulie, Sparky and I had made this trip together every year since Paul got his driver's license. However this would be the first trip without Sparky, it almost seemed sinful. He had gone off to Ohio State University, it was a doctor he hoped to be some day. And apparently he was uncommonly gifted at biology, since he told us that this year he would be staying in Columbus to spend the break with his *'fiancée's'* family. *"Oh brother,* looks like he'll be the first," I thought to myself. Walking over to the counter I set my dirty dishes into the sink, and peeked out the window. Yep, it was Paulie, or should I say *'Seaman Paul Michael Pulchoski,'* trotting up to the back door, no doubt in search of breakfast number two. My buddies were the most famous *chowhounds* in New England, *legends* really. I'll wager that there was not a supper table in fifty square miles that they had not visited at least once! There was a sharp rap at the wooden screen door and then Paul invited himself inside.

"Morning all," he said with that booming, happy voice of his. Paul was the type that made friends easily. People just liked him right away, like a big, goofy footed puppy.

"Hey Paulie," I answered and walked over to give him a hug and an enthusiastic, *but cautious* thump or two on the back. Ever since that one summer with his sister Sandy I had been expecting an ass whipping sooner or later. But to my pleasant surprise, she had proven to be quite discrete over the years, which only magnified my guilt in the eyes of the Lord I suspected.

"Ah well, life's lessons are chosen for us, our part is the learning, *that's the hard part after all,"* I thought to myself.

"Hey Peepers," he replied, thumping me much harder than I expected?

Coughing up a little of my breakfast I choked out, "EASY big guy, save some of me for Kenny to manhandle!" Paul ignored me and walked over to mother and hugged her while she sat at the table.

"Hello Paul, you're looking well son, how's your family?"

"Their all fine Mrs. Kelly, just fine, Mom said to say hello."

"Do you have any bacon to go with this porridge on the stove," he asked leaning over the pot of oatmeal?

"You know I do Mr. Pulchoski, I'll fry some up for you straight away, take a seat now," Mom said getting up from her chair.

"Thanks Mrs. 'K'," Paul replied swinging his leg over the back of a chair and sitting down.

He tucked a napkin into his shirt collar making an amusing little bib for himself and waited to be served. I have to admit, the Navy seemed to be working for him, and he looked really good, healthy and strong. They must have worked him pretty hard at boot camp because he was at least forty pounds leaner and in the best shape I had ever seen him in. Good for him,

I bet he would make those roughneck hooligans at the *'PizzaBurger'* think twice before they ever messed with him again, or any of us for that matter. I smiled and brought him a glass of milk and a banana, taking a seat next to him. We chatted for another thirty minutes or so while he ate and then excused ourselves to gather my gym bag containing a change of clothes and a few possibles for our little trip. Shannon ran into my room, as we were finishing and jumped onto my bed.

"Ethan, will you be home tomorrow," she asked?

"I will."

"Ethan," she said coyly, "can I sleep in your room while you are gone?"

"Yeah sure squirt, just leave it dry as you found it ya *wee chiesller,*" I teased her, and swatted her with one of the pillows. She laughed and then stuck her tongue out at Paul, who then returned the left handed gesture of endearment. We all went out through the living room towards the kitchen together, and my mother was waiting with a sack full of sandwiches and fruit for the road.

"There you go boys, at least you'll have one healthy meal between now and Sunday," she said sarcastically.

"Thanks Mrs. 'K', " Paul said peeking in the large grocery bag and removing a *'Granny Smith'* apple.

"Where does he put it all," Mom said shaking her head and giggling.

"OK, we're off," I said kissing my mother and sister goodbye. Mother hugged Paul as well and pinched his ear. Paul made an attempt to hug Shannon, but she squealed and kicked him good and hard in the shin.

"OWWW, you little sh----- ahhh, sorry Mrs. Kelly, *but she started it,"* he said, pointing at Shannon who was now hiding behind me.

"On you're way now boys, on your way," Mom said tiredly.

"And make sure you drive safely Paulie, remember, that's my first born in the seat next to you!"

"Oh, and give my best to your mother and dad," she called after us as we jogged to the car.

Jumping into his '66 Mustang like Batman and Robin, Paul fired up the motor and we left a little rubber in the drive as we backed into the street, the road trip officially on. I turned around in the seat and watched my waiving mother and sister getting smaller and smaller as we approached the four-way stop at Elm and Spruce. We both stuck our hands out our windows and waived as Paul cruised through the intersection, honking his horn in a farewell salute.

Kenny was waiting for us on the parkway in front of his house, sitting on his duffel bag. He was in his usual spring attire, gabardine slacks, a stylish polo shirt, and freshly polished penny loafers, by far the best dresser of the group. He certainly put the two of us to shame, what with Paul in his Navy dailies and a buzz cut, and me in jeans, tee shirt, sneakers and a shaggy mop of sandy brown hair, at least a couple months overdue on a trimming!

"Dudes, what took you," he asked?

"No, let me guess, Paul had to strap on the feedbag again!"

"No I didn't," Paul said, louder than an innocent man would need to.

"Dude, there's oatmeal on your shirt goofball," Kenny said pointing at Paul as he tossed his bag and himself into the back while I held the door open and the seat forward for him.

I jumped in after Kenny and closed the car door. Ken waived to his Dad who was watching us from the bay window, a large Chinese Elm in front of the house casting a morning shadow across the porch. His Dad waived back and then walked away carrying Kenny's little brother, letting the drapes fall back to cover the window.

"Drive on swabbie," Ken said, and the *'three amigos'* were on the road again.

We went through town past the State Capital building and then hopped on Interstate 87 heading south towards Cooperstown, about seventeen miles outside of Oneonta. I reached over to the radio and switched it on, Led Zeppelin's *'Black Dog'* blared from Paul's newly installed quadraphonic stereo system, it was *bitchin!* I quickly made a mental note, have to compose a list of frequently used words that may be inappropriate for fledgling priests, *and do it soon Ethan*

(hearing my mother's voice in my head)! We rode along a while just listening to the music and looking out the windows, watching the brilliant colors flash by, drinking in the countryside without any conversation at all. It was Kenny who broke the silence just as the local DJ finished telling all of New York State, *'that was The Beatles and Revolution, can you believe these guys are really breaking up,'*

"Hey, what's in the bag Kelly?" He didn't wait for an answer and grabbed the shopping bag from between Paul and I, and started rummaging through it. Finding an apple to snack on he took a loud bite and then pulled out his second course, a homemade chicken salad sandwich. And that was that, the feeding frenzy was on, and by the time we reached the turn off for Cooperstown the only thing left uneaten was the paper shopping bag, and Paul was searching *that* for potato chip crumbs!

"Man, I gotta take a whiz," Paul said, fidgeting uneasily in his seat.

"Yeah, me too," I added.

"That makes it unanimous, I need to piss like a race horse," Kenny chimed in from the back, wrinkling his nose and grimacing.

"We'll whip into 'Jackie's Place' just before town and hit the head," Paul said, he was Navy now, so he said *'head'* instead of bathroom? We all tried thinking *dry* thoughts until we got to our destination, ETA approximately nine minutes according to the sailor in the driver's seat. But then the rain started, *of course!* By the time we pulled up to *'Jackie's Place'* it was pouring, and we were climbing over one another trying to get out of the car and into the restroom. We hit the front door with a crash and ran past Jackie herself and a handful of startled patrons on our way to the potty.

"Hi Jackie"

"Yo Jackie"

"Hey Jackie," we said in unison, racing past her in a all fired hurry.

"What the----," she started to say, but we were in the bathroom before we could hear the rest. The three of us surrounded the toilet like we were at a campfire, fiddling with our pants, Paul had a tough time navigating those thirteen buttons. Then we had ourselves a *group pee.*

"Good thing we aren't chicks, we'd have to try this squatting," Kenny said sheepishly.

"Quit your yapping Einstein, it's affecting your aim," Paul snapped! We heard the door open behind us and Jackie peeked in, she was just in time to hear our *'group sigh'* of relief.

"AHHHHHH..."

"Good Lord boys, were you raised by wolves," she asked sarcastically? She rolled a mop and water pail just inside the door, "make sure you use this and leave my bathroom as clean as you found it," she said giggling and shaking her head.

"Now I've seen everything, wait till Father hears about this one," she said laughing harder now.

"SORRY JACKIE," we all said together, as we finished our business.

"Hey, *watch the pants Paulie,"* Kenny quipped!

"Shut up doofus," Paul quipped back, starting the thirteen button drill in reverse!

"We're idiots, this will be all over town in an hour," I said reaching for the mop and pail.

"I wonder what the lunch special is today," Kenny and Paul said at the same time, punching each other in the arm while I swabbed the deck.

"You guys can't possibly be hungry already," I said straightening up and pushing the hair back out of my face.

"*Shut up Ethan, we're on vacation,*" Paulie shot back, drying his hands with a paper towel.

I set the mop back in the pail and the three of us exited the bathroom and went back into the diner. As we walked through the swinging doors we were greeted by Jackie and her staff as well as two good-natured locals seated at the counter, arms raised high, in a full on *'apple juice salute.'*

"*Well done boys,* **well done,**" Jackie said, barely getting the words out through her belly laugh.

The three of us just blushed and took seats at the counter next to the locals, what a way to start the trip! "*Well,* at least Uncle Chuck wasn't here to record this for *posterity* in Ethan Kelly's *'book of dumb ass stunts',*" I thought out loud to myself, there was *that* to be thankful for. "*Oh man, another word for the list!*"

Seven

("...it ain't me it ain't me, I ain't no Senator's
son no, it ain't me, it ain't me, I ain't no
fortunate one"...CCR)

Cooperstown, New York, April 1969
Spring Break

Paul threw the Mustang into reverse and started to carefully back out of his spot in front of the diner, while Kenny worked on his smile with a toothpick in the back seat. I couldn't believe it was still raining so hard, I also couldn't believe that those two had put away a short stack of buttermilk hotcakes apiece either. *Ah well, the legend continues!*

"HEY, WATCH OUT PAULIE," Ken hollered, pulling his knees up to his chest, preparing for impact!

"OH SHIT," Paul exclaimed! He hit the brakes and we all slumped forward in our seats as an old geezer in a brand new lily white Dodge Ram crawled past us, absolutely oblivious to the close call.

"Sorry Ethan," he added sheepishly, looking over at me, shrugging his shoulders and grinning.

"I'm counting on you to make sure that there is a special place in Hell for *'A-holes'* like that," Paul said through gritted teeth!

"Don't think that'll be *my* call buddy"

"Well you better make some noise about it then, or it won't be Father Kelly I'll be calling ya, it'll be Father *WANKER!*"

"Good one Paulie," Kenny chimed in.

"You know, it's a full time job praying for both you heathen *Eejits!*"

"Be thankful that we're not out in this downpour, catching our death putting your bumper into the trunk," I added for good measure.

"*Man*, you were a lot more fun when you were just a *plain old sinner* like the rest of us," Kenny said coolly, tossing his toothpick at me from the backseat. Paul pulled out of the drive and we rode the rest of the way into town in silence. As we turned onto the main drag the rain started to let up some.

"About time," Paul muttered under his breath. He slowed down to coast past the 'Hall of Fame' so that we could get a good look,

"There it is, the place where the great ones come to live forever," I said.

"OH YEAH," we said in chorus. We looked back at one another and grinned like grade school kids. Kenny slapped Paul on the shoulder and said, "Let's get to your Aunt's place and get settled, *peanut*." Kenny really emphasized the *'peanut'* part, which he knew drove Paul absolutely nuts, no pun intended!

"*In your ear Kenny,* I got your peanut, I got you peanut *hangin* right here Paley," he said sarcastically from over his shoulder!

Peanut was what his Aunt Ester had always called him. I think it was because as a newborn he was so dimpled, and had a head full of wispy white hair, just like a *ten-pound* peanut shell she would say. She and her husband Bill had lived just around the corner from 'Doubleday Field' since he retired in 1950. He had been a steeplejack for 35 years in New York City, and had walked the *'high iron'* during the construction of the Empire State Building, way back in the day! They had taken his savings and bought a nice and big Victorian home on Primrose Avenue. Several birch and elm trees, as well as Uncle Billy's prize-winning rose-garden, and a huge wrap around porch surrounded it. The home was much larger then the two of them really needed, having never had children of their own. But they kept it full of life with a cross-eyed German Shepard named 'Prince,' two cats named 'Harley and Reilly,' and a wise cracking cockatiel named 'Clifford' who ruled the roost. Aunt Ester referred to the gaggle of pets as her *'home team.'* It was comforting to know that she had them around, what with Uncle Billy having passed this Thanksgiving last. This was where we always stayed on our annual trips to officially celebrate the start of yet another baseball season. You just can't beat 'Spring Training' in Cooperstown, the town is quaint and beautiful, and besides the Hall, there was usually an *'old-timers'* game on the first Saturday of April at Doubleday Field. If you were lucky you might get a chance to watch and meet legends like *'Stan the Man Musial,' 'Pee Wee Reese,' 'Gil Hodges,'* or maybe even *'DiMaggio'* himself! Imagine that, the *Yankee Clipper's* name on my ball glove, now that would be Heaven on Earth for true! I had read in the Gazette just before supper, that Yogi would be in town this week, and I hoped to get him so sign our gloves, Dad's and mine. *Man,* if I could pull that off, *oh man!* The first thing I would do when I got home would be lay out on Da's spot in the yard an tell him all about it. Paul honked the horn as we pulled into the drive. Aunt Ester waived at us from her rocker on the porch as she rose to greet us.

"Hello boys," she said with that gravely, whiskey voice of hers. "Come over here *'peanut'* and give your Auntie some sugar!"

"*Ahhh*, Aunt Essie," Paul whined.

She swatted him on the shoulder with her hand and the flesh on her heavy arm wagged back and forth. Then she grabbed his face with both her chubby little hands as he stooped down to have his cheek bussed. Aunt Ester kissed her nephew and then *reset* her dentures. Those things were always coming undone. You really had to pay close attention when she spoke to you with all the clicking and clacking and what not.

"OK you two, come and get yours as well," she said gesturing to Ken and I.

"*Oh MAN*, this always freaks me *OUT*," Ken said under his breath.

We walked over and submitted to the ritual greeting. I laughed out loud as I trailed behind Kenny, actually looking forward to my turn at a geriatric wet kiss, they always tickled and made me shudder. It reminded me of my own Great Aunt Helen who would pucker up from across the room and track me down with her eyes closed. And although I could never prove it, I was convinced that she had her own sonar, just like a vampire–bat. So in comparison, Aunt Essie's little busses were not so bad. At least Aunt Essie didn't have a moustache like Sparky's Aunt Florence. Now that was uncomfortably weird!

"Ethan Kelly, you're a head taller than the last time I saw you," she said resetting her smile after kissing me hello!

"I declare you boys are growing like weeds!"

"I hope you're hungry, I've been cooking all morning you know." We could smell the pot roast and the candied yams from the porch as we walked into the parlor.

"I could eat," said Ken cheerfully.

"Me too," Paul chimed in.

"Good Grief," I said bewildered, knowing that those two were not just being polite! We lugged are bags into the guest rooms and went to wash up for yet another meal, *oh brother!*

Sitting in a rocker on the front porch after supper, I closed my eyes and enjoyed the sound of the light *drizzle* hitting the awning. The guys were helping with the dishes and keeping Aunt Essie in stitches with their tales from the neighborhood, as well as Paul's hilarious imitation of his drill instructor from boot camp. I yawned and stretched in the chair and looked at my watch, it was four in the afternoon. I was looking forward to getting over to the *Hall* and wandering through all of the displays, and memorabilia. Things like the Babe's uniform, and the last baseball he ever autographed, not to mention Ty Cobb's cleats! I wondered if there would be any blood on those things, what with all the stories of his tendency to spike opponents on the base-paths? Sure, we had seen most of these things over and over through the years, but for my friends and I, each visit was like the first. Maybe this was how if felt to be *'in love'* I thought? Nah, *what a dope Ethan*, there had to be more to loving an actual person, after all, they could love you back! But even so, I hoped that if I were ever to have an opportunity to fall in love, it would come with this same wonderful, *toasty warm* feeling. You know, the one that rushes through your body like a hot shower on a cold December morning. Or the *giddy* anticipation you experience while you count the minutes before Christmas morning. Or the rush you feel through your body when someone just *gets you.* You discover how good it feels to *not have to be anyone else but YOU!* Of course, baseball may not inspire those things in everyone, but no matter how old we got, the love for the game was always fresh as the day our Dad's first taught us to catch and throw a hardball. Yeah man, it was still very cool.

"*Dude*, quit your daydreaming and let's hit it, we're burning daylight," Kenny said, swatting the crossed leg off of my knee as he passed by.

"Yeah, let's go Father Kelly, before they elect you Pope," Paul added, following Ken to the *Stang.*

"Leave the poor boy alone, you ruffians, he doesn't have to go, he can stay here with me and watch the television," Aunt Essie said, taking a stance behind my rocker.

"You want to stay behind and take it easy Ethan dear?"

"No ma'am, I'm fine, couldn't miss the Hall, I've been waiting all year for this!"

"Alright dear, you run along and catch up with the others, I'll be fine here," she said pouting, making me feel a little like I *should* hang back and keep her company. Then she shot me a smile and winked saying, "I'm just pulling your leg boy, *land sakes, young people are so gullible!*" She laughed and laughed as I jumped into the shotgun seat and closed the door behind me.

"Glad you could make it Ethan, thought you might have stayed behind in *geezerville* to catch Ed Sullivan," Paul said sarcastically.

"Ed Sullivan's on Sunday nights stupid," Kenny said, correcting Paul's mistake.

"All right Einstein, just because TV Guide's the only thing you ever read," Paul chided back.

We slowed down to cruise past a couple of local girls walking toward the intersection. Kenny stuck his head out the window, *"Ladies,* plenty of room back here for you, need a lift?" Not the most original line, but appropriate given the weather conditions, and it usually worked in a small town like this as well. The two girls giggled and stopped to chat, the taller of the two catching Paul's eye right away. "Are you going by *'Mickey's Place'* on Main Street," the tall brunette asked?

"We are now," Kenny answered for the car!

"OK, you guys look harmless," the girl said, whispering something into her friend's ear.

"I'm Rebecca and this is Bridget," she said gesturing to her shy blonde friend.

"Well I'm Ken and the big man at the wheel is Paul, and the silent one next to him is Ethan," Kenny said making the introductions.

"Oh yeah, Ethan is going to be a priest, so you don't have to worry much about him," he added grinning.

"Scoot up and let the girls in doofus," Paul said tapping me on the arm with his finger.

"Uh, sorry," I said weakly, scooting forward in my seat and opening the door.

The two of them climbed in back and I closed the door behind them. Paul put the car on gear and off we went on our little detour before the Hall. Paul fiddled with the pile of eight track tapes on the floor and selected a little Santana for the ride over to "Mickey's." Nothing like some hot Latin licks to warm up the honeys he always said. I had to admit, it did get the blood pumping, but I only had his word for the rest.

"Nice, I love Carlos Santana," Rebecca said from the back, she was sitting behind Paulie. Ken had maneuvered himself between the two girls before

we had even pulled away from the curb, the boy was quicker than greased lightning!

"Yeah, he's one of my favorites too," Paul said.

"*Hey man,* I heard that there was going to be a big-ass festival or concert somewhere around here, later this year," Ken said. He had already managed to work in his patented *'yawning move,'* and had positioned an arm around each girl. They leaned forward in the seat and looked at one another.

"*Oh my God,*" Bridget mouthed to her friend as they looked back at Kenny with a peripheral glance. Rebecca just waived her friend off and leaned back in her seat.

"Yeah, I heard that too, it's supposed to be at some farm near Woodstock, Nester's farm I think," Rebecca said chewing loudly on a stick of gum.

"*Bitchin,*" Kenny said using only his coolest vocabulary.

"Yeah, I think I heard that Santana will be there, and Jimi Hendrix, and The Who, hey, maybe the Beatles will show up," Bridget said excitedly!

"*Nah,* the Beatles are breaking up, we heard that on the way down here," Paul said glancing back over his shoulder.

"Yeah, well you never know," I said hopefully, trying to be supportive, Bridget *was* awfully cute!

"Shut up Kelly, you don't know *jack,*" Kenny scolded!

He was right of course, I really wasn't much of an authority on this subject, and even less of one when it came to girls. I suddenly had the feeling that I was about to be ditched. Let's see, I'm with a sailor on leave, and a major horn-dog, **yep**, they're gonna to send me into a drug store for sodas or something and then ditch me as soon as I get out of the car. I thought about it for a minute, was there any way out of this situation? *Hmmm,* not likely, at least not without tipping their hand. Thereby risking a decent *ass kicking,* or, at the very least an *atomic-wedgy.* Spoiling my buddies' chance at *making out* with some of the local talent would be sorta un-cool I reasoned. So, I decided that discretion would be the better part of valor, opting for the *'silence is golden'* path, and prepared myself for the inevitable. These guys were going to earn me tons of extra credit in the *prayer department* back at Holy Cross, they were a virtual warehouse of material!

"*Hey,* who's thirsty," Kenny said grinning ear to ear, *oh brother, that didn't take long!* Paul pulled up to the curb in front of the five and dime. He put the Mustang in park and reached into his jeans pulling out a couple of bucks.

"Ethan, you're closest, be a pal and run in and get us some root beers," he said, winking at me. I looked at the money in my hand, four dollars, exactly the price of admission at the Hall of Fame up the street, gee what a surprise!

"Yeah, *OK*, I'll be *RIGHT BACK*," I said, shooting him the three-fingered *'boy scout'* salute, hoping he could *'read between the lines.'* Now technically I didn't actually *say the word*, but it was implied, so I felt compelled to find a way to work it on there. Thinking to myself, *"he does see it all ya know, **damn it!"** Oh man*, there's another one, this was just going to be one of those days! Jumping out onto the sidewalk I closed the door behind me. I could see Rebecca climbing into my vacated seat through the reflection in the storefront window. I smiled to myself and went inside hearing the car peel out, they couldn't even wait for me to get out of earshot, *my pals!*

Walking up towards 25 Main Street and the Hall, I chewed an Abba-Zabba candy-bar and sipped on some Hires Root Beer. Fortunately the rain had not started up again, even though the clouds were dark and fat with water. The wind was blowing the maple trees along the parkway in a northerly direction up the street, almost as if they were guiding me to my destination. I turned up the collar on my jacket and tossed the half empty root beer bottle into the waste barrel next to a newspaper stand. And there it was, big as life across the street, the brick shrine that was the focus of our trip. Well, at least it still was for me at this juncture I thought, smiling to myself. I paid my four bucks and went inside, the building smelled of old leather, and horsehide, it was wonderful. Soaking up all of the ambiance, I went immediately to the Yankee shrine and counted up all of the championship pennants that hung from the ceiling. I looked at all the team photos, 'the Bronx Bombers,' 'Murder's row,' as well as pictures of all the great ones like, 'DiMaggio,' 'Ruth,' and 'Gehrig.' This was always my first stop, and I touched the glass of each display twice, once for me and once for Da, he was with me, I felt pretty sure of that. It was a long time before I checked my watch, and I was not surprised to learn that I had killed three hours roaming from room to room.

It was nearly 9pm and I could see that the place was getting ready to close. Nine o'clock was pretty late in a small town and I'm sure that most of these people had supper waiting for them, so I made my way towards the exit. Stepping out into the night I caught a chill as the wind hit me in the face. It was just starting to rain again as well, and the guys were nowhere in sight. I thought for sure that they would have been back by now, ***crap,*** now what was I going to do! It was not that far of a walk, but it was beginning to rain pretty darn hard. I didn't want to call Aunt Essie because she couldn't see worth a flip in the daytime much less at night and in a rainstorm, Lord above, I was *screwed*. Oh boy, two more for the list, I was turning into Paul! I decided to wait it out at the coffee shop across the street, at least I would be warm and I had enough dough on me for some pie and a cup of coffee. The bells attached to the door jingled lively as I waked in and I stamped my feet and shook off the weather while I removed my jacket.

"Sit anywhere son," the elderly waitress said as she tidied the booth in the corner. I sat at the counter and turned the big white ceramic cup right-side up to indicate that I was ready to be served. I checked out the pies and cakes in the revolving display case to my left and set my sights on a piece of coconut cream pie.

"Coffee," the waitress asked, already pouring?

"Yes ma'am" I reached for the creamer and the sugar bowl, guiltily scanning for Uncle Chuck, just in case.

"You hungry?"

"That pie there looks pretty good, I'll have that."

"The banana cream or the coconut cream?"

"Coconut please," I said smiling back at her. Actually it was more of a grin, why was I so awkward around women I wondered?

"Coconut it is, last piece, made it myself you know," she said giving me a quick wink.

I stirred my coffee and blew on it a little while I took a sip, sweet and creamy, just the way I like it! The rain was hitting the window pretty hard now almost falling sideways in all of the wind. I wondered where the guys were, but shrugged it off, wherever they were they were dryer and warmer then I was, *a lot* warmer I suspected.

"You going to be alright in this rain son, you want to call someone for a ride," the waitress asked, concerned?

"Do you think it will rain much longer," I asked?

"I expect so, maybe you should call someone."

"Yeah, guess you're right, where is the payphone?"

"It's in the back by the john, can't miss it"

"Thanks," I said and took another sip of my coffee.

I walked over to the front door and looked out through the glass to see if Paul had pulled up in front of the Hall across the street. I mean, he knew what time they closed the place and he knew I was on foot. No luck though, the museum looked deserted, so I walked over to the payphone, digging for a dime in my pocket on the way. I dialed Aunt Essie's number and she picked up on the tenth ring.

"Hello," she said softly, I could hear Prince barking in the background.

"Hi Aunt Essie, it's Ethan."

"Oh Ethan, I'm glad you called, your Mother and Uncle Liam are here."

"What," I said surprised?

"Is everything alright, is Shannon OK, why are they there, what's the problem, what's going on any---?"

I was cut off in mid sentence by the sound of my Uncle Liam's voice, "Sonny, where are you and the boys now," he asked? His voice was very business like and it didn't make me feel very comfortable. I told him where I was and that the fellas were out on a date, sort of. Uncle Liam said that he would be by straight away, and he would tell all about it when he got there. I hung up the phone, went back to the counter and sat down. *"What on Earth was going on here,"* I wondered to myself. My face must have given me away, and the waitress returned asking, "Everything OK young man?" I looked up startled and said, "Oh, yeah, no problem, *nothing really.*"

"Well, you don't look like everything is OK." "Did you find a way home anyway?"

"Yes ma'am, there's someone coming right over."

"Good! Well then, eat your pie before your ride gets here," she said sliding the desert plate a little closer to me. I really had lost my appetite since the phone call, but I wolfed down the slice in record time, more to please the waitress than anything else. I finished off the coffee as well and declined on a refill. Uncle Liam pulled up out front in his big blue Caddie and tooted his horn.

"Gotta run, thanks for the snack," I said waiving goodbye, leaving the folding money for the tab on the counter, and a buck and a half *tip* in quarters in the saucer.

"Hi Uncle Liam," I said climbing into the front seat next to him.

"Hello Ethan son, this weather's a fright boy, you could catch your death."

"No need to worry, I was waiting out the rain in the diner, it was plenty warm in there Uncle."

"Ah, you're right of course sonny, good thinking."

"So what brings you and Mother out here when I'm due to be home tomorrow?" My Uncle didn't answer right away and that bothered me. *"Uncle,* is there something wrong, is everyone OK, *what's up anyways,"* I asked a little sterner than was polite from a child to his elder.

"Ethan, don't worry son, everyone is health and happy, there are no emergencies that brought us here," he said calmly.

"Well then what's so important that it couldn't wait until I returned home to tell me about?"

"Truth is Ethan it was your mother that insisted we come today, if it were left to me I would have waited until tomorrow," he said waiving his hand in the air in a dismissing manner.

"What's she all fired up about Uncle?"

"You got some mail today sonny, and she wanted to open it because it was from the Selective Service Bureau, you know, the draft board!"

"What the... But I'm in college, I'm supposed to be exempt from service as long as I'm a full time student, right?"

"That's what I tried to tell her, but she wouldn't listen to reason, you know how it is when she gets her Irish up!" That was true enough, mother was uncommon stubborn when she was angry, scared, or confused.

"Is everything well at school boy, I mean you're not flunking out are ye?"

"No sir, nothing like that, I can't imagine what this is all about," I said chewing a little on my thumbnail.

"Well, not to worry, there's nothing to be gained in that, for now I think your Mom would just be feeling better if you were at home." I nodded without answering, looking out the window at the driving rain, thinking to myself, *"my gosh,* these seats were posh, more like sitting on a sofa than riding in a car." I guess I should have been worrying some, but I just tuned everything out and we rode in silence back to Aunt Essie's.

Paul's car was in the drive and we pulled in behind it. We ran up to the house and shed our goulashes and coats on the mud-porch. Everyone was sitting at the dining room table, Mother and Aunt Essie were drinking tea and the guys were eating chocolate cake. I waived at the fellas and walked over to my mother. Leaning over I kissed her on the top of her head and pulled a chair up next to her. "Uncle Liam filled me in on your afternoon," I said, looking at her, my chin resting on my folded arms as they hugged the back of the chair that I was straddling.

"I see," she said cool, calm, and collected.

A *ruse* I suspected, I sensed that she was on her emotional edge. I waited for her to say something else, but she just sipped her tea and stared back. This was a crucial moment, because the wrong word on my part would start an avalanche of Gaelic of which I would only understand half. Being a veteran of many mother/son discussions since Da passed, I knew to be *quick to listen and slow to speak,* like the good book instructed. I raised an eyebrow slightly, trying to get her to smile and make the first move. That was the key to surviving one of her moods. Don't give her anything to tee off on. She put her hand to her mouth slowly, pretending to dab the corners of her mouth with the cloth napkin. I relaxed and smiled, game set and match, I had won the waiting game.

"*Darn you Ethan Kelly,* I came here to be mad at you!"

"Why would be getting a letter like this from the government son," she asked, waiving the envelope in front of me?

"Come now my dear, I'm sure the boy is not a radical," Uncle Liam said reassuringly.

"*Liam,* I'm asking Ethan, now let him answer for himself!" She looked back my way and studied my face, wrinkling her nose and squinting slightly.

"Well?"

"Well what Mom?"

"Are ye bad mouthing the President, God Bless Him, are you sitting in with all that *hippity yippity* rabble on campus?" That was it for Kenny, he couldn't control himself and he had an Uncle Chuck *'through the nose'* moment, colorfully complete with milk and cake.

"*Good gravy,*" Aunt Essie exclaimed, stepping up behind Ken and patting him hard on the back as he choked up his little snack.

"Are you going to be OK," she asked.

"Yeah, *yeah,* **urrgg,** I'll be fine," Kenny said, clearing his throat and blowing his nose into Aunt Essie's linen.

"I'll just get you some water," she said, walking quickly to the kitchen, Prince getting up from his blanket to follow.

I got up and got out of the way, walking with Mother and Uncle Liam into the parlor where we sat ourselves on the sofa. I assured my mother that I had not become a subversive in any way and that my grades were quite good actually. We would just have to wait until Monday to straighten this whole thing out, there had to be a logical explanation after all. My Mom seemed to be surrendering to our reasonable argument, my Uncle's and mine, and the mood around the house lightened somewhat. Aunt Essie and the guys joined us in the parlor and we decided to play crazy-eights, Aunt Essie's favorite card game. While she and Mother were getting the table set up for the game, I picked up the envelope and took a close look at it. *UNITED STATES of AMERICA: SELECTIVE SERVICE BUREAU* it read, so official, almost made me feel important. I tore open the envelope, removed the letter, and unfolded it carefully. Walking over to the reading lamp by the recliner I sat down and read it for the first time. *GREETINGS* the letter began, the rest was a blur of unrecognizable acronyms, confusing explanations and unbelievable instructions. None of it really registering, except for the last sentence, which simply read, *'You are ordered to report to the U.S. ARMY induction center, Buffalo New York, 23 May, 1969 where you will receive further instructions.'*

I looked over at my family and friends, they were laughing and teasing Kenny about his little episode. I made eye contact with my mother and smiled at her, folding the letter and placing it back into the envelope. There would be no sense in discussing this now, no good could come of it, no need to spoil the evening. I would wait until I could speak to someone in authority on Monday. I planned on getting up early that day and finding someone to assure us that this was all some innocent paperwork snafu. This was obviously a terrible, terrible mistake, some machine had been programmed incorrectly, something like that. I was only nineteen after all, and a future priest for goodness sake! What good would I be a jungle ten thousand miles away? I would never carry a weapon, I could never take a life, kill another human being, that was just nuts. I looked over at Paul and wondered what the future held for him, I mean he was already in the service, would he be going to Viet Nam? Did everyone who received these kind of notices end up on the other side of the world? I was getting a headache just thinking about it, and shook my head a little to clear away the pictures forming in my mind. I got up to join the others at the dining room table.

"Don't start without me," I called over to Aunt Essie who was shuffling the cards.

"You all right sonny," Mother asked?

"Yeah Mom, I'm fine ma'am," I replied.

"I'm just gonna grab a soda from the fridge," I said, rubbing her shoulder as I passed by.

Opening the refrigerator, I stuck my head deep inside and felt the cold air on my face. Grabbing a Coke, I straightened up and closed the door. Paul was standing right next to me, it startled me and I almost dropped the bottle of pop.

"What did it say Ethan?"

"Nothing, it was just a clerical thing, you know, they needed my social security number and student ID number, stuff like that," I answered unconvincingly, taking a long drink of Coca-Cola. Paul stared me down for a couple of seconds, making me a little uncomfortable.

"WHAT," I said sharply.

"Don't *bullshit* me Ethan, what was in the letter, or do I need to kick your ass and read it myself?" I swallowed hard and handed him the envelope. He didn't need to open it, the information was all over my face. My friend put his big hands on my shoulders and leaned forward so that our foreheads touched.

"We'll make some calls when we get home buddy, I got a couple mates in admin that can steer us to the right people."

"Don't worry, we'll work it out Peepers, you're the good one in the group, I'm sure God has better plans for you than busting your hump in some rice paddy," Paul said mussing my hair.

"Dude, you really need a haircut," he said making a face! I laughed and wiped a tear from the corner of my eye, then put the ice-cold pop bottle to my head to compose myself.

"You gonna be OK?"

"Yeah Paulie, I'll be fine, thanks ye heathen, I knew I wasn't wasting my prayers on you," I said slapping him on the shoulder. He laughed and put his arm around me as we walked back to join everyone else. Just before we reached the kitchen door Paul pulled me close to him and whispered in my ear, *"Ethan, I know about Sandy... I've always known."*

I stopped breathing and froze, waiting for the hammer to fall.

"It's cool with me, she was gonna lose it sooner or later anyway, better it was you than some loser!"

"Besides, now I have a *'get out of Hell free card'* and a *'guaranteed pass'* at confession for as long as *you* live," he said, laughing his ass off as we went through the door and sat at the table with the others. Oh man, *ass*, that's another one for the list, this pious stuff is really hard!

Eight

("...Oh great Googamooga, can't ya hear me talkin
to ya, just a ball of confusion"...the Temptations)

Oceanside, California, February, 1968
Camp Pendleton

Staff Sergeant Percy Marquette shook his head slowly as he watched
his graduating class of *spanking new* Marines toss their caps, brake ranks
and rush to meet family and friends for an afternoon of celebrating and
inebriating. His latest platoon of *'nubies'* was raw at best, and worse still,
no way were these kids ready for what they were in for. And what they were
in for, was patiently waiting for them, just a 13-hour plane ride from sunny
southern California. Most of these boys would nap quietly the entire flight.
But they were about to lose their innocence with regard to humanity, and
none of them would ever sleep quite as soundly after their tour, *he knew* this
to be true. Nobody knew that better than Sgt. Marquette, nobody. He had
barely escaped the madness himself following two tours *'in country.'* The
Lord or more accurately fate (Percy no longer believed in a God) had stepped
in when his mother passed on. The whole thing actually saved his life he
remembered. The trip home, the time with family and friends had broken the
spell he had fallen under. The *'death spell'* that consumes some warriors by
siphoning off all ties with their human soul, as they became *'one'* with their

own precision, with their craft, killing. It was a blood lust from which some men, *boys really*, never recovered.

"Hey Gunny, come with us to Diego on liberty, *ese*" hollered Pfc, Arturo *"Junior"* Martinez. He was standing with a small crowd of *'homeboys'* from his east LA neighborhood. Percy took notice of how the group sort of wore their own kind of uniforms, colorful plaid Pendleton shirts worn un-tucked, bandanas, an occasional hairnet and dozens of tattoos depicting *Jesus*, crucifixes, spider webs, and topless women.

"You go on ahead *'meat'* knock yourselves out!"

"But, **hey now**, y'all be sure that your little butts are back in my barracks by 1600 hours come this Monday," Sgt. Marquette shouted back!

"Your *bad ass* Uncle in the east has plans for each of you sorry *cherries!*"

Percy snapped to a quick attention and shot the lot of them a crisp salute, turning on his heels sharply, heading for his Quonset hut and the peaceful serenity of his desk and the air conditioner. He still had a stack of graduation certificates to sign, stamp, and run over to Division.

"Aye Aye, Gunnery Sergeant," Junior shouted, returning the salute while running as fast as he could in reverse trying to catch up with his crew and keep from being left behind. Percy stopped, turned and placed his hands on his hips, watching all of them climb into a steady stream of Chevy's. There were Impalas, Monte Carlos, Chevelle SS's, and a couple of chopped '56 and '57 wagons as well. He stood there and watched as they peeled out, laying rubber through the lot on their way out. He made a mental note to hold Junior personally responsible for this little break in the UCMJ (uniform code of military justice).

"Why do I always get all the *'beaners'*," he asked himself out loud? Now, Percy was not a prejudiced man or a racist by any means, he simply used the same term the *boots* themselves used whenever they referred to one another. At least it was the only term in *English* that he recognized. His last three classes consisted of primarily Hispanics, with an occasional white boy tossed in for seasoning. There never were many *'brothers'* at this camp, but hey, they were pretty close to the OJ, home of the *'mouse'* and his *amusement house*. Where you weren't likely to see a black man *'or dwarf'* for that matter, within ten yards of Miss Snow's lily-white behind! However, he wished that the brass would integrate the boots stateside rather than throw them together in the field. That never really worked out so well. Better to work out the colliding *race* issues here than *under fire* he thought.

"Ah the hell with it," he said under his breath, and started back towards his office.

As he walked, he pulled out the letter from his shirt pocket and opened it again. Re-reading the orders, he saw that they hadn't changed since this morning, surrendering to the fact that he would be serving a third tour, shipping out with this latest batch of *'sweet peas'* in the coming days. Fucking *'Charlie'* had really stirred things up with all that *'TET'* shit a couple of weeks ago. They were still pulling bodies off the wire at the firebase near Khe Sanh. And it was more of the same in Saigon and Hue and a hundred other towns, villages, hamlets, and forward bases from Da Nang to the DMZ. It hadn't been much of a military victory for the dinks so far, they were losing good men by the thousands as KIA's. But it was a real bitch for the big *'Green machine'* as well. Those little folk had been at war for the past twenty years, between the Frenchies and us. And they had darn near tunneled under every square inch of the country. NVA General Giap's plan was ambitious to say the least, involving tens of thousands in a simultaneous assault on as much of the South as they could reach. Where we used the air to rain death on as much of the North as possible, they used their tunnel system to appear and disappear from under our very noses in alarming numbers.

So even though the casualty figures were heavily in our favor, the fact that this event was playing out all over the USA on the evening news was having a severe effect on the supporters of the war effort. The peace movement was running at full speed and even the hard line hawks in Washington were starting to soften their stanch stands. There were rumors that Johnson might bow out of the presidential race in November. And the peaceniks were starting to trip over each other stepping up to the bully pulpit. Senator Eugene McCarthy was making a lot of noise saying all of the things that the hippies and radicals wanted to hear. But Percy's money was on Bobby Kennedy as a dark horse, it just made sense to him. *Hell,* Dr.King seemed to be a good choice too, but *no way* the country was ready for that much change!

Reaching his destination, Percy entered the hut, hung his cap on the rack inside the door, and walked over to the desk, flopping into his chair. Grabbing a clipboard full of certificates, he leaned back and put his feet up on the extended leaf. He glanced at the thick wad of papers and scowled, tossing the clipboard back onto the desktop, the loud thud resonating off the aluminum walls and ceiling.

"Damn it Gunny," said a voice from the rear of the hut!" Are you going to pout about those orders all the way to Monday?"

Lance Corpora, Lawrence A. Polen (the 'A' was for asshole if you asked anyone in Alpha Company) strode in from his bunk still in his stocking feet, rubbing the sleep from his eyes. Corporal Polen the exact opposite of his platoon Sergeant, was a thin pencil necked wiener, that sounded as if he could double for the Deputy Sheriff in Mayberry. He had made his grade because he was the only one in the outfit that didn't speak English as a second language. And he had mastered the military art of acronym-speak. In other words he was the poster child for *BORING!*

"*That will be all the familiar talk from **you** Mister,*" snapped Percy. He shot a menacing glare the corporal's way causing him to swallow so hard it made his pronounced Adam's apple waiver as if attached to a coiled spring.

"Uh, sorry Gunny, no offense," Corporal Polen stammered.

"Put your jump boots back on son, and ***get me a cup of coffee,***" Gunny ordered! He smiled as he watched his Corporal trip over himself trying to set a land speed record for obedience.

"*Shoot,* why couldn't all white boys jump through hoops like this, too bad this power didn't extend beyond the Corp," Percy thought out loud.

Cpl. Polen returned with the coffee and waited for Gunny to take a sip and nod approvingly before he dared return to his rack to finish his nap. Sergeant Marquette walked over to the window and looked out into the compound. There was the usual abundance of activity that preceded a full-scale deployment. All the equipment and specialty personnel (artillery, supply, motor pool, etc...) would be shipping out from San Diego bound for Okinawa and then the Republic of Viet Nam. The bulk of the grunt personnel, the rifle companies that would spend the next 13 months humping through jungles and rice paddies, would be bused to Los Angeles International Airport, where they would cram onto converted commercial jets assigned to special military duty. Percy took a long sip from his cup of coffee, and closed his eyes, the setting sun warming his face as it shined through the window.

"Man," he said softly to himself. "I'm gonna miss this *candy ass's* coffee," he said looking back over his shoulder at the form laying on the cot in the back of the hut. He lifted his cup in a genuine gesture of gratitude and walked back to the pile of papers on his desk, time to get back to work.

The music was loud as usual at these kinds of places. Strip clubs worked the same everywhere. Sure, some were higher class, but in the end, the girls got naked, you got drunk and dry humped, the house got your money, and you left with yourself and the lie that you'd end up telling the guys back home, about your '*from the pages of Penthouse*' night with three *hot* exotic dancers and one *nasty* little chimp! Junior Martinez was being carried out to his cousin Sal's Impala by a couple guys from his outfit. He was pretty drunk, but he was a happy drunk, and giggling all the way to the car.

"*Yo, ese,* did you see me with that chick?"

"*Man,* that *chica* in there was loving all of PFC 'ME,' *horale!*" Junior said, drooling just a little on himself as well as his buddy's arm.

"Shit Junior, can you keep your spit to yourself, you drunken wetback," shouted PFC Wesley Hightower.

"Hey, fuck you white boy, cut Junior some slack man," hollered PFC Angel Gonzalez from the other side of the load they were carrying to the car.

"Hey, *hey*, he don't mean nothin by it Angel," Junior said, slurring the words so much they didn't sound like English or Spanish, just *'Spanglish'* gibberish.

"Oh man, he's gonna puke," Hightower got out just as Junior *'ralphed'* all over his cousin's fine wheels.

"AYIEE, my *RIDE*, watch my **RIDE** *mensa, ah chingaso,* **mira this mess** ***homey,***" said Junior's cousin Sal. He walked over and kicked his tire, and then kicked at Junior as well, who was sitting on the curb with his escorts on either side propping him up. He wiped his face on Hightower's blouse and started laughing hysterically.

"God Damn It Junior, this is not funny, do you *read me* asshole," Hightower screamed, jumping to his feet, letting his friend tip over into the gutter, still laughing.

"Come on man, get up," Angel said, lifting his buddy by the shoulders.

Junior stood up and attempted to straighten his tie and discovered it was missing. He had a vague recollection of a girl working it off of him during a lap dance. Who then proceeded to amaze his group with her ability to stand the thin side of the tie straight up in her fist, and then take a good ten inches of it into her mouth, backing off slowly leaving it in tack and shimmering in the dim light of the bar. It was a work of art that they all appreciated to the tune of twenty bucks and one standard issue dress tie. It would cost Junior much more in blood, sweat and tears once Gunny got wind of the episode, and he always did. He just knew everything, that's why the boots called him Sherlock when he wasn't looking.

"Just get him in the back dudes, I need to drive you all back to LA, this night is OVER," said Sal disgustedly!

"Come on man, *RAPIDO cavacho*!"

"Alright, don't get your panties in a bunch *Pedro*," Hightower said, all Mexican's were *Pedro* to him. He and Angel worked Junior into the back seat and then crawled in on either side.

"Junior, I swear, if you puke in my car ***I'll shoot you myself!***" Sal said reaching under the seat and waiving a short barreled .38 over his shoulder, watching the three of them in the rearview mirror! His cousin just nodded and snickered quietly in a semi state of consciousness.

"Don't worry Sal, we'll watch him," Angel said from the back.

"Yeah, well you better dudes, or I'll shoot you too!" Sal fired up the motor and started to pull away when another Marine ran up to the car. He wasn't drunk like most of the others and Sal recognized him as the cousin of his sister-in-law Theresa.

"Hey ese, you trying to get wounded here and miss the party in Nam," Sal said sarcastically?

"Sorry, can I ride back with you to LA, my family is coming to see me tomorrow from Fresno before we ship out," the young Marine asked.

"Get in fool, before someone else gets the same idea, *come on we're outta here!*"

"I'm in, let's go joe," the Marine said smiling. Sal stepped on the gas and they moved quickly away from the "Gaslight" district just as the shore patrol was driving up to clean house.

"That was a close one," said Hightower from the back.

"*Oh man*, Junior really stinks homey! Crack open the windows and let in some fresh air," pleaded Angel and Sal in unison. They all cranked down the glass as fast as they could, sucking in lungs full of the clean, crisp ocean air as fast as they could.

"Whew, *fuchie capesta*," Sal said holding his nose from behind the wheel.

"We'll need to stop at a filling station before we get to LA and hose this *chongo* off," he continued.

"Works for me," chimed in Hightower, pushing Junior's head off his shoulder and over to Angel's side of the car.

"Hey man, what's with that," Angel protested.

"Look, he's one of you guys, I don't want a lap full of frijoles half way to LA, OK?"

"*Fuck you* Hightower," Angel shot back.

"Yeah, *fuck you gordo*," Sal added, waiving the .38 again and raising his eyebrows rapidly in the rear-view mirror for Hightower to see, *he did*. The car was quiet all the way to Long Beach when Angel said, *"Horale, ese*, I got to take a leak, you know?"

"Yeah, OK," Sal said and pulled over to the shoulder on the 405 near Lakewood Avenue. Angel squeezed out from the back as Sal leaned forward in his seat.

"Be right back dude," Angel said rapping the roof of the car as he ran into the ice plants to relieve himself. Sal flicked his zippo and lit up a cigarette, his face illuminated in the firelight for a moment. He took a long drag and exhaled the smoke out the open window.

"Hey, white boy, is my cousin still breathing back there or what?"

"Yeah, he's cool."

Sal looked over at his passenger seated next to him. The young Marine was fast asleep leaning against the door, his head propped up on the window. He reached over and poked him lightly in the arm.

"Hey, Mitchell, wake up man, you need to pee," he asked?

Pfc Mitchell Rojas stirred and opened his eyes. "Where are we man?"

"Dude, we're on the freeway beautifying America, got anything you want to contribute?" Sal teased, talking as his cigarette dangled from his mouth.

"No, I'm OK for now," Mitchell said sleepily.

He was tired from the late hour and not the late partying. That wasn't his style, he had always saved all of his money for his family, just like when he would boost in the summers. He missed his wife and children, he even missed his job at the Checkerboard Square feed company in Fresno. Mitchell had worked hard to become a real member of this nation, and had studied and studied to become a citizen. So he did not think twice about answering the call to arms when his draft notice came Christmas last. It would be his honor to serve. His family was so proud, so very proud. He truly believed that all things were gifts from God, and that the ones you do not understand, maybe even *especially* the ones that you don't understand, are blessings of some sort. And while he did not fully understand the politics of his new country's need for his sacrifice, it was enough to know that they were counting on him, that God was counting on him. His faith had always been strong, but after the miracle six years ago in the melon fields, he had stopped questioning God's will, his guidance of his life, and started to embrace the challenges, changes, and people that were brought in and out of his life. There was just so much peace to be had by turning his life over to his Lord. He didn't have the language skills to explain it, but he had the ability to show it by virtue of the way that he lived his life. Lead by example, that was what his personal ministry was all about, no? What he witnessed with that little girl so many years ago was the true power of unconditional love. And the reward for accepting his role in that event was the life of his beautiful son Miguel, praise God!

"Hey Hightower, where do you think they'll send in the Nam," he asked, turning around in his seat to face his buddy?

"I don't know man, all I know is we fly outta LA sometime next week, and land in someplace called Da Nang, from there who knows."

"You think we'll stay together as a unit," Mitchell asked, anxious for Hightower to agree?

"Man, you ask too many questions," the big man from Texas said, waiving his hand at Mitchell as if dismissing him.

"I heard that we might see action from the *get go*," said Angel as he climbed back into the car.

73

"Shut up Angel, you don't know shit man, none of us do," Hightower shot back.

"Eat me Hightower, we're Marines, you know that they're gonna send us somewhere *hot*, that's the drill ain't it," Angel said looking out the window as Sal pulled back onto the freeway.

"Shut up ALL of ya, I'm trying think dry thoughts down here," said a weak voice from the floorboards in the back.

Man, I gotta take a whiz," Junior said, starting to giggle again as he rejoined the *living* for a few moments of clarity.

"God Damn It JUNIOR," Sal said whipping back onto the shoulder and turning to aim the pistol at his cousin. Mitchell shoved open the door and Hightower jumped out pulling Junior with him as Sal fired a couple of rounds into the upholstery to show everyone that he was serious.

"Get over into those pucker bushes boy and do your nasty little business before the law dogs get out here on us," Hightower barked at Junior!

Junior stumbled towards the ice plants trying to pull open his pants to relieve himself, laughing uncontrollably as he weaved towards his goal. Angel and Hightower ran after him, helped him drop his drawers, holding him upright while he did his business. They opted to let him dress himself, leaning against the car, watching the comedy unfold. Twenty minutes later they were back on the road to Los Angeles, to spend a last weekend with family and loved ones before the short journey into hell.

Sergeant Marquette looked at his Timex, it was 13:30 hours on this cloudy Monday afternoon. He decided that he would stroll over to the barracks in fifteen minutes or so for a nose count and a lockerbox inspection. It always tickled him to see what kind of contraband the boots would try and sneak past him after a weekend of drinking and whoring. He had sent Corporal Polen over ahead of him get a lay of the land so to speak, **OK**, to spy to be precise. He knew that would spook the troops, and that it would cause them to relocate their prizes (garter belts, panties, Playboy's, and various other assorted pornography) to hastily chosen secondary locations. But there were only so many places to hide treasure in a Marine barracks, and Percy knew them ALL!

Looking out the window, he saw PFC's Hightower and Gonzalez *walking* Junior Martinez rapidly toward the barracks. Percy smiled broadly, *"well at least this tour was gonna begin with a little comedy,"* he muttered to himself. He placed his cap on his head and exited the hut, walking at a brisk pace to the barracks next door.

"ATTENTION ON DECK," screeched Corporal Polen!

The barracks snapped to attention at the foot of their bunks, chests out, chins in, like good Marines. Gunny walked the line slowly, looking from one side of the aisle to the other, a slow sweep of the area. He stopped in front of PFC Martinez's rack and turned to face him slowly. Junior was still looped from the weekend. And while his body was technically *at attention,* his eyes were definitely *at ease,* both of them so crossed it almost made Percy seasick just standing next to him.

"Private Martinez," Gunny asked sweetly.

"Are you in there somewhere son?" Junior did not answer right away, he started to make some noises, but there were no actual words. Gunny looked to either side of his favorite *'meat,'* settling on PFC Hightower, walking over to him and standing nose to nose. *"WHAT HAVE YOU DONE TO MY MARINE, MAGGOT,"* Gunny screamed, spittle spattering all over Hightower's face!

"Gunnery Sergeant, the Private had nothing to do with his condition, **Gunnery Sergeant!"**

"YOU CALL THIS NOTHING, LOOK AT THIS MESS!" Before Percy could take a verbal run at Angel as well, the uncomfortably silent barracks was filled with the sound of a tremendous stomach rumbling.

"Oh shit," said PFC Gonzalez, breaking formation and lifting the lid to Junior's locker box. Hightower was a millisecond behind his buddy as he spun Junior 180 degrees and bent him over the target, *just* in the nick of time. Percy watched in awe at the precision of this teamwork as his favorite *'meat'* emptied his stomach contents onto all of the personal items in his sacred locker box.

"JESUS H. CHRIST, what kind of happy horseshit is this people?"

"I want this place spic and span in exactly 30 minutes, do you read me ladies," Gunny screamed at the barracks in general!

"30 MINUTES, by my Timex," he said holding up his arm and pointing to his wrist. Sgt. Marquette spun on his heel and stormed out of the barracks.

"Dismiss this train wreck," he said to Corporal Polen as he passed him exiting the room!

"DISMISSED," stammered Lance Corporal as he ran off to catch up with Gunny on the way back to the office. Percy stopped to let Polen catch up with him.

"You know something Larry, if those guys cover for each other half that well in the bush, maybe we'll bring more than half of them home."

"Ahhhh, what do you mean **we** Gunny, my orders were for Camp Lejeune in North Carolina," Polen said nervously, smiling weakly.

"Funny thing about orders Corporal, only the bad ones are written in concrete, *only the bad ones boy!*" Gunny put on his shades and changed direction for the commissary, he guessed he'd get a cold drink before going back and kicking Junior's butt for **GP**. This was a nice distraction from the reality of shipping out, he might as well get some mileage out of these clowns before the truth sets in.

Nine

("...hello darkness my old friend, I've come to talk
with you again"...Simon & Garfunkle)

Boston, Massachusetts, May, 1968
<u>Holy Cross University</u>

Thud, thud, thud, the sound of a baseball bouncing off of a wall could
be heard resonating down the hall of the dorm. A half naked student leaning
against the wall, a bath towel wrapped around his waist maintaining his
modesty was sweet-talking someone over the community telephone.

"Hey man, knock of the noise will ya," he hollered at the unknown
antagonist!

Thud, thud, thud, **THUD,** "UP YOURS!" *Thud, thud, thud, thud,* came
the reply. I recognized the mystery voice as my roommate Sean, and I knew
the hallway *'Romeo'* as well, one Wilson Walter Woodbury. A real piece of
work, *chock full* of money, opportunities he didn't have to earn, and *himself!*
I smiled to myself, watching this familiar scene unfold, as I made my way
toward our room.

"*HEY ANDREWS*, I said knock it *OFF!*"

Thud, thud, thud, ***CRASH,*** the sound of shattering glass startled both
Wilson and myself. That wasn't a good sign, because I knew it meant that

77

my short fused friend would be coming after young Wilson like a screaming banshee. Deducing that there would be only a small window of opportunity to defuse this situation, I formulated a plan of action quickly. Taking off on a dead run I flew passed Wilson, grabbing his towel in the process.

"*KELLY*, you asshole," screeched Mr. Woodbury, frantically trying to cover himself with the telephone handset.

I made a mental note to only use the phone in the Library from now on! Reaching the door to my room a millisecond later, I was just in time to intercept Sean exiting in the opposite direction. He had the great equalizer in hand, a Louisville Slugger, the one with Pete Rose's autograph burned into the wood, his favorite *piece of ash* as he referred to it.

"Outta my way roomie, it's a rude bashing that wanker is asking for today," Sean said through clenched teeth, trying to get passed me, dressed in only his BVD's and a *ginney tee*. I stood my ground and used my height and weight advantage to block my friend's way.

"Move it Ethan, or you'll be getting a wood shampoo as well!"

"Take it easy ya *eejit*, take it easy, I handled it for ye," I said showing him the wet towel.

Sean settled down a second and peeked around me, just in time to catch a glimpse of Wilson's skinny backside as he disappeared into his room three doors down. Sean howled with laughter, doubling over, resting the bat across his knees. He straightened up and put his arm around my shoulder leading the way into our room. I looked back down the hall as I closed the door, checking for any sign of a counter attack. Sean and Wilson had been feuding since day one, so you could never be too careful. I turned in time to see Sean walk over to the busted out window and stick his fool head through the larger than expected hole. That baseball must have been tied to a brick given the severity of the damage. Of course he paid no attention to the jagged pieces of glass hanging all around his noggin, typical!

"YO, Weezer, toss up me ball over dere," he said pointing toward the commons. A big, bushy haired freshman, who we all called Weezer (he suffered from asthma), waived up to him and trotted off to fetch the baseball from the bright green lawn.

"That's a good lad Weez, chuck it on up here!" The big freshman picked up the ball, and did his best to imitate Koufax's wind up, then threw the ball to Sean with surprising accuracy and velocity.

"How was that Sean," he said, huffing and puffing after his ten-yard jog from the commons back to the stoop?

Chester Oliver Williams, Weezer's given name, was sort of a local celebrity around here. To say that there was a LOT of him to love would be an understatement of colossal proportions. But where the Lord gives us certain personal challenges, he also gives us certain gifts to balance things out. All you just had to do was figure out what they were, sort of like a twisted egg hunt. Our buddy Weezer must have been peeking while the bunny was busy hiding the eggs, because he was blessed with many more gifts than challenges. First of all he had a heart and a spirit that matched his amazing girth, and if there were a picture here you'd be saying WOW right about now! And, he was an uncommon genius with regard to anything mathematical, which made him a popular addition to most of the campus cliques, especially around mid terms and finals.

Let's face it, EVERYONE struggles with math. Only those gifted enough to speak it like a foreign language faired well, at least from my limited experience. It's funny how petty idiosyncrasies can be happily overlooked in exchange for free tutoring, if not for outright ghost written homework, at a modest price of course. If those weren't blessings enough, he also had the voice of an angel, one that rivaled any Irish tenor my parents ever dragged me to hear. Have you ever listened to a sound so incredibly sweet that if actually brought tears to your eyes?

"Nice throw Weezer, you holding out on the team big man," Sean said laughing? Chet laughed as well and waived him off, settling back onto the stoop and his pile of books and papers. Sean stepped over me as he moved from the window, I was busy picking up the larger pieces of glass from the floor. He walked over to his un-made bed and flopped down into the molded center, tossing the baseball up in the air and catching it as he landed with a squeaky thud.

"Just leave it Ethan, what it's to you anyway, you're otta here today aren't ya," Sean said nastily. So, the crummy mood continued, he had been pouting ever since he found out about the draft notice, and he grew more sullen with each passing day.

"Gimme a break Sean, its not like I enlisted ya know!"

"Yeah, well maybe if you had swallowed your pigheaded *Kelly* pride, and let Weezer take your trig and physics mid-terms you wouldn't have lost your deferment, now would ya knucklehead!"

He got me with that one, it was true, I could have skated on Weezer's good nature and kept my grade point average out of the red zone, but it just didn't seem right. Who knew that the Feds were watching so closely anyway? Mother and Uncle Liam had argued and pleaded my case with some world class whining all the way to our State Senator, striking out on three pitches. At least they swung for the fence each time, I was so proud of them. Worse still, it turned out that tapping Paulie's *'connections'* was a real bad idea, earning me a fast track to the Marine Corps instead of a chance at stateside duty with the National Guard. At least my family was able to arrange through the same State Senator for me to enter the service as a conscientious objector, where I would be trained as a medical corpsman. I had hoped that I might serve as a chaplain, but not being ordained seemed to be a deal killer. So, here I was, two days away from reporting to Buffalo for induction and then taking a bus ride to North Carolina and Camp Legjune.

"Let's call a truce OK Sean, I don't want to leave on a sour note buddy," I pleaded with my friend.

"I'll be back to school before you know it, a year or so tops," I said, failing to convince even myself.

"Yeah, whatever Ethan, you know how that goes, once things change they're never the same!"

"Not fair Sean, you know me better than that," I replied with a little attitude of my own.

"Ahhhhhh," was all the response he could manage, resuming his solo game of catch.

I had a notion that he actually felt left out somehow, that he maybe even toyed with the idea of following along, maybe even enlisting. Sean Andrews was a scrapper that was for true, but to his credit, he was more of a realist and philosopher of sorts. While he didn't run with the radical crowd, he did pay attention to their words and attended some of their protest rallies. And although he was raised as I was, in a strict Irish Catholic environment, taught from birth to respect honor, duty, family, God and Country. He was at just the right age to be led in whatever direction that caught the beat of his heart. Like most of us, he was just one inspiration or kiss away from jumping into a cause with both feet. I walked over and sat at the foot of his bed, catching the ball on it's way down with my right hand. Sean folded his arms and just stared at the ceiling defiantly.

"I thought we talked this all out at the boozer last night?"

"We did, but yesterday it was only talk, and today is today." I could think of nothing comforting to say, and tossed the ball up for him to catch.

"I need to get my stuff together, my Uncle will be here any time to drive me to Albany."

"Why don't you come and spend a couple of days with us Sean, I'll show you around, maybe run over to the Hall, you've never been?"

"Nah Ethan, that's time for your family and friends, they don't need a stranger in the house."

"Don't be such a knob Sean, your one in the same and you know it!"

"You've talked to my Mom and sister on the phone more than I have, so it's time they have a face to put with the voice."

"Yeah, ya think so?"

"Yeah, I think so," I said throwing some balled up socks at him, disrupting his concentration, causing the ball to hit right between the eyes.

"Ahhh, DAMN IT, Ethan ya eejit," he said jumping up from his bed, starting to take a run at me.

"**THE GLASS**, *the glass, watch out for the broken glass,*" I said warning him about the hazard before he ran through it in his stocking feet.

"You're a lucky man Ethan Kelly, I was gonna brain ya!" Weezer knocked loudly and stuck his head in the door at just the right moment.

"Hey Kelly, your Dad's outside, said to tell you to shake a leg."

"That's my uncle, Weez, tell him I'll be right down."

"OK, hey Andrews, better watch your step, Wilson's in the hall with a couple of balloons that I'm pretty sure aren't filled with water," Weezer added, giggling as he exited.

"*Oh man,* I'll run interference and stall Uncle Liam while you get dressed and pack a bag, and be quick about it or we'll hear all about it on the way," I said to Sean, tossing his duffel to him and grabbing my own. He shot me a quick okey-doke as he rolled back onto his bed, feet in the air, pulling on his trousers both legs at once. I slammed the door behind me hoping to startle Wilson into dropping at least one of his tainted missiles. I spotted him just outside of the lavatory, one balloon visible, and the other one presumably in his other hand behind his back.

"Where's that weasel roommate of yours Kelly," he asked sneering? Walking slowly, giving Sean time to get ready and figure out his next move, I nodded at Wilson.

"He'll be along any minute."

"Well, he'll be spending the rest of the day bathing in tomato juice when I finish with him," Wilson said, gently massaging the visible green balloon in his throwing hand.

"Don't you bet your life on it Willie boy, don't you bet your life," I said teasing, he hated when we called him that. Wilson sneered at me when all of the sudden there was a loud crash, more breaking glass! Weezer shouted from down the hall, "There he goes, that crazy son of a bitch jumped out the window!"

"Oh SHIT," yelled Wilson, and he took off on a dash down the hall heading for the front door, dropping the balloon he was holding behind him. *WHEW*, that was rank, he must have drank a whole six pack to come up with that much urine, *yukky*!

"Which way did he go Weez," Wilson screamed at Chester?

"Around the corner and over toward the Library I think," Chet replied, trying to keep a straight face. Wilson let out like his pants were on fire and disappeared around the corner. About that time the door to our dorm room opened and out strolled Master Andrews, duffel over his shoulder and a Dr. Pepper in his hand.

"Shall we go Mr. Kelly," he said nonchalantly.

"Indeed," I said coolly. And we walked over to meet Uncle Liam by his big Cadillac. Sean stopped over to high-five Weezer on the way, and they congratulated each other on a fine piece of deception.

"Later big man," Sean said saluting his co-conspirator.

"Pleasure working with ya, Andrews, you're a natural," Weezer said, returning the gesture.

"Come on boys, get your things in the trunk and lets go," Uncle Liam said, in a hurry as usual.

We threw in our duffels and hopped in the car, Sean in back and me at shotgun. I settled into the seat and looked around the campus as we drove towards the exit onto the main thoroughfare. This place was not home, but I already missed it like it was. The reality of my situation had not fully set in yet, but I knew it was coming, maybe when I hugged my family goodbye in Buffalo, maybe when I arrived at boot camp, or maybe when the plane landed in Viet Nam, sooner or later it was coming.

"Ethan, who's the chiseller in the back of me car now," my uncle asked?

"That's the famous Sean Andrews Uncle Liam, of the Long Island Andrews, wealthy merchants so I'm told," I said laying it on thick.

Uncle Liam glanced at Sean in the rear view mirror and studied him for a moment. The whole truth was that the Andrews family actually was a very large and successful shipping family, with a dozen merchant vessels sailing back and forth between New York and Portsmouth, England. Sean was the only child of Patrick Michael Andrews IV, a third generation merchant seaman that made his bones during the Second World War, freighting everything from food and medical supplies to ammunition and equipment to the allies. His shipping line was one of the few if not the only company to suffer zero losses during that period. Patrick Andrews took that reputation and built a small empire through the fifties and sixties, and Sean was his unenthusiastic heir apparent.

"*Ach,* he doesn't look too bright now does he," Uncle Liam commented snickering.

"He'll surprise you Uncle, he'll surprise you," I said, knowing that Sean was undoubtedly flipping my uncle off from behind his seat.

"Pleasure to meet you too Mr. Kelly sir, a real pleasure it is," Sean said far too politely.

I could see that this might be a long trip, so I scooted down in my seat and laid my head back against the soft cushioned rest. Closing my eyes, I suddenly wished I had taken the train, and I programmed myself to dream of my last trip home. I wanted to dream about that girl who had tugged at my heartstrings without even knowing it. I couldn't remember her name to save my life, but I would never forget her face! Those eyes, that soft sweet voice, the giggle that made me sigh out loud, and the smell of lilac. I took that vision into a deep sleep, knowing that my uncle must have been looking at me and wondering if I had gone completely daft, he may be right.

Ten

("...Trust in the Lord with all your heart, And do
not lean on your own understanding"...Proverbs 3:5)

Firebaugh, California, May, 1968

Tina could see that he was still taunting her, watching his reflection in the window. The morning light felt warm on her face as it beamed through the trees from her side of the big yellow school bus. She closed her eyes hoping that the action would also drown out the noise behind her, it didn't.

"*Tina, Tina, jellybeana, she's a witch just like Serena, twitch her nose and blink her eyes, and she will make the dead bods rise,*" sang a large curly headed sixth grader from across the aisle.

He laughed out loud and jabbed the kid next to him with his elbow. Hector smiled weakly, managing *not* to laugh along with the older boy who was responsible for all the commotion. He leaned forward, his head touching the seat in front of him. Hector tried to get Tina's attention and communicate with his eyes that he was only going along with the teasing to keep from getting pounded himself. Let's face it, being a ten-year-old and a minority in an overwhelmingly white public school was hard enough, no use rocking the boat by taking sides here. Besides, he knew that Tina was safe enough, the whole town watched after her anyway.

"**Hey now,** knock that crap off little man, do I need to stop this bus and write your name on the *giz list*," hollered our driver. The *giz list* was not someplace you wanted end up, unless of course you craved extra homework and didn't need recess in your life.

"No sir," Davie Myers said, sitting back down glaring at Tina.

Lionel Dupree had been driving this bus for the last couple of years, ever since he returned from his tour in Viet Nam. Not a particularly large man, in fact he was not much bigger than the Myers kid, who was pretty big for his age, standing in at five foot six inches. But it wasn't his stature that kept the peace, it was the look in his eyes. A look that projected scary images of unconscionable horrors and unknown demons, Lionel wasn't someone to mess with or cross, you just knew that. But the *look* was all he ever needed, nobody ever pushed him beyond that and once the situation was cooled, he was back to the happy-go-lucky fella that all the teachers and parents knew and loved.

"What about you Hector, are we cool?"

"Yes sir," Hector mumbled.

"That's better, we're cool babies, *we're cool*, **right**," Lionel said, a big smile contradicting a menacing stare!

Tina turned her head towards the aisle, opened her eyes and looked directly at Davie and Hector. She smiled at them, and the curly haired bully started to say something, but suddenly just looked down at his shoes instead. Hector leaned back and smiled over at his little friend from around the big sixth grader. The bus lurched forward as it pulled away from the curb and continued the five-mile trip to Nestle Avenue Elementary School. Tina twisted 180 degrees in her seat, pulled her knees up and tucked her feet underneath her. She lay her head on the thinly covered backrest and watched the world pass by the window. Focusing her attention on the telephone lines, she concentrated intensely, a game she liked to play because it made her tummy tingle, like a roller coaster she imagined, although she had never actually ridden one. She smiled and giggled to herself, her little head bouncing lightly on the backrest in time with the rhythm of the road.

"What a weirdo," Davie Myers mumbled to himself, watching the little girl out of the corner of his eye.

"Shut up Davie," Hector said under his breath, hoping he had not actually been heard, silently cursing his sudden burst of courage! "Right on little brown brother, *right on*," Lionel said, flashing his big toothy grin at Hector through the rear-view mirror. It was 8:15 in the morning, the day just starting for most, just ending for some, and quite possibly the last day on earth for one.

Victor Lopez finished topping off his pick-up truck and tapped the nozzle of the gas pump on the rim of the tank. Turning slowly to his left he re-hung the handle and hose with one hand while he spun the gas cap back in place with the other.

"*Oh man*, I better wash up," he said out loud, catching a whiff of his hands and frowning.

His wife Maria really hated the smell of gasoline and seeing as he was headed home for a late breakfast he thought that he would wash up early for her sake. Victor and a small crew of day laborers had been out all night baling hay in the cool of the darkness, a common practice. It's a process that needs to be performed while there is plenty of moisture in the air in order to keep the bales tight and neat. Then, after a couple days drying in the hot sun, he would return with a new crew and a bale wagon to collect the bundles. In the mean time he was tired, hungry, and anxious to get home to the hot meal that he knew Maria would have waiting for him. *Lord above*, how he loved that woman, she was so much more than he deserved, he knew that. But, to his credit, he had made it his personal mission to give her the best life that he could manage, and to fill it with as much happiness as she could possibly stand.

He never did understand how such a beautiful woman could fall in love with such an ordinary man as himself. His mother had tried to explain once, that it was all part of God's plan, to bring two people together, to give them the opportunity to recognize his gift of *one for the other*. And occasionally, if the two were listening to their own hearts, if they were able to acknowledge the instincts that only they could feel, then the seed that was planted would grow into a love everlasting. Victor was thankful that he had listened to his heart that day so many years ago, and had not let his mind convince him that he was otherwise unworthy. He had seen a light in Maria's eyes, a sparkle, that felt as though the Lord was winking at him, whispering, here is your destiny. He wasn't sure whether or not she had the same experience, but he was pretty sure that it was God who kept putting them together in spite of life's many obstacles. To be perfectly honest, there was really no reason for them to be together, other than they were meant to be together. He smiled to himself as he climbed into the truck and closed the door. *Yeah*, he would go home and have a mighty fine breakfast, take a nice hot shower, and hopefully, if his son was napping or suitably occupied, maybe even make love to his wife before dashing off around the ranch the rest of the day checking up on this and that. He reached across the bench seat to the passenger side and patted his daughter's favorite picture book.

"Hop on Pop," he said softly.

"Never fails!"

Waving to the clerk inside the filling station, Victor started the engine and pulled away, the bells ringing twice as the tires rolled over the trip cord on the ground. He switched on the radio and listened to Richie Valens singing *"Oh Donna, Oh Donna…"*

"To bad this guy is dead, he could have been big as the Beatles man," Victor thought out loud.

Turning out of the driveway and onto the highway, he merged easily with the light Monday morning traffic. It was already hot out and he drove with the window down, his arm cocked at a forty-five degree angle, half in and half out of the pick-up. Even with his dark brown complexion he had a visible *'trucker's tan'* going. It was par for the course given the long hours he spent behind the wheel of one vehicle or another. He shot a one-handed wave at several passing cars and trucks, as was the custom in these small farming communities, Hell, everyone knew everyone else around here anyway. Victor looked out through his windshield and saw the big blue sky spreading across it.

"Man, its gonna be another gorgeous day," he said aloud to nobody in particular.

"Gracias Father," he said, lifting his crucifix to his lips and kissing it, then stuffing it back into his shirt. The view in every direction was the same, pale blue sky and scattered white, wispy clouds. It really was a nice day in the making. Victor saw the school bus up ahead, it was waiting to turn right onto Nestle Avenue. He sped up and then rolled slowly along side, knowing that his daughter would be in her usual seat on the driver's side of the bus. Sure enough, there she was, he spotted her long dark hair with the pink headband on top, pulling her hair back away from her face. He tooted his horn lightly and leaned across to the passenger side of the pick-up, waving to his little girl. Tina looked over and saw her dad and turned in her seat, getting up onto her knees. She placed both of her hands against the window palms flush, and bounced up and down excitedly in her seat. "Papa, *Papa*," she said lightly rapping on the window with both hands.

"OK now, sit on down baby girl before you hurt yourself," Lionel said sternly but with a smile.

Tina sat back down on her heels and leaned her face towards the window, resting her forehead on the glass. Victor continued to wave, waiting at the traffic stop, and watched as his daughter settled back down into her seat. She leaned back a bit and put her two index fingers up to the glass, tracing out the shape of a heart with them. Looking straight into her father's eyes through the glass, she said to him, *"Te adoro Papa."* Even though he couldn't actually hear her, he could read her meaning and the words on her face, and he smiled brightly. He blew her a kiss as the stoplight changed to green and she pretended to catch it and put into her coat pocket. The bus then lurched forward and turned onto Nestle Avenue continuing the journey toward the elementary school. Victor sat back up and slowly cruised through the intersection, about ten seconds and five horn blasts later than he probably should have. He flashed the angry motorist behind him a *'peace sign,'* and then checked his look in the rear-view mirror, adjusting the brim of his hat. Settling his arm back into position on the open window he tapped his fingers to the beat of 'The House of the Rising Sun' by Eric Burden and *The Animals.*

Maria looked up at the cow hanging on the wall, the clock in its belly read 8:30, her husband would be along any time now. She walked over to the fridge and pulled out a bowl full of fresh eggs and set it on the counter near the stove. Opening the oven door she pulled out a heavy iron skillet and set it on the front burner. She turned to fetch some milk for the scrambled eggs and stopped suddenly, returned to the stove, and moved the skillet to a back burner, remembering that her son was able to climb up and reach things now.

"*Mensa, Maria,*" she said out loud, scolding herself, no use tempting fate she thought.

Maria started to switch on the burner and then decided to give Victor a few more minutes to arrive. Besides, everyone knows that breakfast is always best right out of the frying pan, *piping hot*, especially the *machaca* that she was planning to serve this morning. It was one of her husband's favorites, he loved to tear the tortillas into pieces and scoop up the delicious mixture of scrambled eggs, onions, cilantro and shredded beef, topped with a fair amount of her home made salsa (she whipped up a fresh batch every day). *Oh,* how she liked to watch him eat, it always made her feel so good seeing him enjoy the things that she prepared. It reminded her how much she loved being a wife, a partner, and a mother. That the life she had was the destiny she had always dreamed of. If you asked her, she would tell you that true love was always in the little things, and she was so grateful that God had sent her a man who understood that, without needing to have it explained to him.

She picked up the bowl of eggs from the countertop and put them back in the fridge to keep them from spoiling in the heat. This house was a blessing and she was grateful, but boy was it remarkably uncomfortable when the swamp cooler wasn't working! A horn honked outside and Maria leaned across the sink to look out the window. It was Randy and Jesus, probably stopping by to pick up something or other from the tool shed. She waved to them as they cruised by the house, a small cloud of dust following the truck. Maria slid the curtains shut to block out the sunlight trying to keep the house as cool as possible. At least there was a merciful little breeze and it blew the gingham curtains back at her as she walked away from the counter.

"Where is that man," she muttered to herself, looking up at the cow clock again. Maria thought about inviting the fellas in for coffee to keep her occupied until Victor came home, well, really to keep her from worrying. She didn't like it when circumstances delayed him, it made her nervous, and it wasn't like him to be late for anything, especially a meal. She changed her mind about the coffee halfway to the kitchen door. She suspected that Victor might be more frisky than hungry this morning after being out in the fields all night, so company was probably not such a good idea. Maria blushed a little thinking about that possibility, well, maybe she was feeling the same way. *Hey*, a pillow can't hug you back, she thought, a girl can only take so much, *right?*

"Mama, my shoes won't tie," Gilbert whined, walking into the room carrying a shoe in each chubby little hand. Her son had slimmed down considerably over the last year or so, finally getting some height to go with his girth. But he was still her little *'gordo'*, and he looked so cute shuffling into the room across the linoleum floor in his socks and a "Mickey Mouse" tee shirt from last summer's vacation to Disneyland.

"Come here *mijo*, mommy will help you fix those old shoes," she said fixing her face into a cute little pout as she knelt down to pick him up. Gilbert ran towards her, slipping along the way, and fell into her waiting arms. His giggles were muffled as his mother held him tightly to her chest, her long hair falling all around him like a shield, leaving only his little feet visible to anyone who might happen upon the scene. She stood up and carried her son to the counter and helped him with his shoes. Placing a shoe on each foot, she spread out the laces and took his hands in hers.

"Alright gordo, you put your hands on top of mine and watch me tie these things," Maria said to her son, looking right into his eyes. Gilbert, tucked his chin down to his chest and nodded his head in the affirmative, his eyes tilted way up to maintain contact with his mother.

"OK, *here we go*, "she said and they started the daily routine together. Maria had played the same learning game with her daughter, and it hadn't taken long for her to master the shoe lacing skill. And both of the children loved the little song she sang whenever she practiced this skill with them.

> *"Lay down the left one, lay down the right*
> *Roll them in the green grass and pull them really tight*
> *Raise them up to heaven and make some loop de loops*
> *Then pull one through the center and knot it up real good*
> *Finish up by cinching up the clump with all your might*
> *Then run along and play away the day until the night"*

Maria and Gilbert sang this song a couple of times before she finally set him down and watched him race out of the kitchen towards the living room.

A second or two later she heard the familiar sound of "Bugs Bunny" coming from the television, and she sat down at the table for a minute to fix herself another cup of instant coffee.

"*Myaaaa*, what's up Doc," she heard Bugs say from the other room. She smiled when she heard her son giggle at what ever was going on in the story. She glanced up at the cow again, Victor was pretty late, and her stomach began to ache a little. Maria got up quickly and went to the kitchen door. She stuck her head outside and hollered over to the tool shed.

"**Hey,** Jesus, Randy, coffee?"

The two men waved to her, nodding an enthusiastic acceptance to her offer, anything to take a break from all this heat! She went to the cupboard to get a couple of cups and switched on the burner under the teakettle, she wanted to keep busy, to keep from thinking bad thoughts. It was 9:38, where was that man anyway?

"*Hola Senora,*" Jesus said knocking on the wooden screen door as he walked inside the house, Randy followed right behind him. They stamped there feet on the doormat before entering, politely cleaning off most of the dirt from their boots. Maria motioned them over to the kitchen table and set the cups out next to the jar of '*Taster's Choice'* and the sugar bowl.

"Thought you guys could use a break from the sun," she said sweetly.

"Muchas gracias Senora," Jesus said holding out his cup for Maria to fill with hot water.

"Yeah, thanks a bunch Mrs. Lopez," said Randy as he ladled in a spoonful of instant coffee into his cup.

"It's no trouble, were you two with Victor last night baling hay?"

"*Si, I was,*" Jesus said stirring his coffee and blowing on the cup before taking a sip.

"I thought he would be here when we drove up, but I didn't see his truck.

"Yeah, he should have beat us here by a good half hour," Randy added.

"Oh, he'll be along, he probably just stopped at the market on the way home, and you know how much he likes to flirt with Louisa," Maria said nonchalantly.

Louisa Sanchez was a seventy-eight year old woman, a five foot nothing ball of fire, with the spunk and energy of a woman not even half her age. *Every* man, who came into the *bodega* was her *boyfriend*, and she loved to sweet-talk them all. She had been at that market for as long as Maria could remember, and probably a good deal longer than that. The thought of Victor standing in line, uncomfortably trying to check out while Louisa chattered away, stealing sideways glances at her husband's tight jeans, almost made her laugh out loud. He always did his best to pose in modestly provocative and exaggerated positions to encourage her attention, entertaining himself and anyone else standing nearby. Maria smiled to herself as she pictured this little scene and silently prayed that this was exactly what was delaying his arrival. She sat down at the table with the two hired hands and chatted idly, sipping coffee and checking the clock, deciding to wait until 10:00 before officially panicking.

Tina watched as her teacher, Mr. Rawlins, wrote the problem on the blackboard. She was good at arithmetic, and she already knew the answer to the long division exercise he was composing.

"Alright, who would like to volunteer to work this for the class," he asked without turning around, admiring his penmanship? The class was silent, nobody was raising their hand, and nobody ever did so he was not surprised. He waited the prescribed thirty seconds before *'volunteering'* someone.

"Hector, would you please come to the blackboard and help me solve this problem?"

The boy tried to make himself disappear, but when he opened his eyes he was still in class and everyone but the teacher was looking right at him. Another prayer falling on deaf ears he thought, too young to realize that the education he was receiving was the real answer to his prayers.

"Yes sir," he said, getting up and slowly trudging up the aisle to join his teacher at the front of the class, preparing himself for the inevitable humiliating experience.

He was poked at with pencils and rulers as he walked the gauntlet, a couple of paper planes and rockets bouncing off of him as he reached the end. Mr. Rawlins turned and handed him the chalk, placing a hand on his shoulder and guiding him to the board. He opened one eye and peeked at the board, then quickly opened the other eye, big and wide. ***HE KNEW THIS ANSWER***, it was the same problem his dad had helped him with the night before! He almost tripped over his own feet in his rush to the blackboard. He turned around and faced the class, a sly grin breaking across his face, they weren't going to get the show they were expecting this morning, no sir! Before Mr. Rawlins could deliver his routine admonishment for failing to work hard enough on homework, Hector turned back around and started to work the problem. He imagined his teacher and classmates silently marveling at the speed at which he ciphered through the steps, chalk dust filling the air, sparks flying from his fingertips. He paused a second for effect, then sprinted to the finish, tempted to autograph the board at the end of his showcase. He turned slowly to smugly look back at all the nay-sayers, and quickly noticed his teacher's wrinkled brow. Instantly he knew the cause, and he spun quickly back to the board and wrote at the top of the problem *'r 3'* he had forgotten to show the remainder, *WHEW,* that was a close one!

"I am surprised, pleasantly, pleasantly surprised," Mr. Rawlins said rubbing his chin whiskers with his left hand. He walked up to the blackboard and stood next to Hector, and placed his hand onto the child's shoulder.

"Well done Mr. Hernandez, well done," Mr. Rawlins said to his pupil.

He held out his hand for Hector to return the chalk, and then circled the problem placing an asterisk or star above it to acknowledge the child's success. Hector beamed as he returned to his desk, the pokes and taunts replaced by pats on the back and high fives. Being a kid was cool, one minute you're the goat and the next the hero, there were no such thing as grudges among children, they all lived in the moment. Too bad that concept dies in all of us somewhere between puberty and death. Tina turned in her seat and clapped her hands rapidly in front of her chest so that only Hector could see, letting her friend know that she was happy for him. Still lost in the moment, he could only manage a shoulder shrug and silly grin in response. Mr. Rawlin's had completed writing a new problem onto the board and was about to ask for the next volunteer when the door opened suddenly and a visitor walked into the room. It was the Principle, Mrs. Titus and she was accompanied by a police officer, more accurately, Sheriff Cardwell. They came to the front of the class and Mrs. Titus whispered something to Mr. Rawlins. The Sheriff looked around the class making everyone a little uncomfortable. He removed his sunglasses and smiled at the children, allowing them all to collectively draw another breath.

"Don't worry kids, nobody's going to jail today," he teased, winking at the class.

"OK people, we're going to break for recess a little early this morning, I'm sure that will not spoil the day for any of you," Mr.Rawlins said with a smile.

"Leave your books open to page 44 and quietly walk to the playground with Mrs. Titus," he continued. The room was filled with the sound of squeaking chairs as everyone slid from behind their desks at the same time. Obeying their teacher's request they quietly and orderly followed the Principle out of the classroom through the door. As they filed by his desk in the front of the room, Mr. Rawlins reached out and touched Tina on the shoulder.

"Tina Lopez, would you please wait here for a minute, the Sheriff would like to ask you something," he said smiling, trying too hard not to make her nervous?

Tina nodded and stood next to her teacher as the rest of her classmates filed by, too happy about escaping the arithmetic lesson to notice she had been kept behind. Only Hector looked back over his shoulder on the way out the door, but he was washed away with the throng of recess minded third graders. When the last child had exited the classroom, Mr. Rawlins walked over and closed the door. He returned to Tina and took her hand and walked her over to a seat in the first row. She sat down and folded her hands in front of her on the desktop and looked at the two men who were leaning against the teacher's desk.

"Tina, I'm sorry about scaring all you kids like this, but I sort of need your help sweetheart," Sheriff Cardwell said in a soft even tone.

She liked the Sheriff, he was a nice man she thought. She had met him shortly after she had helped Hector's sister Rosa with her baby's birth. She remembered the day she first saw him because he had driven to her house with Senora Donnelly in the back of his police car. She was afraid that maybe he had come to take away all the mommies, and she was scared for her own. But, as it turned out, Mrs. Donnelly was in the back seat because Sheriff Cardwell's blue-eyed Husky *Daisy* was sleeping in the front seat. Tina loved that dog, and her family was given one of her puppies as a present at Christmas, much to the dismay of *El Guappo*, the cat. She had named the puppy "Dustin" because his tail was always wagging, dusting whatever was trailing behind him. Senora Donnelly had told her family that the Sheriff would always be nearby if ever they needed him, he was there to make sure that Tina would always be safe. And since then, whenever a stranger appeared at the house with a sad story or a need, you could be certain that a Deputy would be along soon afterward. It never occurred to Tina that they needed protection of that kind, but her mother was much happier with the attention, that was obvious. She no longer jumped when the phone or the doorbell rang. Tina continued to stare at the two men, waiting for one of them to speak, to tell her what this visit was all about, and to tell her why she wasn't out playing in the sun with her friends.

"Listen honey, something happened this morning," the Sheriff continued.

"Ah hell," Sheriff Cardwell said curtly, walking away toward the door, one hand on his hip, his hat in the other. He slapped his hat against his leg and turned back to face the little girl.

"Look, Tina, Mr. and Mrs. Donnelly asked me to come get you because someone needs your help."

"I say, let the bastard die, he deserves to die, but damn it, there are some extenuating circumstances that are difficult to explain."

"All I know is that the Donnelly's are good people and they must have a good reason to send for you baby girl," Sheriff Cardwell finished.

Tina just stared at him, understanding nothing except the reference to the Donnelly's. Her teacher started to ask say something, but the Sheriff waved him off and walked over to Tina, taking a knee in front of the desk she was sitting at.

"*Listen,* I have a Deputy going over to your house right now to pick up your Momma, and she will meet us at the hospital. But we need to get going because there really isn't much time, at least I don't think that there is," the Sheriff said, his eyebrows raising while he thought about that for a moment.

Tina nodded and scooted out from behind the desk, taking the Sheriff's hand. They walked toward the door hand in hand, Sheriff Cardwell placing his cap back on his head. He took the sunglasses out of his pocket and placed them over his eyes as they walked out of the building and into the bright morning sun. He opened the passenger door of the car and helped the little girl inside, making sure to adjust the seatbelt to fit her small frame. Hopping into the driver's side of the patrol car he drove off with the lights flashing but no siren. Hector watched the car race away from behind the chain-link fence, wondering what was going on?

Maria picked up the cups and put them in the sink, she turned on the water and rinsed them out, placing them on the drying rack on the counter. It was well past 10:00 and she was in an official panic now. She had asked Jesus and Randy to drive around and see if they could find Victor. She had almost shoved them out the door, shouting for them to get going and to call as soon as they found him. She tried to block all of the awful thoughts going through her mind, deciding instead to concentrate on how she would *kill* him herself if he weren't already dead!

"*Darn you Panson,* there are telephones on every street corner, and I know you have an ashtray full of coins because you don't smoke," she cried out loud to herself. Gilbert walked into the kitchen and stood next to his mother, looking up at her, trying to decide if he should start crying as well. She took her hand away from her eyes and picked up her son, hugging him tightly and swaying her body from side to side as if they were dancing. The doorbell suddenly rang and Maria swung Gilbert onto her hip and carried him quickly into the front room. She could see Deputy Grady at the door through the screen. He removed his sunglasses and his hat as she approached the door.

"Excuse me Mrs. Lopez, the Sheriff asked me to stop by," he said a little too nervously for her comfort.

"**WHAT,** *what is it,* where is my husband, what do you know," she said rapidly and excitedly, her eyes moist and pleading. Her tone had startled her son and he started to cry, with that face kids make when they are more confused and scared than hurt or angry.

"**Shhh,** *shhhhh,* mijo, lo ciento baby, *lo ciento,*" she said trying to quiet her son and steady her nerves at the same time. She looked back at Deputy

Grady from over her son's little shoulder and waited for him to answer her. He just stood there, not exactly sure what to say next, he really didn't know too much, and didn't want that to show, typical rookie behavior.

"WELL?"

"Oh, *right,* I'm sorry maam, *yeah,* well the Sheriff asked me to stop by and fetch you over to the ER at the County Trauma Center," he stammered, embarrassed that this little woman was intimidating him more than she should be able to. Deputy Grady leaned closer to the screen as Maria ran back into the house, disappearing from his view.

"Mrs. Lopez, maam, we need to get a move on," he said reaching for the door handle to follow after her. Before he could turn the knob, Maria came crashing through the door, knocking him back a couple of steps. She was half way to his patrol car by the time he recovered enough to chase after her. She stopped in the middle of the lawn, fixing Gilberts baseball cap onto his head to shield his eyes from the sun.

"Let's GO Grady, lets go, Victor is probably bleeding on some table somewhere, lets *GO!"*

The Deputy opened the car door and then closed it behind them as soon as she was seated. He ran around to his side and hopped in, turning the engine over and fastening his seatbelt simultaneously. He fumbled with his sunglasses and Maria swatted him on his arm, *"Come **ON** Grady,* step on it, where is the *'thingy'* that turns on the lights and siren anyway," she said anxiously.

"Take it easy will ya, we don't even know what the emergency is anyway!"

"Well, use your *talkie walkie,* short wave telephone in a car, or whatever you call this thing in the middle here and ***find out!"*** Maria stamped both her feet on the floorboards and leaned back hard against the seat, *"Ohhhhh, will you just hurry please!"* Gilbert peeked out from behind his mother's hair and looked over at the frustrated deputy. He reached out with his little hand and offered the poor man a cookie. Deputy Grady looked over and let a smile replace his frown for a millisecond then reached over, taking the cookie, and winked at the child.

"Thanks, I need this." Maria turned her head to see what was going on.

"Oh for goodness sake, I only have patience for one baby this morning, OK?"

"We're on our way now, don't worry," he said as he picked up the radio mike and called into dispatch to report his status.

"One Charlie Seven to dispatch, I picked up the Lopez woman, she has a small boy with her, and we're in route to County Trauma, ETA ten minutes, over."

"One Charlie Seven, acknowledged, meet One David One on tack one, copy."

"Roger that, ten-four."

"What did all of that mean," Maria asked?

"It means that we will arrive at the hospital in about ten minutes," Deputy Grady said.

"What about my husband, what did you find out?"

"Hold your horses will ya, I've got to contact the Sheriff, maybe he can help you with that one," Grady quipped tiredly. Maria, said nothing and just stared out the window, fighting the urge to chew on her thumbnail. Grady switched the dial on his radio and put the mike to his mouth.

"One David One, One David One, One Charlie Seven, over."

The radio squawked at him a second or two and then Sheriff Cardwell's voice came over the wireless.

"One Charlie Seven, what's your twenty son, over."

"Avenue C, crossing 10th street, ETA seven minutes, over.'

"Ask him, ask him," Maria pleaded.

"One David One, Sheriff, Mrs. Lopez is concerned about this call, do you have information about the whereabouts of her husband Victor, over?"

"One David One, kinda dicey out here right now Grady, tell Mrs. Lopez that I'll bring her up to date when you arrive. Oh, and let her know that her daughter is here as well, that she is just fine, over and out."

"One Charlie Seven, roger that, out."

"Sorry Mrs. Lopez, you'll just have to wait a few minutes."

Maria didn't answer, she was already praying. When she heard that Tina was with the Sheriff her worst fears were confirmed. She knew that Victor had been in a terrible accident and that he was either dying or dead already. Why else would the Sheriff have picked up her daughter and sent for her as well, why else would they be racing to the hospital. She sat in silence the rest of the trip, time seemingly standing still, she was no longer interested in arriving so quickly. She could feel her faith leaving her, and she tried to fight it, to cling to hope against hope that the Lord would be merciful. But the darker side was winning and she was falling into a depression that was cold and bleak. Just as she was about to surrender, to abandon all of the blessings that she had come to know and to love, Gilbert dropped a cookie down her blouse and he went fishing for it. She watched passively as his little arm disappeared inside her shirt, searching for his lost treat. She turned her head, catching Deputy Grady looking at her strangely and snapped out of *her* trance. She pulled her son's arm out of her shirt, cookie in hand, and quickly buttoned up her blouse, snapping Deputy Grady out of *his* trance. He cleared his throat and smiled weakly, she smiled back and shook her head. *"Pigs,"* she thought. Men were all the same, if breasts had any more power women would rule the world.

"We're here," Grady said coming to an abrupt stop at the entrance to the Emergency Room.

There were several patrol cars around as well as an ambulance, a fire truck, and some news vans. Whatever was going on, it looked like it might make the six o'clock news, there were trucks from channels four, two and seven that she could see. Grady opened her door and she and Gilbert got out of the car. A small crowd of people standing around the entrance turned quickly, and leveled their attention on Maria and her son. Grady put his arm around her and the baby and shielded them from the microphones and cameras as they made their way to the automatic doors.

"Officer, *Officer*, what can you tell us, who is this woman, is she the one, *is she the one*," a short red-headed newswoman demanded rudely, standing way inside of his comfort zone.

Grady ignored everything and everyone as he bullied his way toward the door and finally into the ER. Once inside the mood became much quieter, almost too quiet given the level of commotion just outside those two doors. Maria looked around for someone or something familiar. At first there was nothing, and then over by yet another set of doors, laid across a chair, was Victor's Levi's Jacket, the same one he had worn to the alfalfa fields last night. She remembered he had it with him because she had to fight with him to take it, he didn't like wearing jackets or heavy coats. She froze when she noticed that it was covered in blood, the entire white wool collar was soaked in thickening red blood. She had not seen that much blood since Rosa Hernandez had given birth on her kitchen floor. Maria walked over to the chair and looked down at the bloody coat, her eyes beginning to moisten again. She tried to hold her composure, she hadn't actually seen Victor yet, and nobody had said anything. Someone came up behind her and put an arm on her shoulder lightly.

"Maria, you need to come with me child," said Alma Donnelly softly. She gently turned Maria around and hugged her and Gilbert, softly brushing Maria's hair with her hand.

"*Maria, MARIA*, look at me, let me know that you are hearing my words." Maria looked at Alma and nodded, more confused than scared at the moment. She was prepared for the worst, and just wanted someone to get on with it.

"Yes," she said weakly.

"OK now, we're going to go into this room over here, and someone will explain all of this to you, do you understand me?"

"OK"

The three of them walked to a second set of automatic doors and Deputy Grady pushed the large button on the wall, causing the doors to slide open. The sign over the door read "Burn Unit" and Maria could feel hers knees get weak, she wasn't sure if she wanted to walk any further. This was not one of the possibilities that she had prepared herself for. She could feel Alma rubbing her shoulders as they walked slowly down the hall, busy people in green clothes looking at them as they passed avoiding any eye contact. She felt as though she had to pee all of the sudden, but that passed quickly and was replaced with an urge to vomit. A tall man in long white lab coat stopped in front of them and said something to Alma, she could hear the sound of their voices, but the words did not register. The tall man smiled at her and then gestured to another set of doors, pushing a button to open them magically. She looked inside and saw Sheriff Cardwell standing at an intersection, his back to them his arms folded in front of him. He turned at the sound of the opening doors and smiled at Alma and Maria. He walked over to them and placed his hands onto Maria's shoulders, and then tussled Gilbert's hair a little.

"I'm sorry for the rush and all the drama, but we had ourselves a situation here that sorta got out of hand quickly."

"Victor, where is Victor, *I,* I saw his jacket in the hall, there was so much blood," she whispered, not really looking at him.

"Come with me Maria, I'll explain everything," he said gently.

He turned and led them down the hall towards the same intersection that he was standing in only a moment ago. As they passed a room on the right, Maria looked over and stopped. Inside the room was Rosa Hernandez, she was sitting on a bed, handcuffed to the rail, a female Deputy standing nearby. Maria turned toward the room and stared inside until Rosa made eye contact. She had been crying, but smiled when she saw Maria, giving her a little wave with her other hand.

"Come on, I'll tell you about that as well," Sheriff Cardwell whispered.

They continued on and turned left at the intersection and Maria stopped again. She gasped, her eyes filling with tears as she handed Gilbert to Alma. She ran to the end of the hall as fast as she could and leaped into her husband's arms, nearly knocking him down. She kissed him over and over, his face, his hands, his face again, and then threw her arms around his neck, clutching at his shirt, her hands closing with so much pressure that she nearly tore through the fabric.

"Where have you been," she whispered, her face buried in the nape of his neck, breathing deeply and drinking in his pheromones.

"Where have you been *Panson,* I was so worried, I thought you were dead!"

"I'm sorry Honey, this all happened so fast, there was nothing I could do," Victor said softly, stroking his wife's long, beautiful hair. She sighed, and then looked up at him suddenly frightened again.

"Where is Tina, Grady said that Tina was here?"

"She's fine Maria, she's fine. She's just been called to serve again. But honestly, I really wonder what the man upstairs was thinking where this one is concerned?"

"What are you talking about Victor, what do you mean, why is everyone acting so strange, why are all the TV people outside?" Sheriff Cardwell walked up to the couple and put his hand on her shoulder.

"Maria, you saw the Hernandez girl in the other room?"

"Yes"

"There was an incident this morning that involved her"

"She went to the free clinic over on Clemons Street, near Avenue F, and walked right like she owned the place," Sheriff Cardwell paused and swallowed before he continued.

"She had a bottle of pop in her hand, or so the receptionist thought. She went right into the office where a Doctor Katz was working at his desk. The receptionist said that she heard them argue, and then it was quiet for a minute or two. Then all of a sudden the Doctor screamed for her to get out, and the door opened and Rosa started to exit. She stopped suddenly and looked right at the girl at the front desk, then told her that she was going to save her a lot of suffering. The receptionist peeked around her and saw that Dr. Katz was standing with his arms out as if he had just been hit with a water balloon, dripping wet with something that smelled familiar. Before it registered in her mind that what she smelled was gasoline, Rosa tossed a lit match into the room, and the place exploded in flames. By the time we arrived, the doctor was out on the wet grass, his clothes and hair still smoking from the fire. Apparently the paramedics were still in route when your husband drove by and saw the poor man run from the building, fully engulfed in flames. He pulled over and tackled him on the grass while the receptionist turned the garden hose on both of them. Rosa just sat on the steps and watched, rocking back and forth in a trance, saying over and over *that's it for you.'* Nobody knew what she was talking about. We didn't get the whole story until we got her in that room over there and she told us about the rape. In the last couple of hours there have been eight other girls that have come forward and testified to being raped by this doctor as well. If these accusations are true, then this guy may have gotten just what he deserved. Oh, I know, I shouldn't say that out loud, I mean I am the Sheriff, but damn it, some of those girls are Tina's age!" Maria looked back at her husband and asked him.

"Where is Tina now?" Victor started to speak when the Sheriff cut in again.

"Maria, your husband rode with that man to the hospital, and prayed with him while he lay dying."

"He confessed to all of these charges in the ambulance and asked for forgiveness, he was delirious, he thought Victor was a priest." Victor spoke up, "I didn't know what to do Maria, but I felt that the Lord wanted me to do something, why else would he send me near that place, at exactly that moment, it's not on the way home?"

"And you thought of Tina?" Victor looked down at his boots, "Yes, God help me, I thought about our daughter, you said yourself that there was no one that we could turn away.'

"Aiye Victor, this man is evil, he might have taken Tina as well, sooner or later!"

"Who are we to judge Maria, he was a man, he was suffering, we had the means to end his suffering, to offer hope?"

"Where *is she* Victor," she asked again.

"In there," Victor pointed to a room across the aisle.

There were two Deputies standing out front and she could see the shape of someone moving behind the frosted glass. She pushed away from her husband and walked past the Sheriff. When she got to the door a large Deputy extended his beefy arm to block her way. Sheriff Cardwell signaled the Deputy to let her in and he turned and opened the heavy wooden door. When she walked in she saw that the screen around the bed was pulled shut and she walked over to it. A nurse had just exited carrying two rolls of gauze and some adhesive tape. She stopped and looked at Maria.

"May I help you," she asked? Maria didn't answer her.

"Excuse me, I don't think you should be in here," she said and looked toward the door at the Deputy standing watch.

He motioned for her to come over to him and pointed toward the Sheriff and she left the room. Maria reached out and slid the curtain open, preparing herself for a hideous site. But when she opened her eyes and looked inside what she saw startled her. The man in the bed was sitting up right, his wrists and ankles shackled to the bed-frame, and his face was wet with tears. But there weren't any signs that this man had been set afire, there were no burns or blisters, no bandages, no drying bloodstains like the ones all over Victor's jacket. He looked absolutely normal, except he was silently sobbing looking down at the small girl at the foot of his bed. Her head was on the blanket, her little hands held onto the man's left foot, she was sleeping peacefully, her soft breathing interrupted only by the rhythmic beeps of the heart monitor that was attached to the patient. Maria looked back at the man, *this doctor,* and this abuser of little girls and women. She really wanted to hate to hate him, she wanted to lash out on the behalf of those girls, she wanted to protect those he hurt, to protect those he might yet hurt, but she couldn't. She was standing in a *holy place*, a place where the Lord was working for his children through his children. She walked over to the man and looked deeply into his eyes, they were raw and red. They stared at one another for a full minute, and then she reached over to him and wiped away a tear.

"I'm sorry," he said weakly.

"I know," she replied "I know."

Maria turned and walked over to her daughter and stroked her hair, the pink headband was pushed up with the angle of her head. Maria pulled it off of her and then leaned over to whisper in her ear.

"Wake up *mijita*, let's go home." Tina stirred a little, yawned and stretched.

She looked back at her mother than over to the man and got up. Taking her mother's hand they turned to walk away. As they started to leave, Tina stopped next to the bed and looked at the hand shackled to the rail. She reached over and took hold of one of his fingers and then looked up into his eyes. She held his gaze for a moment and then let go of his finger, she smiled and waved to him. Doctor Murray Katz felt the pressure in his chest and he leaned his head back against the pillow. He closed his eyes tightly but the heart attack he was expecting did not come. What came instead was a feeling he didn't recognize, one he had never experienced, a feeling that up till now he never believed in, for the first time in his life he felt love and the awesome power behind it. He listened as the door closed and locked behind his visitor and savior. The man he had been was dead, the man he would be, began his new life with two new words, repentance and forgiveness.

Victor huddled with his family near the nurse's station in the trauma center's burn unit. He watched the people going about their business, and noticed that they were trying too hard not to notice them. He could hear the noise outside the burn unit, every time someone came in or went out. He knew that things were going to be different now. They were not going to be able to hide in plain sight any longer. He looked over at Alma Donnelly, she was talking with Sheriff Cardwell and her husband Arthur. They glanced his way periodically and smiled reassuringly. He knew that they were talking about them, trying to figure out a way that this could all go away. But this was too much, this was catnip to all the media lurking outside waiting for a chance to tempt them with the promise of riches, in order to exploit this phenomenon whatever way they could. No, he wouldn't let them do that, he would take his family and run again, find somewhere to start again, perhaps the Donnelly's could help, and he prayed that they would find a way.

He looked down at his family. They were all stretched out on the small uncomfortable sofa. Gilbert resting his head on Tina's lap, Tina resting her head on Maria's lap and Maria sound asleep on his shoulder. There was no shoulder for Victor to rest on, but he was in good hands, and he continued to pray for deliverance from this situation. He remembered what his mother had taught him as a boy, follow your heart son, and keep your faith strong. Everyone and everything that comes into your life is part of God's plan for you, pay attention to the signs and listen to the spirit that guides you. Your mind may be your most powerful tool, *keep it sharp*, but it's your heart that has dominion over you, and can keep you from hurting yourself and others with that powerfully, sharp mind. Pretty smart for someone who never finished school he thought. He thought about his mother for a moment and pictured her smiling face. He decided that the true measure of a person's life was the way in which they would be remembered. Remembered by those who loved them, and by those who did not.

Victor yawned and looked at his watch, it was 12:45, past his normal lunchtime, and he was starving, he had already missed one meal today. As soon as the dust settled on this he was taking them all to A&W for burgers and root beer, he could picture that frosty mug and began to salivate. He kissed his wife on the top of her head and leaned his head back against the wall. He hoped he had done the right thing today, it felt like the right thing, time would tell.

Eleven

("...And, tell me over and over and over again
my friend, you don't believe, we're on the eve of
destruction"...Barry McGuire)

An Hoa, Republic of Viet Nam, November, 1968
<u>*Somewhere near Dodge City*</u>

They had been out humping the bush since daybreak after dropping in at the LZ about four or five clicks from the area known as Dodge City. It was a 36 square kilometer area south of DaNang and about twenty or so kilometers from where they had started from in An Hoa. The NVA and Mr. Charlie were thought to be thick in this place and the brass had decided that the Marines would be cleaning house big-time here. They had seen nothing but water buffalo, bugs, and skeeters all day, and then the daily downpour came at sunset. The rain would fall in big fat drops so thick that you could not see but a foot or two in any direction. And with the humidity, you actually were sweating as well. It was no wonder that the chicks here had such beautiful skin. If someone were to bottle this place, they'd make a fortune selling the world's greatest moisturizer.

"Just like back home in Biloxi, Mississippi," JoJo Cole would say in his smart-ass tone. He was a real pain, but usually he was more funny than irritating, and that was a nice diversion from the steady diet of fear and boredom. It was shortly after the rain stopped and the night fell that things got interesting, not the first encounter for most of them, but the last for some of them.

Junior lay very still in the tall elephant grass. He stared up at the night sky, a pitch-black backdrop freckled brilliantly by a million twinkling stars. It was the most beautiful sight he had ever seen. You would never get a chance to see something like this in east LA he thought. The corners of his mouth began to pull his face up into a smile. It was the kind of smile that he usually saved for his kid sisters (Sonja and Leticia), his Mom and Grandpop, his *Tia* Irma's homemade tamales, and of course, the current Playmate of the Month.

He lay there, quiet and still, sweating bullets in the heat of the night, watching the stars blink back at him. A shooting star suddenly passed by quickly, falling from the sky like a ripe apple from a tree. The giggle that was about to escape his lips was stifled, as a large hand slapped over his mouth. Junior's eyes snapped wide open almost bugging out of his head with the fear that he was about to be wasted by a VC *'crawler'*. He sighed, a loud exhale through his nose as he recognized Hightower. The huge Texan's face, camouflaged with alternating stripes of olive green and black paint, was an inch from his daydreaming friend's. Hightower didn't speak, but Junior understood his meaning by the look in his eyes. He was to be very quiet, make no sound. Obviously they were not alone! Junior blinked an affirmative to his buddy's warning, placing one hand over Hightower's and reaching for his M16 with the other. Wesley Hightower had been sent out on a solo recon after the firefight about a half-hour before. He let go of Junior's face and rolled to his right, crawling quickly to where Gunny and Davis, the radio operator were hunkered.

"What's you got for me boy," Sgt. Marquette whispered loudly?

Hightower slid in close beside the two men and removed his helmet. He took the sweat towel from around his neck, dried the top of his head and replaced the heavy Kevlar hat back onto his head.

"We're in deep shit Gunny, Charlie is crawling all around us, I had to grease one just to get back here," he said still trying to catch is breath.

"I don't know where that dip shit butter bar was trying to lead us, but he damn sure fucked things up real good this time!" Sergeant Marquette looked back at the frustrated grunt and scowled at him. He was about to reprimand him when a sing-song voice broke the hushed silence.

"Hell white boy, show some respect for the dead, he's one of you ain't he, all that pretty blond hair, crying shame, that's what that is, mother fuckin cryin shame," said PFC Joseph Cole from the other side of the muddy ditch.

"*CAN IT JoJo*, you trying to draw fire down on this position boy," Gunny spat back at the soldier in a harsh whisper, his teeth clenched tightly!

"Son, that kind of talk ain't gonna get us outta this jam now is it?"

"I know your momma didn't teach you none of them words."

They stared back at the bloody remains of Lieutenant Daniel Sheridan, their recently deceased platoon leader. He had been the latest in a string of 90-day wonders that routinely showed up in country. These young officers were commonly referred to as '*butter bars*' because of the cloth rank insignia on their uniforms (shiny gold lieutenant bars weren't a very good idea in the field). However among the combat vets the term was used more sarcastically, depicting the fact that these newbies didn't know shit, and that meant they were a danger to whoever had to follow them. Typically you saluted and *yes sir'd* these guys but took direction from your platoon sergeant, the seasoned leadership in the field.

"Sorry Sergeant Percy. I didn't mean nothin by it," JoJo said flatly.

"Boy don't you get familiar with me, I ain't no kin to you. Refer to me as sergeant or gunny, do not call me by my Christian name, you hear!"

"Yes sergeant, loud and clear," JoJo replied, getting up onto one knee and looking more alert.

"Wesley, get your redneck Texas ass over here and give me some details son," Gunny said still glaring at JoJo.

Junior watched and listened to all of this while trying to be aware of every noise and movement around him. It was these times when all of your senses were heightened, when you could hear centipede's footsteps, or a mouse fart. Still lying on his back, he released the safety with his right index finger and held the M16 a little tighter. Maybe not the wisest maneuver given these close quarters, but better ready and steady, than cautious and nauseous he decided. Junior smiled remembering the cadence drill from boot camp, "*this my rifle, this is my gun, this ones for business, this ones for fun,*" they would chant over and over while marching around the barracks in their skivvies one hand shouldering their M16 and the other holding their *johnson*. Tonight Junior and the rest of the platoon kept both hands on the business end of their M16's. He turned his head to the right and could see Gunny talking into the radio handset, Hightower, Davis and Cole kneeling around him, each of them scanning the bush looking for signs of Mr. Charlie.

He set his gaze on the body of Lieutenant Sheridan and studied the stillness of it; it was almost like looking at a painting, like it wasn't real. He turned his head to the left and suddenly everything was real again. Only five feet from where he rested in the muddy grass was another body. This one wasn't in quite so peaceful a position as the lieutenant's had been. This one was all turned and twisted, badly bruised, missing a part or two here and there, gizzards and giblets hanging from it's middle and such, like a turkey freshly slaughtered for the feast. This one, not even an hour before, had been telling Junior a joke about the Easter Bunny, Cupid and the Tooth Fairy standing at the urinal in the officers latrine. He couldn't remember the punch-line, all he could remember was that he had been walking through this muck right next to this one when the mortar round slammed into the ground directly in front of them.

All he could remember was the ringing in his ears and the searing pain in his head as he rolled from side to side trying to make it stop. Seeing the tracers light up the night, whizzing by him, brilliant green and red streaks of light, it was almost beautiful. He could not hear the incoming rounds or the screams of the guys around him, the urgent directions hollered by his platoon sergeant, or the *thump thump thump* of tree-line mortar rounds as they rained deadly razor sharp *fleshettes* onto the ground and into the mud or bodies of the targets they found. All he could remember was that this twisted mass of flesh and bone lying near him had been his friend since day one at boot camp. The guy had been with him through thick and thin, had carried his drunken behind out of many a tight spot, held him by the collar while he puked into his locker-box, and studied with him late after taps to help him get ready for his GED test. All he could remember was that this one was his friend, Angel Martinez. Junior, Angel, and Hightower were tight, the three amigos baby. Junior turned his head away and looked at the night sky again. Somehow it wasn't as beautiful anymore. Someone was going to pay for this alright, *oh yeah*, someone was going to pay. Junior pulled back the lever on his weapon putting a round into the chamber, and set the switch to automatic. Most definitely, there was going to be some payback tonight!

The Huey banked to the left slightly and then leveled out flying at one hundred and fifteen knots, about one hundred meters above the trees below. It was a clear morning, not a cloud in the sky and nothing much happening below either from what the Air Cavalry Captain could see from his jockey seat. He adjusted the frequency on the radio located in the center of the control console and put a hand to his ear. They usually flew with the side doors open and so there was always a lot of racket to talk over.

"Foxhunt leader to posse, we're getting close girls, we'll circle once and drop in two at a time for extraction, Medi-Vacs first as usual," Captain Wallace barked into the headset microphone.

"Lock and load, and try not to grease any of the good guys y'all. I don't want to have to write any more FF letters home, OK?" he pleaded.

FF letters were sent to families explaining that they're loved ones had been killed or wounded by friendly fire. Captain Wallace wondered if any of these letters were ever actually mailed, as they had to be cleared by the brass first, and given the current popularity of the war, well?

"Roger that boss man, we have removed the blindfold from Corporal Parrish as instructed, that should help, but we aren't responsible for those crossed eyes of his," joked the last of the eight Huey pilots to check in.

"Real funny Garvey, that'll cost you a Bud or two when we get back, over," Captain Wallace replied. The sun was rising fast and high behind the squadron of Huey helicopters as they raced above the tree line toward the battle weary marines just a few minutes ahead. The shadows of the helicopters stretched long and lean across the countryside as they flew in formation, like a small pack of wild *'mechanical'* ducks heading south for the winter. Small arms fire began peppering the sky around the Hueys and they climbed another hundred meters to a safer altitude.

"Foxhunt leader to Recon leader, pop some smoke Gunny, we're getting close, over," Captain Wallace said into his com-set. No reply, he repeated his order.

"Foxhunt leader to Recon leader, I say again, blow some smoke, do you copy, over?" There was a little loud crackling in his ear, but the Huey pilot could hear a response coming.

"Recon leader, to Foxhunt leader, little busy down here, this will be a hot LZ, I repeat, this will be a hot LZ, over," came the voice of Sergeant Percy Marquette.

"Roger that Gunny, what's the current situation, over."

"Charlie has us pinned in a rice paddy about 300 yards from the original LZ, you'll have to hover, too wet to land. Got two KIA's, five badly wounded, and fifteen of Uncle Sam's nephews keeping the dinks off of their buddies, they're cold, hungry, and anxious, me included, over," Percy said into the radio, the sound of automatic weapons blaring in the background.

"Roger that Gunny, keep your heads down, we're coming in with the mini guns first and spraying the perimeter, do you copy, over?"

"Aye-aye Captain, give em hell sir, out!"

Captain Wallace looked over at his co-pilot and nodded, he then looked back over his shoulder at the door-gunner on the M60 gun that was side-mounted in the belly of the helicopter. A twenty year-old Private smiled at him chewing nervously on a thick wad of bubble gum and gave him the thumbs up sign. The Huey pilot turned back around in his seat and looked straight ahead at the hilly countryside, knowing that they were about to clear those hills and descend into a hornets nest of live fire and confusion. He held his breath a second and prayed for mercy for all, and for forgiveness for the lives he would take this day.

"Foxhunt leader to posse, you all heard the man, we got ants at the picnic."

"*Butch, Duke, and Sundance*, follow me in over the rise and lay into the area around the red smoke yonder, copy?"

The three Huey pilots all acknowledged their receipt of the orders as they followed Captain Wallace over the rise in an attack formation. The red smoke of a hot LZ could be seen just to the left of their position. The ground-fire was heavy and they all hoped that Charlie did not have any RPG's (rocket propelled grenades). If God had heard his prayers, then they would only have to deal with small arms weapons, Captain Wallace reassured himself. He angled his helicopter toward the ground, the business side of the Huey ablaze with the action of the murderous fire from the M60 gun, hundreds of shell casings falling to the earth as the deadly projectiles sought out targets on the ground below. In a few minutes he and his crew will have put more minerals into the area than a thousand years of natural evolution. The Hueys circled in and out of the area surrounding the billowing red smoke for about fifteen minutes, cutting down grass, trees, bushes, and whatever or whoever crossed the path of their deadly purpose. When Captain Wallace decided that the risk was minimal he ordered in the Medi-Vacs. The choppers tasked with providing cover for the pick up circled the area looking for signs of trouble. They darted around the perimeter, in close and then out wide just in case Charlie was trying to set up a mortar attack on the LZ. This morning their luck was good, or more precisely, Captain Wallace's prayers had been heard.

"Foxhunt leader to Recon leader, how's it going down there Gunny, over?"

"Going fine Captain, just what the doctor ordered sir!"

"Roger that Gunny, just another day at the office."

The Huey gun-ships continued to patrol the perimeter while the Medi-vacs hovered near the rice paddy and the grunts carried their dead and wounded to the aircraft. Junior and Hightower were zipping up the body bag that held their buddy Angel, the wind from the helicopter rotors flattening the tall grass all around them. Junior was looking at his hands, they were covered with Angel's blood after picking up what was left of him and stuffing it all into that heavy rubber bag. He was clenching his fists so tight that the blood oozed up from between his fingers, his body shook violently with frustrated anger, he finally screamed as loud as he could, *"Nooooooo!"* Only Hightower could hear the cry, muffled by the racket of the hovering aircraft. Junior fell to his knees sitting back on the heels of his jump-boots, he slumped forward, arms resting on his thighs, and put his face into his bloody hands. He sobbed uncontrollably in that spot as Hightower stood over him, his big paw stroking his friend's head and neck. The helicopter may have drowned out the sound of Junior's anguish, but everyone looking out of the transport upon the scene could feel the weight of his frustration and desperation carried through the air in his silent primal scream. This was a life changing moment for everyone, how could it be any less. The memory of this action would haunt each of them, it would make men or monsters, only time would tell. In these few moments they had been exposed to the cruelest of diseases, *hatred*, a cancer that closed minds and hardened hearts. Cruel given that it was self-inflicted, and came with a cure that was always at hand. Cruel in that the cure was difficult to administer, because it required a change of heart, a willingness to forgive.

"*Yo, Hightower*, pick up Junior and let's go man, let the corpsmen take Angel onto the sandman's sled," JoJo pleaded with the big Texan. Wesley looked over at JoJo and fought the urge to frag the smart-ass prick.

"*Yeah, OK*," he said, and he leaned over to help Junior get to his feet.

"Lets go, lets go, lets go," yelled the door-gunner, waiving them toward the Medi-Vac nearest them. Junior did not want to leave without Angel, and he struggled a bit with Hightower at first.

"*Leave him man*, the corpsmen are right behind us, they'll put him on the transport Junior. You want to get us all slicked you dumb-ass wetback," JoJo yelled at the distraught marine! Hightower put is beefy arms around his buddy from behind and picked him up off of his feet, kicking and screaming.

"*Put me down ya big ape*, I'm not leaving Angel here for the dinks!"

"Shut up Junior, look the corpsmen are right here, see!"

"Hold still or I'll roll you up in a body bag like a burrito you crazy beaner. You can sweat in it all the way back to An Hoa for all I care," Hightower shouted to his friend over the beating of the chopper's rotor blades.

"*Yeah*, *damn skippy*," JoJo added sarcastically.

"Shut your trap JoJo, I don't need any of your jive nigger bullshit right now," Hightower fired back at his least favorite marine.

"Who you callin nigger **JIM**, you better watch I don't bust a cap in your big white behind while you run back to the chopper, *that's right*, you heard me," JoJo sassed back, looking around to see if he had enough witnesses.

"You jerk-offs better be on that transport in ten *God damn* seconds or I'll bag and tag each of your sorry asses and write your mommas myself, now *MOVE OUT*," shouted Sergeant Marquette as he ran up on the trio of squabbling grunts.

He motioned to the corpsmen to pick up Angel's body and take him back to the helicopter. He turned to see if the three loud mouths had started for the transport as he ordered, fully prepared to shoot whoever was still standing where he last saw them. They were already at the chopper and

Hightower was shoving Junior through the side door. Percy followed the corpsmen back to their ride, about three or four strides behind them. They were about five yards from the waiting chopper when the whole area erupted in small arms fire. Rounds were bouncing off of the helicopters, the trees and audibly ripping through the thick elephant grass making a sound like tearing wrapping paper. Percy let out a holler as he felt the bullet rip into his right hamstring muscle. Stopping dead in his tracks, he collapsed onto his left knee. Turning instinctively he opened fire in the general direction of the enemy. The door-gunner opened fire as well, covering Percy with hundreds of hot shell casings, each of them burning him wherever they made contact with his uncovered skin.

"Oh shit," he exclaimed rolling to his left to get out of the way of the hot little bastards.

As the corpsmen lifted Angel onto the chopper the man holding the litter on the outside of the helicopter took two rounds in the back. He dropped his end of the litter and then Angel's lifeless body, was hit by four or five rounds as well, the body bag ripping into tattered pieces. Percy scrambled to his feet, the pain in his leg nearly causing him to pass out. He grabbed the fallen corpsman and pulled him to his feet, shoving him as close to the hovering chopper as he could. The other corpsman and one of Percy's marines from the platoon, PFC Scotty Jenkins, grabbed the unconscious man and dragged him into the helicopter. Percy turned back around, reloaded his M16 with a fresh clip and continued to return fire.

"Come on Gunny, gimmie your hand man, **hey**, *gimmie your hand*," yelled Jenkins to his wounded platoon sergeant. Percy couldn't hear him over the rotor noise and his chattering weapon.

"GUNNY, GUNNY!"

Percy looked back over his shoulder, his weapon becoming almost too hot to hold, the smell of cordite filling his nostrils. He tried to blink the sweat from his eyes, not wanting to lift a hand from his M16 and risk being over run by Charlie. The dinks couldn't be more than a hundred feet from his position now. Looking around he could see that this was the last chopper still on the ground. He could hear Jenkins urging him to get moving, he could hear Mr. Charlie shouting at him as well. He was bleeding badly and he knew the only thing keeping him on his feet was the adrenaline pumping swiftly through his body.

"Gunny, take my hand man," Jenkins pleaded, one foot on the skid, leaning halfway out of the chopper, clinging to the airframe with one hand.

Percy turned back towards the enemy and squeezed off the last of his clip then dropped his weapon. He turned to reach for the soldier's hand but the chopper had drifted up, just out of his reach. He tried to stand but the strength was gone from him, his right leg too badly damaged. He was ready to surrender to his fate when the helicopter skid appeared in front of his eyes and a pair of strong hands grabbed onto him. Jenkins pulled with all of his might on his sergeant's shoulders and dragged him onto the skid below him. The corpsman holding onto his legs raised a hand to the pilot and signaled for him to take off. The young pilot lifted the chopper from the ground gently so as not to drop the precious cargo. As it climbed, Jenkins and the corpsman struggled with the task of pulling Percy into the aircraft. The chopper pitched suddenly to the right, sending everyone sliding toward the open door. The door-gunner slipped from his perch, his weapon tilting skyward, spraying the air with hot lead, mercifully, missing the rotors blades. Finally gaining control, the pilot leveled out the helicopter.

The door-gunner unhooked himself from the airframe and grabbed the two body bags before they slipped out the side door. He dragged the Lieutenant Sheridan's and Angel's bodies back to the center of the aircraft and then went over to help PFC Jenkins and the corpsman. The chopper continued to climb as the three of them worked on bringing Percy into the hold of the aircraft. Small arms rounds struck the bottom of the helicopter and a few ricocheted around the hold, but no one was hit. Jenkins looked down at his sergeant and the two of them made eye contact. Strangely, Percy noticed that this kid looked a lot like his Aunt Charlotte's boy Henry. It was funny that he would be thinking like that right this minute, but he did. He smiled up at Jenkins, a big toothy grin. It was a smile that he hadn't used in a very, very long time. Scotty Jenkins looked back at the Gunnery Sergeant and returned the smile. "What was this big goofy face all about, he wondered, it just seemed so absurd?" Jenkins tried to stay serious, but Gunny just looked so damn funny, and that 'Buckwheat' smile was so big, he couldn't stop the giggles, this was so ridiculous!

"*Jesus Christ, Gunny*, you are one crazy mutha, you know that," he said laughing out loud. Looking back over his shoulder while he struggled to get a better grip on Sergeant Marquette, he saw that the other two guys were looking at him kind of strange as well.

"It's OK fellas, I think that Gunny might have a feather up his non-com ass," he said, breaking into a deep belly laugh.

PFC Jenkins turned around to get back to the business of hauling Gunny into the chopper, when the round hit him square in the face, his head exploded like a ripe melon hitting the pavement. The corpsman and the door-gunner fell backward, as the weight they were supporting became lighter by half. Gunnery Sergeant Percy Marquette fell back to the earth watching the chopper get smaller and smaller as he waited for impact and the sweet relief of death. He laughed out loud right up until the moment he hit the ground and closed his eyes on this life forever.

Hightower kept looking out the helicopter from over the shoulder of the door-gunner who was tethered to the airframe. He was drawing some irritated looks from the guy so he sat back down on his helmet, pulling his knees close to him. He looked across at Junior and JoJo, they must have made up because Junior was fast asleep on JoJo's shoulder. He and JoJo made eye contact and acknowledged one another with a nod of the head. Hightower peeked around the center bar and looked into the cockpit of the Huey. The two guys flying the chopper were shaking around in the buffeting turbulence as badly as everyone else, there was no such thing, as 'first class' on a bird like this. You were lucky to get off these things with both your kidneys still operating.

"*Hey man*, did everyone off the ground back there," Hightower shouted at the lieutenant in the pilot seat? There was no reply.

"*Excuse me sir*, did we get everybody?"

The pilot looked back at Hightower and gave him the *'OK'* sign, touching his thumb and index finger together forming a letter *'O'* sort of.

"*Yeah, I think so*," he shouted his voice half stuttering with all the turbulence. Somehow that response didn't make Hightower feel any better, there just wasn't enough *smile in his style*. He stared back out the open door and watched the countryside whiz by.

"Kinda hard to figure all this shit out, *ain't it*," JoJo said loudly from across the way.

Wesley looked at him and sort of nodded in agreement, he didn't want to hear any of JoJo's usual bullshit, but he was much too tired to protest.

"Yeah, one minute we're in hell, and the next we're flying back to a warm cot, three squares and all the jack we can drink or weed we can toke, a real vacation, *right?*"

JoJo looked down at his bleeding arm, he must have taken a little shrapnel during the shit storm back at the hot LZ.

"*Lord, will you look at that*. Looks like Mr. Charlie has done bought old JoJo some RR in Saigon. Gonna be some mighty fine split-tail there mother fucker, *fine, fine, fine*, and ole JoJo's gonna be gettin his groove on baby," he said closing his tired eyes and smiling broadly.

The door-gunner seemed amused by JoJo's performance as he laughed out loud. "*Fuckin A man, Fuckin A*," he said in agreement. Hightower watched JoJo's head roll around with the turbulence, thinking to himself how different everyone was and then again, how they were all the same. Back in the world none of these guys would ever have come together, at least not on their own they wouldn't. *In country*, the rules were different. In country you made new rules and they were all about survival baby. In country it wasn't your race, color, or religion that was important. It was a man's heart, guts, and nerve that they were measured by. The conditions here were equalizing, it made them all the same. Everyone watched after everyone else because everyone had the same thing to lose, their life, and it made brothers of the oddest couples. After all, they were just a bunch of kids tossed together from all walks of life, except maybe the usual privileged few. They were expected to do the unthinkable, the down right unconscionable. These teams of misfits, when idle and inert, were only a danger to themselves really. But when stirred and shaken they came together in an extremely volatile mixture, one that the enemy came to fear. Fear was the catalyst, the motivator, and the glue that held them together. Hightower wondered for a moment if they would carry that closeness back to the world with them. Then he snorted a sigh and shook his head.

"No way," he said in a loud whisper…*"**No way!**"*

"*What you lookin at motherfucker,* you thinkin about kissin me or something, you big ass gorilla," JoJo said tiredly from under his tipped helmet.

"Shut up JoJo, don't you ever give your mouth a rest man, I know my ears could use one right about now?"

"Fuck you Wesley!"

"Fuck you Joseph!"

"Hey, fuck both of you *mensas*, I'm trying to get some beauty sleep here *cabrons*, cut me a break OK," Junior said still resting on JoJo's shoulder.

"Junior, get your greasy enchilada ass off of me and go sit by your girlfriend over there," JoJo said pointing over at Hightower!

"*Man, JoJo* I was just getting comfortable," Junior whined as he crawled over to Hightower's side of the chopper.

"Scoot over gordo, I need to crash here next to my *carnal*," Junior said to Hightower, pointing to the exhausted marine next to him. He curled up on the space next to the big Texan, tucking his hands between his knees and resting his head on a stack of flack jackets.

"Mitchell, hey, Mitchell, you still alive under that hat *baboso*?"

Mitchell Rojas peeked out from under his tipped helmet and smiled weakly.

"Yo Junior, I'm still here homeboy," he said.

"*Horale*! *Hey man*, you see Angel get it today?"

"Quiet Junior, leave it be *ese*, go back to sleep and remember the smiles man, not the bag of parts in the Huey back there," Mitchell said, pointing over his shoulder with his thumb.

"Amen brother Rojas, Amen to that," JoJo said from behind his closed tired eyes.

"Nite-nite homeys," Junior said, closing his eyes and falling quickly back to sleep.

Junior decided to deal with Angel's death later, *they all would*, right now, they just wanted to enjoy the relative safety of the moment. Junior's buddies leaned their heads back against the airframe and followed his lead, choosing slumber for the duration of the bumpy ride back to An Hoa. What they *didn't know* about Gunny or Jenkins was a blessing for now. There would be plenty of time to deal with that mess later.

Twelve

("...Sittin on the dock of the bay, watching the tide roll away. Sittin on the dock of the bay, wasting time"...Otis Redding)

Da Nang, Republic of Viet Nam, 7 December 1968

1:30am

"I'll see your half a buck and raise you a fiver, *jack*, what do you think about that, huh," said Lance Corporal Larry Polen, slapping a *'low five'* to his table neighbor, Corpsman Tony Yamamoka. They toasted his bold move by downing jelly-jar shots of JD, Larry managing to spill most of it into his lap. Knowing him, I was inclined to believe that the act was more deliberate than accidental; he really was kind of a weenie [Mental note here, *'weenie'* as an adjective was not a candidate for *'the list'*, unless of course it was meant as an insult!]. Now five dollars was a pretty hefty bet for this group, it wasn't like we were the Rockefellers playing at some posh club or anything close to that. No, we were just a rag tag gaggle of bored out of our mind jar-heads killing time, idly filling in the hours before the next bout of insanity.

"What are you so proud of Larry, you got nothing on top and I know you ain't got nothing underneath. Hell half of Saigon knows that, you know how women talk boy," snarled Lt. JG Aaron Walker, one of the five Medi-Vac pilots assigned to this FSSB (force service support group) unit. He wasn't exactly the poster boy example of military *esprit de corps*. Tall for a chopper

115

pilot, too tall if you stayed close to the rules, always out of uniform, trade mark colored shades, hair over the collar, and an ever-present five o'clock shadow. To say the least he was a tad unconventional, to say the most he was a royal pain in the keester for the CO. He glared at Cpl. Polen from over the top of his rectangle cut, rose colored shades, rocking back and forth on the Coca-Cola crate he was sitting on, watching to see if he flinched. Larry Polen, the polar opposite of the man across from him did not twitch a muscle, barely drew breath from what I could see, drummed the fingers of his right hand on his three down cards.

"You *in* or *out*." He asked cool, calm, and collected?

Now I had seen this act a hundred times since arriving at this duty station a month ago, but I had to admit it never ceased to amaze me how this mouse of a man *ALWAYS* bested this self-centered lout. Apparently common sense was an option on the *Walker* model, which came standard with beauty, brawn and bravado.

"*Ah man*, he's not bluffing, he has to have trips under there, I'm out," said Lt. Walker as he shoved his hand towards the center, letting out an audible sigh of frustration. "Your play Ethan, maybe you can pull a couple more hearts from down under to go with the three you have topside and flush this weasel out!"

"*Aaron*, you folded with a pair of kings and queens showing, Polen doesn't have squat, *are ya completely daft man*," I hollered at the Lieutenant Junior Grade!

"*You tell him Irish,*" yelled 2nd Lt. Carla Cardinale, one of the surgical nurses and a regular at these card games. "What an *'maroon'* Walker," Carla said, borrowing a line from Bugs Bunny.

"And you have the nerve to bag on poor Larry about his tiny stones, gimme a break," she laughed!

"Up yours dishwater," LT Walker snapped back, weakly taking aim at her hair color.

"In your dreams buddy, you should be so lucky," Carla shot back as she peeked at her hole cards one more time.

"Come on Ethan, its your bet, are you in or out," she said, skillfully shielding her slightly bent hole cards with her right hand?

I stared at the pair of eight's that I had showing, laying unimpressively next to a duce of hearts, a ten of diamonds, and the ace of clubs. Now I knew that my pair of eight's had another sibling underneath and that three of a kind was a pretty darn good hand in seven-card stud. But, Cpl. Polen was awfully confident at this wee hour of the morning sitting on such a seemingly cold hand. And I was suddenly feeling very guilty about questioning Aaron Walker's instincts! I peeked at my hole cards one more time, shielding them nicely, ala nurse Carla. Nope, looked like my silent prayer had gone unanswered, the water had not changed to wine, and neither of my other two cards had changed into an eight. So I decided to use the sense that the good lord had given me.

"I fold," I said pushing my cards toward the pile of script in the center of the small table.

"*Yeah*, well if the altar boy here is nervous than so am I, count me out," said Tony Yamamoka, tossing his cards, out of turn, into the pile as well.

Tony and I had been flying together with this Evac Squadron since the day we arrived in country six weeks ago. He was a good-natured guy, around my age, a foot shorter than I was but built like a power lifter, which came in handy given the duty we had pulled. Hopping off of helicopters and scampering around the countryside hauling wounded and worse back and forth had been a literal baptism of fire. Having someone like Tony around made the task tolerable. He would crack jokes the whole time we were under fire, carrying litters as fast and as gently as we could to the safety of the chopper and then racing back into the insanity to fetch another poor soul. He was able to keep us focused on what was at our fingertips, helped block out whatever was happening around us. In the process, making our entire world about six meters in diameter during the seven or eight, 2 to 3 minute dashes we performed routinely on each rescue mission. It was a gift he had, that was for true, one that I thanked God for each and every day.

"What is up with you guys, did someone hang a sign out front declaring this a '*testosterone free zone*' or what," Carla sighed. She looked at her cards again, she knew she had nothing, but she wanted to still be in when that weenie Larry Polen had to fold. And now he was going to take the biggest pot of the night and there was nothing she could do about it! She was pretty sure that *his nothing* was bigger than *her nothing*, so she leaned back against the tent support and pushed her cards into the pot with both hands.

"Take it Larry, looks like you're the only one at the table with testicles tonight, at least I have a natural excuse," she said looking disgustedly at Tony and me.   Lance Cpl. Polen reached across the table and wrapped his two skinny arms around the pile of script, chits, i.o.u.'s, and losing hands. He pulled them into his personal comfort zone, a triumphant grin spreading across his thin taut face.

"Pleasure doing business with y'all, I think this will be enough to turn in on tonight gents. Oh, and let's not forget the generous contribution from the fairer sex as well, thank you kindly nurse Carla," Larry Polen said slow and sweet, like pouring cold molasses from a mason jar.

"That's *Lt. Cardianle* to you stumpy, and I hope you choke on it!"

"Now, now, let's not get *catty* **'lieutenant'** nurse Carla," Cpl. Polen shot back.

Carla scrunched down low in her folding chair, extended her left leg as far as she could and kicked Larry in the balls under the table.

"*Oooooooooo*, you bitch," squealed Cpl. Polen frantically reaching for his groin, spilling his treasures all over the tarpon floor and slamming his forehead onto the table.

"*Meeeeooowwwww*," she giggled as she got up and walked towards the door.

"See you ladies in the morning, I'm gonna catch some sack time before reveille. Hope I didn't scramble those eggs Larry, *nitey nite sweet pea*!" Lt. JG Aaron Walker hopped up on that cue and trotted after Nurse Carla.

"Good night girls, I think my luck is about to change, don't wait up," he said confidently as he went out the door into the dank night air.

The rickety wood framed door slammed behind him making a loud slapping noise that woke our newest roommate from his light slumber. Mitchell Rojas had joined the outfit a week before, replacing one of our door gunners, Rollie Lopez, who had been rotated back to the world after fifteen months in Viet Nam. Rollie (his real name was Raul), had been on the *'short'* list for so long, that he had started to have the local street urchins take the first bite of his candy bars, just in case, what a nerd! Actually it was a well-known fact that the *'shorter'* you got, the more superstitious you became, it was all relative. That kind of behavior would have really bothered me a lifetime ago, but since my battlefield inauguration, a scant two hours after arriving in country, I had become a numb to it all, if not down right callused.

That was a harsh day in my short life to date. Twenty of us, *'newbies'* they called us, were standing by a transport waiting to board when a loud explosion shook the ground and peppered us with debris and shrapnel. A jeep that was parked across the road from us, jumped straight up into the air, a good fifteen or twenty feet. I had been watching that very jeep the whole time I was standing in line with the others, getting a visual lay of the land so to speak. There had been two soldiers sitting in the front when a kid wearing a Red Sox jacket, a little boy maybe nine or ten years old, walked up to them carrying a puppy dog. I was watching as the driver reached down to pet the animal when the satchel charge strapped to the child went off. It had been concealed under the foul garment. I could remember later thinking callously. *I hate the Red Sox!* The explosion left a six-foot crater in the ground, the jeep a crumbled mess, and it's occupants scattered around the perimeter in torn and tattered pieces, the child and puppy vaporized. If that weren't chaos enough, three of the newbies standing the very same line as Tony and I had been killed by the shrapnel that sprayed across the road in our direction. They had been in this country for one hundred twenty-seven minutes, just long enough to become a statistic for replay on the six o'clock news back home. My ears rang for days, but I had sustained no other physical injury. But I did learn lesson number one on day number one in country, and that was that *nobody* was guaranteed a tomorrow! So, as far as Rollie's superstitions were concerned, I understood all to well.

Mitchell was nothing like his predecessor, he was in fact the exact opposite when it came to personalities. Rollie was robust, full of life, the first in line for whatever the in-crowd was up for, and Mitchell was shy, quiet and unassuming, the kind of guy that wouldn't say crap if he had a mouthful. At least this was the man that we had come to know over the last eight days. Not exactly what you would expect from someone tasked with blowing the crud out of anything or anyone that got near the Medi-Vac or it's crew. Now that I think about it, I had wondered right from the start how someone like him drew such hazardous duty. I mean he was not much bigger than the weapon he wielded. And if you added up the stacks of ammo boxes with the 50MM machine gun, the weaponry out weighed him by at least a hundred pounds. If it were not for the fact that he was tied to the airframe when he fired the gun, the chattering weapon would have dragged him around behind it as it recoiled wildly.

"Hey man, what's with all the noise amigos," Mitchell asked sleepily, looking in my direction.

"Games just ending Mitch, go back to sleep," I said.

"Yeah, OK," he replied, rolling over, turning his back to the room.

"Thanks for the contribution to the Cpl. Polen retirement fund fellow marines," Larry said while he scooped all of his winnings into his helmet. He tucked the hat under his arm and made his way out of the tent and towards the non-com quarters. Tony threw an open canteen at him, and a stream of water arced across the doorway as the canteen hit the canvas wall.

"EAT ME LARRY," Tony yelled from his bunk, bending over to unlace his jump boots, getting ready for lights out.

I walked over to my own bunk after I tugged on the chain from the ceiling outlet and cut the juice to the bulb. The new day had officially begun a couple of hours ago, but it sort of ran into the day before, which had sort of run into the week before. Lesson number two in country had come over time, I had discovered during the last six weeks that warfare was ninety-five percent agonizing boredom, accentuated by five percent of sheer terror. Secretly, down deep, I was rooting for boredom to win out over terror in the months to come. I scooted my jump boots underneath my cot, knelt beside it, and genuflected. I prepared to recite the prayer that I had said every night since I was a small boy. My Grandmother had taught it to my mother and she had taught it to Shannon and I. Of course each generation added a little something of their own, but it was basically the same as when Grandmother brought it over from her village in Ireland. I cleared my throat and listened for Tony and Mitchell, they had heard this so often, they had started to whisper along with me a couple of nights ago. I wasn't sure if they knew that I knew, but no matter, the Lord accepts even the curious converts.

> *If you're hearing me Lord, if you have some time*
> *Let me thank you for your blessings so kind*
> *Let me praise you for the grace that you give*
> *Let me share your love wherever I live*
> *God bless Mothers and Fathers and Grandparents too*
> *Aunties and Uncles and friends old and new*
> *Puppy dogs, kitty cats, the whole petting zoo*
> *Father just love us till we come home to you*
> *Amen*

I genuflected once more and crawled into my rack.

"Thanks Ethan," whispered Tony from across the tent.

"Si, *gracias ese*, gracias la Senor," yawned a weary Mitchell Rojas.

"No worries bunkies," I said, pulling the heavy wool blanket up to my chin so I could sweat myself to sleep.

3:30am

WOOSH, THUMP, THUMP, THUMP...The tent was suddenly illuminated with brilliant white light as the flares exploded high overhead. We all hit the floor and rolled under our cots, pulling our helmets onto our heads as quickly as we could. Holding our breath we waited for the mortar rounds to start falling in and around the camp. One minute, two minutes, three than five, no sound, the light beginning to fade as the flares burned out. We continued to wait for the all clear signal, you never knew about these things. Sometimes Charlie just like to mess your our minds. Another few minutes still nothing, finally it was pitch black out and then one by one, lights began to flicker on around the camp. Yep, Mr. Charlie was just messin with us again, but better *messed with* than *messed up* I thought. We got back into bed without saying a word to one another, sadly these kinds of shows had become routine.

6:30am

Reveille came a little later here than back at boot camp. There was no rush lately, we hadn't had any casualties to speak of for a couple of weeks, thank God! Once the PA system finished its announcement I turned onto by back and stared at the ceiling for a second. I had kicked off the wool blanket in my sleep trying to escape the home made sauna and lay there in my government-issue skivvies, bathed in sweat. My tongue felt like it was wrapped in bacon and I made that smacking noise everyone does when they first wake up. Jack Daniel's was not as smooth as Jameson was, but then good whiskey was always better than fair bourbon Uncle Chuck would say. I swung my legs out over the edge of my cot and let my bare feet come in contact with the canvas floor. Tony and Mitchell were already back from the latrine and showers and were lacing up their boots.

"Get enough rest there buzz," Tony said sarcastically.

Apparently I may have been snoring ever so slightly, a trait I picked up from my mother oddly enough? My mother loved to sleep, and she could sleep through an earthquake I reckoned. But the woman would snore softly on her back and drool slightly on her stomach. Da used to say he would have to buy stock in Sears Roebuck with all the pillowcases he bought each year. The only way she slept peacefully and with out incident was tucked snuggly onto my father's shoulder. That was the best way to fall asleep with a woman my Da once told me. But sonny he said, after a while the blood settles in your arm and it's the pins and needle treatment for ye. Oh Ethan, the tingling so intense it could drive a person daft enough to chew his own arm off. Not that I'd ever need the advise personally, but I stored it away to share with others should the opportunity ever present itself!

"Slept like a baby *Yama-lama-ding-dong*," I teased back. He wasn't amused and patted his sidearm to let me know. Sometimes you could joke with Tony and sometimes it was dangerous, he definitely had a chip on his shoulder from way back somewhere in life?

"Chow time homeboys, let's go see what the mess sergeant backed over for breakfast," Mitchell said, distracting our tense roommate. Tony smiled at Mitchell's joke mostly because it was unusual for Mitchell to speak at all.

"OK Mitchy boy, let's eat," he replied as he finished tying his bootlace. "You coming Ethan?"

"I'll be right along, need to brush this rug off of my tongue and take a cool shower, save me some road kill you guys!"

I grabbed my shaving kit, my towel and some fresh underwear and followed my two friends out of the tent. They went east to the mess tent and I went west to the showers, it was already hot out, this would be my first Christmas away from home, my first Christmas without snow, this whole Viet Nam experience would be a series of firsts and lasts I reckoned.

8:30am

After some fairly decent chow in the breakfast mess, we went about our daily chores. We took about twenty minutes to square away our quarters and then went over to the chopper to check our gear. Tony and I sorted through the first aid kits and took inventory, making sure none of the meds or any other essentials had grown legs in the night and found their way into some junkie's locker box. Occasionally Mr. Charlie himself would sneak in and walk off with whatever they could, they had people suffering as well, it was hard to blame them. Mitchell uncovered and cleaned his weapon, sitting cross-legged in the chopper; he broke down the gun and cleaned it like he was bathing his child. It always amazed me how beautiful fine machinery could be, and how ugly a purpose it could have. Being an objector I did not carry a weapon, but I understood the necessity for them in man's world.

"This is one bad ass gun Ethan," Mitchell said to me as he oiled the barrel of the weapon. "I can grease dozens of dinks with this mutha *ese*! It's a beautiful thing man, a beautiful thing."

"Come on Mitch, you know it bothers me when you talk like that," I said preaching.

"It's not really you, those are just words you heard from someone else, I can see it on your face that you're not comfortable saying them."

"Leave him be Ethan, we need him sharp and dangerous man, *you don't want to screw up his aim do you*," Tony scolded me!

"That's not what I meant to do," I started to reply.

"YEAH, BUT YOU ARE FUCKING WITH HIS HEAD, *SO KNOCK IT OFF*," Tony said getting right in my face.

Lesson number three in country, war is war and peace is peace, and never the twain shall meet. I had pushed his fear button and I knew it, so I quietly backed down and continued inventorying the meds bag. Tony stood there watching me, waiting for me to kick this up a notch, I had more sense than that. We needed to be tight as a unit and fighting amongst ourselves wasn't a good tactic in that regard.

"Sorry guys, I'll try and leave the preaching for Sunday's after I get my collar," I said. "And hopefully before I get my wings," I added trying to get Tony to ease up a bit.

"Man, how did you end up here anyway," Tony said disgustedly, shoving me playfully as he walked past me heading aft to check the stokes?

"I was drafted, just like you!"

"Hey Ethan," Mitchell said in a loud whisper. I looked over his way.
"Yeah?"

"I'm sorry amigo, but he's right ya know. I gotta keep my head in the game, for all of us. I want to get home and see my Louisa and my little boy Miguel, ya know?"

"I know Mitch, forgive me, bad habit of mine. I feel like I can read people, it's weird.

Sometimes I feel as though I can see right into a person's heart, know just what they are feeling. I don't know if its intuition or wishful thinking, but whatever it is, it's very real." Mitchell nodded and looked out the door to see where Tony was.

"It's funny Mitchell, I have had this sense all of my life. I knew that my father was going to die, I knew that I would be coming here, and I know that I will be going home. These weren't hunches, I KNEW THEM, like reading tomorrow's newspaper?" I looked at my friend and I could see he was looking at me strangely.

"Sorry Mitch, maybe it's the road kill from breakfast talking, don't pay any attention to me, I'm just rambling," I said getting back to my work.

"No ese, *I too believe* that God works through people, I've seen this myself, I have. *Madre Dios Ethan*, it was a miracle, we all saw it. I watched Him save my Miguel with the heart of another child. I watched while my woman, my Louisa held our dead baby in her arms and sobbed. I watched this tiny *nina,* maybe only a couple years older than my son, come to her and bring him back with a kiss and a smile. I saw this Ethan, *I saw this myself,*" he said in a low voice, his eyes moist and glassy. Mitchell sniffled and wiped his eyes and face with his shirtsleeve. He stood up and placed the butt of the big gun on the floor of the chopper and pulled hard on the breech several times quickly, working the oil into the weapon. "I know that story sounds weird, maybe even silly. But its true *ese*, it really happened to us. One day maybe you'll come see us after we get back to the world, when you become '*Father Kelly*' you'll come and bless my home and my family, OK?"

"Sure Mitch, sure, it'll be my pleasure buddy," I replied, watching him re-cover the machine gun and jump out of the aircraft.

"I'm hittin the head homey," Mitchell said, slapping my shoulder as he passed by. I nodded in acknowledgement and zipped the meds bag closed.

"Let's go to the drugstore Tony, inventory says that we're light three morphine set ups and some liquid stitches (super glue).

11:45am

I can barely stand the humidity, just breathing starts the sweat glands into overdrive! It would be almost bearable if there were just a hint of a breeze, but no such luck, the air hung dank and dead calm. At least Mr. Charlie had sense enough to stay underground safe in the cool womb of mother earth. While we interlopers' sweltered topside, the elements working on draining the might from our fight so to speak. Tony was reading a stack of Fantastic Four comics in his underwear on his bunk. He had a green sweat towel over his head under his Orioles baseball cap. Mitchell was lying on his bunk fully dressed, both his arms crossed over his face cat napping. He didn't look near as uncomfortable as the rest of us, barely sweating at all.

"Hey Mitchell, how do you do that man," I asked, hoping he was still awake?

"It's not hard amigo, I learned this as a child working in the lettuce fields. You just wear an undershirt beneath a long sleeved shirt, a bandana around your neck, and keep your head and eyes covered. You will sweat like everyone else, but the layer of clothing underneath stays nice and damp, keeping your body temperature from rising and your energy and strength from escaping into the air."

"Gracias man!"

"Por nada homey."

"Chow time boys," Tony said as he pulled on his pants.

"How can you eat in heat like this," I asked?

They didn't call him Tony Baloney for nothing; the man had a stomach made of cast iron! I think that he would have been a fine addition to the eating machines I left back in Albany. I do believe that Paulie and Kenny would have been proud of this character!

"I can eat anything, anywhere, anytime, as long as there is gravy or Tabasco at the table, then *whatever* they're serving is one of my favorites!" Tony said with more than a little pride.

Tony slipped on his unlaced boots and grabbed a shirt from the clothesline we had running down the center of the tent. You had to keep the line inside because it rained at least three times a day around here. He gave the shirt a quick sniff. As long as it didn't smell like vomit, it was wearable. The rules of etiquette were slightly different in the forward areas. Mitch and I trudged slowly after him. I wonder what the mess sergeant had run over for lunch?

2:30pm

"Any mail today Lt. Walker," Mitchell and I asked in unison as we passed his quarters? Aaron Walker was sitting out front in on a lawn chair in a swimsuit and a surfer tee shirt, you know, the kind the Beach Boys wore, wide red and white horizontal stripes. He looked more like he was on vacation in Malibu then flying Hueys in Viet *damn* Nam, pardon my French, now there's another entry for the list! I had already added at least five pages since arriving. Why, by the end of my tour there may be multiple volumes! I decided then and there all future entries would be mental only.

"Sorry girls, your momma didn't send no cookies this week Kelly. *Oh yeah*, and she didn't send any tacos either Rojas," Lt. Walker said acidly! We must have disturbed his beauty nap so we apologized.

"Sorry dude, didn't mean to frazzle your karma, *like wow man*," we chimed in together, running the rest of the way in case Aaron had a rock nearby. We slowed down as we reached the tent and looked back over our shoulders to see if he was following, nope, *safe!*

"Now what do you want to do, it won't be suppertime for another couple of hours," Mitchell asked.

These slow periods between actions were murder, oh not actual murder that came with the actions, but no less deadly to the general moral of the unit. We had finished a days work in about three hours this morning and we didn't want to get too far ahead or we'd have nothing to do tomorrow. I looked through the screen window over at Tony who was sitting on my locker box.

"Hey, three flies up?"

"Yeah, I'm in," he replied.

"What's that," Mitchell asked?

"Baseball my Spanish friend, that's baseball!"

"I'm Mexican, and don't you need bases and a field and a whole bunch of other guys to play this game?"

"Ahhh, that's the beauty of this game. It's so simple, you can adjust it to fit any situation. It is quite possibly the most perfect game God ever created, aside from foot races of course, *but those are no fun*, nothing to swing a bat at," I explained.

Tony came out of the tent with our gloves (I had two, Da's and mine), a couple of balls and our only bat, a 34 that I had bought at the PX in Da Nang. We headed toward the other side of the camp just past the mess tent and the post-op area. And as we passed by the nurses quarters Lt. Carla jumped out of her bunk and ran after us.

"I'm playing too," she yelled.

"Oh wait a sec, lemme get my Dodger cap," she hollered, stopping quickly to lean back inside of her tent and lift her baseball cap from its perch over the door.

"OK, now I'm ready!"

"You're killing me Nurse Carla, I mean the Dodgers, *really?* Oh well, praise God it wasn't a RedSox cap you went back for, cause then there would be trouble for sure!"

"In your ear Kelly, you Yankee fans are all the same, the Babe's been dead for years, and Mantle was over rated, ya big Irish goofball," she taunted back. I ignored her insults and looked over at Mitchell.

"You see Mitchy my boy, only baseball could breath the life back into a day as dull as this. Stay close to me son, and I'll be teaching about a whole new world," I said to him as put my arm around his shoulder and blathered on about Yogi, DiMaggio and Mantle.

5:00pm

The game had ended in a tie, not because an equal number of runs had been scored by each side, but because Tony had pulled his 45 automatic and threatened to shoot the next batter that scored during our last inning rally. The game was called in the name of pacifism or sheer cowardice, you choose, never the less nobody was killed and everyone won, seemed like the right call given the circumstances. I guess you could say Tony was a sore loser, a good thing in wartime, a not so good thing in peacetime, hopefully he would outgrow it by the time we rotated home! We tossed all of the gear into the tent as we passed by, then went to the latrine to wash up for supper. I wonder what the mess sergeant had run over for dinner tonight?

7:30pm

I rolled over onto my stomach in my bunk and continued writing my letter to my little sister.

"So, like I said, I really like the picture of you and mom sitting on the front porch steps at home, thanks for sending it to me. And no, I have not seen any rats the size of small dogs over here. But as long as the subject of dogs has come up. Yes it is true, some of the local people raise dogs for food. I was kind of grossed out by it at first, but then it's not like there is a supermarket just around the corner over here either. People do what they need to in order to survive and provide for their families. I learned real quickly that families are the same everywhere. They may look different, dress different, talk different, and eat different foods, but they all act the same. The kids all giggle the same way as you and I did, and the parents all smile the same way that Mom and Da do. I mean did, oh, I'm sorry Shannon, sometimes I still think Da is here with us. Don't say anything to Mom or Uncle Liam, but sometimes I talk with Da. When its dark and quiet, and I'm pretty sure everyone is sleeping or occupied, I kind of chat with him. I don't actually hear him answer me at least not with words that I can actually hear, but I swear girl, I can sometimes feel an answer inside of me. I mean I feel all warm and I

shudder like someone has walked right through me, and it makes me smile, makes me feel like I've just been hugged. I wish I was home with all of you right now, I wish I could hug you and tuck you in like I did before all of this. But don't worry ye wee chiseller, I'll be home soon enough and I'll make up for all of the nights I've missed. Keep up with your studies sis, and help Mom as best you can, at least try not to drive her completely mad! Kiss and hug everyone for me, and tell Mom there is a letter for her on the way as well. Merry Christmas, XOXOXOXO, your loving brother Ethan"

I blew on the ink a little to make sure it was dry enough to fold and place into an envelope. After reading it through once more I folded it neatly as was my custom, and then slipped it into the pre-addressed envelope. I gave the mail a little kiss and then placed it on top of my locker box so I would remember to give it to Cpl. Polen when he came over for the nightly card game. Looking at my watch I saw that the gang would start arriving within the hour, I decided I had time for a short catnap, maybe it would improve my luck.

9:30pm

Sleepily I swiped at my face, something was tickling my nose. I opened my eyes but there was something covering them. Reaching up I pulled off the obstruction, it was one of Tony's scummy sweat socks, beautiful, I had slept through the start of the game, and been poisoned at the same time! I tossed the sock at Tony who was busy looking at the five cards in his hand.

"Look what the cat dragged in," Tony said ducking in time for the sock to fly past him and onto Mitchell's cot.

"Smooth Yamamoka, now I've got the tweener seat," I whined!

"You snooze, you loose, you know the house rules Ethan," Larry Polen said smugly.

The tweener seat was the chair between Nurse Carla and Aaron Walker. Whoever sat there was subjected to all of his grab ass thrusts and her less than lady like parries. It was a constant battle with them and pointless really, as she always ended up with him at the conclusion of the night. In the mean time I would be pinched and jabbed black and blue, talked through and kissed over the entire game. I looked at Aaron and decided my plea would fall onto deaf ears with him, so, I turned Carla's way.

"Hey Lieutenant, would you mind changing seats with me tonight? I mean we both know you two are gonna leave here together anyway, can't we just dispense with the Passion play this once, please," I begged, wearing my most convincing altar boy expression? She looked at me for a long time, holding up the game.

"Hey Carla, are you in or out," snapped Cpl. Polen?

She ignored him and continued to look at me, rocking her head from shoulder to shoulder like a puppy. She put her cards down and then placed both her hands on my face and kissed me softly on my mouth.

"Nope," she said pulling away from me.

"He cheats when I sit next to him. He keeps trying to look at my whole cards while he tries to cop a feel," she added.

"OK *Larrykins*, I'm in, whatcha got there sweet pea?" Larry showed his trips and Carla showed him the finger, it was going to be a long night!

11:30pm

The game broke up early tonight, Cpl. Polen's lucky streak was still on and when three of the four cards he drew were aces to go with the one he was holding, Tony decided he had to be cheating. It didn't matter that Tony had been dealing, he was sure that Larry was just sneaky enough to pull it off. So before Tony could find his sidearm and permanently even the odds at the game, Nurse Carla, in a rare showing of compassion, leaped across the table and dragged the protesting Corporal out of the tent and off to the safety of anywhere but here! Actually, by the look on Larry's face, I believe that he may have been more frightened of Lt. Carla than Tony. After all, Tony was mostly talk when it came to idle threats, and Carla, *well*? Aaron was right behind the two of them, and so the game was officially cancelled, there was no way he and Carla would be leaving her tent before reveille! Tony switched out the light and hopped onto his cot, "Goodnight girls!"

"Night Tony, night Ethan," Mitchell said pulling his blanket up to his chin.

"G'night all," I answered.

"Hey Ethan, don't forget the prayer *ese*," Mitchell said in the dark.

"I won't Mitchy, in a minute OK?"

"OK, *hey Ethan*, are you really going to be a priest when you get back to the world?"

"Yeah, think so, why do you ask?"

"Well, *that's just it*. Why do you want to be one of those guys?" I suddenly realized that nobody had ever asked me that before, "Good question Mitchy, I've wondered *why* myself many times."

"It sort of comes to this. My whole life I have been taught that God is in my life. As I grew up I began to actually feel that he was, and didn't need to be told as often. And now, at this point in my life, I can really feel Him here with me."

"There is a purpose for me, and I can't say for certain that as a priest it will be revealed, but it's where my faith seems to be leading me."

"So to answer your question, *yeah*, I really am going to be a priest when I get back to the world, when *we all* get back to the world."

"Horale Father Kelly, *horale*."

"Hey Kelly, you know, I don't think that you can pitch in the majors if you're in the clergy, too many Sunday games," Tony teased.

"You're right about that Tony, but I didn't really have a decent curveball anyway."

"That's right, and your fastball was weak too ya noodle armed geek," he said.

"Love you too Tony boy," I teased back weakly, I thought my fastball was pretty good!

"Ethan, will you add my family to the prayer tonight," Mitchell asked?

"Sure, you know I will."

"Hey Mitchell, tell me more about the time your boy was revived?"

"He wasn't revived *ese*, he was returned Ethan, returned from the dead, no doctors, no treatment, he was returned to us by *la Senor*!"

"I felt Him there with us Ethan. Just like you said you could feel him in your life now. He was in that little girl that day, I think that he is still with her."

I started the nightly prayer and was sure to add a request to bless and keep Mitchell's family in the Lords good graces. The fellas prayed along with me, reciting the parts that they remembered, and I wondered when we were through about the things that Mitchell had talked about. I made a mental note to find some time tomorrow to chat with him more about it. Like as not, we were in for yet another ho- hum day. I held my arm up to the screened window and squinted trying to make out the time. It was 11:55pm, lights out at the end of this day; I wonder what the mess sergeant will run over for breakfast tomorrow?

Thirteen

("...Do not withhold good from those to whom it is due. When it is in your power to do it"...Proverbs 3:27)

<u>*San Francisco, California, 10 December 1968*</u>

KC Littleton stared at the cup of yogurt in front of her and then glanced over to her neighbor's desk and studied the corned beef on rye and two dill pickle spears, fresh from the *'Brooklyn Deli'* over in North Beach. She was three weeks into a *do or die* diet, determined to be ready for the paper's New Years Eve party this year! She had already bought the perfect black sequined gown from Sac's Fifth Avenue and the cutest shoes ever, so she just *had* to be strong. Visibly shuddering she reached for the yogurt and started stirring the fruit up from the bottom of the cup. Oh well she thought, it *was* strawberry, her favorite right? KC lifted a spoonful to her face then took one more sideways peek at the sandwich.

"*Oh what the hell*," she said under her breath, and scooted over to Jordan Chen's desk on her four-wheeled wooden chair. Looking around guiltily, she lifted the top slice of the sandwich and removed a generous helping of corned beef and stuffed it into her yogurt cup. Then after licking the mustard off of her fingers, she hastily reassembled the huge sandwich, mashing the pieces together and gently patting the top as if to say, *'hey, thanks a lot!'* She then rolled quietly back to her desk, using her spoon to fold the meat in with

130

her dairy lunch as nonchalantly as possible. Gross you say, maybe, but to someone who hadn't eaten a regular meal in weeks, it was *five star baby!* KC scooped a spoonful into her mouth and closed her eyes, a look of shear ecstasy spreading across her face.

"Oh God, this is *sooooo* good, almost better than, *now what was that called again*, oh yeah, sex," she muttered softly.

It was totally unladylike, but she didn't care, she just chewed the corned beef slowly, savoring each and every morsel. Actually, it had been a tad longer than her current diet since she had experienced that little bit of human distraction. Alright, alright, it had been much longer. **OK, OK, OK**, maybe it had been a whole **YEAR** longer! Who had time for boyfriends and relationships with this job anyways? And forget about one night stands, not to brag or anything, but she was really good, and men were like puppies once she took them home. The only way to get rid of them was to stop feeding the poor babies and then change her telephone number and the locks on her doors. What a *'catch 22'* situation, by New Years Eve she would be the perfect *bait weight,* but she'd only be trolling for nibbles, life really sucked! She took another spoonful of her odd concoction and pushed off from her desk with her right foot, spinning the chair in a series of 360-degree turns.

"*WEEEEE,*" she squealed, this weird mixture was actually pretty good, and she was already fantasizing about how to market the stuff. Now, what could she call it?

"*OOOH I know,*" she whispered to herself.

"*Fruit Crème a la Boeuf,*" she said in her most flagrant French accent. Isn't it queer she thought, how even the most disgusting phrase can sound positively regal *en Francias?*

"Enjoying yourself KC," asked Jordan Chen, leaning back against the side of his desk, arms folded in front of him? She stuck out her leg and stopped her spin in mid revolution, her back to him and the spoon still in her mouth. She started to mumble a response and bit down on the spoon, which flipped the handle up into her face, causing a decent amount of pain when her teeth slipped from the spoon to her tongue.

"**OWWW**, *shit Jordan*, don't sneak up on me like that, you know I hate when you do that!"

"Sorry *shrimp*, guess I should have known better than to leave all that temptation on my desk while I washed up for lunch," Jordan said, sitting down and examining his significantly smaller *'Mile High'* from the deli.

"Hey I told you to stop calling me that too! For Christ's sake Jordan, I'm three inches taller than you *Kato*, and that's without the heels!"

"OK, OK, truce, no more ribbing about your name Miss *LITTLEton* and no more quips about the *Green Hornet's driver*, deal?"

"*DEAL*, now hurry up and cut that sandwich in half, I'm starving over here," KC said finishing her yogurt concoction as fast as she could.

"My God KC, how can someone so beautiful be such an *oinker* when it comes to food?"

"No wonder it's been so long between dates for you!"

"*Oh*, and by the way, I don't look anything like Bruce Lee so stop stereotyping me and my people! Didn't they teach you any social skills at Radcliffe," he asked, handing her half of his sandwich, stopping to count his fingers, making sure that he got them all back!

KC grunted a response as she took a healthy bite, savoring the experience like it would be her last. Watching her eat was more like reading a romance novel; she didn't consume her food so much as she actually seemed to make love to it. Jordan marveled at the way she would chew and then sensually lick the Russian dressing that ran down her arm from the palm of her hand. Breaking his trance, he closed is mouth and cleared his throat, getting back to his lunch and sorting through the papers on his desk.

"So what's got you so cranky today KC, you nearly snapped my head off before I left for lunch!" Taking a sip of her diet cola she spun her chair in his direction and answered him.

"I don't know Jordan, do I really need an excuse to abuse you darling?"

Slowly crossing her legs, she made sure to bat her eyelashes that cute and coy way that he liked so much. Then she placed her chin onto her laced together fingers and stared at him until he was obviously uncomfortable. To be honest, this was really unfair. It was a near lethal dose of sex appeal, especially where Jordan was concerned. The tossed hair, her cute freckled face resting daintily on her delicate hands, her arms raised and tucked in close to her body, causing the maximum amount of cleavage to be revealed through her sheer cream blouse. Oh my gosh she thought, this might actually kill him, *huh*, he should be so lucky! The two of them had dated early in her career at the *Daily News*, and it had gotten pretty serious she had thought. But proving true to his gender, he was really only interested in an *open relationship*, a fact he revealed one night about a year ago when she ran into he and *a friend* at her favorite Italian restaurant in North Beach's *Little Italy*. After introducing her as a *colleague from the paper* to his friend, she decided to totally swear off men, for a little while anyway!

"Come on KC, I thought we were past all of that," Jordan said, involuntarily watching her pose for him, twitching the ankle of her crossed leg steadily and rhythmically.

"Yeah, *well I am*, but I can see that you're not," she said sarcastically, sitting straight up in her chair and turning back to her desk. She started humming *'Just You Wait Henry Higgins'* from *'My Fair Lady'* and turned a page in the newspaper that she was studying. She had been reading up on a series of stories from a local paper in Bakersfield about the capture of a serial rapist. There had been some rather odd circumstances surrounding the event. It was some sort of religious phenomenon, something to that effect. Jordan interrupted her concentration when he tossed his table scraps into the waste bin and opened his can of soda with a loud pop.

"Do you mind," she snapped, giving the paper a good shake as she leaned back in her chair using it as a shield between the two of them. She continued to read when she saw a pencil appear at the top of the paper. Jordan slowly scrunched the newspaper down and looked at her from over the top.

"Come on Kathy (KC was short for Katherine Charlotte), be nice, what has the boss man got you working on anyway?"

KC lowered the paper into her lap and stared at him for a moment, God he was cute she thought. Shaking herself back into reality she turned the paper to page eight and folded it in half. She pointed to the piece about the serial rapist and tapped it with her index finger.

"That's it right there, no big deal, just a follow up on some dirt bag that got cuffed and scuffed down in Fresno," she said matter of fact like. He walked over to her desk and stood behind her. KC turned quickly and socked him in the arm, hard enough to make him flinch.

"And I told you not to call me that, we're not that close anymore, get it," she snapped, spinning back to face her desk.

"*Ouch*, you're a real piece of work KC, a real piece of work, you know that," he snapped back, rubbing his arm where she had made contact with her bony little fist. Jordan read over her shoulder for a second or two and then returned to his desk.

"See, now that wasn't so hard, was it? Why do you have to make such a drama out of everything KC, I mean really, it's getting to be a drag you know?"

She ignored him and went back to reading the story. She smiled to herself and secretly thanked him for *just being himself*, reminding her how lucky she was to have broken free of his spell before any real damage could have been done to her heart. KC was one of those people that protected themselves with a hard shell, one that shielded her softer, truer, secret self from the big bad world.

"Hmmmm," she uttered softly, "This Murray Katz guy had quite a little racket going," she continued talking to herself.

"You say something," Jordan asked?

"No, just thinking out loud."

KC read on and circled the paragraph about the fire and the arrest. There were no photos of the guy in bandages at his arraignment; he looked pretty normal to her? But the story said that one of his victims had been arrested for setting him and the clinic on fire, *what gives*, she thought. KC read the article a third time looking for facts that she may have missed, she hadn't missed anything. She opened the Fresno newspaper and read the related articles there as well, none of them seemed to touch on this anomaly, and she wondered why. She unhooked the handset from her telephone and dialed extension 51 and waited.

"Mr. Williams office," a cheery voice answered.

"Hi Connie, its KC, is Brian in?"

"Sure, he just got out of a meeting, let me check and see if he's free, hold on."

KC drummed her fingers on the photo of Murray Katz in the Bakersfield newspaper.

"What's your story morning glory," she whispered to herself.

"KC, I'll connect you now," Connie said into her ear.

"Thanks."

"Yeah KC, what do you need," her editor said, sounding busy and tired.

"Hi Boss, I know you're busy, this won't take a minute."

"Come on KC, get to the point, I'm actually busy this morning."

"OK, listen, I've been researching that piece you asked me to look into on the serial rapist in Fresno."

"Yeah, and?"

"Well, I think I have found something inconsistent here. I'm not exactly sure what, but my gut is telling me that something is pretty *hinky* about the facts, something nice and juicy!" she said enthusiastically.

"Really, like what? Whatever it is you better be darn sure about it. I just don't have the budget to let you chase after butterflies every time your stomach turns!"

"NO, it's not like that boss, I really think that there is a story there, gimme a day or two to check things out, OK?" There was an uncomfortably long silence before she heard her editor answer.

"You're really *sure* about this hunch of yours?"

"Yeah Brian, I really am!"

"OK, take a couple days and run this down. But no airfare, drive down there and stay in a cheap motel this time KC, not the Ritz Carlton like your last assignment!" As if there actually *was* a Ritz Carlton in Fresno California, what a nerd!

"Don't worry chief, I'll stick to the Holiday Inn's of the world this trip."

"Do you need a photographer for the piece," he asked?

She thought about it a minute, not likely she thought, but then her instincts corrected her snap decision.

"Yeah, I think that might be a good idea, who's available?"

"Take Jay with you, I think he just finished his assignment with your pal Saundra on the Wine Country."

Saundra Callaway was no friend of hers, she was in fact the queen bitch of San Francisco journalism, but Jay was a pretty cool guy and fun to travel with, so this was a good teaming she thought.

"Great, I'll give him a call and make the travel plans, I'll have the itinerary on Connie's desk in half an hour, thanks a lot Brian."

"Good hunting girl, bring me back a winner, we could use a check in the win column right about now, and be careful," he said, the line disconnecting.

KC scribbled a quick note onto a scrap piece of paper and turned in her chair to get up. She stuck her tongue out at Jordan and went off to find her photographer Jay Namura. A transplanted Hawaiian, Jay was a fish out of water wherever he went. Now he wasn't gay, not in the least, but if she ever needed to send someone into that world undercover for a story, he would be the first one she recruited. The man was fussy about his attire, was eclectic in his taste toward food, wine and décor, and had the most beautiful posture she had ever come across. Hell, if she were a man, she was pretty sure that *she* would be gay on him. At least then she would always know which wine to order with the entree. But all of that aside, he was a really cool guy to hang with. He knew just enough facts about just enough topics to be engaging and fun in most conversations, which was perfect given that they would be trapped in her close quartered VW van for about four hours on the way to Fresno.

KC squinted in the sunlight as she tried to scan the road map lying across the wheel that she was also trying to steer with. She adjusted her sunglasses by wrinkling her nose and worked one arm over the left side of the map. Her eyes darting from the road to the map about fifty times she finally ascertained that they were about seventy miles from Fresno on Interstate 15, at least she was pretty sure. Her traveling companion had talked himself to sleep about an hour ago and was resting peacefully with his head rhythmically bouncing on the window to his right. KC wadded up the open map and tossed it into the back of the van before it flew into her face and caused an accident. She pulled her knees up and steered with them for a second while she peeled off her jacket, it was getting warm now that the sun was full up and they were out of the gloomy overcast skies of the Bay Area. The van swerved a little towards the shoulder and KC grabbed the wheel and quickly compensated, causing Jay's head to smack the window hard enough to wake him.

"Hey, watch the road speedy," he said rubbing his noggin and looking at her from under his arm!

"Sorry, I was a little hot in that jacket," she said apologizing.

"We almost there," Jay asked?

"Yeah, we're close, about an hour or so by my calculations."

"What's the plan when we hit town anyway?"

"I want to stop by the District Attorney's office and ask about the status of the case. Find out who is representing Mr. Katz, and then go by the lock up and see if I can interview the arresting officer."

"*WHOA, WHOA*, when were you planning to feed me anyway? You know I can't create my special magic on an empty stomach!"

"Give me a break Jay, I only need you to shoot pictures of the dirt bag himself, not for any of these yokels. I'll drop you at the hotel and you can check us in and run up a tab with room service, OK?"

"Alright, but you're going to have to upgrade us from the Holiday Inn sweetheart, I am not going to subject my delicate palate to their sort of low brow cuisine, I mean really!"

"Oh man Jay, you know Brian has us on a shoestring budget this trip!"

"Look KC, we always produce beautiful work together, *always right?* I'm sure that he'll look the other way after we bring home the winner he's hoping for."

"Yeah but Jay, *it's my ass*, beauty or no beauty, a budget's a budget!"

"*Awww*, come on KC, it's only money, small price to pay for beauty," he said, winking at her and putting on his designer shades. KC hung her head in submission and shook it slowly.

"This better be one hell of a hunch KC girl," she murmured, straightening up and grasping the wheel firmly, her knuckles turning white with the tension.

After she dropped off Jay along with the bags and equipment at the local Sheraton *(oh God)*, KC skillfully wove the VW through the mid-week traffic towards the downtown section of the small city, located in the heart of California's agricultural district. Straining her eyes trying to read the street addresses on the buildings, while carefully trying to avoid a fender bender in the process, she finally came upon her destination, 13374 Broadway, the Superior Court building which housed the offices of the District Attorney. She pulled into the driveway and took the ticket from the machine, which prompted the mechanical arm to raise and allow her entry. She exited her vehicle and locked the door behind her, a girl couldn't be too careful, right? Entering from the street side of the building she felt the rush of cool air as the large glass door closed behind her. She walked towards the reception counter manned by uniformed Marshals, and inquired as to the floor of the District Attorney's office.

"That would be the third floor ma'am, you can get the room number from the directory on the wall next to the elevator," the Marshal said politely.

That pleasant exchange put her in a better frame of mind and her *kinder* instincts took over, guaranteeing that the next person she ran into would be met a big beautiful smile. She scanned the directory, found the room number, and pushed the arrow pointing *up* and waited for the next car. The bell rang and the doors opened in front of her, and she stepped aside as a group people wearing jurors badges exited, no doubt heading for the cafeteria for a coffee break. She got in and pressed the big number three on the panel and watched her reflection appear in the shiny stainless steel doors as soon as they closed shut. She adjusted her skirt after giving her pantyhose a tug or two and then fine-tuned her short-cropped hair. The bell rang again, announcing her arrival, and KC exited the elevator. She walked right up to the reception desk and introduced herself.

"Hi, I'm KC Littleton from the San Francisco Daily News, I believe I have a 10:30 appointment with a Mr. Jeffery," she said with a great big smile.

"Hello, yes, well let me check with his secretary, please have a seat while I announce you," the pretty young woman said as she directed KC with her hand toward the set of rather large leather *Queen Ann* chairs stationed against the wall across from the mahogany counter. She walked over and sat down, sitting toward the front of the chair and not leaning back, she didn't expect to be waiting long. KC watched the receptionist dialing on the PBX and smiled at her again when they made eye contact. She looked around the lobby and nodded her head approvingly, nice set up she thought, top cabin all the way.

"Miss Littleton, I'm afraid that Mr. Jeffery is tied up in conference at the moment, would you like to wait or re-schedule?"

"Oh, I really do need to speak with him today, this morning actually, I have several other stops to make and I will only be in town for a couple of days. May I ask how long he might be tied up, maybe I could come back this afternoon?"

"Let me check with his office, one moment please," the receptionist said, her tone and demeanor changing slightly, and her cheerful smile was absent this time.

"OK, thank you so much," KC replied, wrinkling her nose suspiciously, watching the young woman sit back down and disappear behind the large countertop.

"This is bullshit," she muttered, loud enough to be heard.

"Brian's office made this appointment yesterday before I even left work for the day, wonder what gives?" she added for good measure.

"I am sorry Miss Littleton, but Mr. Jeffery will be tied up the rest of the day. However his Supervisor will be happy to meet with you in his absence if that will be good enough for you?"

"Oh yes, that would be wonderful, please thank her for me," KC said, making a mental note to find out why Mr. David Jeffery would be ducking her?

The receptionist returned to her call for a moment and then came from around the counter to escort KC to her revised appointment. They walked through the paneled double doors and entered the inner-sanctum of the halls of justice in Fresno California. It was a maze of hip high cubicles with scads of people smartly dressed running around busy as beavers, filing this and typing that. They turned a corner and passed a water cooler and a small table that contained a percolator full of coffee and some Styrofoam cups. Finally they stopped at a good-sized secretarial desk, complete with a side table where a rather large and new IBM select-writer was perched. The young woman introduced KC and then excused herself, walking back the same way they had just come. KC looked over the woman sitting behind the desk and quickly extended her hand.

"Hello, I'm KC Littleton, I am very grateful for a chance to meet with...?"

"Hi, I'm Lois, and you'll be meeting with Mrs. Hall, Lou Ann Hall, she is the Supervising ADA (assistant district attorney).

"Let me just tell her that you're here, I'll just be a sec," Lois said, knocking lightly on the door and disappearing into the office behind her. She reappeared instantly and motioned for KC to go on inside.

"Thanks," KC said as she passed her and walked into the ADA's office.

"Hello Miss Littleton, please have a seat, I am Lou Ann Hall, what can we do for you today?"

KC walked over to one of the two chairs in front of the woman's desk and sat down. She suddenly wished she had buttoned the top button of her blouse before she had entered, that information-coaxing tactic wouldn't be very effective now.

"Hi, Mrs. Hall, thank you so much for seeing me on such short notice."

The woman leaned forward in her seat, placed her elbows on her desktop, laced her fingers together slowly and rested her chin on the knuckles of her folded hands.

"Now, what has brought someone from the great *San Francisco Daily News* all the way to the sticks today?" KC snickered nervously under the woman's cool gaze and cleared her throat.

"Um, really Mrs. Hall, we are not out here looking for dirt or anything like that. Actually I am doing some follow up for a piece I am writing about sex offenders, and I wanted to do some research on the case your office is prosecuting against a Dr. Murray Katz." she explained. KC didn't like the way the supervising ADA was scowling at her. She waited a reasonable amount of time for a response, and when none came, she continued.

"I would really appreciate any information you could share with me so that I can use it as reference material to profile his crimes and compare them with other cases that I have been researching." KC new that she was lying, actually she was a pretty good liar when the need arose, but she wasn't sure that Mrs. Hall was buying any of it.

"Mrs. Hall, ma'am, have I said anything wrong here," KC inquired?

"No dear, not at all, but I am afraid that we will not be able to help you, that case is still under investigation."

"I understand that Mrs. Hall, but are you sure that I couldn't just tag along with the detectives that are working the case, just be a fly on the wall so to speak?"

"Young lady, we do not try our cases in the newspapers around here!"

"This isn't San Francisco! We're not as liberal with our respect for the constitutional rights of our citizens under the law," the ADA snapped!

KC looked sheepishly back at the woman and frowned; obviously she had struck a nerve, but why? This was an open and shut case according to the known facts as far as she read them. The guy had been abusing women and girls through his capacity as a doctor in a free clinic, as a trusted member of the community for goodness sake. Why would the District Attorney's office care if her paper ran a piece about their stoic persecution of such a terrible man? It didn't make sense to her and that bothered her, and KC Littleton did not like loose ends, they screwed up her nightly hibernation!

"I apologize if I gave you the impression that I would be anything but professional with regard to any reference to your office or its investigation. Nothing could be further from the truth, I am just doing some basic research, and this case has some similarities to others that I have been looking into," KC said in as soft a tone as she could muster.

"Never the less, as I have said we are not able to share any information with you or any other publication at this time. Perhaps once the case is closed we can send you whatever data you may require," ADA Hall said, also in a softer tone.

"*Look*, I apologize for my harsh tone, but you must understand, this particular case has been a personal nightmare for me as well as many others. We're embarrassed, angry and frightened that something like this could happen in our community, this isn't the big city, we don't expect that kind of behavior, we're not used to that kind of evil," she finished.

"I understand how you feel Lou Ann. You know, we aren't *accustomed* to this kind of thing any better in the *big city*," KC said, trying to sound consoling and not angry, which is what she was after the woman attacked her sensibilities.

"I guess maybe I should go now. Thank you for seeing me, and again, my apologies."

KC walked to ward the door and then stopped when the ADA called to her.

"Miss Littleton, for what it's worth, I really would like to help you, but my hands are tied."

"However, our Police Department did not actually arrest Dr. Katz. He is in the custody of the local Sheriff's Department."

"You might try talking to Sheriff Cardwell over in Firebaugh, it's not far from here, he may be able to fill you in on things that I am not free to talk about." Lou Ann Hall offered all too sweetly.

KC shot the woman a crooked little smile.

"Thanks," she said, sourly, getting up slowly to walk out the door. Once out of the room she went quickly to the elevator. As she waited for the elevator to arrive, a hand touched her on the shoulder, startling her. It was Lou Ann Hall.

"One more thing KC, a request really," she said. Mrs. Hall looked at her for a moment before continuing. The bell rang suddenly and the doors opened to an empty car. KC reached inside with her hand and held the doors open. She ignored the buzzers clambering inside the elevator letting her know in no uncertain terms that she wasn't the only person anxious to go up or down.

"Yes," KC said, looking back at the supervising ADA?

Lou Ann Hall reached out and gently rubbed KC's arm, smiling at her as she did so.

"I'm sure you are very good at your job, I can see that in your eyes."

"But I suspect that you're also kind, and have a conscience. I can see that in your eyes as well. When you finish gathering your information, and you have all the facts that you need, *please*, leave the child out of your story, *there's no need to include her*," ADA Hall said, her eyes betraying her sincerity. She didn't wait for an answer. She just turned and walked away quickly, back toward her office. KC was perplexed and she knew her face probably gave that away easily.

"Hey wait a minute! What child, *what's the deal anyway*," KC called after her.

There was no reply, ADA Hall had already turned the corner and disappeared. The urgent buzzing requests kept coming, and KC finally entered the elevator and watched the stainless steel doors close. She looked back at her reflection and noted the puzzled look on her face. She reached for the cross she wore around her neck, not really knowing why. It was an involuntary reflex she had whenever she was nervous.

"What was all *that* about," she wondered out loud. The bell rang and the doors opened, she passed sideways like a crab through the herd of people entering and made her way out of the building. Suddenly this assignment gotten very interesting, this girl loved a good mystery, what reporter didn't, and she was world class nosy! KC smiled and put on her sunglasses as she exited the building into the bright noonday sun.

"*Beautiful day*," she said to a stranger passing her, as she turned right toward the parking lot. Taking out a spiral note pad she jotted down a couple key thoughts, then listened to her stomach growl.

"Hope Jay is still hungry, *I'm starved!*"

Fourteen

("...There is, a house, in New Orleans, they call the rising sun. And it's been the ruin of many a poor boy, in God, I know, I've won"...Eric Burden and the Animals)

Da Nang, Republic of Viet Nam, 24 December 1968

I turned slowly, doing a 360-degree sweep of the compound with my two eyes. Squinting against the bright morning sunlight, I mentally inventoried all the local flora and fauna, paying particularly close attention to the tall tropical palms, and noticing how very still everything was in the absence of even the hint of a breeze. Stopping my circular traverse of the camp at the zero degree point, I tilted my head back, closed my eyes and let the sunlight finish evaporating the water from my face. The rain had stopped only ten minutes before and already my clothes were dry to the touch. I almost felt refreshed, like I just got dressed. But I knew this feeling wouldn't last long, my clothes would be soaked again soon, only this time from the inside out. The humidity in this country, especially at this time of year would make August in Mississippi seem positively *Eden* like!

I removed my helmet and pulled the green terry towel from around my neck and covered my head like an Arab nomad, then replaced the hard hat back on its perch. This was the only shade that didn't require me to compete with the local indigenous personnel of the insect variety, i.e. mosquitoes, centipedes, and various other *yucky creepy crawlies* (as my sister would say), for a dark, cool piece of real estate. Reason enough for my shamefully miserable attitude I suppose, but today I just had an old fashioned case of the homesick blues.

I found myself wishing for the polar opposite of *here*, a nice *freezing* New England winter. I stood next to the mess tent and watched as the evidence of this morning's downpour vaporized into steam, and I suddenly found myself longing for the snow back home in Albany, New York. I missed the cold crisp air; the white puffs of my heated breath that came with each exhale as I walked out each morning to fetch the newspaper, dressed in only my pj's and slippers. And I missed my mother's hot cocoa and on special occasions, her hot cider with the cinnamon sticks for stirring. I missed her freshly baked bread and the heavenly aroma that wafted through the house when she cooked for us. I missed her cabbage soup and Grandmother's Mulligan stew, and I even missed the god-awful porridge that Mom would whip up each morning for breakfast. *"This will stick to your ribs sonny, and it'll put hair on your chest boy,"* she would say encouragingly. Of course I would always answer back, *"and will it do the same for Shannon Ma?"* And then not surprisingly, my left handed quip would prompt her to swat me smartly on the back of my head, playfully scolding me, *"don't you be sassing your mother ye silly goose!"* Basically, I just missed being home, and I was struggling to keep my joy in tact in spite of this incredibly hot and sticky day. *But hey now,* it was Christmas Eve after all, and everyone was bound to be feeling at least as homesick as me. I was going to have to dig pretty darn deep to find a little of *old St. Nick's* good cheer in me, and then somehow find a way to share it, without getting beat up in the process! I was fairly certain that nobody would be role playing as *Santa Claus* around here, not with this weather. Anyone fool enough to dress up in a furry wool suit and long whiskers in this heat would just be asking for a *section eight* (psychiatric discharge)! *No sir*, we were just going to have to rely on a healthy dose of fellowship, administered the plain old-fashioned way, person to person. I was pretty sure that there was still time enough to salvage some *Christmas spirit* between now and tomorrow morning!

"Hey *Nancy*, you've got mail squirt," hollered Lt. Walker from his tacky, multi-colored, webbed chaise lounge chair, located in front of his quarters, carefully positioned for the optimum tanning experience, of course.

"Come on, shake a leg, before the ink runs in this heat!"

"Be right there," I yelled back, walking a little faster, while trying not to raise my body temperature too much, it was still a long time before the relative cool of night. When I reached him, Aaron Walker tipped his Chicago Cub's baseball cap up with his index finger, and looked at me from behind the turquoise lenses of his latest pair of *groovy* shades.

"Way to *haul ass* Kelly, good thing the tent wasn't on fire!"

"*Oops*, will ya look at that," he said checking his wrist watch.

"You're just in time for cocktails!" It was ten o'clock in the morning, I thought, *good golly miss molly!*

"Pull up a chair and read me all the news from home," he ordered, genuinely interested.

"Where was it you were from again, *Paduchaville, right?*"

I took the letter from his hand and started to answer, "Well, *I ah*, ya see, umm..."

"Oh come on dude, it's a slow mail day, nobody else got much of anything, looks like you're the main attraction Irish!"

He was right of course; it would be bad form not to share with the outfit on a shutout day like this one. Besides, the envelope was pretty thick, so I suspected that there were at least a couple of letters in there. Probably one from Mom, one from Shannon, and maybe one from Uncle Chuck, his were everyone's favorite. And if I knew my mother, there was bound to be a decent amount of Christmas cheer within these pages, at least enough to pass around the camp. *Ahhh*, and nobody could fling the blarney like my Uncle Charles, why the man could blather on for days! My mother had always said that she was fairly certain that when he died it would be in mid sentence! Nurse Carla really fancied hearing his letters, and would always playfully ask if he were single when I finished reading them. When I said no, she would tease me mercilessly, asking if there were any *other* Kelly men of marrying age, *wink wink*, or at least any that *weren't* planning on becoming cops, jockeys, or *priests*, that is! She always drew a blush from me with that one, and then she would kiss me on the top of my head as she walked away. I was discovering that chastity was going to be a real challenge, *what was that girl's name on the train again,* **darn it?**

"Yeah, OK," I said unfolding a lawn chair and sitting across from Lt. Walker.

"What'll it be Ethan, warm gin, warm beer, or whatever this brown stuff is," Aaron asked, swirling a tumbler full of an amber colored liquid in front of his face, trying to ascertain the nature of the contents. He squinted at the glass as he held it high over his head, directly in the path of the sun's rays, then, quickly tossed the contents onto the ground at the base of his tent.

"*Whoops,*" he said, quickly sitting up straight.

"Remember Ethan lad, discretion **is always** the better part of valor my young friend," he said rolling his eyes toward the newly formed puddle on the ground.

"Now that I think about it, I seem to recall Nurse Carla being too tired to walk *all the way* over to the latrine last night," he said, rolling his eyes in the opposite direction, indicating the path to said restroom, located about one hundred fifty yards to the east.

"Think I'll pass on the beverage offer lieutenant," I said.

"Thanks just the same."

"Not a problem Ethan my boy, *more for me*," he said pulling a Budweiser from the stainless steel cooler. Inside there were about a dozen or so cans, floating in tepid water, that may have been ice about an hour ago.

"Alright, now, so what does Mom have to say today," he asked, popping the can of beer open with the church key hanging from a chain around his neck. The white frothy foam oozed out of the opening and Lt. Walker slurped it up noisily taking a nice long swig.

"*Ahhhhhhh, mother's milk,*" he said closing his eyes, a big smile slowly spreading ear to ear across his lean, square jawed face.

"Sorry, go on, continue please, *continue*," he said with a wave of his hand while he leaned back in the lounge chair and wiggled himself into a comfortable listening position. I cleared my throat and started to read Mom's letter first:

"Dearest Ethan, I am hoping that this letter finds you safely in the Lord's care and good graces. We're all missing you so much son, myself most of all. Your sister Shannon brought home a stray pup yesterday. Your uncle Liam says that it's a jack terrier, or a russell terrier, or some such name, I really don't know for certain? And she wanted to call the little nibbler Ethan; of course I would have none of it. Can you imagine I asked her, having to swat that poor pooch with a rolled up newspaper whenever it misbehaved and then be scolding it, calling it by your brother's name, it just wouldn't be proper I said to her. So, she decided to call him Paulie instead, I guess you'll have to be explaining that one to your poor friend when you see him next. You know, I ran into his mother at the market the other day, I was buying some mutton for Sunday supper. And she told me that young Paul had gone to Viet Nam as well. Do you see him often when you're working over there? I hope so, that would be nice I think"

"Ethan, your Mom is a **nutbar**, does she think that you're away at summer camp? Is she even remotely aware that it's the *USMC* not the *YMCA* that you belong to for now? And isn't your buddy Paul a swabbie on a flat top somewhere," Lt. Walker complained, lobbing rhetorical questions at me in rapid succession?

"Well, she's not exactly up on the military lingo, in fact she still thinks the Marine Corps is an extension of the *Boy Scouts*, for kids that can no longer fit into their short britches of course!"

"God bless civilians," he said toasting my mother and finishing off his first brew of our little story hour.

I turned the page over and continued with the news from home. Mother went on about the lawn being too long and wishing I was home to take care of that. She complained profusely about Shannon and her shenanigans and then asked me to forgive her blathering, reminding me how much she loved the two of us. Lieutenant Walker laughed out loud at her reference to the presidential race back home. She was alarmed that Nixon could likely win the election, "can you believe it sonny, an Episcopalian in the White House, and saints preserve us!" She ended the letter with her usual flair, and actually brought an uncharacteristic tear to the eye of our arrogant young chopper pilot, when she prayed for us all. I think it was the fact that she mentioned each and every one of my buddies by name, including Lt. Walker.

"That was nice Ethan, but if you tell anyone that I got a little misty here, I'll super glue your hand to your pecker, *are we clear on that,*" he said curtly. He showed me the same glare that Timmy Mahoney would give me, right before he socked me in the snout whenever I pushed his patience on the playground.

"*Lighten up ace*, you should be much more worried about what I can do to your reputation around here, stud," Carla said from behind my chair. She must have walked up while I was reading, very sneaky qualities this nurse possessed! She unfolded another beach chair and set it next to the cooler beside Arron Walker.

"Nobody knows your dirty little secrets like I do baby," she said with a wicked little smile, as she took a sip from the beer he handed to her.

"Cool it Carla, we got a crowd forming here," Aaron said, indicating the arrival of my roommate Mitchell and Lance Cpl. Larry Polen. Lieutenant Walker tossed a beer to each of them as they pulled up a seat joining the three of us.

"*Hey carnal*, heard you got a letter today *Holmes*, I could use a little slice of the world right about now *ese*," Mitchell said, taking a sip of his beer. Mitchell always looked funny with a beer in his hand, he had such a baby face. Sure, he may have been twenty-five, older than everyone here but Aaron Walker, but he only looked fifteen, *if that!*

"Yeah Kelly, gotta share the wealth, you know the code," Cpl. Polen chimed in.

"Alright, everyone keep your shirts on," I said, reassembling the pages into their original order. Presently I went ahead and read my mom's letter over again and then read Shannon's, it was short but sweet. Shannon did manage to explain how she came to name the puppy Paulie. "He's so soft and furry, just like Paulie!" I took a little time to explain that remark to my captive audience.

"*Oh man*, Paulie used to get so mad whenever we were at the community pool in the summertime, and Shannon would sneak behind him with her doll's hairbrush and comb his back, it was classic! He would chase her around the pool, threatening all kinds of mayhem, and then lose her when she dived into the water, my sister could swim circles around any of us. After about five minutes of flailing around in the pool trying to catch my tadpole of a sibling, he would eddy over to the side, pull himself out of the pool and onto the deck, and lay flat on his back breathing heavily, plotting his revenge. It was a regular ritual with those two, but harmless, and one that provided a ton of belly laughs for the neighborhood!"

Then, much to Carla's delight I pulled out a couple pages from my Uncle Chuck. Her eyes sparkled like lights on a Christmas tree, and she scooted her chair closer to me so as not miss a single word! Pausing slightly for effect, I began to read his letter trying my best to impersonate my Uncle, using the thickest Irish/Gaelic accent that I could muster:

"So boy, they went and made a soldier of ye did they. Well, so long as they know that you're the good Lord's soldier first, as are we all, aye right? Well now, about your Uncle Liam, oh sonny, he's as batty as ever he is. Still harassing that poor State Senator over your Da's wake and now he has taken to writing to the President of these United States, his Lordship himself!

My uncle went on to tell us all about the family happenings, who had done what to whom, the complete unabridged diary of the Kelly clan, including all their usual shenanigans. And he did so in that delightfully entertaining fashion of which everyone had grown so fond. I never knew my Uncle Chuck to let an audience down, not ever! When I finished reading I looked up and caught Carla wiping away tear with her shirtsleeve. I folded the pages neatly and returned them to the colorful airmail envelope, looking around at everyone as I stuffed it into my shirt pocket.

"I think I'm gonna go and write my Dad a letter," Carla said, getting up and walking slowly toward her quarters. She gave my hair a tug as she passed, then stopped suddenly, "*Ethan*, can I have the letter until tomorrow, I want to have something to open in the morning. I promise I'll give it back at breakfast, OK?" I didn't hesitate, or even turn in my chair, I just pulled out the envelope and held it over my shoulder. I felt her fingers brush my hand as she took it, and then she kissed my on the top of my head, "Thanks," was all she said.

"No worries lieutenant, *Merry Christmas*," I said softly, as I watched the fellas give me the business with their mime performance of me fraternizing with an officer. The camp's public address system suddenly broke up our quiet time, loudly announcing a scramble. *ShowTime,* we all thought simultaneously, as we swiftly scrambled to our feet and took off in multiple directions, frantically but methodically preparing to move out!

Tony and I jumped up into the chopper as the engines whined and the rotors began to slowly spin, wobbling dangerously until they reached a suitable RPM. I tossed the meds bag to Tony. He stowed it under beneath the stokes and litters. Mitchell pulled the cover off the 50MM machine gun hanging in the doorway and then strapped himself into the shoulder harness tethered to the airframe. He gave the breech a good hard tug, making him officially *locked and loaded*. I didn't like that thing, but secretly I was glad it was there, my faith not being as strong as it could be I guess?

"Saddle up girls, we're outta here," Lt. Walker shouted over the noise, tapping the top of his head, signaling that we we're lifting off.

"What's the story LT, where are we headed," Tony hollered leaning into the front cab of the helicopter. The sergeant seated in the second chair, the co-pilot's seat, leaned back and shouted over his shoulder, *"couple of minor GSW's (gun shot wounds), squad of riflemen about twenty clicks northeast of Da Nang need to be extracted from a cold LZ. It'll be us and two-niner-bravo in for the pick up, Butch and Sundance will be running cover for us."* Sergeant Dixon then went back to reading the checklist on his clipboard, and Tony returned to take his seat in the hold with Mitchell and me.

"What did we pull this time Tony," I asked as the chopper lifted off the ground just seconds after two-niner-bravo had done likewise.

"No biggie, picking up some grunts a little north of here, just Band-Aids and kissing boo boos, *that's all*," he said giving us the universal signal for a boring run by stroking the airspace above his lap with his clenched fist.

"Ay Dios mio, you're bad *ese*, you're bad," Mitchell said with a grin on his face.

I turned and looked out the doorway so as to hide my own grin and the blush spreading across my face. The choppers leveled out as they flew into formation, the fast moving air providing some comfort by drying the sweat from our faces. I was tempted to remove my heavy, uncomfortable flak jacket for the ride to the LZ, but changed my mind when I caught a glimpse of Mitchell kissing his crucifix and then his weapon. There was not much of an updraft on this run so the ride was pretty smooth, meaning we weren't bouncing around the hold, loosening all of our teeth in the process. About 20 minutes out we sighted the green smoke indicating a safe landing zone.

"*Well*, there was that to be thankful for," I thought to myself, saying a quick prayer for us all.

I didn't think anyone would mind. Our escorts flew past us in a hurry, on their way to reconnoiter the position before we set down. I could hear Lt. Walker talking with the ground and took a peek out the door to get a read on the situation below. From what I could see, everything looked pretty quiet; at least we wouldn't be sprinting around, dodging bullets and *whatnot* on this trip. Sergeant Dixon got our attention by slapping the thin metal barrier between the cockpit and us.

"Get set," he shouted, showing us the thumbs down sign with both hands, shaking them vigorously.

I grabbed the front end of a litter in my right hand and squatted on my heels waiting for the skids to touch the ground. Tony was right behind me with the opposite end of the litter in his left hand, his right hand holding onto the meds bag slung over his right shoulder and tucked securely under his arm. I looked up and watched Mitchell scan the area, sweeping his weapon from side to side, the butt firm against his shoulder, his right index finger resting lightly on the trigger guard, and the rest of his hand gripping the stock with white knuckle intensity.

"*OK, here we go again,*" I said under my breath, as the skids touched down, and *poof*, Tony and I were on our way, *what a team!*

Three sweaty marines jumped into the helicopter at the same time that we jumped out. We made a beeline for a group of four grunts crouching over two men lying in the grass on their backs. They were directly in front of us about thirty meters from the chopper.

"OVER HERE," yelled an arm-waving Corporal, he was missing his helmet and his head was bleeding from a nasty gash dangerously close to his left eye. Tony and I covered the distance in about ten seconds and set our stuff down next to the nearest body.

"Whatta we got here," asked Tony, quickly checking under the field bandage of the nearest horizontal marine, not waiting for a response from anyone.

"*Oh boy*, it's a large caliber gun shot wound to the shoulder," he said turning the soldier gently.

"Looks like the round went right through him! His clavicle's busted, and we got a compound fracture of the humorous as well. Good thing this kid passed out!"

"Best give him a little morphine though, we don't want him coming to on the return flight and freaking out, *right,*" he asked rhetorically.

I nodded my head in agreement, "Yeah, a small dose though, and let's sling his arm before we transport him, better he doesn't get a look at what's left of his arm, OK?" Tony held the syringe between his teeth as he removed the cap from the pre-set dose of morphine with one hand and felt for a nice thick vein with the other. Once the drug was administered Tony and I lifted the man onto the litter and let two of his buddies tote him back to the chopper.

"Hey," I yelled after them, "Bring back another litter for this guy," I said pointing to the next patient.

"WELL, it's about God damn time, I can see that I'm gonna have to ride in the *back* of the bus again! Even way out here there ain't no justice for the black man," shouted the wounded marine next to Tony.

"Hold still buddy, let me take a look at you. And I think that you meant to say *equality* didn't you," Tony said in a low tone that made me a little nervous.

"Who are you, *the Chinese Clarence Darrow*? Shut the fuck up and get me on that helo, *chop chop*!" I grabbed Tony's hand as he reached for his side arm and stared him down, communicating with him telepathically, pleading with him to cool it! Tony stood down for the moment, and scooted closer to the injured man to get a better look at the damage. I silently gave thanks for the fact that God saved fools from themselves, especially on holy days, at least that was my story for today, and I was sticking too it!

"Just for shits and giggles, I'm Japanese! And for the record, **you** shut the fuck up before your big mouth interferes with my field diagnosis and I mistakenly amputate *your johnson*!" Apparently this marine was not much for church and such, as he proceeded to get right back into my fellow corpsman's face.

"Let's go *bitch*, wrap a towel around my foot and get me to that transport!"

"Hold your horses *Sambo*, this looks pretty god damn bad here," Tony said clenching his teeth and ripping open the wounded marine's pants leg with a little too much gusto.

"Ohhhhh, *mother fucker*, that hurt! And who you calling *Sambo*, stumpy?"

"You know what, out a respect for that very sharp K-bar in your hand and for Mr. Johnson here, I'm gonna forget about your racist comment for now," the wounded marine said calmly through clenched teeth, placing his helmet in his lap and looking over at me for moral support.

"You seen and heard it all, right Opie," he continued, making eye contact with me?

"There is a lot of trauma here Ethan," Tony said to me as he continued to work.

"I'll need to set a tourniquet here, and then we'll need to see about cauterizing this wound or he's gonna bleed out on the ride back. *Man, this is one ugly wound Ethan!*"

"You don't need to tell me Doc, I know exactly what I got going on here. Check this out mother fucker," the black marine said proudly, jerking his right leg from Tony's grip and twirling his foot quickly in small circles, spraying us both with blood and mud.

"Just look at this mess, look what Charlie's done to Momma Cole's middle boy JoJo? The son-of-a-bitches done shot off my three favorite toes! They fucked up a perfectly good pair of Uncle Sam's boots too!"

"**What** are the boys in the neighborhood gonna call me now, *step and a half?*"

"*Oh man*, I'm gonna have to live with that handle all the way to judgment day!"

"Probably be limping around like *Amos McCoy* all the live long day as well, *Lord have mercy, this is pitiful,* **pit-I-ful!**"

I couldn't help but snort out a chuckle at this guy's comic delivery, he was smooth enough to be on The Ed Sullivan Show I thought to myself.

"Give it a rest JoJo," yelled a big marine through a thick southern drawl. He was standing just to the left of me, actually he was kneeling, his shoulder leaning against his M16, his large hands holding the weapon firmly in place, butt end down in the dirt. *Oh my gosh*, this guy was huge, he was almost as tall on his knees as the guy who was standing next to him was.

"That's right *Holmes*, let the doc do his thing man, so we can all get outta this shit before the dinks pick up our trail," said the smaller marine.

"You can just kiss my black ass *poncho*! If you had been awake on your watch Mr. Charlie wouldn't have been able to sucker punch us like he done," said their wounded comrade, spitting the words out through obvious pain.

"He's right Junior, this one's on you man," the big man said, turning his head and spitting a healthy stream of tobacco juice into the elephant grass.

"You tell him Wesley, you tell him!"

"**Owwww, goddamn-it this hurts!**"

"Come on doc, give me something man," JoJo pleaded with my partner.

Tony was already swabbing a nice thick vein with a cotton-ball soaked in alcohol, prepping JoJo's arm for a morphine injection. He jammed in the needle skillfully and administered a healthy dose. The effect was immediate, and the agitated marine became visibly loose and sedate as the drug ran through his bloodstream and he succumbed to the warm peaceful feeling that was engulfing him.

"*Ohhhh man*, that shit is good doc, put a few of those in my pocket for later my little Oriental brother," JoJo said to Tony in a singsong kind of voice.

"*Oh yeah*, you know what Junior, this stuff almost makes up for your dumb ass, you freaky little wetback motherfucker," JoJo continued, as he lay very still and wagged his finger at the sky above him.

"*A viente, cabron* (same to you, bastard)," Junior replied, smiling and slinging his rifle onto his shoulder. "Come on Texas, let's pick this fool up and get on the chopper," Junior hollered at his buddy, slapping him on the shoulder as he walked to where we had laid JoJo out on a litter.

"Come on Hightower, *rapido gordo, ariba!*"

The big Texan grunted as he picked himself up and trotted over to join his buddy. The two of them grabbed the litter and started jogging towards the helicopter. Tony and I ran along side of them, my partner holding the IV bag with the lactated ringers while I carried the fallen soldier's weapon and helmet. JoJo was in another world trying to sing what sounded to me like '*Baby love*' by the Supremes. He was way too out of it to enunciate anything recognizable, but I was pretty sure that he had the tune down. By the time we reached the helo, all five of us were singing the song at the top of our lungs. I suddenly had a crazy thought, except for all the blood and death stuff, I could actually see where my mother *might* confuse the USMC with the YMCA, maybe a little, *maybe*.

"*Madre Dios, ola carnal*," Mitchell shouted at the marine they called Junior as we scooted JoJo into the chopper hold. Junior and the big Texan carried their buddy into the center of the aircraft and set the litter down.

"*Hey, homeboy*, we wondered where you got transferred to," Junior said, as he duck walked over to his friend manning the heavy machine gun. He stood up and embraced Mitchell, slapping him vigorously on the back with both hands. Their heads bumped together sending their helmets crashing to the deck in the process. Tony scooped the hats up and placed them one at a time back onto their heads, "*You guys may still need these*," he said, turning back to help me secure the litters to the deck for the return run.

"Junior, leave the poor guy alone! Let him do his job man. *How ya doin Rojas*," Hightower shouted over the rotor noise as the helicopter started to leave the ground. Mitchell waved back at Hightower and gave him the thumbs up sign, "I'm cool Wesley, good to see you *ese!*"

"Likewise runt, *hey*, did you hear about Gunny and Scotty Jenkins," asked Hightower?

"*Oh man*, that was fucked up *Holmes*. We should have gone back and got him *man*, I'm really pissed about that," Junior lamented, slamming his palms hard against the deck.

"Do you mind, I was talking to Mitchell," Hightower said, sneering at Junior. I could see that these three guys had a history, and frankly I was enjoying their little reunion. Too bad JoJo was unconscious, I was pretty sure he would have added a real comedic, if not explosive element to the group dynamic.

"Yeah man, I heard about them just before I transferred to this FSSB. I didn't know Scotty too good, he was pretty new, but I really miss the Gunny, he was good people ya know," Mitchell said loudly, his head resting on his arm which was lying across the top of the big swaying weapon.

"*Horale,*" Junior said in agreement.

On that note, everyone settled into a silence that lasted the remainder of the return flight. While we all bounced around in place as the helicopter battled with the thermal updrafts, I studied the faces and posture of our passengers. I noticed that there was a comfortable familiarity about the small group. It wasn't that they were anything alike as individuals, not even close, but there was something about them, about the way they looked at things, at one another, as if they were reading each other's thoughts. And then it dawned on me just what it was that I was picking up on. In fact, I realized that I had some of the same feelings myself, within my own circle, within our own outfit.

These guys had been molded into a close order unit, *a team*, fused together by bullets, blood, and boredom, they were a family, by circumstance more than choice, but family none the less, you could feel it on the air. Now I understood what the term *brother's in arms* really meant, it was cool, very cool.

We routinely landed back at the FSSB, everything was SOP. Tony and I rushed our charges over to triage so that they could be racked and stacked according to the severity of their wounds. Then we went back to the rig and cleaned up the mess, washing the mud, blood, and people bits out of the hold, finally stowing the gear and refilling the meds. Afterwards it was a tepid shower, some fresh clothes to sweat in and a visit to the mess tent for a nourishing, bland helping of whatever *cookie* had run over this morning. *Oh man*, there wasn't much anyone of us wouldn't have given for a gallon jar of Tabasco, *anything* to add some taste to these meals!

"Hey doc, over here," called Junior, he was seated at a table near the coffee dispenser. I walked over to join him, and saw that he was with his buddy Hightower as well as my roommate Mitchell. Setting my tray on the table beside Mitchell I stepped over the bench to work my way into a seat next to him.

"Scoot over some Mitchell," I said, squeezing in at the busy table. Even though chow had officially ended an hour or so ago the joint was still hoping with stragglers and tourists. We tended to refer to all of the people *passing through* camp (military and civilian alike) as tourists. Kind of gave the place sort of a resort feeling if you let your imagination run freely. The mess tent had a tendency to stay crowded, what with people trying to escape the heat and all. The large screened in area was a favorite shady spot for most of us. Combine a cool drink with the two big fans that oscillated at either end of the structure, moving the air and keeping it from stagnating, and well sir, that was just little slice of Heaven. Just close your eyes and you were on the beach in Atlantic City, or shore side at Lake George.

The three marines sat there drinking coffee, their empty trays stacked clumsily between them in the center of the table. They must have been positively starved because there wasn't a noticeable scrap left anywhere that I could see. Not even a hint of the lumpy brown stuff (gravy I thought…hoped) that smothered our beloved mess sergeant's entrée of the day (meatloaf I wondered…prayed).

"*How's JoJo doc*, he gonna be OK," Junior asked, sipping his coffee as I took my seat.

I wasn't comfortable when the guys in the field referred to me as *doc*, it wasn't right, I was no doctor, I was just an ambulance attendant chasing through the weeds and tall grass looking for anyone who couldn't run on their own. I started to say something then stopped, I had grown tired of correcting people, and besides they called anyone with a Red Cross on their helmet *doc*. Of course that insignia may have meant a little more to me than most, as it was a symbol of my faith as well. I smiled to myself wondering how many times I had been caught frantically reciting *Psalm 23 (the Lord is my Shepard…)*,while running like heck with Tony through muck, mire, and gunfire.

"*Hey, doc*, where you at man," Junior asked, snapping his fingers in front of my face, breaking my trance?

"Sorry, what did you say?"

"JoJo, what do you know *ese*?"

"*Oh… right*, last I saw he was in the OR getting treated. It'll likely be a while, you'll just have to wait and see. I'm pretty sure he'll be in recovery in a couple of hours. Unless there are problems and they need to fly him to the base hospital in Da Nang?" I answered.

Junior didn't say the words, but his eyes spoke for him. I waited a minute longer for an audible response and then added, "*You know what*, soon as I wolf down this chow I'll go look in on him for you," I said reassuringly. Junior smiled at me from over his coffee mug.

"Thanks doc." He set down his mug and nudged Mitchell with his elbow.

"What's your name anyway doc?"

"Kelly," I said.

"No man, your Christian name?"

"Sorry, its *Ethan*, Ethan Kelly," I replied apologetically.

"Thanks for pulling us out back there, and for putting up with JoJo's bullshit," Hightower said in his pleasant southern drawl.

"You know, he don't mean nothin by it, it's just his way. Hell, everybody deals with fear a little different, you know how it is," he added astutely.

"Not a problem, he wasn't that bad really, I've had worse experiences. I'd rather deal with a witty smart-ass than a stiff any day of the week," I said with a mouth full of food.

Good thing I wasn't at the supper table back home or I would have been pinched under the table by now. *Hmm*, I guess just by thinking of it I had already been virtually pinched anyway. I shook my head and smiled to myself, unknowingly thinking out loud, *"man, what awesome powers Mom's possess!"*

"Yo, *daydreamer*," Junior said snapping his fingers again.

"I'm *Arturo*, Arturo Martinez, but people just call me Junior. Not because my pop's name is Arturo too, but because I'm usually the shortest guy in the room," he said, standing up to proudly show off his five foot five inch frame.

"The big redneck over there is Wesley Hightower. But he'll answer to *gordo, cabron,* or just plain old *maricon*, as well. But I suggest you call him by those names with a running start," Junior laughed.

"*Shut up Junior!* Look man; don't waste your time listening to this sorry wetback. Just call me Hightower, sort of fits my frame, as you can see." I reached across the table and shook his enormous paw. He was right about the name and the frame, this was the biggest guy I'd ever seen.

"Nice to meet you guys," I said letting go of Hightower's hand. "You had to have been a football player Hightower, am I right," I asked? Hightower must have been more humble then he let on, as he sort of blushed a little at my inquiry.

"In High School I was, never got to play past that though. I needed to help my family with the ranch and such. Course, then I went and got myself drafted just because I *wasn't* going to college. Which, I could have been if Daddy hadn't been feeling so poorly. I'd have taken me take that scholarship to UT, and played ball for the Longhorns! But then the letter came and it seemed that Uncle Sam needed me a might more than Daddy did, I shoulda kept playing ball I reckon."

"Bet you were good," I said, shoveling the last of the mystery meat into my mouth, trying to chew it without actually tasting it.

"Oh man Ethan, if he played football anything like he kills dinks, then he would have been a, *what do you call that*, um, umm, oh yeah, an All-American, *horale!*" Junior said with genuine pride.

"CAN IT Junior," Hightower said, getting up from the table to refill his coffee mug.

"I'm gonna go check in with the CO and see how soon we can get back to our unit," Wesley said, waving as he walked out of the mess tent. Junior and Mitchell waved back and then turned to me, waiting for me to say something next I guessed.

"So, you two know each other from, *where*," I asked, conducting the conversation, using my fork as a baton? I wasn't in any hurry to wait out the rest of the superheated holiday lying in my bunk, re-reading letters and weeks old sports pages.

"Me, Junior, and Hightower were in boot camp together back in California. We didn't meet up with JoJo until we got here, almost eight months ago," answered Mitchell.

"Yeah, we been through some serious shit together ese, *serious*. But were still here, not like some of the others," Junior said, staring out the screen at the people milling around the camp doing this and that.

His look became distant and the smile had faded from his face, prompting me to be weary. I had been here long enough to know that combat vets generally had short fuses and large charges, so I decided to be comfortably on edge with Mr. Martinez. Junior turned back from gazing out the window and caught me watching him.

"Something on your mind," he asked?

"No, just thinking about getting some seconds," I said, it was the first thing to pop into my head, and I was hoping I wouldn't have to get up and actually do it, if Junior called my bluff.

"***What are you nuts cabron***, that stuff will kill you deader than Charlie will," Junior gasped, clutching his heart, and laughing his ass off!

Making a mental entry into my *swear word diary*, I snickered weakly along with him, grateful to have dodged a gastro-intestinal bullet. I looked over at Mitchell and he was grinning as well. After a minute or two, Mitchell continued to fill me in on their history from boot camp. He told me about the time Junior's cousin Sal tried to shoot him for stinking up his *cherry ride* after a graduation drunk in San Diego. He talked about his mates, Hightower, Angel, and Scotty as well as some others. But, he talked mostly about their Gunnery Sergeant, how this man had taken a real interest in them, encouraging them and building them into men. How the gunny had been like a father to some of the guys that passed through, on their way to whatever the future held, Junior included.

"He used to ride Junior really hard sometimes. But then I would see them talking afterwards, when they thought nobody was around. I'd see him put his arm around *homeboy*, get him in a play headlock, make him laugh like a little kid, while giving him a couple dozen nuggies. He found Junior's smile, the streets had taken that from him a long time ago, but he found it, and gave it back," Mitchell said, his voice trailing off. I looked over at Junior, he was silent, listening intently, and stirring his cold coffee.

"*Man*, then we lost Gunny a few weeks back, just before I transferred to this outfit. He shouldn't have been here ya know, he didn't have to come back here he'd already done his time and then some. You know, not a day goes by I don't think about him, he took care of us out here, like we were his own kids man," Mitchell added, looking over at Junior, nodding his head knowingly. That was all the spark that Junior needed to go off, he slammed his fist onto the table and yelled as loud as he could.

"That was *fucked up man*, I mean really *fucked up*," his likeable demeanor changing instantly into a state of fury, like someone had flipped a switch.

"*Easy Holmes, **callate,*** be cool hombre, *be cool*," Mitchell said, standing up to calm his friend, coaxing him to sit back down. And just as suddenly it was over, Junior's rage switched off like someone just turned out the light in the room. Mitchell looked over at me and indicated with a slow nod that it was OK, that everything was under control.

"We were pretty close you know, all of us from that class I mean," Mitchell said in an even tone.

"The Gunny was even able to keep us all together as a unit for about the first four months in country. Then slowly the Corps began to split us up, transferring us from one Rifle Company to the next, filling needs here and there, as guys rotated back to the world either in a seat or in a box. There were just eight of us still together when Gunny, *ah,* I mean, Sergeant Marquette got himself killed last month. And Scotty, well, he got it with the Gunny, trying to haul him into a *helo* during a running firefight at a hot landing zone. They had to ID him from his tags because the dinks had shot his face off. *The gunny man*, he got left behind after he fell a couple hundred feet back to the ground. That's what's eating at Junior, he didn't get a chance to say good-bye, that was hard for him, still is," Mitchell said, squeezing his buddy's shoulder with his right hand.

"*That's all I want to say about that.*"

I nodded at Mitchell like I understood, *but I didn't really*. Yes, I had seen death before, here and at home. But I had never lost someone so close, so quickly and so violently. The nearest I came was losing my own Father, but

I had a long time to prepare for his death. And when his time came, it was more of a relief than a shock. God help me, I was actually happy that his suffering was over, and more selfishly, that *my* suffering was over. I had time to rationalize, to come to a peaceful understanding that he would always be with me. I could feel my eyes getting moist, so looking down at my feet, I pretended like I was scratching an itch and rubbed at my face.

"That's rough Mitchell, I can't even imagine what that must have been like," I said softly.

Junior suddenly stood up and started laughing, "*Que pesado* (this is boring) ese, let's grab Hightower and catch a ride into Da Nang, raise a little Christmas hell, *no?*"

"What do you think *carnal, **feliz navidad**,*" Junior said, climbing off of the bench and pulling Mitchell up by his shoulders.

"Ah, I don't know, what about you Ethan, you want to come with us," Mitchell almost pleaded with me. I sensed that he wasn't too anxious about hanging out and partying with his buddies. I also suspected that they could be quite a handful when it came to raising hell. Even still, that town was no place for a fledgling man of God, I knew that much. I was still young, dumb and full of cum, and I didn't need to be brazenly subjecting myself to Satan's softer temptations, especially not on Christmas Eve!

"*Naw*, I don't think so Mitchell, *that's not for me*, you know that. Why don't you guys stay here and we'll see if we can scare up a poker game, I'm sure Carla and Larry will be up for it." Mitchell started to answer, but Junior cut him off.

"Thanks but no thanks doc, ***that's*** not for *PFC Me*. Besides, JoJo told Hightower about a couple places he knows, and I want to treat my *homeboy* here to an early Christmas present," he said with a wicked little smile.

"*Aye Dios mio*," Mitchell said weakly, as they walked away together.

Junior planted one arm firmly around his buddy, and with the other he waved good-bye to me from over his own shoulder, never glancing back in my direction. I felt a little guilty about leaving Mitchell in Junior's care, but he was a grown man I reasoned. I got up and bused the table, watching the two of them cross the camp towards the hospital, "must be checking up on JoJo," I muttered.

It was getting pretty late, and I was more than a little worried about Mitchell. He wasn't much of a party boy from what I could see, and he was with some dangerous company in that respect, that was for sure. Alcohol, loneliness, and battle fatigue made for quite a witch's brew. Add in a few random elements, like women, and let's see, oh yeah, more women, and the mixture could be positively lethal! It wasn't hard to guess where those guys would be hanging out tonight, or what was on the party menu. I just hoped that Mitchell would be able to stand his ground under the kind of peer pressure that I knew Junior was going to lay on him. Goading him into tagging along for whatever mischief he was planning.

I shook my head and turned over onto my side in my bunk, trying to keep my mind on my book. I was reading *Robinson Crusoe* by Daniel Defoe for the *umpteenth time*, one of Da's favorites. I had just reached the part where he decides to name his newfound savage friend *Friday*. It was one of the best parts of the story. There was a soft knock at the door and I closed the book and tilted my head back towards the sound. Tony, who was playing gin rummy with Cpl. Polen at the card table, spoke up and answered for the tent, "Come on in, it ain't like it's locked or anything!" Lieutenant Cardinale walked in wearing a bathrobe over her khakis and tee shirt. She went over to where Larry Polen was seated and looked over his shoulder scanning the cards in his hand.

"Still on that hot streak, are ya Larry? Hope you guys aren't playing for serious coin," she said winking at Tony.

"*Oh CRAP,* you're making it real hard not to shoot you Larry," Tony said in disgust, putting down the Queen of Diamonds as his discard. Larry scooped it up and then laid down his hand, a colorful display of Kings, Queens, and Jacks, *"GIN!"*

"*Goddamn it,"* Tony shouted, tossing his cards at the corporal. Larry picked them up and started counting his points.

"Let's see, that's 20 for the gin, *oh wow,* and another 84 in your hand. At a nickel a point that brings tonight's total to $17.80, looks like Christmas has come early for old Larry!"

"I tried to tell you that was coming Tony," Carla said grinning at the frustrated corpsman.

"Well why didn't you just say so lieutenant?"

"What am I supposed to do, read your mind or something?"

"HEY, be nice now, it'll be Christmas in about an hour or so," she replied, pulling a chair over next to my bunk.

"I'm *Buddhist* Carla. I don't believe in Santa you crazy bitch!"

"*Come on Larry,* shuffle and deal, you're not leaving here until I win all my money back, pencil neck!" Tony and Larry continued with their card game and I rolled over to see what had brought our visitor out at such a late hour.

"I thought you would be all tucked in, counting sheep, trying to fall asleep so that Santa wouldn't pass over your tent tonight," I teased, smiling at her, and hugging my book like it was my faithful childhood companion, *Buster* the beat up teddy bear. Good thing I had given him to Shannon some time ago, otherwise it would have been *Ethan, the beat up corpsman* out here! She smiled back and then leaned forward in her seat.

"Have you guys seen Aaron tonight," she asked?

I shook my head, "Nope, not once since we got back from the evac this afternoon, why do you ask?"

"I don't know, just have this queer feeling and it's keeping me up. I thought he would have stopped by before now, *you know*, to wish me a Merry Christmas," she said with a weak grin.

"*Hey*," she said, quickly changing the subject. "Who was that tall drink of water you and Mitchell were eating with at chow earlier," she asked, putting back on her tomboy armor?

"That was a buddy of one of the GSW's we brought in today, his name is Hightower."

"That fits I guess, what about the other guy, the beaner?"

"That was Junior Martinez, he's a real piece of work. Turns out Mitchell and those two were boots together in California. Mitchell transferred from their outfit to ours after they got shot up awhile back. They lost their sergeant and another guy in the process, sounded pretty hairy."

"*Where is* Mitchell tonight anyways, he's always such a homebody, I just noticed he wasn't here?"

"Junior dragged him along for some R&R in Da Nang with Hightower and few others."

"You think Aaron might have gone with them," she asked, her frightened, little girl voice returning for a second?

"Might have, they were looking for someone resourceful to help them score a ride into the city."

"*That rat bastard*, stood me up to go out whoring with the boys," she said, slapping her thighs hard enough to attract Tony's attention.

"Man troubles Nurse Carla, *I could have told you **that** was coming*," he teased sarcastically.

"Shut up Yama-whatever, I wasn't talking to you!"

"Look who's forgetting about Christmas being just around the corner now," Tony said chuckling.

"*OK Tony*, I surrender, give me a break here will ya!"

She turned back and looked me directly in the eyes, "Listen Ethan, I'm a little worried, women's intuition stuff ya know? Do you mind if I just sit here with you for a little while? Maybe you can read to me from that book, it'll keep my mind from conjuring up all sorts of horrible things."

"*Yeah*, sure Carla, I used to read this to my sister all the time. She liked it mostly because I would change my voice to fit each of the different characters. It was like acting in a one man play."

"I'd like that Ethan," she said scooting the chair closer to my bunk. I sat up and crossed my legs Indian style and placed the book in my lap.

"*Oh*, and just so you know, if none of those horrible scenarios plays out with Aaron, I am going to beat the *bejesus* outta that man when I see him next!" I nodded at her in mock support and started to read Chapter One...

I was awakened by a commotion outside of the tent, a jeep or a taxi I wasn't sure which, had screeched to a sudden stop a few yards away. I must have dosed off while reading the book to Carla. I rolled my head from side to side, waiting for my eyes to adjust to the darkness. I noticed that I was leaning against a tent support, the book face down on the bunk to my right. Sprawled out on my bunk to my left, was Lieutenant Cardinale fast asleep. My heavy wool blanket covered all of her body except her feet, which were snugly tucked into my lap keeping her cold feet nice and warm. My legs were still crossed Indian style and I was feeling the stiffness in my joints.

I gently lifted Carla's feet out of my lap and started to get up, my knees ached from being stuck in that position for hours. And my feet were suffering from the absence of decent circulation. When they finally touched the ground it was as if a thousand needles were being pushed into them. I stamped around in the dark quarters trying to hasten the flow of blood and a return to normalcy. I could hear shouting in the compound, but I couldn't make out any words, whoever it was, they were moving in a direction away from our quarters. I pulled on my jump boots and started for the door.

"Where are you going," a little voice said from behind me. I turned around and saw Carla propped up on one elbow, rubbing her eyes with her little fist.

"It's probably nothing, go back to sleep," I whispered.

She started to lie back down when the shouting outside returned, a little louder and closer this time. I recognized Junior's voice right away, he was talking fast and he was obviously agitated. Then Hightower's deep voice broke through the silent night.

"Shut up Junior, you'll wake the whole camp stupid. Let's get him into his tent and see how bad it is," he said in a loud whisper.

The door to the tent burst open as Aaron Walker and Wesley Hightower entered quickly, carrying an unconscious Mitchell Rojas over to his bunk in the corner. Junior Martinez was right behind them, toting my roommate's helmet and boots. He tossed them carelessly onto the card table with a loud thud, and looked over at me.

"*We got trouble ese, get your medicine bag Ethan, homeboy is hurt man,*" he said excitedly, pointing over at Mitchell's bunk.

I rubbed my eyes roughly then slapped myself awake with both hands, focusing on the scene that was unfolding around me. Things were happening fast and furious, a real frenzy, but oddly, my mind was processing it all silently and in slow motion. I did a slow 360-degree turn in the spot I was standing in. I noticed that Carla was missing, no longer curled up on my bunk. Hightower rushed by me with a handful of bloody towels, Aaron Walker was kneeling beside Mitchell's bunk holding a flashlight above his head and over the shoulder of Tony Yamamoka, who was sitting on the edge of the bed in his olive colored skivvies. He was tending to our roommate, doing what he was trained to do. Junior hovered around them, pacing back and forth erratically, pulling his sweat soaked hair back with one hand and dragging his other hand repeatedly across his pant leg, trying to remove the blood before it became a permanent stain. Tony turned towards me and I could see that he was yelling something at me, but I could only see his lips moving, I heard no sound. Suddenly someone shoved passed me, knocking me out of the way in the process. And then a sharp, familiar pain wrestled me from the hold of my hysterical paralysis. It was Nurse Carla, and she had pinched me good and hard, twisting my nipple through my tee shirt. She reached up and yanked me down by my ear lobe to her five foot three inch eye level.

"You want to get in the game here Ethan," she hissed!

I rapidly blinked back at her, fluttering my eyes like a prom queen, and jerked free from her hold.

"Owww, goddamn-it Carla," I swore, rubbing my ear and chest like a chimp in the circus.

The chaos of the moment surrounded me now as all of my senses came back on line simultaneously. The bulk of the action was over at Mitchell's bunk, and I could see that one of the surgeons had taken Tony's place at Mitchell's side and was frantically working. Carla must have fetched him; he must have been the *fullback* that ran through me a moment ago. And considering the severity of the pain in my shoulder, Hightower must have been blocking for him! I moved closer to get a better look without getting in the way, when a bloody hand reached back toward me and grabbed my wrist.

"*Here*, take this bandage and put a lot of pressure *right here*, right where my hand is now," shouted the surgeon, who I recognized immediately as Captain Fornell.

"Yes sir," I replied quickly, dropping to my knees and scooting in next to Mitchell.

I got a fast peek at what looked like a pretty deep stab wound to the abdomen, and then slapped the bandage over the nasty gash and pressed down with a considerable amount of pressure. Now I had done this at least a dozen times in the field, but working on someone that I knew was very different. Now I was scared, and I had to fight with myself to ignore the instinct to cut and run. I felt Mitchell reach down with his hands and place them over my own. He was trying to speak to me, but his voice was soft and low, and I couldn't hear him over all the commotion in the room. I leaned forward trying to make eye contact with him, but Tony and the doctor were in front of me, blocking my line of vision. I watched Tony run an IV with lactated ringers while Dr. Fornell ran his stethoscope across Mitchell's chest and abdomen, listening closely, trying to determine if any of Mitchell's vital organs had been punctured or lacerated. Captain Fornell called for Carla and whispered something in her ear that sent her running out of the tent a second later, Lt. Walker following quickly after her. Meanwhile, Tony wrapped a BP sleeve around Mitchell's arm and started squeezing the pump to inflate it. Like a well choreographed dance, Captain Fornell positioned his stethoscope over the main artery on Mitchell's left arm and waited for Tony to open the valve so that he could get a good read.

"We're running out of time people, *come on Carla*, where are you sweetheart," Capt. Fornell said tersely, mostly to himself. Mitchell started to shudder and flail around in his bunk, and it was difficult to keep the bandage on the wound, his body was so slick with all of the blood and fluids.

"He's crashing Doc," Tony shouted, trying to hold Mitchell still, leaning onto his shoulders with all of his weight. Mitchell's hands still held onto mine, but his grip was getting noticeably weaker.

"Hold on Mitchy, hang in there buddy," I said in a loud whisper, repositioning my hands and the blood soaked bandage over the wound, applying more pressure with my tired arms. I prayed for God to give us a little more time, to give Mitchell's body a little more strength. But there was so much blood, and it was leaking out of him much faster than the IV could replace it.

"CARLA, where's that goddamn plasma," the Doc shouted at the ceiling, his frustration visibly and audibly apparent!

Junior was on his knees muttering to himself and getting in the way, trying to scooch in closer to his friend.

"Somebody get this man out of my way," Captain Fornell ordered.

"Aye Aye sir," Hightower said, gently picking Junior up and walking him over to my bunk. Junior didn't offer much resistance, he was totally out of it, and emotionally drained.

"Come on Junior, let the man work, we'll wait over here," Hightower said, sitting down next to his buddy who had curled up into a fetal position on my cot.

A small crowd had gathered outside the tent, about ten or fifteen people, standing around in their skivvies and pj's, watching our little drama unfold. It got very quiet as we all waited for the cavalry to arrive with the plasma and mobile surgical kit, a few minutes feeling like a few hours. All of a sudden, Mitchell's weak, raspy voice broke through the uncomfortable silence, and he choked out my name.

"Ethan, Father are you here?" I looked at him and saw that his eyes were open.

He was looking up at the ceiling, watching the lamp swing, slowly casting shadows back and forth across the room. He drew in two quick breaths and then blinked his eyes.

"Bless me Father for I have sinned," he coughed swallowing hard.

"It's been a while since my last confession," he whispered to the air. I caught a glimpse of his face and watched a tear roll down his cheek.

*"Oh **fuck me**,"* I thought out loud.

I wasn't prepared for this, this was *sacrilegious*, I wasn't actually a real priest yet. How could I take his confession? I lowered my head and wiped my sweaty brow on my bare arm, trying to keep the pressure constant on my dying friend's wound.

"Father, are you there?"

Now it was my turn to swallow hard, *"Yes my son, I am here."*

I glanced over at Tony he closed his eyes and bowed his head. I looked down at Captain Fornell, he was sitting cross-legged on the floor, his elbows resting on his knees, his face buried in his hands. The room became very small, like there was only space for Mitchell and myself.

"Father... Ethan, please help me," he drew in a couple more quick, shallow breaths, *" help me give thanks for His love and forgiveness."*

"The Lord be with you Mitchell Rojas."

"And also with you Father"

"What is your good confession my son?"

"I tried help him. I tried to help Junior Father. I fucked up homey... I fucked up!"

"It's enough that you tried my son, God's grace is with you."

Mitchell closed his eyes and coughed hard, I could feel that his bleeding had slowed considerably. His color was pale, even in this light. His body shuddered again and Captain Fornell rose from the deck and put his finger to Mitchell's neck, checking his carotid artery for a pulse. Mitchell opened his eyes and drew in a long deep breath through his nose then let it out slowly, startling the doctor.

"Ethan, my wife, my boy, Father, please," he whispered.

"Yeah, Mitchy, what about em?"

I waited for a reply, but none came, just a long silence instead. Mitchell lay very still, his eyes still open, his chest no longer rising and falling with any breath.

"Peace be with you Mitchell Rojas, go with God my friend."

"Via con Dios, mi carnal, via con Dios," I heard Junior whimpering from across the room.

Captain Fornell started to reach over and close Mitchell's eyes when the cavalry arrived. Carla set the surgical kit at the doctor's feet and tossed Tony a fresh bag of plasma. Energized by the possibility of working a miracle, the small team of medical personnel went to work. The Captain pushed me aside and started to prep Mitchell's body for one *last stand*, while Tony started chest compressions and Carla quickly inserted a breathing tube down his throat and attached the respirator bag. I slowly walked backwards toward my bunk to stand with Hightower and Junior, my hands still covered with Mitchell's blood.

"He's dead ain't he hoss," Hightower asked?

"Yeah."

"They ain't gonna bring him back are they?"

"Nope"

"What the hell happened tonight," I asked without turning around to face either of them?

"What can I say, it was stupid, really, really stupid. We got drunk, went to one of JoJo's coochie houses, tried to get Mitchell to loosen up a little. He must come from a dry county in California, cause he didn't but sip on one beer the whole night. And there was no way we were gonna get him to follow us inside with the women. So he just sat out front on an old rumble seat and sipped that warm beer, flipping through an Archie comic book that belonged to a kid of one of the girl's."

"Cut to the chase Wesley, how did he get knifed?"

"Well sir, Junior got into an argument with this whore, over what she thought she had earned. You know how the women are over here, when one starts hollering they *ALL* start hollering, shrieking really, in that VC gibberish where they sound more like cats fighting in the alley! It got so loud that Mitchell must have thought that we were in trouble, so he busted in the joint like John Wayne. As soon as he walked in the door, that girl's momma, she stabbed him with a bayonet that she was using to chop up some cabbage. That's the whole story, I swear," Hightower said shaking his head.

I was really angry, and I was tempted to go off on both of them, not to mention Lt. Walker who should have known better, but all I could think of was Mitchell's last words. I had taken his confession, and it was *he* had asked for forgiveness, *for letting down his friends.* His last moments on this earth were all about forgiveness, about his love for his family, about his love for his friends, about his love for his God. I was cut deeply and to the heart by my friend's selfless act of contrition, and my angry emotions were instantly replaced by a desire to reach out, just as Mitchell had.

I turned around slowly and made eye contact with Hightower, stepping closer to him. His body tensed for an instant, his thick muscled arms flexing, in anticipation of defending himself. He eased a bit when he realized that I wasn't getting ready to charge at him. I reached down and touched his shoulder, then looked down at Junior. He was so quiet, lying there on his side, rocking slowly back and forth. I knelt beside my bunk and sat back on my heels. He looked up at me with wet eyes, his hands clasped together as if in prayer, biting down on his thumbs that were wedged between his teeth. I heard the team giving up in the background.

"*That's it*, time of death, 00:07, 25 December 1968, Merry Christmas everyone," Captain Fornell said to whoever was keeping the official record. I put my head down and rubbed my eyes with my thumb and four fingers.

"*You know what*, his last thoughts were of his family and his friends. He prayed for you guys, for all of us," I said, still rubbing my tired eyes.

"*Lo ciento, por favor, **ay Dios mio**, lo ciento mi amigo, lo ciento,*" Junior moaned, clutching the wool blanket and weeping into it. I looked up at Junior and watched him dealing with his anguish.

"If you really mean that Junior, then honor the faith he had in you by having some faith yourself. Take some of the love that Mitchell showed us all tonight and use it! Change your heart; share it with yourself and everyone you know. Whatever you do man, don't take this war home with you *ese*. Leave it all here, let it just die here man."

"It's easy to hate, it's much harder to forgive. Take Mitchell's gift with you and do likewise, *forgive everyone of everything*, start with yourself buddy!"

I stood up and turned to look back toward Mitchell's bunk. He was lying there alone now, his wool blanket pulled up over his face. I had always thought that it was queer how people were so frightened by the peaceful face of death. And I remembered a poem my Da used to recite at times like these, when someone near and dear had passed, or was near to passing. It went like something like this:

Like a dark and silent specter…he stands and waits for me
Neither smile nor frown upon his face…am I allowed to see
Blessed by some and cursed by others…and feared by nearly all
He's ne'er afraid in dark, nor light…to show his deathly pall
If I'm alone and deep in pain…if life I cannot see
I'll sooth myself with silent prayers…it's me he's come to see

I looked over at Carla, her back was to me, and she was busily packing away the equipment and supplies. I watched as Tony walked over to her and put his arm around her. She leaned her head onto his shoulder while she kept on working. Captain Fornell passed by me and nodded, and then stepped into the doorway to speak with the SP's who were standing by, waiting for the facts. Lieutenant Walker strode over to where Carla and Tony were standing. He stood behind them for a second or two and then stepped forward embracing them both with his two big arms.

I took a deep breath and then glanced back over my shoulder at Hightower and Junior. Then I looked straight up at the ceiling and exhaled deeply. I closed my eyes and prayed silently for the strength to follow the same advice I had just given Junior. I wondered how the news would be delivered to Mitchell's family, but knew instinctively that it would be cold, coming from strangers, or worse still by way of a form letter. There wasn't much I could do about it though, because it would be at least a year before they cut me loose from here. I remembered Mitchell's story about his boy being healed by a little girl.

"Pity you weren't here tonight, we coulda used you," I said softly to myself, regretting my tone as soon as I said it.

I decided that I would write his family and tell them about how well he had lived. Tell them that it was his family that he called for in his final moments. Maybe I would visit with them one day, so there could be a face with the name, someone real to hug, somebody who had been there with him at the end. I think Mitchell would like that, actually I knew that he would. Hadn't he had asked me only a few weeks ago to come see him after all this craziness, after I got my official collar. Maybe I would go, maybe. But a year was a long time over here. For all I knew someone might have to write a similar letter to my own family. Shaking that thought off, I walked over to my three friends were huddled, and joined them in a group hug. Right about now I needed a little love myself.

PART TWO

1968-1973

Knowledge, human catnip...

Fifteen

("...You can't always get what you
want, but if you try sometimes you get
what you need"...Rolling Stones)

Boston, Massachusetts, 18 February 1973

Winters in Boston could be harsh, *not Buffalo harsh*, but harsh enough to make you dream about sailing the Caribbean on a 48 foot Catamaran with a freezer full of ice cream sandwiches and a fridge full of cold ones, *Rolling Rock* preferably. Now that I think about it, that dream had been one of my favorites back in the Nam, a recurring one as a matter of fact, only then I was trying to escape the heat. I shook my head to clear my mind and continued to check my look in the vanity mirror. I had been killing some time in the small groom's chambers, admiring my stiff new collar, while I waited for everyone to arrive.

These sorts of occasions were typically without ceremony, but my mother would have none of that. She had convinced (some might prefer coerced as a more accurate adjective) Father McKenzie that a proper blessing was needed before I left home to begin my internship at Saint John's Cathedral in Fresno California. He capitulated of course, and she took it from there, planning this small gathering of several dozen humans, mostly family and close friends. I smiled to myself as I remembered that day a week ago last.

The good Father sat at our kitchen table drinking tea with milk, and read the details of Mother's little event. As he held out his cup for a refill, he said to mother, "Can you do *nothing* on a small scale Margaret Mary?"

"The saints preserve us, next you'll be asking me to invite the Bishop himself to preside over this send off you're arranging for young Ethan."

"Don't be giving her any ideas now Father, don't be giving her any ideas," I said to him. Mother poured more tea into our parish priest's cup and stuck her tongue out at me. Now that was a Kodak moment, and as you can see I did manage to record it for posterity. Meanwhile, back at the ranch, I looked at my watch, it was nearly time to get this little party started. I peeked out of the door and surveyed the room, knowing that we were still missing an important guest, one whom I would not want to start without. So, I returned to my chair and sat back down. I didn't actually need to *look* for him, if he were here I'd have *heard* him by now, we all would have. The man did not speak so much as he bellowed, and he had never in his life successfully sneaked into any room. My big friend was like a goofy footed puppy on a freshly waxed floor, nobody would miss his entrance! I looked at my watch again and decided I would stall as long as I could, he would be here soon, I knew that we could count on him, we always had.

Paul Pulchoski lifted the collar of his P-coat and pulled it close around his neck, the bitter cold cutting through all the layers of clothing that he was wearing. He still loved that old P-coat, even though he had been out of the Navy for over a year now. It wasn't the most practical of accoutrements but its sentimental value was high, as was his tolerance for pain. He stopped for a second to stamp his feet and see if he could hasten the circulation to his extremities. As usual, he was running a just little late, and to make matters worse, he had had to **walk** almost the entire way from *Flynn's Tavern* on Beacon Street, all the way over to the *Cathedral of the Holy Cross* on Dartmouth Street. It seemed that last night's record snowfall had made the roads unsafe for man or beast, much less automobiles. His slightly labored exhales billowed up in front of his rosy-cheeked face in great clouds as he stopped to catch his breath and check the time on his wristwatch. He could still make it he thought, but he'd have to cover the next couple of blocks in less than 15 minutes.

"Damn it Paulie, you're gonna have to haul ass," he said to himself encouragingly.

"That's a lofty goal," he thought out loud.

"Fast even for Kenny Wong, that skinny rat bastard," he continued, finishing his thought. Paul smiled to himself contemplating the pun made at his buddy's expense, then resumed his *race pace*. Yeah, he'd make it all right he was highly motivated, after all this was a big day in their best friend's life. How often does someone get ordained as a priest in the Holy Roman Catholic Church anyways? Well, not *exactly* ordained yet, I was only a year into St. John's Seminary in Brighton since my graduation from Holy Cross University. Now it was time to begin my *novice internship* serving a neighborhood parish. The road to priesthood would take another couple of years before my actual vows. I remember explaining the whole process to Paul and Kenny one afternoon while the three of us shot hoops in Kenny's parent's backyard.

"It's sorta like being Jim Reed on Adam 12," I said referencing a popular TV show from when we were kids.

"I'm like this rookie cop, on probation see," I explained.

"Sure, I get the uniform, the gun, the shield, *you know*, only it's a hassock, a collar, and a Bible. *And,* then I have to ride along with a veteran, *like Malloy*, and he makes sure I don't make any dumb bunny mistakes in the course of doing my duty. Then he grades me see, and if I hack it on the streets, then I get to swear in as a member of the force, *get it?*" I finished, searching their expressions for a sign that they understood. I was met with blank stares and slow nods, and was about to try a different tack when Kenny's Mom appeared with a tray of food and lemonade. Boy, was I relieved to see her, because the only other example I could think of was *'The Mod Squad'* and that would have meant that one of us would have to have been *'Julie.'* And since Paul and Ken could both pound me, that plum role would have fallen to *moi* ! Oh, and speaking of food, I always loved eating at Ken's house. I never knew what we were going to have next it was all so exotic and new to me. Now Paulie would push whatever was served, around on his plate, test smelling the food and nibbling at the edges, where I would just leap right in and go for broke. Once he was convinced I wasn't going to die, he would join the feeding frenzy, old man Wong leading the charge, his chopsticks like deadly weapons in the hands of a real Kung Fu master! *No sir*, Kenny's mother never disappointed us with any meal, they were always *top shelf*, even if we couldn't pronounce their proper names. Ken and I would laugh until our stomachs hurt watching his Mom squish Paul's cheeks together with her tiny hands trying to help him with the difficult diphthongs. He reminded us of Chumley the Walrus from the Tennessee Tuxedo cartoon show.

Paul checked his watch as he ran, *well, trotted*, OK, OK, as he walked really, really fast. Surprisingly, he was making pretty good time, he could have even slowed down a bit without a risk of slipping his schedule, but he didn't. He knew if he was even one second late, my mother would box his ears for sure, no doubt that was the real motivation here! He finally arrived at his destination, slightly winded but none worse for the wear. He had covered the distance in twelve minutes flat, an accomplishment that would be shared repeatedly during the reception afterward, *"this should be good for at least a pint or two,"* he whispered to himself, panting slightly. Paul held onto the rail at the base of the stairs and looked up to the arched entrance. He walked up the steep steps to the old cathedral and opened the huge wooden door. It creaked loudly as the hinges struggled with the weather and the enormous weight. Whatever lubrication may have existed, had frozen over a long time ago.

"So much for sneaking in at the last minute," he said, closing the door as quickly as he could. The foyer and receiving hall was packed with people, all of them friends, family, and colleagues of one Ethan Matthew Kelly, *who*, by day's end, would be forever known around here simply as Father Kelly.

"Stealth as ever Paulie, smooth buddy, *smooooooth*," Kenny Wong taunted from across the room, shifting his three-year-old daughter from his right arm to his left. She was so cute, dressed in her white chiffon Sunday school dress with the pink lace and the little matching hat and gloves. You'd never guess the kind of world-class profanity that sweet, innocent child was capable of delivering.

"Shhhhh, you don't have to shout KT, she'll hear you ya know!"

"Yeah well, then I've got some bad news for you," Kenny said grinning. He raised his free hand to his face, slowly extending his index finger along side his right eye, and pointing to the small figure standing behind Paul.

"Man," Paul whined, turning around slowly to face the music.

And there she was, Margaret Mary Kelly, all five-feet-two inches of her (in heels no less), standing just behind the uncomfortable *center of attention*. Her two fists were planted firmly at the waist of her smart navy blue suit, and she cast a glare at Paul that could curdle milk!

"*OH*, we *all* heard you Paul Michael Pulchoski! You weren't hard to miss, barreling through those two great doors dere! Now, what have you to say for yourself boy," demanded Maggie Kelly.

Paul began to stammer out a reply but my mother cut him off sharply.

"Come on now, ***out with it!***"

"*Yeah* Uncle Paulie, *out wit it you wiener*," a tiny voice scolded in the background.

Paul didn't have to look back to see who's voice it was, he knew it was Kenny's little girl Sophia. He watched the child's mother swat her husband on his powerful bicep, and then reach for her daughter.

"*Sophie*, that's not nice baby, no potty mouths allowed in God's house! *Come on honey*, let me have her," Kenny's wife Carolyn said, coming to Paul's rescue before her precious little chatterbox could ***really*** start in on him!

"*Ow*, I didn't say anything," Kenny said chuckling, mock flinching slightly. He handed the child to his better half, and they smiled at one another knowingly. They never encouraged her misbehavior in fact they were really good at lovingly disciplining her with time outs whenever she got out of line. The two of them were textbook terrific parents. But, *occasionally*, Sophie's timing and delivery were just *too funny* to ignore. Carolyn once confided in me and said that sometimes she would have to duck into a closet and bury her face in coat to mute her laughter, after sitting Sophie in the corner as discipline for similar verbal infractions. Enjoying their daughter's natural comedic timing was a secret vice that they shared between them, harmless really, probably not even a real sin, I'd have to check on that sometime. They had a great marriage too, even though most people around here would have bet big money against it. Their beginning was truly a clash of cultures, and I shamefully take pride in the fact that it was me who brought them together in the first place. I had known Carolyn Haughtner since we were five years old. Her family had been neighbors of my Uncle Liam when he had first settled in Lancaster County, Pennsylvania, *Amish country*. She and her four brothers (two sets of twins) would come and play with all the Kelly clan at our family gatherings and we became good friends over the years. She was a lot like Kenny in many ways. They were both the eldest children in their families, and they instinctively accepted the role of shepherding the younger kids. They were loving and respectful of their parents, but they were fiercely independent as well, almost to a fault at times. Not pig headed mind you, but to say they *disliked* losing at anything would be a gross understatement. If I had a nickel for every time Kenny came close to pounding me for not taking some game seriously enough, I could have paid my way to Rome to visit the Holy Father at the Vatican! *Well now,* at some point during the years when we were all growing up together, I got the notion that the two of them should meet. I don't know when or why, maybe it came to me in a dream, it really doesn't matter, I can't remember anyway. The fact is for whatever reason I managed to badger my Da into letting me bring Ken along with us one summer, to the annual Kelly gathering at Uncle Liam's. And it was there that the future couple first met. *On the surface*, they were polite enough to one another, showing just the right amount of disinterest. But just beneath the surface you'd swear that you could feel something in the air, like when you stood next to a power line. It was electric, like two magnets moving quickly across a table toward one another. It was the way she would look away whenever he caught her watching him. It was the uncharacteristic boldness of my normally shy and reserved friend, as he blatantly sought out reasons to be near her. It was what it must be like to witness the miracle of life, watching the cells divide and grow into something wonderful, only in this case, it was moment begetting moment. It was the fulfillment of a promise, bringing together two halves to make a whole. It was quite simply God's commitment to deliver our heart's desire. This one and that one, opposite yet the same, designed to fit together, one half completing the other, their differences being the real strength of their bond. It was so natural it seemed unnatural, and they almost missed it entirely, because as strongly as they were drawn to one another, their families seemed to repel one another. The parents were too firmly rooted in long practiced traditions and beliefs to allow their children to break from the mold and fall in love with one another. Their cultures did not encourage, much less allow for change or compromise. And, in their defense, they were only trying to do what they thought was best for their babies. But in the end, after lots of prayer I might add, it was love that overcame the fear of spoiling the bloodlines. The same love that compelled these parents to *circle their wagons* so to speak, and protect their selfishly close-minded sensibilities, eventually took on a different shape. The same love that was all about honor, tradition, and logical acceptance of the way things are, slowly changed and became more about acceptance and understanding. Because love isn't logical, *it's magical*, and when Ken's mother saw how genuinely happy this foreign girl made her son, how Carolyn seemed to bring out the very best in him, then the changes in attitudes started. Then the barriers began to come down, brick by brick, row by row. It was a beautiful thing to watch a grand merging of cultures it was. Luckily they had the English language in common, because I suspect it might have taken considerably longer to get the parents together if they had to bridge the culture gaps in Chinese and German! I remembered giving them the little poem that I wrote describing their epic courtship. It was shortly after I had come home from my tour of duty, the day before their wedding actually. If I remember right it had been a left-handed parody of Allan Sherman's ode to summer camp, and I had entitled it, pseudo-intellectually of course *"When East, Meets West."* I know, I know, *it's crap*, but it seemed clever at the time. I must have written it during a bout with malaria, or during a mortar attack, or after one of Lieutenant Arron Walker's prized Havana cigars (those always made me light-headed). In any event, I was obviously working a few cards short of a full deck when I penned this.

I think it sort of went a little like this…

> *"Hello mudda, hello fadda*
> *Look I brung you, a new dotta*
> *She's a white chick, but no loser*
> *No I didn't meet her at some college boozer"*

Not exactly *Shelly or Keats*, and it kind of got a lot cornier as it went along, but my heart was in the right place I think. Besides, as I recall, Carolyn kissed me for it, Ken socked me for it, and the three of us decided it would be better kept just between us. *Oh yeah*, we also decided that I was pretty much the nerd of the century. Well, so much for any literary aspirations I may have had, *cest la vie!*

"That's pretty low Kenny, teaching Sophie to *dis me* like that, I'm hurt man!"

"***Its not me***, you know that Shannon teaches her all that sassy stuff whenever she baby-sits!"

"*Ahrrgg*, you two are impossible, I'm going to get Sophie some punch," Carolyn Wong said, turning quickly on her heels and heading toward the refreshment table in the hall.

"Now you've gone and done it," Kenny snapped at Paul.

Before Paulie could fire off another quip at Kenny, my mother reached up and got hold of his ear.

"*Will you be ignoring me in God's own house Mr. Pulchoski?* I may be a wee girl but I can still pack quite a wallop mister," mother said in a harsh but playful whisper. I watched and listened to all of the commotion with sinful glee, peering out of the crack in the slightly ajar door that separated the groom's chambers from the Church's large foyer. I couldn't help snickering to myself as I watched my friends deal with their predicament, "*better you than me,*" I whispered to myself, covering my mouth with both hands to mute my chuckling. My sinful delight in their suffering was dealt with swiftly when the door opened quickly into my face and I received an eyeful of heavily enameled wood.

"*Oww, what the...*"

"Careful Peepers, remember where you are brother dear," my sister Shannon said sweetly but sarcastically.

"Father Mac sent me to fetch you so that we can get this over with and onto the party!" I looked at her with one eye closed in an exaggerated wink, my head tilted slightly, vigorously rubbing my sore eye, and answered back, "*Aye, what?*" Even with only one eye working, I couldn't help but notice how beautiful my little sister had become. She was almost sixteen now and she grew to look more and more like those pictures of our mother when she was young, the ones of her and Da when they were courting. Shannon had mother's lovely figure and beautiful auburn hair, and she had inherited a little of Da's height, so at five feet eight and in her modest heels, she appeared statuesque, positively regal.

"I'll be along in a minute girl, just tell Father Mac that I need to get a little more comfortable with this collar," I said running my fingers across the new addition to my wardrobe. Shannon walked over to me, wet her fingers and pushed the hair out of my eyes, then took a look at where the door had hit me.

"*Ah Ethan*, let me put a little make-up on that eye," she said reaching into her handbag for her compact.

"We can't have you standing up to be blessed in front of God and the Church with a shiner now can we!" Reaching up I touched my sore eye, and I didn't need to look to know that she was right of course. But *make-up*, on *my* face, *Lord above*, that had to be at least a venal sin, I just prayed that neither Paul nor Kenny walked in at this moment!

"Alright girl, do your business, but be quick about it, the walls have eyes and ears ya know!" We both chuckled at the situation and Shannon applied the paste expeditiously but gently.

"There, good as new, I'll tell Father that you'll be out in a minute," she said. Turning to leave she stopped after a couple of steps. She spun around and looked at me, her gloved hands clasped in front of her face, her eyes beginning to glisten. She walked quickly over to me and hugged me like she had the day I went away to Viet Nam. We stood there holding each other for a moment, then she stepped back and struck a real grown up pose, her arms folded in front of her.

"*I'm so proud of you Ethan*, Mother's proud of you too. And you know Da's watching now as well. He's up dere, telling Jesus himself what a great kid he made, and that if it hadn't been for the calling, you'd have been the next Whitey Ford!" I just stared back at her, I didn't have the right words to fit the moment so I tried to say it all with my look.

"Now you promise me that no matter what, you'll be here when my wedding day comes. I'll not have anyone else say the words and give me away, do you promise?"

"I promise Shannon, I will."

"Pinky swear," she added, as she held out her hand with her littlest finger extended. I walked over to her and we hooked our pinky fingers together.

"One two three, this I swear to thee," we said together, quickly pulling our hands back. "Now go on, I'll be right out," I said to her.

Shannon blew me a little kiss and walked out of the room. I went to the door and closed it gently behind her, then walked over to the vanity. Leaning forward I placed my palms onto the table and looked at my reflection closely in the mirror. The make-up my attentive little sister had applied was hardly noticeable and that was a relief that made me smile. I stared into the mirror, and looking back at me was a man, someone that I had only just begun to know. I could see in his eyes the memories of someone who had lived beyond his years. I could see incredible happiness and equally incredible sorrows. There were issues yet to deal with, things to set right, hearts to heal, much to learn, and the challenge of the unknown in front of him. I was actually taking the next step toward a calling that I was sure was real, but of which

I was totally uncertain. I closed my eyes and the movie in my head started again, *"The Ethan Kelly Story."* And I let it run for a few seconds, the memories as vivid as the days that they were initially experienced. I could feel my face smile, smirk, and then frown. My eyes became moist and then dry again as the short story played on in my mind. The last few frames that I watched were a replay of the day Pfc. Mitchell Rojas died. When it was over, I opened my eyes slowly. The man in the mirror was looking back at me knowingly. I stood up straight and reached into my coat pocket and pulled out the envelope. Removing the letter from inside, I unfolded the pages and scanned the words that I had read a dozen times since receiving it. They were words of pain and praise, of love and bitterness, of anguish and hope. It was those last words of hope that compelled me to seek out the author and do what I could to ease the pain. This letter had reminded me of a promise I had made on the other side of the world to a man that I hardly knew. I folded the pages and returned them to the envelope and then put it back into my coat pocket. I looked in the mirror again and the man was smiling at me, it had taken me five years to answer this letter. *"A promise is a promise,"* I said to the man, to myself, and I turned to join the others. I reached the door, turned the knob and opened it. The whole room turned to face me as I walked into the foyer and I swallowed hard, and smiled, quite embarrassed as they applauded.

"It's about time Ethan, *I mean Father Kelly*, we were about to send out a search party," Paulie said to me beaming, happy to see me but more happy to be rescued from mother's wrath.

"It's a little early for the Father reference Paulie," I said, although I had to admit, it sounded good, *comfortable*, just like Paul's P-coat!

"Ah, so what are we supposed to call you then, *rookie?"* he said laughing.

"Hey, wait a minute! Is that *make-up* on your face?"

I ignored the comment out of self-defense and quickly looked down to find Sophie Wong standing next to me, holding onto my pinky finger. She held a Dixie cup filled with fruit punch in her other hand and together we walked toward the Church and the start of chapter one in my new life as Father Kelly...

Sixteen

<u>*Firebaugh, California, 12 December 1968*</u>

Alma Donnelly wet her thumb and turned the page in the magazine that she was reading. Actually, she was just flipping through it while she waited impatiently for her visitor to arrive, *her unplanned visitor*. She didn't like surprises very much they interrupted her daily routines and schedules. It was order and discipline that had always been the cornerstones of her adult life. So this morning's telephone call from some pushy newspaper journalist had put an unwelcome wrinkle into her smoothly planned day. Feeling a little agitated by the lien on her personal freedom to come and go as she pleased, Alma uncrossed her legs and slapped the magazine onto her lap.

"Damn it, where is that woman anyway," she said to herself, looking over to the crystal timepiece perched at the edge of the exquisite mahogany coffee table in front of her.

"*RUTH*, please bring the tea service and set it here in the living room," she called to her housekeeper. Alma looked once again toward the timepiece, "I'll give her five more minutes," she muttered to herself, leaning back on the sofa. She picked up the magazine, crossed her legs and stared once again at the National Geographic, November 1966 issue.

"Excuse me madam, shall I set the tray here in the center, or would you prefer nearer to you?"

"Oh thank you Ruth dear, over here by me if you please," Alma said sweetly.

"As you wish madam," Ruth said politely as she gracefully placed the serving tray on the table next to her employer.

"Will that be all Mrs. Donnelly?"

"Yes dear, thank you."

Ruth turned and exited the room while Alma fussed with the flower arrangement on the silver tea set. One of Alma's most favorite pastimes was working in her garden, and she and Arthur had a fabulous one. This rural area had some of the most fertile soil on Earth, and she spent many joyous hours tilling that soil, raising her beautiful roses and wildflowers. She would wake early with her husband each morning, and after breakfast would go out into the garden to cut a basket full of flowers for the house. She loved the way they brightened up the home and the wonderfully fresh and fragrant scent that lingered throughout the day. Her smile was returning along with her usual sunny disposition when she heard the doorbell chime. Smoothing her skirt, she sat up straight and then reclined back against the sofa, waiting for her guest to be announced. She could hear the sound of heels on the hardwood floors in the hall, on again and off again as they went from runner to runner.

"Excuse me madam, Miss Katherine Littleton," Ruth announced to the room.

"*KC, please,*" Miss Littleton pleaded, extending her hand as she entered the room and walked towards the sofa. Alma stood up, smiled and reached to take her visitor's hand.

"Alright then, KC it is, a pleasure I'm sure," Alma said, gesturing toward the sofa, indicating for the young woman to sit beside her.

"I hope you don't mind, I arranged for tea, do you take milk, or sweetener?"

"Thank you so much, I'm a coffee girl myself, *but when in Rome, right,*" KC said, trying to lighten the tense mood a bit. She accepted the cup and saucer from Mrs. Donnelly and politely took a sip.

"Yes, *well*, what is it that I can do for you Miss Littleton? *Forgive me, I mean KC?*"

KC pursed her lips and gently blew on her tea, watching Alma from over the brim of the cup as she took another sip. She studied the woman's face and posture, trying to get an indication of how much she knew about the purpose of her visit. She had suspected that Alma may have been briefed from the get go, she had sensed as much from the tone of Alma's voice.

"My goodness, this tea is really quite good, I may have to convert," she exclaimed!

"*Poor Juan Valdez*, this just might put him out of business," KC added, jokingly referring to the popular television ad as she attempted to make friends.

"I'm happy you're enjoying the tea dear, but really, I have quite a busy day ahead, so may we please get to the purpose of your visit," Alma said as politely as she could, given her frustration.

"*Uhmm*, I'm sorry, yes of course," KC said clearing her throat.

"Mrs. Donnelly, my paper is working on a piece about violent crimes against women in California. Its a four part series and I am here doing some research on the Arroyo Grande Clinic case, the one involving Dr. Murray Katz and all of those young women and little girls, you've heard of it right?"

"Of course I have, *dreadful*, but how could I possibly help you with your research?"

"Forgive me, I can understand your confusion, I should have done a better job of explaining," KC said setting her cup down on the table and reaching into her purse for her spiral notepad. Quickly flipping back several pages, she stopped and tapped her pencil on the place where she wanted to start.

"In the course of my interviews with police, prosecutors, and various witnesses I have come across several facts that seem to contradict other facts, and a few things that honestly just do not make any sense at all," she continued, scratching her head with the eraser of her pencil and wincing at the notepad.

"For one thing, are you aware that no one has been allowed to see or interview the accused since his arrest?

"Oh, and given all the print coverage that exists on this case, it just seems odd that there is only one candid and *fuzzy* photo of him since his arrest. It was taken as he walked from a police van to the courthouse for his arraignment. And his cuffed hands were up blocking his face at that!"

"Why all the smoke and mirrors you think?"

"All of this secrecy makes someone like me very curious," KC said, trying to analyze Alma's facial expression for a telltale reaction, but there was none, this lady was cool as a cucumber, she thought!

"That is all quite fascinating Miss Littleton, but what does it have to do with your visit to my home?" KC looked back down at her notepad, circled something with her pencil and then placed the eraser on her pursed lips.

"You know, I was having lunch yesterday in the cafeteria at the very same hospital where Dr. Katz had been taken for treatment after the fire. I was trying to make heads or tails of this puzzle and choke down a plate of tuna surprise, when someone, a nurse, sat beside me and noticed a news article that I was reading," she said, pausing a moment for effect.

She looked over at Alma and smiled, silently studying her reaction, and then she was rewarded for her patience. Mrs. Donnelly blinked several times and then loudly and nervously cleared her throat. KC thought to herself, *she flinched!* Not wanting to give the woman any time to regain her composure KC let out a little more line before she set the hook.

"The nurse, her name was Dorothy Mahoney, *but she said to call her Dot,* excused herself for intruding and for looking over my shoulder. She said that she couldn't help but recognize the article that I was reading. Dot said that she had been there, that she was one of the ER nurses on duty that day," KC continued, growing more confident in the ultimate success of this visit. She decided that now was the time to set the hook and reel this woman in, sensing that there would be very little struggle, hell, Alma Donnelly would probably jump right in the boat!

"Dot told me a story Mrs. Donnelly, actually it sounded more like a fairytale, but you were in it Alma, and that is why I'm here," KC said as she helped herself to a refill from the beautiful silver tea service.

Alma Donnelly sat still like a deer caught in the headlights; her eyes revealing her secret struggle between fight or flight. She watched the young journalist doctoring her tea with milk. Remaining silent she stalled for time as her mind worked vigorously at devising a believable explanation, one that would satisfy the reporter and still protect the Lopez family. The seconds passed slowly, agonizingly so, and Alma could almost hear her eyelids open and close as she blinked in time with her thought process. Finally, she spoke.

"What exactly do you want to hear from me Miss Littleton?"

KC Littleton forced herself to suppress a victory smile and set her cup back onto its saucer.

"KC, please," she started. *"And may I call you Alma,"* she asked sincerely? Mrs. Donnelly nodded in agreement.

"Alright then, *Alma,* what I want is to understand what apparently *you all understand already,* about what really happened that day. I think that you know exactly why I am having such trouble gaining access to the truth surrounding Dr. Katz's case. But more than that, I think that you have a story that may be far more interesting than the one that I came here to research. The question is, are you willing to share it with the world," KC said, leaning forward to rest her arms on her knees?

Alma sat for moment or two and looked out the bay window, beyond the lawn and the drive, out at the endless hectors of farmland. From where she was sitting she could see the fruits of her husband's life work, the lettuce fields, the strawberry fields, the radish and carrot fields, all of it green and lush and vibrant. She thought about all of the people she had come to know and whom she had befriended over the many years that they had lived in this valley. They had become more than just employers or *patrons*; they had become family to them all. And now she was about to betray their trust, not of her own volition, but in an attempt to control the damage. Alma turned and looked at KC and searched her face for a sign of compassion. She breathed in deeply and tried to see if she could feel a sense of justice within the young woman's character. And to her great surprise, that is *exactly* what she felt, and it caused her to smile brightly, catching the young journalist completely off guard. KC sat up straight and leaned back against the sofa.

"*What had just happened here,*" she wondered to herself? She wasn't sure what is was, but she could feel *something* in the air, and she smiled back at Alma, although she didn't understand from where the smile came?

"Alright dear, I'll tell you what I can, where would you like to begin?"

Nestle Avenue Elementary School
Morning Recess, 9:20am

The bell rang loudly and the hoard of little people scurried toward the door and out to the playground.

"*WALK*, all of you, I don't want to have to spend my coffee break treating your little skinned knees," shouted Miss Miller, the substitute teacher filling in for Mr. Rawlins today.

It was a nanosecond late as the last of the children exited through the door and the words fell silently to the ground, unheard. The lines quickly formed at the tetherball courts and the handball courts. Several girls were already playing hopscotch on the yellow lined blacktop, and all the *cool boys* had already chosen sides and were about to roll the first pitch on the kick-ball field. It was just another day at Nobel Elementary School. The entire student-body was positively giddy, anticipating the pending break for Christmas vacation.

Hector Hernandez stood out in right field painfully aware that the bases were loaded and secretly hoping against hope that nobody would kick him a fly ball to catch. He wasn't the most gifted athlete on the field, and he didn't want to drop a ball and give Davy Myers another reason to bag on him! It wasn't like it would just stay at school, he had to ride the bus with him too, and that was too much grief in one day for him to bear. Hector would actually pray each night for a miracle, one where he would wake up in the morning and be six feet tall. Then he would pound the daylights out of that kid. But for now he would settle for a little blessed coordination, *'come onnnnnn God'*, he whispered to himself!

As it happened, today God was on Davy's side, and Hector could feel his breakfast churning around in his stomach as he tracked the high fly ball coming his way. His little feet propelled him left then right, forward then back in quick static movements as he tried to position himself under the rapidly descending rubber ball. Just when he thought he was going to make the catch, the bright sun peeked out from over the falling object and blinded him. The ball came down squarely on his *Charlie Brown like* noggin and it bounced another twenty feet behind him before he regained his sight and figured out which way to run! Never in the history of childhood had any little boy wished harder to be invisible. Hector tried to block out all of the noise, the jeers and the taunts, that were being hurled his way, and ran after the still rolling ball. By the time he reached it all four runs had scored, and he had personally allowed the first grand slam in the history of Alfred E. Nobel Elementary School to be scored against his team, *Los Gatos Grande*. Whose captain by the way, was on his way out to right field to pound him at this very moment!

"IT WASN'"T MY FAULT DAVY, I LOST IT IN THE SUN," Hector shouted as he ran as fast as he could in the opposite direction!

Tina Lopez sat Indian style on the grass and watched as first Hector then Davy passed her, grinning widely at the little comedy. She wasn't worried about Hector, he could run circles around Davy, *that gordo*, she thought to herself. She got to her feet as soon as the first bell rang and started walking back toward the classroom. As she walked through centerfield, Hector flew past her in a dead run, seeking the safety of Mr. Rawlins' classroom. Davy ran by a few seconds later, already out of breath.

"You'll never catch him," Tina sang out loud as he passed her.

"Shut up freak," Davy said, turning to face her while running backward.

A second later he tripped over his own shoelaces and fell onto his behind on the hot blacktop. Putting out his hands to break his fall, Davy skinned a couple layers of epidermis off of his palms. He shouted an expletive beyond his years as he watched the *strawberries* on his hands brighten with his blood, and picked himself up, more embarrassed than hurt. Tina walked up to him slowly and stopped to see how badly he was hurt. As she reached out to take his hand Davy jumped back away from her.

"Get away from me *Freakenstein*, I don't want you touching me, you little witch," he said harshly, an inkling of fear in his eyes.

"I won't hurt you Davy, let me see," Tina pleaded softly.

"No way, get away from me," Davy shouted from over his shoulder as he ran toward the Boys Room to clean himself up.

Tina watched him run away and disappear into the restroom next to the drinking fountains. She felt the eyes of the other children on her as they looked on from a safe distance. Some of the kids at school could be cruel, not all of them mind you, but some. They would call her names and avoid her, or leave her out of games and activities. But she didn't mind very much, she had her share of close friends, like Hector, who always made her laugh, and her best friend Wendy who knew all the words to every Beatle's song. They would sing together on the bus to and from school for as long as the driver would stand for it. So their stares did not bother her as much as one might think. But she was growing up, and was becoming more and more aware that people were uncomfortable around her, maybe even a little afraid. That was just silly she thought. Most people did not even know her, only of her.

Her parents had explained that her gift was one from God, and that it was given to her to share with everyone. It was not important for her, not for anyone for that matter, to understand this thing, only that they accept it. *And*, child that she was, she faithfully and innocently accepted what she was told as truth. Her faith was in her parents love for her, and her parents had placed their faith in God's love for them all. She knew instinctively that they were right of course, and in her faith she knew no fear. Whatever it was that passed through her to those who suffered was not harmful to anyone, she knew that. There was not any transfer of pain she was not empathetic in that way. There was never a shared consciousness between she and whomever she touched. She could neither read their minds or their hearts. There was only *the dream*, the compulsion to sleep and wait for Grandfather to come and sing to her, to watch over her, until such time that her mother or father came to wake her and take her home. Tina closed her eyes and took a deep cleansing breath and then raised her arms high over her head and twirled around in a circle. She giggled and called after Davy Myers even though he was no longer in plain view.

"That's OK *gordo*, it wasn't bad, you'll be OK."

She turned and smiled at the other kids, the excitement over for the moment, and they all continued on toward their classrooms, only a little faster now, as they had the second bell to beat!

Seventeen

*("...She's some kind of demon messing in the glue. If
you don't watch out it'll stick to you. To you, what
kind of fool are you? Strange brew -- kill what's
inside of you."...Cream)*

<u>*San Francisco, California, 13 December 1968*</u>

"I don't care what you stumbled on KC, I told you we haven't the budget
for witch-hunts," Brian Williams shouted into the telephone receiver! The
voice of his tenacious little *wildcat of a news hound* could be heard pleading
her case from across the room, even with the handset firmly pressed against
his aching ear! Brian took the phone and pounded the handset several times
on his desktop and then returned it to his ear, his head resting in his free
hand, his fingers slowly massaging his throbbing migraine.

"*kc, kc, KC, **KaaaCeee**, will you let me get a word in edge wise, **please**,
I'm exhausted just listening to you!*" Brian said, imploring his favorite pain in
the ass to shut up long enough for him to change his mind. The attack on
his peace of mind was relentless and he knew that in the end he would find
himself pleading *her* case in the big man's office. Grover Cleveland Gateway,
the founding father of their grand old publication, was still a pretty tough
customer, even at the ripe old age of eighty-one. Twenty years past the age
of sensible retirement, the cagey old man had the energy and keen mind
of someone fifty years his junior! He had made his bones in the newspaper
business at the turn of the century, covering the assassination of President

William McKinley on the sixth of September, nineteen hundred and one for the New York Times. Then after a twenty-five year career, moving back and forth between New York (Times) and Chicago (Tribune), his life took a major detour.

This was the time when he came into great wealth upon the death of his estranged father in nineteen hundred and twenty-seven. Timing being everything in life, he pulled the bulk of his father's fortune from Wall Street and invested heavily in California real estate. Relocating his growing family to San Francisco, the jewel of the Great Golden State in nineteen hundred and twenty-eight, he started the *San Francisco Daily News*, establishing himself as editor and chief, it was a life long dream come true! As he was an only child with no surviving family beyond his own, he answered to no one for his actions or decisions. The fact that the fortune was his solely had allowed him to avoid the annoying pitfalls of dealing with nagging, criticizing, and kibitzing well-intentioned relatives.

The only criticism would come from the highbrow financial circles that he disdained anyway. And ironically, on his newspaper's first birthday, he would report on the crash of the very market that they worshiped, *their safe haven*, the one that he had chosen to abandon against their counsel, leaving those arrogant fools behind to mock him. *This* was the man that Brian was going to have to negotiate with in support of his fledgling reporter's hunch. But Brian knew KC well enough to accept the fact that she rarely cried wolf. If there *were* a story of National interest to be found in *Hooterville*, she would nose it out, no matter how many people she had to drive insane in the process. He smiled to himself and picked up the receiver again, after having placed it under a magazine to mute her non-stop chatter while he gave the aspirin he had popped a chance to work it's magic. He waited for the right moment, and when she paused slightly to draw a breath he jumped in.

"OK, OK, I surrender! Let me call you back in a half hour, I need to go see the old man on this one KC. You know he's the only one that can over ride the bean counter's edicts. Lucky for you he treats you like a kid sister, it must be that crooked little smile of yours," he said, finally squeezing in a whole sentence before she started yammering again.

He listened to her impatiently as she offered him her advice on how to pitch the story. Brian checked his wristwatch restlessly as he hemming and hawing as she spoke. He'd have to hurry up and end this call so he could catch GCG before he went into Chinatown for his daily dose of *Chow Mei Fun*. The old man was a well-known noodle fiend all over the city.

"Gotta go kid, I'm on deadline here, I'll call you back at the hotel, so stay near a phone for the next hour or so," he said quickly, his face following

the handset to it's cradle as he hung up the phone, his last word fading on the air. *Success*, he thought, he finally got the last word!

Brian exited the elevator on the eleventh floor and walked into the large reception area of the newspaper's executive offices. He was greeted with a smile from a young intern named Abby, who was working the reception desk, and he returned her polite gesture.

"Good morning Mr. Williams," the young woman said cheerfully.

"Morning Abby, how are things young lady?"

"Aced my Psych final," she replied, pantomiming an over the top swiping of her forehead, indicating her relief.

"*Good for you!* I believe Mr. Gateway is expecting me."

"Sure, I'll just buzz Mrs. Harris and let her know that you are out here, just a sec OK?"

Brian nodded and relaxed in a slightly modified parade-rest stance, as his hands were folded in front of him while he waited to be waived on in. A minute later Abby answered the phone ringing in front of her and then looked up at Brian and winked, "You can go on in now, see ya round the water cooler," she said sweetly.

"Thanks," he answered back as he walked past her desk and into the long hallway lined in rich, dark mahogany.

He passed the power wall of framed front pages depicting several significant historical events of the last forty or so years. Brian paused a second as he looked at the most recent addition, the sorrowful photo of a dying Robert Kennedy, his bleeding head cradled in the arms of an unknown immigrant busboy on the kitchen floor of the Ambassador Hotel in Los Angeles. His eyes traversed up the page to the headline that simply read, *"NOT AGAIN."* Clearing his throat and straightening his tie, Brian walked up to the desk of Francine Harris, the long time executive secretary to Grover Gateway. She met his arrival with her usual professionalism, not too stiff, but not too casual either.

"Hello Brain, good to see you again," she said greeting him.

"Nice to see you as well Frankie, thanks for squeezing me in on such short notice."

"Not at all, Mr. Gateway should be off the phone in a moment, have a seat."

"Can I get you some coffee or tea?"

"Oh no, I'm fine, please don't fuss over me, *really*, I'll probably only be a few minutes anyway," he said, hoping that his assumption would not turn out to be prophetic. Frankie smiled back at him and nodded, and returned to her work. A minute later Grover Gateway appeared at the open door to the right of her desk.

"Brian, come on in son! Now what do we need to discuss so urgently this morning anyway," he asked, placing his hand on Brian's shoulder and leading him into his office.

"Frankie, make sure to hold all my calls until we finish. Oh, and call ahead to *Wah Lee's* and order me the usual, OK?" Mr. Gateway said without looking back at his secretary, following his visitor into the room, closing the door behind him.

"Sit down Brian, sit down, and let's chat about what that wildcat of ours is up to."

"Well sir, I really don't have all the details yet, but she is definitely excited about something. Its tied to this serial rapist case in Fresno. Honestly sir, you know how she is, sometimes I wonder if she's worth the aggravation, and you can quote me on that," the frustrated managing editor said.

"But, then again, we can't argue with success, she's become one of the best investigative reporters in the Bay Area, if not the State. You called that one sir I never would have believed that was possible. What exactly did you see in her that made you so certain that she could cut it? Grover Gateway leaned back in his big leather chair, it squeaked slightly as he rocked slowly and finally he answered.

"You remember the piece she did a couple years ago, when you had her working the entertainment desk? *By the way, what were you thinking anyway, I meant to call you out on that one, you're lucky I nap more than I used to!"*

"Anyway, it was the story about that silent film actress who had been arrested for allegedly ignoring an enormous stack of parking citations, and then battled the SFPD physically when they came to serve her papers. KC could have had a lot of easy fun at that poor woman's expense, just like everyone else in this town did. But instead, she treated her with respect, and stuck to reporting the facts in a light that subtly championed the cause of the aging and prideful actress. If I remember right, *and I do*, the city not only backed off on their right to prosecute, they actually went after the slum lord who owned the building where she lived and gently coaxed him into providing assigned parking to all tenants so that she could park her beat up, old Studebaker off the street," Mr. Gateway concluded, snickering to himself, and slapping his open palm to his desktop to emphasize his point.

"*RESPECT*, that's what I saw Brian, a genuine respect of others. I saw in her a sense of compassion that compelled her to avoid the easy angle on an easy mark, *and instead*, put her effort into ferreting out the real story, the more meaningful story. The one that all of the others had missed in their hurry to be first, in their hurry *to scoop one another*. And in their haste they missed the opportunity to be *extraordinary*, to write a piece that people would respond to, that would effect change."

"Now ***that's*** real instinct boy, that's a heart that rules the mind," Mr. Gateway finished, staring down his managing editor, giving him a single nod of his head. Brian was at a loss for words.

As usual his boss had sucked all of the energy out of the room and used it to build a soapbox to stand on. He fought the urge to roll his eyes at Grover Gateway's lengthy retort, *for Christ sake*, he thought, the man could have just said that he liked her style, why did everything have to be... Brian shook off his mental detour and re-established eye contact with his boss.

"Yes sir, I do remember that story now that you remind me, it was a great piece. I don't know if I'd go as far as getting KC fitted for a halo yet or dust off the mantel for her Pulitzer, but I do agree that she has turned out be something pretty special," he said, studying Mr. Gateway's face for a reaction. Feeling confident that he hadn't been too flippant in his response, Brian started to continue with the purpose of his visit.

"And its those instincts that you mentioned that have brought me here this morning," he continued, shifting in his chair as he spoke.

"KC called in about an hour ago, very excited about something she's uncovered while on assignment down in Fresno."

"*Fresno,*" Mr. Gateway said raising an eyebrow. "Is she on that Katz case, the one where the *sicko* was attacked by one of his own victims?"

"Yeah, that's the one," Brian answered, not surprised at how current his boss was.

"Hmmm, go on then, what is she onto?"

"She got suspicious while pressing for details about the arrest and everyone seemed to clam up."

"She found out that this Katz fella is in lock up at the hospital in a sealed off ward. Nobody goes in or out without clearance and escort, and no press is allowed anywhere near the place. She said it's like a fortress over there."

"*Well*, he's probably in pretty bad shape given the fact that his victim ***set him on fire***," Gateway said sarcastically.

"Yeah, well that's the thing, *he should be*, but KC seems to think that may not be the case."

"And she knows this, *how?*"

"She met some nurse while having lunch in the hospital cafeteria, and the woman told her an interesting story."

"*Do tell...*" Grover Gateway said, leaning back in his chair, touching his fingertips together lightly.

"Yes sir, *well*, the woman claimed to have witnessed something that she couldn't explain." "A real *miracle* she called it."

"***Oh please Brian,*** don't tell me you're spending my money on an excursion into fantasyland!"

"No sir, I don't think so. Like you said earlier, KC has real instincts and she's convinced that there is a much bigger story here."

"When she called, she said that she had followed up on a few leads that she got from this nurse, and she hit pay dirt on the first call!"

"It's a fascinating tale this person told her sir, *nationally fascinating.*"

"And Grover, nobody else has picked up on this angle, not anyone, not anywhere. *We* would scoop every paper in the state, *hell*, the country!" Brian said, a sly grin projecting his eagerness.

He watched a smile begin to spread from corner to corner on Grover Gateway's heavily lined face. Then he leaned back in his chair, relaxing for the first time since he arrived at the meeting, his own face beginning to mirror the same smirk that was beaming at him from across the desk between them.

"You know what, I'm famished! How do you feel about Chinese noodles anyway Mr. Williams?"

Eighteen

("...Pleasant words are a honeycomb, sweet to the soul and healing to the bones."...Proverbs 16:24)

Los Angeles, California, April 1969

The telephone rang and rang in the outer office of the Monsignor, Father Pablo Villa Cruz. But the shrill bells fell on deaf ears, echoing fruitlessly down the long corridors of the Archdioceses of Los Angeles. It was already half past eight in the evening, well after vespers and too late to reach anyone at their desks. Everyone had either gone home or had moved on to the rectory to settle in for the night. Whoever it was would have to call back in the morning, as the good Father did not like those confounded answering contraptions. It was his notion that those machines just encouraged people to be annoying and disrespectful of the privacy of others.

"If I wanted to take calls at all hours I would buy a recliner and live in my office," he would say whenever his assistants pleaded with him to join the twentieth century. The infernal ringing finally subsided and the disturbing vibrations died a natural death as they faded into nothingness. Whoever it was and whatever they wanted would be dealt with tomorrow.

Fresno, California, April 1969

"*Goddamn it*," Father Willet said slamming down the receiver onto the cradle. He quickly genuflected and repented for his outburst and blasphemy.

"*Forgive me Lord*, but that old man just gets my goat," he said looking to the heavens, talking more at himself than actually praying.

He was of course, speaking of Monsignor Villa Cruz, the very man that he had apprenticed under, and who had placed him in charge of his own parish at a very early age. Father William Willet had been at Saint John's for nearly thirty years now and had become something of a neighborhood icon in the process of building his congregation.

He was known affectionately among the parishioners as *Wee Billy*, although you would never actually hear that term of endearment uttered in his presence. Standing in at a whopping, five feet two inches, he was small only in physical stature, as he had the heart of a giant. Father Willet had arrived at Saint John's Cathedral during a time when the political climate of the rural countryside was sleepy and quite, almost dull for a young priest, looking to prove to God that he had called the right man into service. But within a couple of years the winds of social change began to blow, *even way out west*, and a great turmoil was on the way.

A natural born cross bearer, and a true champion for underdogs and lost causes, Father Willet put himself at the forefront of each new movement. First, he campaigned for American support to China after the invasion by Japan. Then, conversely, he supported with equal vigor, the rights of Japanese Americans in relocation camps like Manzanar. He took a brief sabbatical when he left Saint John's Cathedral for two years, from 1950 to 1952 to serve his country in Korea as a chaplain with the United States Army. Later, he stood side by side with illegal aliens in their struggle for basic rights as human beings.

He had even started his own *freedom riding* campaign in support of Rosa Parks, the courageous Negro woman who stood her ground in Jackson Mississippi. He viewed discrimination in the country as a national plague, one that was multi-racial, multi-cultural, and multi-faith. It always amazed him whenever he included an historical lesson in his sermon, watching the puzzled looks from the pews as he spoke of the plight of the early Chinese and Irish immigrants. For many people in the congregation, *color* was the common denominator when factoring the problems of segregation and discrimination. The equation his congregation subscribed to read this way, *brown and black divided by white.* **That** was how people defined the social norm around here.

It never occurred to any of them that ignorance and hate could actually be color-blind. The truth, according to Father Willet, was that evil was an equal opportunity spoiler, and it flourished in the hearts of those who could not love beyond themselves. Why do people treat love like the *good china*, only bringing it out on special occasions? Was it so hard to understand that it was in the everyday dishes where love could be found? This would be a lesson that he would spend the rest of his career and his life teaching to his flock. In his mind, love was the simple answer to all the hard questions where God's children were concerned. Now he was finding time to organize peaceful demonstrations in protest of the war in Viet Nam, applying those principles of love that he believed in so passionately.

However, the crowning achievement of his long service to date was probably the community-sponsored school that he began for the children of migrant farm workers, those who were in the country illegally. These children by law, up until very recently, were not permitted to attend State funded public schools. Sure, the local cities usually allowed the kids to enroll if they could provide a permanent address within their district, and to be honest, most of the time the State officials would look the other way. But in Father Willet's eyes, just because there were loop holes to squeeze through didn't excuse the legislature from punishing hard working immigrant families, albeit unofficial immigrants, in a nation of immigrants. For goodness sake, our founding fathers themselves arrived at Plymouth Rock without papers!

"*Everyone* has the right to learn, to have the opportunity to read and write, to take their best shot in life, to provide for themselves, and for their family, its as basic as it gets people" he would preach to his flock at each and every mass.

"Remember, it is pleasing to God to give cheerfully, *not just when its easy*, but when it's hard, *much more so when it's hard!*"

"Did not our Lord Jesus, indiscriminately save the souls of us all?"

"So who are we to decide who is privileged and who is not," he would beseech them one and all.

Not everyone was happy to hear these words as they cut deep and required personal reflection. Nor were many pleased by his activist approach in serving the Church. The *haves* were as uncomfortable in the light as the have-nots. Neither wanted attention drawn to them, preferring to hide in the comfortable shadows of their silence, afraid to stand and be noticed for their capitulation. Shamefully, this *look the other way attitude* became the accepted norm for many years, a form of segregation that was not unlike the situation a thousand miles to the east in the nation's Deep South. Prayerfully, he might reach enough of them to inspire changes.

Father Willet sat in the floral Queen Anne chair next to his bed and stared at the silent telephone. He had taken a moment to reflect on his mission with this Church, and then shook himself out of his daydream and cleared his throat. He picked up his address book and thumbed to the section he wanted and looked up the number to his old friend Grover Gateway. He knew that he was risking an official reprimand from the Archdiocese in LA for going outside the family to settle this issue. But he also knew that the Church hierarchy moved at a snails pace when it came to real decision-making. Especially when the matter at hand just might provide a platform for a certain old ladder climber to acquire the red robe of a Cardinal, the aspiration of a lifetime!

The aging priest reached over and lifted the receiver from the telephone cradle and spun rotary dial with a shaking hand. He leaned back in the chair as the dial ratcheted laboriously back to its starting place and he waited for the ring on the other end of the line. Picking up the newspaper from his lap and adjusting his glasses, he started to read the article again, *'there could be no other explanation, what I saw was a miracle, an honest to God miracle,'* the article said, quoting Nurse Mahoney, as she described her encounter with the *'angel of the valley.'*

Father Willet slowly shook his head, feeling deeply for the child and her family, their quiet and simple lives being altered forever. They would be exploited by the curiosity of the masses, as well as the greed of those who would look to profit by her existence. But it was her safety that he was most concerned for. The Church could be quite imposing when dealing with matters of spiritual abnormalities. He feared that what could not be explained away might have to be put away, out of sight out of mind if you will. The Church, the Government, they were cut from the same cloth, entities unto themselves really, it has always been so he thought. He set the paper down, removed his glasses and listened to the ringing in his ear.

Finally from the other end, "**Hello**, who is it," inquired a gruff voice.

"GG, it's me Billy, do you have a minute for an old friend," Father Willet asked tiredly.

"You are aware of the late hour, are you not, old friend?"

"Spare me the pious platitudes Grover, I need your help so put the phone up to your good ear!"

"**Now there's** a voice that I recognize, what can I do for you Billy boy, *I mean Father*, forgive me."

"These stories your paper is running, the *'angel of the valley'* stories."

"Yes?"

"GG, how much do you personally know about this child?"

"Why do you ask, where are you going with this Billy, you're making the hair on my neck stand up?"

"I want to come see you Grover, and I want to bring Arthur with me."

"*Arthur?* Do you mean Arthur Donnelly?"

"Yes" Father Willet closed his eyes and crossed his fingers while he waited for a reply. A couple minutes of uncomfortable silence ensued and then Grover Gateway spoke.

"When can you be here?"

Fresno, California, April 1969

The loud banging on the door of her hotel room, **BAM BAM BAM**, awakened KC. She pulled the pillow out from under her, placed it snuggly over her ears groaning a muffled response.

"GO AWAY..."

"Come on KC, I've been beating on this door for ten minutes, I'm gonna get arrested if you don't open up soon," Jay Namura pleaded from the hall.

KC peeked out from under the pillow at the nightstand. What was left of the alarm clock was scattered all over the table, pieces of dull black plastic and clear bits of Plexiglas. She squinted at the small bit of devastation trying to mentally piece together the puzzle that was the night before. She felt around under the tangled mass of sheets and blankets, fumbling for a possible clue in the alleged murder of the alarm clock. Lying close to her on the bed was what appeared to be a fairly heavy police issue flashlight.

"*Yep,*" she mumbled aloud, "*this would do it.*"

"WHAT TIME IS IT," she yelled from her nest of twisted blankets and sheets.

"It's time to **GO NOW**, KC, it's already past nine o'clock babe," Jay replied through the door.

"*OH crap,*" she exclaimed softly, in a horse whisper. She rose up onto all fours and tried to kick her way out of the blanket cocoon she had made during the night. Finally she was able to roll out of bed and onto her feet.

"Just a sec Jay, I'm throwing on a robe," she hollered in the direction of the door. She was fully clothed already, but she didn't want him to see her in the same clothes she was wearing the night before. Passing the mirror on the dresser she caught a glimpse of herself.

"*Ugh, good thing I kept this short haircut,*" she said to herself as she tried to flatten a severe case of pillow head. She reached the door and fumbled with the three locks for a moment before finally letting in her favorite sidekick, photographer, and oft time partner in crime.

"Christ Kathy, you're a real treat in the morning, no wonder you're still single!"

"Shut up, and call down to the desk for some room service, we won't have time to stop for breakfast anywhere now." she said to her partner.

"The usual?" he asked.

"*Yeah, yeah,* coffee, coffee, coffee, three eggs, scrambled, bacon crisp, sausage links, home fries, an English muffin and strawberry jam. Tell them not forget the jam this time!"

"OK, I'm gonna shower and stuff, make yourself at home," she said disappearing into the bathroom, closing the door most of the way.

"Jeez, how does she live like this," Jay muttered to himself as he cleared a spot on the little sofa, sat down and dialed the front desk.

"Hello, yes, I'd like to order breakfast for room 222, Miss Katherine Littleton," he said into the handset. He heard the shower start and the toilet flush almost simultaneously. Curious he thought.

"*How did she do that?*" He snapped back to attention as a voice spoke to him from the front desk.

"Oh, OK, that'll be fine," he said raising an eyebrow. The desk clerk seemed to know what she wanted before he even had asked, apparently KC had made an impression on the staff.

"HEY JAY, don't forget to remind them not to forget the jam," KC yelled from the bathroom, her wet head and soapy face peeking around the door.

"**I WILL**, now get back in the shower before you trip and crack your skull, crazy woman," Jay yelled back at her.

"Did you get that," he asked into the telephone receiver?

"Good, fifteen minutes then, thank you," Jay said hanging up the telephone.

KC emerged from the bath with her head wrapped in a thick white towel, in that turban-like fashion that all girls master at birth, a matching terrycloth robe, and freshly painted toes. The toe thing was her signature morning ritual. She NEVER left home with naked toenails, even if she were wearing sweat socks and sneakers! She went over to the dresser and selected a nice pair of blue/black slacks and a cute cream-colored long sleeve blouse to go with the beautiful spring day that was blooming just outside the window. She sat down at the little table near the window and waited for her food to arrive, working an emery board over her already perfect nails.

"Well, today's the big day, aye Jay," she said smiling.

"Looks like it," he said while he fussed with his equipment, checking each bag to be certain that he hadn't forgotten or misplaced anything. He affixed a telephoto lens onto his 35mm Nikon and peered through the eyepiece, focusing in on his lead reporter. KC smiled a fake cheesy smile and batted her eyelashes.

"Sweet," Jay uttered as he broke the camera back down into its separate pieces and returned them to their case. "So, how long will we have with this guy anyway," he asked watching her finish her sprucing?

"Not sure, we're only in there because of old man Gateway and his money, I mean influence," she replied.

"It doesn't really matter though, nobody else will be getting this story, so snap as many pics as you can, and get close up, we want to have our own experts look over his condition to corroborate Miss Mahoney's account of the alleged miracle."

"*Check*, up close and personal, gotcha!"

"Hey KC, tell me again why we haven't shot any footage of that kid you've been talking to for the last month or so, I don't get it?"

"It's complicated Jay, I didn't understand it myself at first. To be honest I still don't really get it very well, but I can tell you this much. That little girl gives me the heebie-jeebies. You know when we're talking she watches me. And it's not so much that she's looking at me, but through me. It feels like she is looking right into me, *seeing it all*, even the stuff I hide from myself. She may act normal, she may look normal, no different than any other kid on the playground, but I'm telling you she's unique in a way that I cannot find the words to explain."

"I want to meet her," Jay said.

"I know you do, and you will, *soon*, I swear. But I need to keep a promise that I made the Donnelly woman, back around Christmas time."

"What promise, you don't make promises, at least promises that you keep," he teased.

"Hey now, be nice," she teased back.

"In return for Alma's personal account of the facts regarding the Arroyo Grande Clinic scandal and the circumstances surrounding the subsequent arrest of Dr. Katz, I agreed to only write *about* the legend but never *name* the legend," KC explained.

"I know what you're thinking, who is this woman and what has she done with your pal KC," she quipped.

"Something like that," Jay said, studying her.

"You're serious aren't you," he asked, realizing the answer before she offered it.

"I am." They stared at one another for a moment when there came a short rap at the door.

"*Room Service,*" the voice said from the other side. Jay got up and let the bell hop in to set up on the table where KC was sitting. He could smell the fried meats and suddenly was famished even though he had already consumed a short stack of buckwheat hotcakes before he had arrived here. He tipped the bellhop a five and sat down opposite KC, helping himself to a sausage link.

"HEY," she said, swatting his hand with her butter knife.

"Sorry," he mumbled, smiling broadly, his mouth full of little bits of sausage, unglamorously clinging to his front teeth. She laughed at his reply and stuck her tongue out at him, totally caked with scrambled egg, they were even now!

Nineteen

("...I finally decided my future lies beyond the yellow brick road..." Elton John)

<u>*Boston, Massachusetts, 19 February 1973*</u>

The smell of pancakes cooking nearly overpowered me! The warm fresh aroma of the batter as it bubbled and tanned on the hot griddle wafted from the kitchen and across to the counter that I was perched on. I watched as the waitress, *Patty her name tag read*, paraded them by me in a steady stream around the diner, covering all points of the compass. There were buttermilk, blueberry, banana, strawberry, buckwheat, and every now and then a golden brown waffle. *Oh Lord not the waffles,* each of them with a gooey pile of sumptuous strawberries and a healthy dollop of home made whipped cream crowning the heavenly concoction! The smells were driving me mad, I had to force myself not to leap onto the next plate that passed me and lick the pat of melting butter right off of a warm stack of hotcakes! Picking up the thick ceramic mug in front of me I took a big gulp of freshly brewed coffee and washed down the saliva before it drooled onto my shirt. Eggs and home fries to the left of me, French toast and sausage to the right, it was almost too much to bear. Just as I was about to surrender to temptation and spear a sausage link dowsed in maple syrup from the plate nearest me, Paulie's booming voice rescued me from my shameful moment of weakness.

"*Ah, Ah, Ah,* Ethan buddy, you want to start your new job doing penance for Oscar Meyer?"

Startled, I stealthily retracted my wandering fork and laid it next to it's brother and sister, the knife and spoon.

"Oh man, this is a heck of a way to start the day. First, I'm last in the pancake queue, and now I'm totally waylaid by a tip toeing grizzly bear!"

Paul laughed and sat at the counter next to me, patting me on the shoulder as he did so. He tossed his P-coat over the two seats next to him and signaled to Patty that he would like some coffee. I looked at him with a furrowed brow turning my face into a question mark. That was of course, as everyone knows, the universal facial expression for *what, why, who, when?* Paul nodded in acknowledgement that my silent message was received and shot me the equally well known *just a sec* signal, the single index finger wave, as he thanked Patty for bringing his coffee and asked for two more as well. He took a quick sip and set his mug down, giving Patty the okey-doke gesture making an *"O"* with his thumb and index finger, thanking her for the mighty fine cup of joe she had brought him. Then he turned to me and said, "Kenny, Carolyn and Shannon are right behind me. I saw them as I walked in, they were parking the car in the lot."

"Oh," I replied, nodding my head.

"Well buddy, are you ready for your trip to sunny California? As for me, I'm just a little nervous about the new job in Chi-town," Paul said.

As fate would have it, today he and I would be flying as far as Chicago together. He had just been hired as an air traffic controller at O'Hare International Airport, and was on his way to a new life of his own. The Navy had been good enough to teach him this trade during his service on board the USS Constellation, while on station in the South China Sea. We had been within a few hundred miles of each other the entire time I was in country with the Marine Corps, and never even knew it.

I grunted and nodded an affirmative reply, then pointed to my cup as Patty breezed by, indicating that I wanted a refill. She blew the hair from her eyes and gave me a look that made me wish that I had been more polite with my request. I mouthed an apology and she smiled weakly, making me feel even more like an ass. I made a mental note to make sure that I absolved myself by leaving an obscenely large tip when we left. I also made *yet another* mental entry onto *the list*, volume three now (major backsliding during finals week in 1972). The tinkling chimes on the front door rattled and rang, turning the heads of a few restless children as they looked to see what the cat dragged in.

"Over here Kenny," Paulie shouted at our friend as he entered the diner with his family and my sister in tow. Ken waived at us and I flagged down Patty to ask about a larger table. She leaned across the counter holding a half-full coffeepot and motioned for me to do likewise.

"A big group just left, I'll have the table bused ASAP, it'll just be a minute Father," she said sweetly.

"Thanks," I said awkwardly. I had forgotten about the collar and was embarrassed by my assumption that she might be interested in me. For a millisecond I thought that I was still just a regular guy, I could see that my new status was going to take some getting used to. Ken and company reached the counter and the hugs and greetings got started.

"Well if it isn't the great Father Kelly, top of the mornin to ye Father, top o' the mornin," Kenny said in his best Irish accent. It wasn't bad for a first generation Chinese American, actually he did a much better German accent, but then he had been practicing that one on Carolyn's parents for a while now. I hugged my buddy and we did the standard *guy* back slap, just to make sure nobody got the impression that we were enjoying the embrace more than we should be. Carolyn nudged in and broke up our hug-fest and kissed me on the cheek. She was holding Sophie as well, so I got a double smooch as the child landed a wet kiss on the other side of my face.

"Hello Ethan, I'm so proud of you," she said, beaming at me.

"Me too, Uncle Ethan, me too," Sophie added, reaching out with both arms for me to take hold of her. Carolyn released her into my arms and Sophie hugged my neck as hard as she could, making her little growling sound, pretending to be the Incredible Hulk. It was a little skill she acquired from her Uncle Paulie, much to her parent's dismay.

"If I had a nickel for every picture that was ruined by that awful face that Paul taught her," Carolyn lamented, swatting Paulie on the shoulder as she said so.

"OK, break it up you two, take the donnybrook outside, let me in there to hug my big brother," Shannon said playfully. Sophie fussed a little as I gently handed her over to her mother, and I stood to embrace my sister. Shannon and I held onto each other for a moment and then she leaned back just enough to up into my eyes. She held my gaze for a second, her eyes clear and sparkling, and then she pushed away from me, retreating a step or two. She stamped her foot just like she did when she was a child and gruffly folded her arms in front of her.

"*Oh*, I am so mad at you Ethan Kelly," she said startling the others and me as well.

"I'm sick and tired of always saying goodbye to you!"

"I want you to promise me that this will be the last time," she said feigning anger, and then smiling to set everyone at ease again. She laughed and poked at me, looked around the room, and made sure that everyone heard her when she added, *"I'm kidding, **I swear**, I'm only kidding."*

I watched her and she saw that I was watching. I knew she wasn't kidding, and she knew that I knew. Shannon went over to Paulie and hugged the big man like he was a six-foot version of Buster, the rag tag teddy bear we shared as kids. Paulie hugged her back, a bewildered look on his gob. He made eye contact with me, an odd if not somewhat guilty expression on his face that said, *"where did that coming from, she hates me!"* Before I could think of what to say to either of them, Patty arrived to brake up our small reunion, and lead us to our freshly cleaned table in the corner of the diner.

"This way folks," she said with a smile. And we all followed her to take our seats like the dutiful and hungry young Americans that we were!

Nearly ninety minutes later and following the feast of the decade, we sat chatting idly while we waited for Patty to bring our check. Kenny was skillfully working over his teeth with a toothpick, which by the way, was fascinating Sophie to no end. And Carolyn was keeping Paul and Shannon in stitches telling the story of the time Ken and Sophie tried to give, *Wilson,* Sophie's black Labrador puppy, his first bath. Sophie had named the puppy Wilson after the *mait're de* at Ken's folk's swanky restaurant. Wilson *the dog* had a white diamond shaped birthmark on his neck that looked very much like a bow tie, so he appeared as though he were wearing a tuxedo round the clock. Not being in on the joke, poor Wilson *the person* never quite understood why the boss's grandchild would always giggle and point his way whenever the family visited the restaurant.

Meanwhile, back at the ranch, Sophie, who had lost interest in her Dad's armature dentistry as well as the dull banter of the other chitchatting adults, had fallen asleep while we weren't looking. She was now napping comfortably curled up in my lap. I looked down at her and watched her breathing softly and smiled to myself. To be honest, I was a little envious of Kenny right at this moment; he just seemed to have it all going for him. Father Mac had warned me that these sorts of doubts and heartaches would come and go throughout the life of a priest. It was normal to envy he said, but it was quite another thing indeed to covet. This was one of the reasons that it took so long to become a priest. It was why novices were given an opportunity to serve before taking their vows. Because giving up the secular life was a difficult decision for everyone, it was meant to be difficult. The call to service was deeply personal, and could be misread in many ways. In order to truly understand whether or not the calling was for you, it was important to count the costs, to understand the sacrifices, as they were to last your entire earthly life.

I looked over at Ken. He had joined in the retelling of the dog-bathing incident and was correcting Carolyn on a couple of key details, bringing even more laughter to the table. I then looked around the diner, it was still pretty busy and I could see that our waitress had her hands full. I decided that the last thing she needed was another *me first* gesture from across the room. I looked out the window and watched the traffic move slowly. It was fairly light as opposed to nonexistent like yesterday in the wake of the blizzard. During the night the snowplows had piled drifts four feet tall on either side of the street, but there were still more pedestrians than autos. Sophie stirred in my lap and nudged her way into a more comfortable position continuing with her nap. As she pushed against my coat I felt the papers inside my breast pocket. Reaching in, I removed them, and unfolded the two-page letter. It was the letter that I had received three years earlier from Mitchell Rojas' wife, Elena. I stared at the letter a moment without reading the words.

I remembered the day it arrived in the mail, re-routed to me from Albany by my Mother. It had come more than a year after I had written to Mitchell's family about his death. To be honest it had been long enough that I had successfully put it all, *put them all,* totally out of my short-term memory. By then I had launched myself into school and the pursuit of this very moment with all of my heart and soul. It was a kind of defense mechanism, I knew that, but it was a really effective one. And up until the day that this letter had arrived, I had managed to put all of that part of my life behind me, securely locked away in a place where it could no longer hurt me. *Now,* I had already read this letter at least a dozen times, but I couldn't resist the urge to read it once more. You know, I had actually tried to reach Elena and her son once or twice, but the letters that I had sent kept coming back stamped in red, *return to sender,* or, *not at this address.* I stroked Sophie's soft black hair and read silently to myself:

Dear Father Ethan,

I wanted to write and tell you how grateful I am for the nice letter that you sent. My Mitchell, he had written to me several times about you and said that one day he would bring you to our home and introduce us all to the gringo Padre that he met in Hell. He told us about the way that you would share your letters with everyone when they were all homesick and blue. He said that you were teaching him to read more better, and fix his English so that he could get a good job and not sweat in the fields anymore. Whenever he wrote about you I could see his face and I knew that he was smiling. When I got the letter from the Marines, the one about him dying, it was cold, only two lines, and it made me feel cold, it made me shudder, like I was standing on a grave. It didn't even sound like they were talking about a person; it was more like they had lost a jeep or something. It made me very sad, it made me very angry, it made me want to hurt them back. Forgive me Father, I know that these are bad thoughts, but you are a priest and who can I confess these things to if not you?

When you're letter came a few weeks later, I was afraid to open it. I didn't open it for many days. But one afternoon, after Miguel, my son, came home from school, I watched him sitting at the table, eating a jelly sandwich. He looked so much like his papa, and I thought of his letters and I went to read them all again. Sitting on top of the stack was your unopened letter and I picked it up and held it for a moment. I decided that it wasn't from the Marines or the Government because the address was hand written, so I opened it. Your words were so sweet, so beautiful; they made my Mitchell, my husband, come to life again. You gave me back my life in the few minutes that it took to read your letter. For this I will never forget you, my prayers will always be with you Father. Please remember me and Miguel to the Lord and the Blessed Virgin when you pray each day and each night. I know that Mitchell is waiting for me in Heaven, I know that I will see him again in his glory.

Peace be with you Father Ethan, forever your sister in Christ,
Elena

I set the letter down and saw that everyone was looking at me. Feeling the wetness on my cheeks I realized that I had been crying. Shannon scooted closer to me and put her arms around me, pulling my head close to hers. She reached up and wiped the tears away from my face with a tissue and took the letter from my hands. I didn't protest, I just held onto Sophie and looked across the table and past Carolyn, out at the snowdrifts in the street. The sun had begun to peek out from behind the heavy cloud cover, and for a moment it seemed like the forecasted storm might not materialize. My face felt warm as the light shined through the big window and I came out of my little trance. By now the letter had made its way around the table and everyone was quiet. Only Paul knew what I was feeling and he respectfully held his tongue, he knew that words only brought the ghosts. I decided to take the advise that I had given to Junior Martinez those many years ago, to leave the war behind me, where it belonged, it had no place here, not now. Our cute but exhausted waitress interrupted the awkward silence thankfully.

"Sorry for the wait folks, here's your check, hope everything was OK," Patty said cheerfully, tearing the slip of paper from her book and putting it on the table in front of me. I started to reach for hit, but Paulie swatted my hand and grabbed it.

"What do you think you're doing, this is all on me," he said reaching past Shannon and pinching my cheek. Paul set the check on the table and leaned forward to free his thick wallet from it's snug housing in his pants pocket. While he was digging for it Kenny reached over and grabbed the check.

"Not so fast ya big ape, this is on the Wong family today, Happy *Belated* Valentine's Day one and all," Ken said with a big grin.

"Thanks Kenny, that's sweet," Shannon said, reaching across the table and squeezing his hand.

"You know, I've been doing pretty well since Pop turned the family business over to my management company. I'm showing him that he didn't waste his money on all that higher education. Me and my Harvard MBA are gonna open high-class Asian restaurants from coast to coast my friends," Kenny said, tugging at the lapels of his Brooks Brothers jacket with pride.

"Show off," Carolyn said teasing her husband lovingly. He reached into his jacket and retrieved a slender, posh, alligator skin billfold and pulled out his Diner's Club Card.

"*Plastic man*, it's the future dudes, mark my words, in thirty years cash will be passé!"

Ken set the card on top of the check and signaled for our waitress to come over. Paul relaxed and settled back into his seat.

"You're the man Kenny-san," he said.

"You're the man!"

"Dude, *I'm Chinese*, not Japanese! Jeez, you've known me your whole life! You've sat at my mother's table and scarfed down gallons of hot and sour soup. My Pop even gave you a Chinese name at your sixth birthday party at his restaurant when the staff sang you the birthday song in Mandarin ya goofball," Ken said exasperated!

"Honey, leave him alone, he didn't mean anything by it," Carolyn said rubbing Paul's shoulder sympathetically. Suddenly a little voice broke through all the huffing and puffing and announced to the table.

"*Uncle Ethan, I have to tinkle!*" Sophie sat up, stretched her little arms in a big girl yawn, and then began rubbing her eyes with tiny fists.

"I'll take her," Shannon said, reaching over to take the child from my lap.

"Come on baby, your Auntie Shannon will I'll take you to the *loo* dear," my sister cooed.

"*Hey*, wait for me," Carolyn said, "I've had four cups of coffee and it's a long drive back to Albany!"

"We're really going to have to make tracks after we drop Ethan and Paul at Logan if we're going to stay ahead of this storm!"

She elbowed Kenny in the stomach, "Scoot over Ken, I really need to pee," she pleaded, pushing at her husband with her two hands and her head.

We all rolled left out of the cramped corner booth so that she could catch up with Shannon and Sophie. I got up right after Shannon and Ken followed me as we started the exit daisy chain. Paul was last to get out and the three of us males gathered up all of the coats while we waited for the women to return. Patty came back with Ken's receipt and waited to retrieve his signature. While he signed the slip I pulled out a twenty-dollar bill from my pocket and set it under an empty juice glass. I didn't want to forget to take care of Patty and make up for my shameful lack of compassion earlier. Shannon waived at us from near the front door and we made our way over to her and then out of the diner. We spilled out onto the sidewalk just as the clouds rolled back in, covering up the sun that had peeked out only moments before. The wind began to blow a little harder and I turned my collar up against the sudden chill. Ken pointed over to the parking lot while I shouldered my duffel bag and followed the crowd to the station wagon.

"You sure you've got room for this bunch, I mean with the storm coming and all," I asked?

"We could just take a cab you know," I said, pointing at Paul and myself.

"Yeah, we could just take a cab," Paul chimed in.

"Don't be silly you two," Carolyn said.

"Yeah, don't be silly Uncle Ethan, *noodle head*," Sophie added.

"Noodle head, that's a new one," I said chuckling.

"Well at least we know she didn't learn it from Shannon, there are more than four letters," Paul teased.

"SHUT IT," Shannon quipped at Paul, socking him hard in the arm.

"Owww! Why are you Irish so gosh-darned hot headed!"

"If it's a donnybrook ya want, I'm just the girl that can give it to ya," Shannon said harshly but playfully, as she walked quickly to catch up with the Wong family.

She turned back after a few strides and stuck her tongue out at Paul before she climbed into the car. And if I'm not mistaken, I believe I saw a wicked little smile on her face as she did so. I made another mental note; Shannon and I were going have a talk soon, that was for sure. I looked over at Paul to study his reaction. He had none, which wasn't unusual, so he was safe for the moment. Ken opened the tailgate of the station wagon and I tossed in my duffel bag, as did Paulie. We had been raised together as boy scouts and had been trained the by the same branch of the service. So we had similar notions about traveling, *light and lean, and the less you carry the less you ferry,* that was our creed. I squeezed in next to Shannon who sat between Paul and me. Ken and Carolyn were up front and Sophie was strapped into a car seat between them.

"OK, everybody comfy," Ken asked?

"Guess we're off to Logan to watch Paul and Ethan take to the friendly skies."

I suddenly detected a familiar odor and immediately looked over at Paul. Shannon was already pinching her nose and looking his way as well.

"Oh man, Paulie," Kenny said from the driver's seat, looking at Paul in the rear view mirror.

"You couldn't cut us a break and let that bad boy go outside!"

"Hey, *it wasn't me, I swear*," Paul exclaimed, raising both hands in the air as if he were surrendering.

A tiny, evil giggle came from the front of the car and I looked that way in time to see Carolyn pinching her nose and pointing at the small bundle of joy sitting next to her. Four doors opened simultaneously and all of the people over three feet tall exited the vehicle holding their breath and gasping for fresh air as soon as their feet touched the snow covered ground.

"Darn it Ken, I told you not to feed her any of your chili and cheese omelet, you know what that stuff does to her," Carolyn whined at her husband. Kenny blushed and looked to the rest of us for support.

"It was just a bite, I swear, *one bite*," he said, pleading his case.

We could hear Sophie giggling loudly from inside the car while we stood around with the doors open and waited for the chill breeze to whip through the vehicle and work its magic. One by one we began to laugh hysterically until finally we had become quite the spectacle.

People began to point at us from inside diner and from the passing cars. Its funny how God works I thought. A little bit ago my heart was aching because I was sad and sorrowful. Now my stomach was aching because I was happy and feeling pretty good about things, standing in the snow, freezing my testicles off alongside my family and friends.

So it's true, God never gives us more than we can handle. I guess that the answers always are in the love.

Twenty

Fresno, California, April 1969

Jay and KC had not said more than two words to one another during the twenty-minute ride from the hotel to the hospital. They had spent that time like the professionals they were, mentally preparing for their assignment, putting on their game faces so to speak. They had already agreed upon the photo layout that they would need for the story. And KC had decided that her questions would focus mainly on the man and not the story around him. She already had all the details she would need to set the stage with facts about the good doctor and his mischief. That angle had been covered after spending countless hours interviewing Dorothy Mahoney, Alma Donnelly, her husband Arthur, as well as various other arresting officers, paramedics, and hospital staff. *No*, the real story, *the one angle* that none of the other publications had stumbled on yet, was the migrant child, the local legend. KC was well prepared to break this story, the only thing she needed to watch for were the wild cards, there were always wild cards to play in this business.

LaTina Marie Lopez *was* the wild card in this game, and she was nestled safely in the hand that KC and her newspaper were holding. KC smiled to herself as she silently reflected on the fruits of all of her hard work and long hours. She felt very comfortable in the position she found herself in. She was in the *catbird's seat* as James Thurber might have put it. She had gathered nearly all of the pieces of the puzzle, and she was certain that this interview with Dr. Katz would produce the last of the border pieces. After today she would be ready to complete the puzzle from the inside out. But first KC needed to see for herself the evidence of this *so-called* miracle. She wanted to see first hand what this entire county had managed to keep secret for so long. She wanted to hear from the monster himself, the account of his spiritual redemption and physical resurrection. Once that was done, once her own curiosity had been satisfied, she would be able to finish this job, and break the story without suffering the pain of moral or social conscience.

After all, this wasn't just another stigmata hoax, or Virgin Mary apparition. This was the real thing, a warm body with a sweet face that people could see and a soft voice that they could hear. It would be the closest thing to an interview with an Apostle or even Christ himself. She started to feel the old adrenaline run, like she always did before one of her stories ran. But this was going to be the *mother of all stories*, it was going to be the biggest byline that she had ever had, a career launcher, a life changer! And yet she was apprehensive for reasons she didn't quite understand. *No*, that wasn't exactly true she thought, *it was the kid*, the little girl had bewitched her somehow. During the time she was recording her talks with the Lopez girl, ten full cassettes of dialog, she and Tina had somehow managed to bond. Without her realizing it, KC had broken her cardinal rule, *never get tight with a mark*, and she was angry with herself for ignoring that basic journalistic axiom. It was that one little rule made the job easy, because you didn't need a conscience with a mark, you could lie straight faced and pat yourself on the back for a job well done! But with a friend, with someone you stupidly allowed yourself to care about, the ethical line between right and wrong became less fuzzy. The lies actually left a bad taste in your mouth, words seasoned with a raging case of social conscience. KC shook that thought out of her head and shuddered visibly.

"You OK Kathy," Jay asked?

"Yeah, I'm fine, looks like we're here," she answered, clearing her throat and pointing to the building.

KC pulled into the Emergency Room lot as she had been instructed to, while Jay finished taking inventory of his equipment. He zipped the camera bag closed just as she turned off the engine, and they exited the Ford Pinto together, racing toward the automatic doors like they just might have an actual emergency to tend to. They weren't wearing their press ID's as per the guidelines of their special privilege, and went directly through the double doors bypassing the insurance/billing desks. Once inside they walked up to the nurse's station, a long chest high counter littered with files and clipboards, and asked for a Detective Sergeant Daniel Jankowski. The young woman behind the counter looked puzzled at their request and was about to say something when a slightly balding gentleman in a blue blazer and gray slacks walked up behind the pair.

"That's OK doll, they're looking for me," the middle aged man in the off the rack suit said in a thick Bronx accent, slightly out of place for this hick central California city. He took hold of KC by her elbow and led her over to a short, uncomfortable couch against the wall. She shot Jay a queer look letting herself be led away by the strange man.

"Detective Jankowski I presume," KC uttered?

"*The one and only*! You two must be the reporters from San Francisco that pulled all the strings to get in to see the *magic Christian*," he said, replying to KC's question.

"*Ahhh*, yeah, that would be us, I guess. And what exactly do you mean by the *Magic Christian* anyway," KC said, squinting at the detective and tilting her head slightly.

"Don't worry, you'll see for yourself soon enough," the detective snickered.

Jay pulled out his Nikon and started to attach the short lens for the portrait shots he and KC had discussed earlier at the hotel. Detective Jankowski stepped over to him picked up the equipment bag and motioned for Jay to return the camera to the bag.

"*Nuh Uh my friend*, no pictures, that's one of the rules on this special visit," he said gruffly. Both KC and Jay started to protest but Jankowski cut them off.

"**NO EXCEPTIONS**, the camera stays on this floor. I'm sorry if that was not made clear to you beforehand, but it's not negotiable, I don't care how much money your boss has to throw around!" Jay gently returned the camera and lens to the bag and the detective zipped it closed and walked toward the nurse's station.

"Keep an eye on this will ya hon, we'll be back for it in just a little bit," he said, winking at the young woman behind the counter and dropping the heavy bag on the counter.

"HEY, watch it, that equipment is delicate AND expensive," Jay shouted. He turned back to face the two stunned reporters.

"SUE ME," Jankowski said sarcastically.

"*So,* are we ready now lady and ummm, *gent?*"

Jay said nothing, he just stared at the man in disbelief, while KC raised both her hands and shook her head in a mock surrender.

"*OK*, let's just get on with this. I'm assuming that there won't be any more surprise conditions to deal with," KC stated rhetorically.

Detective Jankowski led the way to the service elevator and held the door for his two charges. They entered the car single file, the detective from hell bringing up the rear as he pushed the button for the sixth floor. KC looked up at the roof of the elevator and noticed her own reflection staring back down at her in the glass. She reached up with her left hand and mussed her hair, giving her short haircut a quick adjustment. When she lowered her head and caught Jankowski giving her the stink eye. She returned the gesture by shooting him her best Harpo Marx impression, complete with the crossed eyes, the cheeks full of air, her tongue extended, as she mimed a real authentic *Bronx cheer!*

"Oh, *that's mature*, you kiss your mother with that face," Detective Jankowski said sarcastically.

KC squinted and moved her lips rapidly, silently mimicking him as the elevator stopped and the doors opened. The wall in front of them announced that they had arrived at the sixth floor in bold black letters. The trio exited the car together, the surly detective squeezing between Jay and KC in order to lead them down the hall to their destination. Jay took in every detail with his photographer's eye, and he elbowed KC, as they were about to turn the corner. Up ahead there was two of Fresno's finest standing on either side of the closed door to room 665. KC stared at the room number as they walked up.

"*Hmmmm*, one door down and I'd have been worried," she whispered so only Jay could hear.

"Know what you mean jellybean, I was thinking the same thing," Jay whispered back, indicating that he had also picked up on the *anti-Christ* reference.

"OK, ground rules," Jankowski started.

"Oh come on, I asked you downstairs if there were going to be any more surprises," KC whined.

"Take it easy doll, nothing out of the ordinary. And these are his attorney's rules, not ours."

"Go on," KC said warily.

"Alright, number one, no pictures, you already know that one. Number two, no tape recording, you were told about that before you arrived, *so hand it over shrimpy*," the detective said, holding out his right hand like a grade school teacher waiting for some kid to spit out her gum. KC started to feign outrage, and then thought better, digging into her purse and removing a small cassette recorder.

"*Ahem*, number three, his attorney will be present during the interview and will advise her client whether or not to answer questions based on the relative impact to his pending trial. Last but not least, number four, DOT NOT TOUCH the prisoner. That's important Miss Littleton; the guy is positively *psycho* about being touched by anyone. He believes that he's already been touched by the hand of God or something like that." Jankowski finished, staring at KC until she made eye contact.

"*I get it, I get it*," she said gruffly, her frustration doing a poor job of camouflaging her nervousness.

"What about you Mac, do you *get it* too," Jankowski directed at Jay Namura?

"Yeah, I'm with ya," Jay replied matter of fact like.

"OK then, you're on," Detective Jankowski said as he signaled for the officer nearest him to open the door. KC and Jay gave each other a reassuring glance and then followed the detective into the room.

The teakettle whistled furiously while Maria waddled as fast as she could down the hall to the kitchen. She was within spitting distance of her delivery date, and this baby couldn't come soon enough for her. Tina and Gilbert had been such easy pregnancies, but this little one had been different from the get go. To begin with, the fact that she had conceived at all had come as a complete shock to her. God forgive her, she had been secretly taking precautions to prevent this very thing from happening. She knew that Victor wouldn't understand, in fact he would probably have been angry given his strong Catholic beliefs. But ever since they discovered that Tina was more than just *their* child, that she had become an instrument of God's will, Maria had been terrified of bringing another baby into the world. Gilbert was already on the way by the time these events began to regularly take place in their lives. Who knew what might be in store for him she wondered? But this new child growing inside her, this one that could have, maybe should have been prevented, she just didn't know what to think. There was nothing to think about anyway, it was coming and she would deal with God's will. But even so, she worried that she would not be strong enough to protect Tina from the wolves *and* care for a growing family as well. She was after all just one woman, and life's demands on her time, her energy, her sanity, were reaching a physical, mental, and spiritual apex.

"Aye Dios mio," Maria said to herself as she reached the screaming teakettle and removed it from the burner. The shrill whistle trailed off into oblivion while she set the steaming water container down on a potholder on the kitchen table. She pulled the chair far enough away from the table to provide enough clearance for her and the baby, and then slowly lowered herself onto the soft cushion. Puffing out her cheeks she let out an audible sigh then drew her sleeve across her brow. Maria made herself a cup of instant coffee and stirred in a little cream from the cow dispenser that Victor had bought for her at the county fair last summer. She watched the dark liquid swirl and then change into the same creamy tan color of a Brach's caramel square. Maria sipped her coffee, thankful for the peace and quiet with the kids in school. She held the cup with both hands in front of her face and blew lightly on the coffee watching the ripples her breath made. She was recalling the argument she and Victor had the night before. Victor had come to bed and snuggled up next to her, rubbing her belly, making a fuss about the coming birth.

"It's going to be somebody's birthday pretty soon," he cooed at her swollen stomach. He really was being really sweet, and she wanted to be as happy as he was, but she wasn't. She was scared, and her hormones were raging, running wild throughout her body. She was hot, she was cold, she was dizzy, and she was inconsolable. She knew it wasn't fair, but she couldn't help it, he would just have to forgive her, and it shamed her knowing that he would do exactly that.

"So which names did you decided on honey," was all he had said.

"IS THAT ALL YOU CAN SAY TO ME PANSON," she yelled at him harshly. Maria hated herself before the echo had even faded against the walls of their small bedroom.

"I DON'T KNOW, OK, I DON'T KNOW," she had wailed and breaking into tears.

Maria closed he eyes and shuddered. She took another sip from her cup and promised herself that she would make it up to him when he came home. Maybe she would call Mrs. Donnelly and ask her to stop by and help her make some *chili verde* and fresh home made tortillas, that was Victor's favorite meal, it would be a good start at making up she thought. She was pretty sure that Alma would be happy to help, besides she thought, the woman wanted to learn how to make tortillas anyway, and now was as good a time as any! Maria smiled to herself at the prospect of making things right and looked at the stack of mail by the fruit bowl. She picked up the stack of bills and sorted through them. She came across an envelope addressed by hand and studied

215

it. The letter was for Tina and it had no return address. She turned it around a couple of times and then set it down on the table in front of her.

She tapped her finger on the envelope and toyed with the thought of opening it first to screen the contents. But she decided that the handwriting was a childish scrawl and that it was probably from one of Tina's little friends. She decided that would leave it for her daughter to open herself, remembering how much fun it was to get mail when she was a child. Still, it was tempting, and she picked up the envelope once more.

"No, *she's getting older*, I can wait," she sighed to herself, and set the letter down.

Detective Jankowski closed the door behind them and KC and Jay walked up to the chairs near the window. A handsome woman with shoulder length blonde hair, dressed in a smart burgundy business suit got up and extended her hand to greet them. She looked to be in her late thirties or early forties KC thought.

"Hello, I'm Helen Walden," she said in a controlled and professional voice.

"I'm part of Dr. Katz' defense team and will advising him during your interview."

"Yes, well, this is Jay Namura and I'm KC Littleton," KC said firmly shaking the woman's hand. Ms. Walden reached over to Jay and shook his hand as well, and motioned for the two of them to take a seat.

"Dr. Katz will be arriving any minute, he's being brought down from another floor," she explained.

"*Oh*, we thought that he was in this room. Why all the secret squirrel activity anyway," KC asked?

"I'm afraid that due to the nature of the case and the sensitivity of certain aspects of the case, it's been necessary to keep Dr. Katz out of the public eye," Ms. Walden answered.

"What aspects," KC pressed.

"Really Miss Littleton, I'm not at liberty to discuss that with you right now. But as I understand it, you're already privy to many details that the mainstream media has been kept in the dark about. I'm certain that once you meet Dr. Katz that you'll be able to put two and two together."

"May I ask the reason for the restriction on photographs," Jay asked.

"Again, Mr. Namura, I believe that you'll have your answer as soon as Dr. Katz arrives." Ms. Walden waived her arm toward a table near the door like she was one of the girls pointing to door number 1, 2, or 3 on *Let's Make A Deal.*

"May I offer you any refreshments," she asked indicating the pot of coffee and tray of juices?

"No thanks, we're good," KC said, answering for both of them.

"As you wish"

With that the door suddenly opened and in walked a uniformed officer followed by Dr. Murray Katz, his hands shackled at the waist in front of him, his ankles bearing similar restraints. Ms. Walden rose and walked over to the doctor and whispered something in his ear. Dr. Katz nodded and the smiled at the pair of reporters, who were now standing, more out of curiosity that courtesy.

Helen Walden made the introductions and everyone sat around the small makeshift conference table in the center of the room. Dr. Katz asked for some apple juice and turned to look directly at KC. It made her uncomfortable to be so near someone who had done such terrible things, and yet she felt no fear or surprisingly any anger. Even with the facts that she possessed about his crimes, when she looked at him all she could feel was pity. Could this really be the same man that Victor Lopez had spoken of? Who, in Victor's words, looked like a 50/50 bar on a hot sidewalk? She studied him closely and watched as he sipped at his juice, which an officer had poured into a Styrofoam cup, making sure that the prisoner had no contact with any metal object.

"I know what you're thinking," Dr. Katz said, breaking the silence and startling KC slightly.

"Excuse me?"

"I know what you're thinking," he repeated.

KC remained silent, not ready to speak, waiting to see what it was he was about to offer.

"I can feel her presence you know. I know that you have been with her."

"Who have I been with doctor?"

"Please Miss, don't insult my intelligence, you've been with my angel, with she who made me." *With she who made him*, what was this lunatic talking about KC wondered.

"I'm afraid you've lost me doctor, *she who made you*, what exactly did this person make you to be," KC asked agitated?

"Come now child, you know what I am saying, *she who made me whole again*, she who provided this chance to make things right. You've sensed the power although you've not yet witnessed it." There was a long, pregnant pause as the monster and KC stared through one another.

"Until now that is," Dr. Katz continued.

"***Look at me Katherine***, is this the face you expected to see!"

Helen Walden leaned toward Dr. Katz. She placed her hand lightly on his arm and whispered in his ear again. The doctor relaxed and returned to the calm composure that he had entered the room with. He sipped at his juice again and then set the cup back on the table. KC blinked repeatedly, she was not comfortable with the familiar way that the doctor had addressed her. Why did he call her by name she wondered was he just well coached?

"Forgive me, I haven't had much contact with anyone since the incident," Dr. Katz said slowly.

"My attorney has informed me that you are well informed about that awful day."

"You've done well to uncover that which has been well guarded, formidable my dear, formidable!"

"I ask you again Miss Littleton, is this the face that you expected to see?"

KC swallowed hard and looked over at Jay. He was also transfixed on the utterly unblemished person of the man they knew to have suffered horrible burns over ninety percent of his body. His flesh should have melted into a form unrecognizable as human. Yet there he was, and Jay's mind was screaming conspiracy. This could not be true, the only logical explanation was that this must be someone pretending to be Murray Katz, but why, to what end, to serve what purpose?

"No doctor, it's not what I had expected at all. Or rather, what I had hoped to see," KC said in a low voice.

"Seeing you suffering and dying from the wounds you received from the poor girl you drove insane with your evil, would have actually been comforting. That would have satisfied my belief in, no, my hope for justice and karma. But, it also would have been wrong, given the things I now know to be true."

Dr. Katz said nothing, showed no emotion as he looked back at KC, absorbing every syllable of her verbal attack. KC wanted to hurl more damning condemnation at him, but just as Maria Lopez had shared when interviewed about that day, KC was unable to feel hate in spite of her mind's urging. The fact was, the doctor had been right all along, Tina was here, in spirit, and KC could feel it. This man who deserved to be hated, who had done so much harm to so many innocent people, *had been forgiven*, and with forgiveness came mercy. She looked at him with her two eyes. She studied him with her mind, processing and re-processing all that she had learned of the man up to this very moment. Then, with her heart she discovered his repentance, it permeated from every pore of his body. She watched as the first tear appeared in the corner of his eye, when he must have recognized that her heart had won over her mind.

"Penny for your thoughts," the doctor said softly.

KC couldn't speak, she began to stammer a reply, but stopped abruptly, she needed to compose herself.

"Get a grip KC," she whispered harshly to herself. She looked away from Dr. Katz and over to Ms. Walden, the woman wasn't even paying attention, she was looking out the window. KC turned quickly to Jay and touched his arm.

"We need to go now," she said firmly.

"We just got here KC, are you letting this nut get to you?"

Clearly Jay was not experiencing the same revelation that she was, but she didn't have the wherewithal to explain it to him this minute.

"It's not like that Jay, I'll fill you in on the way back to the hotel, we just need to go now!"

"Ms. Walden, thank you for helping to arrange this, my editor will be contacting your office soon I'm sure."

"*Ah, OK.* Are you quite sure you're finished here," Helen Walden asked dumbfounded? It was obvious that this woman was no more in tune with the moment than Jay was, KC thought to herself.

"Yes, I have what I came for, thanks again," KC said standing, tugging at Jay's sleeve in the process.

She looked back at Dr. Katz reluctantly and nodded at him, drawing in her lips and biting down on them.

"Thank you for seeing us doctor," she said weakly.

Murray Katz stood and extended his shackled hand as far as he could and offered it to KC.

"I'm sorry," he said, his hazel eyes clear but moist. KC took his hand and squeezed his fingers, *"I know,"* she said, smiling as she turned to leave.

Elena Rojas tucked Miguel in, then kissed the sleeping child lightly on the forehead and turned out the light. She tiptoed down the hall to the tiny living room and sat down on the second hand sofa that she had bought only a month ago with some of the money that Mitchell's life insurance policy had provided. Every day since his death had been a repeat of the day before where her heartache was concerned. She looked up at the wall that the television was set against. There were four framed pictures of her family surrounding a wooden crucifix. The one on top was her favorite. It was of she and Mitchell at their wedding, taken just before he playfully squished cake all over her face. She loved the big smile on his face and the light in his eyes. The picture to the left of the cross was of Miguel when he was only a year old. It was taken six months after that child witch had saved him from death in the melon fields.

The picture to the right of the cross was of the three of them. It had been taken at the strawberry festival in Bakersfield, a year before Mitchell had received his draft notice. And the picture underneath the cross was of Mitchell. It was the same picture that every mother, wife and girlfriend of a US soldier had in their home. He looked so fine in his Marine Corps dress-blues posing against the backdrop of the American flag, unfurled proudly behind him in the photo. She looked and looked at the picture for over an hour. The light from the television flickered erratically around the otherwise darkened room. The images from the TV were reflected in Elena's brown eyes, even though she was not actually watching the screen.

Presently, she got up from her spot on the sofa and walked over to the television. She reached into her apron, removed an envelope and set it down on top of the old black and white TV. She smiled as she ran her finger over the name on the envelope, Father Ethan Kelly. Then she reached up and removed the picture of Mitchell from the wall and held it close to her. Turning slowly she walked down the hall to the bathroom. She stopped and closed Miguel's door before she went in and set the picture on the sink. Elena looked at herself in the vanity mirror and pulled her long black hair back into a ponytail, securing it with a blue beaded tie that was sitting by the faucet. She turned and adjusted the bathtub faucets to just the right setting and let the water run while she undressed. Carefully, she folded her clothes and placed them neatly on the turned down seat of the toilet. Then she twisted the faucet knobs counter clock wise to shut off the flowing water. She gingerly dipped her toe into the tub and tested the water temperature it was perfect.

She stepped into the tub and lowered herself gently, letting the hot water rush over her naked body, feeling it surround her, embrace her with its wonderful sensations. She reached down with her two hands and cupped her breasts, it had been so long since anyone but she had done so. Elena leaned her head back against the tub enclosure and closed her eyes. She was remembering the last time she and Mitchell had made love. It had been so long ago, but the memory was strong and the vision in her mind was vivid. She caressed herself softly and slowly, biting down gently on her lower lip. Elena began to breathe deeply, rocking her head slowly from side to side, whispering Mitchell's name again and again. Then she suddenly stopped, opened her eyes and sat up straight. She reached up with both hands and removed the cross from around her neck, pulling it gently over her head, careful not let it get snagged in her long hair. Slowly she let the jewelry curl into a ball inside her open palm and then placing her hand outside the tub she let the cross and chain fall to the tiled floor. Elena Rojas leaned forward a little further and retrieved the picture of her fallen husband. She brought the picture to her lips she kissed it softly, and then in a swift motion smashed the frame on the edge of porcelain tub, the glass shattering into dozens of large and small bits. Selecting a piece that suited her intentions, she leaned back gently against the bathtub. She lowered her hands down into the hot water, and under the surface she used the sharp piece of glass to slice deeply into her flesh. She made no sound. The expression on her face could only be described as one of peace and determination. She let the glass fall silently to the bottom of the tub, the water already turning a sickening shade of red as her open veins poured out her life's blood. Slowly she slipped away into unconsciousness, to the *nowhere place* that the weak too often escaped to, whenever they chose this path. On the wet floor, under the shards of broken glass, the image of Mitchell Rojas stared up at the ceiling. The only light left in the small room being the dim luminance of a forty-watt bulb above. The light of his life, his beautiful Elena, no longer shone.

Twenty-one

("...It is better to be of humble spirit with the lowly, than to divide the spoil with the Proud..." Proverbs 16:19)

San Francisco, California, November 1969

He watched the gulls swooping and gliding only a few yards in front of him. They soared on the stiff ocean breeze and then turned sharply back into the wind. The swift maneuver allowed the graceful birds to nearly hover as they scanned the retreating surf below for their supper. Looking for signs of scurrying sand crabs, small minnows or unlucky mackerel deposited close to shore by the breaking waves, they took turns diving into the shallow backwash. Father Willet tossed the last few chips that remained on his paper plate to the sand below, chuckling to himself softly as the gulls raced one another to reach his bit of charity, screeching, honking, and carrying on the way that they do.

"They're you go you noisy little beggars, eat hearty now," he called down at the sand, as the wind blew the hood of his jacket back off of his head. What was left of his hair went flying every which way in a cascade of salt and pepper. He reached up behind his neck and pulled the hood back over his head, making sure to cinch the cords tight and push the *stay* beads up to hold the hood in place.

"Getting damn cold out here," he said out loud to himself as he checked his wristwatch for the time.

"I'll second that," replied Arthur Donnelly, as he walked up behind the shivering priest, visibly startling him.

"*Oh for goodness sake Arthur,* you nearly frightened me to death," Father Willet said, his right hand spread wide against his chest. "How does someone your size manage to sneak up on anyone anyway?" Father Willet held out his hand for his friend to shake, which he did vigorously, and the two men exchanged a warm greeting.

"You're just getting old Billy, *hell so am I,*" Arthur said laughing as he did so.

"I suppose you're right of course. *Hey,* at least nobody has to wipe our chins at supper," Father Willet teased affectionately.

"Well, that *is* a blessing Billy boy! I'm pretty sure my Alma wouldn't put up with that for long anyway," Arthur added chuckling.

"Give her a little more credit Artie, the poor woman's a saint and you know it! And for the record, she's been cleaning up after you for years, you old geezer," Father Billy said cheerfully.

He covered his mouth with his hand, attempting to hide the evil little grin that his eyes had already betrayed. The two men walked together past the restaurant and toward the end of the pier. When they reached the end, they both leaned forward on the rail and stared out across the bay at Alcatraz. They were silent for several minutes, just watching the water and enduring the strong onshore breeze. It was only just two in the afternoon, but sunshine and heat were scarce in San Francisco in late November, especially with the fog, the constant cloud cover, and what not.

"At least it not raining," they said together.

Arthur punched his friend lightly in the arm, *"Owe me a coke,"* he said, just like they did when they were kids. Billy Willet and Artie Donnelly had grown up in the same Brooklyn neighborhood some fifty years earlier.

They had survived the Great Depression together living just one floor from one another in the same brownstone apartment building, not far from Ebbet's Field. In a time when there wasn't much of anything to go around except hard times, the boys had managed to keep out of any real trouble. A feat accomplished mostly by the grace of God, but also due to a truly fanatical love for the game of baseball. As children Artie and Billy would skip school when the Dodgers were at home and stand outside the ballpark listening to the game from the sidewalk below. They would make up stats while they listened to the public address system announce each batter, and the crowd cheer and jeer, inning after inning. After awhile they would pester passing field ushers through the wooden fence for the score and actual details of the game. Sometimes they would have to duck into an alley, avoiding a beat cop or truant officer who might stroll by on his rounds. Only to reappear on the sidewalk after they disappeared around the corner, just in time to hear the crowd roar again. They would eat their sack lunches of bread and cheese and then stand outside old man Valenti's fruit stand looking as pitiful as they could until he tossed them an apple or a pear to share. It may not have been a day at the *Ritz* as outings went, but beggars couldn't be choosers. It didn't matter though, they were happy just to be near all the action. At home they had had to endure the prejudices of their fathers, who had brought the timeless feud between the English and the Irish with them to the new country.

Artie Donnelly's family had immigrated to the USA from Ireland in nineteen hundred and fifteen, right in the middle of World War One. They had left behind a life of abject poverty, trouble, and sorrow in the little village of Shannonbridge, County Offaly, and set all of their hopes and dreams on a new start in America. Billy Willet's family had arrived only a few weeks earlier from Great Britain, Manchester to be exact. And in the twenty some years that their families lived as neighbors in the same building, their fathers had not said ten civil words to one another. Pigheaded as that may have been, the feud did not keep the two boys from becoming fast friends. The two lads together were actually quite a sight. Artie being a whole head and set of shoulders taller than *wee Billy*, a fact that William Willet would have fought over if he heard it said out loud. Actually in contrast to the obvious physical realities, *of the two*, it was the fiery, ill-tempered William Willet that was known as the fearsome part of this odd pairing. Whenever there was a threat of trouble, it was young Billy who would take charge, telling Arthur to stand tall and look as menacing as possible, while he himself would act as manic as possible. This defensive tactic would save them from countless beatings over the years. They were the oddest of pairings and became the most steadfast of friends, the original *eek and meek*.

In nineteen hundred and thirty-five the boy's lives went in completely opposite directions. In a bizarre twist of fate, the mild mannered and gentle Arthur Donnelly applied to and was accepted to West Point. While the cantankerous and brash William Willet entered St. John's Seminary in Boston Massachusetts. Years later, after having served unknowingly within fifty miles of one another during the Korean War, the two friends were reunited. It was when Arthur and his new bride Alma attended Mass at St. John's Cathedral in Fresno California for the very first time since moving east from Rochester New York. As fate would have it, this also happened to be the first solo Mass performed by the Church's newest recruit, one Father William Willet. And keeping true to his passionate nature, the new parish priest inadvertently introduced the flock to his less than perfect style of communication (a style that they would grow to love in the years to come) when he spontaneously bellowed in front of God and the congregation, *"Well I'll be a monkey's uncle, look what that damn cat dragged into my Church"* after spotting his childhood friend sitting in the second row. Following a collective gasp from several parishioners, and a smattering of finger pointing and turning heads, Arthur Donnelly replied with equal gusto.

"For pity sake Billy, they're going to have to change the color of your collar to yellow and give these poor people fair warning!"

Their little exchange inspired a fifteen-minute giggle fest that would forever endear the two of them within the community that in the end, they would each devote their lives to…

"You need to start punching me in the other arm you big ape, this one's plum wore out," exclaimed Father Willet.

"And for your information, you can't have any coke, *diabetes*, remember?"

"Oh yeah, *sorry*…Say, when is this Grover fella supposed to be here anyway," Arthur asked impatiently, folding his big arms in front of him, as he started to feel the chill.

"He should be along any minute, he likes to make an entrance, keep your shirt on *King Kong.*"

"Oh hell Billy, he's probably sitting at the bar in the restaurant watching us freeze our tails off while he sips a Brandy Alexander!"

"Maybe…we'll give a few more minutes before we go inside and wait. Actually, I could go for a toddy right about now myself, my knees are starting to knock!"

"You been following that series of articles that his newspaper has been running for the last couple of months," Arthur asked?

"You know I have Arthur, *don't be coy*, it's why we're here, *right*," Father Willet snapped.

"Sorry, no offense Artie, I'm just old and cold," said Father Willet, apologizing for his snit.

"None taken, I've known you too long to be cut by that sharp tongue of yours," Arthur replied, waving his hand as if to erase the remark from an imaginary list.

"To be honest, I am surprised that Grover has been able to keep this tight a lid on everything and still get the Katz story out," he continued.

"Well, so far so good, but people are starting to get nervous, I don't like it," Arthur said, picking at his fingernails with his pocketknife.

"You know, I was actually hoping that they could have broken the Katz story without having to mention her at all," Father Willet said, more to himself than to his friend.

"*Come on Billy*, you knew that wouldn't be possible under those circumstances. Why, that man was lit up like a tikki torch and he still has a better complexion than you or I do. Too many people saw that happen, that's a fact that is going to be hard to hide for very long. No, the most we can hope for is that your friend Grover will continue to bury the details in the back pages. She doesn't need to be front page news anyway," Arthur said as he turned his back to the wind and leaned against the pier railing.

"We'll see," Father Willet said.

"But, beyond the legions of curious cats we may have another problem, a potentially dangerous problem," Father Billy added, turning to face his old friend.

"What other problem," Arthur asked?

"That son of a bitch, Villa Cruz," hissed Father Willet.

"*Billy*, your vows, remember? You might want to tone it down a little bit, I hear tell that the Almighty is omni-present," Arthur teased. Father Willet ignored his friend's comic retort.

"That old bastard is going to try and use the Lopez girl to further his own career, I just know it! He desperately wants a red Cardinal's robe. And he could very well make quite a name for himself with this child, a name that could echo within the halls of the Vatican itself one day!"

"*What are you raving about,*" Arthur asked, exasperated?

"Don't you see, he wants to preside center stage in front of the world, and unveil the first legitimate miracle worker of the modern era? Not since Christ himself or the twelve Apostles have people witnessed occurrences of this magnitude, *the raising of the dead for Heaven's sake!* And now, given the speed of modern communications, her image and her story could be broadcast around the globe, possibly compelling millions to seek the faith in the process. You have no idea what catnip that is to a power miser such as Monsignor Villa Cruz," Father Billy lamented.

"*My God*, with the right kind of spin, he might actually parlay this into a campaign to become the next Pontiff," Father Willet said in a hushed voice, as if he were afraid of being overheard.

Arthur stared at his friend as he slowly began to comprehend the possible consequences of such a future. Not so much for the Church or its hierarchy, he didn't pretend to understand the politics of such a succession. But he did understand the possible reality such a future brought for a scared little girl. Tina Lopez would be robbed of any chance for a normal life, *well*, normal within the confines of her infamous abilities. The kind of normal life that he, Alma, and Billy had tried to provide for nearly ten years now, ever since that day in his melon fields. Remarkably, her secret had remained in tack in spite of the increasingly frequent occurrences within the central valley community.

Up until now the rumors remained safely within the boundaries of a relatively small social circle. The good Father championed the cause, keeping the faithful in line and Tina's anonymity in place. But the Katz trial had exposed them all to the penetrating light of the mainstream media, tempting some with instant celebrity. Folks were folks, and the two friends knew it was only a matter of time before someone would falter and jump at a chance at fifteen minutes of fame. Now, they're only hope was with a man who had made a career of being *first to the punch*. A lifelong newshound, whose photograph might as well be in every dictionary right next to the word journalist.

"So what do you think Billy boy, can we count on your friend to support the cause?"

"I don't know Arthur, I just don't know."

Before Arthur Donnelly could utter another **what if** question, the two men caught site of Grover Gateway walking toward them. He was wearing a long overcoat that hung below his knees. A full head of wispy brown hair blew backwards in the strong wind, his hands stuffed deep into his coat pockets. Arthur watched in amazement as this nearly ninety year-old man made is way toward them briskly, taking long sure strides. He marveled at the shape the man was in, feeling a slight pang of envy as he strode up to meet them. Grover Gateway arrived where they were standing and extended his hand to Father Willet.

"*Billy*, good to see you again my friend," he said, giving Father Willet's hand a good tug.

"Good to see you to Grover, you're looking well. I see you're still baffling the medical community with your incredible health. Is it possible that you are actually getting younger as you age," Father Willet replied, blatantly schmoozing!

"This is my closest friend in the whole wide world, Arthur Donnelly," he continued, introducing the big man to Grover Gateway.

"It's a pleasure sir. I hope you don't mind, but I did a bit of research. You're quite the land baron around these parts, or so the county records indicate," Grover said, complimenting his new acquaintance on his good fortune.

"It's a living," Arthur replied, shaking the man's hand heartily.

Grover reached into his breast pocket and removed an ornately decorated silver flask. He skillfully uncorked the container and offered it to Father Willet.

"Little edge against the chill Billy," he asked his collared friend.

"Don't mind if I do," Father Willet replied, taking up the flask and helping himself to a nice long swig. Wiping his mouth on the sleeve of his jacket he handed the flask to Arthur.

"Artie?" Arthur took the flask and raised it in his benefactor's direction.

"To your health gentlemen! You're a fine American Grover Gateway, a real life saver," he said, taking a healthy pull as well.

"*Ahhhhh,* mother's milk," Arthur exclaimed as he handed the flask back to Grover. The elder of the three took a man sized swallow of his own, then recapped the flask and returned it to his coat pocket.

"All right now, let's get down to it," Grover Gateway said decisively.

"Gentlemen, I am not one to come to a meeting unprepared. You should know that I am well aware of the history of the situation that brought us here today." Grover turned his gaze toward Father Willet exclusively.

"I am also keenly aware of your concern about that **holier than thou** pop n jay, Villa Cruz in Los Angeles," he said, directing that comment at the good Father.

"He is the reason that I chose to meet out here in the open, among the screeching birds and barking seals. Too many eyes and ears inside small rooms and public buildings if you know what I mean," Grover said, looking at each of the men for a moment to make sure they got his meaning.

"Look, Grover, I appreciate the fact that you're well known for your preparation and attention to detail, but really, I…" The old newsman held up his hand cutting Father Willet short.

"Don't get preachy with me Billy, you'll ruin my generous mood," Grover snapped.

"I am not without compassion, and I share your dislike for the Monsignor."

"*Meaning,*" Father Willet said slowly, a little miffed at being slighted, his face turning into a giant question mark?

"Meaning, I want to help. I have no desire to drag a ten year-old child through the gutter of public scrutiny and curiosity. Besides, I don't believe in miracles, I'm too old and too bossy," he said, winking at the two men.

"The fact is I have spoken at length with KC, my girl on the scene. It appears that now *she* believes in them enough for the both of us! Apparently that child has bewitched her somehow, I don't know, you tell me," the old man said scratching his forehead, then running his fingers through his thick hair.

"You and your '*angel of the valley*' may have ruined my best reporter, it's a damn shame," Grover said acidly. Arthur and Father Billy stared at the man trying to get a read as to whether or not he was kidding!

228

"*What the hell*, right is right, and I'm getting too close to finding out for myself who had the better plan, Christ or Milton," exclaimed Grover Gateway, waving his hand at the two of them in a flamboyant gesture of surrender. Arthur glanced over at Billy with a puzzled look on his face.

"John Milton," Father Willet said answering his friend's silent query.

"The author of '*Paradise Lost,*' a famous novel about English penal colonies in Australia," he further explained. Arthur nodded as if he might have heard of it, but he had not, and he waited for his friend to continue.

"There is a wonderful line from the book, one that's quoted often."

"It goes something like this, *I would rather rule in Hell than serve in Heaven.*"

"Mr. Gateway seems to be unsure of the folly of such a statement. Perhaps he will seek my counsel one day before he takes that leap into purgatory," Father Willet finished, shooting a sideways glance in Grover Gateway's direction.

"Oh, I see," said Arthur meekly.

"So, are you with us Grover, or are you here to tell us that you have a higher responsibility to the masses?" the priest asked, raising an eyebrow suspiciously.

"Do find yourself compelled to keep the world in the know at any cost, just because *they have the **right** to know?*"

Father Willet found himself in a stare down with the powerful old tycoon, waiting for the axe to fall. The savvy old newsman pulled the remnants of a cigar from his pocket, a *Corona-Corona*, and then tucked his head in close to his body, shielding the stogy as he lit the far end. He drew deeply on the cigar as he puffed it back to life, the bright red ash glowing and then changing to a deep crimson color. He removed the stumpy cigar from his mouth and let out a long plume of the fragrant smoke. Placing the cigar between his teeth he bit down hard on the thick, tightly rolled, deep chocolate brown stogy.

"OK, here's the plan as I see it," Grover said breaking the uncomfortable pregnant pause. Stepping in real close to the two men, he placed a hand on each of their shoulders. He had to reach a bit to get to Arthur's.

"Stoop on down here Goliath," he said to Arthur Donnelly.

"*First*, you let me deal with Villa Cruz. I have some contacts who you're better off not knowing. And I'm sure that they will able to redirect the Monsignor's curious nature." Grover studied the queer look on Father Willet's face.

"Don't worry Billy, it's nothing sinister, just an exchange money is all. The Vatican is a business like any other, and for the right price any obstacle can be dealt with, *right?*" Father Willet smirked and nodded his head in agreement. It was a reality that bothered him a little, still holding on to the notion that serving the Lord was a completely spiritual vocation.

"*Second*, KC will continue her feature on the Katz incident, but we'll continue to keep the Lopez girl's name under wraps. We'll have to print the facts, *all of them*, and let the piece run its course. But believe me, in the court of public opinion, without a name or a face to reference people will lose interest quickly. We'll concentrate more on the gory details of that rat bastard's exploits, he should fry for his crimes anyway as far as I'm concerned!"

"*Third*, I want to provide some security for the Lopez family, to keep the competition from stumbling onto KC's trail of informants and witnesses, *agreed*," Grover asked, making eye contact with both men? They nodded a silent affirmative. Arthur waved his hand in front of his face trying to minimize the effect of the smoldering cigar.

"*Oh,* sorry," Grover said, taking the cigar from his mouth and smashing it out on his overcoat. Placing it back in his pocket he said smiling, "I'll save that for later."

"Thanks, I was getting a little light headed," said Arthur, using his pinky finger to remove a little crust from the corner of his eye.

"OK, *fourth*, and last. Billy, you and your friend here are going to need to make sure that there won't be any more leaks from your community!"

"There can't be another nurse who saw *this* or a cop who saw *that* coming forward, eager to tell what they know. Whatever you have to do to assure that doesn't happen again, I suggest you do it. Maybe that fella down your way, Sheriff Cardwell, can help you two keep the lid on this for a little while longer. Trust me, if *any* of this gets to the TV guys, then it's over, all bets are off! I'll release this story so fast it'll make your heads spin! I can't risk my paper's credibility and allow the television affiliates to paint a picture of deceit and collusion on the face of the *by God* San Francisco Daily News! That cannot happen gentlemen, are we clear?" They exchanged glances and *harrumphed* an agreement in old man speak. Grover Gateway stamped his feet on the wooden deck and shoved his hands into his coat pockets shivering slightly.

"*Man its cold out here! Who's idea was this anyway,*" he asked jokingly.

"Come on, I'll buy the first round boys," he offered. That being said, the *three wise men* started toward the restaurant and the comfort of a leather booth and a few whiskeys between them.

Twenty-two

*("...If I leave here tomorrow, will you still remember
me. Well I must be traveling on now, cause there's too
many places I gotta be ...Freebird, Lynyrd Skynyrd")*

<u>*Chicago, Illinois, 19, February 1973*</u>

"Ladies and gentlemen, we're starting our approach to O'Hare
International Airport. Please return to your seats and fasten your seatbelts as
soon as the indicators are activated. On behalf of the crew and myself, thank
you for choosing United," the captain's voice announced over the intercom.
The speakers crackled once again and he continued.

"We should be on the ground in approximately twenty minutes. The
current time in Chicago is 4:15pm."

"Flight crew, prepare for landing."

Paul pushed the button on the arm of his seat, raising the backrest to
a 90-degree angle. He nudged me with his elbow, waking me from a really
good nap.

"Come on Ethan, we're getting ready to land, and I need to piss like a
racehorse," Paul said in an urgent tone.

I tightened up my entire upper torso and went into a big boy stretch,
hyper-extending my flexed arms, my hands curled into hard fists as I slowly
rose, rudely wakened from my peaceful slumber. I blinked my eyes rapidly
and rubbed them vigorously with my balled up fists until I reached a semi-

conscious state. The pillow I had been hugging had fallen to the floor in front of me and I leaned forward to retrieve it.

"You can take the teddy bear away from the man, but you can't take the boy away from the teddy bear," I murmured.

"Hey, that should be a tee-shirt," I said out loud as I sat back upright. While I fumbled with the armrest searching for the button to raise my seat, Paul jabbed me again, this time a little harder. He was half standing, his butt wedged firmly up against the tiny defenseless window.

"MOVE IT ETHAN, before I have an accident doofus!"

"Alright already," I said, scooting out of my seat and back out into the aisle a couple of steps giving Paulie a clear path.

He maneuvered quickly past me and raced up the aisle toward the forward head. A old man a few rows ahead must have had a similar need, as he started to creep out into the aisle, a dangerous move considering the Rhino barreling down on him.

"COMIN THROUGH," Paul hollered as he passed the poor man on a dead run, knocking him back into his seat in the process!

"SORRY," he yelled without looking back, disappearing into the small bathroom, the little red occupied sign appearing instantly!

I shook my head and walked over to the old gentleman, helping him to collect himself after the crash.

"I'm very sorry sir, my friend there had a bit of an emergency, too much coffee," I said apologetically.

The agitated old man was starting to read me the riot act when he noticed the collar around my neck. He cleared his throat as he swallowed a boatload of profanities, which Paul had legitimately earned by the way, and managed to mumble, "Thank you Father, no harm done," as he settled back into his seat. I patted him lightly on the shoulder and walked back to our seats to wait for Paul to return. Opening the overhead locker I retrieved our jackets, and tossed Paul's P-coat onto his seat. I turned just in time to catch him walking up to the poor old fella that he had freight trained. He stopped and tried to apologize, but the old guy was having none of it. Suddenly the man's even smaller wife began to wail on Paulie with a big red purse and he had to run for his life!

"*HEY, stifle crazy lady, STIFLE*," Paul exclaimed, back-peddling down the aisle toward me.

"*Smooth Yogi,*" I said teasing my bearish friend.

"EAT ME," Paul replied with gusto, drawing a few stink eyes from our closest neighbors as he belittled a priest.

"What are you people gawking at? He's not my father, he's my brother," Paul whined, defending his *God given* right to chop me at will. He shrugged his shoulders at me as he passed by me to his seat.

"You're a piece of work," I said chuckling as I sat down beside him.

"Aw, give it a rest will ya Ethan. ***When you gotta go, you gotta go!***"

"*Nuf said*," I replied, as we fastened our safety belts simultaneously.

Paul raised the plastic window shade and we watched as the plane descended toward the airport. We could faintly see downtown Chicago and the lake beyond as we flew over the suburban neighborhoods of Aurora Illinois. I leaned back in my seat and closed my eyes, involuntarily fiddling with the crucifix underneath my shirt. Take offs and landings were huge issues for me. Once I was airborne I was OK, but I never quite trusted the physics of something so big falling from the sky and transforming itself from plane to bus, it just didn't make sense to me! I could feel Paul staring at me in disgust.

"Why are you such a sissy about this Ethan," he asked, almost spitting the words at me.

"Where's your faith *Father Scaredycat*? You think that the boss is going to let anything happen to his golden boy," he asked teasing me. He was right of course; I really should set a better example. It couldn't be very comforting to watch a priest *panic-pray* the rosary on an airplane. I opened my eyes and turned my head toward my buddy.

"Thanks for the pep talk Paulie."

"Don't mention it," he replied, snapping his fingers as he scootched deeper into his seat and leaned his big head back against the cushioned rest. We sat quietly for a moment and then I added, "By the way, I swear by all that is holy, if Sophie Wong ever calls me *Father Scaredycat* I'm coming back here to pound you!" Paul snickered with eyes closed, as quoted the Sundance Kid from the movie we both loved, *"You just keep thinking Butch, that's what you're good at!"*

The Boeing 727 touched down with surprising ease, little puffs of white smoke emanating from the tires when the rubber met the tarmac. I watched all of the heads around me bounce to and fro as the plane raced down the runway, decelerating rapidly to an eventual crawl. As soon as we reached the end of the runway and made a slow right turn toward the terminal, the scurrying began. It always amazed me the way everyone would race one another just to be first off of the plane.

"Welcome to Chicago, we hope that your flight was a pleasant one. And thank you for flying the friendly skies of United," the captain said routinely.

Paul was setting his watch to Central Standard Time, but I had decided to wait until I got to California before I did likewise, *why do it twice*, I thought.

Besides, my arithmetic skills were still pretty good, so figured I could just do the math until then.

"What time is your connecting flight to LA," Paul asked, holding his wrist up to his ear, making sure that his watch was actually ticking.

"7:30pm," I replied.

"You want to grab an early supper together then," he asked?

"Sure, that sounds good. Let's find a bar and get a bratwurst and a beer," I said, suddenly very hungry.

"You're playing my song Ethan Kelly," Paul replied, rubbing his palms together vigorously as if he were trying to start a fire with a couple of sticks.

"That'll be grand, brats and beers it is then," I said, confirming our plan!

The plane stopped suddenly, sending everyone forward then back abruptly. Paul and I remained seated and watched the pageant of hurried travelers push and shove one another as they raced to deplane. Paulie nodded his head toward the frenzied mob, *"NERDS,"* he said, his mouth twisting in a mild snarl.

"Yeah," I said in agreement, as I leaned back and waited for the aisles to clear.

At last the steady stream of passengers began to thin out and we got to our feet to make our way off of United Flight 218. As we reached the front of the airplane, a cheerful stewardess smiled broadly and thanked us for our patronage, just as she had been trained to do.

"Thank you sir, enjoy your stay," she said to Paul. He nodded a *'you're welcome'* response, and squeezed past her, out of the plane.

"Thank you Father, enjoy your stay," she repeated to me, looking a little tired and anxious to leave herself.

"You're welcome, and thank you Miss," I replied, following Paul into the rolling corridor.

We exited into the terminal and looked around trying get our bearings quickly among the hustle and bustle of hundreds of others trying to do exactly the same.

"This way," Paul said, leading toward the first boozer that he spied. We sprinted ahead and walked into a loud place called *Chicago Bob's*. The pane glass was decorated in colorful lettering belting out they're slogan, Dogs/ Brew& Baseball.

"This is the place," Paulie announced, tilting his head backward and sniffing the air. The aromas of sausage sizzling, sauerkraut pickling, hot peppers steeping, and beer flowing was almost too much for him to bear.

"Ahh Ethan, this must be what Heaven smells like," he said with reverence, his hand over his heart like he was reciting the pledge of allegiance.

"Easy Paulie, let's not frighten the natives," I teased.

We settled in at the bar and ordered a couple dogs each and a pint of Guinness. Paul and I watched the bartender closely as he drew the pints, making certain that he did not ruin the pour by being hasty. When he set the pints in front of us, we waited patiently for the stout to settle and for the creamy foam to collect at the brim of the glass. Then we picked up our libations and clinked the glasses together as we were accustomed to doing at such occasions.

"SLANITE," we toasted one another simultaneously, which is *cheers* in Gaelic basically. Then we tipped our drinks up to our gobs and gulped down half the refreshment before returning the glasses to the bar top.

A moment later our meal arrived, the thick bratwurst nestled snuggly in the soft bun, smothered in sauerkraut and peppers, a few wafer thin garlic slices adorning the top of the colorful feast. Paul reached across the bar and felt underneath for the condiments, and fished out a large yellow squeeze bottle filled with French's mustard. He squirted a healthy slathering onto his dogs, handed me the mustard, and I did likewise. We ate in silence, finishing the first Guinness and ordering a second with our mouths full. No Irishman worth his salt would ever leave an establishment before drinking at least two pints of the black stuff or one shot of whiskey, either Bushmill's or Jameson, it would just be rude! Paul checked his watch as we savored the second pint and I watched a little of the boxing match that was playing on the small TV behind the bar.

"Hey, it's almost six o'clock Ethan," he said to me.

"I need to be getting on down the road, and you need to see about catching your next flight."

"Guess so," I replied, finishing my Guinness.

"I still have better that an hour to kill, I think I'll stay right here and have another pint," I said, signaling the barman that I was ready for another.

"Suit yourself, but I need to git! I still have to check in at the hotel and I have an early orientation in the morning," he said gathering his coat and gloves.

"OH MAN, I have to start apartment hunting as well, there goes the weekend I guess," Paul said, slapping his hand to his forehead.

"YIKES, sounds like your up against it alright," I said sympathetically. He stood up and put a twenty dollar bill on the bar, waving his hand at me before I could launch a protest.

"Suppers on me Ethan, I'm a working man now!"

"Kenny picked up the check at breakfast, remember, and besides, they don't pay priests squat," he added, slapping me on the back.

I got up and pushed his outstretched hand away, throwing my arms around my buddy's huge shoulders. We hugged one another for longer than

235

the other patrons seemed to be comfortable with and then pushed away, each of us raising a fist to dab the moisture from our eyes before anyone could notice. Both of us sniffled loudly and then dragged our sleeves across our noses, then pointed an index finger at each other. We were so smooth it must have looked choreographed.

"Have a good trip," Paul said back peddling toward the door.

"Yeah, you too," I said, nodding my head, placing both hands at my waist.

"I'll call your Mom later and get the number where you're staying in California," he said as he reached the door.

"OK"

"Good luck Ethan, I mean *Father Kelly*," Paul said as he turned and walked away toward the baggage claim area.

I waived to him but he didn't see me. Then I turned back to the bar and sat down. My third Guinness was waiting for me patiently, the foam already settled, the drink calling to me. I reached for the glass and raised it toward my own reflection in the mirror behind the bar.

"*Slainte* Paulie, *Go mbeannaí Dia duit* (may God bless you), I said to myself, toasting my buddy's future. The barman walked up and set a shot of whiskey down in front of me.

"Oh no, I didn't order this," I said puzzled.

"Compliments of the lady in the corner booth," he said pointing toward the red booth over my shoulder. I turned slightly in my chair.

"Thank you," I said to the woman I could not see.

"My pleasure, it's the least I can do," a sweet, *familiar* voice said from behind the high cushion of the booth.

I sat there staring at the hand that held onto a tall pilsner beer glass. She slowly wiped the moisture from the glass with her slender index finger and suddenly a memory started to bubble to the surface in my brain. Before I could grasp onto it, the woman picked up her glass and it disappeared from my view as she took a drink.

"How have you been Ethan," the mystery voice asked?

"*Excuse me,*" I said, stalling for time as I tried to put a face and name with the voice I was sure that I knew.

The woman's legs suddenly appeared as she swung them out from under the table and stood up. As she rose to her full height, all five feet two inches of her, it all came to me in a flood of recognition. There before me stood none other than Lieutenant Cardinale, *Nurse Carla*, my second favorite smart-aleck in the whole wide world, next to my sister Shannon of course.

"*Carla?* Oh my God, I can't believe it's you," I exclaimed.

She nearly sprinted over to me and jumped up into my arms. I leaned forward to embrace her and lifted her right off of the ground when I stood back up, her little high-heeled feet dangling in space. I set her down after a moment or two and she enthusiastically kissed me hello right on the mouth before she noticed the collar was wearing.

"OH SHIT, I'm so sorry Ethan, *I mean Father*, oh man, I should have known! *Oh stupid Carla,* stupid, stupid," she rambled, scolding herself, flustered beyond a quick composure.

"OH MAN, I said shit to a priest, forgive me Ethan, ***DAMN IT,*** I mean Father," she said, continuing to dig a deeper hole. I put my finger to her lips before she got any deeper.

"That's alright Carla, no offense, apology accepted."

Nurse Carla lowered her face into her left hand and massaged her eyes with her thumb and four fingers.

"Ethan Kelly, of all the gin joints in all the towns, I had to run into you here," she said, borrowing a line from *Casablanca* and doing her best Humphrey Bogart impression.

"You know, I was actually thinking of you just now, it's weird, you always seemed to be around whenever I needed a shoulder or a friendly ear."

"Really," I said, legitimately surprised and flattered by her comment.

"Yeah, really!"

"I'm on my way to New York City to intern over at Manhattan General, in the ER no less, go figure," she informed me.

"I'm a doctor now, can you believe it?"

"I'll bet you thought that I would end up raising Arron Walker's brats," she teased sarcastically, poking me in the side as she did so.

"No I didn't, really Carla I swear!"

"WOW, a doctor, I'm really proud of you. But to be honest, I'm not surprised, you always were the sharpest knife in the drawer," I replied, congratulating her.

"Ethan, if it weren't for that collar I'd swear that you were flirting with me," she teased, flashing me that beautiful smile I remembered so fondly. I blushed a little bit, *OK a lot*, she always could push my buttons, and she hadn't lost the knack any over the years. She reached around me and picked up my drinks, "Do you have a little time," she asked?

"Please say yes, I really want to catch up with you," she pleaded.

"Please, please, please?"

I nodded an okey-doke and we walked back to her booth. I stood next to the table and waited for her to seat herself, admiring the fact that she was still as pretty as I remembered. She was one of the few bright spots from that dark period of my brief history on Earth. I seated my self and played with the shot glass in front of me. She reached across the table and covered my hands with her own.

"It's so wonderful to see you again Ethan. It's OK to call you by your name right? Or is that against the rules or something? "she asked sweetly.

"Yeah, it's alright Carla, priests are people too," I assured her with a smile.

"Oh good!" she replied, wiping her brow with her sleeve.

"Alright then," she added, checking her watch.

"Listen, I've got a seven o'clock flight so we need to cram as many current events as we can into a half hour, you first!"

I started from the day we said goodbye in Saigon and then walked her quickly through the events of the last four years of my life. I told her about my new assignment in California and I even told her about my plans to find Mitchell's family and return the St. Christopher's medal that he gave me back to his son. I asked her if she knew where all of the others had ended up and if they kept in touch with each other. She told me that Arron Walker had become a successful stockbroker, and was living in San Diego California the last she heard. She told me that Corporal Larry Polen had been killed in action shortly after I had shipped out. And she didn't know much about anyone else.

"Oh, I do know something about that big guy from Texas, what was his name, *Hightower?*"

"It turns out that he is a cop in Los Angeles. I ran into him while I was attending school at UCLA. Actually, he sort of ran into me when he stopped me for doing 50 in a 35 zone. He did waive the ticket in favor of lunch at a local burger joint though. The poor man didn't have a chance once I turned on the charm. You remember how effective that can be, *don't you Father,*" she teased.

We finished our drinks and glanced at our watches, agreeing it was time to scoot. She made me write down every phone number and address that I knew so that she could stay in touch. Then we walked out of Chicago Bob's together and onto the causeway.

"Oh, I wish we had more time Ethan," Carla said, reaching up and cupping my face with her two little hands.

"I know, but you have my Mom's number in Albany. When I come to visit I'll call you and we meet in the city. You can show me all around the Big Apple," I said cheerfully.

"OK, it's a date!"

She put her arms around my middle and buried her face in my chest, embracing me a tightly as she could. Then she stepped back, kissed her finger and put it to my lips. She turned, waved goodbye and walked away. I watched her for a minute or so and then turned to walk in the opposite direction. I missed her already!

<u>*Albany, New York, 20 February 1973*</u>

Kenny Wong turned into the driveway of his home on Newcastle Avenue in a posh neighborhood just three blocks from where he had grown up. It was nearly seven o'clock in the evening and he was looking forward to a nice meal and some quiet time with his little family. The day had been a long one, having had to make up for lost time due to spending the day taking care of Ethan and Paulie. He didn't mind though, the fellas were his brothers by choice, as much a part of his family as was he in theirs. He pulled up to the garage, put the car in park, and then got out to raise the heavy wooden door.

"Man it's freezing," he said aloud to no one in particular.

Ken didn't like the cold much, which kind of made one wonder why he never relocated to Florida or California. Actually, if you knew Ken you knew that he was devoted to his family and that he would never stray very far. He had always accepted the fact that he would be the responsible child, designated to care for his parents and preside over family business. This was a strong tradition in the Asian culture, one that was not spoiled by the decadence of the west and their adopted country. He jumped back into the car and pulled into the garage, shutting off the engine when the hanging tennis ball touched the windshield.

"Thanks Mr. Kelly," he said to himself.

My father had taught all three of us how to drive because Ken and Paul's parents were too new to the English language, having immigrated from China and Poland respectively. The hanging tennis ball routine was developed after Paulie drove Da's Camaro through the wall of our garage while learning how to park the car. It was one of the few times I ever saw Da cry in front of anyone without a Kelly surname!

Ken gathered his briefcase and overcoat from the back seat and walked out of the garage, balancing everything in one hand while he pulled the heavy door closed with the other. He walked toward the back service porch and suddenly felt all itchy on his neck, like he was coming down with a case of the hives or something like that. Something was not right, he always got this feeling when something was wrong, it was as if he could feel the bad vibrations floating on the air. He took the stairs up to the porch two at a time and opened the door leading to the mudroom. He stomped his feet to get the snow off of his rubbers and sat at the bench to remove them from his shoes.

"Carolyn," he called out. No answer. He stood up and let himself into the house through the kitchen door.

"CAROLYN," he called out again, louder still. Ken didn't like this at all. He could smell supper cooking and he could see the pots and pans on the stovetop, as well as something through the oven window.

"What the hell," Kenny said to himself.

"CAROLYN, SOPHIE, where are you guys," he hollered, hoping that they were just playing with him, hiding in the closet waiting to jump out and say BOO!

He lifted the lids on the pots sitting on the stove. They were still warm but the burners had all been turned off. It looked like some peas and carrots and some mashed potatoes, no gravy pan yet that he could see. Kenny put his finger in the mashed potatoes and scooped up a taste. He looked around quickly, if his wife were here that would have brought her running. She always socked him whenever he would do that little maneuver. He walked over to the oven and peeked inside, meatloaf, and the oven was switched off as well, curious? He set his briefcase and coat down on the kitchen counter and walked out into the dining room. The table was set, and there was bread, butter and condiments on the lazy Susan. Kenny was never one to panic, but he was beginning to move from annoyed to concerned.

"HEY, is anybody home," he called out to the house?

He jogged up the stairs and checked each bedroom and bath, nothing. Everything was neat and clean, there just weren't any people around? Ken sat down on Sophie's bed and did some mental gymnastics. OK, what did he know? The food was warm so they couldn't have been gone long. They only had one car, so they couldn't have gone far. The appliances had been turned off and nothing had been spilled so they hadn't been in any hurry. So where could they be logically?

"The neighbors," he said to himself. Carolyn probably went next door to the Anderson's to borrow a cup of sugar or something he reasoned. Ken walked back into his bedroom and picked up the telephone. He dialed Fred and Lori's number and waited for an answer. After the eleventh ring he hung up the phone.

"What the f____..." he started to exclaim when he noticed the note. It was right there on his pillow. He picked it up and read...

'Hi honey, sorry about dinner. Sophie got a real bad nosebleed and I couldn't get it to stop. Lori and Fred are giving us a ride to the emergency room. I'm sure

its nothing, you know how she has been picking at her nose lately. We should be home soon, an hour tops. Love you…C'

Kenny let out a sigh and stretched out on their bed. He looked up at the ceiling and scanned the little acoustic bumps for a minute trying to make out shapes and figures in the jumbled mess. After awhile, he yawned and stretched, then swung his legs over the side of the bed and leaped to his feet.

"Well, I don't want to eat alone," he muttered.

So he picked his car keys off of the bed where he had dropped them and trotted down the stairs. He re-checked the oven and stove on his way out, making sure that everything was turned off, then did his arrival routine in reverse, ending with pulling his rubbers over his shoes on the service porch. The drive to Memorial Hospital was short, only about fifteen minutes. He had no problem finding a parking space because it was after normal business hours. He locked his car and walked toward the building, passing the Anderson's station wagon along the way.

"Good, everyone's still here," he thought to himself. When he reached the entrance to the building he let himself in trough the double glass doors. The waiting room was nearly empty so he had no problem locating Fred and Lori Anderson.

"Hey you two, thanks for coming to the rescue," Kenny said to his neighbors.

"Have you been here long?"

"Just a little while, no more than an hour," Fred answered.

"So what's going on, where's Carolyn and Sophie," Kenny pressed gently.

"Hi Lori," he added.

"Hi"

"We don't really know much Ken. Your daughter's nose was bleeding pretty badly. They took her in right away," Fred explained.

"Carolyn went in with her and we haven't seen them since."

"We heard them once, sounded like Sophie was unhappy with something."

"Like what?"

"I'm not sure, but I know it involved needles because Sophie was screaming bloody murder about not wanting a shot!"

"Oh man, I hate that," Ken said wincing as he pictured his frightened little girl.

"I think I'll just go up to the desk and see what's what. There are probably a ton of forms to fill out anyway," Kenny said calmly.

As he walked over to the reception desk, the double doors to the ER opened automatically and out walked Carolyn, a tall man in green scrubs walking beside her, his arm around her shoulders. He could see that his wife was visibly shaken. She had not even noticed that he was just six feet in front of her.

"Carolyn," he said softly. She looked up but did not acknowledge him right away.

"Honey," he said, silently questioning the doctor with the look on his face.

"Mr. Wong?"

"Yes," Ken said without looking at him, reaching out and stroking his wife's hair.

"Mr. Wong, why don't we sit over here and chat for a minute," said the stranger in green.

He released his hold on Carolyn Wong and her husband stepped up and walked her over to a small sofa against the wall. They sat down together and Carolyn looked at Ken blankly and mouthed something that he did not understand.

"Mr. Wong, I am Doctor Meade, I'm the attending on duty tonight," the man in green said slowly. Ken nodded an acknowledgement and held his wife, softly caressing her shoulder as he waited for the doctor to continue.

"Mr. Wong, may I call you Ken?"

Kenny nodded an affirmative.

"Ken, your daughter is a very sick little girl. The nosebleed was not caused by any object or excessive irritation on her part. I suspect that it is symptomatic of a serious blood disorder. We did some preliminary test, removed some fluid from her spine and drew several vials of blood for the lab to process."

"What are you testing for," Kenny asked, his growing concern evident in the tone of his voice.

"I don't want to say just yet. I don't want to alarm you without cause."

"Don't BS me doctor! If you're trying not to frighten us forget about it, it's too late!"

"Listen, I'm not a specialist, but I am fairly certain that your daughter may have leukemia."

"I'm sorry," Doctor Meade said, reaching across and patting Ken on the knee.

The words echoed off of all the walls, and the doctor's voice became fainter and fainter as Ken rolled the word around in his brain, leukemia… leukemia. He didn't like the sound of it. The word sounded like something that you spit out after a coughing fit. He knew instinctively that this was not good news, he knew just enough about the disease to be scared, to be petrified. He was fighting off the urge to be angry, to lash out at the world, at God, at anyone close enough to ease the pain that was growing in his stomach. Ken could feel the tears forming and falling from the corners of his eyes, and he fought to stay in control of his emotions, like he always did. He needed to see Sophie; he needed to hug his baby, to tell her that Daddy was going to make everything better. He just wanted to go home and pretend that none of this was real.

"Mr. Wong, Ken, do you understand everything that I have explained to you?"

Ken snapped back into the present and looked up at the doctor.

"I'm sorry doctor, I lost you after the word leukemia, you were saying," Ken asked, regaining his composure?

"I said that the lab tests would take a few days to complete. In the mean time I would like to refer you to a specialist in oncology."

"Yes, of course," Ken said evenly.

"Until we know more I suggest you take your family home and make them as comfortable as possible," Doctor Meade said with a smile.

"Sophie is very young and will need a lot of reassurance and positive re-enforcement. She is a smart little girl, and I believe that she intuitively knows that there is something wrong with her. She'll be looking to you and Carolyn for strength and support. I cannot stress strongly enough the importance of keeping her life as normal a possible."

"Are you following me with all of this," the doctor asked?

"I get you doc, can we see her now?"

"Of course, the nurse is just removing the gauze from her nose and probably feeding her some Jell-O and orange juice. Come on I'll take you to her," Doctor Meade said standing and gesturing for Ken and Carolyn to do likewise. Ken stood and helped Carolyn to her feet, she was moving a little slow.

"Snap out of it babe, let's get the baby and go home."

Carolyn nodded in agreement and smiled, her strength returning and her eyes becoming clearer. As soon as they entered the ER they saw Sophie sitting up on a gurney dressed in her overall and sneakers. Her long hair was braided into a ponytail with a red ribbon tied around the end. She was spooning Jell-O into her mouth when she spotted her parents. Sophie raised her hand quickly to waive and sprayed the cherry gelatin all over the wall and the nurse.

"Hi Daddy," she said happily, the trauma of the exam already forgotten.

"They sticked me with needles two times," she exclaimed!

"But you were very brave sweetie, and you got Jell-O for being such a big girl," the nurse said lovingly, glancing at the parents with a smile and a knowing look in her eye.

"I only cried a little bit Daddy, can we go home now?"

"You betcha sweetheart, let's go home," Ken said scooping his daughter up into his arms, causing her to squeal with delight.

"Can we bring nurse Betty home with us," Sophie asked looking back over her Dad's shoulder at the nice woman who had been taking care of her?

"Not this time honey, maybe next time, OK," Ken replied, looking over at Carolyn who gave him a thumb's up and a big smile.

"Giddy up Daddy, Hi Ho Server," Sophie said kicking her heels into Ken's ribs like she were riding a horse!

"*Silver* honey, it's Hi Ho *Silver*," Ken said correcting his daughter.

"OK, Hi Ho **Server**," she said again.

"OK, whatever, I'm ready to go home now," he said surrendering.

He reached out and shook Doctor Meade's hand and then did the same for Nurse Betty, thanking them for their support. Ken then reached for Carolyn's hand and the three of them walked out of the hospital together into an unknown and unwanted future.

Twenty-three

(..."In my little town, I grew up believing, God
keeps his eye on us all"... Paul Simon)

<u>*Los Angeles, California, January 1970*</u>

Pablo Villa Cruz, Monsignor to the Catholic Church, and the Archdioceses of Los Angeles, sat deep in one of the two wing-backed Queen Ann chairs in the rectory study. He gazed intensely into the fire blazing in the hearth, the flickering firelight reflecting in the lenses of his bifocals. He had been sitting for the better part of the last hour contemplating and stewing over the letter that lay in his lap. The priest reached up with his left hand and grabbed his face just below the eyes. He squeezed in with his thumb and four fingers and dragged his hand slowly downward, stretching the flesh as he did so. His hand passed down over his mouth, then around his chin, across the length of his neck, stopping finally just below his throat and at the top of his breastplate.

He removed the hand from his chest and reached for the fine bone china teacup setting on the table next to the chair. The cup was empty and cold to the touch so he turned and poured more hot tea from the matching cozy covered teapot. He picked up the cup and saucer and lifted the cup to his lips. Blowing lightly across the brim of the cup he sipped the strong Earl Grey tea and then returned the set to the table. Father Villa Cruz settled back into a comfortable thinking position in the chair and placed the tips of his fingers together, flexing them back and forth against each other as he continued to vex over the news from Rome.

"This is unacceptable, but undeniable," he whispered to himself.

"I know that radical peasant *Father Willet* is connected with this somehow," he continued, talking to the fireplace and the empty room.

He picked up the letter, and unfolded it as he adjusted his specs. Moving his arms forward and back until his eyes focused just right, he began to read it one more time. The Monsignor mouthed the words as he read, a habit from childhood. English was of course his second language and even after so many years in this country, he still had to go slow in order to keep from misinterpreting words and phrases. Reciting the words as he read them seemed to keep him at a pace that prevented him from making careless mistakes.

The letter was from his dear friend, His Holiness, Cardinal Giancarlo Pavongatta. He and Carlo began their service to God and the Holy Roman Church at the same time, in Sicily during World War Two. They had been young priests together at the *Basilica Cattredrale* in Messina, shortly before the Americans landed on the island and taking control of Palermo in July of 1943. One year later, in July of 1944, the Americans would capture Rome after successfully landing at Anzio in January. By April of the following year, 1945, that *bidonista* (swindler) Mussolini and his whore Carlotta Petacci would be shot and hung by their feet, on display in the Piazzale Loreta in Milan. Once the war was over, the two friends were summoned back to Rome, and from there; their lives went in very different directions.

Carlo, who came from a politically influential family in Rome, took an assignment at the Holy City as a researcher for the Vatican Secret Archives. While Pablo, a child from modest beginnings in the sprawling countryside of Tuscany accepted a post on the other side of the world in the United States, at St Paul's Cathedral in Buffalo New York. There he diligently wheeled and dealed his way to a position of power within the Church, where he was eventually elevated to Bishop and assigned to the Archdioceses of Los Angeles on the opposite side of the country. It was a move that he welcomed though, given the perpetual warm climate and absence of mountains of snow. Father Villa Cruz began to read:

My Dear Friend Pablolito,

How sad it is that we cannot sit on the veranda and share a glass of wine like in the old days. I miss those simpler times, the spirited debates, the warm conversation, the food, bella mia, the food Pablo. Do you remember Sister

Demarco? I tell you that woman was a genius in the kitchen! Oh Pablo, the ciapino, and the linguini with clams, Madre Dio, we should have petitioned her name to the council for sainthood! If only I could have stolen her when we left Sicily and brought her with me to Rome, the Council of Cardinals might have appointed me the youngest Pontiff in history. I tease Pablo, I tease, and not a word of this should pass your lips! Can you imagine the penance for such a boastful remark? Ah, but enough reminiscing, we have business you and I.

Pablo, these letters you have been sending me of the accounts of this child are remarkable. In all my years of research in this area of study, this is the most excited I have been about truly witnessing a miracle. Unlike like the Stigmata claims and the healing waters or even the paranormal apparitions of Holy Mother Mary's image supposedly hovering in photos of random occurrences, this phenomenon has been documented flawlessly. The film footage that your agents were able to take of the girl raising that bastardo doctor from the dead, and actually reversing the effects of his horrible burns, was more than incredible, it was nearly unbelievable! My friend, I will always be allied to your aspiration to reach the College of Cardinals, but I must tell you. This film is dangerous, and your desire to share knowledge of the child with the world is wrong headed. Pablo, this letter is not to protect you from discovery by the College, it is to rebuke you in their name. In fact, I've been ordered to intervene on behalf of the Church and petition you to abandon this plan of action. My friend I'm to inform you that you've been recalled to the Holy City to appear before the College of Cardinals on this matter. Until these arrangements can be arranged, you are directed to cease with your pursuit of this child and disavow any knowledge of her existence. Distance yourself from her Pablo, this child no longer exists in the eyes of the faith. If you are careful and do as you are told there is a good chance that you will suffer no hindrance to your hopes and dreams for the future. Settle your business in California my friend and get yourself to Rome as quickly as possible. I will anxiously await your reply, your brother in Christ, Carlo.

Father Villa Cruz set the letter back in his lap and removed his glasses. He pinched the bridge of his nose where the heavy frames had rested, leaving deep indentations. He closed his eyes and slowly shook his head. "Who has put you to this Carlo," he wondered. "Who is it that has the ear of the Church, and how high does this person reach?" He would have to comply of course, but **before God** he would find out the reason for the Church's reluctance to capitalize on this. He had seen this film, and he had talked with that devil Katz. Father Villa Cruz knew the child was for true, *he knew it!* And to his mind, if she were carefully managed, the Holy Church might convert tens of millions with the kind of hope and promise that the *angel of the valley* could bring into the living rooms of the world, courtesy of the mainstream media!

He leaned back in the comfy chair and settled in for a nice peaceful siesta, it would be the first of the New Year for him. Perhaps he would see things more clearly in an hour or so? A moment later he was fast asleep, a low hum of a snore permeating the airspace of the peaceful study.

Firebaugh, California, January 1970

KC pressed down on the little arm at the left of the steering wheel of her rented Plymouth Duster. The blinker sprang to life and started its loud rhythmic cadence of clicking and clacking as she exited the Freeway onto Central Avenue. She was getting weary of the long commutes from San Francisco to *Hooterville*, but the extra effort had been paying big dividends with regard to her career. Her star was rising in the world of newsprint and in fact she was starting to get offers from the glitzy folk in the TV biz! She decided that she would wait a little while before she sprang that one on Brian and Grover. Her series on serial killers and violent offenders had been extremely popular having been picked up by the major papers up and down the coast of California, as well as a couple of neighboring states as well.

The timing of her work couldn't have more perfect, her stories coming out just ahead of the Manson crap in LA. She was being regularly interviewed and quoted as an expert in bizarre senseless crimes, and to be honest, she was enjoying all the attention. Her last piece had compared the two men, one psycho to another. Dr. Murray Katz and Charles Manson were sort of the Frick and Frack of psychopaths. Charlie's bizarre nature, flagrant actions, and apparent absence of remorse starkly contrasted Dr. Katz's obvious repentance and controlled, articulate, and gracious social demeanor. It was actually difficult to determine who was the most frightening, the lunatic or the liar? KC's money was on the liar. It was her contention that one could see a lunatic's moves and follow his trail, he could be tracked and plotted. But a truly gifted liar was clever, careful, not easily followed, not easily caught. A lunatic can be seen easily, all you have to do is pay attention. However, a gifted liar is cleverly camouflaged and is able to walk among us. She turned onto Central Avenue and went back under the overpass, heading toward Avenue C and the small home of Victor and Maria Lopez. She had been invited for supper a while back and she saw this as a chance to see how the family dynamic worked given all the commotion. Victor Lopez had been a hard sell, but apparently Arthur Donnelly had convinced him that she was no threat, and after all, she had kept her word about leaving the little girl out of the limelight. She patted herself on the back *daily* for that little triumph. She had no idea that it was the *Big Kahuna* himself, Grover Gateway who was running interference for her, as he wrestled with his journalistic instincts and his recent acceptance of his own mortality.

Anyway, KC thought that this would be a good chance to quiz Maria Lopez a bit more and also have some alone time with Tina. KC remembered the last time she had scheduled an interview with Tina's mother. She had arranged to meet with Maria at her home one morning, quite early, so as to avoid any interruptions by the kids and the husband. You know, talk woman to woman so to speak, while Maria puttered around the house doing chores and what not.

However, when KC arrived at her doorstep she was greeted by pandemonium. As t turned out, KC had scheduled the interview on the very day that it was Maria's turn to be the neighborhood mommy for about 5 or 6 infants and rug rats! There wouldn't be one free minute that day to chat, much less for KC to jot down any notes, as she was instantly drafted into Maria's one woman army. The children whined and cried, crawled and squirmed, ate and pooped all over the modest little home on the range! While there may not have been much time to devote to a meaningful interview, the two women did get a chance to know one another, and Maria was so happy to have help for a change. To be honest, though KC may have done a fair share of whining herself, she secretly kind of dug the experience. She was at the *late* nesting age, 32 or 28 depending on who was asking! And the allure of motherhood was never too far from her collective sub-conscious.

"All I need is a man that I can trust with my heart," she would say to herself occasionally, whenever this mood would wash over her. And therein lay the problem. She had become quite jaded from her extensive dating experiences, and had difficulty using the words **man** and **trust** in the same sentence! The two words just didn't sound right together, at least not without sounding like an oxymoron anyway. KC shuddered and shook off her little mental detour.

"GET YOUR HORMONES IN LINE KC GIRL," she said out loud!

"What'd you say," Jay Namura asked sleepily, waking from a catnap in the seat next to her?

"Nothing, just forget it," she snapped back at him! She felt an instant pang of guilt and apologized, "Sorry Jay-man," she said, shrugging her shoulders and rolling her eyes.

"Is it *THAT* time of the month already," he teased, pretending to flip open a notepad and count the days on a pretend calendar.

"How often do you go through this anyway? I mean they do call them *periods* right, like they might happen periodically? Or in your case does it mean that you just have them **PERIOD!**"

"SHUT UP," KC yelled, turning toward Jay completely and slugging him with both fists, the old one-two punch. Jay covered up like an experienced boxed and protected his face.

"HEY crazy lady, the wheel, keep your hands on the *the freaking steering wheel OK!*"

"Watch the road will ya, *WATCH THE ROAD!*"

"OH SHIT," KC exclaimed, turning back quickly and grabbing the steering wheel to avoid veering off into the opposing lane of traffic. The rental car swerved sharply back to the right of the road as she regained control of the vehicle.

"You OK Jay," she asked huffing and puffing, her heart racing while she slowed down to the speed limit.

"Still here, but that right cross of yours is gonna leave a mark," he replied checking out the purple bruise that was forming on his bicep.

"Sorry sweetie, but you know how crazy I get when my friend is visiting," KC said, blowing her hair from her eyes, and blushing slightly.

"Was that an apology or an excuse?"

"*JAAAYYY*, COME ON!"

"OK, OK, I forgive you! Now calm down before we get to the house. You'll scare everyone with that **MADD BITCH** routine. For crying out loud girl, sometimes you worry me," Jay said shaking his head. KC reached up and tilted the rear view mirror toward her and checked her look.

"Oh my gosh," she said, alarmed by her own reflection.

"Take the wheel a minute will ya Jay," she asked letting go, without waiting for a reply.

She fixed her short hair by combing it with her hand, and then picked up a tissue from the seat and dabbed the tears from the corners of her eyes.

"You're a real piece of work Kathy, I don't know how you managed to make it to the ripe old age of 33," Jay lamented.

"*32, I'm 32 Jay!*"

"Yeah, *whatever*"

"Just for the record though, you were 32 last year. I remember because that lamer Jordan surprised you with 32 roses at your desk in front of everyone and you didn't speak to him for a week!"

"I laughed my ass off. I never did understand your attraction to that wiener anyway. Especially not with all of this available to you," Jay said, holding the steering wheel with his left hand and waving his right down the length of his body. KC turned her head slowly toward her best friend and gave him the evil eye.

"I'm 32 Jay, **GET IT?**"

"Meooooww," Jay replied, letting loose of the wheel and sliding back to his side of the car.

"And for *your* information, Jordan is ancient history. That was a low blow by the way, I told you my *friend* was visiting. We're supposed to have an understanding during times like these, right? It's you be nice to me, and I won't *KILL YOU!*"

"Peace, I stand corrected on both counts," Jay replied, raising both hands to surrender. KC nodded and returned her full attention to the road. They remained silent until she pulled into the long dirt driveway that led to the Lopez home.

"We're here," KC said as they drove slowly along the rural access road.

"Good thing we stopped in Gilroy and had the car washed," Jay teased while he cranked up the window to keep the cloud of dust from filling the inside of the car.

KC decided not to react to his little breach of their truce and kept her eyes on the road. Jay removed a pack of Juicy Fruit from his pocket and offered KC a stick of gum. She nodded her head and signaled for him to unwrap it for her. Then she opened her mouth and Jay stuck the gum between her teeth.

"Thanks"

"My pleasure"

As they pulled up near the house KC noticed that the Donnelly's were here as well, she recognized their big Cadillac El Dorado parked in front. Arthur Donnelly broke the unwritten law that only small men drive all big ass cars. At six feet four inches a car that size actually suited the man. KC pulled up behind the big Chevy and shut off the engine.

"Remember Jay, only shoot group photos of the family. No pictures of Tina alone, not even one of me and her together," KC reminded her photographer.

"Yeah, yeah, I got it. *I don't get it,* but I got it," said Jay sarcastically. With that said, the two of them walked up to the front porch and climbed the three steps to the door. Alma Donnelly answered the door on the first knock, opening the wooden screen to let them into the house.

"Hello KC dear, so nice to see you again," Alma said, placing her hands on KC's shoulders and busing her on each cheek.

"I'm sorry dear, I don't believe I know your friend," Alma continued, nodding toward Jay.

"Excuse my manners Mrs. Donnelly, this is my associate Jay Namura," KC said politely.

"Mr. Namura, a pleasure I'm sure," Alma said, extending her hand for Jay to shake.

"*Jay*, please, and the pleasure's all mine," he replied as he took her hand and shook in gently.

"Well, come on in and meet everybody else, won't you," Alma asked, taking Jay by the arm and leading him toward the small living room.

"Come along dear," she said over her shoulder to KC. Jay looked back over his own shoulder at her, "She called me your *friend*," he teased in a whisper.

"SHUT UP," KC mouthed at him, threatening him with a clenched fist!

After all of the introductions were finished, the small crowd seated themselves around the table for supper. Victor took his place at the head of the table to proudly preside over the little gathering.

"Senor, would you like to say the blessing," he respectfully asked of Arthur Donnelly?

"Oh no Victor, this is your home, please by all means," Arthur answered with equal respect.

Victor reached up and took the hand of the people seated beside him, and everyone did likewise in preparation for saying grace. Jay leaned in close to KC and whispered in her ear.

"I'm not sure the Buddha would approve of this little bit of treason," he teased. KC stomped on his foot with the heel of her pump and Jay instantly bowed his head and bit his lips, stifling the scream that was about to escape his mouth.

"Father God, we thank you for this meal we are about to receive. We thank you for the many blessings that you grant us, for each may we be truly grateful. We thank you for the health of everyone here tonight. And we thank you for the love that you give to us, to wear and to share. Lord, for all of these things and more we offer praise and thanksgiving. In Christ's name we pray, amen," Victor said, his enunciation nearly perfect. He only rolled his R's on the word receive. Then KC genuflected along with everyone, else except Jay who drew the line at symbolism, and they all repeated the *amen* part right after Victor.

"Let's EAT," exclaimed Gilbert in a squeaky voice. He was seated on a stack of telephone books right next to his mother.

"Quiet *mijo*," Maria said softly, playfully scolding her anxious and hungry son.

They all enjoyed a bountiful meal that featured a collision of two cultures. There were taquitos, rice and beans served along side of fried chicken, mashed potatoes and gravy, sweet baby peas and corn on the cob. Add in the iced tea and the coffee and peach cobbler afterward and it was a veritable feast!

The conversation remained light during the meal and Jay did manage to get up and take a few candid group shots of everyone sitting around the table and enjoying themselves. He even let Victor snap a couple, which was a major coup for Jay as he was positively anal about his equipment! KC noticed that Arthur and Alma were more like family than employers, and how much the children seemed to love them. It was the main reason that she had agreed to all of the secrecy in the first place. Her naturally blabby instincts had been trumped by Alma Donnelly's sincerity that day nearly a year ago when they had first met together at the Donnelly home.

KC looked over at Tina who was seated next to her father. The little girl had not said a word during supper, but she didn't appear to be upset either. However KC's sixth sense told her that something was amiss, that something was on the child's mind. She didn't have to wait long to investigate her instinct. While Alma and Maria cleared the table and the men went onto the front porch to stretch, belch, and Lord knows what else, Tina came over to her and took her hand. She didn't say any words, but with her eyes asked KC to follow her. They went through the kitchen and out the back door, and out into the small yard. Tina looked back over her shoulder and waived at her mother who was watching them from the kitchen window. The two of them walked up to the tire swing hanging from a thick low branch on the elm tree near the garage. Tina let go of KC's hand and jumped up into the middle of the swing. She twirled around in it for a minute or so, and then dragged her shoes on the grass, slowing herself to a stop. She looked at KC as she lay on her stomach inside the tire. Then she reached behind her back and removed an envelope from the back pocket of her jeans, and she held it out to KC.

"I got this," she said in a voice smaller than her age.

"I see that, what is it," KC asked sweetly?

"It's a letter silly," said Tina, looking at KC like she might be a little slow.

"Oh, do you want me to read it to you?"

"*No*, mama said that I should show it to you."

"She did?"

"Yes"

"Have you read it?"

"Yes"

"Who is it from?"

"From the burned up man."

"What did he say?"

Tina didn't answer right away. She just kicked at the ground and started to twirl the swing again.

"Tina, what did the man say?"

"I don't know"

KC reached over and stopped the swing from twirling. Why was this fifteen-year-old kid acting like a five-year-old? She held out her hand and Tina gave the letter to her. KC looked back at the house and saw Maria working at the sink and watching them through the window.

"Aunt Alma says we can't show the letter to Papa," said Tina matter of factly.

KC did not reply, she just walked over to a set of lawn chairs under the elm tree and sat down in the nearest one. She looked at the envelope and her heart sank when she read the return address.

"*What fresh Hell is this,*" she whispered out loud.

KC opened the envelope and pulled out the one page letter and read silently to herself. When she finished she looked back at the house and then read the letter again. When she finished the second time she leaned back in the lawn chair and was startled to discover that Alma and Maria were seated in the two chairs across from her.

"What do you make of that," asked Alma?

"I don't know what to think Mrs. Donnelly, but I can understand why you don't want to show it to Victor," KC said, rubbing her temples with one hand and handing the letter to Alma with the other.

"It wasn't threatening or inappropriate in any way other than it was sent to her at all. But it did give me the *heebie jeebies*, I can't explain it, but it did?"

"You know, it was actually quite sweet in a way, almost loving. WAIT, that's what's so weird, he loves her! *Oh my God, he loves her,*" KC exclaimed in a harsh whisper.

"***Yes***, that's what I was reading between the lines as well," Mrs. Donnelly agreed, slapping her knee with the hand that held the letter!

"*Aye Dios mio,*" Maria said, rocking in her chair and wrenching a dishtowel in her hands. Tina walked over to her mother and crawled up into her lap. She looked over at KC and smiled.

"He won't hurt me like the others," she said softly.

"What sweetie," KC asked, looking back at the girl?

Tina pulled the gold cross and chain from her mother's blouse and fiddled with it.

"He won't hurt me like the others," she repeated.

KC got up and strode quickly over to Maria and Tina. She knelt down in front of the chair and reached out and abruptly took the cross and chain from the little girl's hands, causing Tina to look back at KC and frown. KC took hold of Tina's shoulders roughly and turned her towards herself. The two of them stared at one another intently while Maria and Alma looked on puzzled.

"Why do you say that Tina," KC demanded?

KC realized at once that she had frightened the child and she immediately relaxed her tone and unscrewed her face, letting go of Tina at the same time.

"I'm sorry honey," she said apologizing.

"Sweetheart, why do you say that he won't hurt you? Who won't hurt you?"

"The burned up man," Tina said calmly, looking KC directly in the eye without blinking her eyes even once. KC almost gasped out loud and looked back over her shoulder at Alma Donnelly who had raised her own hand to her mouth to silence herself as well.

"Honey, why did the burned up man write to you," KC pressed gently?

Tina didn't answer. She just looked at KC for a full two minutes. It was an uncomfortable pause, but KC kept silent, she felt an answer coming.

"That day, the day that Jesus asked me to pray with the burned up man, and I did, Papa said it was OK. Then it got hot, it got really, really hot and I sweated and then I got sleepy. When I woke up, Mama was with me and we went home. The burned up man was crying, but he wasn't burned up no more," Tina said smiling as she recounted the day at the hospital.

She picked up her mother's crucifix and began fiddling with it again. The three adults sat speechless for a couple minutes. There didn't seem to be much else to say, nobody had a clue as to what Tina was trying to communicate or what Dr. Katz's letter really meant, not a clue.

"He wants me to come see him, he needs to know something, I have to tell him something," Tina said suddenly, breaking the silence. KC looked at the child puzzled.

"What baby, what does he want to know, what do you have to tell him?"

Tina let go of the cross and chain and it fell back into Maria's blouse. Tina leaned forward towards KC, bending and flexing her index finger repeatedly at the joints, indicating for KC to scoot in closer. Katherine Littleton moved in close to the girl, they were face-to-face, nearly nose-to-nose. Tina reached up to KC's face and placed her hands on her cheeks, pushing them in slightly so that KC involuntarily made a fish face. Tina leaned in further and kissed KC on her forehead, a slow, soft, loving, kiss. Not a child's kiss, it was more like a mother's kiss, it made KC feel awkward. Then she pulled back away a little and looked into KC's eyes saying sweetly, "All better."

KC started to say something when she suddenly realized that the terrible cramps that she had been suffering from ever since she got her period in Gilroy, nearly six and a half hours ago, *were gone!* Not just feeling better gone either, *but gone-gone*, like they had never existed gone. She hadn't felt this relaxed since before puberty, this was too weird? She looked at Tina and she was smiling at her.

"Will you take me to see the burned up man?" the girl asked.

KC swallowed hard and replied.

"Why honey, why do you want to go see this man," KC pleaded.

Tina leaned in close to KC's face again.

"It's a secret..."

Twenty-four

(…"Saturday nights the night for fightin, get a little
action in"… Elton John & Bernie Taupin)

<u>*Manhattan, New York, March 1973*</u>

"You are new to this city are you not Missy," the cab driver asked, trying to make eye contact with his passenger via the rear view mirror?

His quiet passenger remained silent, staring out the window at the passing cavalcade of bright lights and neon signs. The driver reached back with his hand and rapped on a Plexiglas barrier laden with holes like a piece of Swiss cheese, that separated the front from the back.

"***HEY***, did you not hear me *missy nurse?*"

Carla Cardinale looked up, startled by the sudden noise.

"Sorry, I guess I was daydreaming," she apologized, smiling meekly.

"Not to worry Missy, I just asked if you were new here, that is all," the driver replied, smiling back at her with his eyes.

"*Oh, right*, I guess it shows doesn't it," she answered, sitting up straight in her seat as if appearing more alert would make her feel more like a local.

Actually, this was only her second cab ride since arriving in the city. Her maiden voyage had been from JFK to the Stanley Arms, and her new apartment on east 78th street, better than a month ago. Newly board certified Dr. Carla Cardinale had spent the last four weeks transitioning into her new job at Manhattan General, working the dayshift while she got the lay of the land. But the honeymoon was over, and tonight she was starting her new rotation on perennial *'new guy'* shift, graveyard, 9pm to 9am. She had been warned ahead of time that the hours were going to be brutal. But she had already had a taste of that during her tour in Nam. And she knew that she would learn more tricks and practice more medicine on this shift than in the cushy daylight hours. She could have stayed in LA to earn her stripes, but Carla needed a change of scenery, of the people in her life. She could no longer deal with the fact that the people she had known all her life saw her in a different light after she came home from the war. She didn't feel different but they all made her feel as though she must be.

"Fuck em," she remembered saying to herself one morning during her senior year while riding the bus from Westwood to Sherman Oaks.

And the very next day she applied for a post at Manhattan General in New York. Sure it was a bold impetuous move, but that was normal for Carla now days. *Hmmm*, maybe she had changed, maybe it was just time to leave the nest. Besides, this hospital was the Mecca for all hard-core ER physicians, and perfect for a combat experienced former nurse turned doctor!

"This is NEW YORK CITY child!" chief resident, Dr. Kendra Kwazie had told her on the day she got her new assignment.

"And dust to dawn belongs to the freaks! It's when they all come out to play their nasty little games, you just wait and see."

"You know, I thought that I had seen it all, with all the foolishness back home in South Africa. But *no sir*, this is the real jungle!"

"The predators here are far more terrifying than lions and what not," said the statuesque doctor.

She accented her point by stabbing her index finger at Carla, and retracting her middle finger back as if pulling a trigger, then letting her thumb fall as if it were the hammer of a pistol. Hence the taxicab tonight, Carla had decided that she would be taking a cab to and from work no matter what the cost! She would eat corn flake sandwiches every day if she had to so that she could afford this luxurious bit of self-preservation. No way was she going walk three blocks **to** the subway station and then three more blocks at the **other end**. New York City was scary enough in the daylight; it could be down right terrifying after dark! And Carla was no shrinking violet, not by a long shot, but let's face it, growing up a *valley girl* in Encino California had not prepared her for all of this action!

"It is OK young woman, Ravi will take good care of you," said the jolly cab driver, laughing loudly as he did so.

"Ahhh, thanks, *Mr...?*"

"Just Ravi, that is all. And what can I call you little one?"

"Carla, nice to meet you Ravi," she answered, smiling back at his eyes in the mirror.

"Hello Carla, the pleasure is mine I am sure. You are a nurse at hospital, *yes?*"

"Not quite, I'm a doctor actually, I work in the emergency room," Carla said, showing off just a little bit.

"*Oh my goodness gracious*, please forgive me doctor, I did not know," Ravi said apologizing in earnest.

"No problem, it's an easy mistake I suppose, I mean I was a nurse for quite a while," she said, accepting his cute apology.

"May I ask you a personal question Ravi?"

"Yes of course," he replied happily.

"Is that an Indian accent I detect?"

"Oh gosh golly, no," *he said alarmingly.*

"No, no, no, no, no...I am Pakistani you see," Ravi said correcting her, pointing at his green card that was swinging from his rear view mirror.

"I'm *so* sorry, I meant no offense, really, I was just curious, I assumed that Ravi was an Indian name," said Carla, apologizing with a run on sentence.

"None taken dear girl. Do not be so silly!"

"*OK*, we are here Miss Doctor Carla," Ravi announced.

Carla opened her purse to take out the twenty that she had budgeted for the cab ride. Ravi rapped on the Plexiglas as he watched her fumble through her bag.

"*No, No* Missy, the first ride is my pleasure, welcome to the neighborhood," said the happy cabbie, as he turned in his seat to properly smile at his new friend. Carla was taken aback by his generous offer and she quickly replied, "**Oh no Ravi**, I don't want to get you into any trouble, please take the money," she said holding the bill up to the glass. Ravi put his hand up and assured her that all was well.

"I am an *independence* contractor, so there are no worries Doctor Carla. Perhaps you will ask for Ravi whenever you need a ride in the future days," he replied proudly. Carla *snap* folded the bill and creased it crisply. She winked at her new Pakistani friend and said.

"You can count on it Ravi, you're now my official yellow cab chauffeur!"

"Very good then, *bye-bye Dr. Carla*," Ravi replied, giving her a two-fingered scout salute as he turned to leave.

"Bye Ravi, and thank you so much, you made my day!"

Carla gathered her purse and coat and exited the taxi. She waived to Ravi as he pulled away from the curb and then she turned and raced through the cold night air up the walkway toward the hospital ER entrance.

Finn's Bar & Grill, East 76th Street NYC

The Yanks were down three to nothing in the sixth inning, and they weren't playing well enough to give Sean a warm fuzzy that they might still catch the Sox tonight. He picked up his whiskey and downed it quickly, setting the heavy shot glass back on the bar top hard enough to attract the bartender's attention.

"Want another Mr. Andrews," the bartender asked politely?

"Nah, don't think so Ernie, I'm going to call it a night I think," Sean replied, reaching into his coat pocket for his wallet. He dug out a fifty-dollar bill and placed it on the bar.

"Why so early, we're only in the sixth, plenty of time for the bombers to come back," Ernie said, scooping up the bill with his right hand, his left hand following closely with an expert swoop of a terrycloth bar rag.

"I'll get your change," Ernie said walking toward the register.

"Keep it *buddy boy*, you know I don't carry anything less than a twenty in my billfold," Sean said, winking back at him.

"And by the by, there's no way the Yanks are gonna catch the Sox tonight, Tiant's on fire, he's struck out 10 already and it's only the sixth, *we're doomed I tell you!*" Sean lamented, reluctantly praising the RedSox ace Louis Tiant.

"Yeah, I guess you're right, I wish that guy would have stayed in Cleveland! Why did he have to come out here and fuck up our playground anyway," Ernie said disgustedly.

Sean smiled to himself as he returned his wallet to his coat pocket.

"Good thing Ethan Kelly isn't here to see this shellacking, it would kill him!" he said softly to himself, suddenly missing his old college roommate.

Sean had actually thought of Ethan quite often over the years, and wished that he had stayed in closer touch. But life is funny that way, just when you feel the most comfortable the winds of change swirl around and rearrange things *as they are* to things *as they will be*. The war had taken Ethan one-way and sent Sean in another. While his best friend had answered the call to serve, even with his deeply personal objections and moral hindrances, Sean had drifted in with the anti-war crowd. Nothing militant mind you, but active dissent nonetheless.

He had marched in Boston, New York and Washington, he had *sat-in* with various groups at campuses up and down the eastern seaboard, and he had written letter after letter to congressmen and senators, even LBJ himself. Sean smiled to himself as he remembered how he used to send a fifty-cent piece in every letter to the President. It was Scotch taped to an index card that read, *"see if you can get the barber to trim those ears next time, it's on me!"* His new cause had consumed so much of his time it was a miracle that he was able to graduate at all. But graduate he did, and with honors none the less. "You're the *only* smart one in *this* room," Ethan used to say whenever he was struggling with his studies, especially mathematics. Sean smiled, remembering his poor friend's pouting face resting on his folded arms, while he lay atop a stack of geometry texts and yellow quad paper. Ethan would just stare at him until he looked up from whatever he was doing and offer to help. Sean sometimes wondered which Irish curse was the worst. *Being too stubborn to ask for help or being too pig-headed to admit that you needed it?*

"You OK Mr. Andrews," Ernie asked as he walked up to him from the other side of the bar?

Sean was leaning forward, his elbows on the bar with his chin resting on top of his laced fingers. Startled, he leaned back and sat up straight.

"*What? **Ahem**,* yeah, no worries Ernie-san, just daydreaming I guess," he replied, just a little embarrassed for being caught lollygagging.

He scooted the barstool back a foot and stood up. He grabbed the lapels of his sport coat and gave them a good tug, making sure the fit was right. Sean looked up into the big mirror behind the bar and checked his look, running his hand back through his blond hair, frowning as he noticed that he could use a trim.

"See ya Ernie," he said, turning to leave.

"Yeah, see ya Mr. Andrews," the bartender replied, giving the standard male head bob to accent the farewell.

"*YEAH, see ya SALLY,*" said a chorus of voices from a booth in the corner. Sean stopped and turned to acknowledge the left-handed salutation, and noticed the three guys in the booth for the first time.

Two of them looked like they had just got off of work, from some Wall Street firm maybe. They were dressed impeccably in their vested pin striped Brooks Brothers suits. No doubt there were two pairs of fine Italian leather resting on their pampered dogs under the table as well. They were also wearing the universally recognized '*we make loads of money, so we're better than you*' smart-ass grins on their gobs. "Oh oh," Sean muttered as he remembered another set of Irish curses he heard somewhere while growing up, "*always assume a snickering man is laughing at you're expense, and never join a donnybrook without tossing the first punch!*" The third of the trio was not like his two dandy friends. This one looked rough and tumble, like a cop or a fireman, definitely blue collar. Sean could tell by the way that he carried himself, and by the steely predator's gaze he wore. There was no fear or hesitation in his look, just anticipation. Sean already liked this fella, pity he was going to have to mess him up!

"Were you talking to me fellas?"

The large steely-eyed fella looked up at Sean from the booth. He studied him a second or two while he drank from his half empty schooner of beer.

He took a long pull on the beer and then set the heavy mug down on the table in front of him.

"We were talking to the Sox loving queer dissing the Yanks and kissing Louis Tiant's ass," said the big man with the crew cut and thick Bronx accent.

He twisted around in the booth and swung his legs out over the end of the seat and stood up. Sean watched him stand up slowly, realizing immediately that he had just bitten off more than he could chew. The fella was six feet five if he was an inch, and he had shoulders wide enough to drape a Persian rug over and then beat it clean with a baseball bat. The big guy folded his beefy arms in front of him and looked Sean up and down carefully.

"*Yep*, that would be you!"

The two Wall Street twins picked up their schooners clinked them together and then tipped them toward Sean in a mock salute. Sean put his hands on his hips, blew out a large puff of air as he sighed deeply. He looked back over his shoulder at Ernie behind the bar. The stout bartender raised his hands and shook his head.

"Don't do it Sean, just go on home buddy," Ernie implored wisely.

"Don't do what Sally?" chided the big man.

"Will ya be dancing for us then Paddy," he added mockingly, turning to walk back to the table. He sit back down across from his friends.

Ernie dropped his head quickly as if it had just been unhinged, his chin resting flush against his chest. He put both hands onto the bar and shook his head slowly. He had seen these kinds of situations played out many times before and he knew all too well what was coming next.

Sean took a step back while the three men, *check that*, while the *fancy boys* and the *big ape* enjoyed a good laugh at his expense. He reached behind the bar and took hold of the beverage dispenser and placed his finger over the end of the nozzle. He squeezed the trigger and sent a long stream of soda water spraying across the aisle toward the three agitators, dousing them good. **NOW** *IT WAS ON!* The three tough guys were soaking wet as they exited the booth with uncommon speed and descended on Sean and his makeshift fire hose. Sean's last conscious memory was the sight of the largest fist in recorded history tracking straight and normal directly toward the bridge of his nose...***LIGHTS OUT!***

Manhattan General Hospital, 10:30pm

"What have got," asked Dr. Carla Cardinale, as the gurney whisked by her on the way to trauma room number three?

"Looks like the losing side in a bar room brawl at *Finn's* over on east 76th."

"Let's see, we got a broken nose, a broken clavicle, multiple contusions, and a couple of missing teeth. Actually, they're not missing, he's still holding them in his right hand!" Carla said with a smile.

"We couldn't get him to turn them loose, like they were the crown jewels or something," the paramedic said as he retracted the side rails of the gurney to prepare to transfer the patient to the treatment table. Carla raced up to join the two paramedics and the triage nurse, Susan Billings, in trauma room three and helped them move the poor man from the gurney to the table.

"On my count…one, two, three," she said and the four of them skillfully scooted the patient onto the table, dragging him by the sheet he was resting on.

Carla gently pulled his swollen eyelids back and flicked a pen light at each eye, watching as the pupils dilated and mentally measuring their responsiveness. Nurse Billings busied herself by attaching the BP sleeve around his arm while Dr. Cardinale went ahead and re-took the man's pulse. She carefully examined his bruised nose and then gently pulled back his upper lip to get a good look at the damage to his smile. He had lost two teeth all right, the two front ones, and she pulled in her lips and bit down on them gently, quickly raising her hand to hide the grin that was forming as she reacted to the goofy face he was making involuntarily.

"*You poor man,*" she said under her breath as she let go of his lip, returning a little bit of dignity to her half conscious patient.

She waited while the paramedic cut open the injured man's shirt and then jumped in to examine his torso for signs of broken ribs and internal trauma. She pushed on him, rolling him onto his side, checking his back and flanks as well. He was clear of any *visible* injuries and the exam of his abdomen did not produce any outward signs of internal bleeding.

"Not *too* bad," she said.

"Looks like whoever did this number on him was concentrating on wiping the smile off of his face," Carla said, shrugging her shoulders.

"He's coming around," announced Nurse Billings, doing her best to hold his hands down on the table as he wrestled with consciousness and unconsciousness.

He groaned, and tried to speak, but understandably, he was having considerable difficulty what with the split lip and missing teeth. It sounded more like he was whistling a tune than saying any words.

"Take it easy pal," Carla said softly but sternly, while she maneuvered her stethoscope around his chest and abdomen, listening as he breathed for telltale signs of leaks and airway restrictions.

"*HEY*, does this guy have a name," she shouted over her shoulder to the two paramedics who were gathering their gear and filling out paperwork?

"Yeah, *umm*, just a sec, yeah, here it is, Andrews, Sean Patrick Andrews," the taller of the two paramedics answered. Sean started to groan and squirm on the table again, trying to get Carla's attention.

"Don't try and talk just yet Mr. Andrews, let us work here, OK," said Carla sweetly, doing her best to calm the frustrated man.

Nurse Billings raised her left hand to scratch the itch on her twitching nose. As soon as she let go of Sean's arm he raised his own hand and gently touched Carla's cheek.

"Call me *Shthhhean* darlin, call me *Shthhhean*," he mumbled and lisped, a weak, pitiful, toothless grin spreading across his sad but cute face.

"*Oh that's just great!* **Susan**, a little help here," Carla called out to Nurse Billings!

"Exactly how drunk was this guy when you picked him up anyway," Carla asked the paramedic team while she continued to administer treatment to her patient?

The two men shrugged at one another invoking the turtle defense, as their necks disappeared between their shoulder blades. Their faces turned into question marks before one of them finally responded. "Beats me," said the smaller paramedic.

"But that's not an alcohol high he's on. We gave him a little dose of morphine in the field. The guy was just a real a mess."

"Yeah, it was a three on one beating he took. When we rolled on the scene the cops were cuffing and scuffing a gorilla with a crew cut and stuffing him into a squad car with two other guys," the larger paramedic added. Carla looked down at her patient and gently moved a lock of blond hair away from his face.

"You're going to be OK fella, I promise," she said softly, looking at the glistening blue eyes that were barely visible behind the swollen tissue surrounding them. Nurse Billings leaned in closer to take a closer look at the patient herself.

"You know what, he's gonna turn out to be pretty cute once we get him cleaned up and a dentist fixes that smile," she said, nodding approvingly.

Susan Billings gently wiped Sean's face with a cool wet cloth, smiling at Carla as she did so. Sean was responding to their care and tried to keep his eyes open and his mind alert, at least as much as he could under the circumstances. He stared up at the two women while they worked. He focused much of his attention on Carla and it was starting to bug her a little. Although his freshly stitched split lip was preventing him from talking, his eyes were managing to send her a clear message.

"*Oh brother*! Why do I attract all the Romeos," she whined.

She scribbled some notes onto Sean's chart, and made a mental note to remember this guy's name, and check in on him later. Anyone who could survive a beating like this, maintain a sense of humor, **and** still have the nads to zoom a pretty girl, was someone she wanted to know!

"Nitey-nite Mr. Andrews, I'll look in on you a little later my dear, but first we need to get to the big finish here," she said, as she administered a small morphine booster, mostly to put him out for the night, but also to spare him the shock of this last phase of his ER experience. As soon as he drifted away to dreamland Carla picked up the tools of the trade and prepared to begin the last procedure.

"*OK champ, **now**, let's see about re-setting this busted beezer!*"

Twenty-five

(..."A prudent man sees evil and hides himself. The naïve proceed and pay the penalty"... Proverbs 27:12)

Fresno, California, June 1970
Superior Court, Division Two

The trial would end much sooner than anyone would have expected. Actually, given the near total absence of any real defense, it would last significantly longer than it needed to. Certainly longer than the accused, *soon to be convicted*, Dr. Murray Katz would have hoped. He had started the proceedings by totally dumbfounding his court appointed attorney by insisting that he enter a plea of guilty to all charges.

"Your Honor, against my better judgment and vehement legal counsel to the contrary, my client wishes to plead guilty to all charges, specific and non specific. Further, the defendant requests that he receive the maximum sentence provided for under the law, and that said sentence be carried out immediately," said an exasperated Peter Roland.

He removed his stylish wire rimmed glasses and held them in his clasped hands in front of him, and waited for the Judge to respond. He didn't have to wait long.

"*NOW SEE HERE COUNSELOR*, I will not have my courtroom turned into a three ring circus while your client grabs for a few cheap headlines at my expense!" said the Honorable, and visibly irritated Benjamin Davis.

"*And you sir*, you will stand before this court and show these proceedings the proper amount of respect! *Do I make myself clear?*" Judge Davis continued, hurling his instructions regarding courtroom decorum at Dr. Katz, who then rose slowly in response to the Judge's demands.

"My apologies Your Honor, I was under the impression that a condemned man needn't bother with mere formalities," Dr. Katz said as acridly as possible.

"*That will be quite enough back sass from you sir!* One more disrespectful comment and I'll have the bailiff muzzle you until you learn some manners!" bellowed Judge Davis.

He stared at the two men for a moment, waiting for the courtroom to become completely silent before proceeding. After a couple of long minutes Judge Davis cleared his throat as he sorted through a stack of manila folders on the bench in front of him.

"That's better," he said without looking up from his busy work.

"No none will be tried and sentenced here today without due process, I hope everyone is clear on that issue?" Judge Davis said, looking up slowly at the courtroom from over the tops of his bifocals.

"Mr. Roland, I am ordering you to sit back down with your client and explain to him that it is in his best interest as well as the best interest of our judicial system that he fully understand the charges against him and then reconsider his plea."

"Yes Your Honor."

"So ordered then."

"Excuse me Your Honor, may I speak?" asked the defendant.

"*No Dr. Katz you may not!*" Judge Davis said, leaning forward on his elbows and glaring at the defendant.

"I want you to sit with your legal counsel and listen closely to what he has to say. I want you to understand that this is a court of law where you will be tried based on the facts regarding the charges brought against you. In this court we will weigh these facts, submitted as evidence in the People's case against you. Here, in this court, *justice will be served!*"

Dr. Katz sat motionless and glared back at the pontificating judge. A smile started to slowly spread across the defendant's face. He could see that he had hit his mark with the gesture and that it was getting the best of the proud but agitated little man in the big black robe.

"I see what you're doing sir, and let me tell you, *I'm too old a dog to fetch that bone!*" Judge Davis quipped, a slight grin appearing on his own face.

"You may very well receive the guilty verdict you seek. You may even receive the harsh punishment that you seek as well. But not without due process, it's the most basic right under the law. And no matter how heinous the charge, EVERYONE is afforded this right. It works for ALL or it works for NO ONE!"

"Do you understand my meaning Dr. Katz?"

"Perfectly"

"Very well, Mr. Roland, you will have ten days to confer with your client and prepare a proper defense."

"Yes Your Honor, thank you sir," replied the attorney, nervously.

"Excuse me Your Honor, point of law if I may," Dr. Katz said quietly from his chair.

Judge Davis looked back at the defendant. He rubbed his mouth with his left hand and then folded his hands in front of him, resting them on the bench.

"What is it now Dr. Katz?" the Judge asked slowly.

"Your Honor, as I understand it, I believe that I am within my rights to fire my attorney for cause, am I not?" Dr. Katz asked.

"Sir, what possible cause could you have for firing this man *this* early in your attorney/client relationship?"

"He's too good Your Honor."

"What?"

"*He's too good*, and I'm fearful that he may find a way for me to avoid justice, and miss the punishment that I rightfully deserve." Dr. Katz explained calmly. Judge Davis sighed audibly and chewed his lower lip slightly before he responded.

"I thought that I had made myself clear earlier Dr. Katz?"

"You let the judicial process deal with the issue of justice, *OK*."

"If it's absolution you seek, save it for your Priest, *or Rabbi in your case.* What the Almighty does with you on the other side is not a concern of this court!"

"Your request is denied! Bailiff, remove the prisoner from the courtroom. *Next case!*" Judge Davis said, dismissing them with just a quick waive of his arm.

With that gesture the courtroom settled down while the defendant and his counsel exited through the side entrance behind the bailiff's desk and into the catacombs of the Superior Court building, where Dr. Katz would be held until after the crowd of reporters, *print and television journalists alike*, thinned out enough for the defendant to be transported discretely to an undisclosed location. Not soon enough as far as Sheriff's Deputy Glenn Grady was concerned, as he was anxious to get home to his family. It had been a long day, and he hated this detail. Besides, this Katz fella gave him the *willies*! He had, ever since the first time he laid eyes on him, back when he had rushed that Lopez woman and her kid over to the County Trauma Center to catch up with her missing husband. That was over a year ago he remembered to himself, during which time he had heard it all.

About the circumstances surrounding the doctor's miraculous recovery, that is. About the Lopez girl and the things that people said she had done, about the things they said she could do. And about the near fanatical protection that Sheriff Cardwell provided for this child. Sheriff Cardwell had spoken everyone who had been there on that day, *personally*. And everyone, *one and all*, had kept the faith where the Lopez girl was concerned, or at least so far as he knew. Deputy Grady glanced in at Dr. Katz through the wire-screened window in the heavy oak door. The doctor was seated in a thick-armed oak chair, his wrists handcuffed to a waist chain, and the waist chain handcuffed to the chair. Grady studied him intently, *"What are you thinking,"* he wondered out loud from his side of the door. Dr. Katz stared at the table without looking up while Deputy Grady watched him through the window. He shifted his eyes left without moving his head and studied the Deputy from the corner of his eye. *"What are you thinking?"* he wondered out loud from his side of the door.

Bakersfield, California, June 1970
Our Lady of Grace, Sanitarium

"How are you this afternoon Rosa?" asked Dr. Fishman, as he seated himself on the sofa next to her.

"I feel great Dr. Lloyd, look, I'm almost finished with this sweater for my little girl," Rosa replied, holding up the tiny sweater that she was crocheting.

"That's terrific my dear, I'm sure it will be a perfect fit!" he said encouragingly.

"How old is she now?" the doctor asked, keeping the dialog moving.

"Oh, she'll be four in December," she replied.

"She is my miracle baby," she added as she went back to crocheting.

"Yes dear, all babies are little miracles aren't they," Dr. Fishman said as he leaned back on the sofa and crossed his legs, totally unaware of how literal Rosa had been with her comment.

"Rosa, I want to chat with you a little about your hearing with the review board yesterday, would that be alright with you?"

"Yes, I guess so," she replied.

"Do you remember what we talked about during the hearing?"

"Yes"

"Can you tell me exactly what you remember?"

"Yes"

"Alright then, tell me what you remember," said the doctor.

"You said that I have been good, and that I am much better now. You said that maybe I could move to a new place where my little girl and my family could come visit me whenever they wanted. That I could live with other girls and go to school and maybe go home when I finish," Rosa recited.

"Very good, what else did we talk about?"

"We talked about being a good mother, and a good daughter, and a good sister. We talked about that day when that man made me loose my mind. We talked about God and forgiveness and we talked about the law and justice," she continued. Rosa set her crochet needles and material down into her lap and looked over at Dr. Fishman. They held each other's gaze for a moment.

"I know what I did was wrong doctor. I know how lucky I am to have this chance to make things right for myself and for my baby. And I am grateful for all the hard work and support that you and the others have provided to me," she said looking directly into his eyes.

"*Madre Dios Dr. Lloyd*, I am truly blessed that this man did not die by my hand," Rosa said, leaning closer to the doctor, looking past him as if he weren't really there.

"Why do you say that?"

"Because, I will not lose my soul doctor"

"She's come to me twice now. First for my Rena, and now for me," Rosa said softly, a small tear escaping her eye.

"Who has come to you Rosa? What exactly do you mean?" Dr. Fishman asked confused.

"The angel Doctor, the angel," she replied with a smile.

"Oh, *I see*, well, I will admit you have had some lucky breaks under the circumstances. Perhaps it's reasonable to assume that there has been a certain amount of divine intervention supporting your providence," Dr. Fishman said, appearing a little uncomfortable with his statement.

Rosa returned to her crocheting and smiled at the doctor. She may not have understood all of his big words, but she was keenly aware of the absence of faith on his part, but she could also sense his curiosity about the strength of hers. It's said that curiosity will inspire study and that study may encourage experience and that experience might lead to knowledge, whereby knowledge and experience combined could yield true wisdom. It's in wisdom where faith is strong.

"Well, thank you for chatting with me today Rosa."

"Of course Dr. Lloyd, you are my doctor, *no?*"

"Yes, I am"

"Rosa, it may take a few days, protocol you know. But I wanted to be the one to tell you that the review board has decided to grant your attorney's petition to transfer you to a minimum-security institution. I suspect that you will be relocating soon, perhaps a just a few weeks," Dr. Fishman said as he reached over to pat his patient gently on her shoulder. Rosa Hernandez continued to work on her daughter's new sweater, pausing only long enough to glance over at Dr. Fishman and nod her head.

"Yes, well, I'll leave you to your crocheting and get on with my rounds. I am very happy for you Rosa, you've come a log way in so short a time, I'm proud of you!" he said, as he stood to walk away.

"Thank you doctor," replied Rosa without looking up.

As the doctor rounded the corner and disappeared, Rosa set her crochet needles back down in her lap. She raised herself just enough to be able to reach under the cushion that she was seating on and pulled out the newspaper. The paper was turned to page twelve and folded to reveal a circled article by Katherine Littleton. Rosa had read the week old newspaper at least a dozen times.

"KATZ Trial Begins AT LAST," the title of the column read.

This woman Katherine Littleton seemed to be talking about someone other than the doctor that Rosa knew. This man, so pious and repentant, this was not the monster who had fathered her child. This was not the same man who cursed at her right up to the moment that she set him on fire. She worried about the article's message, its central question, *'how much forgiveness'.*

Rosa's faith was being tested while Satan worked in her head, tempting her with schemes to allow her a second chance to take her revenge. For two years she had played the role of the dimwitted remorseful wetback that she was certain everyone saw her as. She had let Satan twist her mind into knots and choke off her compassion, replacing it with cunning and a single purpose. Now, the fruits of her deception were soon to be realized with her eminent transfer to a minimal security institution back in Fresno. Once there she would be able to see her family before she finished what she started, ridding the world of that bastard *KATZ!* And this time she'd remain close by and make sure that he stayed dead! Rosa's faith was still strong as ever, only now it was in her own deadly precision. She got up, hid the newspaper inside her straw crochet bag and walked quietly back to her room.

Fresno, California, June 1970
<u>County Trauma Center</u>

Deputy Grady and Sheriff Cardwell flanked the prisoner, each of them holding a fistful of the man's two arms while they rode up to the sixth floor together. Grady was a little uncomfortable given the Sheriff's sour mood. He knew that he wasn't angry with *him*, it was just that being close enough to strangle this a-hole Katz and not being able to *do the world a favor* was a little frustrating for the boss.

"There's no reason to squeeze so hard officer, I assure you I'm not going anywhere," Dr. Katz said, complaining about the finger bruises that he could feel forming underneath the Sheriff's ever tightening grip.

"SHUT UP!" Sheriff Cardwell said with more than a *little venom* in his voice.

Dr. Katz sucked in his cheeks and bit down on the flesh between his teeth to stifle a response that he knew would bring on a bruise-less beating.

"Sorry," he said.

"I said shut up!" the Sheriff said, as he chopped the prisoner in the side, between the pelvic bone and the last rib. It was hard enough to hurt but not leave a mark. Dr. Katz grimaced but remained upright. The bell chimed as they reached their destination and the doors opened automatically.

"This is our stop sir," Grady said to his boss.

"I know Grady, I can read," the Sheriff replied sarcastically.

The three men exited the elevator and proceeded to the converted private room where Dr. Katz had been staying since his arrest. Deputy Grady waived at the guard outside the door and the man stepped out of the way. As they walked inside Sheriff Cardwell immediately saw a very pregnant Maria Lopez sitting uncomfortably in a straight back chair by the window. Standing next to her was little Tina. She was dressed in pair of jeans with two grass stains on the knees, and a colorful tee shirt, red and white striped like the Beach Boys used to wear a few years back. He noticed for the first time that the little girl was beginning to blossom into a young lady. He also noticed that his prisoner was noticing as well. Sheriff Cardwell gave heavy chain around the doctor's waist a hard tug and started to say something, but before he could get out a word Dr. Katz spoke, "I've been waiting to talk to you for a very long time," he said to Tina, as she continued to stand by her mother.

"What the hell are you two doing here and who the hell let you in?" demanded Sheriff Cardwell.

"I'm afraid that was my fault," said a voice from behind the three men.

Sheriff Cardwell turned to look but he already recognized the voice.

"Alma, what on earth?" the Sheriff blurted out.

"Trust me Roger, it will be alright," Alma said to the Sheriff.

"Go ahead honey, say your piece," Alma said to Tina who was still holding her mother's hand.

The little girl walked a couple paces forward and then stopped in front of Dr. Katz. She tugged on his waist chain indicating that she wanted him to squat down to her level. Dr. Katz looked over at the Sheriff for a yes or no. Roger Cardwell nodded his head and the prisoner knelt beside the child. Tina leaned close to him, cupped her little hand to his ear and whispered something only he could hear. When she was finished, she stepped back and looked at the man. He returned her gaze for a moment and then Dr. Katz stood up slowly.

"When?" he asked.

"Very soon," Tina said with a little voice.

"Very, very, soon."

"ALRIGHT, WHAT THE HELL?" said Sheriff Cardwell, pulling Dr. Katz back closer to him, scanning all the faces in the room for clues to *whatever* was happening here.

Tina smiled up at the Sheriff and called him down to her level with her twitching finger. Sheriff Cardwell squatted down and leaned forward on one knee. He looked at the little girl and tipped his hat up with his index finger.

"Well?"

Tina walked up to him and cupped her hand around his ear then whispered into it. Roger Cardwell listened, squinted, and then squished up his face, making him look just like an English bulldog.

"A secret, oh for the love of Pete!"

Twenty-six

*(..."Is this the little girl I carried, is this the little boy
at play. I don't remember growing older, when did
they"... Sunrise Sunset/Fiddler on the Roof)*

San Francisco, California, December 1970

Katherine "KC" Littleton smiled to herself as she read the freshly
painted lettering on the leaded glass that topped the door leading to her
new office. Apparently the successful coverage of the Katz trial and the
amazing popularity of her serial pieces surrounding the *Angel of the Valley*
were paying huge dividends. Her career had really blossomed, and *for the
moment,* she was San Francisco's most celebrated print journalist. Actually,
the last eighteen months had passed by so fast and in such a rush, that she
barely even remembered celebrating Christmas or her birthday, which just
happened to be on the same day.

KC could hardly believe how quickly *fame* had been thrust upon her,
and to be honest, she was wondering just when it's mating phenomenon,
fortune would be following? She had been equally surprised to discover how
much she actually loathed all of the attention. As a youngster she was always
imaging herself basking in the limelight of such notoriety and celebrity, a
real star, just like Marilyn Monroe or Raquel Welch. She was convinced that
it would just be *super cool* to be worshiped and admired like that. But, when
all was said and done, all of the attention just turned out to be a drag! The
telephone screamed at her from the top of her shiny new mahogany desk, and

KC quickly answered it on the first ring. *"It's your dime, talk to me,"* she said, causing a slight peak in the arrogance section of the manners meter.

"Damn it KC, will you please try and answer the phone just a little more professionally? I was hoping that some upward mobility might inspire a change in attitude. I mean you did promise that you'd at least try at the Christmas party, *I have witnesses you know!"* Brian Williams said totally exasperated.

"First of all, I was pretty drunk when I made that promise **Bri,**" KC said, just warming up.

"And by the way, I think I also promised to baby-sit your kids until they started college!" she added quickly.

"Secondly, the level of my professional demeanor is commensurate with the level of my paycheck. It's a simple socioeconomic equation really, raise the latter and you get the former!" she said, tossing that one in for good measure.

"Thirdly, is that a word? *Never mind,* and most of all, I don't **want** to change Brian, I like me just how I am. *Oh,* and for the record, so do over a million subscribers!" KC finished, giggling into the receiver.

She had turned 180 degrees in her high-backed leather chair and looked down towards Brian's corner office. She could actually see her managing editor sitting at his desk, cradling his head with one hand and holding the telephone receiver to his ear with the other. All of the offices that were along the perimeter of the building had walls that were half-conventional and half glass, as was the style of the day for newspapers and high finance institutions. Given the fact that old man Gateway was never far from either medium, it was not surprising that The San Francisco Daily News would be structured in such a fashion.

"Alright hotshot, I give, just hang up and trot on down to my office so we can chat a bit about the angle on the Katz sentencing. And we want to talk a little about your latest submission for the *'Angel'* series," Brian said, changing the subject back to business.

"What do you mean *we,* you have a mouse in your pocket or something?" KC teased.

"The boss will be joining us KC," Brian replied, nonplussed.

"He's coming down here?"

"Yes, it's his building, I guess he can meet wherever he wants."

"Yeah I know, I'm just surprised, that's all," she said apprehensively.

"See you in five minutes, OK...*KC?"* Brian asked rhetorically. As soon as KC started to answer she heard the click in her ear as Brian hung up.

"This last word kick of his is starting to annoy me," she muttered to herself.

She replaced the receiver to the cradle and opened her desk drawer and pulled out a hairbrush. She turned the 8 by 10 of her parents that was perched prominently on her desktop toward her, and straightened out her hair with a few quick strokes. She had been letting her hair grow out ever since she started spending time with the Lopez family. Tina and Maria had such beautiful long hair, and she admired how feminine they looked wearing it that way. KC had been wearing her hair short for a very long time now, and she thought that it suited her, both professionally and personally. She had always been a bit of a tomboy, and lets face it, she had chosen a career that was classically dominated by the male of the species. But oh how she loved sparing with the boys and competing with them at *their* game, even if she did have to work twice as hard to get any real recognition. She especially liked seeing their pouting faces when she whipped them on their home field. But the victories didn't come free, the cost had been her identity. It was one day shortly after she had started at the paper, when Mr. Gateway himself had pulled her aside.

"Not exactly what you thought it would be, is it young lady?" he asked, chewing on an unlit cigar.

"Listen, this may not help you any, but let me give you just a little bit of advise," he continued.

KC remembered thinking to herself, *"Great, I'm getting fired on my second day on the job!"*

"To hunt with wolves you have to be a wolf, at the very least be as cunning and as deadly."

"*Otherwise*, it means living outside of the pack, trying to survive on scraps. And KC darlin, nobody survives long on scraps. Do you get my meaning, *girl?*" he had asked, giving her shoulder the same kind of gentle squeeze that her own father always had.

That was the nudge that inspired her new attitude that spawned the *sassy lassie, one of the guy's* personas that had brought her to this point in her career. But it was only an act after all she had always known that. And after spending so much time with people from outside of her world, from outside of her job and sparse social circle, with women who seemingly needed no pretense to be happy, KC began to sense of part of her that she had set aside long ago. She couldn't put her finger on it, but something was changing, she could sense as much, it gave her a queer feeling, bittersweet in a way that she didn't understand. For now, whatever it was, it manifested itself in a shoulder length hairstyle that she hadn't worn since college. And she loved it, even if it was a lot of extra work, it made her feel like a girl again! Frankly she was getting a little tired of dressing for success and acting so hip and sophisticated. The hell with Gloria Stienim, Helen Gurly Brown and all those pabulum dependent NOW freaks that needed Cosmo to tell them about what they *weren't* missing, now she just wanted to look pretty!

"That'll do," she said to herself. KC got up and put on her tweed jacket over the cream blouse that was tucked neatly into her denim jeans. She had selected her country casual look for moving day into her new office, but suddenly she wished she had worn a skirt.

"Wow," she thought, "Where did that come from," she giggled to herself, and she headed down to Brian's office at a quick step pace. When she reached the end of the hall, she waved at Connie and mouthed, "He's waiting for me," as she walked passed her and into Brian's office. He was already sitting at the big round conference table, scratching his head with a pencil and drumming his fingers on the tabletop.

"Ahem," KC said, announcing herself.

"Have a seat KC, I knew you were here, I could feel my blood pressure go up as soon as you entered my air space," he said without looking up from the papers in front of him.

"Thanks Bri, I'll take that as a compliment. And don't worry, it'll be our little secret, I always knew you had a thing for me," she wisecracked. Brian ignored her comments and continued reading.

"Where's Mr. Big?" KC tossed in after a moment of uncomfortable silence.

"He'll be down in a minute KC, keep your shirt on."

"OK, but you better cool it with the innuendoes, Connie can hear us ya know," KC replied winking.

"*I HEARD THAT KC,* leave the poor man alone!" Connie hollered from the other room.

"SORRY," KC hollered back.

"Are you through," Brian asked, looking at her from across the table. KC nodded an affirmative and scooted her chair in closer to the table.

"I just finished reading your *'Angel'* piece for the second time. It's great stuff KC, I wouldn't change a word, nice work," Brain said complementing her in earnest.

"Thanks Bri, these pieces almost write themselves really," replied KC.

"You think that one of these days I could meet this kid?" Brian asked.

KC studied him for a moment before she answered. "*Gee,* I don't know Brian, I'll ask the next time that I see the Lopez family," she answered.

"Why all the interest all of the sudden?" she inquired.

"I don't know really, but I feel sort of drawn to her, I can't explain it, does that make sense?"

"More than you Brian, more than you know," she said, reaching across the table and patting his hand.

"I hope I'm not interrupting a tender moment here?" Grover Gateway asked as he entered the office, taking the seat next to KC. Brian drew his hand back quickly and KC sat up straight in her chair, each of them acting as if they had just been caught by the teacher passing a note in class.

"I was just telling KC how much I enjoyed the last *'Angel'* installment, you've seen it of course," Brian said, straightening his tie and composing himself. Mr. Gateway transferred his gaze to KC.

"Yes, nice piece of writing Katherine, really. And by the way, I wanted to thank you again for being such a sport what with all of the constraints that we saddled you with on this story. Although I think that by now you have a pretty good understanding of why those close to Tina are so concerned with her anonymity, *am I right?*"

KC cleared her throat and answered meekly, "Yes sir."

"Good, I'm glad that we're on the same page!

"Alright, let's shift gears a minute here and talk about the Katz trial. KC, when do you think this blasted farce will end anyway?" Gateway asked forcefully.

"I can't see it dragging on much longer sir, couple week's tops," she answered.

"I'm pretty sure that His Honor, as well as most of the high and low ranking city, county, and State officials have drained every bit of free airtime and cheap publicity that there is to be had. Besides, I can sense that the public is losing interest. To be honest, if it were not for Katz's connection to Tina Lopez, and the angle that we're saving for later, I would be as well," KC added, while she doodled a series of cursive L's on her steno-pad.

"*I see*, am I keeping you from something KC?" Grover Gateway asked, appearing a little annoyed at her lack of focus.

"NO, *no sir*, she's just a little tired is all. Didn't turn her piece in until late last night," Brian explained on KC's behalf, kicking her under the table as he did so.

"*Owww, what the hell!*" KC exclaimed.

"Is there something you two want to share with the world?" Mr. Gateway asked.

"*NO! Oh God no,*" KC said emphatically, glaring at Brian as she said so.

"Really, Mr. Gateway, Brian is just trying to protect me from myself, it's become a habit with him. He's more like a big brother to me than a boss sometimes," KC continued, her demeanor significantly softer.

"Thanks Brian, but I can take care of myself, you know that," she said to her editor who was busy straightening out everything within his reach at the table like some crazed obsessive-compulsive.

"I know KC, just trying to help," he said without looking at her. Once everything was in place Brian leaned back in his chair and brushed some imaginary micro dust from his shirtsleeve.

"Are you quite finished Mr. Williams," Grover Gateway asked his managing editor?

"Ahem," Brian cleared his throat loudly and nodded a silent affirmative.

"Please continue Miss Littleton," said Mr. Gateway.

"Well, my sources tell me that each side will be delivering closing arguments late next week and that the jury should be sent out to deliberate shortly afterward. Nobody is expecting a long deliberation, especially with Christmas is just around the corner. So I am guessing a week or two tops," KC said, rapping her pencil on her steno-pad in a *pa dump pump* cadence. All she was missing was a cymbal crash to complete the standard ending that accompanied the punch line to most comics' snappy routines.

"When do you think he will be sentenced then…assuming of course he is convicted?" Mr. Gateway asked. KC didn't waste any time answering his question.

"It wouldn't surprise me at all if the judge sentences Dr. Katz in the same breath with which he reads the verdict. It's what Katz wants, it's what the people want, and maybe even what God wants as well."

Mr. Gateway nodded his head slowly, looking from face to face and then once around Brian's office.

"You may be right young lady. But to my mind there is something fundamentally wrong with being so sure that someone needs to die. I know the arguments that support such a policy, and I recognize and understand the emotions that fuel them. But that doesn't relieve the stomachache I get every time I read a headline that begins, *'So and So Executed Today'...*" The three journalists sat in silence as Grover Gateway's words fell to the ground and disappeared into the carpeting.

"Well, changing the subject to more pleasant matters, KC do you know what a *Quinceanera* is?" asked Mr. Gateway.

"No sir, I can't say as I do," she answered, frowning and shaking her head.

"It's a Mexican ritual, I don't know, maybe all Latinos practice it as well, more of a celebration really, like a party. It's given for girls when they turn fifteen, sort of a rite of passage if you will, to celebrate the change from little girl to young woman."

"It's actually quite festive, lots of food, music, and dancing, and so colorful KC, they're just beautiful," Mr. Gateway explained.

He appeared as if he were actually watching a reply of just such a party as he spoke. KC and Brian waited for a moment as they watched the old gentleman sit trancelike, and then KC broke the awkward silence by waving her hand in front of the big boss's face, and snapping her fingers.

"Excuse me, sir, we're over here," she said playfully. Brian rolled his eyes and lowered his head to his hands, expecting them both to be summarily executed for KC's brashness.

Snapping out of his little daydream, Mr. Gateway acknowledged her gesture, "*Yes, well*, the point is KC, you've been invited to attend the Tina Lopez's *Quinceanera*." he explained.

"Really? I'd be honored to attend sir, when is it anyway?" KC replied, slightly puzzled.

"I thought you would say that, so I already accepted on your behalf," Mr. Gateway said.

He reached into his coat pocket and pulled out a note and his glasses.

"Let's see here, ah, here we are. Looks like the first weekend in January. Will you be able to free up your calendar?"

"Of course I will"

"By the way, was it Maria or Alma Donnelly who invited me?" asked KC.

"Does it matter?" asked Mr. Gateway.

"No, just curious," she replied.

"Neither, it was Tina herself," he said, handing her the note.

KC looked at the invitation, written beautifully in long hand on a piece of notebook paper. It simply read:

Dear KC,
Thank you for being my friend, please come to my Quinceanera, it would make me so happy!
Love,
Tina
P.S. Please bring Jay too he's so funny!

KC set the note down and smiled at Mr. Gateway from across the table.

"Thanks," she said, folding the note carefully and putting it into her notebook."

"Listen, could we chat a little about Dr. Katz while we're all together. You know he's talked to her don't you?" KC asked them both. The puzzled look on their faces was all the answer she needed.

"Let me tell you a story…"

Fresno, California, December 1970
Heritage House Rehabilitation Center

Rosa Hernandez sat quietly in the chair across from the large desk and waited for Mrs. Delgado to return. She had stepped out to get them both coffee and said that she would just be a minute. Rosa liked the woman, she was short and round and had a pleasant way about her, made her feel very comfortable when she spoke to her. Rosa looked at the wooden placard with the gold lettering that read *SUPERVISOR*. She glanced around the desktop as well and took a mental inventory. Everything was neatly arranged, pictures facing toward Mrs. Delgado, telephone easily within reach, a coaster for her cup, and one manila folder in the center, a chrome-plated Paper-Mate pen setting on top of the file. Rosa was tempted to get up and go around the desk to see who was in the pictures. But she thought better of it, she wanted to make friends with this woman, she would need her trust in the coming days.

"Here we are," announced a warm and happy voice from behind.

Mrs. Delgado carefully set her oversized ceramic cup onto the strategically placed coaster on her desk and then turned to hand Rosa a Styrofoam cup.

"Cream, no sugar, just like you asked for," Mrs. Delgado said sweetly.

Rosa took the cup and blew over the brim to cool her drink before she attempted to take a sip. She breathed in deeply, enjoying the aroma of the freshly brewed coffee, and smiled at Mrs. Delgado.

"Thank you ma'am," Rosa said.

"Oh, you're quite welcome dear, and call me Celeste, everyone else does," Mrs. Delgado said happily.

"OK, thank you Celeste," Rosa quickly replied, taking a sip of coffee in the process.

"Hmmm, this is good," she said nodding her head in appreciation.

"Its French roast, my sister Annette sends it to me from San Francisco every month, I just love her!" Celeste said shrugging her shoulders and grinning like a little girl.

Rosa took another sip and settled back in her chair while she watched Celeste Delgado open up the file in front of her.

"Rosa, I must say it has been a real pleasure to have you with us this past six months or so. I mean that sincerely dear, you have been a model client for us," Celeste said, complimenting her.

"Thank you"

"I see that you are applying for the work furlough program through the court," Celeste continued.

"Yes"

"Rosa, I'll be honest with you, obtaining an unsupervised work furlough will be difficult at best. Perhaps we can find something for you here at the facility?"

"That would be nice Mrs. Delgado, I mean Celeste," Rosa replied.

"Good, I'll check with services this morning for you."

"Excuse me ma'am, but can I still apply for the furlough as well?"

Celeste sat back in her chair, almost disappearing from site when she did so.

"Yes of course you may dear. But it will take time and like I said, it will be difficult."

"I understand ma'am, I am just anxious to start living a normal life again. I have a baby at home that I love so much and a family that misses me," Rosa said, laying it on thick.

"Yes dear, I understand that, it must be awful to be separated from your child," replied Celeste sincerely.

"I'll tell you what, let's give this work arrangement a try around here. See how much responsibility you can handle while you petition the court. If all goes well here at Heritage House I'll write you a letter of recommendation myself, what do you say!" she asked excitedly.

"That would be great ma'am, I mean Celeste, thank you, gracias senora, gracias!"

Mrs. Delgado picked up her coffee and took a long sip, then jotted a few lines down on the paper inside Rosa's file. She looked up and smiled at Rosa while she picked up the phone. She dialed a four-digit extension and waited for someone to answer. Rosa sat patiently, sipping her coffee and listening intently.

"Good morning Pat, this is Celeste Delgado, how are you dear?"

"Oh that's just wonderful. Listen I need you to do me a favor dear. There is a client that I would like to put on staff in the kitchen. Let's start her this afternoon and see how she works out, thanks Pat. I'll send her over shortly, bye bye."

"There, you're all set to go!" Celeste said beaming.

"Thanks Ma'am, I don't know what else to say, thank you very much," Rosa said, standing to shake Mrs. Delgado's hand.

"My pleasure Rosa, I'm sure this will work out for everyone," Celeste said shaking Rosa's hand.

"How about a refill before you run off to your first day on the job?" Celeste asked cheerfully.

"Yes, please," replied Rosa, handing over her cup.

"I'll just be a minute. Oh I just love it when things work out, don't you," Mrs. Delgado said as she trotted out of the office.

"OK, thanks again," Rosa said.

She waited a second for Mrs. Delgado to clear the room before she beamed broadly to herself. Phase one was complete she had arrived in Fresno. Phase two was now in place, creating a pathway to phase three, Dr. Katz. *"This going to be a cinch,"* she muttered to herself.

San Francisco, California, December 1970
Oceanaire Apartments

"OPEN UP JAY," KC shouted through the door to her friend's apartment.

She had been knocking for ten minutes and was getting totally frustrated because she knew he was in there! KC rang the bell once more and then searched her key ring for the right key.

"Ah ha," she exclaimed as she found the correct quickset key and inserted it into the lock. KC let herself in and went straight for the kitchen, all of this knocking and shouting had built up a sudden appetite, and she knew that Jay always had a well-stocked fridge.

"Finding what you need?" Jay asked sarcastically from behind the breakfast counter.

"I'm getting there," KC said bent over with her head still in the fridge. "Hey, how old is this chicken salad anyway?"

"It's left over from lunch yesterday, and by the way, nice ass sweetheart," Jay answered in the same sarcastic tone.

KC stood up with her arms full toting a loaf of bread, a Tupperware container with chicken salad and a jar of Miracle Whip. She kicked the fridge door closed with her foot and set all of the stuff onto the counter.

"In your dreams buddy, and you could at least put shirt ya know," KC retorted.

"That's not *all* I could put on," Jay said, rolling his eyes downward. KC rose up on her tiptoes and peeked over the counter.

"*Oh gross, JAY!* I didn't need to see that, *I'm eating goddamn it!*" KC whined, making a mental note never to sit on that barstool again.

"Excuse me, I thought this was *my* apartment! You could have called first or knocked maybe, you *have* heard of those things right?"

"*I did call, I did knock.* Hell Jay, I knocked loud enough that half of your neighbors answered their doors!" KC exclaimed while she made her sandwich. She suddenly pointed at him with the knife she was spreading Miracle Whip with, leaving a trail from her plate to Jay's smooth chest.

"So what had you so engrossed that you could hear any of that, *hmmm,*" she asked sharply. Jay scrapped the Miracle Whip from his chest and licked it off of his finger. He started to answer when he was interrupted by a voice from the hall.

"Are you coming back to bed or what?" asked an equally naked female from the doorway. Jay turned toward the voice, "I'll be back in a minute sweetie, go on back to bed and keep the sheets warm for me baby," Jay said calmly.

"Oh pooh!" pouted the young woman, as she turned to do as she was told.

"Oh, I see schools out," KC teased.

"Can it Kathy, I don't meddle in your love life do I," Jay snapped.

"That's too easy, *I don't have a love life.* Besides, you're my best friend so I have an inalienable right to meddle in your private life and live vicariously through you if I need to!" KC lamented, taking a huge bite of her chicken salad sandwich. Jay pulled on her arm and brought the sandwich close to his face so he could take a bite as well.

"HEY," she said, pulling the tasty morsel back to her side of the counter.

Jay wiped his mouth with the back of his hand and asked her with his mouthful, "So what's so important that you had to make a house-call?"

"I was just in the neighborhood and got hungry. Seeing as I was financially embarrassed at the moment I decided to drop in on my favorite cheap restaurant, *Chez Jay!"* KC explained.

"Besides, I wanted to let you know that I wanted to leave for Fresno earlier than we had planned to. Oh, and I met with Brian and Mr. Gateway this morning, we went over the angle for closing out the Katz story, and I wanted to share that with you too. By the way, we're invited to Tina Lopez's birthday party in January, I think she might have a crush on you buddy!"

"I'll check my calendar and see what's what," he said.

"What makes you say she has a crush on me?" he asked shyly.

"She thinks you're funny…and she hasn't even seen you naked, go figure!" KC teased.

"Listen, we'll all understand if you have more *pressing* affairs!" she sassed further.

"OK enough already!" Jay pleaded.

"Look, *mi casa su casa* buddy, you know that, but Kathy, the timing, *aye yi yi!"* Jay said.

"I know, I'm sorry," KC said sincerely.

"Listen sport, let's talk about this over dinner tonight, my treat!"

"We'll go to that place you like so much, over in North Beach. What was it, oh yeah, *The Stinking Rose*, no?" Jay asked anxiously.

"Yeah OK, what time?"

"I'll pick you up at your place at eight, I'll even do a *grappa* shot or two with you. But you'll have to drive me home if I do, you know that stuff blinds me!" he said.

"It's a date, *but leave the junior miss behind OK*, otherwise I'll have to charge you a dollar and a half an hour to sit with her!" KC said teasing her friend.

"Deal!"

"Now scram! And take your lunch with you while I go finish mine!" Jay said, winking at her, and grabbing a pillow from the sofa to cover up while she passed by him.

"Did you just go swimming or something, I mean I heard that men sorta…"

"OUT KC! *See*, this is why we never became a couple, you're such a smart ass!" Jay hollered, swatting her with the pillow and pushing her out the door.

Jay could hear her giggle all the way down the hall. KC turned and waved to her friend, as the door slammed shut. Walking backward she hollered, "*Bye bye*, thanks for the lunch and the show, I'll be sure to tell all my friends about this place!"

Twenty-seven

(..."Children's children are a crown to the aged, and parents are the pride of their children"... Proverbs 17:6)

Firebaugh, California, Friday, 9 January 1970
<u>*Home of the Lopez Family*</u>

Maria was beside herself with all of the preparations. Thank God for Mrs. Donnelley and her family and friends, she would never have been able to pull this off without them. She looked over at her husband as he ate his breakfast and read the newspaper. Maria walked over to him and refilled his cup, kissing the top of his head as she did so.

"Victor, do you think that you will have time to stop at the Emporium and pick up the decorations for

"The Quinceanera?" she asked sweetly, but with a stern look on her face. She was ready to pounce should he give her any answer other than YES!

Victor gave her a sideways glance and took notice of the look on her face, recognizing this tactic of hers. He decided that today was probably not a good day to joke around with her so he refolded the paper and sat up straight in the chair. He picked up the freshly filled cup and blew across the brim before taking a careful sip.

"Woman, you make the best coffee in the county," he said with a big smile.

"Don't play with me Victor, there's too much to do *baboso!* Now, will you pick up the decorations or not?" she said scolding him a little.

"Yeah, yeah, of course I will baby cakes, I know what a big deal this is," he answered quickly, taking another long sip of his coffee. He looked over his shoulder at the cow clock on the wall.

"YIKES...It's already eight, I need to skeedaddle before I **DO** have a problem making that pick up later this afternoon," Victor exclaimed, draining his cup and jumping up from the table. He grabbed his jacket from the back of the chair and rushed toward the door.

"HEY, HEY, are you forgetting something *Panson?*" Maria said, holding his keys in one hand and his lunchbox in the other.

Victor stopped and rolled his eyes, and then walked quickly over to where she was standing by the sink. Maria quickly put both items behind her back, closed her eyes and puckered up. Her husband smiled at her coyly even though she couldn't see it, and kissed his wife softly on her waiting lips.

"Hmmm," he muttered as he stood up straight. She opened her eyes, smiling, and started to hand him his things.

"Did you just have some bacon, cause I could definitely taste bacon on that kiss," Victor teased.

"AYIE!" she exclaimed, tossing his keys on the floor and swinging his lunchbox at him.

Victor raised his arms to parry the attack and pulled his wife close to him. She squirmed at first and then settled down in his embrace. Victor kissed the top of her head and then released her, taking the lunchbox with him and stooping to retrieve his keys.

"*Shhh*, you'll wake the baby," he said as he turned to walk out the back door.

Maria leaned back against the counter, put her left hand up and spread her fingers across her forehead. Then in one long fluid motion she raked her hand through her long black hair, pulling all of it back so tight she could barely close her eyes. As soon as she finished the sweep of her scalp from the top of her head to the base of her neck, she filled her cheeks with air, and puffing them out, exhaled with a heavy sigh.

"*He's right,*" she said out loud.

There was no need to disturb the peace and quiet just yet. That would come soon enough. Pushing back against the kitchen counter with her behind, Maria propelled herself out of the kitchen and toward the kid's room to peek in on the latest addition to her brood, little *Cynthia Louise*. The child had been an earlier than expected present last month, born in the last hour of Christmas day, two weeks premature. Praise God there weren't any complications to speak of. Maria just figured that Cynthia was as eager to be born, as *she* was to deliver, *sometimes nine months is a really, really, really, long time!*

Quietly tiptoeing up to the bassinet that set snuggly yet serenely between the two twin beds that the other children slept in, she looked down on her sleeping baby. Maria really had to force herself to resist the urge to bend down and kiss her, and instead, took in a lung full of that sweet newborn scent. After a minute or two she slowly backed out of the room, closing the door behind her, but only halfway. Maria had never been comfortable completely separating herself from the children when they were infants. She was always in tune with their breathing patterns, as well as all the little cooing noises and squawks they made. These were the *all's clear indicators* that mother's counted on for their own peace of mind.

As Maria slowly walked back toward the kitchen she silently scolded herself for the hard time she had given Victor about this child being her last. He had been so patient after all, waiting so long after Gilbert until she was ready to try again. Maria knew that he was going outside his faith and his Catholic beliefs just to be supportive of her fears. She also knew that Victor had taken a little heat from some of the men in the community for seemingly not being *in control* of his family. A machismo/cultural thing among Latinos, a matter of respect, she understood that. It really was a socially brave thing that he did for her, and she loved him dearly for it. It had been a long seven years since the birth of her son, but she knew that he understood her fears. Even he would tell her time and again that she had done nothing that called for his forgiveness, she still prayed for it. She prayed that God might open her heart to his will, tell her that she was just being silly, there was nothing to worry about. But she was just so nervous about having another *special child*. As far as she was concerned one was quite enough thank you!

Maria was so thankful that Gilbert seemed to be normal and unencumbered with any special talent or gift, beyond being a terrific finger painter and a champion chowhound that is. And even though she had already convinced herself that this new baby would be normal as well, she would still watch closely for any sign otherwise! On the way back to the kitchen Maria routinely stopped by her room and grabbed the basket of dirty laundry. Lugging the heavy container back with her, she set it on top of the washer, and then went back into the kitchen to pour herself a nice hot cup of coffee. She sat down at the small table, added some cream to her cup and stirred it slowly. Then reaching across the table she picked up a spiral notebook and flipped it open to the page marked with the paper clip. She sipped her coffee while she read over her planning notes for Tina's Quinceanera.

Looking over the guest list again, she began to separate the names into two sections, one for the Mass, and one for the Reception. The Mass was normally reserved for immediate family only, but she and Victor had added a few people who had become honorary family members over the past couple of years. Namely, the Donnelly's, Alma and Arthur, to whom the Lopez family owed a huge debt of gratitude for the many blessings they enjoyed due to the opportunities that the wonderful couple provided. And of course she had to add Sheriff Cardwell, he had been so supportive of their special needs since Tina's calling had become well known in the county. Last but not least, they had added that newspaper reporter from San Francisco, KC and her funny friend Jay. Maria had been somewhat surprised at how fond she had become of her during the last year or so. She remembered how scared she had been when Alma Donnelly had first explained how they would need the protection of a sympathetic media source to secure Tina's anonymity.

Maria had never been one to trust anyone outside the family or community, but Alma had convinced her that it was the only hope they had at keeping the lid on everything, especially after the incident with Dr. Katz. As it happened, Senor Donnelly's best friend in life, their parish priest Father Willet, was blessed with some very influential contacts in life, in addition to the Lord God Almighty that is! Turns out that Father Billy had made a powerful friend in Senor Grover Gateway, someone he had met during his time in Korea in the early nineteen fifties. Through this gringo's newspaper, *The San Francisco Daily News*, the family had been able to arrange to protect Tina from premature exposure in exchange for the exclusive rights to their story. They all knew that one day the whole truth would have to come out, *truth percolates they say.* And so they agreed that when that time came, Senor Gateway's newspaper would carry the story to the world. But that would be after Tina was grown up and able to deal with the inevitable media blitz that would accompany the sensational tale.

Maria would rather have disappeared again, just as they had on many other occasions whenever their secret began to leak out into whatever community they were living in. Before anyone could put a name with Tina's face, she and Victor would pack up the family and they would leave quietly, like a band of gypsies, and start over again as quietly as possible, in some small town along the melon circuit. Those had been rough days, but even so, she longed for the peace and quiet of blending in with the scenery. However, that kind of life wasn't very fair to the children, to her, or to Victor, *to anyone really*. Everybody deserved a future, something to look forward to, to plan for, and somewhere where roots might grow. She finished adding to the extended family list for the Holy Mass and started looking over the reception list, it was huge! If it weren't for the Donnelly's generosity she and Victor would be witling it down considerably right now. Maria took another sip and making a sour face quickly set the cup of ice-cold coffee back down on the table.

"Mensa," she said to herself as she choked down the icky liquid and pushed the cup away from her.

Leaning forward she placed her elbows on the table, one hand folded into another, and rested her chin on her fist. She turned her head and looked out the window over the sink. Smiling, she remembered fondly her own Quinceanera. She closed her eyes and imagined the reception with all the dancing and wonderful dishes that everyone enjoyed. Maria could remember every person by name that made up her court of *Damas* and *Chambelones*, which for all intents and purposes were very much like bridesmaids and groomsmen at a wedding. And she blushed a little bit as she remembered her dance with her special *Chambelon.*

She wondered if Tina had someone special in mind that she wanted to bestow that honor to. It never even occurred to her that her daughter might have those kinds of thoughts? Shifting her attention away from that thought for the moment, she concentrated on the memory of the beautiful white gown that her mother had made for her, the very gown that she would now hand down to Tina. There was still a lot to do before Saturday, and she wasn't going to get any of it done sitting there and daydreaming. Sitting up straight, Maria picked up her pencil and jotted down a quick note:

1. Call Alma about the VFW hall for the reception
2. Call KC and confirm
3. Call florist for Tina's bouquet and headdress
4. Make tamales, rice, and beans for supper.
5. Break out the red dress. Tonight the *Panson* gets lucky!!

Firebaugh, California, Friday, 9 January 1970
<u>*Home of Arthur and Alma Donnelly*</u>

"Arthur, I don't have a thing to wear," Alma Donnelly shouted to her husband as she stared into an apartment-sized closet filled to capacity. Arthur Donnelly lowered the newspaper into his lap. And leaning his head straight back, he bellowed from his comfy chair.

"You've got to be kidding!" There was the usual momentary lapse between responses and then her reply came a decibel louder still.

"NOPE!"

Arthur sat there un-phased; it was after all the reply that he was expecting. He reached over to his wallet sitting on the table next to his chair and gently patted it, as if to say, *"don't worry old friend, I'll be with you every step of the way."*

He picked up the newspaper and folded it neatly, setting it back into the magazine rack next to the chair. He stood, did an about face, and walked out of the sitting room heading toward the closet and source of all the commotion. Arthur stealthily entered the closet while his wife noisily rifled through her awesome selection of clothing, hanger by hanger. As she admired a rose colored pants suit that she had taken off the rung, Arthur moved up behind her and pulled her close to him. He leaned over and gave his wife a kiss on the top of her head, it was quite a stretch as well given he was better than a foot taller than she.

"You're going to have to get on your knees cowboy, if you're after what I think you're after," Alma said, teasing her husband as she felt his body announcing his intentions through the shear material of her blouse. Arthur smiled and pulled her closer.

"You're still a pistol dear, *God I'm a lucky man!*" She let her outfit fall to the floor and turned in her husband's embrace to welcome him properly. He held her close and they sort of slow danced in the closet for a moment before Alma spoke.

"You know Arthur, I never in a million years imagined my life would turn out like this," she said dreamily.

"How do you mean?" he asked.

"You know, all this wealth and good fortune," she replied, as they continued to dance sans music.

"Don't take this the wrong way honey, but sometimes I envy Maria Lopez and her life."

"Really?"

"Yes"

"Oh," he said, not really wanting to go where he knew this conversation was heading.

"Oh I know it's nobody's fault, but sometimes I beat myself up for not being able to give you children," she said, squeezing his lead hand with hers and bunching up his shirt with the other as she pulled the material in with the fist she was making.

"Let's not open old wounds honey, I'm happy with the life that you have made for me, don't you know that?" he asked rhetorically.

"Thank you dear," she replied cooing.

"It's just this big party for Tina, I wish it could have been for a daughter of our own. I think I would have been a good mother," Alma said, drying a tear on her husband's shirt before it ran down her cheek.

"Of course you would have Alma, I know you would have," Arthur said consoling his wife.

"Don't you know that Tina looks at you as if you were family, just like her mother and father do?" He could feel Alma nodding *yes* on his chest as they swayed from side to side, walking in tiny circles, as they continued with their closet waltz.

"So stop placing yourself on the outside of this shindig woman, you're as much a part of this as anyone else in the Lopez family. Be happy and be proud, just as if she were one of our own. I know that I'll be smiling large, as proud of her as if she had grown up right here with us!"

Alma stopped moving and looked up at her husband. She reached up and pinched some of the gray hair protruding from the open collar of his button down cowboy shirt. She tugged on the small tuft and pulled him down to her eye level and kissed him like she used to when they were young.

"*Hmmm*, daddy likes," Arthur swooned.

"Daddy ain't seen nothing yet," Alma said in her best Mae West impression.

Fresno, California, Friday, 9 January 1970
<u>*Holiday Inn*</u>

KC Littleton was seated at the small round, cheap looking walnut veneered table that decorated all the rooms in this dive, and thumbed through the 'Q' volume of the Encyclopedia Britannica. Wetting her finger she thumbed through the pages until she found what she was looking for.

"*Quinceanera,*" she said out loud, trying to phonetically pronounce the unfamiliar word. KC repeated the word several times, never quite grasping the correct intonation of roll of the letter 'r '.

"*Ah, screw it,*" she muttered and then went on to read about the history of the celebration. Suddenly there was a loud knock at the door.

"**Come on in Jay,**" she hollered without looking back.

"Doesn't work that way Kathy, I don't have a key," he yelled through the closed door. KC rolled her eyes and turned the book over to hold her place then she got up to open the door for her friend.

"What took you so long?" she whined, letting him into the room. Jay walked over and sat on the end of the queen-sized bed and glanced over at the table where she was sitting.

"What are you reading?"

"Just trying to see what kind of party this is," she replied.

292

"Yeah, so?"

"So, I think we definitely brought the wrong clothes, way too casual for this thing. Maria called and left a message at the desk letting us know that we're expected at the Mass as well."

"*What Mass*, I thought that this was a sweet sixteen party," Jay complained.

"Well it's not," KC snapped back at him.

"We've got a little shopping to do my friend, and I mean a whole outfit, shoes and everything!" she added emphatically.

"Oh man, I hate shopping with you KC, you're worse than my mother," Jay whined, throwing himself back on the bed and pulling the covers up over his head.

"Get over it crybaby!" she quipped.

"Let's go, we only have a couple hours before the stores close! And get off of my bed you retard, you're totally messing up the hospital corners!" Jay frantically tossed off the blankets and stood up, straightening out his shirt in the process. The two of them reached the door at the same time and Jay squeezed by her quickly, squishing her into the doorjamb as he passed by.

"*Damn it Jay,*" KC hollered after him, grabbing an ice cube from the bucket on the table and tossing it at him as he ran down the hall.

"Just for that dinner's on you as well," she yelled over her shoulder as she pulled the heavy door closed behind her.

"*Yeah, yeah, yeah...*" came his faint reply from around the corridor.

Fresno, California, Saturday, 10 January 1970
<u>*Saint John's Cathedral*</u>

Father William Willet daintily dabbed the corners of his mouth as he wiped away the remnants of the most amazing breakfast he had ever experienced. The eggs Florentine, the perfectly glazed Canadian bacon, the prociutto sliced ever so thin with capers and Pecorino cheese, and the freshly baked focochia bread, *mama mia*, he had to have been a Roman in a past life! He giggled to himself as he got up from the table and walked to the kitchen. Peeking his head just inside the swinging doors, he looked for Sister Demarco and waved at her when she caught sight of him.

"Sister, how can I thank you for such a meal. I am so happy that you decided to stay with us instead of returning to Sicily," Father Willet said, praising her.

"I thank God each day for arranging for Father Villa Cruz to agree to allow you serve our Lord here in the countryside where you are comfortable, instead of the metropolis that is Los Angeles," he added, laying it on thick.

"Prego Padre, Prego," replied Sister Ruth Demarco.

"Is my pleasure to serve at Saint John's, you are all so nice to me," Sister Demarco added humbly.

"Yes, well, I must be off now to welcome all the guests for the Lopez girl's Quinceanera. They should be arriving momentarily," he said, clasping his hands as if praying and turning to leave.

"Si Father, the *misa de accion de gracias*, I understand," said Sister Demarco, nodding knowingly.

"That's right Sister, *the thanksgiving mass*, very much like the tradition in your country I expect," the priest replied.

"Si Father, similar, yes."

"Well, thank you again for the wonderful breakfast. I am tempted to skip the reception and come back to the rectory for the evening meal," said Father Willet, trying **not** to sound as serious as he really was.

Sister Demarco waved as he left the kitchen and then went back to finishing her chores for the morning. Father Willet sighed and then made his way back to his office to change into his official garments for the ceremony. As he walked down the corridor he looked outside at the courtyard and noticed that the family was already starting to arrive. He picked up his pace and hurried along, waving to the Donnelly's when they spotted him from outside.

"I'll be along in two shakes of a lamb's tail," he shouted from the other side of the glass.

Arthur Donnelly gave him the thumbs up sign and turned to direct the new arrivals to the front of the Church where Father Willet would greet everyone as they walked in. Then the ushers or *Chambelones* would seat everyone on either side of the altar. The process was very much like that of a wedding, except of course there was only one family represented and there was no groom.

Alma and Arthur found Victor out in front of the Church holding baby Cynthia, with little Gilbert standing quietly beside him.

"Where are the girls?" asked Mr. Donnelly.

"They are already inside, Maria is helping Tina get ready," Victor answered.

"Oh I wanted to see her before the ceremony," Alma said disappointed.

"Go on inside Mrs. Donnelly, I know Maria would be happy to have your help. Tina is so nervous, I'm sure she would be happy to see you too," Victor said encouraging her.

"Yes Alma, go on. Like I said, she's your little girl too!" Arthur added with a smile.

"Thank you, I believe I will do just that! Do you think that you men can handle everything else without us"" Alma asked jokingly as she patted little Gilbert on the head. She turned to walk away and Gilbert ran after her, catching her at the first step. Alma stopped and took his hand and the two of them disappeared into the Church.

"Looks like it's just you and me Victor," Arthur said, gesturing toward the steps.

"Guess so," Victor replied, as the two men and a baby walked up to station themselves at the doorway.

Already a small crowd was waiting at the top of the stairs, and Victor walked over to address the elders in Spanish. He thanked everyone for coming and asked to please wait a moment until the *Chambelones* were ready to begin seating them. The five young men were busy waiting for their own mother's to finish straightening their ties and slicking down their hair. One by one they took their places at the top of the stairs and waited for the priest to arrive to begin the procession and ceremony. By now there was quite a crowd, about one hundred people had gathered out in front of the Church at the base of the stairs. The large doors behind Arthur opened, and out walked Father Willet, in his grand official splendor. The two friends greeted one another and then Father Willet walked over to Victor and placed his hand on his shoulder.

"Welcome Victor, this is a proud day for you," he said to the father of the Quinceanera.

"Thank you Father, gracias Senor," Victor replied.

"Well then, let's get this party started," Father Willet said cheerfully. He took his place next to Victor and Arthur, ten nodded to the *Chambelones* to begin to lead the people toward the doors.

The crowd began to pass by the three men to be greeted and seated, the music from the organ accompanying the process as the doors were propped open. Victor introduced each family member and guest to Arthur and Father Willet as they passed and the two elders smiled and did their best to make everyone feel welcome. As the line of people thinned to the last few, Arthur caught sight of KC and Jay as they made their way up the stairs. He jabbed Father Willet with his elbow and nodded toward the two reporters.

"That's our gal from Grover's paper," he said under his breath to the priest. Father Willet gave them a sideways glance, not wanting to be impolite to Victor's Tia Ramona and her family. He nodded back atArthur and continued speaking with each person as they passed by him. He paused for a moment and held the hand of a small boy that was with Victor's aunt.

"I know this boy," he said looking back at Victor, a puzzled look on his face as he tried to place the face.

"What is your name child?" the priest asked. The little boy did not answer.

"Como se llama nino?" he asked again in Spanish.

"Mi nombre es Miguel senor," the little boy answered softly. Father Willet looked over at Victor, "Is this who I think it is?" he asked.

"Si Father, it is the child that Tina brought back in the fields," Victor answered.

The priest nodded slowly and gently held the little boy's hand. He looked down at the shy child and made the sign of the Holy Trinity with his hand in front of him.

"Via con Dios nino," Father Willet said softly.

"Gracias Padre," Miguel answered as Tia Ramona took his hand and led him into the church. Father Willet watched them walk away, not taking his eyes off of the boy until they disappeared into the building.

Finally the two representatives from the San Francisco Daily News were standing in front of the three men. Victor introduced them to his parish priest, "Father, these are our new friends, KC and Jay. They have been very good to Tina and she asked for them to be here personally," he said with a smile.

"I am very pleased to meet you my children," Father Willet said, reaching out to take each of their hands individually with both of his.

"Your Grace," KC said, trying to curtsey as she had seen women do in the old movies.

She looked up at Victor and saw him shaking his head, no.

"Oh…excuse me, I mean *Your Worship*," she said correcting herself and curtseying again.

"Ditto," Jay said, bowing low like a Vaudeville actor.

Father Willet squinted and looked over at Arthur Donnelly with an *'are you seeing this'* expression on his face. Arthur shrugged his shoulders and raised his hand, stifling a giggle. Meanwhile, KC and Jay had straightened up and were standing face to face with the priest.

"Hope we did that right, we practiced for a good fifteen minutes in the parking lot before we came up here," Jay said proudly.

"Yes of course you did! I can honestly say that I have never been greeted in such a grand manner, never in my thirty years as a priest," Father Willet said praising them.

"Shall we all go in now? I believe everyone is waiting on us," he said, putting a hand at the small of KC and Jay's backs, ushering the two of them into the Church personally. He smiled to himself thinking, ***"First that wonderful meal and now this! Oh Lord, I do love my work, I surely do!"***

Twenty-eight

(..."Evil men do not understand justice,
but those who seek the Lord understand
all things"... Proverbs 28:5)

Fresno, California, February 1971
Golden State Penitentiary

The lights flickered off then on again inside of Dr. Murray Katz's private cell, located in the isolation ward of the newly completed State Prison facility. Not bad digs actually, for someone who had caused so *much* pain to so *many*. However he wasn't planning to be here long, not if his prayers were answered, as he fully expected them to be. To his amazement, Murray Katz had discovered that he liked praying, *a lot*. He found it soothing, therapeutic even, and it allowed him to sleep at night without the voices. Murray hated those voices, they had brought him nothing but trouble from his earliest recollections. They taunted him, goaded him, *dug and dug and dug* at him until at last he capitulated, doing all the despicable things they wanted him to do. They were insatiable, lustful, devoid of any compassion or humanity, and they were relentless.

"*Don't be such a pussy Murray, she wants it, she needs it man, give her wants she craves...NOW!"*

The convicted felon sat at the small desk in the corner, perched on a ridiculously small four-legged stool and studied the papers that were scattered in front of him. He held two sheets up against his face with his left hand, while he skimmed a third with the index finger of his right hand, re-reading the letter a second time, savoring each word as if they were golden morsels from Heaven's own banquet table. He smiled involuntarily, and then chuckled softly to himself. He could hardly believe his luck, *"prayer really does work,"* he thought.

"So, the kid had been right all along."

Dr. Katz stood and carried the letter back to his bunk and then flopped down onto it. Lying on his back, he held the letter above his head and read out loud:

"By order of the Superior Court of the County of Santa Barbara, and the People of the State of California: Murray Armstrong Katz, for crimes committed against the People for which you have been duly convicted, you are hereby sentenced to die by a lethal dose of poisonous cyanide gas in the death chamber housed at Golden State Penitentiary. Sentence to be lawfully carried out at 12:00pm PST, 20 December 1973, pending any and all appeals. May God have mercy on your soul."

So here it was at last, the very ending he had lobbied for all along, to the utter dismay of his legal representation. This case was a career launching opportunity, and his young and energetic attorney was well aware of it. The trial was second only to Charlie Manson and his girls with regard to the National coverage in the mainstream media. Katz recalled a particular conversation with the erstwhile Peter Roland with a certain cynical glee. It had gone something like this.

*"**What are you crazy**, have you completely lost your mind here! Look, Dr. Katz, I am more than confident that we can avoid the death penalty all together. Let's face it; the girl who committed suicide had many reasons besides her alleged encounter with you to put her over the edge. Hell, I've got affidavits from informants that swear that at least four braseros have been doing her since she was thirteen, and two of them are her first cousins! The only real damage is the link by blood to the Hernandez child. But after her attack on you, I'm reasonably certain that we can have you serving a minimal sentence in an institution where you will likely walk in less than five years,"* Peter had explained rather excitedly. To which the good Doctor had replied.

"I am crazy Peter, like a fox as they say. I *want* the death penalty and let me tell you why. By *trying* to escape what I *rightfully* deserve I will alienate myself from the very people I'll need to save me from the fate I seek," Katz remembered saying slowly. He paused a moment as he reminisced to lay the papers on his chest and get comfortable, closing his eyes and sighing deeply as he did so. He remembered Peter Roland rolling his eyes and looking at him as if he were the dumbest Jew on Earth.

"But Doctor..."

"ZIP IT PETER!"

His attorney reacted as if his High School football coach had just kicked him in the ass. Folding his arms and cocking his head to one side, his facial expression saying, *"Are you talking to me buddy!"*

"Let me finish and I swear, it will all be clear," he had said, assuring the flustered young lawyer that he had a plausible plan.

Dr. Katz remembered watching the young man for several minutes before continuing. Studying him, he looked for that *something* that every defense counsel possesses. That crooked little smile they all have, the one that always appears just when they realize that they've worked the system to its limits. And a client walks, *right or wrong*, true testament to their outlandish skills.

"Look, my insistence that I pay the ultimate price for crimes that I freely admit to committing is the key to my strategy. It will be through remorse and repentance that I earn a shot at cheating the hangman on appeal. The trump card was the Lopez girl and her ill-fated miracle. That was the twisted bit of luck with which I will eventually arrange for my freedom. That little girl is my ace in the hole. She has the world in the palm of her hand and she doesn't even know it. And she's safely in my pocket as well, and she doesn't know that either!"

And there it was, the moment that Dr. Katz had been waiting for. The light came on behind Peter Roland's big brown eyes, erasing his dull expression. And a crooked little smile slowly spread across his face, subtle, barely noticeable, and silently acknowledged by two co-conspirators, out to set justice back by one guilty man.

Dr. Katz took the papers from his chest and let them fall to the floor beside his bunk. Then he rolled onto his side facing the wall and pulled his knees up into a fetal position and closed his eyes. He prayed just loud enough that the walking boss might hear him and propagate the pious illusion. He needed them all for a little while longer, and then he would be free to show that little girl just how grateful he could be.

Sausalito, California, February 1971
Stinson Beach

KC cupped her hands together and blew a lung full of warm air into them, trying to keep from totally freezing to death. *What was I thinking* she kept asking herself, looking out at the small black stick figure that was waving to her from the ocean as he straddled his surfboard? She waved back to him, thankful that he could not see her face or read her lips from that far out. This was the LAST time that she would let Jay set her up on a blind date! She wondered where Jay had met this whack job, but then again, Jay made friends easily and probably ran into this guy at a taco stand and somehow surmised that this would be the perfect man for her...*NOT!*

To be fair, this guy was cute, coming and going, and he wasn't totally stupid, even for a *California Dude.* If she were sixteen again and totally inexperienced, could be this guy might be able to teach her a thing or two. *But come on*, standing on the beach at this ungodly hour in a freezing wind, watching someone try to impress her with daring feats of fancy like cutbacks, drop-ins, and duck dives was not exactly her idea of a dream date. Jay was going to pay for this, KC had already decided that much this morning. She sat down on the cold sand and wrapped the blanket completely around her, leaving only her eyes exposed to the frigid conditions.

She stared out at the ocean, way beyond what's his name, and started constructing her last piece on the fate of one Murray Katz, former doctor and current convicted rapist and murderer. She let her mind wander, back to the day the verdict came in. KC remembered being in such a good mood, having just spent a wonderful weekend with her new extended family in Firebaugh. Prior to arriving at the courthouse to witness the end of the Katz trial, she and Jay had attended Tina Lopez's Quinceanera, dancing and laughing their way into the hearts of every one of her cousins, aunts, uncles, and friends. She smiled as she relived the warm memories, the reverent ceremony, the lively party, the way Jay butchered the Spanish language, and the food, *my God* the food.

She had made an absolute pig of herself. There wasn't a dish she didn't try twice and not a recipe that she didn't take home! The whole event had taken her back to happier days as a child, before her parent's divorce and the break up of her own family. She had fond memories of birthday parties and trick-or-treating in the neighborhood on Halloween with hundreds of kids dragging pillowcases behind them. The cotton slipcovers heavy with the tasty little treasures they had spent the evening collecting. It had been a long time since she had been made to feel so welcome, so unconditionally loved, and she liked it! KC was surprised at how much she really did miss it. Someday, somehow she was going to have that again in her life, for herself, for her own family, just wait and see.

KC shook her head vigorously, trying to stay focused on the angle she was planning to close out the Katz story. That man was such a puzzle to her, she couldn't explain it, but somehow he just didn't seem right. She had watched during the trial as he ignored every opportunity to save himself by using the system in his favor. She new of his attorney, he had a reputation to be ruthless in the pursuit of his craft, and yet he seemed to be just going through the motions, *dull and listless* in his performance. It was as if he and Dr. Katz were deliberately trying to through the game, offering no defense whatsoever. As if they had been counting on the mercy of the people they could not have made a larger miscalculation. And then, when the day finally came, and the Judge asked the jury for their verdict, she could have sworn she saw Murray Katz smiling as the foreman spoke.

This behavior was so contrary to the pious man she had seen talking with Tina Lopez. His actions seemed to defy the words that she had read in his letters to the little girl. *What is his angle* she thought, what good could come from is death, *what did he really want from this child?* She couldn't help vexing over these feelings that she was having, maybe it was intuition, she didn't know; whatever it was it was giving here a stomachache. KC decided to title this last installment as *'Community Closure.'* The somber tone of the verdict and finality of the sentence would be the salve that healed the open wounds of so many. It all seemed fitting, it all seemed just, and yet, she felt as though she could sense a softening in the court of public opinion. She had noticed an increase in sympathetic letters to the editor, letters that cried mercy for the poor wretch who had been *touched* by *the angel of the valley.*

"Stick to the facts KC," she said loud enough to hear her own voice over the howling of the wind and the pounding of the surf. In the end she knew that is exactly what she would do, it was what she was trained to do, and she was uncommon good at it.

"Oh oh," she said as she noticed her date running toward her from out of the waves. His surfboard tucked under one arm he used his free hand to reach behind his back and pull the long cord down freeing himself from the confinement of his wetsuit.

"HEY, so what'd ya think," he shouted as he walked toward her?

"Narley," KC replied, trying to sound hip, and interested at the same time.

"Wanna give it a try," he asked, giving his head a shake, spraying her with saltwater. KC pulled the blanket tighter and closed up the only opening that exposed the fact that there was a person underneath.

"NOT ESCPECIALLY," she replied muttered sarcastically.

"What I *REALLY* want is some hot coffee and a stack of buttermilk pancakes. You think you can pull that off? I'm really much better company when I'm warm and fed, I swear," KC added cheerfully, deciding she would at least try and be nice.

After all, it wasn't this guy's fault that he wasn't her type, it Jay's for not knowing better! *He would be getting his later* she thought out loud, giggling softly at the prospect of making him pay.

"Sorry, I didn't hear that last part," asked Joe Surfer?

"Never mind, so are we on for pancakes or what," she asked, peeking out from under the blanket, smiling and overtly batting her eyes to be cute?

"Yeah, sure," he answered, holding out his hand, offering to help her up from the ground.

"OH NO you don't! I'm not budging from this spot in this frozen hurricane! You're going to have to bring the mountain to Mohammad," she explained in no uncertain terms.

"Yeah but my Vette is way up the hill in the lot! You want me to drive out here on the sand to pick you up?"

KC didn't respond she just disappeared back under the blanket.

Joe Surfer turned and stared the long walk back to his car, *"What a bitch,"* he muttered not so quietly. KC giggled and scrunched into a smaller, warmer ball under the blanket.

"You'll be sorry," she sang to herself.

"I'm gonna eat my weight in pancakes and sausage buddy!"

Fresno, California, February 1971
Golden State Penitentiary: Personnel Office

"So this was Warden Simons' great idea," whined Officer Vaughn as she skimmed over the work order in front of her.

As one of the few females on the administrative staff, one would think that she might be a little more discrete in her sarcastic criticism of their reformation-minded warden's latest initiative. That clearly was not Ginger Vaughn's style. She was as *no-nonsense* a person as there ever was. Standing in at an even six feet and with shoulders any linebacker would be envious of, she could be an imposing figure at first glance, and she wasn't about to take crap from anyone, regardless of rank or sex. This shared work program with the local halfway houses and minimum-security institutions just seemed risky to her.

And bringing a female, any female, inside to work in the kitchen could only mean trouble in the long run. At the very least it was going to put more stress on her and her coworkers, Ginger was certain of at least that much! She ran her finger down the page and studied the names and the photos beside them. None of these people seemed dangerous, but then how would she know, there were no records provided with the list. There was no time to complain much, the new program had been implemented without any feedback from the rank and file, so all she could do was salute and execute. She divided the small group of women into three groups of three and then assembled them in the team room with their assigned duty officers.

"OK ladies, welcome to Golden State," Officer Vaughn said in a voice that clashed with her physique. The nine women in the room all nodded in unison and sat quietly waiting for instructions.

"I'm Officer Vaughn, and I'll be in command of this detail," Ginger continued.

"I've broken you into three teams, red, white, and blue. Red Team will be with Officer Tandy, and you will be working in the prep area of the kitchen. White Team will be with Officer Dolenz, and will be working clean up and sanitation. Blue Team will be with me, and will be working the special meals area, preparing the trays for the shut-ins," explained Officer Vaughn. She looked from face to face, nodding at each duty Officer as they went to stand with their team.

"Two rules ladies"

"**ONE**…nobody leaves the sight of their duty officer. When one of you has to go, you all will go together, no exceptions."

"**TWO**…there is to zero contact with the inmate population. That means ZERO, no eye contact, note passing, or singing a happy tune. If one of you ladies messes up, then all of you will go back to your specific institution. You will not be compensated for services, and you will be restricted from further work furlough privileges indefinitely," Officer Vaughn said, making eye contact with everyone as she did so.

"Are we clear on these rules?"

Again, each head nodded in unison.

"Come on people, make me feel wanted, how about a *'yes Officer Vaughn'* so I can brag to my kids how important I am around here," she said, smiling and betraying a little of her outside of work personality.

"Yes Officer Vaughn," the women chimed in together, genuinely returning the smile.

"OK then, thank you ladies. Red and White teams through that door," she said pointing to the heavy wooden door on her right.

"Blue Team follow me, that's Fowler, Lindsey, and Hernandez," said Officer Vaughn, reading off the names on her list.

The three women walked through the double doors on the left while Officer Vaughn held them open from the other side. Ginger sized up her team as they filed by. She didn't see anyone she couldn't easily take if there was any trouble. The team stopped and waited for her to catch up and the four of them walked briskly down the hall toward their workstation for the day. When they arrived at the small kitchen set aside for the special clients or inmates, they were introduced to the manager in charge.

He spent a few minutes explaining their responsibilities and checking out the talent. He got a couple of sideways glances from the two white girls, but was totally ignored by the cute little Mexican girl. He didn't care, sooner or later she'd need him to keep this cushy job, he could wait. Until then he would just give her the shit jobs, scraping trays and unloading the superheated dryer. Yeah, she'd come around sooner or later. Nobody did those jobs long if they didn't have to. He nodded to Officer Vaughn indicating that orientation was over, and went about getting each of them started. Ginger Vaughn took a seat at a small table in the back of the room and poured herself a cup of coffee.

As Rosa Hernandez followed the horny little manager, she noticed the chalkboard on the wall. On it were columns of prisoner numbers with coded meal selections next to them. Reading the board quickly as they passed by, she saw it, M1423166. She couldn't believe her luck, she had found him one the very first day. This was going to be easy, this really was going to be a cinch!

"What are you laughing at," the small horny manager spat out at her, certain it was him.

"Nothing senor, por favor, lo ciento," she said sweetly, realizing that she might need this guy sooner or later. His demeanor changed quickly and he smiled broadly, revealing a couple of gold teeth. He ran his hand down the back of her shirt, letting his fingers gently probe for her bra strap.

"Maybe you can help me at the grill," he said snickering huskily. Rosa didn't move or object she just stood there while he pawed at her.

"HEY, RUDY, you want to keep that hand mister," shouted Officer Vaughn from across the room, coming to Rosa's rescue! The startled kitchen manager jumped back away from his prey, then walked reluctantly, but obediently back to the grill. Officer Vaughn walked up to Rosa and placed a hand on her shoulder.

"Are you OK," she asked gently.

Rosa nodded sheepishly as if she were embarrassed.

"Si, gracias senora, gracias," she said, lowering her head and walking up to the stack of dirty trays.

Ginger Vaughn shot a disgusted look at the little bastard working at the grill. She put one hand on her nightstick and pointed at him with the other, her meaning loud and clear. Rosa looked over her shoulder at each of them and smiled to herself, she had made two friends today!

Twenty-nine

(..."A prudent man sees evil and hides
himself. The naïve proceed and pay
the penalty"... Proverbs 27:12)

Fresno, California, 20 February 1973
<u>*Greyhound Bus Terminal*</u>

"Thanks for meeting me at the bus terminal Father, *but really*, I could
have just taken a taxi," I said looking over at Father Willet, trying to keep the
hair out of my face as it blew every which way.

It was obvious that I had arrived totally unprepared for the drastic change
in weather, having just come from the ice and snow of a typical East Coast
winter to this veritable heat wave in sunny California. I had only been to the
State twice before. Each time I had been just passing through San Francisco,
going to and coming from my tour of duty with the Marine Corps. As I recall,
on those occasions the weather had been nothing like this. In fact it had been
rather cold and dank, not actually raining, but ominously threatening to.
The hot wind that we were driving through today, reminded me a little bit
of Vietnam, minus the awful humidity of course. I found myself shamefully
wishing that the Church had provided Father Willet with a slightly more
luxurious automobile, at least one with air conditioning! As it was, I was
happy enough just to know that the ride would be a short one.

"Just a couple of miles more Ethan my boy," he said loudly over the sound of the wind whipping into the car from his open window.

"You won't even have time to break a decent sweat," he added, smiling as he watched me shed my jacket and coat.

"*Hey,* why don't you crank on that handle on the door next to you and help me turn up the *air conditioning* to high!" he said laughing.

Now my hair was really flying and I ran my fingers through it, holding as much of it as I could behind me. I glanced over at Father Willet and caught him giving me the once over with his eyes; a snap inspection just like the DI's did back in boot camp. Before he could say anything though, I quickly interjected, "I think the second thing I'll do once I get settled into my room, is stop by the local barber and see about getting this mop cut properly!"

"That would be a nice gesture Ethan, after all you're a priest not a pop star," said Father Willet, returning his attention to the road in front of him.

"By the way, you would have been hard pressed to find a taxi anywhere out here. And even if you did, you would have had to take out a loan to afford the ride!" he said, cracking himself up in the process.

"As you can plainly see, taxis just aren't practical in these wide open spaces son," he explained, as he swept his index finger across the span of the windshield, pointing to acre upon acre of what seemed like an endless expanse of fertile farmland.

The countryside was dotted by an occasional cluster of modest homes, barns, silos, and tool sheds, all of it efficiently connected by lonely four-way stops and railroad crossings. This was an America I had only read about in some of John Steinbeck's California novels like *The Grapes of Wrath, The Long Valley, and Tortilla Flat,* each of them completely foreign to my East Coast upbringing and prejudices. I leaned forward in my seat and scanned the scenery on each side of the road from the vantage point of the large Buick windshield. There was not a mountain or hill in sight, just mile after mile of tilled soil, crops of some kind or another, and large sections of land that reminded me of Paulie's backyard, wild and over grown. Father Willet identified those sections as alfalfa, or hay.

"*What the live stock eats boy, you know horses and cows and such,*" he said, bewildered I seemed so perplexed at such common knowledge.

"*I get it,*" I said, nodding my head in an affirmative response, trying to convince him that I wasn't a total idiot.

And although I now knew the name of the crop, those patches of green and yellow alfalfa just looked like weeds to me. We rode along in silence for a moment or two before he slowed to a stop at one of the four-way intersections. There was a large blue and white tractor stopped across the street. It was headed in the direction from whence we came, and its headlights were on even though it was the middle of the day. Both vehicles entered the intersection at the same time after checking for cross traffic traveling east and west. Father Willet waved at the driver sitting high up in the enclosed cab of the big machine at it passed. The barely visible driver waved back at us from behind the tinted glass.

I could see a transistor radio swinging from the rear view mirror just above the driver's head. I watched in awe as the tractor went by, the huge farm vehicle dwarfing the small sedan we were traveling in. It filled the window space as it rolled by, blocking out the hot sun for a moment and providing some cool relief in the process. I turned around in my seat as far as I could and watched it disappear in the rear window, the big tires leaving behind an interesting trail of soft soil on the road as it fell from between the thick rubber tread. As we sped up, I leaned back in my seat and I looked over at Father Willet squinting as the sun reflected off of the windshield of a passing car.

"Looks like were going to have to stop at the Emporium and get you a pair of sunglasses young Ethan," Father Willet said without looking my way.

"Those blue eyes of yours will give you fits out here," he added.

"Roger that," I said without thinking.

"Excuse me?"

"Sorry, I was just agreeing with you," I said, hoping to leave it at that.

"Oh that's right, you're a veteran aren't you," the Father asked rhetorically. He glanced over at me, and then quickly shifted his eyes back to the road.

"Yes sir, it's no big thing though," I replied, praying that he would not press any further.

"I understand son, I see a few ghosts from time to time myself," he said softly.

"Thanks Father," I said without looking at him.

"We'll just tell everyone that crooked finger on your hand and the scars around it are from some old football injury, does that work for you?" he asked. I could feel his eyes on me but I continued to stare out the windshield. I covered my left hand with my right and stared even more intensely at the passing scenery.

"That will be just fine Father, thank you sir."

"Not to worry son," he replied, reaching over and wiping away a tear from the corner of my eye before it had a chance to run down my cheek.

"Must be all this damn wind," he said, as he dried his palm on the fabric of the front seat cushion.

"Maybe I'll just roll up my window a tad, and see if I can keep that mop of yours out of your eyes."

"Don't want anyone thinking I reduced you to tears on the first day now do we," he teased, giving my shoulder a good whack. I smiled to myself and snorted a reply.

"No sir, we wouldn't want that!"

<u>*Albany, New York, 20 February 1973*</u>

"**Shannon Elizabeth Kelly**! *Supper has been ready for ten minutes now girl, come to the table before it chills to ice!*" bellowed Maggie Kelly from the kitchen.

Shannon lay on her bed putting the finishing touches on a letter to her brother when her mother's shrill voice interrupted the peace and quiet she had been enjoying. Her Mom's resonated powerfully off of all four walls in her little room. She tossed her writing tablet and pink inked pen onto the floor then flipped over onto her stomach, burying her face in her pillow as she screamed out a reply meant only for her ears. Why the woman couldn't just walk the twenty or thirty feet from the kitchen to her room was a frustrating mystery to her. She flipped over again and quickly sat up swinging her legs out over the side of her bed. Red faced and winded from her primal response, she straightened her hair with her hands and called back to her mother.

"COMING!"

"Well, that's a nice surprise now," Mrs. Kelly said as her daughter walked into the kitchen to take her place at the table.

They were having most of their meals in the kitchen now that there was just the two of them. It's just much more practical, and easier to clean up afterwards, her mother would say. But Shannon knew that she was really just lonely for the old days. When the four of them would sit around the big table in the other room and enjoy a grand meal and some raucous chatter. Her mother seemed to have aged considerably after her Father's death and then Ethan's horrible experiences in the war. She was so happy when he came home, but now he was gone again, and she was becoming more and more irritable as she prepared herself for Shannon's inevitable turn to leave the nest.

"What's a nice surprise?" Shannon asked as she sat in the chair opposite her mother at the small kitchen table.

"I didn't have to come fetch you, that's what!"

"Oh Mother, don't be silly!"

"Silly am I? If you were in here helping me prepare these meals there would be no need to call or to fetch, *now would there!*" snapped Maggie

weakly. Shannon knew when she was out matched so she held her tongue and placed her napkin in her lap.

"It's your turn to say grace girl, so get on with it," Maggie said genuflecting.

"We thank thee Father for this meal, we thank thee Father for thy grace, we thank thee Father for your love, Forgive us Father while we stuff our face!"

"SHANNON!"

"Sorry…"

"In Christ's name we pray to Heaven above…Amen."

"Must you always try my patience so girl? Honestly, the things that come out of your insolent gob!" Maggie Kelly said as she dished boiled potatoes onto her daughter's plate.

Shannon looked at her mother and smiled impishly showing both rows of teeth in the process. It wasn't that the humor of the moment was lost on Maggie Kelly. She just knew that if she gave Shannon an inch, it would be a mile she would be taking next. Maggie finished serving up her daughter's supper and started to attend to her own plate. She reached for the ceramic gravy boat she had bought at the flea market in Hudson Falls last year, and poured the rich brown mushroom concoction over her potatoes and beef brisket, the tasty mixture steaming, still piping hot from the stovetop.

"Did you finish the letter to your brother, girl?"

"Yes ma'am, I did ma'am," Shannon said with a mouthful of brisket.

"Shannon, I swear by all that's holy, I don't know how you're going to find a husband with manners like those?" her mother lamented.

Shannon shrugged her shoulders and shoveled half a boiled potato into her mouth, letting her actions say all that she cared to on the subject. The fact was she already knew who her future husband would be, so she wasn't worried. She had seen it all in a dream when she was twelve, and knew for certain that she was destined to marry this fella.

She had convinced herself that that this bit of magic had been a real glimpse of the future. Well, perhaps a real glimpse from the perspective of a *puppy love struck* twelve year old anyway. She had even imagined that she had seen the faces of her children. Real or imagined, premonition or a fantasy, either way it was a sweet thought to carry around in her heart, and it kept the lonely child from sailing away on a breeze of melancholy and self pity. Once she had actually told him as much, although it was not likely that he understood her to be serious, she was a child after all. She smiled to herself as she thought of Ethan reading all about this in her letter, and she wished that she could be a fly on the wall for that moment.

"What are you grinning about Shannon? You look as though you just saw a fairy or something?" Shannon snapped of her little daydream and started chewing her food again.

"*Nufing Mom,*" she mumbled while she chewed.

"*Better I keep this a deep dark secret for now,*" she thought.

"*Especially from mother!*"

It was a good idea, even though she was dying to mess with her mind a little. Shannon picked up her glass of milk and took a couple big swallows. She started to raise her arm to wipe her mouth with her shirtsleeve, but thought better of it, and reached down into her lap for her napkin. She raised it to her face and dabbed her mouth delicately just like a proper lady should, and then gently returned the napkin to her lap. She looked over to her mother and smiled triumphantly, like she had just won a gold medal at the Olympics or something, and waited for a gesture of approval.

"Alright Shannon, *I thank you for that.* I suppose there may be hope for you yet, *ye wee chisller!*" Maggie Kelly said, winking at her playful child.

"I hope your brother calls soon so we know he arrived safely. I don't like California. I've read such awful things. All the hippies and radicals, and those horrid stories about motorcycle gangs hopped up on drugs and strong drink, I just don't like it."

"Don't worry none Mom, he survived Vietnam, I think he can handle California!

"Besides, you know Ethan, he'll call Mom, *he always calls,*" Shannon said reaching across the table to pat her mother's arm. Maggie Kelly smiled at her daughter and then narrowed her eyes and wrinkled her nose as she followed the trail of gravy from Shannon's plate to the sleeve of her nice white blouse.

"*Oh Shannon,*" Maggie said shaking her head slowly.

"*My poor grandchildren,*" she said with a sigh.

Fresno, California, 20 February 1973
<u>*Saint John's Cathedral*</u>

I finished unpacking my bags and placing all of my stuff in the small chest of drawers near the bed, and the tall armoire in the corner of the little rectory room.

"*At least there's a private bathroom!*" I said out loud to myself.

I had envisioned a more communal setting and I had to admit I was relieved to discover that I had been wrong. I had had my fill of community showers and open latrines while in the military. So I was happy to learn that my new vocation would provide some basic personal amenities...nice! Father Willet had said to stop by his office when I was settled and we would tour the facility and he would introduce me to everyone on staff. The Church itself was magnificent, built way more than a hundred years ago I suspected. It had that unique Spanish influence that I had read about when I was studying up on the region after learning of my assignment here. I had asked Father Willet on the drive over whether or not there were any of the old adobe missions nearby, the sort that California was famous. He said that there were at least a couple and that when time permitted he would show them to me.

"We'll make a day of it Ethan!" he had said.

I put my coat back on and stopped a second in the bathroom to make sure I was presentable, then went out into the hall to get my bearings. I started walking back the way we had come, retracing my steps, and feeling more confident as I recognized landmarks along the way.

"Once a boy scout, always a Boy Scout," I muttered to myself, making a left at the intersection of corridors.

As I continued on toward Father Willet's office, I thought about how and when I would bring up the subject of the Rojas family. I already knew that they attended this Church, Mitchell had told me about this place several times, always speaking affectionately of Father Willet. One day while we were hanging up sweaty tees to dry in the hot breeze, Mitchell had said, *"You know ese, some call him Wee Billy, but not to be mean. Everyone loves that little guy man! His heart es muy grande carnal, muy grande! Oh, and don't let his cussing give you the wrong idea, everyone has vices, even priests I think."*

I remember pondering that at the time and wondering if Father Willet also kept a secret list of colorful language for personal penance. I had to admit I was able to understand why everyone was so enamored with him. He had a presence and charm that captivated you right away. Within seconds of meeting him you had the impression that you had known him for years, and you felt comfortable right away. I was pretty sure that this was the Holy Spirit at work, and I found myself hoping that I could emulate him in time.

Arriving at his office I saw that the door was open. I knocked on it anyway before I entered and Father Willet waved me in pointing to the two chairs in front of his desk. I chose one and sat down, crossing my legs *guy style*, one ankle resting over one knee (Kenny, Paulie, and I had always giggled whenever we saw men cross their legs like women, it wasn't natural, how they could do that without squishing the boys we wondered).

I looked around the room while I waited for Father Willet to finish with whatever he was doing. I really liked the feel of the room, with the floor to ceiling bookcases built into all four walls, and the large multi-paned window that looked out onto the courtyard. In the center of the yard there was a huge Elm tree hovering over a beautiful stone fountain of water. Accentuating the pathways leading to the courtyard were dozens of colorful rose bushes, a ring of rod iron and redwood benches completed the peaceful setting. I assumed that this was where most people took pictures of brides and grooms, and newly christened children after each ceremony had been performed.

"Well Ethan, are you all settled in?" Father Willet said, leaning back in his big leather chair, smiling at me, his hands clasped at his chest, fingers laced.

"Yes sir, I am sir," I replied, slowly nodding my head with a suave *so what's next* frown on my face, trying a bit too hard to appear older and worldlier.

"Great," he said, opening a manila folder that was setting in front of him. Reaching over to his right Father Willet picked up his spectacles, skillfully running the wire frames one side at a time over his ears, being careful not to snag what hair was left on his head in the process.

"OK, well, I've read your file here and I must say I am impressed with your work so far at Seminary. There are high marks here and several glowing evaluations from your professors and advisors in these pages."

"Thank you sir," I replied, trying to appear relaxed, although it was my nature to be less so whenever people praised me for any reason.

"I'm curious though, what made you specifically ask for an assignment to this Church?"

"I don't know what you mean sir," I lied, and poorly at that.

"Oh come now Ethan, let's not start out on the wrong foot here, you were doing so well. This isn't a test boy, there's no hidden agenda or anything sinister like that."

"I'm just curious why someone who could have gone *anywhere* in the whole wide world, chose here, of all places?" Father Willet asked, giving his clean-shaven face a good rub with the thumb and four fingers of his right hand, seemingly searching for whisker evidence of a five o'clock shadow.

I cleared my throat, realizing that the moment to bring up **my** hidden Rojas agenda had suddenly presented itself. I stifled a smile as I thought to myself, *"I don't know why anyone makes plans at all, clearly everything happens in God's time!"*

"Forgive me Father, I apologize for my lack of faith in your compassion. I did have a reason for choosing this Church for my internship," I explained.

Uncrossing my legs I stood up and began to walk slowly around the room, running my fingers over the hundreds of books resting on the shelves, *volume by volume*. I stopped when I reached the window and stared out at the courtyard.

"It's beautiful," I said, watching as a sparrow landed on one of the redwood benches.

"Yes it is," Father Willet replied, watching me closely. I paused for a moment and listed to the muted singing of the birds through the paned window.

"I had this friend in Vietnam. He was from out here, attended this Church actually."

"Is that so?"

"Yes"

I watched the sparrow on the bench fly away and another one drop down from the Elm tree to takes its place.

"I didn't know him long, but then you make friends *quickly* or *not at all* under those circumstances, ya know?"

"I know what you mean son, believe me, *I know what you mean.*"

"He was a good guy this friend of mine. He made us all smile whenever he smiled. It was sorta like you could see right through him, right into his beating heart whenever he smiled. His joy was so pure, so powerful, so transparent, that it was positively contagious! Have you ever known anyone like that Father, *have you ever?*" I asked, suddenly aware that my voice was well above a normal conversational tone.

Father Willet rose from his chair and walked over to the end of his desk and leaned back against it leisurely.

"Yes Ethan, I have had the pleasure of meeting people like your friend on many occasions in my life. It's one of the perks of the business we're in I think."

"*As you say*, I imagine it's sorta like what Christ himself said in the Beatitudes of Matthew 5:8, **blessed are the pure in heart for they shall see God.**" I kept silent and unconsciously raised my left hand to my face and began to nibble on the knuckle of my disfigured index finger.

"Ethan, What happened to this good friend of yours?"

I started tracing the square panes of glass with my finger, still watching the sparrow on the bench as it mechanically turned and twisted it's head, searching here and there for shelter, food or whatnot.

"He didn't make it," I said in a flat tone.

"I see"

"I watched him die, his bloody hands on mine while I tried to keep his guts inside of him. I took his confession Father, I know that I shouldn't have, but I did just the same!" I said, confessing a bit myself.

"*Nonsense Ethan*, God just gave you a battlefield promotion is all"

"I'm sure that your friend appreciated your comfort in his final hour. He didn't die alone son, he knew love in life and you showed him love in death.

Mark my words, one day you'll meet again on the streets of glory, and he'll have a chance to say to what he couldn't on that day, you both will."

"Wait and see boy, you just wait and see!" said Father Willet softly.

"Thank you Father, *do you really think so Father?*"

"I do"

"Thanks, I actually feel a little better already."

"Good…confession is good for the soul I hear," he said smiling.

"Now, is he is the reason you came here to St. John's?"

"Yes, sort of"

"*Sort of,* what does that mean?"

I turned around to look at the priest, and we held each other's gaze until I decided I was ready to tell him everything. Walking back to the chair, I sat down and spent the next hour telling him all about Mitchell Rojas, Junior Martinez, Carla Cardinale, Arron Walker, Tony Yamamoka, Wesley Hightower, and Larry Pollen. I even told him about JoJo *whatever his last name was,* except I left out all of the swear words, *my list was full enough already!* Everything that I had put out of my mind for the past four years came bubbling out of me as I recanted a part of my life that I swore I would bury forever.

Father Willet listened intently and expressionless, but I could see in his eyes that he more than understood. Perhaps my coming here wasn't really ***all*** my idea after all. I was beginning to feel as though this little detour in life may have been chosen ***for me***. When I finished telling my story I leaned back in the chair and reached into my coat pocket and pulled out the letter from Elena Rojas. I handed it over to Father Willet, watching him as he opened it and read it twice. He set the letter down after a moment or two of silence and removed his specs, pinching the bridge of his nose between his eyes with his thumb and forefinger. He looked up at me but before he could speak there was a light rap on the door that broke through the pensive moment.

"Excuse me Father, my apologies young man, but supper will be served in the dining hall in fifteen minutes," said a very old and very small nun standing in the doorway dressed in a traditional black habit.

"Thank you Sister Demarco, we will be along in a moment," Father Willet replied.

"*Oh, my manners!* Sister, this young man is our new novice from Boston, Father Ethan Kelly," he said introducing me to the aged woman.

"A pleasure sir, I'm sure," she said sweetly in a thick Italian accent. She folded her hands in front of her and bowed slightly. I stood up and turned toward her.

"The pleasures mine Sister, and I'm from New York, not Boston, Albany actually," I said, correcting Father Willet innocently.

"*Ahhh*, yes, well, supper will be served shortly gentleman," said Sister Demarco as she turned to go about her business.

Father Willet and I returned to our seats as soon as she disappeared from view.

"Wonderful woman that Ruth Demarco," Father Willet said smiling. He leaned forward and motioned for me to do likewise, as if was worried we might be overheard.

"I'll be honest with you Ethan. I stole this nun from a most disagreeable and powerful priest about ten years ago. I'm sure that you must have met him when you passed through the Archdiocese in Los Angeles, Father Villa Cruz." I looked back at Father Willet, certain that my face gave away my puzzlement.

"I'm sorry Father. I'm not reading you," I said.

"*Father Villa Cruz,* you would remember him, believe me! He kind of reminds you of Brando's character, Vito Corleone in *The Godfather, you saw the film I'm sure!*" Father Willet said trying to lead me to a recollection.

"*Yes, YES*, I do remember him, he did most of his talking with hand gestures, and his accent was so thick I really only understood the single syllable words when he spoke." I said, recalling a brief encounter with the man.

"That's him!"

"Anyway, Sister Ruth Demarco had arrived in Los Angels during one of Father Villa Cruz's absences, he was away visiting a childhood friend at the Vatican at the time."

"I happened to be attending a conference in town and staying at the Archdiocese while in Los Angeles. The first night Sister Demarco was there, she happened to be assigned to prepare the evening meal for all of us."

"Ethan, *my goodness*, if abstaining from this woman's cooking became the eighth sacrament, I would have to leave the priesthood!"

"I can deal with the poverty and the celibacy, but *mama mia*, can this Sister **COOK!**" Father Willet said, cupping his face in his two hands. I put my hand to my mouth to restrain a giggle as listened to him continue with his story/confession.

"*So what happened next?*" I begged.

"After the meal I nonchalantly strolled by the kitchen, pretending to be lost in the unfamiliar building. When I finally found Sister Demarco she was sitting at a small table eating a small portion of the meal she had prepared. I introduced myself, thanked her for the wonderful supper, and *ever so innocently* inquired as to what her situation might be here at the Archdiocese. When she let it slip that she was actually confused as to why she had been reassigned so far away from her home in Sicily. I offered to help her see about sorting things out as soon as possible. The next morning I worked over the Archdiocese' administrative staff with some patented *Father Billy* fast talking and arranged to have Sister Demarco assigned to St. John's before Father Villa Cruz returned to the USA."

"But she's been here ten years, I thought you said that she wanted to go home to Sicily?" I asked, confused.

"Yes, well, she did at first, but after a few months here and some skillful introductions to fellow humble Christian souls like herself, Sister Demarco gradually became accustomed to our small town life. It was much closer to the life she had in Sicily, *and*, here in America we had Supermarkets and soap operas, she calls them her stories." Father Willet explained with a big grin.

I leaned back in my chair and grinned back at the sly old devil, understanding better why he was so well loved by one and all. A priest that could work both sides of the street, too bad a man of the cloth couldn't run for office, Father Willet was a natural!

"So, you see, everybody's happy, except of course Father Villa Cruz, and I happily do penance for that every week right up until the day the Lord calls me to my reward!"

"Good story Father, I guess we better get to the dining hall before she has to holler after us."

"Yeah, OK, in a minute Ethan, I sort of got side tracked here," he said, returning his attention to the letter from Mitchell's wife Elena.

"I did know this couple Ethan, they started coming to Mass here in 1962 I think."

"Ethan, how much did Mitchell tell you about his life here in the states?"

"Not much, just the usual family and high school stuff. Oh, and he had some interesting stories from boot camp as well," I said, chuckling.

"What did he tell you about his family?" Father Willet asked.

I shrugged my shoulders while I thought about it for a second.

"He showed us wedding pictures and vacation pictures of Disneyland and such. Oh, and he showed us a couple pictures of his son. I think he said his name was Miguel." I answered.

"*That's it*, nothing unusual or strange?" said Father Willet, pressing just a little bit.

"Yeah, that was about it." I said, and then quickly raised my index finger in a *wait a minute* gesture.

"No, now that you mention it I do remember one thing?"

"Yes?"

"There was one night when he babbled on about his son surviving some kind of accident. He said that and an *angel* had brought him back from the dead. I just figured his kid must have drowned or something and had been revived. I could see how some people might mistake that for a miracle." Father Willet looked at me for a moment and then leaned forward on his elbows.

"It was much more than that son," he said slowly, staring at me with an intensity that made me uncomfortable.

"Elena Rojas killed herself in 1969 Ethan, shortly after she buried her husband. That's why you never received a reply to any of your other letters."

I sat there, stunned, totally unprepared for this bit of news. The shock turned to anger, as I got thoroughly pissed at myself for not seeing this coming. I mean I had witnessed enough grief first hand to understand how powerful a malady it was to one's sanity. It ranked right up there next to jealousy and hate. I had watched it age my mother prematurely and I had seen it leave a vibrant young man like Junior Martinez in a near catatonic state. So why was I so surprised by this revelation?

"How Father?" I muttered, unsure why I asked.

"*Does it matter?* It was just awful, that poor child finding her like that," Father Willet said, wincing as he said the words.

"I told her I would come Father, I promised Mitchell I would come, but I waited four years to do it."

"I took care of me first, it was selfish and look what happened," I said scolding myself.

"*Stop that Ethan!*"

"Don't be throwing yourself a *pity party* on my turf young man!" said Father Willet, doing a bit of scolding as well.

"No one can take the blame for someone else's weakness or action."

"Elena Rojas was a good woman and a fine mother, but in the end it was her faith that was weak. In the end she let Satan tempt her with grief and allowed herself to accept his solution. She abandoned her child and the living in exchange for a false peace and an eternity of damnation!" he said in the terse tone of some delivering a *fire and brimstone* sermon.

"I'm sorry Ethan for sounding so cold and heartless. It's not that I don't feel for her pain and suffering. But I can't allow you to rationalize an understanding and acceptance for the path that she chose. You will counsel and pray with people during your career that will be facing the same kind of decisions. You must understand, these passion plays are ancient, each one unique and each one the same, all of them merely a variation of the same theme. It is only the ending that is negotiable, based solely on the path that one chooses."

"*Son*, if you learn nothing else from me during your time here, remember this. No matter how tempting it is to believe otherwise, *right is right, wrong is wrong, and sin is sin!*"

"It really is as black and white as that. The only shades of gray and colorful contrasts that come into play are our mortal attempts to deny that simple axiom. Scholars have written volumes about the tenants of free will. How that wholly human ability is what separates us from the angels above, is what makes life so deliciously interesting and unpredictable, and is in the final analysis, what makes us so very wise and scholarly. To my mind Ethan, from my experience and many years seniority, I've come to realize that from the very beginning God has taught us the way, and when we strayed too far he would punish us accordingly, by letting us deal with the consequences of our free will actions. After all Ethan, Eve didn't leave the garden alone, *now did she?*"

I thought a few minutes about his diatribe, studying his face as he studied mine. I liked the way he called me son, and I found myself enjoying his company, but his theology was going to take some time for me to digest. I decided that I wanted to step back and zero in on the reason I had come here.

"Where is Miguel now Father?"

"*Ahhh*, I was hoping you would ask me that," Father Willet said, suddenly smiling again.

"He's a bitter and confused boy right now Ethan. Only a couple months from thirteen, I'm sure you remember how confusing a time that can be under normal circumstances."

"I have tried to stay close to him, but I'm not as sexy an influence as the gang-bangers that surround his small world are. Maybe someone younger can reach him, someone that has the advantage of knowing the father that he worshiped?" the elder priest said, sizing me up as I listened patiently.

"I'm hoping that with your help we might be able to keep him from growing into a hateful young man. That path will only lead to things I don't care to think much about," he said shuddering, as if just hit by an Arctic wind.

He started to say something else when he quickly turned toward the doorway and held up his hand for me to be silent. He sniffed at the air and closed his eyes, a large grin spreading across his face.

"*Oh my*...sausage and peppers tonight, you're in for a real treat," he said, swimming in the heavenly aroma that had already filled the hall and was beginning to fill his office as well. He got up from his chair and walked around his desk quickly. He took my arm, and led me toward the doorway.

"*Let's hurry son,* we don't want to rude now do we?" he said anxiously.

"I'm sure that Sister Demarco has worked hard on your *welcome to St. John's supper.* We can talk more about the Rojas boy over dinner!" he said, licking his lips as he spoke.

I decided while we were walking that I wanted to know all there was to know about Elena's suicide and Miguel's miracle. Hopefully Father Willet would be more talkative after a good meal and several glasses of wine. Here I hoped my Irish heritage would serve me well. By the time I finished toasting the twelve apostles, *one at a time* of course, then the seven sacraments likewise, I'll have learned every secret kept hidden in the old Brit's closet.

I guess Mitchell was right about one thing; even priests had their vices! Mine happened to be sneakiness this week. Being a young man there were plenty of others, but I tended to keep them in check with prayer. I suppose that I could have tried to blame shift and point to influences like MAD Magazine and the Spy vs. Spy frames for my sinful conspiracies against clean living, but...not *really*, it was all me! All men sin to one degree or another, even priests!

Thirty

(…"she goes running for the shelter of her mother's little helper…doctor please some more these, outside the door, she took four more"… Rolling Stones)

<u>*Albany, New York, June 1973*</u>

Apparently June gloom was going to be kind of late this summer, as it was just down right *hot* outside! Even the shade provided little comfort with the humidity hovering around ninety percent. Maggie Kelly rose up from her crouch and wiped the sweat from her brow with the back of her gardening glove.

"Good thing Shannon wasn't around to catch me doing that," Maggie said under her breath.

She would have had to eat crow for at least a week considering how often she scolded her daughter for doing such un-ladylike things! She sat back on her heels and rested a moment, giving the small spade in her left hand a little spin. She looked up at the cloudless blue sky, shading her eyes with her free hand and attempted to determine the time by the location of the sun. After calculating the sun's position for a few seconds, she soon tired of squinting and twisted her right arm to read the face of her watch.

"Phooey!" she exclaimed.

It was already noon and she had puttered away the entire morning digging in the garden, completely throwing off her household schedule. She scolded herself as she gathered her tools and tossed them into the yellow wheel barrel, got up and maneuvered it toward the backyard and the tool shed. She removed her gloves and placed them neatly on top of all the spades and hand tillers. Then she turned on her heel and walked quickly across the yard to the house, reciting a litany of chores that she had planned.

"I guess I'll have put off that nice hot bath I was dreaming of until after supper," Maggie muttered to herself. And with that thought she entered the kitchen through the back door and walked up to the sink to wash her hands. She reached up and gave the white ceramic handles marked 'H' and 'C' respectively, a gentle twist and let the warm water run over her hands. As she reached for the cake of soap in the small dish setting on the windowsill a sharp rap on the kitchen door startled her.

"Hello the house," Kenny Wong hollered, trying to make out shapes through the heavily screened door. Maggie quickly shut off the water and grabbed a dishtowel from the counter.

"Ken Wong, *is that you sonny?*" she asked.

"Yes ma'am, it is," he replied.

"Come on in boy, it's hot outside," Maggie said, motioning for him to enter the house with her right hand.

Kenny opened the wooden screen door and walked into the house, turning around quickly to make sure that the door didn't slam shut behind him. Mrs. Kelly met him halfway near the small kitchen table and gave him a hug. She pointed toward a chair and invited him to sit down.

"This is a nice surprise Kenny, sit down and I'll get you a cold glass lemonade," she said with a smile. Ken held up his hand.

"That's OK Mrs. Kelly, don't bother, I'm not really thirsty anyway," he pleaded.

"Nonsense, it's a million degrees out there and your sweating as well. You just sit right there while I pour you a tall glass," Maggie insisted. Kenny had known this woman his whole life, so he knew when to shut up and surrender. Mrs. Kelly walked over and handed Ken the ice-cold refreshment and he took a long greedy drink.

"There, you see, I told you that would hit the spot sonny," Maggie said beaming.

"Yes ma'am, thank you," Ken replied, wiping his mouth with the back of his hand.

"So what brings you by this afternoon, did Ethan tell you to look in on us from time to time?"

"*You know he did ma'am,*" Kenny answered. Maggie nodded and smiled.

"Mrs. Kelly, I was wondering if I could get Ethan's telephone number in California?" Kenny asked. Maggie studied his face a moment before she answered.

"Sure Ken, let me get it from the bureau dear," she said.

Walking slowly toward Kenny she touched his shoulder as she passed by and went into the other room. Ken tensed up when she walked by and quickly picked up his glass and took another long drink. He closed his eyes tightly trying to remain in control of his emotions. He didn't want to break down in front of this woman. He set his glass down and waited for Mrs. Kelly to return. A moment later a small piece of paper floated down to the table in front of him. He felt his body tense up when two hands suddenly appeared, giving his shoulders a good hard squeeze.

"What's the matter sonny?" Maggie asked with the soft soothing voice that she always used when someone was hurting.

Ken spun around in his chair, his eyes red and moist and buried his head in Mrs. Kelly's apron, allowing himself to be cradled and comforted while he shamefully cried like a child. Maggie held him like that for a good five minutes, letting him get it all out. She knew how fiercely proud young Ken was, and she realized that a fair amount of the tears were dedicated to his frustration at being human. As soon as his shoulders stopped heaving and the sobbing turned to a whimper, Maggie released her hold on him and pulled a chair close to his.

"OK boy, now tell what this is all about," she said softly.

Ken sniffled and reached for a napkin from the holder on the table. He blew his nose loudly and then rubbed the paper napkin vigorously across his nose making sure that all was clear. The he wadded up the paper and stuck it into his pocket. He finally looked up from the floor and at Mrs. Kelly. He swallowed hard before speaking. He didn't want to lose it again.

"It's my little girl," he started.

"Something is the matter with Sophia, was she in an accident dear?" Maggie asked too quickly.

"No, there was no accident," Ken continued.

He could sense that Mrs. Kelly's concern and curiosity was getting ready to go onto autopilot. And he didn't want to play twenty questions while she tried to guess the nature of his daughter's situation. He held up his hand to silence her before she could start a rapid salvo of probing questions.

"Please, Mrs. Kelly, let me finish," Ken said. Maggie pulled her lips in and bit down on them and then leaned back in her chair.

"We found out a few months ago that Sophie has leukemia," Ken said calmly. Maggie remained quiet and still, but her eyes were beginning to glisten.

"We didn't tell anyone outside of the family until now because there was all this testing to do and we were sorta hoping that they would find out they made a mistake or something," Ken said, pausing to take another drink from his glass.

"Let me get you some more lemonade," Maggie said standing.

Ken waved his hand while he drank, indicating that he was fine, and Maggie sat back down, folding her hands in her lap as she did so.

"Well, the testing quickly turned to treatment, and then everything began to happen *so fast* Mrs. Kelly. It seemed like every week we were dealing with life or death decisions. We had to deal with minor victories and major setbacks, but mostly we had to deal with feeling helpless and useless." Ken paused and took an audible breath, then continued.

"Maybe I should have come here sooner, I don't know, but I really need Ethan's support. Of course I'd like for him to pray for Sophie, but I need him to pray for Carolyn too, maybe he could talk to the two of them. I don't know what else to say, and Sophie loves him so much. She even cries for him sometimes in her sleep. She's not doing so well Mrs. Kelly, and I'm scared that I might lose them both ma'am," Ken said, his eyes beginning to tear up again. Maggie started to reach across to him but he waved her off and crossed his arms in front of him.

"I'm OK, I'm OK," he said forcefully.

Maggie slowly sat back in her chair and waited for him to continue.

"Sophie has had all the chemo therapy that her little body can stand. I'm afraid that the cure is killing her faster than the disease. Her doctors are not optimistic ma'am."

"And Carolyn can barely function now. She's taking some pretty potent mother's little helpers, Secobarbitol I think, and some Valium to get through the day, and then Secanol to help her to sleep at night!" Ken said, his voice betraying his disapproval.

"I don't know if I am going to be able to hold us all together, I feel like I'm losing my mind!" The room became suddenly very quiet, and after a several minutes of awkward silence Maggie spoke.

"What can we do to help sonny," she asked softly.

Ken did not resist when she reached out to hold his hand. They looked at one another and then Ken silently mouthed, *"I don't know."*

Maggie Kelly stood suddenly, and Ken could see that her *Irish* was up.

"Well then!" she said loudly.

"If it's a fight the devil wants, then it's a fight he'll get by God!" she proclaimed shaking her fist at the kitchen ceiling.

"The first thing we're going to do is get rid of all these frowns and long faces. The devil likes nothing better than a room full of sad people," she continued, reaching over and gently wiping Ken's tear stained face with her hands. She put an index finger at each corner of his mouth and pulled them up into a smile.

"There, that's more like it I'll reckon," she said, admiring her work. She took her hands away from his face and leaned back in her chair.

"Sonny, I know that this hard. You know that we went through much the same when Ethan's father passed." Maggie went on.

"So it's from experience that I urge you to embrace this tragedy and treat your child, your wife, and your whole family with joy and love, skip the sorrow and pity'" she said firmly, watching his reaction closely before continuing.

"My Edward lived more during those last two years than most men do in a lifetime, *we made sure of that!*"

"Every day was his birthday, the Fourth of July, and Christmas Eve, all rolled into one. Not materially mind you, but personally, we made him feel special each and every day. We surrounded him with our love and devotion, so that when the cancer made him weak, he never felt alone. And neither did we," Maggie said with pride in her voice.

"We were united as a family, and made sure that the devil never got a finger-hold on my husband's soul. There was always a hand to hold, a cheek to kiss, or a warm embrace nearby."

"Look Sonny…*Kenny*, I beg you, leave all of your pain here at this table today. There will be plenty of time for grief afterward, *if death is God's will*," she said, holding Ken's hand, stroking it gently.

"Don't let the devil steal your joy son. Look at Sophie and Carolyn and focus on everything positive about your feelings for them. Then let it flow from you boy! The devil has nothing in his arsenal more powerful than love. Fill your heart with it, and lead your family with a joyful spirit, and you will be able to find peace in whatever future that God has in store," Maggie said as she knelt beside her son's friend.

"I don't know ma'am, *I don't know if I can*," Ken whispered. Maggie Kelly suddenly slapped both hands up to Kenny's face and held them there tightly.

"Of course you can boy, of course you can! And I'll be right here with ye to make sure!" she said sternly.

Ken took a deep breath and then let out slowly. Taking hold of Mrs. Kelly's wrists, he gently pulled her hands away from his face, and they held each other's gaze for a moment.

"Will you come with me to talk with Carolyn, and maybe my parents as well ma'am?" Ken asked softly.

Maggie put her hands on Ken's knee and pushed herself up to stand before him.

"*You know I will sonny,*" she answered.

"But why don't you try calling Ethan first while I leave a note for Shannon," she added, scratching her nose as she looked around for a pencil and paper.

Ken stood and picked up the scrap of paper with Ethan's number and walked into the living room. He stopped in the hall and looked back to see Mrs. Kelly standing at the counter, scribbling out a note. He turned back and noticed the wall in the hallway. It was almost completely covered with framed family photographs. He focused on one near the light switch. It was a picture of Ken, Paul and Ethan as children. They were running around the backyard while Mr. Kelly squirted them with the garden hose. He smiled to himself as he remembered that day. They had been playing *Combat*, pretending to be characters from the TV show. He was always Kirby, and Paulie was always Little John, while Ethan traded back and forth between Sgt. Saunders and *Cage*, the French guy. Anyway, they had sneaked up on Ethan's Dad while he was washing his treasured Camaro.

He had caught sight of us in the car's side mirror as we crawled on our bellies in the grass toward him. Mr. Kelly had waited until we were good and close and then dowsed us good with the hose. Apparently Mrs. Kelly had been watching from the kitchen window and she took advantage of the Kodak moment. Kenny removed the framed picture from the wall and carried it with him into the living room. He sat down in Mr. Kelly's comfy chair and picked up the telephone. Setting the photo in his lap he started dialing Ethan's number. He was glad that he came here today, he was relieved to be calling in the cavalry, and he was grateful that the Lord reminded him daily that he needn't be alone, not ***ever!***

"Hello?" a stranger's voice said in his ear.

"Hi, may I speak with Ethan Kelly, I mean Father Kelly, please?" Ken asked, quickly correcting himself.

"Let me check and see if he's here, I'll be back in a sec," replied the cheery stranger.

"Thank you," Ken said. He looked back down at the photo in his lap and smiled, "*Man*, I was a good lookin kid," he said whispering to himself.

Firebaugh, California, June 1973

The blue 67' Chevelle sat in the alley behind Hal's Liquor store with the engine idling. The driver with the red bandana around his head and the dark glasses, sat motionless as he looked straight ahead out the tinted windshield.

The passenger was turned around in his seat looking at the two kids sitting in the back. They were both around eleven or twelve years old, and they were scared. But they weren't about to let Smiley see that so they sat there stone faced and waited for him to finish talking.

"So what's it gonna be *Holmes*?" Smiley said, showing his gold tooth as he grinned at the two children. He swatted the back of his seat hard enough to assure their complete attention. Smiley got off on the fear he instilled in their eyes.

"*COME ON*, we ain't got all day!" he snarled.

Miguel Rojas looked over at his friend Mark and shrugged his shoulders, silently asking with his eyes if he were in or out. Mark's eyes darted back and forth from Miguel to Smiley and then he frantically grabbed at the handle and opened the door. Tripping over his own feet on the way out, he lay sprawled on the dirt road for a moment. He was waiting for Smiley to get out and drag him back into the car, after he kicked the shit out of him first of course. But nobody came after him. There were no punches or kicks. And after a moment or two he sat up and looked around at the car.

The rear door was still open and Miguel and Smiley were just staring at him, no laughing, no snide comments. Mark got up and waited a second longer for Smiley to make a move, and then he turned on his heels and ran as fast as he could down the alley toward home. Miguel watched his friend leave an impressive trail of dust as he fled home to safety, for now. He wished he had a home to flee to, but all he had was a bunk at St. Anthony's Boys Home. It was the only family that he had since his mother had killed herself, and nobody there gave a shit about a homeless wetback, at least that's what he had convinced himself. This was going to be his chance to get back with people he could relate to. People who spoke his language, who ate his food, who knew his pain, *toda por familia!*

"Well, what about you *ese*? You gonna run home to mama too?" Smiley asked, his chin resting on his arm on the back of the seat.

"My mother is dead, I have nobody to run to," Miguel spat out at him.

"That's tough *nino*, life sucks don't it?" Smiley said acidly.

"So, why don't you just do like I told you, and Raymond and me will take you with us back to LA man, we'll be your new family, OK?"

Miguel stared back without saying a word. The young man with the gold tooth took a quick look around and then opened the glove box. He pulled out something covered with a handkerchief and handed it across the seat to Miguel. The boy removed the handkerchief and studied the gun that rested in his lap. It was small but it was heavy, he had never seen one up close, only on TV and in movies. He picked it up and held it in the palm of his hand.

"OK ese, remember, keep the pistol in your pants behind your back. Walk in and go up to the counter. The old man won't be expecting any trouble from someone so little and so cute," Smiley said grinning.

He reached back and squeezed Miguel's cheeks together with one hand, swatting his partner on the shoulder with the other.

"*Mira Ray, mira,* look at this face, he looks like an angel Holmes," Smiley said proudly. Raymond turned his head slightly and nodded in agreement.

"*OK, listen up nino!* When the old dude leans over the counter to help you, that's when you pull your piece an put two in his eye, ***BANG BANG!***" Smiley said loudly, accentuating his meaning by pointing his index finger at his own eye. Miguel sat motionless and listened to his instructions.

"*You get it mijo,*" Smiley asked.

"*Si Smiley, I get it,*" Miguel replied.

"Good, that's really good. OK I'll come in as soon as I hear the shots and empty the register. If we don't hear any shots two minutes after you go in there, we'll figure that you chickened out and we'll leave. But, we'll come find you later and then I'll put two in your eye, *comprendo ese?*" Smiley said threatening the child.

"Si Smiley, I get it," Miguel answered.

"OK, out you go," Smiley said, reaching back and opening the same door that Mark had escaped from only moments ago.

Miguel leaned forward and stuffed the weapon in his pants behind him, un-tucking his shirt to help conceal it. He scooted over to the edge of the seat, swung his legs out the door and hopped out. He looked back at Smiley and then walked toward the screen door in back. He could hear a fan blowing inside as he opened the squeaky door and stepped inside. He looked back through the screen and saw Smiley holding up two fingers, two minutes, two shots, he got it. Miguel listened to a woman singing a song Spanish on the radio as he walked slowly up the aisle toward to front of the store.

He looked from side to side and silently inventoried the products on the shelves. Boxes of Cheeze–its and cans of Spaghetti-O's, he found himself feeling hungry. When he got to the place where the Hostess pies were displayed he stopped for a second. He touched the colorful purple wrapper on a berry pie, wishing that he had only come into the store to swipe one. He could a pair of feel eyes on him and he looked over and saw an old man sitting behind the counter. He was reading a newspaper and sipping on a cup of coffee. There was a radio just above him. It sat next to a little TV that was turned off. Miguel let go of the pie and started walking toward him. One minute he thought to himself, only one minute to go. In one minute the old man's life ends, in one-minute Miguel's new life begins.

"So, what can I get for you nino," the old man asked smiling down at the boy.

Miguel wished that the old guy he was meaner, maybe even yelled at him. He said nothing, just walked up to the counter and motioned for the old man to come closer with a smile and a wiggling index finger. The sweet old grandpa leaned closer across the glass countertop, resting one hand on the glass and reaching up to turn down the volume on the radio with the other. *Twenty seconds, fifteen seconds, ten seconds...*

"Well," the old man asked softly.

Miguel reached behind his back, lifted his shirttail and tugged the pistol free from its hiding place. He raised it quickly and pointed it directly at the old gentleman's face. He squeezed the trigger and the weapon exploded with a flash as the projectile entered the startled man's head through his left eye. Miguel squeezed the trigger a second time as he was told, but the next bullet missed the old man and slammed into a pint of Jack Daniel's behind the counter, shattering glass and splashing the contents all over the floor. Miguel just stood there, frozen in his tracks. He stared at the old man lying flat on his back through the glass case that separated them. The store became silent as the echo of the shots fired diminished. Miguel could hear someone running in from the back and listened as the screen door slammed shut.

"Aye Dios, I didn't think you had it in you *ese,"* Smiley shouted as he leaped over the counter and started emptying the cash register after prying it open with a large screwdriver.

He kicked the old man onto his side, giving himself some room to work. He scooped the bills from the drawer and the coins from the trays. He snapped open a grocery sack and put some booze and cigars in the bag along with the money.

"Go on *ese,* pick yourself out a prize, but hurry up, we gotta split man!" Smiley shouted.

Miguel stood there for a minute and then walked over to the Hostess pies. He grabbed a berry pie and two apple ones as well, and then shuddered when Smiley suddenly stepped behind him. Miguel handed the pistol to the older boy, looking up at him for direction. The little boy moved very slowly, still in a state of shock. Smiley took the weapon and held it in his hand for a moment, *thinking,* looking back and forth at the gun and at Miguel.

Finally Smiley put the gun in the bag with the money and the loot, grabbed Miguel by the shirt and dragged him toward the back door. Miguel stumbled over his own feet trying to keep up with his new friend, dropping the apple pies along the way. Smiley pushed Miguel into the back seat and slammed the door shut. He jumped into the front next to Raymond and closed his door as Raymond peeled out of the alley toward the highway. Breathing heavily, Smiley looked back at Miguel and gave him a nod. Miguel nodded back as Smiley turned back to face the front and look out the windshield.

"You're OK *homeboy*, **DAMN**, you're OK son," he said to Miguel without looking back. Miguel said nothing, as he raised the pie to his mouth and tore open the wrapper with his teeth.

Thirty-one

(…"One is the loneliest number that you'll ever do,
two can be as bad as one, it's the loneliest number
since the number one, ahhh"…Three Dog Night)

Chicago, Illinois, June 1973
<u>*O'Hare Airport, Air Traffic Control Tower*</u>

.

Paul Pulchoski sat quietly but restlessly beside his assigned trainer and watched him go through the motions, painfully explaining each tiny detail of every little aspect of the job at hand. Paul half expected a lesson on how to stir his coffee, which was sitting temptingly on a table behind them, well out of reach. He remembered learning that embarrassing lesson on day one.

"NO DRINKS NEAR THE EQUIPMENT RETARD!" the shift supervisor had shouted from across the room, running his hand over his crew cut.

"You have got to be NAVY! Why is it that all of you squids think that if the deck ain't pitching and rolling the job's child's play?"

Supervisor Tim Tunney had added sarcastically. Paul smiled to himself, replaying the memory and ignoring the page turning geek that sat beside him rambling on about the protocol for reporting the weather to flight crews. He was a little miffed about being handed the weather as his first duty station. Actually, if he were a glory hound it might have even pissed him off. But he didn't vex over it, for pity sake, it was an easy job, the shifts were shorter than he was used to and the pay was MUCH better than what Uncle Sam was dishing out. An added bonus was the fact that he no longer had to deal with bigheaded fighter jocks trying to one up each other in a game of *who's got the bigger dick!* No-sir-ree-bob, he was playing with the friendly skies crowd now. Every one of them content with a smooth ride all the way to retirement, save the waves for Hawaii man, keep the job as smooth as glass!

"Hey, are you paying attention to me fella," Barry Lewis whined.

Paul looked over at the little shit next to him and straightened up. Mostly out of respect for the fact that this was a twenty-year veteran after all. But also because of the respect the man had for himself and the job. Sure, he didn't have the sexiest role in the tower, and why he had never done anything else in that room besides the weather station Paul couldn't venture to guess. But Barry was all over his job, and his enthusiasm and respect for his role was apparent if not downright catching. Paul cleared his throat and stifled an urge to salute the little man.

"Sorry Barry, I was concentrating on the report of this front forming out over the lake," he lied, pointing at the print out on the table to the left of his trainer.

"Really," Barry said, his eyes lighting up like a first grade teacher whom had just taught a kid their ABCs. He reached over and patted his pupil lightly on the shoulder, and Paul quickly looked up to make sure nobody was watching them.

"Oh my, is Supervisor Tunney coming this way," Barry asked anxiously, nearly putting his face right onto the screen in front of him. Much too close to actually read anything, but it might pass for deep concentration at a glance.

"Coasts clear Mr. Lewis," Paul whispered, trying to hold in a chuckle.

"Whew, that was a close one," Barry said.

"I'm retiring soon you know, wouldn't want any marks in my file to mess up my pension," he added, turning a page and getting back to business.

"Don't worry Barry, I've got your back," Paul said reassuringly, turning his attention back to the task at hand.

"Thanks," Barry whispered.

"Ahem, yes, well, now let's chat about this cold front shall we?" Barry Lewis said loud enough for all the nearby stations to hear.

Paul listened closely to his partner ramble on, stealing a glance at his watch, four hours to quitting time. It was gonna be tough, but he'd make it all right. He had to, it was Tuesday and he had a ticket to the White Sox/ Yankees game a Cominskey Park. No better way to spend a summer night he thought. Well maybe with a girlfriend, if he had a girlfriend that is. Ah what the hell, plenty of time for that, after all, he just got to town, *right!*

Besides, the Yanks were in town and he had a ticket to the game. Girls didn't get baseball anyway, well most girls that is. Shannon Kelly was an exception, but then again he never thought of her as a girl, she was like his kid sister, his rotten little kid sister. Of course, she didn't look like a kid sister the last time he saw her. Paul shook that thought out his mind.

"Too bad Ethan and Kenny weren't around to catch the game with him. Man that would be just like old times," he murmured.

"Hey, are you listening to me fella?" whined Barry Lewis.

Albany, New York, June 1973

He closed his tired eyes, fighting to stay awake and in relative control of his emotions at the tail end of what had been a terribly long and frustrating day. Patiently listening to the phone ring for the sixth time halfway across the country in Chicago, Kenny decided to calm himself by reciting Ralph Cramden's mantra for self control, *"pins and needles, needles and pins, a happy man is that grins."* Then, donning a big clown-like smile, one displaying both rows, top and bottom, he counted to ten through clenched teeth and then exhaled deeply. At that very instant a sleepy voice answered just before ring number seven, unwittingly saving the wall-phone in Albany, from certain annihilation.

"Hello, who is this, it's...*oh man it's 2am*, **what the hell?**" the groggy voice complained.

"Paulie, wake up dude, it's me, Ken."

Paul rose up onto his elbow, bracing the phone between his shoulder and his ear while he rubbed the sleep out of his eyes with his knuckles.

"Kenny...what's going on man, who died anyway?" he replied, unaware of the insensitivity of his remark. Ken leaned back against the kitchen counter and played with the long cord of the wall phone. He sighed heavily, letting Paul's unintentional faux pas go, and then spoke slowly into the receiver.

"Nobody died Paul, not yet anyway," Ken said softly, not wanting to sound annoyed with his friend.

He paused a moment to collect his thoughts, weary from a day of consoling and being consoled. Heartache and grief turned out to be way too much work. Those emotions just sucked the energy right out of him. No wonder God pushed love and joy so hard in scripture, compared to the alternatives, that load was like carrying a sack of feathers. Right now he was just plain old dog-tired after spending the better part of the night talking things over with Mrs. Kelly and then Ethan. He could have just plopped down on the sofa and slept until he smelled coffee brewing, but he wanted to update Paul first. He wanted to close the *amigo-loop* so to speak, and finish connecting the dots that linked him to those nearest and dearest.

"It's the Christian thing to do," he thought to himself.

Now, you couldn't exactly call Ken Wong a *religious* man, he had no patience for that kind of piety. But he was most definitely a righteous man, with a faith that some might be surprised by. Actually it was only by circumstance that he was a Catholic at all. His parent's success had afforded them an opportunity to live wherever and however they chose. And his mother had fallen in love with the beautiful Adirondacks long before she had ever met his father. She had come east from San Francisco California to attend Union College in nearby Schenectady New York, a school she had selected because it was the furthest one from home to have accepted her application.

This headstrong determined little girl had grown into a determined and formidable young woman. She had planned her life in her dreams, knowing every detail of her future, from with whom she would live and where, right down to the number of children she would raise. And as seemingly preordained, shortly after graduation she married the man of her dreams. A quiet and reserved accounting major, Kenny's Mom had known the instant she laid eyes on him that they were destined to be together forever. His poor Dad never knew what hit him he had been thunderstruck! But it must have been what the Lord had intended, because his Dad reminded his children daily how much he thanked his lucky stars for the joss that brought their mother into his life.

The newlyweds spent the first few years building a small business together, and when their nest egg had grown to the right size, they decided it was time to raise a family together. Ken's Mom was very specific about choosing their home. It had to be the one she dreamed of each night. She would be able to look out any window and embrace each of the four seasons in all their glory. There would be tree-lined streets that grew taller year after year, just as her future sons and daughters would. And they would be surrounded by other families, with lots and lots of children for her future kids to mix with. Ken's Mom didn't look at the world as a gathering of countries. She saw the world as an endless series of neighborhoods.

She was a passionate visionary who truly believed in the family of man. And so, one by one, and year after year, Ken and his siblings arrived to fill the rooms of the old Victorian house his folks had picked over all of the others on the block. He and his brothers and sisters may have been Chinese by heritage, but as far Rebecca and Samuel Wong were concerned they would be American by choice. By virtue of where he had been born, Ken found himself raised in a white society by parents who taught their children to respect both cultures, and have the courage to choose their own way. So, alongside all his neighborhood pals he struggled with the Catechism and the *penguins* (nuns) with their heavy wooden rulers and became as good a Catholic as any of them. He had grown into a strong young man, one who fit easily into both worlds.

This rearing was the foundation upon which he built his personal fortress and from where he would draw his strength in the coming days, weeks, and months. He would get through this; he would get his family through this, because he knew he wasn't alone. Kenny believed in the Holy Trinity, *the Father, the Son, and the Holy Ghost,* just as the nuns had conditioned him to. But they were still a concept larger than life to him. He had yet to recognize them as his constant companions and source of strength and peace.

For the *personal things* he always relied on his own *Earthly Trinity* if you will. It was Ken, Paul, and Ethan, one for all and all for one, just like the three musketeers. Now that he had brought Ethan up to speed, it was time to include Paulie. Maybe with the neighborhood triumvirate united in spirit he would be able to survive God's will, whatever that might be. Ken's knees were starting to ache a little from standing for so long, so he reached out with his stocking foot and pulled a kitchen chair toward him. Taking a seat and lightening his load a notch he started with the last update for the day.

"Its Sophie man, she's really sick Paulie," Kenny said through a yawn.

"Sick like what, measles, pneumonia, what's wrong with our baby girl dude?" Paulie asked, suddenly wide awake.

"OUR baby..."

"Yeah, I love her as much as you do. And you know how much she loves her Uncle Paulie. I'm her big ass, fuzzy, six-foot teddy-bear man!" Paul could feel Kenny smiling through the telephone cord, and it eased a little of the tension.

"You're right, you're right, you're absolutely right, *what was I thinking,*" Kenny said, grateful for the comfort that his buddy's voice brought.

"That's better!"

"Seriously Ken, what's wrong," Paul asked, unable to mask the fear in his voice.

"It's bad Paulie...*leukemia man.*"

Paul started to repeat the word but choked on it. Ken waited for him to finish his coughing fit and choke out his reply.

"Are they sure about that Ken, I mean you guys have talked to lots of doctors and specialists, right?" Ken ignored his impulse to snap back defensively and paused a moment before answering his friend.

"We're sure, Carolyn and I have been through the ringer on this Paulie. Everything that can be done is being done, but the cure is turning out to be just as bad *if not worse* than the sickness." The two friends remained silent for a little while and then Ken continued.

"She's so small Paulie, and brave, *oh my gosh Paul, I'm so proud of her.*"

"You should see how she is with all these tests and treatments. She's a million times tougher than any of us!" Ken went on, his voice quavering slightly.

"She's Daddy's little girl, buddy-boy, I'd expect no less," Paul said, verbally patting his friend on the back.

"What can I do?"

"Pray for her dude, get out of bed tonight and hit your knees Paulie."

"You know I will Kenny, *I'm on it!*"

"Is that all?"

"That's all that's left man."

"What about Ethan, you talk to him too?"

"Yeah, earlier, I suspect he's lighting candles like a mad man. Hope he doesn't burn down the church." Kenny said attempting to lighten the mood just a little.

"That figures, he always was a closet pyromaniac. You remember when we caught him melting army-men behind Shannon's playhouse with his Dad's lighter. *He said it was a flame thrower,*" Paul said, chuckling as he recalled the childhood memory. He listened to Kenny laughing tiredly on the other end, and wiped the tear running down his cheek on the sleeve of his Roy Rogers jammies.

"Jesus Kenny... Jesus."

"Exactly..."

Fresno, California, June 1973
Saint John's Cathedral

Dressed in short sleeves and collars to match the summer weather, Father Willet and I strolled together through the church courtyard and gardens. And a fine morning it was, with the warmth of the sun at our backs as we passed the fountain, making our way along the redbrick path toward the dining hall for breakfast. At 7am the sun's rays produced a comfortable heat, not enough to cause one to break a sweat, but just enough to take the chill out of the early morning air. Father Billy stopped beside a group of rose bushes and leaned toward, taking in the wonderful scent of the blooming yellow buds.

"Have you ever noticed how some smells can conjure up certain memories?" Father Billy asked, looking up at his young novice.

I nodded but not in earnest, my mind being three thousand miles away this morning. After speaking with Kenny Wong until the wee hours about poor Sophie's troubles, my heart was aching. There would be no sleeping after that phone call. I had prayed for a good hour afterward, and then spent the remaining couple hours before dawn, wrestling with my conscience over my duty to the Church and my loyalty to my friend. There was much work to be done here at St. John's that was for certain. But I desperately wanted to be available to Ken, Carolyn and little Sophia.

They were my family after all, or as good as, and I felt as though they needed me, even if all I could do was pray and be a warm body to hug, punch, and cry on. I could sense that Father Willet had noticed I was not altogether with him this morning. Apparently the absence of a quick verbal reply had given me a way. He remained silent though, opting to wait a moment before inquiring as to what might be occupying my mind. I knew that he was anxious to discuss several pressing matters this morning. It was why we were strolling around the grounds in the first place. Father Willet did his best thinking out of doors he always said. He felt as though God could hear him better without all the obstructions that a building carries.

"God's got the ultimate open door policy Ethan, and I take him up on it daily, *so should you!*" he would say joyfully to anyone and everyone.

"Don't be timid about knocking on the Almighty's door, especially when you're struggling."

"Say perhaps with your conscious or whatnot."

Although I had only been at St. John's for a few months, I had come to know Father Billy's mannerisms, *his style*, and his routines quite well. So I decided to wait him out and let him lead me down the path to discovery in his own way. I suspected that his strategy was to divert my attention from the problems I was keeping to myself by leading me into a discussion of a pressing or urgent matter. Then while I concentrated on the decoy issue, and answered his many questions, he'd suddenly change the subject and mood with a compassionate, *what's the trouble son?*

"Ethan, let's sit a minute in the shade, do you mind?" he asked.

"You know, the older I get the more sensitive I am to the bright sunshine it seems." Father Willet said, gesturing toward the bench under the tall Cypress tree near the fountain.

"Absolutely Father, after you sir," I replied, waving him on ahead.

The two of us sat down and made ourselves comfortable, occupying opposite ends of the smooth wooden bench.

"Tell me Ethan, how are things with the Rojas boy, *Miguel.*"

The old priest asked me. I raised my left hand, and scratched behind my left ear with my index finger, and thought for a minute before answering him. I had been mentoring Mitchell's son for a couple of months now over at Saint Anthony's home for wayward boys. It was only a few short blocks or so from the church. Miguel and I spent most of that time just getting acquainted. With me all the while trying and trying to establish some sort of bond, anything that might help him to open up just a little bit. I explored the usual common ground, sports, television, books, and movies. I even tried talking about girls, a subject for which I claimed no expertise.

Nothing I came up seemed to put a dent in the hard shell of silence that he protected himself with. Miguel would invoke the turtle defense with every question that I asked by overtly shrugging his shoulders, which reminded me of a turtle pulling its head into its shell to protect itself from bad things. There were bad things that he was afraid of, I sensed that much. I just didn't know what they were. Even with my limited skills, courtesy Psych 101 at Holy Cross, I could see that the boy was going to need a lot more than a pair of sensitive ears to help him overcome what was eating at him. And in my wholly unqualified opinion, the root cause for all the stonewalling that I was dealing with had to be the emotional and psychological strain associated with the violent deaths of his parents. I suddenly felt Father Willet's eyes on me and realized that I had zoned out for longer than I had realized.

"Uh, sorry sir, I was just thinking about my answer," I stammered.

"The thing is I'm not exactly sure what I can do for him. I mean I want to help him, desperately so, but I can't seem to get inside of his defenses."

"Does he run when he sees you coming son?"

"No"

"Does he cry, kick, or scream when you walk with him, or talk to him?"

"No, of course not," I answered, puzzled by his questions.

"*None of that*, the child does none of those things whenever you spend time together?"

"No sir, not a one."

"Well then Ethan, you *are* making progress son, you *are* getting through. You have to learn to recognize even the tiniest gains my boy," Father Willet said, reaching across the bench and swatting my knee good and hard.

I flinched slightly and rubbed away the smarting sensation where his thick palm had made solid contact with my flesh through the thin gabardine material of my slacks.

"Yes sir, well I guess I was looking for more obvious clues of a breakthrough," I replied puzzled.

"Look, the boy just needs to know that people aren't going to abandon him. He needs a little stability in his life is all," Father Willet explained. He leaned back on the bench and watched the breeze gently move the Cypress branches, the spade shaped leaves fluttering back and forth like waving hands.

"Yes sir, that's true I suspect, but I don't think he'll get that from the orphanage. He's been in four foster homes already and each time he's been sent back because his total silence freaks out the families he's placed with."

"That's true enough, but what else can we do son? The Church cannot adopt him, he must find a way to fit back in among the living. I'm counting on you to inspire him to do just that Ethan."

"Otherwise, I'm afraid it will be the streets for him eventually. And he's a prime target for those *cholo* gangsters that cruise the local fields, taco stands, and burger joints looking for kids to recruit and take back to LA or San Diego. He'll wind up in a chop shop, prison, or worse if we don't get through to him," Father Billy said harshly through clenched teeth, barely keeping his famous temper in check.

He was right of course, and I wanted to do all that I could to keep Mitchell's little boy from a fate that the old priest had described. Hell, it was the least I could do, but my mind was spinning since the phone call from Kenny. All I could think of was going home and doing what I could for Sophie. I loved that child as if she were my own, just like Paulie did, just like my mother did, just like we all did. We were all family, connected, if not by blood than by love, and one was as strong as the other. I could feel Father Willet's eyes on me again.

"***Ethan**, where **is** your mind this morning?*" he asked curtly.

And there it was, he had chosen his moment and he had caught me off guard. Now I would have to deal with this in the open, just as he had planned. The man was a true master at his craft. I had much to learn from him, very, very much indeed. Timing is everything they say, and it wasn't my time or his, it was God's.

"Forgive me Father," I answered quickly. "Of course I understand the urgency where Miguel is concerned. And believe me I'm motivated to do whatever I'm capable of. Even push myself beyond my abilities. With God's grace and your guidance perhaps we can make a difference in his life, at least as far as getting him a fair start at it."

"*But?*" he asked slowly, waiting for the caveat to my little speech.

"Excuse me?" I asked.

"***But** Ethan, but, but,* but! Come on out with it boy! What has got you in such a mental tizzy this morning?"

"It's my buddy Ken back home, *He ummm*, he has a little girl. Well, actually, he and his wife, Carolyn, they have a little girl, her name is Sophia. We all call her Sophie, and she is the cutest, silliest, smartest, most adorable little pain in the backside that there has ever been," I said, my voice creaking just a little.

"She sounds precious," Father Willet said softly.

"She is sir," I replied.

"She also sounds like a handful," he added.

"*Yes sir, she is sir,*" I answered, smiling.

I all of a sudden recalled one of her stunts not so long ago. She had filled Paul's coat pocket with rollie-pollies from the backyard. And when Paul put on his coat to leave he reached into his pocket and pulled out a fist full of what he thought were Raisinettes. Paulie always had *something* left over in his pockets. Needless to say there was quite a commotion once he started chewing, and Sophie stood behind the closet door chuckling away hysterically, her little hand covering her mouth to mute the sound. I had been in the kitchen drinking coffee and watched it all unfold. From the moment she tiptoed in from the yard to the instant she streaked through the house, her Uncle Paul in hot pursuit, if only I had had a camera!

"Ethan, so what is the matter son?" Father Willet asked, placing his heavy hand on my shoulder. I looked away for a second and then turned back to look him in the eyes directly, showing more composure than I felt.

"Well it turns out that Sophie is terribly ill Father. Ken says she has leukemia, and that she's not taking well to the treatment."

We stared at one another for a moment and then Father Willet stood and moved away from the bench, leaning back on his hands as he walked. He stopped and then turned back toward me.

"We've a lot to pray for then, don't we Ethan," he said.

"Yes sir, we do sir," I replied.

"You want to go home for a while, don't you son?" he asked.

"Yes sir, if that would be convenient sir," I asked.

"It would not be convenient, but it is important," he answered quickly.

Father Willet looked pensively at me for a couple of minutes. I could see that he was struggling with something. It was painted on his face with the expressions he was making, drawing in his lips and rolling them under his teeth. He turned his back to me for a moment and appeared to be arguing with himself. And before I got too uncomfortable with his queer behavior he turned back toward me.

"Ethan, how much do you remember of the story Miguel's father told you in Viet Nam? He asked, standing in front of me with his hands clasped behind his back.

"I don't know what you mean Father," I answered.

"Did not his father tell you of Miguel's experience as an infant, *in the fields, **of his death?***" Father Willet asked curtly. I flinched a little, startled by the tenacity of his questioning.

"Yes sir, he did, but I just assumed someone did mouth to mouth on the baby. I mean in the heat of battle sometimes quick thinking can seem like a miracle, especially when someone is revived like that," I said, speaking faster than I had intended to. Father Billy looked at the ground and then sat beside me on the bench.

"There is more to that story Ethan, a lot more," he said to me while he leaned forward on his knees with his forearms, clasping his hands in front of him.

"I want you to come with me today and meet someone," he said without looking at me.

"OK," I replied, leaning forward on my knees, copying the same posture he had taken, as both of us stared out at the fountain.

"We'd be taking you into our confidence Ethan, it's important that you understand that," he asked.

I winced as I thought about his words, nodding my head slowly, not exactly sure what he was trying to tell me or how I should react. All I knew for sure was that he was being very sincere, I could feel it in the air.

"What are you trying to say Father? I don't understand the cloak and dagger act," I asked rudely, immediately sorry for my tone of voice.

"Patience my son, for whatever reasons, for God's reasons, these are times when prayers may be answered, when they can be answered," Father Willet said, his eyes on me now as he spoke.

"I have to make a call before I can take you to this person, but trust me, by days end you will understand as I do."

"Yes, but…" I started to reply. Father Willet held his finger to his lips and silently shushed me.

"Trust me Ethan…trust me," he said softly. The elder priest sat up and leaned toward me, placing his beefy arm around me, giving my shoulders a good shake.

"You're a good friend Ethan…" Father Willet started to say, when suddenly he turned his face into the breeze, just like an aircraft carrier turns into the wind to launch its squadrons. He sniffed the air and then turned back towards me.

"Ahhh, do you smell that boy? If I'm not mistaken that would be Sister Ruth's famous *Heuvous Rancheros* and *Texas French Toast,"* he said excitedly. He rose quickly and started walking briskly down the redbrick path toward the dining hall, shouting back over his shoulder to me.

"I do my best thinking at mealtime son, **last one to the table pours the coffee!"**

Thirty-two

*(..."murder by numbers, one, two, three. It's easy as
saying your ABC's"...The Police)*

Los Angeles, California, June 1973

This wasn't like anyplace he had ever been before, there was nothing
familiar about anything, not a thing really, and yet for the first time in his
life Miguel Rojas felt *at home.* He lay motionless on a twin size mattress on
the floor of a small bedroom, watching the shadows from the tree branches
outside the window creep across the ceiling slowly as the time passed. He
wasn't sure how long he had been lying there, an hour maybe two, he wasn't
certain if the sun was rising or setting. All he knew for sure was that he had
crashed at this house with Smiley and Raymond just the other night. The
last 48 hours had been surreal as his mind dealt with the trauma of his first
murder. Not that he actually considered his action to be murder. He was a
child after all, and did not understand such harsh terms. But he knew what
he did was wrong, he had retained at least that much of a link to his mother
and father.

Sometimes, like now, he would remember them, and dream of his
mother's warm smile and her soft voice. He could remember the sweet, fresh
smell of lilac, reminding him of the wildflower meadow across the road from
their home, where he would play after a cool spring shower. Miguel closed his
eyes, leaned his head back on his clasped hands, and took in a deep breath

through his nose. He remembered this fragrance on his mother whenever she held him close, comforting him when he was scared or feeling small. Vague memories of his father pushed their way to the surface and he remembered the way his beard would gently scratch his face whenever he kissed him.

Miguel smiled reflexively remembering his father's deep, gravelly laugh, the one that the whole neighborhood could hear whenever the two of them would wrestle on the grass outside, while his mother would sit on a lawn chair and giggle at them as she snapped green beans for supper. Papa would grab an ankle and a wrist and spin Miguel round and round in circles until he was too dizzy to stand, and then tickle him until he laughed so hard he would nearly pee his pants.

Those were the happy times. He loved remembering all of those things. These were the good dreams, but they didn't come as often as they used to. They were sinking deeper and deeper into the confines of his lonely soul. Slowly they were being replaced by other thoughts, ugly thoughts, dreams that left him cold, hurt, and angry. He was alone now, they weren't here anymore, they had left him, *both of them*, neither bothering to say goodbye, or even ask if he wanted to come along. Why didn't the *angel* save them as she had him? He knew the stories everyone knew them. People would whisper and secretly point at him whenever he walked by.

He was the first, he was the freak, they wouldn't even call him by name any longer. The mean kids in the neighborhood would stand across the street, raise their arms high in the air and shout *"Lazareth, come forth!"* Then they would laugh and scamper away, or sometimes they would taunt him further, waiting until he could take no more. Then bolt when Miguel started hurling rocks, stones, dirt clods, whatever was handy, after them.

"Rotten little bastards, I know who you are! I'm going to call each of your mothers right now!" his mother would shout after them, coming to his rescue.

She would pick him up and carry him back into the safety of the house with a handful of cookies, a glass of cold milk, and a little peace and quiet. Well, Mama wasn't here now, to protect him from the nasty voices that taunted his sleep, saying evil things, urging evil deeds. And Papa wasn't here to stand guard over his room, to wait until he closed his eyes before he turned out the light. They could be but for her. "Why him, why all the others, why not them," Miguel's mind screamed, his eyes tightly squeezed shut, his body bathed in a cold sweat.

"HEY FLOHO (lazy)," shouted a booming voice from the doorway, followed by the loud banging sound of a heavy hand slapping the wall. Startled, Miguel leapt straight up in his bed, frantically gathering the covers and sheets around him, forming a wad of linen that became an instant

security blanket. As his eyes became adjusted to the dim light they focused on the figure outlined by the hall light. It was Smiley, dressed in jeans, a wife beater tee shirt, standing barefoot in the doorway.

"Come on *ese*, get you little ass out of bed, we got things to do today Holmes," Smiley said, waving a spatula caked with whatever he was cooking. He paused a second to lick the food off of the kitchen tool and then turned to leave.

"Better hurry up, food won't be on the table long, me and Raymond are pretty hungry," he said from over his shoulder.

Miguel listened to Smiley laughing as he walked away, then got out of bed and tossed the bedding back onto the little mattress. He bent down to pick up his sneakers with the crusty socks tucked into them. Since he had slept in his clothes dressing was a matter of sitting down and pulling on his hardening socks and lacing up his worn out Ked's. Now he could smell the eggs, chorizo, the hot coffee, and all of the sudden he was starving. He rubbed the sleep out of his eyes and walked out of the room. As he passed the bathroom in the hall he noticed the light was on so he stepped in to do his business. Miguel was used to the regiment of St. Anthony's and was conditioned to do things in a certain order.

He could see that tings would be different here, wherever here was. So he quickly relieved himself, washed up at the sink and dried his hands and face on surprisingly clean towels. Given the company he was keeping, that **was** a real surprise! He turned the light out as he left the bathroom and walked toward the kitchen, following the wonderful aroma of the sizzling chorizo and eggs. He took notice of the house and its contents as he walked and was puzzled. This was a very nice place, not at what he was expecting. To be honest, it didn't look like the kind of place where Smiley and his friend Raymond would be welcome, where *he* would be welcome?

Miguel passed by a table at the end of the hall filled with picture frames, each containing photos of grown ups and kids, a family. He recognized Smiley in one of them. He was much younger, with a head full of curly brown hair, and he was sitting under a tree with a cop dog, *what do ya call it*, a German shepherd. The big dog didn't look too ferocious though, especially since it was busy licking Smiley's face. As Miguel entered the kitchen he was surprised to see Smiley and Raymond sitting at a large kitchen table with two other people that he didn't recognize. There was a large woman in a long house dress standing over the stove. Her back was to him but he could see that she was wearing an apron and was stirring and fussing with whatever she had cooking on the range. Nobody even looked up from the table when he walked in. They were much too busy wolfing down the food that was in front of them. The two unfamiliar guys with Smiley didn't look much older than Miguel himself. They were dressed as if they were going to school or something. And they had much better table manners than Smiley and Raymond. At least they were using utensils, while the two older *vatos* just tore tortillas and scooped with their fingers.

"Sit down mijo and I'll bring you some huevos con papas," the old woman said, startling Miguel. He stood frozen for a moment and then walked over to the table and sat in the empty chair beside Raymond.

"Whew, *usted apesta*, you stink *ese*," Raymond said scooting away from Miguel, pinching his nose and hiding a grin. Miguel crossed his ankles and tucked his feet under his chair, looking down at the table, ignoring the chuckles from the others and staring down at the checkered tablecloth.

"Dejelo solo, oso grande," scolded the old woman, telling the *'big bear'* to leave Miguel alone. She swatted Raymond with a wooden spoon for good measure as she brought Miguel's breakfast to the table.

"Owww, Mama, what did I do," whined the menacing gang-banger, rubbing his arm where the heavy spoon had left a noticeable mark. He and Smiley might run the streets and the neighborhood, but this home belonged to her, and *nobody* messed with Mama's turf, **NOBODY!** Miguel stifled a smirk when he saw Smiley giving him the stink-eye and concentrated on his breakfast.

"That's better," the old woman said, slowly pointing the wooden at each person sitting around the table.

"Now you boys hurry up and finish eating."

"You two have to get to school," she said, directing her attention to the two younger boys.

"And I have to get to work. I don't know what you and Smiley have to do today Raymond, but it had better be something besides watch TV and empty my refrigerator!"

"Si Mama," Raymond said, nodding an acknowledgement, returning his attention to his plate.

"And take that rag off of your head at my table," she added, grabbing the dark wool cap as she walked back to the stove.

"No wonder your Popi went back to Mexico esay," Smiley teased under his breath, pushing half-chewed eggs back into his mouth as he choked back a laugh.

"Popi didn't run out on us Holmes, he got dead in Viet Nam man, *you know that!"* Raymond hissed back.

"Yeah, yeah, I forgot," Smiley said surrendering. He looked over at Miguel and winked.

Miguel picked up his fork and started to eat, looking around the room as he shoveled food slowly into his mouth. It wasn't the same as Beaver Cleaver's house, but it wasn't St. Anthony's either. It had been a long time since he had sat at a table in a home where people didn't tease or stare. It had been a long time since he was treated like one of the family instead of one of the have-nots. He looked over at Raymond and then over his shoulder at the old woman rinsing the heavy iron skillet in the sink. She looked too old to be Raymond's mother. Maybe she was his grandmother? Sure, and Raymond's Popi was her son. No matter really, Miguel felt a new connection between him and Raymond. His own Papa had died in that same place, maybe they knew each other, and maybe they were friends. Maybe God had brought he and Raymond together to be brothers, maybe the old man in the *Mercado* had to die, maybe it was God's will. The old woman appeared behind Miguel and placed her hands gently on his shoulders.

"Raymond told me about your poor mama *mijo*. You stay here with us while he and Smiley look for your Uncle. These boys know everyone around here, it won't take them long to find your family. Until then you're part of our family, OK?" the old woman said, giving his shoulders a good squeeze.

"Todo para la familia, comprendo mijo?" she added, smiling.

Miguel didn't answer with words, he just nodded his head slowly. The old woman removed her hands from his shoulders and mussed his hair as she turned to leave the room.

"I'm going to get ready for work," she announced.

"Felix, Anthony, you clean those plates then get going, you'll be late for the bus if you don't hurry, *muchachos rapidos!*" she said as she left the kitchen.

Smiley looked over his shoulder as he drained the last drop of coffee from his cup, making sure that the old woman was out of earshot. Turning back to the table he dismissed the two younger boys with an evil glare. Felix and Anthony did not any more coaxing than that to take their leave. And faster than you would think possible their plates were cleaned, rinsed and stacked in the plastic drainer. The two of them were out the door and at the bus stop before Smiley had a chance to growl at them. Smiley leaned back in his chair, put a cigarette in his mouth and struck a match to light it. Before he finished his first drag a shrill voice shouted from down the hall.

"I TOLD YOU SMILEY, NO SMOKING IN MY HOUSE!"

"Aye Dios mio, the old bat has a second face under her hair. I swear, nothing gets by her," Smiley lamented, then called back down the hall.

"Si senora, me pordona por favor," he said apologetically, loud enough so that she could hear each word, and then under his breath, *"coma la mierda y muera a vieja musaraña* (eat shit and die old shrew).

345

Raymond giggled at his friend's weak defiance of his grandmother's house rules and got up to rinse off his dish in the sink. Smiley leaned across the table and tapped Miguel's plate with a butter knife.

"Hey, when you finish that food, I want you to get in the shower and wash the stink off of you, OK?"

"We'll get you some clean clothes from Felix's and Anthony's room and then we'll take around and show the neighborhood. We'll take you out to the clubhouse homeboy. You can meet your new family Holmes. We got work for you little man. Just remember, Smiley can burn you anytime if you don't cut it on the streets. I got the gun, and I got the story. Mess with me and you'll answer to the law for the old man you did. They'll fry your little ass for sure. They'll lock you in a dark little cage and wait until you grow big enough to sit in the chair and be strapped down. Then they'll dip you in water, strap on a leather hat and send so much electricity through you that the lights will dim all over LA while your eyeballs are poached liked eggs in their sockets."

Smiley leaned back in his chair and laughed as he took the cigarette from his mouth and placed it behind his ear.

"Shut up and leave him alone," Raymond snapped.

"Fuck you," Smiley snapped back.

The knife made a cold slashing sound as it swiftly whipped past Miguel's face and settled at Smiley's throat, Raymond's hand clenched so tight around the handle that the veins on the back of his hand looked as if they might burst at any moment. Smiley sat silent and motionless, daring not to even swallow for fear of losing his Adam's apple against the dangerously sharp blade. Raymond moved his face very slowly up to his friend's, their noses almost touching.

"You better take that back Holmes?" Raymond whispered, his breath punctuating the intent behind his question.

Smiley answered with his eyes, rolling them up then down in an affirmative motion, his only safe move at the moment. Raymond adjusted the angle of the blade slightly and then gently dragged it up Smiley's neck and over his chin, letting it rest just under his lower lip.

"This is my house *ese*, this is my family. And this kid is my prospect, from now on he is my brother, *usted entiende a mi amigo* (do you understand my friend)?" Raymond asked softly.

Smiley answered with his eyes again, this time with less fear in them and more anger. The knife came away from his face as quickly as it had appeared and Raymond seated himself between Miguel and Smiley. He put his arms around both of them just as his *abuela* (grandmother) reappeared.

"OK, what's going on in here?" she asked suspiciously.

"Nothing Mama, we're cool, *ain't we fellas?*" Raymond answered reassuringly.

"It's all good Mrs. Hanna, we're just gonna take the kid around and see what we can see today," Smiley added, reaching around Raymond and playfully socking Miguel in the arm.

"Well, see that you take good care of this child. Dinner's at six like always, don't be late," said Mrs. Hanna.

She walked over, kissed each one of them on the head and then left for work, the screen door slamming behind her. Raymond scooted the chair back and then stood. He grabbed Miguel by the collar and gently helped him up from the table. Spinning him 180 degrees he pushed him toward the hall, giving him a little kick in the seat of the pants as he did so.

"You heard Smiley, get in the shower and wash the stink off of you," he said playfully, not even a hint of the previous tense moment in his voice.

"Leave your dirty clothes in the hamper, I'll set some of Felix's stuff outside the door for you," he hollered as Miguel disappeared around the corner.

Halfway down the hall Miguel stopped and tiptoed back to the doorway. He listened first for any trouble then peeked around the corner. He had half expected to see Raymond on the floor with a knife in his chest. Instead he saw Smiley and Raymond hugging each other, apologizing to each other, it was just too weird. He saw the look in each of their eyes just moments ago. There was death in their expressions.

This scene was made no sense in his mind it was not logical. This was either total fear, or complete forgiveness. He was too young to understand that they were one in the same. So this was his new family, so this is what he sold his soul for when he killed that old man. He shouldn't be here he thought. The old man in the bodega, his father, his mother, they all might alive today if he were not. She ruined everything! With the touch of her hand she changed the fate of so many innocent people. He was innocent no longer. He would never be innocent again.

Fresno, California, June 1973
<u>*St. Anthony's Home for Boys*</u>

Sheriff Cardwell drove up the long driveway following the slight curve as it led him to the front of the administration building. He shut of the engine and climbed out of his blazing hot patrol car. The A/C had been on the fritz for a last couple of days, just in time for the end of June gloom and the start of a really hot summer. He wiped the sweat off his brow with his forearm before placing his hat on his head. Then he walked the thirty feet up to the eight stairs that led to the entrance to the building. He looked at the large wood placard on the lawn, it read, *"Enter with Love, Leave with Peace."* He smiled a sad smile and shook his head, and took the steps two at a time. He had come to talk about one of the exceptions to that signpost today.

"Good morning Sheriff," greeted the young novice sweetly. She was seated at a small reception desk, dressed in the white habit of a novice nun, with the softhead covering, and small shiny crucifix resting just below her neckline on the white material. She was no more than nineteen or twenty and must have been new because he did not recognize her.

"Morning Miss, I'd like to see Father Phillips, he's expecting me," the Sheriff replied.

"Sure, I'll just ring his office and tell him you're here. Would you mind signing the visitor book for me please?" she asked, sliding the clipboard toward the Sheriff while she picked up the telephone handset.

Sheriff Cardwell leaned over and filled in the blanks on the next open line on the form, his name, who he was here to see, and the time that he arrived, stuff like that. He pushed the pen and clipboard back toward the young lady and stepped back waiting for her to finish her phone call. She glanced at the clipboard and looked up at the Sheriff and smiled, nodding her thanks for his cooperation.

"Ok Father, I'll tell him," she said, hanging up the phone.

"Sheriff, Father Phillips asked if you wouldn't mind waiting ten or fifteen minutes, he is dealing with a small crisis at the moment?"

"I think I can manage that little girl, I'll just sit right over there," he replied, pointing with his hat toward the small receiving room dotted with a few chairs and a sofa.

"Great...um, would you like some coffee while you wait?" the young novice asked.

"You read my mind girl. Oh damn it, *where are my manners!* I can't keep calling you this and that, what is you name anyway young lady?" the Sheriff asked through a gruff chuckle.

"Oh, right, I'm Taylor, I'm new here, but I guess you could tell that already," she answered sweetly and held out her hand. Sheriff Cardwell shook her hand gently.

"Pleasure to meet you Taylor, and I take cream and sugar with my coffee, if that's not too much trouble."

"Not a problem Sheriff, I'll be right back," Taylor said, scooting her chair back and standing.

She was a tall girl, at least five feet ten inches, and Sheriff Cardwell could tell that she had the shape of an athlete even with the heavy cotton habit she wore.

"Taylor that's an odd name for a girl isn't it," he asked as she walked away from the desk. She turned and answered him.

"Yeah, kind of I guess. I'm named for my Dad's younger brother. He died when they were kids. I guess Dad was sorta expecting a son, someone to carry on the family name and burn up the basketball court, you know. He never did get his son, he got five daughters instead, all of us near six feet, and each of us with a boys name, *Andie-Bobbie-Nikki-Randie-and me*. He did get a darn good basketball team though," Taylor said, rattling off her explanation with "Valley Girl" precision.

"Us girls could whip any five boys in the neighborhood by at least twenty points!" Taylor boasted in a prideful tone. With that she spun gracefully on her heel and whisked off to fetch the Sheriff's cup of coffee.

"Well I'll be," Sheriff Cardwell said smiling as he sat on the sofa and reached for the sports page of morning paper. As soon as he had refolded the paper to display the baseball box scores Father Phillips appeared in front of him.

"Sorry to keep you waiting Roger, bit of a mystery around here this morning I'm afraid," the Priest said, standing just in front of the Sheriff, a small coffee table separating them. Roger Cardwell quickly glanced at the box scores and checked on the Dodgers. He said a silent YAHOO to himself after reading that they had beat the hated Giants 4 to 2, and set the paper down.

"Yeah, well, I think I can help you with that little mystery Padre, I mean if it involves a missing Hispanic boy, around twelve or thirteen," the Sheriff said, standing, and extending his hand for the priest to shake. Father Phillips reached out and shook the Sheriff's hand weakly.

"Oh my Lord, what has he done?" he asked, lowering himself into the chair behind him, still holding onto the Sheriff's hand.

Just then Taylor returned with the Sheriff's cup of steaming hot coffee, which Father Phillips intercepted, taking a long drink of the hot beverage. Taylor held her tongue and gave Sheriff Cardwell an apologetic glance. Roger Cardwell held up his hand and reassured her.

"It's alright Taylor, I think he needs it more than I do just now. As a matter of fact, why don't you go to his office and fetch *'some medicine'* from the top right drawer of his desk, he'll be needing some of that as well."

"The bottom right drawer," Father Phillips said, correcting him. "I moved it last month, it's my own little security system," he added with a crooked little smile.

"Right, bottom right drawer then," Sheriff Cardwell repeated.

"I'll find it, what kind of medicine is it?" she asked as she turned to leave.

"You'll know it when you see it," the Sheriff replied, waving her on as he sat back down on the sofa across from Father Phillips.

"It's Miguel Rojas," the priest started.

"We discovered he was missing two nights ago. I called around to the few families that I remembered had housed him after his mother died, but no one has seen him. I also called St. John's and checked with Father Willet. Miguel has been seeing a novice priest there named Kelly, I was hoping that maybe the boy had gone there, I mean he and the young priest seemed to be making friends," Father Phillips explained.

"Well...what did they have to say at St. John's?" asked the Sheriff.

"Nothing yet, neither of them were available when I called, I left word for them to get back to me straight away."

"Why are you here anyway Roger? Do you know something about Miguel's absence?"

"*Padre*, two days ago a liquor store in town was held up. It was Hal's Liquor over on Tenth Avenue, the one across from the *do-it-yourself* car wash. Well, the owner, old man Gerado, *you know him*, Alfredo Gerado, everyone calls him Fredo since the *'Godfather'* came out," Sheriff Cardwell explained, searching the priest's face for an expression of acknowledgement. Father Phillips nodded and pursed his lips, waiting for the rest of the story, already anticipating the ending.

"Yeah, well, somebody shot old Fredo through the left eye, blowing his brains out all over the bourbon and rye section of the liquor display, it was a real mess!"

Father Phillips closed his eyes and leaned back in the chair, grasping the armrests tight enough to turn his knuckles white.

"I've got two witnesses from the car wash that saw a blue Chevy peel out from behind the store with two male Hispanic adults up front and a small Hispanic boy in back," Sheriff Cardwell continued. He paused for a moment allowing the priest some time to digest the facts before he gave him the final bit of information.

"Father, I also have a boy that has come forward and testified that he was with Miguel Rojas two days ago. The boy claims that he and Miguel were at Hal's Liquor with two men in a blue supped up Chevy. He knew them only as Smiley and Holmes, but by his description we think the one named Smiley is a loser named Richard Taquitz, a known gang member from Los Angeles. The boy claims that the two men took them there to rob the store as an initiation to join their club in LA."

Sheriff Cardwell studied the priest's face and could see that all of the pieces were falling into place. His posture had slackened and he released his hold on the armrests and folded his hands in his lap, preparing to surrender to the fact that the end of this story was going to implicate poor Miguel in a particularly heinous crime.

"My young witness says that he ran away, but that Miguel stayed behind in the car. He says that he stopped running when he realized nobody was chasing him. And that he went back as far as the alley and watched from behind a fence. He saw the man named Smiley hand something that looked like a gun to Miguel and that Miguel stuffed it into the back of his pants and went into the store. A few minutes later he heard two loud shots and watched Smiley race into the store. A couple minutes later they both came back out, jumped into the car. The car sped away with the tires squealing and that was that. The kid ran home from there and only came forward after his older sister had recognized the description of the blue Chevy as the one she had seen her brother in the day of the murder. She had told her mother and she brought her son in with a no nonsense edict that he come clean with the facts, or jail would be the least of his worries!"

Father Phillips pondered all of what he had just heard for a moment before replying. As he was about to speak Taylor returned with the *medicine bottle*.

"Is this what you were expecting," she asked sheepishly, holding up a half empty bottle of twenty-five year-old scotch.

"That's the right stuff young lady, just hand it on over here," Sheriff Cardwell answered.

Taylor handed the bottle of spirits to the sheriff and went back to her desk to busy herself. Roger Cardwell unscrewed the cap and poured tow fingers worth into the priest's coffee and sat back down on the sofa. Father Phillips took a sip and then set the cup on the table.

"Thanks Roger," he said quietly.

"My pleasure Tim," the Sheriff replied.

"It appears we have solved the mystery of our AWOL charge," the priest said slowly.

"Maybe, Father, do you believe him capable of doing such a thing?" asked Sheriff Cardwell.

"Yes. I'm sorry to say that I am. Roger, you know who this boy is don't you?" Father Phillips asked in reply, surprised that the Sheriff had missed so obvious a connection.

"No, can't say as I do, should I?" the Sheriff replied, genuinely stumped.

"His parents were *Mitchell and Elena Rojas*. She committed suicide shortly after burying her husband in 1969. He had been killed in action in Viet Nam shortly before or after Christmas, I can't remember which, it doesn't matter though," Father Phillips explained, studying the man's face as he began to connect the dots.

"Roger, **remember**, Miguel was her first miracle, the dead baby that began everything!"

Sheriff Cardwell sat and rubbed his face with the thumb and four fingers of his left hand, squeezing his cheeks and then pulling his skin tight and down over his chin and along his neck until he reached his chest.

"*I'll be damned*, I can't believe I missed that. Hell, I'm getting too old for the job Tim!" Sheriff Cardwell said, scolding himself. He scooted forward on the sofa and rested his forearms on his knees.

"We need to find this boy. He's in bad company, on a dangerous track. I want to talk with everyone who knows or knows of this child. Let's start with this priest over at St. John's, the novice working with Father Billy, what was his name again?"

"Ethan Kelly, do you want me to come with you?"

"Yeah, that would be helpful Tim, I mean Father. That would be helpful."

"Alright then, let me clear my morning and then we can dash off," Father Phillips replied, walking over to Taylor to give her instructions for the rest of the day. He reached down to pick up the cup from the table. Sheriff Cardwell intercepted his hand.

"You can leave that Padre, I think I'll finish this off if you don't mind, maybe it will improve my memory!"

Los Angeles, California, June 1973

They continued cruising the Hollywood strip, giving Miguel a lay of the land and an education in the social amenities of the local street peoples. Miguel had spent the last several hours mixing with gang-bangers, junkies, dealers, and whores. Smiley and Raymond seemed to be well connected in this town, everyone they met treated them with respect, and Miguel liked that. He wasn't used to being accepted by so many people so readily. He knew it wasn't him, so it had to be the company that he was keeping. The *cholos* were easy to spot everyone wearing the same sort of uniform, the colorful Pendelton shirts, the bright bandanas or the netted hair. Body art really fascinated the boy and he enjoyed hearing the stories behind each one, almost as much as the owners of the tattoos enjoyed telling them. The dealers were harder to recognize, they seemed to live in the shadows, but they also bowed to his two new friends, his two new *carnals,* when they came up to the car and chatted through the window to Smiley and Raymond.

The junkies were scary, and Miguel didn't like any of them. They talked too fast and they had crazy eyes. They were always wiping at their mouth and were constantly looking over their shoulders as if they were expecting someone or something to pounce on them at any moment. And although he was shy and a little embarrassed, he liked the whores best of all. They were sparkly and smelled nice, and they all made a fuss over him, kissing and hugging him, messing up his hair and flirting a just little bit, cautiously looking to Smiley and Raymond for their reactions. Miguel was old enough to know what sex was all about and he was as curious as the next pre-teen. But these women, girls really, seemed more like sisters to him, and for the moment he showed no interest beyond that. Raymond turned into an alley just past the Pantages Theater and shut off the engine.

"Well Holmes, what do you think of *Hollyweird*," he asked laughing.

"It's good, very good I think," Miguel replied, speaking more than two words in a row for the first time since he killed that old man in Fresno.

"You bet you ass it's good," Smiley said gruffly, reaching back and playfully swatting Miguel on the head.

"I think Jasmine kinda liked you back there, don't you Ray?" Smiley teased.

"Oh yeah man, I think she wants a little piece of our sugar-baby, big time!" Ray said playing along. Miguel blushed, kicked the front seat and looked out the window.

"You mensas are loco in the cabesa, she was just being nice is all," Miguel said, trying to hide his rosy cheeks. Smiley and Raymond howled with laughter for a good five minutes until Miguel could take no more, joining in with them, laughing so hard his eyes began to tear.

"OK, OK, that's enough, my stomach is starting to hurt," Raymond said, as he worked at quieting down and regaining composure.

"Speaking of my stomach, I could use a cheeseburger man, how about you guys?" Raymond asked, looking back and forth from Smiley to Miguel.

"Well we definitely missed supper at your Mom's chongo, so, count me in ese," Smiley said, wiping his eyes with the palms of his hands.

"Me too," chimed in Miguel, wiping the tears from his eyes with the back of his hands.

Raymond turned in his seat and started the car, looking back at Miguel in the rearview mirror and winking. Miguel smiled back, feeling alive for the first time in years. He felt like he belonged, like he was wanted finally, somewhere, and by someone!

"Where to, McDonald's?" Raymond asked as they cleared the driveway and entered back onto Sunset.

"No way man, McDonald's is for the **Black and Whites**. Let's go over to *'Fat Boys'* on Vine Street, that's where a homeboy can get a decent burger, and a jalapeno too...*horale*," Smiley shouted.

"OK, we're gone!" Raymond said, stepping on the gas, accelerating through the intersection on a yellow light. The blue Chevy wasn't exceeding the speed limit and a yellow light infraction was kind of a weenie thing to cite, but it had been a slow night and Officer Wesley Hightower was bored. He started the patrol car, flipped on his Christmas tree lights overhead, and trailed after the vehicle. Smiley saw the cop car first and turned quickly back to Miguel in the back seat. He handed him the gun from the glove box and put his finger to his lips, indicating that he wanted the boy to remain quiet.

"Put that under your jacket homey, and be cool, don't say anything, we'll tell the asshole that you can't talk, that you're...what do that call that?" he asked looking over at Raymond.

"Mute," Raymond said, slowing down and starting to pull over to the curb.

"Yeah, mute, you're mute OK," Smiley said to Miguel as he turned slowly back and faced front.

Officer Hightower positioned his spotlight at the rear view mirror of the car in front of him. He unfastened his safety belt and opened the car door, putting one foot outside on the ground while he spoke into the mike of his radio.

"One Adam 21, wants and warrants on California License XYX232, over," he relayed to dispatch.

A squelched female voice repeated his request and instructed him to stand by, standard operating procedure so far. Wesley looked out the windshield and counted noses, he saw two adult males and one child in the car. He looked at the license plate again and confirmed that the tags were current. This would just be a courtesy stop, he would let them off with a warning, then call in a ten-seven and get some chow. He yawned as the radio spoke back to him in police code. There were no wants or warrants on the vehicle.

"Ten-four dispatch, thanks, over," he replied.

Stepping out of his car, he rose to his full and imposing six-foot four-inch height. He put his nightstick through the chrome holder on his utility belt and unsnapped the leather restraint on his weapon. He walked slowly up to the car, shining his flashlight into the vehicle to confirm his estimate the occupants. Just as he thought, two adult males and one small boy, maybe ten or eleven, didn't matter really, they would be on their way so enough. Hightower walked up to the driver's window and bent down slightly, his hand resting on the butt of his weapon.

"Evening gentleman, can I see you license and registration please," he asked Raymond.

"Uh, yeah sure sir," Raymond said reaching for his wallet and motioning for Smiley to get the registration out of the glove box. Hightower watched closely as the passenger opened the glove box, ignoring the child in the back seat. Smiley handed Raymond the envelope with his registration and then Raymond handed it to Hightower along with his driver's license.

"Uh, what exactly did I do sir?" Raymond asked politely trying not to arouse any unnecessary suspicion. Hightower removed his hand from his weapon and held the flashlight while he read the license and registration.

"I pulled you over for running a caution light sir. I'm not going to cite you tonight. I just wanted to warn you that although it's technically legal, in this part of town it's not very safe. I've seen too many bad accidents around here because people are always in such a hurry. Believe me, if you had seen some of the stuff I have, ninety seconds at a stop light is a small price to pay for your safety," he said, returning the documents to Raymond.

"Thanks officer, I'll remember that next time," Raymond said, handing the envelope to Smiley while he leaned over and tucked hi wallet back into his pants pocket. Hightower tapped the door on the driver's side with his large hand.

"You folks have a nice evening," he said as he started to walk away.

Wesley stopped suddenly as he turned to walk back to his patrol car. Looking down he saw the child in the back seat and paused a second to smile at him. In that instant his brain had just enough time to register the fact that he was in mortal danger. Pressed against the window was the unmistakable image of the barrel of a very large handgun. Before the second hand of his watch could tick another notch clockwise, the window shattered, one deafening explosion after another filling the quiet night, each projectile entering Hightower's torso in close proximity to one another, in an alarmingly rapid succession. Officer Wesley Hightower, combat veteran, and by God war hero, was dead before his body hit the pavement, his lifeless eyes remaining open to stare up at the stars, the image of the boy's face etched onto his pupils for eternity.

"WHAT THE FUCK!" screamed Raymond?

Smiley jumped into the back seat and wrestled the gun from Miguel's hands. He swatted the boy hard and sent him crashing against the door.

"GO,GO,GO!" shouted Smiley, shoving Raymond on the shoulder as he looked down at the dead cop.

Raymond started the car and pulled away from the curb slowly, then sped up steadily as if nothing had happened. There were surprisingly few cars around and nobody seemed to be paying much attention to them. He looked in his mirror and noticed that the streetlights were all out where they had been parked. It was very dark except for the cop car's lights. The body was lying in the street just outside of the range of the headlights. They turned the corner and headed for the nearest freeway on ramp. He turned in the seat slightly to find Miguel cowering against the door and Smiley stuffing the gun under the seat.

"Did you see that *Raymond,* I never seen anything like that man!" Smiley said excitedly.

He reached over and pulled Miguel away from the door. The boy was shaking with fright, certain that Smiley was going to kill him and toss his body out of the moving car. He tried to push away from Smiley but the man was too strong for him.

"Hey, Hey, settle down mi mijo, I'm not gonna hurt you," Smiley said calmly. He pulled the scared child close to him and cradled him in his tattooed arms.

"Be cool ese, you're a man today, with huevous of steel!" Smiley said proudly. "Did you see that Raymond, Madre Dios, he's a natural, a natural man," Smiley repeated over and over while he held Miguel, unconsciously rocking the child lovingly.

"I saw Holmes, but we gotta get rid of this car **RIGHT NOW**, you know!" Raymond shouted, looking nervously in all the mirrors for any sign of pursuit.

"Hey man, what about Swami's, he's new and the cops don't know about him yet. I think his chop shop is over in Pasadena. Pull over and I'll call him, his guys can chop this ride into a thousand pieces, no one will find ever find any of it. And the plates were from some car in Diego man so they can't trace us that way either," Smiley explained knowledgeably.

Raymond nodded and took the next exit, stopping at a payphone in front of a darkened drugstore. Smiley got out and went to make the call. Raymond turned and looked at Miguel. The boy was sitting still, his eyes stained with dried tears; he wouldn't look up at him. Raymond reached into the back seat and tapped the child gently on the leg. Miguel looked up and made eye contact with Raymond, they said nothing to one another for a moment.

"It'll be OK kid. I don't know what you was thinking, maybe you was just trying to protect us, I don't know. But it'll be OK, you know."

"Man, you really don't know nothin bout nothin, do you?" Raymond said softly.

They both looked out the window at Smiley talking on the telephone. He looked up and gave them a *'thumbs up'* sign while he finished up his call. Smiley hung up and trotted back to the car and hopped into the shotgun seat. He shut the door behind him and gestured for Raymond to get going.

"Swami says to bring the car on in tonight, he'll have some one at the shop with another car for us," Smiley said. He turned back towards Miguel.

"Come on up here and sit with us little man, I'm not too comfortable with such a dangerous dude sitting behind me!" he said through a laugh.

Miguel climbed over the seat and settled in between the two men. He felt safe again, he felt like he belonged again. He felt no remorse for the man he had just killed, people died around him all the time, he was getting used to it.

Thirty-three

(…"For the wisdom of this world is foolishness in God's sight"…1 Corinthians 3:19)

Firebaugh, California, June 1973

"That'll be six fifty even," said the kid from behind the glass.

He sniffled and then scratched his nose with the back of his hand while he waited for me to cough up the dough. I dug deep into my pants pocket and pulled out a small wad of bills. I don't know why, but I never have liked carrying a wallet on me, it just sorta made me feel lopsided whenever I sat down.

"Just a sec," I replied as I unfolded the neatly creased bills.

They were mostly singles mixed with an occasional fiver and one lonely ten spot. And of course there was also my emergency twenty, my *mad money,* as my mother would say. I counted out seven singles and handed them over the counter to the kid with the pocked marked face. He raked in the bills and then slid five dimes back across the Formica countertop along with a large box loaded with the burgers, chips, and shakes that I had ordered.

"Thanks a lot," I said cheerfully as I carefully checked the contents, making sure there were no mistakes.

Father Willet could be positively Neanderthal about meals! The kid gave me a courtesy grunt and looked over my shoulder at the next person in line. Scooping up our little picnic I turned to walk over to where I had left Father Willet and Victor Lopez. They waved when they saw me coming, sitting in the shade of a large oak tree at a round concrete table. The table was at the far side of the hamburger stand facing the alfalfa fields instead of the highway. As I walked up to the table I returned their waves with a head bob, setting our lunch down gently. Raising my hand I licked off some of the shake that had dripped onto my hand.

"OK, that's three chocolate shakes, two cheeseburgers, one without onions, and one pastrami, sandwich, extra mustard, extra pickles," I announced as I sat down next to Victor. Father Willet handed out the food to each of us and then paused to say grace.

"Bless us O Lord for these gifts, thy bounty, for all of your blessings may we be truly thankful, Amen," he said, genuflecting quickly afterward.

Victor and I did likewise and then went after the wrapping around our burgers like children on Christmas morning. Father Willet ate like no other person I had ever encountered, and that included my Uncle Richard who was a well-known chowhound all over New York State! He wasn't ravenous actually, but he wasn't gentle either. And the sounds that came from him as he enjoyed his meal could be described as, to say the least, happy sounds, and to say the most, sounds of shear ecstasy. Victor must have had several meals with the good Father over the years, because he didn't seem to even notice the commotion. In fact, as I looked around I noticed that I seemed to be the only one a tad uncomfortable with the all the noise. I chalked it up to small town living and started in on my own meal. Victor started rummaging around in the box looking for something. Assuming he was looking for the ketchup bottle I reached across the table and slid it toward him.

"No, thank you *Senor*, I was looking for a jalapeno," he said with a big grin on his face.

I must have had a funny look on my face because Father Willet began to chuckle, setting his sandwich down on the napkin in front of him. Picking up his milkshake he took a hard sip to keep him from choking.

"A jalapeno is a hot pepper Ethan, you probably don't see many of those in Boston," he said.

"You should try one, it'll be a memorable experience, I promise," he added with a sly grin. Victor Lopez began to laugh as well, confirming my suspicions that I probably should pass on his suggestion. He got up and went up to the counter and brought back a small bowl of fat green peppers. Victor sat back down and bit into one of them, the aroma that wafted my way actually made my eyes sting.

"*Whew*, dodged a bullet there Ethan old pal," I thought to myself.

Victor and Father Willet got a good laugh at the face I was making and I laughed along with them, just to be polite of course. There was no way I was going to try one of those green gut bombs. Maggie Kelly didn't raise no fool!

"So, what do you think of this place Ethan," the old priest asked between bites.

"It's nice I guess, but is it always this hot?" I replied.

"*Oh yeah*, during the summer it stays around ninety degrees or so," Victor said, answering for Father Willet.

"Sometimes, after the Santa Ana winds blow, we'll get a heat wave that'll make you feel like you're standing inside a blast furnace or something," he added, alternating between bites of his burger and the hot pepper.

"Well I hope that on those days we can wear shorts with these hassocks, otherwise I may just melt away," I teased.

Father Willet flashed me a mustard enhanced smile, chewing and swallowing quickly, trying to get out a quick reply.

"No shorts my boy, but the Archdiocese does allow us to wear short sleeves and forego the heavy wool jackets.

Of course we still have to wear the robes for Mass, but they're made of thick cotton fabric and it's nobody's business what we wear underneath, now is it?" he said with a wink, teasing me back just a little. Using his fingers he scooped up the last bits of pastrami scattered on his napkin and ate them, licking his fingers clean as he did so.

"*Well*, that hit the spot," he said, working his face into an exaggerated frown and nodding his head slowly indicating his satisfaction. Victor and I nodded in agreement and busily worked at finishing our own meals while Father Willet picked at our fries and polished off his shake.

"Father says that you have been helping Miguel," Victor said as he chewed and wiped at his mouth with a napkin. He seemed to be studying me as he waited for my reply.

"I'm not too sure how much help I've been, but at least he's started to talk to me about some things. I mean it's not exactly a breakthrough, but it's a start," I answered.

"Don't sell yourself short Ethan, that boy hasn't had an actual conversation with anyone that I know of since the day he found his mother stone dead in the bathtub," Father Willet said, tossing in his two cents.

"If you say so sir," I replied, not wanting to get into a debate over the matter.

It wasn't what we were here for anyway. I was just anxious to dispense with the introductions and get to the real purpose of this meeting. But of course we were on Father Willet's schedule, and so I would have to be as patient as possible. On the way over to meet Victor for lunch, the old priest had told me the story of the Lopez family and the gift that their daughter possessed. He explained about the very delicate truce he had brokered between their small community and the rest of the world.

He told me about all of the personal and professional sacrifices that were being made in support of this child's well being. When he finished, I understood at once why she needed to be protected, because the world does not honor their heroes, they exploit them, and in the end they consume them. And now I was ashamed because I was here to exploit her myself. I was here to beg mercy for the life of Kenny's baby girl, even if it meant to risk the anonymity that had been so carefully been preserved for this blessed young lady. Victor looked up from his hamburger and caught me staring at him as he ate. We made eye contact and smiled sheepishly at one another, like people do when they're not sure exactly what to say.

"Yes I do say so, "Father Willet said in an exaggerated tone. He stared at me for a moment and then sighed heavily, throwing his arms up into the air in a gesture of frustration.

"Confound it boy, now I forgot what I was going to say!"

The old priest crossed his arms and looked skyward. He uncrossed one arm and raised it to his face, cradling his chin and mouth with the thumb and four fingers of his free hand.

"Let me see now, *oh yes*, like I was saying Victor, young Ethan here just may be able to help that boy rejoin the human race after all."

"That would be very good Father Billy...*Ethan*," Victor said earnestly, looking in my direction.

The look on his face told me that he was a step or two ahead of Father Willet. It was obvious that he knew we weren't here to chitchat about my meager accomplishments with an unfortunate orphan. In fact, Victor seemed rather amused with Father Willet's lame attempt at beating around the bush. I decided that Victor must have been a defensive back on his High School football team, because he didn't seem fooled by any tricky passing route.

"So what do you want me to do for him Father?" asked Victor.

"Well, nothing really. I mean Ethan seems to have things under control where Miguel is concerned," Father Willet said, stumbling around that darn bush.

"No Father, not for Miguel, we have already done for Miguel what God intended," said Victor.

"For Ethan Father, for the pain on his face, for the hurt in his eyes," he added, leaning forward on the table, resting his chin the knuckles of his clasped hands.

I could feel tears begin to well up in my eyes, and I fought the urge to let them flow. I was just about to surrender to the moment and blubber out my selfish request of his family when Father Willet reached across the table and put his hand on mine. His look froze the words in my throat and he spoke for me.

"Ethan's brother, *well*, his brother in Christ actually, has a child that is suffering. A little girl who is losing a battle that no child should have to fight," Father Willet explained gently.

"He learned of this only just the other day. And it was all I could do to keep him from running like the wind all the way home to New York, where all he would be able to offer would be prayer and benediction!" Father Willet said, pressing down harder on my hand and squeezing it tightly, while he looked at Victor Lopez with an intensity that I was unprepared for.

"*My friend*, you and I know that there is someone among us, who may offer much more," he said slowly, reaching across the table with his free hand and grasping the sleeve of Victor's shirt.

I swallowed hard as I watched Victor's face contort while he bit at his lips and wrestled with the unasked request. I prayed as hard as I could in silence for the Lord to spare Sophie through this one father's compassion toward another father. I knew instinctively that there was a bond between them, a bond that all fathers' share by virtue of being a father. And for a moment I found myself envious of that connection between them, of that fraternity.

For an instant I felt as though perhaps this may have been a destiny that I had not considered thoroughly enough. And in that instant her face came into my mind's eye again, *what was her name*! I could feel Victor thinking as he studied my face, perhaps searching for a hint of what sort of man my friend Kenny might be, or perhaps for assurance that the cause was as just, as the risk would be. Suddenly, Father Willet ended the tense pause with a healthy belch, and the air around the table was thick with the aroma of pastrami, pickles, and mustard!

"Sorry lads, it's hard to keep a good meal down," he said laughing heartily.

Victor and I joined him in a good belly laugh and after we were all in tears, not to mention the center of attraction at the small hamburger stand, Victor stood and walked around the concrete table to sit beside me. He leaned forward on the table, resting on his forearms and turned his head to look at me, the bright sun at his back. Squinting, I bent down to put his head between the sun's rays and my eyes and waited for him to speak.

"OK, let's go to my house, and talk to my Maria. If she is good with this, then we can talk about what must be done," he said as he leaned into me and bumped his shoulder into mine.

"Shouldn't we be talking to your daughter," I asked meekly.

"We will Father Ethan, *we will*. But first we must talk to the others, the others must agree."

"The others…I don't understand," I replied, my puzzled look giving away my instant curiosity.

"I'll explain it to you on the way to Victor's," Father Willet chimed in, getting up abruptly, patting us each on the back as he did so.

"Yeah, but…"

"*No but's Ethan*, it's getting hot out here and I'm starting to sweat under all this cotton," Father Willet said, hurrying me along. We stood and bussed our table before heading toward the lot.

"We'll follow you Victor," Father Willet shouted as we walked in opposite directions toward our vehicles. Victor nodded and waved, putting on his sunglasses as he opened the front door of his pickup truck.

"Hand me the keys Ethan, I'll drive from here," the old priest said walking quickly to the driver's side of the car.

I tossed him the keys over the roof of the car and then climbed into the hot vehicle. Father Willet hopped into the driver's seat and turned over the engine, rolling down his window at the same time.

"Might as well turn on the air conditioning full blast," he said, indicating that he wanted me to roll down my window as well. I cranked on the handle and looked back at Father Willet.

"Who are the others anyway?" I asked.

"You'll meet them Ethan, one revelation at a time son, one revelation at a time," he answered as we sped off after Victor's pickup.

Albany, New York, June 1973

Carolyn Wong sat on the hard, straight-backed couch in Doctor Lewis' waiting room. The busy medical assistant looked up at her from behind the glass partition and smiled politely. Carolyn smiled back and looked up at the clock from over the top of the current People Magazine. It was 2pm and Sophie had been in with the doctor for over an hour now. This wasn't a good sign as far as she was concerned. Every trip to hospital brought a mixture of hope and disappointment, with the scales tipping steadily on the side of heartache. She wished that Kenny was here with them today, but he had to work. The insurance was no longer supporting every option since the failure of the first bone marrow transplant to yield a substantial remission.

The bills were beginning to pile up as she and Ken did everything that they could to provide Sophie with the best care and try to make her as comfortable as possible. Carolyn knew that time was running out, she had been told no less than a thousand times that this disease worked fast and furious in children Sophie's age, but she didn't dare give up hope, she couldn't! She looked back at the magazine and wondered why everyone was smiling and laughing. The images of all those happy carefree people suddenly turned her very sullen and she threw the magazine onto the table in front of her.

"Are you alright Mrs. Wong?" asked the woman behind the glass.

"Oh, yes, I'm OK...*sorry*," Carolyn said, embarrassed that anyone had witnessed her little snit.

"I'm sure doctor will only be a few more minutes. I'll go and get you an update."

"Thank you..." Carolyn shouted at her shadow as it disappeared behind a fast closing door.

"Thank you," she repeated in a whisper. The medical assistant returned and leaned out over the counter from behind the glass.

"Doctor says that you can come back if you like, he's just finishing up, exam room two. By the way, we haven't met, I'm Judy," said the woman pleasantly.

Carolyn picked up her purse and got up, smiling at the woman as she walked toward the door. She suddenly noticed how young the woman was, just a girl really. She couldn't be more that nineteen or twenty, and she quite pretty, her long hair pulled back in a thick ponytail.

"Thank you Judy," Carolyn said as she passed by and walked to room number two.

"That's OK," Judy replied, sitting back down at her desk.

Carolyn opened the door and peeked inside. "Hello, hello, it's just me, mommy," she announced sweetly.

Doctor Lewis was sitting on a small rolling stool writing in Sophie's chart. While her tiny daughter sat on the end of a big table with the white cotton covering, her little legs swinging, the heels of her sneakers kicking the underside of the metal examination table making a considerable amount of noise.

"Sophie, stop that, you're making Doctor Lewis crazy!" Carolyn said, weakly scolding her little girl.

Sophie looked at her mother and stopped, her wet eyes revealing more than Carolyn wanted to accept. She walked over to Sophie and sat beside her, gently pulling her close. A healthy Sophia Wong would have jumped off of the table and challenged her mother to a game of tag. But today Sophie was content to melt into her mother's safe embrace. She was far too tired for a game of tag today. Doctor Lewis clicked his ballpoint pen and returned it to his coat pocket. He flipped the chart closed and held it to his chest with his crossed arms. He looked up at the two others in the room with him and paused for a moment before speaking. Sighing audibly, he scooted over to them on the rolling stool and playfully but gently pinched Sophie's tummy.

"My littlest patient was so brave today! Did she tell you how many ouchies we chased away," Doctor Lewis asked with a forced smile.

Sophie pulled closer to her mother pressing her face into Carolyn's breast. The wool cap she wore to cover her balding head came off and she began to cry. She didn't like what was happening to her, she didn't like her hair falling out. The kid's made fun of her, and her mother would cry when she thought that Sophie could not hear her or see her. Carolyn put the wool cap back on her daughter's head, rocking her as she wept.

"So what's the bad news Doctor Lewis?" Carolyn asked in a monotone voice. She wanted to cry too but she was out of tears, she was just numb.

"Well?" she pushed, looking at Doctor Lewis, trying to apologize for her attitude with her eyes.

"Her white count is dangerously low. I really wish that you would reconsider about another round of chemo. Granted, it'll be rough but it could be what puts us over the top in this battle," said Doctor Lewis compassionately.

Carolyn could feel the tears welling up, but they were angry tears, tears of frustration, not anguish or sorrow. She looked Doctor Lewis directly in the eyes and paused a second before answering.

"What do you me by *us* buddy?" she said in an icy tone.

"Will you be having any of this poisonous cocktail yourself this time?"

"Will you be there when she screams for hours from the pain, until her body is so fatigued that she mercifully passes out for a little while, only to wake and start it all over again?"

"Will you be combing your hair out in clumps and walking around town looking like a freak?"

"Tell me Doctor Lewis, is that what you meant by *us* getting over the top with more of your medicines?" Carolyn said, almost spitting the words out of her mouth. The harangued doctor hung his head and spoke at the floor in reply.

"I'm sorry Carolyn. That could have been said better."

"I'm not trying to be a cheerleader, or belittle Sophie's suffering, or yours, truly I'm not."

"I just want to help. I just want to offer up all of the support that there is. Believe it or not, this is painful for me too. I don't want to quit on Sophie. I don't want to say that's it, I'm powerless, and I've tried everything! I would feel like I'm letting her down, like I'm letting you all down."

Carolyn stopped rocking Sophie, and picked her sleeping daughter up into her arms.

"Help us off this table will ya, I want to take her home now, Ken will be worried about us," she said as the doctor helped her scoot off the table and move toward the door.

"You're a good man Doctor Lewis...*Brad*. And I'm sorry for going off on you like that, you didn't deserve any of that. I'm weary, I'm scared, and I'm angry at the world...but that's me, I have to deal with that. I'll talk with Ken when I get home about what you said, we'll be in touch," she said, apologizing as she capitulated.

"Thanks," Doctor Lewis replied with a weak smile.

"*Hey*...do you really want to help like you said?" Carolyn asked, turning back to look at him from over her shoulder.

"Yes...I really do."

"Then set aside your wisdom, skills, and experience...and love her, just pray for her Brad."

"*OK, but...*"

"Please don't say anything more. This ***one time*** have faith in something larger than yourself. Love my child enough to pray for her, and trust in God's will, I swear, she'll be in good hands...

Firebaugh, California, June 1973

"Hey, whose the cute guy with Father Billy?" KC asked Maria Lopez as they watched the three men walk toward the house from the kitchen window.

"I don't know Kathy, I've never seen him, but you're right he is cute... needs a haircut though," Maria replied, teasing her favorite visitor.

"Shhhhh, quiet, they're coming in," KC whispered, hurrying to sit back down at the kitchen table. The two women tried to appear uninterested as the men walked in through the screen door.

"*LUCY, I'm home!*" shouted Victor, he just loved pretending to be Ricky Ricardo, and he was convinced that it always put Maria in the mood. This was his new ploy as the *'Hop on Pop'* tactic had lost its allure about a year ago. But that was OK, he was always looking for ways to keep the spark alive in their marriage, because Maria knew how to keep the fire stoked once the flames started!

"*Ola Amado,*" Maria said, greeting her husband.

"We have company for dinner tonight. Father Billy's here, and this is Father Ethan," Victor said, introducing their guests.

"Maria, always nice to see you dear," Father Willet said, extending his hand.

"And KC, what a pleasant surprise, I didn't know that you were here. I thought that you would be in Fresno covering the murder of Dr. Katz, what was it now, *oh yes*, poisoned wasn't he?" asked Father Willet.

"I will be, and yes he was, *poisoned I mean*," KC answered.

"Really, how?"

"Looks like the same girl who tried to get him at his clinic came back to finish the job. The poor kid is even nuttier than the doc was."

"Pity, oh my, where are my manners...Ladies, this is Ethan Kelly, our new novice at St. John's. He is here from New York, State that is, Albany I believe," the Father said, making his introductions.

"Ethan, this is Victor's wife Maria, and the cute little spitfire over here is KC Littleton from the San Francisco Daily News.

"Pleased to meet you," I said, trying not to notice how pretty KC was. She reminded me a little of Nurse Carla, smart, sure, small, sassy, and sexy... the five S's.

"Senor," answered Maria Lopez, offering her hand. I reached out and pressed her fingers gently in my hand, respectfully acknowledging her station as the woman of the house and our gracious host. KC walked up to me and shook my hand as well, making sure to cover my hand with both of hers.

"Pleasure is all mine...*Father Kelly* is it?"

"Yes, well not quite, but that why I'm here after all," I answered, trying not appear as awkward as I felt.

"Just my luck, the good ones are always taken, *damn it!*...Sorry, I mean *darn it!*" KC replied.

"No offense Father," she apologized.

"None taken," I assured her.

"Why don't you all go into the living room while I make some fresh coffee," Maria said, waving us all toward the hall and out of the kitchen.

"Sure, follow me everyone," Victor said leading the way.

We all made our way into the living room and found a place to sit. As I took a seat on one end of the sofa, KC raced Father Willet to join me, making sure to place herself in between us in the process. I looked over at her and she gave me a shy schoolgirl grin. I guess I left an *s* out of the earlier description of her, make that the six *S's*.

"Sorry, I always sit here when I visit," she explained, wincing at her own explanation. I could have sworn I heard her mumble *"stupid, stupid, stupid"* to herself when she looked away.

Father Willet took the seat at the opposite end of the small couch.

"Well, isn't this cozy," he said cheerfully. KC smiled at him weakly and placed her folded hands in her lap, making sure to look over at Victor while stealing sideways glances at me intermittently.

"So, what brings the Catholic cavalry out to Hacienda Lopez today," KC asked sarcastically.

"KC," Victor said, scolding her as if she were his own daughter.

"That's alright Victor, I grown accustomed to little Miss Smarty pants here," Father Willet replied.

"Yeah, I didn't mean anything by it, give me a break Victor. Oh, and I already have a Dad thank you!" KC playfully snapped.

"Madre Dios, you will turn my daughter and my wife into a *loca mujer* just like you, pray for us Father," Victor teased back, equally enjoying the playful exchange between them.

"Who's loca *Poppi?*" asked a soft voice from the hall.

"You will be if you keep talking to this crazy woman," Victor said to the voice in the hall while he pointed a finger at KC. KC stuck her tongue out at Victor, then leaned back hard against the couch, crossing her arms and legs at the same time.

"Come out here and meet our guests *mija,*" Victor said to the voice in the hall.

A moment later a beautiful young girl walked into the room slowly. She was all of fifteen or sixteen but she carried herself with a grace beyond her years. Her dark hair was long and it fell over her shoulders and halfway down her back. And her eyes were the color of a root beer hard candy, more amber than brown. She smiled at her father and then suddenly darted toward the couch and jumped in between KC and I. She looked shyly at me and then scooted KC over toward Father Willet with a twist of her hips. So there we sat, snug as a bug in a rug. I hadn't felt this confined since my Marine Corp boot camp where they stacked us like cordwood in line after line, nut to butt as they say in the Navy.

"Aiye Dios, why couldn't I have had all sons," Victor playfully lamented.

Maria appeared with the coffee as Tina and KC giggled together.

"I see you have met our daughter," Maria said as she set the coffee tray on the table and prepared to serve.

"Not yet Mama," Tina informed her mother.

"No? Victor, *por favor*, don't embarrass me in front of the nice young priest," Maria said, teasing her husband.

"I was just getting to that. Senor Ethan, *I mean Father Ethan*, this is our daughter LaTina."

"Mija, this is Father Kelly, from New York," Victor said introducing me to his daughter.

"Senor," Tina said softly, scooting closer to KC and folding her hands in her lap.

"Nice to meet you," I said, wondering to myself why was it that all girls used that same move. They all neatly laced their fingers together and placed their clasped hands in their laps whenever they meant to be coy, curious, very curious?

I studied Tina for a moment and then looked over at Victor as his wife handed him a cup of coffee. I was about to speak when KC jumped up off of the couch and looked directly at me, her hands on her hips in a stance assertive enough to make me a little uncomfortable. Then she suddenly turned toward Victor and then Father Willet, her mouth slightly agape and her gaze penetrating.

"You told him, didn't you?" she shouted accusingly.

"Oh my gosh, you told him! You told him everything didn't you!" she continued, getting more and more agitated with each word she uttered. She didn't wait for a response from either of the other men and she aimed her paranoia back at me.

"What do you want anyway? Are you even really a priest, do you have an ID or something? I can't believe this, did either of you even bother to check this guy out?" she said, really starting to get worked up.

"KC, sit down please, let me explain," Father Willet said, trying to calm her.

"I don't want to sit down, I think that we should call Grover or Mr. Donnelly, this doesn't feel right," she shouted, beginning to rant and rave a little.

"KC, we will call them in due time, first let me tell you why I brought Ethan here with me," Father Willet pleaded.

"No, no, no, I want..." KC stopped in mid-sentence, feeling a tug on her shirtsleeve.

She looked down and saw that Tina had moved to the edge of the couch and that she was crying. KC sat back down next to the girl and put an arm around her shoulders. Lowering her voice she spoke directly to Father Willet.

"OK, I want to know what's going on."

Before the priest could answer Tina moved away from KC and stood up. She walked over to her father and turned to kneel beside his chair facing the others on the couch. Maria Lopez stood next to her husband on the other side of the chair, looking down at her family. KC leaned back and crossed her arms, still defiant, but tamed by the calm yet serious look on Tina's face.

"*Poppi*, I can help the little girl, I want to. But I will need to go to her soon, there is not much time."

My hand went quickly to my face to cover my mouth and prevent the gasp that was rushing to escape my lips. I looked right at Tina, searching her face for an answer. How could she know about this, what kind of trick was it? Suddenly I found myself as agitated as KC had been and I kept looking back and forth between Victor and Father Willet. There had to be an explanation, there just had to be. We all sat in silence, the coffee cooling in our cups, not a word from anyone for a good two minutes, and then, "OK, *I'll bite*, who's Sophia?" KC asked.

Thirty-four

*(...something happening here, what it is ain't exactly
clear, there's a man with a gun over there, a tellin
me I got to beware""...Buffalo Springfield)*

Los Angeles, California, 3 July 1973

High overhead two commercial airliners raced across a cloudless sky toward the tarmac at LAX, like two giant sprinters running in a dead heat. Their shadows silhouetted on the neighborhoods below, trailed the aircraft by a length or two, rapidly changing shape as they slithered along each irregularly shaped structures on the ground below. The *405 freeway* loomed just ahead of the fast approaching airplanes, and Junior imagined the busy highway to be the finish line with invisible tape strung tautly from El Segundo to Culver City, just waiting for a winner to cross. He leaned forward in the driver's seat, wedging his head precariously between the wheel and the windshield trying to see if could make the call without causing an accident in the process.

"TWA by a nose," Junior said out aloud as the two planes cleared the freeway and roared on past him on their way to touchdown safely a mile or so in the distance.

Junior Martinez had always loved airplanes, which was easy to understand given the fact that he had grown up in east LA watching them pass overhead day in and day out. He even had dreamed of being a pilot someday, but that dream had faded when the streets took control of his every day. It wasn't that he was alone or had no family to lean on. He *did* have a family, a *good* one, and a very *large* one. But all around him, entwining each intersection of every avenue of opportunity, getting in between family and new friends, playgrounds, parks, schools, and churches, were the streets. Asphalt serpents that served more as boundaries and barriers than safe passage to anyplace in particular.

They loomed outside of every home, every school, every market, and every library, *everywhere*. Essentially dividing entire neighborhoods into virtual petri dishes, where children were swallowed by tough talking predators. They were the protectors of the turf, the guardians of *the way it was baby!* All of the neighborhoods were their families, *todo por familia*, and nobody left the family easily. The local streets and avenues of much of east LA had been carved into social sectors lorded over by various colorfully named gangs who warred with each other over whom would have dominion over whom. They offered safety in numbers against racism outside the hood, against the police, and all too often against one another. It was violence and intimidation they used to assure that fragile comfort zone and foster their trade in drugs, petty theft and grand larceny. Crime paid well, and the take was always in cash, but when they paid, they paid in blood.

To his mind there were but three choices in the end. Capitulate and adapt to the life they offered, die, or escape. Junior learned to keep his dreams to himself, he decided early on that he would escape. His older brother Julio had once told him, just before he was shot to death while standing in line at a Dairy Queen, for what no one knows to this day, *"keep a low tone and mean stare mijo, and maybe you might slip away before anyone knows you are gone."* The streets made widows of children too young to be mothers. The streets made parents old before their time. The streets were Satan's playground, where hope was sacrificed daily for lies, and where love was reserved for special occasions, like births and deaths. *Love made you weak*, hate made you strong, and like any street kid could tell you, you had to be strong to survive.

This was Junior Martinez' reality, at least it was until the day that he was drafted. And this would have been the reality that he returned to had it not been for the people that came into his life, the people that God had brought into his life. When he returned home from the killing fields of Southeast Asia he was determined not to trade one hell for another, even if it was his home turf. He had seen too many friends die thousands of miles from their homes and families. He had no intention of watching any more die outside his own front door or in his own backyard. These were the thoughts running through his mind as he drove into the parking lot of Los Angeles International Airport. He took the ticket that the turnstile offered and the bar raised so that he could drive past and into the lot. He stopped abruptly as a car began to back out of a plum space right in front of the entrance on the first level of the parking structure. Junior put the time stamped ticket stub between his teeth and pulled in as soon as the other car was clear.

"Damn, that was lucky *Holmes*," he said, congratulating himself.

He set the ticket stub on the dashboard and got out of his car, depressing the inside door lock with his thumb before he slammed the door shut. Instantly he felt a panic attack coming on as he patted his pants pockets for his car keys and scanned the front seat with his eyes.

"Aiye baboso," he said, scolding himself in a harsh whisper.

"Ah, here they are," he said out loud, relieved to find the ring of keys setting on top of the car.

He scooped them up in his hand and stuffed them into his pants pocket and started walking fast toward the airport terminals. *"Why does everyone always rush at airports,"* he thought. Why was he rushing, he was at least an hour early to meet JoJo's flight. He shrugged and walked a little faster, crossing the busy street, dodging taxicabs and shuttles, and avoiding the throng of travelers heavily laden with suitcases and whatnot. He looked up at the signpost in front of him and searched for a clue as to where the Delta flights would be coming in. Giving up after a minute or two he walked up to someone official looking to ask for help.

"Say buddy, you know where I need to go to meet my friend flying in from Alabama," he asked.

"Just a second sir," the skycap answered.

"OK, yeah, well he's supposed to be here at two o'clock, but I don't know which way to walk, this place is a lot bigger than I thought," Junior continued.

"Just wait one minute sir, let me finish here," the skycap replied testily.

"Oh yeah, sorry, I'll just stand over here," Junior said apologizing, and stepping off to one side to give the poor guy some room to toss a half dozens bags onto a cart while some old woman waited, checking her wristwatch every five seconds.

"Oh, I hope I don't miss my flight," she said loud enough for everyone within earshot to hear. It was a not so subtle rebuke that was received with an unexpected grace by the skycap. The big man gently placed the last bag on the cart and removed his cap to wipe his brow.

"There you go ma'am," he said as he returned his cap to his head.

"Walter, come on over here son and help this nice lady run over to gate number 4 so she can catch her flight without any worry," he said to a younger man standing to Junior's left. The young man walked up to the old lady and offered his arm to escort her to her airplane.

"This way ma'am," the young man said politely.

"Oh my," the old woman exclaimed, suddenly embarrassed by her left handed snub.

"Your bags are checked and will be sent to your plane in plenty of time, don't worry about a thing now," the big skycap said assuredly. The old woman waved to him from over her shoulder as she and her young escort passed through the sliding automatic doors.

"You got a rough job man. Is everybody that loco?" Junior asked.

"No, not everybody, but enough to make for a long day five of the six days that I work here," the skycap said with a little sigh.

"But hey, it's puts food on the table and is putting my daughter through UCLA, so I don't complain none. Wouldn't be right to whine about the good fortune the Lord's blessed me with anyhow," he added.

"Now, what can I do for you?"

Junior smiled and repeated his question. The big man put both his hands behind his lower back and massaged his aching muscles while he directed Junior to the correct gate, then tipped his cap at him as he turned to walk away. Junior stopped after a couple steps and turned to run after the skycap. He dug into his pocket and fished out his wallet, pulling out a five-dollar bill.

"Hey, wait up man," he called after the skycap. The big man stopped and turned to see what the commotion was about.

"Yes sir, is there something else?" he asked as Junior reached him.

"Yeah, here take this," he said, handing the fiver to the surprised skycap.

"The old lady shoulda done this, *but let me OK*, one workin man to another," Junior said, slapping the skycap on his beefy arm.

The big dude looked Junior over and then noticed the patch on his sleeve, *US Postal Service*. He shook his head in an affirmative manner and smiled, "OK brother, thanks, that means a lot," he said taking the money, folding it and placing it gently into his coat pocket.

He waved at Junior then turned and continued on his way. Junior waved back then looked at his watch, surprising himself at how much time had passed since the last time he checked. He really did need to run now to meet JoJo's plane. The last thing he wanted to do was be late and have that grumpy old so and so searching the airport hollering his name at the top of his lungs! He thought to himself about the last time they had all been together while he jogged toward gate number seven and Delta Flight 2121 from Montgomery Alabama.

Tonight they would all meet for supper in Hollywood, JoJo had always wanted to see Hollywood, so everyone agreed to meet at some steakhouse out there. He was looking forward to seeing JoJo, Carla, and Lt. Walker. He was surprised when he found out that those two had never married. In fact they were both of their spouses had come with them to attend the funeral. He was also looking forward to meeting Wesley's mom and his brother's and sisters as well.

"It'll be a good thing, all of us together again," he thought as he ran.

He was sorry that Larry Polen wouldn't be there, he had not heard until Carla told him that he didn't make it back from the Nam. He was disappointed that Ethan Kelly wasn't able to come as well, he really had wanted to show him that he had done alright since the war. He raised his hand to his face and wiped away a tear falling from his eye as he wished that Mitchell could have been here for this reunion as well. So many memories from so short a time together, but these were people with whom he shared an uncommon experience. They had each survived when many others had not. The fear that bonded them in conflict had turned to a love that would last a lifetime. They were all family now, *todo por familia*. Wesley Hightower may have left this life far to soon as far as everybody was concerned, but Junior took comfort in knowing that Wesley would live forever in his heart, as the hero he was, as the brother he would forever be.

San Francisco, California, 3 July 1973

Tina watched as the huge airplane pulled close to the glass and the funny looking rolling tunnel thing attached itself to the side of the plane. She jumped just a little as the aircraft jerked to a stop, and then sat down on the seat between KC and I. She looked over at me and then crossed her legs, smoothing the material of her dress over her knees with her hands.

"I am not so sure I want to get on that thing," she said nervously.

"Don't worry about it kiddo, I fly these things all the time, nothing to it," KC said without looking up from here copy of the SF Daily News.

Tina looked my way again, pulling in her lips and biting down on them. I patted her hand reassuringly.

"I'll be OK Tina," I said.

"You want to know what I do to keep from getting too nervous?" I asked. She shook her head slowly, still biting on her lips. I smiled at her, amused by her innocence.

"I sing to myself," I said, inviting her to keep the conversation going and forget about watching the plane outside.

"You sing...What do you *sing* Father?" she asked, looking at me as if I suddenly grew another head.

"I sing the same song every time. That one by Herman's Hermit's, you know, *Mrs. Brown you've got a lovely daughter.*" She stared at me for a moment then burst out laughing, startling KC in the process.

"***What**, what's so funny?*" KC asked, seemingly irritated by the attention we were drawing to ourselves.

"You're a nut!" Tina told me still laughing.

"No, *really*, it works. Here try it with me," I said.

"*Father Ethan, you're not really...*" KC started to say, whispering harshly through clenched teeth.

"*Oh no Father, no!*" Tina pleaded, holding her stomach as it began to cramp from laughing so hard.

Standing up and turning to face my two traveling companions, as well as the rest of the airport around gate B7, I cleared my throat, tested my pitch with a few *me me me's*, and then:

Mrs. Brown you've got a lovely daughter
Girls as sharp as her are somethin' rare
But it's sad, she doesn't love me now
She's made it clear enough it ain't no good to pine
She wants to return those things I bought her
Tell her she can keep them just the same
Things have changed, she doesn't love me now
She's made it clear enough it ain't no good to pine

KC and Tina shrank in their seats as I serenaded them with my totally tone deaf rendition, made all the more embarrassing by the worst English accent ever attempted. I stopped after the second verse, confident that I had diverted Tina's attention enough to board the plane without incident.

"There, you see, who could be nervous with this kind of entertainment so readily available!"

The two of them looked at me cross-eyed and then were overcome with a near terminal case of the giggles.

"*Alright*, everyone's a critic," I said in a mock whine. I sat back down while a few of the kinder of souls applauded graciously.

"Thank you, thank you," I said acknowledging my new fans.

"You are a nut Father Kelly," Tina finally said, sitting up straight, dabbing the tears from her eyes with a soft tissue from her bag.

"Ditto! That goes double for me," KC said, tossing in her two cents.

She shook her newspaper and then raised it up to hide behind it. Just as I looked away I caught her peek out from around the paper and noticed the warm smile on her face and the twinkle in her eye. If I didn't know better I might have thought that I had detected a little spark there.

"UNITED AIRLINES Flight 17 for Albany New York will now begin boarding. Please have your boarding pass ready and we will begin seating those in first class as well as those passengers with special needs," announced a pleasant voice over the loudspeaker.

"That's us boys and girls, first class all the way, courtesy big daddy Gateway and the San Francisco Daily News," KC said as she stood and gathered her things.

Tina tensed up a bit, slowly standing, then turning back to retrieve her purse and magazine from her chair. She waited for me to stand and then we walked after KC who was already standing in line waiting to file past the counter attendant. Tina and I joined her and waited our turn to pass by the attendant and enter the jet way.

"Thank you for choosing United, have a wonderful flight," the pretty woman in the red and blue uniform said as we passed by her. She needed to tug a little harder than expected at Tina's boarding pass to collect it, as the young traveler was reluctant to give it up, uncomfortable with anything that seemed out of the ordinary.

"It's OK Tina, it's just like trading an *A* ticket at Disneyland for one of the cooler *E* ticket rides," KC said reassuringly. She let go of the pass and followed KC down the jet way, looking back over her shoulder to make sure I was right behind them.

We reached the door of the aircraft and entered slowly while Tina checked everything out. Her head seemingly rotating 360 degrees as she inventoried each and every unfamiliar dial, latch, button, and flashing light as we reached the aisle. The first class cabin was divided into pairs of oversized seats on each side of the plane. KC and Tina sat on the right with KC taking the window seat, and I sat in the aisle seat just across from Tina. We got settled and waited for the slow parade of passengers to finish filing past us as they filled the empty seats from stem to stern on the big airplane. Finally the steady stream of people ended and the stewardess started to walk the aisles and close all of the overhead compartments. You could hear them banging shut from the back, the noise getting louder as she made her way forward.

A voice crackled over the intercom as the Captain welcomed us aboard, letting us know what our arrival time would be. Afterward the Lead Flight Attendant took over to tell us the rules and regulations of air travel and to give our safety instructions. Tina sat very still during the lecture, only glancing in my direction once. She absolutely avoided looking out of the window by KC and otherwise stared straight ahead, keeping her breathing slow and steady. I suspected she was praying, and I didn't want to interrupt her concentration, so I decided to follow her lead and say a little prayer of my own. I closed my eyes and recited Psalm 23 as was my custom to do daily, and then said the Lord's Prayer as well. Afterward, I thanked God for bringing this child into our lives, for the gift that he had given to her, and for his grace that was allowing me to bring her gift to our precious little Sophie. I opened my eyes, a soothing feeling of utter peace settling my heart and my nerves. I smiled involuntarily and then looked over at Tina, only to find that she was already looking my way. She had been watching me, and she smiled at me when our eyes met.

"Have faith Father, we're not too late, I swear," she said softly and sweetly.

The intercom crackled again, "Flight crew prepare for take off," squawked the Captain's voice. The huge plane jerked slightly then began to back up slowly. Tina tensed a little and I could see just a trace of nervousness in her eyes. The plane turned sharply to the right and then paused before moving forward. I glanced over at KC, she was scrunched down in her seat to get a good look out the window as we taxied toward the runway. The plane bounced slightly on its big tires and we picked up a little speed and I could see Tina's shoulders tense in anticipation of the take off. I reached across the aisle and took her little hand in mine and she held onto it gratefully.

The plane slowed and made a sharp left turn onto the runway and came to a stop. Overhead the seatbelt and no smoking lights came on with a loud bell tone and at that moment the jet engines began to whine louder and louder and the pilots swiftly increased the RPMs. The plane began to sway with the force of the engines while we were held in place by the strong brakes. And then the brakes were released and in a heartbeat the huge aircraft raced down the runway, faster and faster and faster.

"*Weeeeeeeeee,*" KC squealed.

"*I love this part!*"

Tina squeezed my hand hard enough to nearly draw blood, but I didn't notice. I was having my own issues with my fear of flying. And then, softly at first, she and I started:

Mrs. Brown you've got a lovely daughter
Girls as sharp as her are somethin' rare
But it's sad, she doesn't love me now
She's made it clear enough it ain't no good to pine
Then, at the top of our lungs...
She wants to return those things I bought her
Tell her she can keep them just the same

Things have changed, she doesn't love me now
She's made it clear enough it ain't no good to pine
The wheels of the Boeing 747 left the ground and we were airborne...

<u>Los Angeles, California, 4 July 1973</u>

The house was very quiet as everyone slept soundly in the wee hours of the morning. Miguel lay awake in his bed and stared at the ceiling shadows from the street light outside. He had not slept well in weeks, not since the night he killed that cop. The voices continued to haunt his nights and he instinctively feared what they might require of him next. He could feel himself losing control of his actions, his mind being led by something or someone inside him. He yearned for his mother's gentle touch and soothing voice. He tried to hum the songs that she would sing to him, but the memories were being driven deeper and deeper into himself, to a place that he could not reach any longer.

He no longer felt safe with Raymond and Smiley, he no longer felt as though they were safe with him. Miguel was getting the traveling Jones, for where he wasn't sure, but the urgency was there to leave now. He rolled over onto his side and faced the wall, the shadows no longer teasing him. But now he could see shapes appearing in the Navajo White paint on the wall in front of him. First his father's face, the one from his Marine picture that used to hang on the wall above the television. Then his mother's face, the one when she was a child like him, with all of the curly black hair and the plump rosy cheeks that accentuated her beautiful smile. He saw the old man's face, the look of utter surprise right before Miguel blew his brains out. He saw the face of that young cop, the big guy. He liked that gringo's face, it was handsome, like a movie star, like John Wayne, a big blonde cowboy. That's why he shot him in the chest, he didn't want to ruin that nice face. He could still see it, the way his dead eyes looked up at the night sky as they had drove away.

Miguel smiled weakly, remembering these events like they were an episode of a television show that he might have watched at some time, like they weren't real, they didn't really happen, did they? And then gradually he saw her face appear in the paint on the wall. She wasn't a child any longer, she had the face of a grown up. He watched as her features became clearer in his mind's eye. He looked closely into eyes that were not there, but which he had seen before. He felt her presence inside of him, he remembered the warmth she brought to his cold hands, his blue lips. He remembered the light she that brought to his dead eyes, and the pain of returning from his peaceful rest.

Why couldn't she have let him be, couldn't she see that to bring him back was wrong. Surely God must have warned her, told her whom it was she was dealing with. So many people have suffered, he has suffered, and so many more will suffer. One day she will suffer as well, pay back is a motherfucker, ***bitch!***

Thirty-five

*(...Another pleasant valley Sunday, charcoal
burning everywhere, rows of houses that are all the
same, and no one seems to care""...The Monkees)*

Albany, New York, 4 July 1973

You know there are all kinds of National celebrations in the world, from Bastille Day in France to May Day in the Soviet Union. Each of them steeped in tradition and pageantry befitting the people and the culture. Here in America, the 4th of July is the *big daddy* of all of our National holidays. *Shoot*, we have lots of holidays dedicated to patting ourselves on the back and honoring those who paid the ultimate price for our freedom. As a people, we have always passionately revered the memory of the men and women who sacrificed so much for the freedom that they provided. We hoped against hope that we would be able to pass that same freedom on to our children, grandchildren, and great grandchildren. But the 4th of July, Independence Day, *well*, that day is special, sort of like all the others rolled into one.

Only Christmas Day could rival this annual event. And from State to State, city-to-city, and town-to-town, the formula for the day was relatively the same everywhere, *freedom, fun, and fireworks equaled FAMILY.* For one day each year we were just one big happy (for the most part) family. A nation of castoffs, thrill seekers and neh'r do wells, *Americans* by hook or crook, *'one for all and all for one'* as Alexandre Dumas said so well of the heroes in his historical romance *'The Three Musketeers'*. We came here from all points on the globe, from as far back as the Stone Age across the land bridge from Asia, to the English and Dutch Pilgrims escaping tyranny in Europe, and as recent as yesterday from wherever, for whatever.

The 4th of July linked us together, *for a day at least*, one huge immigrant family celebrating the annual family reunion if you will. Toss a dart at a map of the United States and wherever it lands, if there are people present of course, you can count on finding at least one barbecue in at least one neighborhood. Sweet aromas filling the afternoon air with such heavenly smells that I guarantee your mouth water with anticipation. And by nightfall the sky would be filled with smoke and brilliant colors, as fireworks are set off at local parks, on street corners, and in dozens of driveways and alleys, all to the delight of young and old alike. If that dart had landed on Albany New York, you could have zoomed in from space right to the backyard of Maggie Kelly and found all of these things in progress. As you came closer the aroma of beef brisket, hot dogs would have met you, and hamburgers cooking slowly over a bed of hot coals. You would have heard the laughter and squeals of children as they raced around the yard in a fierce game of freeze tag, complete with the sounds of barking dogs in close pursuit, and hollering adults warning them all to stay clear of the BBQ! And then as you floated down to Earth, you would have been snapped out of your dreamlike state by the cold spray from the Mr. Wiggle water toy set up in the driveway to cool off all the sweaty little freeze-taggers. That would be my neighborhood, my home, my people, my family, and my pleasure to share with all you, whoever you are.

"OK, OK, if this wiffle ball hits me one more time I swear I'm going to cook it next to your hotdog, *you hear me Joshua Bennett!*" Paul Pulchoski hollered from his station at the grill. He tipped a beer bottle up to his lips and took a long drink, searching the yard for the culprit of the latest barrage of toys to be hurled his way.

"I didn't see this much action during my whole tour," Paulie muttered to himself, turning over a couple of hamburgers and rolling a line of wieners on the grill. He smiled large as he breathed in the aroma of the cooking meat, then looked around quickly before he stabbed one of the wieners and devoured it in three bites.

"*Ooooooowwww, **CRAP**, hot, hot,*" he squealed, hopping and twirling about the grill like a wounded pelican, performing his version of the *ouchie dance* for one and all. He hurriedly scooped up his beer, nearly spilling it in the process, and proceeded to drain it in record time, more to salve his radiating tongue than quench his thirst.

"Smooth ya big hairy ox," Kenny said sarcastically as he walked up to his friend to check on him.

"Gimmie a break will ya, I'm starving over here," Paulie whined as he popped open another beer with the church key hanging from the chain around his neck.

"See you wore only your very best trinkets *Princess*," Kenny teased.

"You got the matching bracelet in your pocket there sweetness," Kenny continued relentlessly.

"Yeah, I got your bracelet, *I got your bracelet hangin right here!*" Paul hurled back at his tormentor, grabbing the inside of his thigh to crudely make his point.

"*Lovely, just lovely*, good thing Mother is busy cutting up the watermelon," Shannon said walking up to the two men as they continued their chop-fest.

"Oh man, see what you made me do Ken," Paulie whispered harshly.

"***Ixnay with the ofanitypay, umboday!***" Paul added quickly, as he rolled his eyes toward Shannon, and then turned to face her.

"Hey Shannon girl, we was just kiddin around, you know how it is," Paul said uncomfortably, wiping the sweat from his brow with his big hairy arm.

"*Uh huh,*" she replied, poking him in the ribs as she passed by and walked over to stand by Kenny.

Kenny put his arm around Shannon and gave her shoulders a little squeeze. He looked over at Paulie to make sure he was watching and then leaned over and kissed her on the cheek. He knew that would get a rise out of his buddy and he squared his shoulders as he prepared himself for Paulie's response. He didn't have to wait long, "*Hey man, you already got bowl full of sugar at home, you don't need to go borrowing no cup around here!*" Paul protested, instantly realizing that he had been trapped into stepping into the light. Kenny released his hold on Shannon and raised his arms animatedly, stepping to the side and then backing away slowly toward the driveway and the water wiggle.

"Don't get mad Hoss, I'm only being nice. Besides I didn't see any brand on this little Philly here," Kenny said in his best southern drawl, laughing so hard he almost choked on the words.

Paul started to make a move toward Ken when he caught Shannon's eye. She smiled at him in a way that instantly froze him in his tracks, his look of rage slowly melting to one of peace in the presence of such beauty and sweetness. He could feel himself smiling back at her and he was suddenly aware that his heart had jumped from his chest to his sleeve. Before either of them could break the awkward silence with a word or a stammer, a whole section of barbecuing wieners lined up on the grill went up in flames.

"**GOOD GRAVY!**" Paul shouted, jumping back from the grill.

He looked at the sizzling and spattering hotdogs, and acting on his first impulse, beat at them frantically with the oversized spatula until the flames died out. Kenny arrived a nanosecond later, soaking wet with the water wiggle in tow. Together they were quite a site, *tweedle dumb and tweedle dumber*, providing everyone with a good belly laugh until Maggie Kelly arrived to shut off the water and Mr. Wiggle dropped onto the smoking grill to sizzle and spatter along side of the unfortunate wieners.

"***Alright***, out of the way *Heckle and Jeckle*, let me see what can be saved for pity sake!" Maggie exclaimed, shoving Paulie and Ken out of her way. The two of them retreated without any fuss and went to stand on the driveway before Maggie decided to swat them both with whatever was handy.

Shannon walked over to stand between them and put her arms over each of their shoulders. She patted them lightly on the back, lowered her head and shook it slowly.

"You guys are too stupid to live," she said slowly, shifting her weight from one barefoot to the other as she stood on the hot concrete of the driveway.

"Shut up Shannon," Kenny said dryly.

"Ditto," Paul added enthusiastically.

Shannon lowered her hands and pinched them both good and hard on their flanks then spun on her heel and ran as fast as she could down the drive and toward the front of the house. Kenny and Paul hollered in pain and then turned to give chase, Paul taking a surprising lead, and Kenny pulling up and stopping at the sound of his wife's voice. He watched Paul and Shannon disappear at the end of the drive as they turned toward the front yard, and then turned to see what was up with Carolyn.

"What it is it honey?'" Kenny said as he started walking toward his wife standing at the sliding glass door. He picked up the pace as he got closer and saw the panic in Carolyn's eyes.

"Are you OK babe? What's wrong, where's Sophie?" Kenny asked in rapid succession.

"Kenny, *come quick*, she won't wake up! She fell asleep about an hour ago on the sofa and now..."

"OK, OK, baby, let's go see," Kenny said reassuringly as he took her by the hand and walked quickly into the house.

Maggie looked on from the barbecue and set the paper plate with the stack of burned meat onto grass at her feet. She wiped her hands on her apron and then trotted off after Ken and Carolyn. She scanned the backyard for Shannon or some other adult to look after the gaggle of kids scurrying all over the place.

"SHANNON KELLY," she shouted, hoping that her daughter would pop up from somewhere to heed the call.

"SHANNON..."

Paul pulled slowly away from Shannon and looked down at her face, her eyes closed and her lips still slightly pursed. It was their first kiss after all, and it had come as such a surprise to him, he had been taken totally off guard. One minute he was chasing her to give the spanking of the decade and the next minute they were kissing on the front steps. Then, just as he was beginning to realize that life was about to change for him, the shrill voice Maggie Kelly wafted into the front yard from the back. Paul's face reddened instantly with guilt, sure that Maggie had witnessed the whole thing and that her Irish would be WAY up! He stood up quickly and looked around the yard, certain that she would round the corner with something heavy enough to whack a few years off of his future.

"Shannon, that's your Mom's hollering after you. You think she saw us?" he asked, a slight stammer to his voice.

Shannon opened her eyes slowly and smiled up at him, reaching for his hand and pulling herself up by it. She stepped in close and hugged him, resting her head on his shoulder, her long auburn hair falling across her face and onto his arm. Paul held her close to him, but kept an eye out for Maggie's inevitable arrival. He ran his hand down her back and over her hair, feeling every ripple and wave, gathering up a fistful when he reached the small of her back. Man she felt good in his arms, like she was a part of him, like she belonged there. It was still a mystery to him, he couldn't remember who kissed who, or WHY? All he knew now was that he was ready to weather any storm Maggie Kelly might bring to make sure that this moment was a beginning and not an ending!

"What did you say Paulie?" Shannon asked softly.

"Your Mom Shannon, I heard your Mom calling for you," Paul said, still scanning the area for Maggie's attack.

"I didn't hear her," Shannon said.

"I know you didn't, we were kinda busy, remember," Paul explained sheepishly.

"By the way, how long have you been saving that up anyway?" Paul asked, gently pulling the hair from in front of her face and looking down at her.

"Since I was twelve," she answered with a giggle.

"*Are you kidding me*, I thought you hated my ass. What about all those practical jokes, the peanut butter in my ear muffs, the ants in my swim trunks, huh, what was all of that about?" he demanded.

"*You're such a dope Paulie!* Don't you know that when a woman pays that much attention to *you* it's to make you notice *her*? What can I say, you grew on me over the years, until one day, *today I guess*, I realized that somewhere along the way I fell in love with you…*get it now Einstein?*" Shannon explained, holding his face gently in her two hands. Paul looked at her for what seemed like a long time, twitching his nose slightly while she squeezed his cheeks together and changing the expression on his face.

"Now what?" he uttered from behind his fish face.

Shannon released his face and stepped back, placing her hands firmly onto her hips, shooting him a look of mock frustration.

"*Now what* is right mister!" she tried to say tersely, unable to suppress the grin forming on her face.

"*SHANNON,*" Maggie Kelly' hollered from the back yard again.

"YIKES, something's wrong!" Shannon exclaimed. She turned quickly and jumped down from the porch, hitting the ground running.

Paul took off after her and they reached the back yard at the same time. The children and a few scattered adults were milling around the yard and they all pointed in unison toward the house when Shannon and Paul arrived. They raced one another to the sliding door and Paul stood aside as Shannon went inside first. He followed close behind and stopped at the dining room table. He slowly put his hands up to Shannon's shoulders and she grabbed onto his hands as they made contact. They looked over at the sofa across from them and saw Maggie on her knees in front of Ken and Carolyn. Kenny cradled Sophie in his arms, the little wool cap covering her head, the few wisps of hair that remained after chemo jutting out over her little ears.

"*Kenny...*" Paul said softly, swallowing the lump that had just formed in his throat.

"*Paul Pulchoski, you get on that telephone and call an ambulance this instant!*" Maggie ordered, wiping at her tear stained face.

Shannon squeezed Paul's hands and then released them as he turned to do what he was told. She walked over to her mother's side and knelt beside her, putting her arm around her. It was the first time Shannon had ever seen her mother lose her composure. She had always been a rock, always maintained her dignity. Even at Da's service, and when the letter had come from the Marines about Ethan being missing, she had remained stoic as ever. This was the first time in her life that she felt as though she could be strong for her. She looked up at Kenny and his family. His Dad and Mom were standing behind the sofa, consoling the grieving couple, Mr. Wong's lips were hard and tight, but his eyes soft and moist. He didn't need to say anything to get across what he was feeling. Mrs. Wong stood with her eyes closed, her lips moving slowly as she prayed silently to herself. Kenny looked up from his daughter's face and tried to call Paul back telepathically, he didn't have the strength to say even one word.

Ken knew that the ambulance was now a useless gesture, he had felt Sophie leave them as soon as he picked her up. It was if she had been holding on until he arrived, it was the only way she had left to say goodbye. Kenny watched as Paul walked back into the doorway of the kitchen, the telephone handset at his ear, the long cord wrapped once around his free hand and hanging down to the floor from the wall-mounted phone. The two friends made eye contact and held each other's gaze for an uncomfortable moment. The house was silent, save a random sniffle, whimper, or sigh. The hollow, phantom sound of a missing heartbeat ran softly in everyone's silent prayer. Paul lowered the handset from his ear, a faint voice fading into the background as he held it in front of him, tears beginning to well in his eyes. He knew Sophie was gone now. This had turned out to be the best and the worst day of his life...

Los Angeles, California, 4 July 1973

The solemn sound of taps and the roar of the twenty-one-gun salute still rang in Carla's ears as she and Sean followed the others to Junior's house. She and her friends, comrades in arms, had just lay their brother to rest. God, she couldn't believe that Wesley had died for something as stupid as a traffic ticket. That wasn't the way a hero was supposed to die, there was no glory in that. Shot by some punk and left to die in a gutter, alone, his weapon still strapped to his side snug its holster. There was no honor in that death, his life was just pissed away, and that made her so mad. She was mad at the killer, at the city, at the society that spawned this scumbag! God help her, she was mad at Wesley for letting this happen! Carla raised her hand and covered her mouth to keep herself from crying again. Sean reached across to her with one hand and squeezed her shoulder while he steered the rental car with the other. She covered his hand with her free hand, while she worked at regaining her composure.

"Easy now Carla girl, you don't want your friend to be looking down on ya from Heaven above and see you blubbering like a wee child, do you?" Sean teased lovingly.

He glanced over at his new bride to see if he could detect the slightest bit of a smile coming to her lips. Carla was quick to oblige as she sniffled loudly, pulling a tissue from the box in her lap and blowing her nose noisily.

"Jesus H. Christ Carla, you honk your beezer like a drunken sailor," Sean said in mock horror.

That one got to her and she snorted loudly as she broke into a hysterical laugh. Sean laughed along with her, thinking to himself how cool it was that a good laugh, or a good cry always made you feel better in the end. It was a curious psychological phenomenon, curious indeed.

"*Stop it Sean Michael Andrews*, you're going to make me pee my pants you brat," Carla shouted, swatting her new husband on the arm as she began to settle down.

She blew her nose once more and stuffed the used tissue into her purse. Carla ran her hands down her thighs smoothing out her skirt. She looked over at Sean as he drove and studied his face a moment. Oh my gosh she thought, it was still hard for her to believe that she was a married woman now. This was by far the most spontaneous thing she had ever done in her life. Attending Wesley Hightower's funeral was nerve racking enough, but having to introduce a total stranger to her parents as her husband was going to be downright terrifying. Scenarios began to flash through her mind like she were watching coming attractions in the movie theater. They played them silently while she pretended to watch the passing scenery as they drove along: They went sort of like…

"Hi Mom, Hi Dad, guess what I did this summer!" or

"A funny thing happened on the way to the hospital" and worst of all…

"Carla: Knock Knock…"

"Mom: Who's there…"

"Carla: betcha…"

"Dad: betcha who…"

"Carla: betcha wondering who this guy is!" Carla closed her eyes and groaned.

"You alright honey?" Sean asked.

"Yeah I'm OK, but you better keep an eye on me tonight, I may get pretty tossed at Junior's place," she answered.

"This about your friend, or are you still vexing over telling Mom and Dad about us?"

"Oh Jesus Sean, promise you won't call them that right away, let me soften them up a bit before you treat them to all that Irish love and stuff, OK?" Carla begged.

"Alright, you have my word, feel better now?"

"Pinky swear," she insisted, holding out the pinky finger of her left hand.

"Pinky swear," answered her husband, extending the pinky finger of his right hand. They locked fingers and counted to three then pulled them apart quickly.

"OK, now help me with these directions in case I lose your pal junior up there. He must be close to home because we're going faster and he's making these LA turns a little too quickly for my New York state of mind!" Sean said a tad sarcastically.

"Oh behave will you, we're almost there according to this little map. Let's see, this is Crenshaw, and we just passed Del Amo, so Sepulveda should be just ahead. We make a right turn there and his place is only a few blocks on the left, piece of cake," Carla said snapping her fingers.

"I'm impressed, I guess all that time dating a helicopter pilot paid some dividends," Sean teased. Carla reached into her purse and pulled out a whistle and blew it softly.

"Foul, we agreed, no ex-bashing, remember?" she protested.

"Sorry, I couldn't resist that one," Sean apologized.

"Yeah, well..."

"Hey, did he always wear that Cub's cap in Vietnam as well, or did he have more hair back then," Sean teased. Carla punched him in the arm and crossed her arms, feeling suddenly protective of her memories of Lieutenant Arron Walker.

"Owww, *hey*, if I had your right hook I may never have met you," Sean said rubbing his arm where she had socked him.

"Yeah, well it wasn't your boxing prowess that caught my eye anyway," she replied.

"What was it then," he asked.

"It was that goofy snaggle toothed grin and the twinkle in your swollen eyes."

"And the fact that even as pitiful as you were, you still had the balls to hit on me!"

"I mean, you couldn't possibly have even seen me, your eyes were so swollen. And I doubt that you could hear my words, much less remember anything I said that night," Carla said, remembering back to the night they met.

"All I know is that sooner or later the Lord introduces you to the person he has chosen for you," Sean said without taking his eyes from the road.

"Then it's in the hands of fate and two free willed hearts, God leaves that part to them," Carla said completing her husband's thought.

"That's amazing, how did you know what I was going to say?" Sean asked excitedly.

"I didn't, I was just repeating what my friend Ethan used to say," she answered.

"*What friend Ethan*, you've never mentioned a friend named Ethan... *Ethan who?*" Sean asked, a looking both curious and shocked at the same time.

"Ethan Kelly, he was a medic in my hospital unit back in Vietnam, why?" Carla answered and asked.

"Oh my God, that's my Ethan! I mean, I know him too, we were roommates at Holy Cross together before he got drafted," Sean said excitedly, slapping the steering wheel with both hands.

"You're kidding me!" she exclaimed.

"No really, I do, I mean it has to be the same Ethan Kelly, you finished his quote word for word! Oh man, I haven't seen him for ages, not since he left school for the Marines. I heard that he went away to Seminary at St. John's in Boston after he came home."

"He did, he did," Carla exclaimed.

"I ran into him in Chicago on my way to New York. He had that priest thing going, you know, the collar and all. We talked for a little while in an airport bar, he was going in the opposite direction, to California actually, Fresno I think," she continued.

"You're kidding, you mean he's out here now? Oh man, honey we have got to see if we can look him up, it'll blow his mind when he sees us together!" Sean said chuckling.

"Oh no, Sean, he's on his way back to New York, a sick friend or something? Junior spoke to him a few days ago to tell him about Wesley."

"I'm sorry honey, maybe we can catch up with him next trip, OK?" she said consolingly.

"*Yeah, next trip*...but that would have been something to see his face after he saw the two of us, that would have been really something," Sean said softly, more to himself then to Carla.

"Turn right here honey, this is Sepulveda," Carla said pointing at the large green street sign hanging over the intersection.

"I see it baby, thanks," Sean answered, making the turn and speeding up to catch Junior before he disappeared into a neighborhood and lost them.

Five minutes later they were parked in front of Junior's cute little ranch style home. Carla looked around the neighborhood as she got out of the car. She loved the manicured lawns and the homey feeling that she got as she took in the sights up and down Hinsdale Street. It was much different than her New York address, but a lot like the home where she grew up. Slowly everyone gathered in the yard as Junior introduced his wife and child to old friends and new friends alike. Carla smiled to herself, holding Sean's hand tightly as Junior brought Mrs. Martinez over to meet them.

"Sweetheart, this is my friend Carla, we used to call her Nurse Carla, and her new husband Sean," he said holding his tiny wife gently by the shoulders.

"Carla, this is my wife Anh, and the little one clinging to her mother is our daughter Amy," he said. The small woman smiled and shook each of their hands and then she and her family worked their way over to the others. Carla watched them walk away and sighed.

"*Junior Martinez I am impressed!* I take back all the sexist remarks I ever said about you."

"All this time I was so certain that all you did over there was take what was easy. Now I come to find that you ended up giving your heart away to someone, and that you were man enough to follow through as well. Good for you Junior, *good for you!*" she muttered to herself.

"You say something babe," Sean asked.

"No, nothing, let's go inside," Carla answered.

Albany, New York, 4 July 1973
<u>*United Airlines Flight 17, in route*</u>

KC Littleton pushed her reading glasses back up the bridge of her nose as she studied the papers scattered all around her. She had been reading her notes from the interview she did with the now infamous Dr. Murray Katz. She wanted to refresh her memory about that awful man before she went to interview the woman now awaiting trail for his murder. KC had met Rosa Hernandez a couple of times during this whole Katz ordeal, and she knew about her connection with Tina from her talks with Alma Donnelly and Maria Lopez. KC picked up a news clipping from 1969 and held it up in front of her face.

It was from the Sacramento Bee, chronicling the events leading to Dr. Katz's arrest and speculating about the circumstances surrounding his alleged accident as well as the mysterious benefactor who supposedly saved him from some horrible fate. KC was alarmed at how close this reporter had come to sniffing out the truth. Shaking her head slowly she furrowed her brow and tried to recall what it was that led her to Tina and the hidden truth, why she had been so lucky when there were so many others equally as nosy and pushy. She was pretty sure it wasn't all the clean living, having spent a far share of her young life wallowing in the dirt with the best of the party girls and free love advocates. Whatever the circumstances or sequence of events that were responsible for putting her on this plane, in this seat with these people, she was eternally grateful. She reached up to scratch her nose and listened to the slow and rhythmic breathing coming from the seat next to her. Tina had fallen asleep shortly after supper had been served and was napping peacefully beside her. KC turned to check on her and caught me staring across the aisle at her. She smiled coyly and removed her glasses. "Checking up on us are you Father Kelly?" she teased.

"Ahh, sorry, I was just…" I stammered.

"She's pretty isn't she," KC said, nodding toward Tina.

"Yes, *I mean NO*, I wasn't looking at her I was…ahhh…" I said, continuing to stammer.

I could feel the little beads of sweat start to form on my scalp. I raised my hand and ran my hand through my hair to keep them from appearing on my forehead, as if that would keep KC from noticing how un-nerved I was.

"Oh, *I see*, then it was me you were looking at," she added, the grin on her face giving away her delight in the way that I had so expertly painted myself into a corner.

The woman should have been a lawyer, as she was always on the attack, nothing escaped her eyes and ears. She caught every movement and syllable, and then processed them at warp speed into an advantage that she wielded with the skill of a master swordsman. Clearly I was out matched here, and I prayed that she would be merciful and let me off with swat instead of a slice.

"NO, I mean of course you're very nice to look at, but honestly, I was just looking in that direction, *at both of you*," I tried to explain, digging a hole in the cornet I had just painted.

"*BOTH* of us, *really Father*, I had no idea!" she said, really giving me the business now. I leaned back in my chair and buried my face in my hands, totally flummoxed and ready to surrender.

"I give up KC, I'm afraid to say another word!" I whimpered playfully.

"Skip it Father, I was just playing with you," she said, softly giggling at our exchange.

"Yeah, well I'd hate to see what happens when you seriously go after someone," I replied, turning my head and smiling at her as I lowered my hands to my lap. She returned the gesture and sat up straight in her seat.

"So what is it?" she asked.

"What is what," I replied.

"*Oh come on*, let's not dance around the issue, unless you want to get your wish and see me get all serious like," she said curtly.

"No really, what do you mean," I replied stubbornly.

"OK, we'll do this your way. What were you daydreaming about when I caught you staring our way?" she said clarifying, giving me time to think.

"Oh, well I was just thinking about whether or not I should have called ahead and told my friends about who I was bringing and why," I said answering her question.

"Do you think that would have made a difference, would they have told you not to come?"

"I don't know, but I'm beginning to think that I should have prepared them for this. I mean what if this doesn't work, maybe I should have let them decide if this was a good thing," I lamented.

"*Give it a rest Father!* I mean nothing is working so far right?

The clock is still ticking and the only hope that little baby has is sitting right here between us! Where's your faith anyway, you're the one with the collar and God's home number. So get with the program and pray the rest of the way to New York that God has at least one more miracle stored in this sleeping child!" scolded KC.

I looked at her and felt my face getting warm as I was rebuked by the most unlikely of people. I had not sensed how strong this woman was, how new her faith was, how *strong* her faith was. I felt ashamed at my weakness in her presence, and yet I drew strength from her as well. I found myself drawn to her, enamored by her courage and her will. I saw in her the same sort of inner strength and playful nature that I had seen in my mother while growing up. Realizing that I was taking too long to reply, and probably sending all the wrong signals, I turned in my chair and sighed deeply.

"Thanks KC, I needed that. Sometimes I wonder if I'm in the right job, this Holy business is a lot harder than I thought."

"I used to think that you just had to be a good listener, but I'm beginning to understand just how much heart it takes to practice the faith."

"It's one thing to claim the faith. It's quite another to live in it each and every day!"

"And even more than that, it's doing your best to share your faith at every opportunity, with courage, conviction, and compassion."

"Recognizing the people that God puts into your life to help you with your purpose, on your path, to wherever it is that God is leading you."

"I think maybe that is what I was looking at a moment ago. I think that I recognized you and Tina for who you are, and why you're here."

I closed my eyes and rested my head on the little white pillow behind me. I could feel KC looking my way, and I was surprised at how nice it felt. I knew instinctively that she was smiling weakly as she digested everything that I had said. And I could feel the gears in her brain working overtime trying to decipher some hidden meaning in my words.

"Are you OK Ethan, I mean Father?" she asked.

"Yeah, I'm good Katherine. I'm just starting that prayer that you ordered," I replied softly.

"Oh…"

Thirty-six

(...Theres a killer on the road, his brain is squirmin'
like a toad, take a long holiday, let your children
play, if ya give this man a ride sweet memory will
die, killer on the road"...The Doors)

Sheriff Cardwell sat uncomfortably behind the wheel of his County issue patrol car, a not so new Ford Fairlane, 67 or 68 maybe. The temperature had to be in the triple digits outside so he opted for comfort over expediency and stayed in the car with the engine running and the air conditioning set on high. He was watching a group of children swat at a low hanging piñata suspended from a large, thick trunked elm tree near several picnic tables, densely packed with all sorts of goodies. He could smell meat cooking on the barbecues that were set up on the opposite end of the tables, and he could swear he smelled a pot of menudo simmering somewhere as well. There were about a dozen or so kids ranging in age from toddlers to pre-teens scurrying around a big Chinese Elm tree, waiting for someone to strike a fatal blow to a large, goofy looking piñata.

The papier-mâché burro was brightly colored red, white, and blue to fit the day, and it swung wildly around all points of the compass as each child took their turn to swat at it while blindfolded. The Sheriff took notice of one kid, a little boy of eight or nine years, as wide as he was tall. The little boy was standing motionless, as still as a statue just a couple yards beyond the majority of the commotion. He seemed to be following the movement of the piñata closely with his eyes only. His head and body did not move as he tracked the chaotic trajectory of the multicolored piñata. Sheriff Cardwell watched him closely, noticing his little hands begin to grip the bat he held tighter and tighter. The kid was getting ready to make a move the Sheriff could sense it. The child's knuckles began to change color as his grip intensified, restricting the blood flow to his little brown fingers and turning his knuckles white. The blank look on his little round face seemed to become more and more determined with each tick of the second hand on the Sheriff's Timex.

"Come on gordo, you can do it!" Sheriff Cardwell whispered to himself, his own knuckles whitening as his grip on the steering wheel tightened while he slowly inched closer to the windshield, anticipating the hefty child's mighty swing.

Suddenly, the little guy made a beeline straight toward the piñata, knocking over a blindfolded little girl along the way. When he reached the faux burro he swung the baseball bat with all of his mighty might. The charged up child struck pay dirt with the sweet spot of his 30 ounce Louisville Slugger, right on Pete Rose's autograph, decapitating the papier-mâché burro and spilling tasty little treats all over the ground. Scads of excited children squealing with delight pounced all over the cellophane wrapped treasures like a gang of hungry linebackers on a slow moving fullback. Sheriff Cardwell swatted the dashboard and leaned back in his seat roughly.

"Good for you!" the Sheriff shouted aloud in his empty vehicle. He sat there laughing to himself and applauding the round little hero when he turned suddenly to his left, startled by a loud rap on the top of the car.

"See anyone out there on the *most wanted list* Sheriff?" teased Father Willet.

The priest smiled broadly as he leaned forward to rest his forearms on the door through the open window. Sheriff Cardwell recoiled slightly and scooted a little to the right in his seat to regain some of his personal comfort zone while the priest looked in on him, grinning like a Cheshire cat.

"Nope, not a one today Billy," the Sheriff replied, snapping his fingers in mock disappointment.

"Well now, that's a blessing in itself I think," the Father answered back, still smiling broadly.

"So what brings you out in this heat today anyway Ralph?" asked Father Willet.

"Actually Billy, I was sort of looking for you," Sheriff Cardwell replied.

"Really? What on earth for?"

"Well, I kind of wanted to talk with you and that young priest I met the other day. What was his name, Kelly or O'Reilly, it was something Irish, I remember that much?" Sheriff Cardwell said, struggling with his short-term memory.

"You mean Ethan, ah, Father Kelly," said the priest.

"Yeah, Father Ethan Kelly, that's it," Sheriff Cardwell said, as he flipped through the spiral notebook that he used for interviews and such. He licked his thumb and started scanning, finding the name after turning only a few pages.

"Well, I'm at your service Ralph, but I'm afraid that Ethan is on his way to New York, family emergency you see. He's with Tina Lopez and that newswoman, what's her name, ah, PJ, no, JT, *oh blast*, I can't remember, my mind is as feeble as yours today," said Father Willet, struggling with his own short-term memory issues.

"You mean **KC**," the Sheriff said smiling, taking his turn at coming to the rescue mentally.

"Yep, that's it, KC, lovely girl, little pushy, but still, just a lovely, lovely girl," Father Willet replied, nodding his head as he did so.

"What's this about Tina Lopez tagging along? Alma and Arthur never mentioned any of this to me," the Sheriff asked, raising an eyebrow indicating his curiosity and suspicion.

It wasn't normal for the Donnelley's or the Lopez's to break with the security measures that everyone had agreed on. He didn't know this Father Kelly at all, and he never trusted KC totally, so this bit of news was disconcerting at the very least. Father Willet could see the soft wispy hairs on the Sheriff's neck and forearms stand as if he were leaning on a power pole or something.

"Nothing sinister Ralph, I promise you. It's just that Ethan received some disturbing news about a family member, his Godchild I think. It was pretty bad news and very sudden from what I could gather," Father Willet tried to explain.

"How does that involve the Lopez girl?" the Sheriff asked insistently.

"How do you think Ralph?" the priest snapped. Sheriff Cardwell's lips pursed as he struggled to keep from snapping back. Father Willet realized instantly that he had over reacted to the Sheriff's obviously fair question and quickly softened his demeanor.

"I'm sorry Ralph, I shouldn't have barked at you like that, I meant no offense," said Father Willet apologizing.

"None taken Billy. But tell me, just what exactly is going on anyway?" Sheriff Cardwell replied.

"Ethan's little Goddaughter is dying of a blood disorder, leukemia I think. And well, I took it upon myself to offer the help of the Lopez girl," Father Willet explained.

"You did that *all* by yourself, without calling the Donnelley's, me, or anyone? Do you think that was wise Billy?" the Sheriff asked softly, his facial expression a mixture of worry and disappointment.

"I have to be honest Ralph, I reacted solely out of compassion for this boy and his family. I know him to be a good man, and I trust him to be discrete, he has integrity Ralph, I swear he does," Father Willet explained, desperately trying to quell Sheriff Cardwell's escalating concern.

"I believe you Billy, *it's everyone else* who'll come in contact with Tina, three thousand miles from here. She'll be pretty far away from her safety net, with only a fledging priest and an over ambitious newspaper reporter to shield here from the grateful and the curious."

"Think about it Billy, if she *does* what you sent her there hoping she would do, *and she will,* maintaining her anonymity will be the least of her worries, *of our worries.* Do you think that Ethan and KC will be able to keep a lid on everything, on everyone, afterward? Can we count on these two young people to get Tina out of there quickly and quietly, and bring her home safely?" Sheriff Cardwell asked, searching his friend's face for a sign of confidence and assurance.

Father Willet stood up straight and did an *'about face',* then turned again quickly to his right. He walked slowly toward the front of the patrol car, turned and circled around the vehicle. Sheriff Cardwell watched him move from window to window along the side of his car, and then through the rear view mirror as he passed behind him. The priest stopped beside the driver's side after one lap around the patrol car, his feet coming to rest inside almost the same impression from where he had started. He turned to face the Sheriff with his arms folded. Raising one hand up to cover his mouth, his face furrowed with a look of deep concentration.

"Yes Ralph, I do, I believe in them both. I can't explain it so that you will feel it like I do. But, there is something about the two of them. My gut tells that they make a good team. You're just going to have to trust me on this one my friend."

"Besides, God has been quite supportive thus far by bringing the right people into Tina's life, keeping her safe from harm. People like you and me, the Donnelley's, KC and Grover, now young Ethan. The cat's already out of the bag mister, let's not lose faith now. *Oh,* and they didn't leave without first getting the blessing of Maria and Victor, I want you to know that as well," Father Willet said, defending his recent decisions and rationalizing his logic. He looked at Sheriff Cardwell and waited for a response. True to his nature the Sheriff grunted and then clicked his teeth with his tongue, like people do when they are trying to giddy up a horse.

"I hope you're right Billy, *I hope you're right*," the Sheriff replied tiredly.

Father Willet lowered his hands to his hips and rose up and down on his tip toes a couple of times, breathing a deep sigh of relief.

"OK Ralph, now what was it you wanted to talk to Ethan and I about in the first place?" the priest asked.

"Come on in here and let's talk where it's nice and cool," he said to his old friend and parish priest. Father Willet circled the car and climbed inside through the passenger door, closing it tightly behind him.

"Oh yes, its much nicer in here," Father Willet said leaning nearer to the vent, and flapping the material of his cotton shirt allowing maximum penetration of cold air.

"Glad you're enjoying it Billy, but seriously, I've got some news that's gonna put a damper on your holiday," said the Sheriff.

"*Oh,* and what would that be?" the priest answered, still enjoying the icy cold air from directly in front of the two vents on his side of the car.

"It's the Rojas boy, Miguel. He's run off from Saint Anthony's, been gone for a few weeks now," Sheriff Cardwell explained.

"That's just awful news! But where could he go, he has no family, he's only a boy after all, how far could he have gone anyway?" Father Willet replied, leaning back in his seat and turning to face the Sheriff.

"I was kind of hoping that either you or Father Kelly would have a clue. Actually Billy, that's not all of it," the Sheriff said, his tone turning more serious.

"*What*...I don't like that look on your face Ralph," replied the priest.

"We think that Miguel may have been involved in the shooting of a drugstore owner in June."

"*NO, I don't believe that at all!* He is only a boy, *twelve years old for pity sake*, who could kill at that age?" snapped Father Willet defiantly, more at the notion that Miguel would be capable of such a thing, than at the Sheriff personally.

"It happens Billy. Maybe not here very often, but elsewhere, in LA and Frisco, *yeah*, it happens a lot I'm afraid. I'm worried that the kid has gotten in with a bad crowd, and I don't like the fact that these guys think that they can come up here and steal our children for their legion of hell-raisers!" the Sheriff said gruffly.

"What can I do?" Father Willet asked quietly, staring out the window now, looking past the Sheriff.

"I need to know what Miguel and Ethan talked about. Maybe the kid mentioned something about these two *cholos* he's been seen hanging around with. I need to know if Ethan remembers any names that I can check on, *anything Billy*, no matter how insignificant it may seem. You gotta give me something to work with before this kid ends up just another skid mark on the streets," Sheriff Cardwell pleaded.

They remained quite for a few moments both of the men just looking out at the children playing in the park in front of them. The sound of the engine idling and the A/C blowing a steady stream of cool air in their faces filled the squad car as the Sheriff waited for the priest to reply. The kids sat scattered in small groups under the shade of the big elm tree, sorting and trading the treasures they had collected from the spilled piñata. The two old friends watched the little trader's silent negotiations, smiling as they remembered simpler times. If you could have read each of their minds they would probably be having the same thought, *"why did life have to change so much with age...**ohhh,** to be young again!"*

"I'll let you in on a little secret Ralph, sometimes I find myself questioning my faith. Not blatantly mind you, like *'what the f---... you know what'*, but significantly, like *WHY this* and *WHY that*," Father Willet confessed to his friend. The Sheriff nodded his head without looking away from the playing children.

"Sometimes I just want to know why, *you know!*"

"Why do innocent children need to suffer, I mean what purpose does it serve, I don't understand? Why do people slip away from good homes to become bad people? What turns a life of hope into a life of despair?"

"Why can't I accept these things as the Lord's will without having to suffer the pain of discovery and misunderstanding? Is my faith really that weak, does this world still reign over my soul in spite of my years of preaching the contrary? Sometimes I just plain don't get it Ralph, and this stiff white collar at the top of my shirt has no more significance than any businessman's necktie!" lamented Father Willet.

Sheriff Cardwell reached across the seat and squeezed his friend's shoulder tightly. He continued doing so for a few seconds before he replied.

"Billy, I'm gonna remind you of something you said to me twenty years ago. Do you remember that time back in 53, it was right after you came back home from Korea? I came to you after service one Sunday, deeply troubled by a shooting that I had been involved in. Do you remember?" the Sheriff asked softly.

"Vaguely, I mean I remember something about you having to shoot a kid during a gas station robbery or something like that," Father Willet replied.

"Yeah, the Texaco station on corner Landers and 17th street, you remember," the Sheriff said, reassuringly. The priest nodded as his memory of the incident became clearer.

"So, anyway, I came to you after service on that Sunday and asked for a minute of your time."

"Yes, I remember, you were very anxious, not your usual standoffish self," Father Willet recalled.

"Yeah, so we went outside and sat on the steps in front of the church. It was an overcast morning and there was a cool, crisp breeze blowing in from the almond field that used to be across the street," Sheriff Cardwell said, continuing with his story.

"Yes, I do remember that," said the priest.

"Well sir, you asked me what was weighing so heavily on my mind and I told you. I remember that you sat there quietly, looking me right in the eyes as I spoke, as if you were reading my thoughts instead of listening to my words."

"I did?"

"Yes... you did."

Sheriff Cardwell paused a moment to let the priest catch up to him on memory lane.

"When I finished getting everything off of my chest you looked right at me and said four words that took all the hurt, frustration, and confusion away...*He still loves you.*"

"If not for those few syllables Billy, I doubt I could have continued as a cop. I would never have become Sheriff, I would never have been here to look after Tina, and I would not be in a position now to try and save young Miguel from a hell he shouldn't be earning," Ralph Cardwell said softly, letting the words fade gently in the cool breeze of the A/C. Father Willet turned in his seat and looked over at the Sheriff.

"So you're telling me that questioning my faith is normal? That in spite of my weakness, in spite of the initial pain His will may bring, in the long run there is a greater good to be considered. And that in the end, in spite of my moments of weakness...*He still loves me...*is that what you're trying to tell me Ralph?"

"Yeah"

"Fair enough...let's see what we can do about saving this boy from himself. You work on saving his hide, Ethan and I will work on saving his soul," Father Willet said, slapping his old friend on the thigh.

"Deal," replied Sheriff Cardwell.

"OK, we'll have to see if we can get a hold of Ethan tomorrow, he won't even get into New York until later this evening, our time anyway."

"But that doesn't mean we can't go over his notes back at St. John's. The Rojas boy's file is sitting on his desk if I remember correctly," said Father Willet.

"Great, let's go," Sheriff Cardwell said, sitting up straight and putting the car into reverse.

"Hey, Ralph, can I turn on the lights and siren?" Father Willet asked excitedly.

"OK, what the hell…"

"RALPH!"

"Sorry…"

Los Angeles, California, 4 July 1973

It was so hot that Miguel could see the heat rise in shimmering waves from the blacktop of the road in front of him. He raised his hand to shield his eyes from the sun's angry glare and looked as far down the road as he could. There wasn't a car or truck in sight, and there hadn't been one for at least a half an hour. He had started walking in the wee hours of the morning, leaving the house while Smiley and Raymond slept peacefully in the living room, the TV on with only a test pattern to watch. Miguel had awakened around 2am to a sound at one of the bedroom windows. It sounded like a cat scratching the pane, trying to get someone's attention to let it inside. He remembered rolling slightly toward the noise and peeking out from under the covers. There wasn't any cat that he could see, but there was a shadow that made him uncomfortable. It seemed to be tracing the area of the window with a darkened finger, not actually touching the glass, but close enough to take a good reading for whatever purpose.

Miguel watched that shadow for several minutes and then stayed motionless in his bed so several minutes after it disappeared. When he was confident that it would not return he got out of bed slowly and tip toed over to the window. He looked around from the cover of the thin lace drapery and satisfied himself that there was nobody in the back yard. He walked slowly out into the hall and then into the living room, being careful not to disturb Raymond and Smiley, he didn't want to have to answer any questions, or have them alert anyone who might be listening from outside. He paused suddenly as he passed by the TV and heard Raymond repositioning himself on the couch. Then, when all was quiet again, he walked over to the front window and peeked out to the street, being careful to come up to the window from around the chair, out of sight from anyone who may be looking inside. He didn't touch or disturb the drapery on the front window, and looked through the material. Even with this slightly obstructed view, he was able to make out the presence of a couple of cars that did not belong on the block. They were obviously police cars, just unmarked, he had seen those kinds of cars when he rode around with Smiley and Raymond. They had made a point of educating him about that particular kind of surveillance.

Miguel slowly backed away from the window and for a moment considered waking the two older gang bangers and warning them of the potential danger to there freedom. But he decided that the police were there for him, to make him pay for the dead cop in the street. Miguel had been waiting for them, he knew that they would find him sooner or later. He decided that they would have to settle on later, and he ran back to his room and packed a small bag. He stopped by the kitchen and put a few groceries into the bag and then opened the cupboard under the sink. He got down on his hands and knees and moved aside the cleaning fluids and accoutrements.

Reaching behind the dripping trap he unlatched the small door that had been cut into the wall as an escape path for emergencies just like this one. The door opened to the back yard, behind a big jacaranda plant. From there a small person could skirt along the side of the house behind the cover of several large bushes to a spot next to the chimney. All he had to do then was crawl under the fence to the yard next door and then hop the fences from yard to yard until he reached the end of the block at Zelza street. After he crossed Zelza, he could jump the chain link fence and walk along the LA River for miles until he came near a highway where he could try and hitch a ride.

That was exactly the tack that Miguel had taken early this morning, and now he was looking for that one long ride that would take him out of the county and back toward his destination. He was going home now, he had things to do now, and time was running out. A small bobtail truck appeared on the horizon, its tall covered bed jiggling in the haze of the sunlight. Miguel raised his arm to his forehead and stuck out his thumb. The truck slowed as it passed him and then came to a stop a hundred or so yards up the road. Miguel turned and ran toward the idling vehicle and slid to a stop at the passenger door, a cloud of dirt swirling all around him as his sneakers gripped the roadside. He climbed up on the running board and looked through the window at the driver, a youngish white guy around Smiley's age. He had long hair, tied back in a ponytail and a bandana around his head. The driver took a long drink from a quart-sized bottle of RC cola and motioned for Miguel to get in the truck. Miguel opened the door with only a little difficulty, and jumped up onto the bench seat.

"Where ya headed little man?" the driver asked.

Miguel motioned ahead with a motion of his head and pointed with his finger.

"Sorry pal, I don't know where that is, you speak English boy?"

Miguel nodded his in an affirmative manner.

"Well?"

"Many miles senor, Fresno, or Mendota maybe," Miguel said, struggling a little with the diction.

"That's quite a trip for a kid your age. Ain't nobody gonna be missing you?" the driver asked. Miguel shook his head no. The driver turned his head and spit out his window, then opened a cooler on the floor of the truck's cab. He reached in and pulled out another RC cola and handed it to Miguel.

"Here, it'll be a long ride and you look thirsty. I can take you as far as Bakersfield, maybe you can call someone to pick you up from there," the driver said, looking at Miguel and waiting for an answer.

"OK," Miguel replied, taking the RC and tucking it between his legs. It was cold and it felt good after the long walk in the hot July sun.

"Name's Curtis, what's yours?" the driver asked.

"Miguel"

"OK Miguel old son, I hope you like country, cause that's what your gonna get a earful of all the way to Bakersfield boy, buckle up now!" Curtis said as he turned the volume up and shoved the truck back into gear.

"This is a good one boy, everybody loves Hank Williams...'*your cheatin heart, will tell on you*'..."

Miguel looked out the open window to his right, enjoying the wind as it hit him straight in his sweaty little face. He sat relaxed in the seat listening to the music playing on the radio and to Curtis sing along as he drove. Then slowly he reached down to the small canvas bag resting on his lap, and felt through the material searching for the last item that he had packed before leaving the house. Pushing several items aside as he identified them by touch, he stopped suddenly, feeling the smooth handle through the canvas material. It was right where he had put it, at the bottom of the small bag. That made him feel better, he had a way home now, and had his tools. Miguel turned and smiled at Curtis who flashed him a peace sign and smiled back, showing both rows of teeth. Miguel felt safe, he had all he needed for now.

Albany, New York, 4 July 1973
Albany International Airport...10pm

Shannon saw us right away and took off in a full on sprint toward the arrival gate. Paul was too slow as he reached out to grab her arm, missing her by a fraction of an inch as she got away.

"Shannon," he called after her.

But she couldn't hear him through her blubbering as she ran towards me, her tears streaking horizontally backward along her jaw, her long hair flying wildly behind her. She ran past several deplaning passengers, trying to zig and zag as best as she could without knocking anyone over. And then she jumped into my arms, just like she did when she was a pup. KC and Tina looked on flabbergasted as the two of us hit the floor and she landed in my lap, her arms tight around my neck, crying and talking a blue streak into the nape of my neck. I couldn't understand a word she was saying and I could feel her tears rolling down my skin and under my collar as I tried to calm her down. But she would have none of it, she just wanted to sit there like she used to until she had cried herself out. I gently smoothed out her hair and whispered softly into her ear.

"*Easy girl*, whatever it is we'll handle it together, shush now, *shhhhh*," I said trying to console her like I always had.

Her crying turned into a whimper, and her blathering began to slow to where I could pick out a word here and there between her heaving shoulders and snorting breaths.

"*E…than…where…were…you…why…did…*" she said struggling with her composure, rubbing her nose on my shoulder.

I was suddenly aware of a small crowd gathering around the two of us, an airline official kneeling beside us, asking if all was well.

"Is the young lady alright sir? *Oh excuse me*, I mean Father?" the puzzled man in the blue and white uniform asked, noticing the large white collar around my neck. I tried to motion with my hand that she was, giving him the universal OK sign with my thumb and index finger.

"*Yes sir, she is sir…*just a tad upset as you can plainly see. Give us minute here and we'll be out of the way straight away, I promise," I said, putting my right hand behind my back to use as a brace so the two of us wouldn't tip over.

The man from the airline moved behind me and put his hands under my arms and tried to help me get up. I held onto Shannon and coaxed her into cooperating, and with only a little struggle, together the three of us made to our feet. Shannon would not let go of me and continued to hold onto me like a giant teddy bear and with some difficulty we made our way over to a seat near the window. As we sat down I saw that KC and Tina had followed us and had taken seats just across from where we settled. I looked over at KC through a tangle of auburn hair and moved as much of it as I could away from my face before I spoke. She was looking at me like I was from Mars and that the *queen invader* had just arrived from planet Looney Tunes! I rolled my eyes and sheepishly returned her gaze, then looked over at Tina. She was much calmer, looking more concerned than shocked.

"You know her I'm guessing," KC asked sarcastically.

"*Of course,* this is my sister, Shannon," I answered.

"You're not exactly seeing her in her best light I'm afraid," I added in my sister's defense.

"Yeah, well…"

"Is she alright?" Tina asked softly.

"I'm not sure, let's give her a minute," I replied. Suddenly Paulie arrived on the scene, slightly out of breath and a little more than just annoyed.

"Oh man, your sister is faster than I remembered," Paul said as he sat down beside us.

He reached over and stroked her hair, leaning in close to her face to see if she was any better.

"Are you OK honey," he asked.

I looked at him cross-eyed. My turn to look puzzled now. Shannon slowly raised her head and took my face into her hands. Her face was tear-stained and her eyes were still wet. She looked at me closely and then sniffled loudly, turning her head and wiping her nose on her sleeve.

"Where have you been Ethan, we waited and waited?" she asked, not waiting for an answer.

"We needed you here…mother needed you, I needed you, Kenny and Sophie needed you Ethan! *We waited and waited…*" she said softly, the tears beginning to flow again.

I looked over at Paul and silently asked him what was wrong. I saw my big friend's eyes begin to moisten and suddenly I knew that we were too late. I went to hug my sister but she twisted away from me and collapsed in Paul's lap. This was unusual, I thought these two were mortal enemies, especially after the peanut butter incident? Paul held her gently and looked over at me apologetically.

"Is someone going to fill us all in on what's going on here?" KC blurted. Paul looked across at the strange woman and then back at me. He nodded his head toward Tina and KC, asking me who these women were with the look on his face.

"Paul Pucholski, this is KC Littleton from San Francisco, and Tina Lopez from Fresno California. Paulie might know San Francisco, but no way he would know Firebaugh, so Fresno seemed like a better place to reference. He waved at the two ladies and then looked back at me.

"Pleasure, I'm sure, now, what's the story?" KC replied, repeating her question. Paul spoke to me from over Shannon's head while she rested quietly on his shoulder. KC and Tina leaned forward in their seats to make sure that they didn't miss any details.

"Wish you had gotten here sooner Ethan, we really needed you," he started.

"Why, what happened, is it Sophie, *are we too late?*" I asked anxiously.

"*Ethan*, Sophie died earlier this afternoon."

"She just went to sleep and never woke up."

"We were at your house, cooking food and horsing around like we do every year. Everyone was having fun, Kenny was his old self, and Carolyn was laughing and carrying on like she hasn't done in months and months. Even Sophie seemed like her old self, ornery as ever, full of sass and vinegar. Then, about 4pm Carolyn started hollering for Kenny, and the next thing you know we're all standing around in your living room, huddled around Kenny and Carolyn while they held the baby. She looked so tiny Ethan, like a doll, I..." Paul couldn't finish his sentence.

Shannon raised her hand, stroking his cheek. I watched my sister and my friend console each other and put two and two together in my mind. I thought to myself how great God is, how he manages to balance sorrow with hope. Here I was, learning of the end of one life so precious to me, and then also learning of a new life just beginning between two people whom I loved with all of my heart. I reached across to place my hand on Shannon's and saw her smile at me from under all that hair.

The pain in my heart was enormous, and I struggled to stay in my faith and not lash out at how unfair this all seemed. I looked over at KC and saw that she was crying softly as well. I reached across the aisle and put my hand on her knee. She covered my hand with both of hers and mouthed a silent *I'm so sorry* from her seat. All of the sudden I felt Tina reach over and cover both our hands with her own. She looked at me with an expression I could not describe. KC picked up on the uncomfortable stare as well, looking up at me as if I had a clue, which I didn't.

"Ethan, why are these people with you anyway," Paul asked.

"Just a second Paul," I snapped.

"What is it Tina?" I asked the teenager.

"Can you take me to her?" she asked.

"What is she talking about," Paul pressed.

"Quiet Paulie, *PLEASE*" I snapped again.

"Can you take me to see her, the little girl, Sophie?" she asked again.

"*What for, **she's dead**!*" Paul exclaimed.

"***PAUL**...just a sec OK!*" I implored.

"*Oh my God*, Ethan, we need to get her to wherever Sophie is, ***RIGHT NOW!***" KC yelled, suddenly cognizant of what Tina was trying to say.

I looked at KC trying to get on her wavelength, but my mind was working too slowly. Too many distractions, Paul's agitation, Sophie's death, my sister's grief, my uncertainty of this power and how I was going to explain it to everyone.

"OK, wait, just wait a sec…are you saying that you can still do this?" I asked Tina, looking deep into her eyes for more than just a verbal response. She nodded her head and then spoke.

"Yes, *I can,*" she said, convincing me not with her tone but with the look in her eyes.

I felt as though God had reached out through those beautiful amber eyes and touched my beating heart. At once I was elated beyond description, and I knew exactly what we had to do.

"Ethan, *Ethan,*" KC said. She was an inch from my face trying to get my attention.

"Yeah, yeah, OK, let's get going, come on!" I said, standing up quickly and then sitting back down again, realizing I had no idea where to go or what to say to Shannon and Paul.

"**GO WHERE?** Come on Ethan what the *HELL* is going on here!" Paul demanded. I looked over at Paul and waited for him to calm down. Shannon had moved from his lap onto a seat next to KC and Tina, and they were talking softly.

"Paul, we've known each other since we were little boys, and we have always been straight with one another. You, me and Kenny, the three musketeers, right?" I began.

He nodded his head slowly.

"Yeah, pals forever, so what? Tell me what these girls are talking about, you guys are scaring me!" he protested.

"Paulie, that girl has a gift that is too fantastic for words."

"They call her the *Angel of the Valley* where she's from, and they mean that literally! I explained, watching his face for a sign of understanding or at least capitulation. I wanted to get this over with because I didn't know what the rules were for an honest to God miracle.

"Typical," I muttered.

"Still trying to outwit the Lord, what a nitwit Ethan," I said under my breath, scolding myself.

"I don't get it," Paul said weakly.

"Look Paul I can't explain it any better than this. If you can take us to where Sophie is, we may be able, *no,* I mean we will be able to help her, do you understand?" I implored.

"Help her how, she's dead Ethan, you understand dead, right," Paul said, annoyed with the thoughts I was putting in his head. I watched him as he worked this over in his mind and then I started to continue.

"OK Paulie, I…" I began, but was interrupted by my sister who leaned across the aisle toward us and tapped Paul on the knee.

"Honey, listen to this girl, look at her and listen to her words, OK? Do it for me, do it for Sophie, please," Shannon pleaded.

Paul looked over at Tina reluctantly and waited for her to speak. She reached across the aisle and placed her hand over Shannon's on his knee and looked deeply into his eyes. They held each other's gaze for only a moment and I could see Paul get that goofy look on his face, the same one he got whenever they charged him for a single cheeseburger when he actually ordered a double.

"Take me to where Sophie is Paul, and we can bring her home tonight," Tina whispered to her new friend. Paul blinked and then muttered, *"What?"*

"Take me to Sophie Paul…please," she asked again. Paul blinked again, shuddered, and then snapped out of his trance.

"We need to jam Ethan, they took Sophie to the hospital hours ago, to the morgue. You know what happens there dude, what if they're all done man?" Paul said, wincing.

"I'm on it," KC shouted as she jumped up and ran to the nearest payphone.

"Which hospital?" she hollered over her shoulder as she ran to the phone. Paul ran after her to help with the phone call while I collected my thoughts and debated over calling Kenny and Carolyn. I held my sister's hand while I went over the pros and cons of the matter and in the end flipped a virtual coin in my head.

"Two out of three," I mumbled to myself as I continued to vacillate over the issue. Finally I decided that it would be better for Sophie to walk back into her home, hand in hand with her Godfathers, than for Kenny and Carolyn to see her walk out of a morgue like some zombie in some gosh darn monster movie.

"OK, we have a vector," KC hollered from the pay phone, flashing me the thumbs up sign. I genuflected and gathered up Shannon, Tina, and all of our stuff and walked briskly to meet up with KC and Paul.

"They took her to County according to the cops," KC explained.

"We called over there and the mortuary is not scheduled to pick her body up until tomorrow," she added.

"OK, let's get out to the street and into Paul's car," I said, slapping my hands together and rubbing them briskly. "Oh man, Ethan, I've got a rental and it's a two seater," Paul said apologetically.

"OK, new plan, we get a cab and you and Shannon follow us," I replied.

"Perfect, let's jam!" Paul said, taking Shannon's hand and starting to walk away quickly. He caught my look immediately. "Am I missing something?" I teased.

"Later Ethan, we'll talk later," Paul answered, tugging on Shannon's hand. She looked back at me and bit her lips like she always did when she had a secret she couldn't keep.

"The bags, what about the bags!" KC exclaimed.

"*Oh, right*, what am I nuts, we'll get em later," she said, answering her own question.

I reached out and took both Tina's and KC's hand and we all ran after Paul and Shannon. KC and I locked eyes for a moment as we ran and I thought I felt her grip on my hand tighten. She smiled at me and I returned the smile, suddenly feeling a butterfly or two flapping away in my stomach.

Albany, New York, 4 July 1973
County General Hospital…11:30pm

All the way over I racked my brain trying to figure out what we were going to say to the hospital personnel to gain access to the morgue and Sophie's body. I prayed and prayed that they had not touched her yet, that they had not started the awful things they do when they prepare people for burial. I was still working on a solution when the cab pulled up to the entrance of the hospital, near the emergency room. There was an ambulance just pulling away as we got out of the cab and KC paid the driver.

"Keep the change," she said tossing the cabbie a twenty-dollar bill for a ten-dollar fare.

"Don't worry, this little excursion is on old money bags," she said, referring to the owner of

her newspaper and our benefactor according to Father Willet, one Grover Gateway. Paul and Shannon walked up to us the cab pulled away.

"Ready?" Paul asked.

"Yeah, let's go," I replied.

"Can anyone think of a good reason for us to be here?" I asked everyone in general.

KC tapped my collar, "Ah yeah, how about last rites maybe, *duh…*" she said sarcastically.

"Oh yeah, right," I replied, pulling my crucifix from under my shirt and letting it hang outside on the black fabric for effect.

"Nice touch," KC said.

"Thanks"

We entered the hospital in masse and walked up to the nurse's station. KC did all the talking naturally.

"Excuse me, but can you direct us to your morgue please. Father Kelly is here to administer last rites to this family's loved one who passed earlier today. We were told that she is being kept here until the mortuary arrives for the remains tomorrow," she said in her most professional tone.

The nurse behind the counter looked us over, not quite buying the story. KC kicked Shannon in the shin while the nurse was looking at me, examining my attire like perhaps I was only pretending to be holy. Shannon picked up on the not so subtle suggestion and started to cry some crocodile tears. The nurse was too tired and busy to deal with all of that noise, and she pointed to the elevator with her pencil.

"Take the lift down to the basement and turn right. Check with the attendant at the desk and he'll help you with you're request," the nurse said with a slight attitude.

"Thank you my dear," I said in my thickest accent.

"Come now child, tears are wasted on the dead, let's pray for poor Sophie instead," I said, pretending to console Shannon, *well sort of pretending*, I suspected a few of those tears were genuine.

The five of us made our way to the elevator and waited for it to arrive after Paul had pressed the button to send for it. We all entered and turned to face the desk while we waited for the doors to close. It seemed like a long wait, especially with the nurse watching us so closely, but at last they closed and we descended the two floors to the basement below. The doors opened and we made a right as we had been told and came upon an empty desk with a still steaming cup of coffee sitting in the center.

"HELLO," KC called out.

"Be right there folks," a man's voice called from around the corner.

I turned to look in the direction of the voice in time to see a tall thin young man of about twenty or twenty-one, pushing a gurney passed two heavy swinging doors. He returned from behind the doors a second later and walked over to us, taking his seat behind the desk and picking up his coffee to take a sip.

"What can I do for you," he asked pleasantly.

"Hi there, this is Father Kelly," KC started, touching my sleeve as she introduced me to the attendant.

"He's here at the request of the family of Sophie Wong to administer last rites and to help her sister here say goodbye," KC continued, taking Tina by the arm and pulling her closer to the two of us.

"*I see.* Well, I'm not Catholic, but isn't it a little unusual to give last rites after the person has already died, I mean the horse has already left the barn so to speak…no offense," the attendant questioned.

"None taken son," I said. "You're right, it is unusual, but not uncommon, and the girl here was not at home when her poor sister passed. So if you don't mind, it would mean a great deal to the child," I pleaded.

"Well, I guess there's no harm in it," the attendant said.

I looked down at his nametag and read it. "Thank you David, God bless you," I said.

"No problem Father, let me just get her ready for you OK. You don't want me to just pull her out of the wall like she wasn't a person," said David the attendant.

"No of course not, that will be nice of you my son," I said to him with a weak smile.

"I'll just be a second, you folks can sit over there on the sofa if you like," David added as he disappeared behind the heavy wooden doors.

Paul and Shannon walked over to the sofa and took David up on his offer, while KC remained close to Tina and me. It wasn't too hard to read her mind. KC was determined to accompany Tina and I when we went in to see Sophie. There was no way she was going to miss this big an exclusive, I knew that much about her from Father Willet briefing before we left Fresno. The doors opened again and David held them for us while we walked slowly into the room. It was much larger than I had imagined and it reeked of formaldehyde.

"Sorry about the smell folks, you'll get used to it," David explained.

"She is right over there on that examination table," he added pointing toward a little shape covered by a blue sheet under a soft white light.

"Thank you," I said, putting my arm around Tina and walking toward the table.

"I'll be right outside, take your time, there's no rush," David said as he exited the room.

KC followed Tina and I and we all stopped a foot or so from the table. I wanted to go over and pull down the sheet and look at Sophie's sweet face, but my feet wouldn't move. I felt a lump forming in my throat and I choked it back, determined to keep my composure and my faith. That was going to be my part in this miracle. Tina inched forward and then turned back to face KC and I.

"Father, will you help me get up on the table with the child?" she asked of me.

I willed my feet to work and walked over to her and took her hand. She raised each leg one at a time behind her and removed her shoes. Then we walked up to the table and I helped her to climb up and lay beside Sophie. A tiny little hand was suddenly exposed and lay there starkly against the cold stainless steel, almost without a shadow from the soft dim light overhead. I swallowed that same lump as it tried to choke me into a crying jag. Tina turned onto her side and put her arm around Sophie's covered body. I could hear her whispering something to my dead Godchild, but I couldn't make out any words. I thought for a moment perhaps she was speaking in tongues, but having never heard anyone do so before, how would I know?

They lay there quietly save the whispering noise. I felt uncomfortable being so near, as if I were intruding somehow. Several minutes passed and the only movement from the table came from Tina's shoulders, rising and falling as she breathed softly and evenly. Still the whispering noise, I tried leaning closer but the volume never changed and still I could not understand any actual words. After several more minutes I felt KC take my hand as she came to stand beside me. She leaned into me and rested her head on my arm, not saying a word. We waited and waited, the clock on the wall now read well past midnight, almost a quarter to one. KC yawned and then wiped the corner of her mouth with my sleeve. She pinched my arm slightly to get my attention. I looked down at her and she wagged a crooked finger at me gesturing for me to stoop down closer to her.

I leaned over and she whispered, *"I really hoped that this would work Ethan, I'm so sorry,"* she said.

KC rose up onto her tiptoes and kissed me on the nose, then turned to walk out of the room. I watched her walk through the doors and then rubbed my nose where she had kissed me. I turned back to look at the two girls on the table in front of me. Tina still lay on her side, her breathing still slow and even, but the whispering noise had changed. I strained my eyes in the dim light trying to detect any changes to what I had been watching for nearly an hour. Nothing seemed to be any different, but the whispering noise had definitely changed. I could swear I that Tina was laughing, but her body gave no indication, her breaths still slow and steady. I stepped a little closer and started to peer over Tina's shoulder and then nearly jumped out of my skin.

"JESUS MARY AND JOSEPH!" I tried to scream, but my heart was up in my throat, I could make no sound I was that scared.

The pale little hand that had lay on the stainless steel table less than an hour ago, was now holding onto a tiny fist full of Tina's long dark hair. I couldn't believe my eyes, but there it was right in front of me. I had not seen Tina move since I lay her next to Sophie, she couldn't have placed that hand in her hair without KC or I noticing it. No, wait, I did turn away when KC left the room, distracted by her kiss and my own thoughts. I breathed a sigh of relief, stepping back a foot or two to return to my job of standing vigil.

"Man, what a weenie Ethan," I said under my breath, shaking my head and chuckling to myself.

"You're not a weenie, *Uncle Paulie is a weenie*," came Sophie's little voice.

It rang in my ear like a cannon shot. I looked up immediately and jumped back ten feet, tripping over my big feet and falling to the ground, knocking over a tray of instruments with a loud bang! Sophie Wong was on her knees leaning over a sleeping Tina Lopez. Her little arms were hanging over Tina's torso and she was clapping hard at my little pratfall.

"Yea, do it again Uncle Ethan, do it again!" she squealed happily. I could not believe what I was seeing, and yet I knew that it was true.

"Oh MAN, GOD ROCKS!" I screamed at the top of my lungs.

David burst into the room, followed closely by Paul, Shannon, and KC.

"What the hell happened?" he hollered, stopping dead in his tracks when he saw Sophie looking back at all of us like we were all nuts.

Paul collapsed next to me on the floor unable to move or speak. Shannon crawled in between us and started to cry. KC walked up to me and absent-mindedly ran her fingers through my hair as she looked on at the miracle in front of us.

"All the time this was just a fantastic story that people kept telling me," she said robotically.

"To be honest, I didn't really believe it...even with the Katz thing, I never really saw it myself, so in the back of my mind I kept thinking hoax," she continued, her nails beginning to dig into my scalp.

"Hey, what are you, part Apache?" I said, pulling my head away from her grasp.

"Sorry," she said in a deadpan voice, squatting to take a seat on the floor beside me.

"Anyone want to take a shot at explaining this?" David asked.

"Yeah, but you better have a seat, it may take a while," KC answered. The attendant sat down right where he was standing, not in any hurry to get nearer to what he was currently rationalizing as a bad dream. He pinched himself as he sat on the cold linoleum, *"Ouch!"* he exclaimed.

Sophie sat up and then waved to all of us sitting on the floor in front of her. She leaned over and kissed the top of Tina's head and then cupped her hand and whispered something into her ear. Then she scooted out from around Tina's sleeping form and turned onto her stomach to lower herself off of the table. Her bare little bottom still showed the tan line from the swimsuit she must have been wearing earlier while she played in the sun in my parent's back yard. She gently lowered herself to the ground, dropping the last few inches onto the floor. Then she spun around and ran at me giggling wildly, leaping into my arms at the last possible moment. I held her squirming little body close to me and breathed her in with all of my senses. Shannon held her little foot against her cheek and then lightly bit at her toes.

"There's that little piggy," she said, playing one of the little games that she and Sophie would play whenever she would baby-sit. I just sat there drinking it all in.

When Paul came to, I handed her over to him so that he could feel the miracle as well. KC leaned into me. She was completely overwhelmed by the moment, as were we all. I put my arm around her and held her close to me. She watched Paul and Shannon play with the happy child from her perch on my chest, while I looked back toward the exam table to find Tina sitting up, watching all of us. She jumped down from the table and walked over to us, taking a seat in front of KC and I. We stared at one another for a moment, listening to Sophie chatter at Shannon and Paulie. Then KC sat up and leaned across to Tina, and while she embraced her with all of her might I closed my eyes and praised the Lord for this day and His way…

Albany, New York, 5 July 1973
The Home of Ken and Carolyn Wong…2am

Ken stubbed his toe on his way to answer the door. He was still asking himself who the hell was ringing his bell at this hour. He hobbled over to the door and cinched the soft tie of his terrycloth robe a little tighter. Carolyn called down to him from the top of the stairs.

"Are you OK honey?" she asked. "I heard you cussing after you banged into something on the way down," she added.

"I'm **FINE** Carolyn, go back to bed while I see who the lunatic is ringing our doorbell at two o'clock in the *God Damn morning!*" Ken said through clenched teeth.

"Oh, you know what Ken, maybe you shouldn't answer the door, maybe it is a lunatic," Carolyn said in her worried tone.

"Maybe it's a burglar," she added.

"A burglar that rings the doorbell, oh for Pete sake Carolyn, give me a break!" Ken snapped.

"Well, at least look through the peephole," she pleaded.

"ALRIGHT!" Kenny peeked through the tiny hole in the door and studied my distorted face, and the shadows of the others that were standing around me.

"It's Ethan babe, his plane must have really been late. Or else he is coming from Maggie's after hearing about Sophia," Ken called up to his wife.

Carolyn came down the stairs and walked up behind her husband as he unlatched the door. He opened the big storm door and looked out at his friend's smiling face in the glow of the porch light. He saw that Ethan was with Paul and Shannon, and couple others that didn't recognize.

"A little early for trick or treat Ethan," Kenny joked weakly. I walked up to him and embraced he and Carolyn together, pulling them so close that I could almost feel them begin to pass through me.

"EASY BOY, I know it's been a little while, I'm guessing that Maggie's told you all about the day we had," Ken managed to wheeze through my bear hug.

"We have something that belongs to you two," I said, releasing them and stepping aside. Kenny and Carolyn gasped as Shannon walked up the steps holding Sophie wrapped in Tina's white wool sweater.

"Mommy!" she squealed.

"Sophia Rose Wong!"

"Oh my God, *Ethan*, what on earth..." Carolyn tried to ask, through her sobs. She gently took her child from Shannon's arms and held her close.

Carolyn kissed Sophie's baby face and hands, and each of her fingers one at a time. She gathered up her hair and filled her lungs with her child's scent, using all of her senses to assure herself that this was indeed her only child. Carolyn walked over to Kenny and the three of them stood together in a fusing embrace. Ken finally looked up at me, asking me to explain without uttering a word. I turned, reached for Tina and held her hand as she walked up to stand in front of me.

"This is how," I said to the two of them.

"Let's go inside and I'll tell you a story," I continued. I turned and looked at the others, making sure to stop on each face, one at a time to make eye contact. Then I turned back to Kenny and Carolyn.

"We'll *all* tell you a story..."

Thirty-seven

<u>*Fresno, California, 5 July 1973*</u>

Smiley licked at the blood oozing from his split lip, and then bent his head to one side to press his mouth against the cotton shirt rising up from his shrugging shoulder. He held his mouth there for as long as he could and applied as much pressure as he could stand to help the wound begin to heal. Not an easy maneuver, especially while sitting with both of his hands cuffed behind him. He watched the big white cop sip his coffee from a Styrofoam cup across the table from him. He was a tough looking dude, big and beefy, with that buzz cut that all the tough pigs liked to wear. The one that made them look more like fullbacks than policemen. Smiley looked him up and down, from the scowl on his face to the clothes on his back. The skinny gray tie with the black horizontal stripes didn't go well with the short sleeve blue shirt that he wore, especially with the dark stains permeating from under the arms. The poor man had worked up quite a sweat *interviewing* him. The cop kept fidgeting with a spiral note pad on the table in front of him. He flipped the pages back and forth but never took his eyes of Smiley. The obstinate little gang-banger just stared right back at the officer, determined not to give him anything, least of all the satisfaction that the big asshole had put a serious hurt on him!

"I got all night Paley," muttered the policeman.

Smiley remained silent, taking the lead in their little psyche dance and smirking at the big cop defiantly. Not the most diplomatic move considering the intensity of the last forty minutes of *interviewing*. The cop reacted as one might expect, instantly throwing the cup full of lukewarm coffee at the grinning little bastard.

"Look at that, you made me spill my coffee smart ass!" the cop shouted.

"Now who's gonna clean this mess...*HUH?*" the officer bellowed, reaching across the table to grab Smiley by the hair.

Smiley leaned back sharply on reflex and avoided the initial contact by the policeman. He then tensed up waiting for the cop's next move, which he figured would be to pick up the telephone book from the floor and start *asking questions* again. It was a good call on Smiley's part as the big man jumped up, kicking his wooden chair backward to the wall behind him, striking it with enough force to rattle the two-way mirror. Smiley half wondered if someone back there had just said *'Oh shit'*, and was maybe on the way to rescue him. Or if they, whoever they might be, just stayed put to catch some more of the show? He sat still and continued to stare down the cop, agitating him to a near melt down state. He braced himself as best that he could for the blow he knew was coming, managing to even through in a *fuck you* grin before the heavy phone book made contact with the side of his head...*LIGHTS OUT!*

Smiley's hearing returned slowly, low frequencies first. He imagined that he could hear a voice, it sounded far away, and it called him by name. Over and over the voice called, the volume never increasing but the clarity improving. The sounds became clearer, second by second, minute by minute, hour by hour. The throbbing pain between his ears kept him from being sure. He had the sensation of being on a really fast roller coaster, twisting and spinning, faster and faster, being tossed from side to side, his neck beginning to ache from the chaotic motion.

"Smiley, HEY, *homey*, you in there man?" the voice asked.

"Come on man, snap out of it you pussy!" the voice said, a little louder now. Smiley felt himself being tossed about harder and harder, damn roller coaster...

"STOP THIS THING!" he shouted in his mind.

Raymond kept on shaking his friend, trying to jostle him back into consciousness. Smiley's eyes opened just a slit, but it was enough to allow him to realize that wasn't on any roller coaster ride. He recognized the dark gray masonry walls and the cold black bars of his cell, he understood now that he tossing and twisting was just someone shaking him vigorously. Suddenly he was back in the here and now, back in his stinking cell, lying on his stinking bunk in a fetal position.

"COME ON! Snap out of it *estupido*!" the voice ordered.

Smiley raised his head a little, or at least he thought that he did. Actually, it was only his eyes that had moved, rolling skyward and locking in on the face of the voice. He smiled weakly as he recognized his *carnal* Raymond.

"Dude, I've been trying to wake you for half an hour man! They really pimped you out homey, you're a real mess *ese*," Raymond said, looking his friend over, taking a mental inventory of the carnage.

Smiley felt Raymond lift his eyelids one at a time. He felt the soothing coolness of the cold washcloth that Raymond put on his swollen bottom lip, and he was extremely grateful for the gesture of brotherly love.

"Damn Smiley, I thought maybe they killed you *esay*," Raymond said as he swapped washcloths with a fresh cold, wet one from the basin across the cell.

Smiley closed his eyes tightly, trying to reduce the throbbing between them as he rolled onto his back, stretching out his legs and flexing all the muscles in his body in the process. It was painful, but it hurt real good, an expression that any athlete would relate to after pushing their body beyond its limit.

"*Owwwww, ohhhhhh*, hey *ese*, am I dead man?" Smiley finally uttered weakly.

"Yeah man, you're dead," Raymond said nonchalantly.

"I knew it!" Smiley replied with a shallow chuckle.

He turned back onto his side and pulled his knees up to his chest, reassuming the fetal position to stop the cramping in his guts. He tucked his hands between his legs and sighed deeply, staring at Raymond who had moved across the cell and sat Indian style with his back against the wall. He looked at his friend for a moment or two before speaking.

"See you got the good cop," he said, observing Raymond's unmarked face.

"*Uh Huh*, Raymond muttered, chewing on his fingernails.

"Why do I always get the bad cop?" Smiley whined rhetorically.

"You don't know when to shut up and kiss ass *baboso*!" Raymond said scolding him.

"*Aye Dios mio*, when am I ever going to learn," Smiley replied, mock scolding himself as well.

"Did you tell them anything homey, you know, about our little friend?" Raymond asked.

"What could I tell, I don't know shit about where that little bastard is man!" Smiley snapped, slapping his bunk with both of his flattened palms.

"Relax homey, I was just asking. That cop put a real hurt on you man, I wouldn't blame you if you squealed a little to stay alive *ese,* I probably would have," Raymond said, trying to calm his nerve rattled friend.

"When we get outta here man, we're gonna find that little shit," Smiley hissed.

"We're gonna find, and we're gonna flush that little turd *ese,* that's what we're doing first thing, OK?" Smiley added, raising his left arm and pointing Raymond's way, without opening his eyes or moving his head.

"Forget about that kid Smiley, he ain't worth the gas or the trouble man. Besides, he don't know nothin, hell, he's only been around a little while *Holmes,*" Raymond argued.

"Forget him my ass!" Smiley shouted. "He's been here long enough to get the chair if the pigs find him first. And if we ain't careful we'll be sitting right next to him when they throw the switch. You think that punk will keep quiet like me *ese,* think about it!" Smiley replied acidly.

"SHUT UP HOLMES!" Raymond snapped in a horse whisper. "We don't know the neighbors man!"

Raymond stood up and walked quickly to the bars and peered left then right. He listened closely for any sign that someone may be near or worse still, paying attention to their arguing. Satisfied that they were alone except for the black dude at the end of the hall, he returned to his spot on the wall next to the basin and sat back down. Smiley opened his eyes and looked across to Raymond.

"We need to find that kid and put him in the past as soon as possible *ese.* We don't need that kind of trouble walkin around. Besides, the kid is loopy anyway. Sooner or later he would have turned on us, just like a peanut brained Doberman. You remember that Jimmy Rockford flick we saw, *'They Only Kill Their Masters',* you remember" It was just like that homey, just like that," Smiley whispered. He rolled over to face the opposite wall, folding his arms and tucking his hands under his arms.

"I'm gonna take a nap now, I'm really tired. Be cool OK, we'll be outta here in a few days, they got nothin to hold us on," Smiley said, falling into a deep sleep before his last syllable faded into the stale air of the holding cell. Raymond stood and walked over to the bunks slowly.

"Horale," he muttered as he stepped over his friend, climbing to the top bunk.

He picked up his small pillow and punched it into a soft cotton covered ball of fluff. He lay down and stuffed the pillow under his right ear, laying his head heavily upon it. A moment later he and Smiley were snoring softly in rhythm. In the darkened cell at the end of the hall the black man switched off the reel-to-reel recorder. The big white cop sitting on the bottom bunk sat up.

"You get all of it?" he asked softly.

"Yeah Sarge, I got it all," the black officer replied.

San Francisco, California, 5 July 1973

Grover Gateway sat deeply in the plush leather chair behind his richly coated mahogany desk. His eyes were trained on a photograph way across the room of himself and former President Roosevelt, Franklin Delano Roosevelt to be specific. But his thoughts were not of any interesting personal experience or historical event. No, this morning his mind was focused exclusively on the bit of news he had received less than an hour ago. Grover Gateway was not a man that liked surprises, although that would seem contrary to the career he had chosen and dedicated his life to. Maybe it would be better to clarify that it was surprises of a personal sort that he so disdained. Being a tad of an obsessive-compulsive by nature, he had spent a great deal of effort to make sure that everything in his own life occurred according to plan, on schedule and unobstructed by fate, a phenomenon that he believed could be avoided, whenever possible.

Grover had always believed that save for acts of God, that most of life's unfortunate mishaps and personal calamities could be seen coming a mile off. And they only befell those that chose not pay any attention to the signs along the way. This was the cause for his current state of mind, the reason that he had sat for nearly an hour ignoring all other matters, mentally grousing with himself for breaking one of his cardinal rules by letting others have control of his own fate. This arrangement that he had allowed himself to be coaxed into because of a lifelong friendship and his soft heart was going to be the cause of some severe consternation he feared. He rocked back in the large swiveling chair and crossed his legs, one knee over the other. He lifted the top leg for a moment and rubbed his calf against the knee of his other leg, gently massaging a slight cramp in the muscle. Grover liked the way the gabardine fabric felt on his skin, it was silky, like the satin sheets on his bed at home, sort of made him feel special, like he was pampering himself ever so slightly. He settled back into a comfortable resting position in the chair, and raised his hands, lacing the fingers together behind his head. KC's excited little telephone call this morning had caught him by surprise, a matter that he would take up with Mr. Williams later.

That kind of news should have come to him through channels, with a helluva lot more details and a contingency plan ready for his review. However, there was no time to worry about protocol issues, he could deal with that later. Right now he was curious, no, he was angry about the fact that he had not heard about any of this from Arthur or Billy, or even that yokel Sheriff in Fresno, what's his name, Cardwell. The news was disturbing in and of itself, but this enormous breach of the security measures that they had all agreed upon was just too much. Grover had kept his part of the bargain, like always. All the others had to do was clear things through his office so that he could arrange for proper security measures. At least they had the smarts to keep his girl KC in the loop, although after listening to her emotional babbling this morning he was wondering how good an idea that may have been. This had to be Billy's doing, it had his signature all over it! That old fool had always been the most reactionary of sorts. And never has a bigger sucker for a hard luck story ever walked the earth! Grover shook his head slowly while he stared at the ceiling tiles.

"*Ahhh*, it's why the old coot became a priest in the first place," he rationalized under his breath.

"Now what...the cat's certainly out of the bag by now," he thought aloud.

Now he was in a quandary regarding what to do next. On the one hand, he could wait and see if KC and this Father Kelly could do the impossible and keep this episode quiet. He thought a minute about what that would mean. First of all, KC and this young priest would have to contain the news of an *actual miracle*, and keep all of the witnesses silent, at least for the moment. He didn't see how that would be possible given the fact that they walked out of a morgue, *hand in hand with a presumably dead child*, in front of God knows how many people! But then again, most of those people were family and or friends of Father Kelly's. The only random elements would be the hospital staff, and at that hour how many could that be? Of course there would be records to un-record, breaches of hospital protocol, and at least two or three local misdemeanors if not actual felonies.

"*God what a mess,*" Grover said aloud as he leaned forward and rested his elbows on the desk in front of him.

He ran his hand over his face, feeling for the beard that he had shaved off earlier. He closed his eyes again and breathed in deeply, letting it out slowly in a heavy sigh. They had dodged a bullet with the Katz incident, and he couldn't see them being so lucky a second time. Grover picked up the pen lying on the manila folder in front of him and started doodling on a yellow legal pad to his right. On the other hand he thought, wrestling with his conscience over a promise to an innocent young girl and his responsibility as a newsman/journalist, as the God damn publisher of a widely circulated, major metropolitan newspaper. It came down to a choice between a handful of close friends and a million and a half loyal subscribers, not to mention his credibility and morality.

"GODDAMN YOU BILLY WILLET!" he bellowed, as he slammed his flat palms hard onto his desk.

"This is one helluva pickle you've put me in old friend," he said to the empty room, rising from his chair.

He walked over to the mini-bar in the corner of his office and pulled a heavy tumbler down from the glass shelf. Opening a decanter of Redbreast Whiskey, his favorite Irish swill, he poured himself two fingers, neat, into the glass. He fancied this witch's brew from Dublin best of all, often times referred to as the Irish iced tea. Raising the tumbler to his lips he sipped at the libation slowly at first, and then tilted back his head and drained the glass. Baring his teeth and licking his lips, he poured himself another, and then walked back to sit behind his desk. He set the tumbler down and looked at his wristwatch. It was 9am California time, which meant it was noon back where KC was in New York. He had told her to call back at one o'clock her time with an assessment of the situation, and that he would instruct her further at that time. Grover decided that he had enough time to call Arthur Donnelly and brief him. Well to be honest, first he was going to kick ass, and then he would brief him! Reaching over to the intercom he buzzed his secretary.

"Francine, get Arthur Donnelly on the horn for me right away, OK?" he ordered.

"Right away chief," replied his long time secretary.

"Damn it Francine, how many times have I asked you to stop calling me that over the years!"

"Too many to count Chief," she answered.

"Oh good grief!"

"If she weren't my sister-in-law I swear, *BANG...ZOOM!*" he explained to his office furniture, doing his best imitation of Ralph Cramden of the Honeymooners, he just loved Jackie Gleason.

Francine Harris giggled to herself as she dialed the Donnelly residence. She loved teasing that man. Served him right she thought, after all, dumping her for her sister was a good enough reason to hound him for life! Grover sat at his desk waiting for the call to Arthur to come through. He picked up a stack of papers from his desk and pretended to scan over them, then tossed them back down. He was too agitated to do any real work. He needed to settle this situation, this battle between his conscience and his instinct. He drummed his fingers on his desk nervously when Francine's voice came over the desktop intercom.

"I have Arthur Donnelly on your private line...*chief*," she said.

"*DAMN IT FRANCIE*...oh, never mind, put him through," Grover said surrendering.

"OK...chief."

The red light lit up on his private line and Grover picked up the handset quickly.

"Arthur?"

"Grover, what a nice surprise, what can I do for you...*chief*?" answered Arthur Donnelly, unable to resist teasing his friend.

"Not you too," Grover whined.

"I'm kidding, I'm only kidding...really, why did you call anyway?" Arthur asked.

"OK, OK, look, we have a real situation here," Grover started.

"What situation?"

"I'll tell you when you get here. I sent a car for you, it'll be out front of your hotel in fifteen minutes," Grover instructed.

"Wait a minute, I'm not even dressed, and besides, how did you know I was in town, I only arrived late last night?" Arthur protested.

"Give me a little credit will you, it's my business to know where all of my interests are at any given time. Did you think I rose to these heights on luck?" Grover answered.

"Now hurry up and get ready, the car is on its way," he ordered, hanging up before his friend had any time to protest further.

Grover looked at his wristwatch again and mentally programmed himself to look again in thirty minutes, estimating the time Arthur would arrive. He was going to lean back and take a power nap before he started in on picking Arthur's brain for answers. He reached over and buzzed his secretary again.

"Francine...I'm taking a little snooze, hold my calls, and buzz me when Arthur arrives, got that?"

"OK chief..."

"Oh brother..." Grover sighed deeply...

Bakersfield, California, 5 July 1973

Miguel waved to Curtis as the truck turned back onto the highway and drove off. He watched it disappear and then walked across the street to the Dairy Queen on the corner. When he got to the window he ordered a cheeseburger and a medium coke, easy on the ice. He hated it when he got a cup full of ice and only a half a cup of soda, just seemed like such a rip off to him. He handed the girl behind the counter the ten that Curtis had given him and she handed him back seven dollars and eighty cents in change. He turned to walk over to one of the stone tables and saw the police cruiser pass slowly by the burger joint. He turned back to face the counter and watched the squad car reflection in the glass. The cop never even looked his way and he turned his head slightly to make sure that the car was continuing on through the light...it did. Miguel took a seat at one of the tables and waited for the counter girl to call him over to pick up his order. He set his little bag under the bench and leaned back against the table, letting the sun warm his face, it felt good, like when he was a little boy playing in the melon fields.

"Hey kid, your food's ready," called the counter-girl.

She slid the paper sack and cup toward him and walked back to the other side to take another order. Miguel pushed himself up and walked over to get his meal. The soda cup was already sweating in the sunlight and he raised it to his forehead and enjoyed the cool wetness. He walked back to his table and unpacked his burger and took a long sip of his coke. Miguel removed the wrapper from his burger and licked the melted cheese from it, then took a big bite, and chewed it slowly. He looked out at the road and wondered where his next ride would come from. He wasn't worried, he would catch one sooner or later. He knew where he was going and it wasn't far now.

His Uncle would be there, old and alone, he would be easy to fool. Miguel reached under the seat with his feet and drew the small bag from under the seat to under the table. He rested his feet on the top of the canvas bag, the nearness of it bringing him some peace of mind, the contents reassuring him of his purpose in life now. He took another big bite and started his slow chewing regiment again. After a couple minutes, he took another long sip to help wash down his meal. He watched as a steady stream of tractor-trailers paraded by on the busy street, the bulk of them merging right onto the Interstate. Yeah, it was going to be easy to find a ride the rest of the way he thought. Miguel smiled weakly and picked up his cheeseburger, hungrily finishing off his meal for the day.

San Francisco, California, 5 July 1973

Grover was startled awake by the long buzzing sound emanating from the intercom on his desk. He pulled his feet off of the top of his desk and sat up quickly. Reaching over and swatting the intercom he answered the irritating summons.

"*Yes, ahhh, yes Francie, what is it?*" he said while he rubbed the hardened sleep from his eyes.

"Arthur Donnelly to see you chief," she answered.

"Send him on in…"

"*OK chief*…you can go right on in Mr. Donnelly," she said, her voice resonating over the intercom. Arthur Donnelly opened the door and entered the office, coming to a stop behind the over stuffed wing chairs that sat across from Grover's huge desk.

"*Grover,*" he said, acknowledging his friend. He removed his Stetson hat and held it in front of him.

"So what's all fired important that you have to send someone to up and fetch me?" he asked.

"Looks like you and Billy have dug us a pretty deep hole my friend!"

"*Whoa there*…wait just one cotton-pickin minute! Just what exactly are you talking about?"

"Are you telling me that you don't know anything about the Lopez girl flying off to New York with Billy's new priest and my girl KC?" Grover asked insistently.

"Good Lord! *What for?*" Arthur asked, stepping around and then collapsing in the chair directly opposite Grover visibly stunned.

"Oh damn, I was hoping that you were trying to keep something from me and that you were secretly in complete control. But you're not that good an actor Artie…this is a Goddamn disaster!" said Grover disappointedly. He got up, returned to the bar, refilled his tumbler and then poured one for Arthur.

"Here, you're going to need this," he said, taking the seat next to Arthur and sipping his whiskey.

"I spoke with KC about an hour ago. She and the girl accompanied Father Kelly back to New York to see what Tina could do about helping his dying Godchild," Grover began. Arthur took a long slow sip of his drink and then held the glass in his lap, waiting for Grover to continue.

"It seems that Billy arranged all of this before the holiday with Victor and Maria. It Billy's little conspiracy cause he knew that you and I would have been too cautious and probably talked the Lopez's out of it. He must have told them that he had already cleared everything with us, they never would have agreed otherwise, I'm fairly certain of that," Grover continued. Arthur nodded his head in agreement.

"So what happened that's got you in such a tizzy?" he asked.

"I'm getting to that...it seems that they arrived too late to see the sick child, she had died while they were in route."

"What a shame, I'm so sorry, *the poor child*," Arthur replied, first shaking his head and then scratching it.

"So if they were too late, where's the problem?" Arthur asked.

"I'll tell you *where* the problem is...Tina brought her **BACK!**" Grover exclaimed.

"In front of five witnesses no less, four of which are not apt to keep their mouths shut! To be perfectly honest, I'm all that confident in KC at this point in time either. She seems to have been personally affected by this experience. She just didn't sound like herself on the telephone, I can't say exactly what it was, but she sounded different, there wasn't any edge to her tone of voice like usual. She sounded too...I don't know, soft I guess is the right word? I'm hoping its just puppy love, you've seen how she looks at that young priest, *God damn trouble maker!*" Grover explained excitedly.

"Alright Grover, don't stroke out over this! Let's think about our options here," Arthur said calmly.

"*OPTIONS!* Arthur I need to decide in one damn hurry what my next move will be. I told you and Billy right up front that if I ever felt that we risked exposure that I was going public *FIRST!*" Grover reminded his friend.

"I have been more than cooperative over the years, but I have a responsibility here, and I have to go with my gut on this. And right now it's screaming to go to print before I wake up tomorrow to read all about this in the New York Times!" he said, pounding his fist on the arm of the chair and spilling a bit of whiskey onto his slacks.

"Take it easy Grover, if they had anything we would have heard all about it on the radio and television by now, don't you think?" Arthur asked trying to reassure the rattled old news-hound.

Grover sat silent for a moment and the relaxed a little.

"Yes...of course, you're right, you're absolutely right. I'm getting too old for this job," he lamented. He reached across the desk and pressed the intercom button.

"Just a minute Arthur...Ahh, Francine, get Williams down here right now!" he shouted into the big plastic box attached to his phone by several thick cords.

"He's in a staff meeting chief," she replied.

"Well get him out of it!" he roared back.

"*Will do.* Keep you pants on chief, the days just started you know," she answered.

Grover rounded his desk and sat back in his big leather chair. He grinned at Arthur, shrugged his shoulders and pointed at the intercom, trying to explain his frustration with the gesture rather than fill the room with expletives. Arthur nodded and smiled, then scooted his chair closer to Grover's desk.

"Look, Grover, I'll bow to your instincts, I owe you that. You've been more than fair, all things considered. But would it hurt to talk to Billy and get his side of the story before we jump to conclusions and set wheels in motion that won't be easy to stop?" Arthur pleaded. He watched Grover's face as he thought this over, spinning his hat nervously in his hands as he did so.

"Francie, would you please get Father Willet on the phone for me," he asked sweetly trying to sound more in control of his emotions, and to make up for his previous tirade.

"That's better...my pleasure chief," she answered just as sweetly.

"When was the last time you spoke with him?" Grover asked.

"Just yesterday, and he didn't mention any of this," Arthur replied.

"Well what did he mention?"

"He said that he helping Ralph Cardwell try and locate a runaway kid. You him, the Rojas boy, we told you about him. The one that started this whole thing, he was the first," Arthur explained.

"So what's he got to do with anything?" Grover asked perplexed.

"Nothing that I know of, at least where Tina is concerned. I doubt that she would even remember him, she was only four or so when that all took place."

"This kid's been in a few scrapes since his folks died. His dad didn't make it back from the war and his mother, *God rest her soul*, killed herself a year or so ago. The Sheriff thinks the boy may know something about the murder of a storeowner, so he's looking for the kid. Billy's new priest, Father Kelly had been working with Miguel, that's his name, Miguel Rojas, and the Sheriff has been picking Billy's brain for clues as to where to start looking for the boy. That's all I know..." Arthur said, leaning back in his chair. Grover stared back at Arthur, a flummoxed look on his face, and shrugged his shoulders. Before he could reply there was a knock on the door and Brian Williams entered the office.

"Excuse me sir, Francine said that you wanted to see me right away," he said, apologizing for intruding. Grover Gateway gestured for him to take a seat.

"Sit down Brian; I need you to do a little covert digging. Check out what the competition may or may not know about a certain incident that may or may not have taken place in upstate New York during the wee hours this morning," Mr. Gateway explained to his managing editor.

"Sir?" Brian replied. The intercom squawked.

"I have Father Willet waiting on line three chief," said Francine Harris.

Grover looked over at Brian and whispered, "I'll explain everything in a few minutes, I've got to take this call," he explained, putting a finger to his lips to shush everyone.

"Hello Billy, we have to talk," Grover Gateway said calmly. He scribbled something on the yellow legal pad and handed it to Brian.

"That's right, I know all about it. Did you hear the news this morning? I mean did you get a call from KC or Father Kelly as well?" Grover probed.

He looked over at Brian and waited for the silent acknowledgement to his note. Brian looked up and nodded, then rose from the chair and excused himself. He handed the legal pad to Arthur as he left. Arthur looked down at it and read the page slowly.

"I'm sending a plane for you this afternoon Billy. I don't care what you're doing with Sheriff Cardwell it will have to wait. We need to put our heads together on this thing TODAY, do you understand?" Grover said, a slight agitation in his voice. He looked over at Arthur and they made eye contact. Arthur looked back down at the yellow paper and read it once more. The message was short and sweet…*"run the story…"*

Firebaugh, California, 6 July 1973

The light from the kerosene lamp dimly lit the small one room apartment. They were way outside of an already small, small town. This was a tenement area, a place where coyotes oppressed the illegals further, renting them shacks for almost half of what they brought in breaking by their backs in the fields. There were no toilets, running water, or convenience stores. There were just long hours, hard work, and plenty of sweat. Not Nirvana by any standard, but when you have nothing, even a little bit is a fortune.

This was where Miguel had begun his life and this is where he had returned. He sat across from the old man on a chrome chair with a torn cushion. A wooden table made from an empty spool of all path telephone cable separated the two of them. The old man smashed out his cigarette in an empty can of snuff, and looked across the table at the child of his niece Elena. The boy looked a lot like his mother, but he could see that he did not have her heart. He looked at the boy knowingly, and Miguel returned his gaze with an equal amount of clairvoyance.

"She told me that you would come back here…one day," the old man said sadly.

Miguel watched him, counted the lines around his eyes, and the wrinkles under his neck. Elena Rojas' Uncle Romero had always been a big man, much larger than the average brasaro that migrated to this country illegally in search of a better life. He had always been larger than life in the eyes of this small community. But time had had worn him down, reducing him to the frail old man that now sat across from his great-nephew.

"Who told you this, *my mother?*" Miguel asked.

"No"

"Who did then?" Miguel demanded. His Great Uncle Romero sat there silently and stared at the boy.

"*Her?* Was it her, *the angel?*" he asked again. Miguel grew weary of the silence, and he could feel his body temperature rise to equal the level of his frustration. The seconds passed slowly.

"*Tell me old man*, did you talk with her, did you talk about me?" Miguel pressed, his agitation increasing noticeably and alarmingly.

"No"

"What does that mean...*no?* Are you loco in the *cabesa*...huh?" Miguel said, smirking at the old man. Uncle Romero held his tongue and continued to stare back at the child, infuriating him further.

"Are you fucking with my head old man...huh *cabrone?*" Miguel snapped, his eyes narrowing. Still no answer from Uncle Romero, he remained stoic, silently defiant with his posture, pushing Miguel to the end that was his fate.

"*ANSWER ME DAMN YOU!*" Miguel demanded in a voice much older than his years.

The two of them sat there neither twitched nor even blinked an eye. Miguel's shoulders were beginning to haunch over, his chest rose and fell slowly with the deep breaths that he was taking. Slow and steady his rage built, his eyes glistening with moisture as they narrowed with his furrowing brow. His nostrils flared as he drew in one deep breath after another, and the, in an instant his rage erupted, sending his body into swift action. Before he could exhaled the last deep breath he had taken in, he had covered the distance between he and his only living relative, plunging his knife deep into the old man's chest. The entry made a sucking sound as he pierced the lung and entered his Uncle's heart. The two of them looked as if they were attached at the waist, they were standing that close. Miguel held onto the handle of the large hunting knife tightly. He could feel his Uncle's blood flow over his fingers, sticky, wet, and warm. Their eyes locked, Uncle Romero remaining defiant to the end, showing no anger or love, just a blank, empty, expressionless face.

He was ready to die like this. *Truthfully*, he had been expecting to die this way. He had seen this day in the eyes of the angel not so many years ago, at his grandson's miracle. He coughed two or three times through his tightly closed mouth, the sound muted and hollow. Miguel watched as the life slowly left the old man's eyes. Uncle Romero dropped to his knees. The hunting knife that was pulled from his body, remaining behind in Miguel's clenched fist. The old man grabbed onto the boy's waist trying to steady himself. He rested his head on his nephew's belly, the knife hanging ominously overhead. Blood dripped slowly from the blade onto his face. He drew in a shallow breath and spoke into Miguel's shirt.

"Perdonar conmigo, mijo," he said (forgive with me son).

Uncle Romero let out a deep sigh and then collapsed against the boy. Miguel stepped back and let his uncle fall to the dirty floor, his face bouncing off of the musty carpet with a muted thud. He stared at the body for a moment, then stooped over and cleaned the blade on his uncle's shirt.

"Forgive what old man?" he whispered.

Thirty-eight

(...Finally, be strong in the Lord, and in the strength of His might. Put on the full armor of God, that you may be able to stand firm against the schemes of the devil."...Ephesians 6:10)

<u>*Fresno, California, September 1973*</u>

I listened to Father Willet enjoy his food, *my God*, how he enjoyed it, almost sinfully so, *one, maybe two* heavy sighs away from actual gluttony. If digestion were as good for the soul as confession I dare say the man would likely be the holiest man to ever walk the earth, *Christ himself excluded*, of course! And if that were true, then Sister Ruth Demarco should be canonized into Sainthood as well. After all, it was her culinary skills that inspired such intense pleasure in the man. I had to admit, *truth be told*, I was fast becoming quite a fan myself. I watched as Father Willet sopped up what marinara sauce remained in his pasta bowl with warm a piece of Sister Ruth's famous ficcocia bread. His eyes rolled back in his head just like a shark, as he devoured the last morsel of his fine meal, a look of complete satisfaction and peace washing over his face.

"Ah Ethan my boy, we may need to petition the archdiocese to re-Christian this church Saint Ruth's...the new patron saint of hungry souls!" he exclaimed, leaning back in his chair and patting his full round belly with both hands. I nodded, silently agreeing with him while I finished chewing the last of my own meal.

"Which reminds me," the elder priest started, picking up his glass and taking a healthy sip of water. "We had better see about sending Sister Ruth on a little vacation before that *venal* pop-n-jay Villa Cruz arrives on Friday," he said, finishing his thought sarcastically.

"Father," I exclaimed. *"Venal?* Sir, do you really believe His Eminence to be corruptible?"

"He's our Bishop! Surely he could not have attained so a high post within the church with such qualities!" I protested naively.

"You are a child Ethan! You know nothing about how the church works do you."

"As much as I love our Lord, and the call to serve in His Holy name, I am cursed with more than my fair share of common sense."

"Ethan, I have lived my whole life within the church. Along the way I've had an opportunity to bare witness to many wonderful things and some *not so* wonderful things as well."

"And I've experienced both personal and professional revelations on my journey through life. Since it is not my place to judge, I won't be passing judgment by sharing doubts or suspicions with you. I will however, share one conclusion that I've drawn from all my experiences."

He leaned nearer to assure himself that I was listening intently.

"And that is this, *the church is a business*, no different than any other. Its business is salvation, so in a sense it is a service organization of sorts. We are in the business of saving souls. We preserve, repair, strengthen, and encourage them. *And*, we also gather and collect them, like so many pennies in a jar. Counting, sorting, and confusing *spiritual* accounting with *Principles of Accounting*, while we divvy up the human race, one nation at a time."

"Now here is where my personal cynicism comes in. This soul saving business as it were; has one big banner beneath which all of the others are listed, and it reads RELIGION," Father Willet explained, taking a moment to read the expression on my face. *Was I listening, or was I only hearing his words,* I saw him wondering, reading the look on his face. He took another sip of his ice water to sooth his straining vocal chords, then continued, satisfied that he had my complete attention.

"Under that heading you'll find the all the others, from Christianity in *ALL* its many forms and denominations, or *divisions*, as the Apostle Paul insinuated in 1st Corinthians. To Judaism, Buddhism, Islam, Hinduism, you name it, they're all one in the same. From the confines of many cannons and theologies, and scores of mystic beliefs, men have organized themselves into religious entities and spiritual cults, both large and small, all around the known world and throughout time as we measure it. They gather together as many people as possible in order to propagate their beliefs into social confabulations of like mined souls."

"And to this day they compete for the right to proclaim their doctrine, belief, their way of life as the *one* true religion for mankind. Sounds a little harsh, I know, *and odd I suppose,* for an ordained priest in the Holy Roman Catholic Church. But trust me my son, I have lived a long time. I've seen first hand the workings of many of the world's religions, and have known personally a thousand people who have lived their lives by those teachings. I have..." Father Willet started to continue, until I interrupted.

"Whoa, whoa, whoa, can you stop and take a breath for just one minute!" I exclaimed.

"Really Father, all this pontificating, *no offense to His Holiness?* Exactly how long have you been saving all of this up?" I asked dizzily. He looked back at me, puzzled at first, and then shrugged his shoulders chuckling, extending his arms palms up as wide as he could.

"I don't know," he giggled. *"I really don't know.* Apparently a long time, I suspect this kind of venom takes years to produce," he said, trying to explain through his laughter.

"All of this inspired by the mere mention of Bishop Villa Cruz? *I don't get it,"* I said perplexed. Father Willet was looking out the window, his expression indicating that his mind was elsewhere for the moment. I waited a couple minutes for him to mentally return to our discussion, and then started to speak.

"Father..." I began.

But this time he cut *me* off, raising his hand, and then standing. He began to pace the floor next to the table, his hands clasped behind him as he walked. When he stopped he was standing beside me. He placed his hands on the back of the tall wooden chair in which I sat, and exhaled deeply through his nose.

"Thanks Ethan. You know, until you said it out loud I hadn't actually realized just how strongly that man has affected me over the years. In a very real sense he represents the point I was trying to make from my soapbox," he said, his mood lighter and less agitated.

"I really don't remember you actually *making a point* Father. Being as I sort of derailed your train of thought with my outburst," I said, apologizing for my interruption.

*"Ahem...**Quite**,"* he replied, clearing his throat, agreeing with me.

"The *point* I was trying to make was that over time every religion out grows its inspiration. And in doing so becomes less divine and more demanding. Eventually building a hierarchical structure towering over its foundation, an inverted pyramid if you will; doomed to topple and self-destruct. Simply

433

put, *too many chiefs and not enough Indians*, does that make sense to you?" he asked.

I'm not sure but I may have nodded in agreement. It was hard to remember because he quickly resumed his theorizing.

"Father Villa Cruz is one of those chiefs that think he who dies with the most feathers in his bonnet sits closer to the Lord at the Heaven's supper table. Because I know him to be this way, I am fearful of his interest in Tina Lopez," Father Willet confessed to me.

Now he had my full attention, I had no idea where he was going with all of this ranting. While it was not unusual for the Bishop to visit, it was curious that he would specifically ask for an audience with the Lopez girl and her parents. Father Willet's concern for the Lopez family made much more sense than his sudden interest in hiding Sister Ruth from His Eminence. Although, hiding Sister Demarco might be a good idea given the circumstances of her assignment to Saint John's, I thought, recalling Father Willet's recanting of the story of her arrival.

"Do you think that he is coming because of the newspaper coverage?" I asked timidly.

"Of course he is!" Father Willet snapped. "Villa Cruz is too smart to be fooled by Grover's attempt to downplay all the rumors, burying them in some exposé on religious hoaxes and fake miracles. Your friend KC may be a talented young woman, but Villa Cruz is cunning beyond her capabilities," Father Willet explained.

"No, he is here to see for himself. You're familiar with the phrase the truth percolates aren't you?" he asked rhetorically. "He'll know the instant meets with her!"

"So what if he does, what harm can he bring to her?" I asked, smugly.

"After he reprimands me for keeping this from the Council of Cardinals, he will seek to have these occurrences validated by the Church. And when they are, and how could they not be, especially after your little escapade in New York, he'll use Tina's new celebrity to earn himself a red robe like the others and politic his way onto the Council. And then my boy, the world beware his rising star, that man truly scares me," Father Willet said sadly in a low tone.

He pulled out the chair next to me and sat down. Leaning forward and resting his elbows on the table, he laced together his fingers and set his chin down upon his knuckles. He turned his head slightly toward me and sighed.

"So tell me Ethan, what was it you wanted to talk about before dinner?" he asked.

I had totally forgotten about all my anxiety after listening to him relate to me all of these fears, doubts, and revelations. Suddenly my little struggle with cold feet and a warming heart seemed unimportant, and I decided to put seeking his council on a back burner for the time being. What was the rush anyway, it wasn't life threatening, although it could be life changing. Still, there were more important matters to tend to. Helping the Sheriff find the Rojas boy was high on my list, and now helping Father Willet fend off this papal opportunist was a close second.

Add in keeping the lid on Sophie's resurrection and then Paulie's recent confession, and my plate was pretty full. At least I was batting .500, *two challenges and two blessings.* Heck that was even better than Mickey Mantle's lifetime batting average! I had to smile, surely my issue could wait I guess, besides, they say absence makes the heart grow fonder don't they? I reached up and patted my breast pocket, reassuring myself that the letter was still in there. I fought the urge to take it out and read it again, to read it to Father Willet and ask him what I should do. It could wait, she could wait, KC would understand...

Albany, New York, September 1973

Shannon stood at the kitchen window and watched her mother as she tended to her flower garden. It was a little warmer than normal for late September, and Maggie Kelly never let a day of sunshine go unobserved or uncelebrated. Smiling to herself Shannon took special notice of her mom's ever present oversized shorts and big straw hat. These items were part of Maggie Kelly's summertime uniform, along with a dozen or so colorfully mixed and matched tops in a variety of styles, from light and breezy blouses to the occasional sleeveless button down. When she would tend the garden on hot summer days like this, her mother would be the highlight of *Rudy's* route, he was our mailman, as well as attract the attention of more than a few of the neighborhood males. Somehow they would collectively decide to water their lawns, wash their cars, or take a stroll at the same time her mother was digging in the flower garden, bending, stretching, and reaching to the delight of one and all. Her Mom was still quite a handsome woman after all, far too young to be a doting old widow. Shannon giggled softly to herself, if her mom only knew what a commotion she was causing, she thought...or maybe she did?

Shannon decided to set that aside for the moment, making a mental note to cautiously check into it some other time. She watched her mom tap at a plastic basin holding a marigold plant with her shovel, freeing the plant so that she could transplant it into the freshly dug soil. As she looked on Shannon could swear that she could sense the presence of her father, and she turned her toward the spot on the lawn where he used to lay in the sun, curing whatever ailed him. He wasn't there of course, but it sure felt like he was. Shannon had always loved the way her parents would carry on with one another, never hiding their love behind a façade of pretence and decorum. They may have been adults but they were childlike in the innocence of their affection toward one another. Even the passage of time was powerless against the strength of the bond between them.

Shannon knew instinctively that her parents would be young at heart forever. She loved that about her folks, and she felt as though today she completely understood their way, especially now that she recognized that same closeness between Paul and herself. It might have been a thunderbolt for him, because let's face it; men are clueless when it comes to reading signs of the heart. But for Shannon, all their years together, from childhood till now, had allowed the seeds God had planted in her heart to blossom into a love so genuine and pure that she could scarcely contain her joy. Shannon knocked at the windowpane to get her mother's attention. Maggie looked up from her crouch in the marigolds and waved at her daughter with a spade still in her hand. Shannon waved back and silently mouthed, *"I'll be right out."* Maggie nodded and rose up, placing her hands on her bare knees and sitting back on her heels. Shannon walked out of the house and toward her carrying a couple of glasses of ice-cold lemonade. She smiled back at her mother who was beaming and squinting in the backdrop of the bright sunlight. Shannon exhaled deeply, puffing out her cheeks as she came closer. It was time to tell her mother about what was on her mind and her heart.

"Hello girl, you're home early aren't you?" Maggie asked sweetly.

"Yes ma'am, I am ma'am," Shannon replied.

"I, um, made some lemonade, "she added, leaning over to hand her mother a glass.

"Tanks Shannon, that was sweet of you dear. Why don't we go over and sip these in the shade," Maggie said, handing back the glass so that she could use both of her hands to push herself up from her knees.

The two women walked over to the patio and seated themselves under the umbrella that stretched out over the round glass topped table. Maggie removed her gardening gloves and let them drop to the cement deck next to her chair. She picked up her glass with one hand and removed her big hat with the other. Fanning herself with the hat she took a nice long drink of the ice-cold lemonade.

"Indian Summer seems to just bring out all the colors in the garden, but Lord above, *the heat!*" Maggie exclaimed. Shannon smiled at her mother and sipped at her drink as well, biding her time for just the right moment to speak her mind.

"*So, what is on that sly little mind of yours,*" her mother asked using her best Sherlock Holmes tone, *Basil Rathbone's* Sherlock Holmes of course. Shannon closed her eyes involuntarily, "Ahhhh, here it comes," she thought, silently choking on her drink.

"I know you daughter," Maggie started. "You had that same look on your face when you brought home that puppy while Ethan was away in that awful place," she continued, pressuring Shannon just a smidgen trying to entice a reaction that she could read. Shannon sat frozen for a moment, still holding her glass to her mouth.

"*Come on girl, out with it!*" Maggie insisted playfully.

"ALRIGHT MOTHER!" Shannon pleaded, taking a second to smooth out her sundress and pull her hair back away from her face.

"Ahh, he's gone and done it hasn't he!" Maggie pressed.

"*He who, done what?*" Shannon exclaimed, feigning bewilderment.

"Why that big old bear of a boyfriend of course. The one that you've been hiding from me for months now, that's who."

"He's gone and asked you to marry him hasn't he?" her mother proclaimed.

"*MOTHER!*"

"So now you'll be wanting to throw away college and chase the fairytale, right?" Maggie said accusingly, doing her best to stifle a smile.

"Mother, how can you possibly know these things when we NEVER talk about this kind of stuff?" Shannon asked, totally flustered, leaning back abruptly in her chair and crossing her arms defensively. Maggie Kelly started to laugh uncontrollably, startling Shannon out of her pout and inspiring her to grin involuntarily like a skinny Cheshire cat.

"Oh Shannon, my darling girl," Maggie sighed, finally gaining control of herself, her composure returning slowly as she wiped the laughing tears from the corner of her eyes with the palms of her hands.

"*Shannon, Shannon, Shannon*...I've seen this coming ever since your twelfth birthday party. I knew that look on your face the instant I saw it. I knew straight away what was growing in your heart, you can't hide that sort of thing from your mum," Maggie said, watching her daughter's face soften, her pout turning into a blush.

"I knew because I had the same look when God revealed your father to me," Maggie added, suddenly looking past her daughter and into her own past, if for only an instant.

"Its different for women than men you know. Men are always so surprised when God introduces them to the one that he has chosen just for them. While we women are more relieved when God reveals to us what we already instinctively suspected, it kind of re-enforces our powers of intuition. Men will always *fall* into love; it's their nature. But for a woman, love needs to grow inside her heart, much like a child grows inside her womb. Women need to nurture love and carry it until that day when its ready to be born, when it will be hers forever and ever no matter what twists and turns life may bring," Maggie said, explaining her own very personal philosophy.

"That's beautiful mother, but is it always that way?" Shannon asked softly, reaching across the glass table and covering her mother's hands with her own.

"I mean what about all the couples that don't last, the divorces, the break ups, has God let these people down somehow?" she asked weakly.

"I don't believe that God lets anyone down girl, its not His way, you know that sure as I do," Maggie said.

"Truth be told, most people who search for love are actually looking for satisfaction. I don't believe that love is something that one finds. I believe that love is something that finds you. And I believe that God means for all of His children to be happy and fulfilled, and to that end he brings people into our lives to help us know happiness and fulfillment. And, in *His* time, he sends along the one that he made just for you."

"All I can say Shannon, is that when this person enters your life you will know instinctively who they are and why they are here. Then it will be up to the two of you to either acknowledge God's gift of one for the other, *or not*, call it fate or whatnot. The Lord only brings you the opportunity for happiness, the rest we have to do for ourselves, for better, for worse, or not at all...it's our choice," Maggie explained, squeezing her daughter's hands and then sitting up straight in her chair. She crossed her arms in front of her, looking intensely back at Shannon.

"I have been watching the two of you ever since that birthday party, wondering if I had really sensed something wonderful."

"I prayed on it everyday too, I mean, it was Paulie after all. I've known that boy since he was a shirt tail kid, and let's face it, I was a little shocked that God might have picked this goofball as the love of my daughter's life," Maggie confessed, slowly shaking her head and chuckling softly.

"Mom...be nice, he turned out OK don't you think?" Shannon protested weakly.

"Of course dear, he's a fine young man, *really*," Maggie answered reassuringly.

"Why with your legs and his shoulders there may be a Kelly quarterbacking the Jets someday," Maggie boasted.

"Um...Pulchowski mom, the Jets would have a Pulchowski playing quarterback in the future," Shannon said, gently correcting her mother.

"*Yes, well,* I just hope that they have enough letters for the poor boy's jersey," her mother teased. The two of them giggled at that thought for a minute, Shannon blushing at the realization that her mother was already contemplating grandchildren, while she hadn't even let Paul reach second base yet!

"You know, I suspected this day was coming when I saw the two of you together the day Sophie Wong passed away. I remember thinking to myself that when God takes a life he always creates a new one right away, *I remember thinking that,*" Maggie said, recalling that dark day.

"But mom, Paul hasn't even asked me anything yet. Well nothing important anyway, mostly questions like *are you gonna finish those fries,* or, *can I have a bite,* stuff like that," Shannon confessed sheepishly.

"Not to worry child, he's planning to, trust me," Maggie replied.

"Actually, I was thinking about asking him myself," Shannon said, thinking out loud.

"SHANNON, don't steal the poor man's moment," her mother scolded.

"Yeah, but mom, he's a little slow in the romance department. I mean I know that the thought is hanging on the tree, ripe and ready to fall, *but he just stands there waiting,* instead of getting out a gosh darn ladder!" Shannon lamented.

"Oh POO! Shannon Kelly, I raised you better than that!" Maggie exclaimed.

"But Mom..."

"But nothing young lady! Look, male egos are a fragile thing at best. The last thing that you want to do is fracture his with your impatience. His ego is critical to his vitality. And believe me child, you'll want to nurture that your whole life together, the benefits are amazing!" Maggie explained, fanning herself a little harder with her straw hat and winking at her daughter.

"MOTHER!" Shannon exclaimed, grinning widely at her mother's provocatively suggestive observation.

"Oh behave girl, it's just a fact of life, enjoy it!" Maggie said giggling.

"Now, as for school, well, why don't we all chat about that in a day or so, there's no need to rush into this, *is there?*" she asked her daughter with a raised eyebrow.

"No ma'am, of course not," Shannon answered, crossing herself.

"Good girl," Maggie replied.

"*Now*, you leave young Paul to me. I'll get him up that ladder in no time, you'll see," Maggie said, raising her glass of lemonade to toast the day's revelations.

"OK then Mother," Shannon replied, raising her own glass, and reaching across to clink it together with her Mom's. The glasses clinked and the ice rattled as they toasted the day and sipped at the watery lemonade.

"By the way girl, not to change the subject too quickly. But how is little Miss Wong anyway? You're still babysitting while Carolyn waits for the new baby to come, right?" Maggie said, inquiring after the Wong family.

"Sophie is doing just grand, you should see her Mom, she's back to her old mischievous self," Shannon replied.

"The saints preserve us, as I live and breathe, I cannot understand how those doctors could have made such a mistake! Imagine putting poor Ken and Carolyn through such hell because of their grievous error. It was criminal I tell you, I'm tempted to go right to the TV people and tell them all about those quacks, give them a real piece of my mind," Maggie said bitterly, her Irish nearly to the boiling point.

"*Oh no mother*, remember we promised Ethan to be Christian about the whole matter. Everyone makes mistakes now, remember to forgive is divine," Shannon said, trying to calm her mom down.

She didn't like lying to her mother, but she had agreed along with everyone else that night at the Wong's, that the less said the better. Nobody wanted to see either girl's life turned inside out, as it could be by the curious and the skeptical. Shannon had been a little worried about the night attendant from the morgue, but apparently his heart was just soft enough, and KC's boss, Mr. Gateway's wallet was just fat enough to keep him silent while he studies abroad in Europe.

"Don't you worry about me young lady; I know how to hold my tongue."

"Besides which, those quacks will be answering for their deeds come judgment day," Maggie added defiantly.

"I know Mom, *I know*," Shannon acknowledged apologetically.

"So when is Carolyn due anyway?" Maggie asked her daughter.

"*Ummm*, January I think. I hope the child arrives on time, the poor girl is so uncomfortable, especially in all this heat. Do you know that I caught her crying the other day, *positively weeping*, because she couldn't tie her own shoes," Shannon answered.

"Oh, poor dear. Women get that way dear. I'm afraid that we're just a bucket full of hormones while we're in that state, you'll see for yourself one day. Maybe I'll take her some of your Grandmother's Mulligan stew later tonight. Will you be coming with me Shannon girl?" Maggie asked.

"Sure Mom, I will," Shannon answered.

The two of them sat in silence for a moment, sipping their lemonades, then suddenly burst into a giggling jag.

"*I...I...*I can't believe it, my babies are all grown up," Maggie said through the giggles.

She dabbed at her eyes and added reflectively, *"I wish your Da could be here to see all of this."*

"He will be mother, he will be," Shannon replied.

"And you'll be asking Ethan to come home to marry the two of you when the time comes," Maggie asked without needing to hear the answer.

"Of course mother, who else but him," Shannon answered.

"Who else indeed," Maggie replied. The two women sat silently for a couple of minutes, letting all that had been said between them sink in completely.

"Oh my goodness, we've a wedding to plan!" Maggie exclaimed.

"Easy mother, hold your horses OK. We still need to lock in the groom, remember" Shannon reminded her mother playfully. Maggie Kelly picked up her glass and drained the last of the lemonade, melting ice and all. Then, setting down the empty glass she wiped her mouth dry with the sleeve of her shirt, just the way Shannon had always done.

"Piece of cake!" she said, smiling and snapping her fingers. *"Piece of cake..."*

Firebaugh, California, September 1973

Tina sat at on the end of her bed brushing her long dark hair. She had pulled it all back and gathered it behind her, and held it in a long ponytail. Then grasping it tightly in her right hand she pulled it back over her shoulder and gently brushed the foot long bundle extending beyond her closed fist. She was really proud of the fact that she never seemed to have problems with split ends. Her hair was naturally lustrous, not too fine, not too thick, and never dry or frizzy. She never had to do more than shampoo, no need for a conditioner as her hair seemed to have just the right amount of natural oils to keep it soft and manageable. Even so, she followed her mother's regiment religiously, one hundred strokes before leaving the house each morning, as well as each night before bed with a soft bristled brush followed by one hundred strokes with a large toothed comb. She was finishing the brushing part when someone knocked on her bedroom door.

"Si," she called out.

"Mija, KC and Jay are here for your TV practice, they're in the living room with your father. Hurry baby, before your Dad starts in with his knock-knock jokes," Maria Lopez pleaded through the closed door.

Her mother no longer just burst in on her, she had stopped that a few years ago, when she was fifteen, right after her Quinceanera. Tina was eighteen now, and turning nineteen in May for goodness sake! KC had told her that it was time for her to step out into the light of day. That she wasn't a little girl anymore, that she could handle whatever came her way, even a little bit of attention from the big bad world! She had been had been under someone else's wing for as long as she could remember. Maybe KC was right she decided, maybe it was time to test her wings.

"Be right there mama," she called out, jumping up from the bed and setting the brush on her bureau, stopping in front of the mirror to take one last look at herself before walking out to meet her guests.

She opened the door and walked slowly down the hall, not wanting to arrive too quickly and appear too anxious. What was it KC had told her about a woman's prerogative? Oh yeah, *always keep them waiting*, she had told her, especially men, keeps you in control, they're so insecure, just a pitiful thing to behold. Tina smiled as she walked, recalling how hard KC had laughed out loud when she had shared this with her.

They had been having lunch together with Jay at a local diner, and KC had been teasing Jay relentlessly about his new girlfriend, *the dancer*. Tina remembered being puzzled when KC made quotation signs with her fingers every time she referred to Jay's new girlfriend *Misty*. She remembered giggling when her mother explained what *kind of dancer* Misty happened to be. And she also remembered her mother swatting her father with a dishtowel when she caught him listening in on their conversation.

"Oh I see, now you're paying attention to me!" her mother had said to her dad.

"Shame one you Panson!" she had said scolding him playfully.

Tina liked KC and Jay, she liked the way they made all of the attention she was getting seem normal, like it was nothing special. They put her at ease, and they seemed to have the same effect on her parents as well.

"Hey, nobody remembers yesterday's headlines," KC would say whenever Tina seemed worried about the phone ringing or a stranger knocking at the door. KC always told her, *"I'm just a phone call away kiddo,"* each time she walked out the door after a visit.

It was just like having a big sister, and it made Tina feel so secure. She had a little trouble thinking of Jay as a big brother though, but that was because she had a little crush on him. Truth be told, she also had a little crush of Father Kelly, but then so did KC. Tina never let on that she knew, but she had seen the way KC looked at him and the way her voice was different whenever she spoke to or of him. She wasn't sure, but she thought she noticed the same behavior from him, but had dismissed the idea; he was a priest after all! Tina walked into the room and saw that Jay and KC were sitting on the sofa. Poppy was in his chair and Mama was standing beside him, stirring some icing in a large ceramic mixing bowl.

"Finally," her mother exclaimed. "Tina, shame on you for keeping your guests waiting," Maria said, scolding her daughter.

"*Lo ciento mama.* I'm just a little nervous. All of this preparation reminds me of cramming for a math test, *ewww!*" Tina said, apologizing and pretending to retch.

"It's OK kiddo, your dad was keeping us entertained," KC chimed in.

"Yeah, I don't think I have ever heard that last *knock-knock* joke before," Jay added, sarcastically.

"I just made it up!" Victor said proudly, snapping his fingers and grinning ear to ear.

"Really," Jay said, turning to look at KC and roll his eyes. KC kicked him under the coffee table and leaned forward to see past him, while he reached down to rub his aching ankle.

"You bitch," Jay mouthed silently at KC, out of sight of all the others.

"It was cute Victor, *really!* Maybe I'll use it sometime in a story or at a party, if that's OK with you?" KC asked politely.

"SURE!" Victor exclaimed.

"You really think it was that good?" he asked, scooting forward in his chair. KC kicked Jay again to get his attention.

"Owwww...*shhhure!*" Jay said through clenched teeth. He slid to his left, getting out of the range of KC's pointy pumps and looked back at her to make sure that she wasn't following.

"Yeah it was great Victor, honest!" he added enthusiastically, turning his head in KC's direction and mouthing "HAPPY!" She stuck her tongue out at him and then leaned back on the sofa and crossed her arms. Tina giggled at their antics and went over to sit on the ottoman in front of her father's chair.

"Come on Papa," Maria said. "Help me ice this cake while these children work," Maria added, coaxing Victor to follow her by handing him the wooden spoon covered thickly coated with chocolate icing. It was all the incentive he needed. Victor, being a notorious chocoholic, and who probably had his picture hanging in every diner and fine restaurant in two counties, was more than happy to oblige. Tina moved to the chair vacated by her dad and sat down.

"OK, what do we need to do?" she asked her two friends.

KC turned and reached into her leather briefcase, pulling out a handful of blue 3 X 5 index cards. She started sorting them and gestured for Jay to go and get his stuff from behind the couch.

"Alright, let's see. I've got a few sample questions here to ask you. Let's pretend that I am the person who will interview you. And Jay is going to set up a camera and some lights to simulate the kind of environment that you will be exposed to," KC started. She paused a second, thinking that she had noticed a puzzled look on Tina's face.

"Stop me if I'm going too fast OK," she said to Tina.

"I'm OK," Tina replied, nodding her head and sitting up straight in the chair.

"Just relax and remember, you're in your own home, you're in charge of what you say or don't say, understand?" KC asked, watching her expression before she continued.

"Yes, I understand," Tina replied.

"There are no rules here Tina, speak your mind, it's your time now," KC said, trying to sooth any frazzled nerves the girl might have.

She observed her for a moment while Jay set up his equipment. KC was in awe at how much Tina grown, not so much in stature, but in her maturity. She looked wise beyond her years, and more importantly she looked comfortable, *no*, she looked eager, like she had something important to say. It wasn't noticeable in her posture, but KC could see it in her eyes, and it made her just a little bit nervous. Jay switched on the lights and adjusted them so that they would be representative of the kind of set that the *Sixty Minutes* crew would bring. He looked at Tina through the eyepiece of the camera on the tripod and focused in on her. Then he looked over at KC and gave her the OK signal, switched the video monitor to play.

"OK Tina, are you ready?" KC asked.

"Yes, I think so. I think that I've been ready for a long time," she answered, sitting very still and looking directly into the red light emanating from the camera in front of her. KC and Jay looked at one another then back at Tina.

"OK then, let's start," KC replied, setting the index cards in her lap. Jay held the session board in front of the camera and said in a loud voice, "Angel of the Valley Interview, take one," then he clapped the board shut and counted down, *"in three, two..."* he said, pointing at KC signaling her to begin.

"Good evening everyone, I'm Diane Sawyer, and this is Sixty Minutes."

"Tonight we may just make history, as we cross over from fantasy to reality, from fiction to fact."

"In this exclusive interview you are going to meet an extraordinarily gentle young lady, whose extraordinary deeds have humbled this reporter beyond words."

"As for her deeds, you'll have to judge for yourselves."

"I promise you, this will be an interview that you will all remember."

"This story will not only pull at your heart, but will challenge your sensibilities."

"It is an old story in a new time...*and all of it true,*" KC said, calmly reading the lead copy that the network had provided for this private rehearsal. Jay fussed a little with the camera angle and switched on another lamp. He signaled KC that he was through and she continued.

"She's called the Angel of the Valley, and angel she may very well be."

"America, meet Tina Lopez," KC announced, while Jay zoomed in slowly on the pretty young girl.

PART THREE

1974

God's not so secret, secret…it's all about the love…:)

Thirty-nine

(...."If I speak with the tongues of men and of angels,
but do not have love, I have become a noisy gong or a
clanging cymbal"...1ˢᵗ Corinthians 13:1)

<u>San Francisco, California, February 1974</u>

"Knock, knock," said KC Littleton softly, pantomiming a rap on the glass portion of her editor's half opened office door. Brian Williams looked up from whatever it was he was reading and gently pulled his bifocals down along the bridge of his nose. Leaning back in his chair he raised his arms and laced his fingers together behind his head. He peered over the top of his glasses, inviting KC to take a seat with a nod of his head. She walked over to one of the *not so comfortable* straight-backed chairs in front of his desk and seated herself delicately, smoothing out her new skirt as she crossed her legs.

"Well, well, well, if it isn't *Miss Pulitzer Prize* herself," Brian said playfully. KC put her hand up behind her head and struck a pose.

"Why, whatever are you talking about?" she said animatedly, batting her eyes and sucking in her cheeks. She quickly slouched back into the chair and limply waved her hand back at her boss.

"Oh, I guess you heard about the Pulitzer thing," KC said feigning like it was no big deal.

"Imagine that! Everyone making such a fuss over little ole me!" she said, exaggerating her look of mock disbelief.

"Yeah, we all heard KC," Brain said, trying to match her nonchalance.

"I KNOW!" KC exclaimed.

"CAN YOU BELIVE IT!" she shouted at the ceiling.

Brian watched the newspapers newest star lean forward in her chair and kick at the carpet as if she were running in place, letting out a rebel yell that was sure to bring security.

"Oh man Brian, I never dreamed I'd come so far so fast," KC said as she settled down and sat back in her chair, leisurely crossing her legs and smoothing out her skirt.

"I'll admit it KC, I had my doubts at first. I mean you were *such* a pain in the ass, and you *NEVER* listened to a word I said," Brian lamented, leaning forward and resting his arms on his desk, hands folded, and his fingers laced.

"But, there was always something about you. Mr. Gateway saw it right off, I didn't," he continued.

"And damn if he wasn't right all along...congratulations Kathy," Brain said smiling, standing and extending his hand across the desk for KC to accept.

KC leaned way forward to shake Brian's hand, her shapely behind neatly displayed through her tight new skirt for everyone looking in on the two of them from the newsroom just beyond the glass walls of his office. Totally unaware of the commotion she was causing she shook her editor's hand and then returned to her seat.

"Thanks boss man," she said, smiling back at him.

"You're welcome," Brian replied.

"I see that celebrity has altered your sense of style a little," Brian said, referring to her new clothes.

"That's quite an outfit, very stylish. What, no more jeans and tee shirts?" he teased.

"This old thing," KC quipped, standing up and doing a slow 360-degree pirouette.

"It was just hanging in the closet gathering dust," she added, feigning a yawn.

"Maybe in Jay's closet," Brain said sarcastically.

"You better be careful what you wear around here. He has his spies everywhere you know. Pretty soon word will get out and the fashion war will be on!" Brian said, grinning at the look of mock horror on KC's face as she raised her hand to her mouth, pretending to gasp.

"You know Jay, he'll drive himself and the rest of us nuts trying to stay one step ahead of you on the style tote board," he said, reminding KC of her friend's competitive compulsions.

KC laughed out loud, "You're right, you're right, you're absolutely right! That guy will tap all of his sources, gay and straight, to make sure that everything that I come up with will just *be so five minutes ago!*" KC replied, dabbing at the giggle tears welling in corner of here eyes.

"Alright, I think that we've picked on poor Jay long enough, especially since he is not here to defend himself," Brian said. He picked up the news copy in front of KC and waggled it in her direction.

"This is what I wanted to talk about Kathy. Maybe you can shed a little light on it, cause I have to tell you, I am way in the dark on this girl, way in the dark!" said Brian, tossing the copy back toward KC. She reached out and picked up the papers, but she didn't need to look at it, she knew what it said.

"Couldn't we spend just a little more time on my award?" she asked sheepishly.

"Kaaaa Ceeee..." Brian growled in a low tone.

"Oh alright! But you have to promise to *hear* me out before you *chew* me out...OK?" KC replied.

"Come on KC, we're talking about the credibility of the San Fran-freaking-cisco Daily News, our bread and butter! Look, we dodged a bullet with that Sixty Minutes interview thanks to your close relationship with the girl and her family, not to mention Grover's likely pact with Satan. *But this...*" Brain said, pointing at the pile of papers in front of her.

"I...ahhh, I know what you're thinking," KC stammered.

"OH NO YOU DON"T EITHER!" Brian replied gruffly.

KC bit at her lip while she stalled for time. She fully intended to tell him the whole truth, she just needed to figure out how to do it without giving the poor man a heart attack! Brian stared at her impatiently, his eyes narrowing, causing his brow to furrow, and his face to be pulled into that expression of his that always made her laugh out loud. She bit her lip a little harder and let out a weak squeal as she diverted her eyes quickly. Now was not the time for a belly aching laughing jag. KC could see that Brian was nearing his boiling point, and she was painfully aware that he was watching her bite at her thumbnail like a child while she searched for the right tack to take.

"Let's go KC, what are you, thirteen?" Brian bellowed, completely frustrated by her stalling antics. She cleared her throat and swallowed hard, then raised her eyes to face him.

"OK, here it is in a nutshell," KC began.

"Oh no you don't! I am not interested in the Reader's Digest version, I want details, ALL the details KC, you get my meaning, right!" Brian fired back at her. KC sighed audibly and folded her hands in her lap.

"Fair enough, the whole *Magilla* coming up," she replied, jerking her head sharply, tossing her long hair over her shoulder and out of the way.

"About a week ago, *no*, it was more like two weeks ago, I got a phone call from that yokel Sheriff in Fresno, you remember him, Cardwell was his name," she began.

"Yeah, so," Brian replied curtly.

"*Well*, he said that he needed to talk with me as soon as possible, that it was important."

"I see, and the good constable was compelled to bring this revelation forward after reading your piece on the Katz murder?" Brian asked sarcastically, his eyes settling on the news copy that his star reporter was holding onto.

"*Please...*Brian, this is serious," KC protested.

"I am aware!" he said gruffly. Brian snapped his fingers several times, then waggled his index finger at KC indicating that he wanted her to hand back the copy she was holding. He held out his hand, "Give it here," he said tiredly. KC handed the news copy over to him. He took it and leaned back in his chair, pushing his glasses up on his nose so that he could read the text.

"Go on," he said without looking up.

KC cleared her throat and continued, "Right, well, as you know, we did that series of articles profiling the Hernandez woman, and the details of her experience with Dr. Katz. We covered all the angles, the subsequent child, her obsession with revenge, the circumstances surrounding her first attempt on the doctor's life, and the inadvertent ties to Tina Lopez," KC explained.

"When you say the first attempt on the doctor's life, you're referring to the fire she started? The one where the Lopez girl supposedly healed the man miraculously," Brain asked, still reading the copy he was holding.

"Yep, *that fire*," KC answered curtly, not appreciating her boss's condescending tone.

"By the way, there is no supposedly about it. That event was genuine, I saw the guy myself, several times. There was never a trace of any injury, not a mark on his body," KC added sharply. Brain ignored her and flipped the page on the copy he was reading.

"You said that there ties, plural, to the Lopez girl. What other contact was there, I don't see any mention of further incidents involving the she and the Hernandez woman?" Brian pressed.

"Tina Lopez was present at the birth of Rosa Hernandez child," answered KC.

"And the relevance of that little fact?" Brian asked.

"The baby was dead in her womb, it should have been still born," KC replied.

"You know this...*how?*"

"By the sworn testimony of two eye-witnesses, Maria Lopez and Mrs. Arthur Donnelly."

Brian set the news copy back onto his desk and sat silently for a couple of minutes. He had laced his fingers together and fashioned a church and steeple with his hands. He rested his chin on the open doors of the church (his thumbs), and the steeple (his raised index fingers) against his nose. He ran the steeple up and down the bridge of his nose while he mentally chewed on what KC had said so far. She watched him as he sat there thinking, she knew that he needed a few minutes to absorb all of the facts as she presented them. She wasn't at all affected by his intense stare. She knew that he wasn't looking at her but past her. They sat together in silence for a good five minutes before either of them spoke again.

"You know, maybe he was never burned at all, maybe we just got played on that one KC. I mean I never did like the fact that we had no real physical evidence supporting all of the talk and conjecture, unsound journalism I remember thinking at the time. But you so adamant and Grover was so convinced, I'm afraid that I was out voted," Brian said, reflecting on his own recollections.

KC held her tongue; she didn't like his tone or his left-handed insinuations. The very idea that she could be duped so easily was insulting.

"Be that as it may Brian, might I remind you that I was present when that girl brought back a stone dead child! I saw that with my own two eyes, and none of your pettifogging will ever convince me otherwise," KC snapped. Brian dismantled the church made of fingers and folded his arms in front of him.

"OK, peace KC, it all happened like you said," he said capitulating.

"So what did Sheriff Cardwell have to say that was so all fired important, that could undermine the stories that we ran on the Hernandez woman and that rat bastard Katz?" he asked. KC puffed out her cheeks and exhaled deeply. She gave her matching jacket a hard tug and then replied.

"Like I said Brian, we ran that series profiling the mindset of a murderer. We chronicled the life of Rosa Hernandez right up to the moment she ultimately succeeded in her quest to avenge herself and all the others by killing Dr. Murray Katz. We told the world about her cunning, and her resolve, and even hinted around her motive being immorally just. The readers ate it up, subscriptions increased; we were getting lots of free play in the mainstream media. *Oh hell*, Time and Newsweek were carrying weekly follow-ups, and the big three networks were running segment after segment. I am even aware of a studio of some renown planning to release a film early next year!" KC said, pausing to take a breath.

"*I know*, it was a great series KC, probably helped you win that Pulitzer. So where's the problem, what did Cardwell have to say that would cast a shadow over your work?" Brian pressed, his tone beginning to sound a bit more frustrated. KC stared back at him silently, and then closed her eyes.

"Dr. Katz isn't dead," she said softly.

"*WHAT!*" Brian whispered harshly.

"He isn't dead. That's what the Sheriff called to say," KC replied.

"What do you mean he isn't dead? You told the world that you saw his corpse lying cold and dead on the coroner's stainless steel examination table for Christ's sake!" Brian shouted, the veins in his neck beginning to bulge. KC got up and began to pace the room nervously. She stopped after only a couple of laps and stood in front of Brian Williams' desk.

"He was dead Brian, I swear to God, he was dead! I watched the medical examiner tilt the table back and insert all these tubes into the man. I even stayed longer than I should have and saw them start to pump all the fluids out of the man's body. HE WAS DEAD!" she exclaimed, frustrated to near tears. Brian stared at KC and rubbed his face, he could feel his five o'clock shadow beginning to form.

"Dead is dead Kathy, how does the sheriff explain that away?" Brian asked calmly.

"It was the girl Brian, she changed all that," she replied.

"*What?* Are you trying to tell me that she worked her black magic and brought him back, is that what you're trying to say KC?" Brian asked, not sure that he wanted an answer.

"Yes sir…I didn't believe it myself at first. Not until I remembered an incident a couple of years ago at the Lopez house. I was there visiting with Alma Donnelly when Tina received a letter from the man, it was really spooky!"

"I remember actually being frightened by the whole experience, by the girl herself. She was maybe ten or so at the time, but a *young ten* if you know what I mean?"

"Not ten going on twenty, but a genuine child."

"The fact that Dr. Katz was even able to get a letter out to her made me angry, and the aura surrounding the content made my skin crawl. It didn't seem to bother Tina though, she had no prejudices toward the man, and I wrote it off as naiveté. But in hindsight I totally misread the situation."

" She didn't see him as I did, as any of us did, she wasn't blinded by hatred or disgust. In her eyes he was a new person, forgiven, saved by her healing hand and the Lord's mercy and salvation."

"Now that I think back on it, from her perspective, it really was a beautiful gesture of gratitude on the doctor's part. I can hardly believe my ears, but you know, it really was! And I remember Tina asking if we would take her to see the man. She *wanted* to talk to him, and when I asked why, she said it was a secret?" KC said, sitting back down in the chair across from her editor. She scratched her head lightly along the center part of her hair, trying to piece together all of the fractured facts that the Sheriff had shared.

"A secret, *a secret*, that reminds me. Sheriff Cardwell told me that Alma and Arthur Donnelly eventually pulled a few strings and arranged for the child to meet with Dr. Katz. He said that while he watched Tina and Katz talk that he experienced the same feeling of foreboding as I had. He said that he also recalled being confused and uncomfortable with familiarity between the two of them," KC said recanting her conversation with Ralph Cardwell.

"You sure that's the term he used, *familiarity?*" Brian asked.

"Yes, why," KC replied.

"I don't know why, the word just seems inappropriate somehow," Brain answered.

"I know what you mean, *weird huh?*" KC said making that cute *I'm so confused* face of hers.

"You know what else is weird?" she asked, before Brian could answer.

"No, what?" he replied.

"Sheriff Cardwell told me that when he asked Tina what it was that she had whispered to the doctor, she had told him that it was a secret!" KC exclaimed, nodding her head affirmatively as if she had just stumbled upon something important. She suddenly sat up very straight and started wagging her index finger at her boss.

"*Oh man Brian, I think I know what the secret was,*" she said excitedly, her eyes beginning to sparkle like they did whenever she laughed out loud or sobbed uncontrollably.

"Well give it up then Kathy," Brian said, scooting to the edge of his seat.

KC got up and started pacing the room again. She always maintained that she could think better while she was on the move. She considered herself more of a guerrilla journalist so to speak. She lapped the room once, passing behind Brian on the straightaway and then pulled up in front of his desk again.

"*YES!*" she shouted, raising her arms to the ceiling and flopping back down in her chair. "It all fits, *I'm such a dope!* I should have suspected this the first day I interviewed Rosa Hernandez, she as much as told me the whole story," KC said, scolding herself.

"Slow down Kathy, I'm having trouble keeping up with your runaway recall," Brian complained.

"You read it yourself, it's all in that news copy right in front of you," she whined.

"It was there all the time, right in front of our noses! Only we read right past the real story and swallowed the hook, the one that I baited all by myself. *What a bunch of nerds!*" KC said, scolding the both of them right into the next dimension. Brian slouched back into his chair and started to chew on his thumbnail. He was trying to ascertain where KC might be headed with all of her ranting, but for the life him he was drawing a blank. KC could see by the look on his face that he was lost, but she patiently waited for a response before she continued. Brian exhaled deeply through his nose.

"Nope, I'm not following you," he answered finally. She could see that he was still crunching hard on the facts so she paused a minute longer to let him mull everything over.

"All right Brian, let's break it down slowly, together, OK?" she said, offering to take the lead. Brian nodded, still chewing on his thumb, past the nail now and onto the cuticle.

"OK"

KC drew in a deep breath and then started in with her theory *slash*, explanation.

"Logically we know that the common denominator in this social equation is Tina Lopez, you agree with that, right?" she asked.

"Depends, how do you mean that?" Brian replied, answering her question with a question.

"Well, let's look at it chronologically. Katz enters Rosa's life, *literally*, Rosa enters Tina's life by giving life, and Tina enters Rosa's life by saving that life. Then Rosa re-enters Katz's life to take his life, while Tina enters Katz's life to save his life. Tina's action changes Katz's life, Rosa action changes her own life, and that's were we went off track," KC explained fervently. Brian screwed his face into an expression of total bewilderment.

"I know you're trying to make a point and lead me somewhere, but for the life of me Kathy, I haven't got a clue!" Brian said stammering, as he shrugged his shoulders and held his arms out wide, palms up. KC reached across his desk, and picked up Brian's coffee cup and took a drink to sooth her parched throat.

"YUCKY! This coffee is stone cold!" she exclaimed, sticking out her tongue and making a face like, she had just bit into a lemon. She leaned forward awkwardly and returned the cup to the desktop.

"Sorry," Brian muttered, smiling sheepishly.

"No worries," KC replied, dabbing at the corners of her mouth with her thumb and forefinger.

"*OK, look,* at this point we went with the obvious scenario and played up the revenge factor where Rosa Hernandez was concerned. We only saw Tina as a random element in these murderous plots and subplots. It was LOGICAL for Rosa to pursue Katz to his death. It was LOGICAL that her mind would be so twisted given the trauma he put her through. And isn't that the very angle we always shoot for? Get the facts, lay them out, draw the conclusion that is easiest to sell, *right?*" she asked, laying out the start of her theory.

"So are you insinuating that Rosa Hernandez really didn't want to kill this bastard?" Brain asked wryly.

"*EXACTLY!* I knew there was a reason I always bragged about you around the water cooler," KC said beaming back at her boss. Brian rolled his eyes and smiled back embarrassed by her remark.

"Yeah, yeah, yeah, so finish your story and help me see how we can spin this in our favor," Brian said hurriedly.

"Alright, alright, keep your pants on, I'm getting to it," she replied.

"*So,* what if we agree for a minute that there really is a God. I'm not sure about where you stand on this personally, but I am a relatively new believer. Translation, I *want* to believe but my heart and mind are still in this world, so, *ashamedly,* my faith is pretty weak," KC said trying to level the field for her theory. She didn't wait for Brian to respond.

"Even after what I witnessed in New York, my human nature is to question everything. It's not a natural response, it is a conditioned one, understand?" she asked, looking back at Brain, waiting for him to reply this time.

"I'm with you," he said.

"And for the record, I believe as well, it's the reason I never fought this story in the first place. I'm no different than any of the faithful. I'm in awe of God's awesome power."

"And the thought of these events, miracles if you will, is like stoking the fire in my belly, makes my own faith stronger," he confessed. KC looked back at her boss, seeing him in a new light, a little smile spreading across her face.

"Really, I had no idea," she said.

"Yeah, well, I keep my private life, you know, private," he replied.

"Yeah...maybe that's the problem with everyone, we keep too many things private. Maria Lopez told me once that her life became so much easier when she learned to live in the light. It took me a long time to understand what she meant. Listening to your little confession really helped me see her point, *thanks.*"

"But, I digress," KC said, scooting forward in her chair.

"So, we agree, God is alive and well."

"Now, what if we add Him into my little equation? What if He is the random element, pulling all the other variables together in such a way as to save lives instead of take lives, *huh...huh!*" KC hypothesized enthusiastically. Brian frowned and chewed on that thought a moment.

"Are you saying that God meant for Rosa Hernandez to kill Murray Katz?" he asked, perplexed by KC's endless string of *what ifs*.

"No, but I think that maybe the only way she was going to get past all the hate was to kill it, *literally*. Of course, being compassionate, God understood that her heart was blinded by hatred, so He came up with a plan. Enter Tina Lopez, the expeditor of Rosa *and* Dr. Katz's salvation. Placed close to each of them by her intervention into their personal fates, Tina found herself in a unique position to be trusted by them both. Neither aware of her connection to the other, each of them changed forever by that connection," KC answered, watching his face for a knowing reaction. It was clear that Brian was trying to keep up with her, so she decided to press on before he had a chance to question her reasoning.

"Interfacing soul to soul if you will, being connected so closely, must have given Tina an insight into the hearts of each. The one who secretly wanted to be forgiven and the one who secretly wanted to forgive, neither of whom would ever realize their desires on their own. This was the part we all missed, well, that I missed for sure. I couldn't forgive him for what he had done to her, so I couldn't see Rosa ever forgiving him either. *Hell*, truth be told, I was rooting for her to do him in!" KC exclaimed, snapping her fingers and crossing her arms.

Brian grunted, nodding his head, indicating that he was following along so far. KC checked her wristwatch; she wanted to finish up before Jay arrived to take her out for a celebration lunch at The Stinking Rose, his favorite Italian restaurant, not hers. She could already taste the linguini and clams, and was looking forward to the grappa afterward. She cleared her throat and her mind and then continued.

"I think that's when all the *secret* talk started. I think that Tina used her spiritual connection to Katz to work God's plan to save them both. Katz's life was spared because of his repentance and the cost would be his involvement in the rescue of Rosa's soul. The day we read his letter to Tina in the back yard, was the day that Katz communicated to her that he knew *what* it was that he was to do. The day that he and Tina met face to face at the hospital in front of Sheriff Cardwell was the day that she told him *when*. From that point on, God just let Rosa make her own way down the path of vengeance, confident she was doing His work. And then when the time came for Rosa to implement her plan to poison the man, Tina intervened by way of Sheriff Cardwell and none other than our own fearless leader, Grover Cleveland

Gateway," KC concluded. Brain sat up when he heard this part and shot KC a *'what the fuck'* look.

"Come on KC, that's way out there, even for you. How do you link Mr. Gateway to all of this?" he asked disbelieving.

"*Simple*, moving Katz at a moment's notice and allowing Rosa within spitting distance of anything remotely connected to her obsession would require somebody to grease a lot of skids, and more importantly, somebody to supply the grease. Who better than a law enforcement insider close to Tina and an endless source of wealth and power likewise attached?" she reasoned, flawlessly.

"You're saying that a duly sworn County Sheriff and revered publisher and journalist conspired to fake the murder of Dr. Katz? And that Grover Gateway then knowingly allowed the newspaper he spent a lifetime building to run stories that he knew were patently false? Is that what you want me to believe KC?" Brian whispered harshly, careful not to speak loud enough to be overheard.

"Yeah, that's pretty much it," KC replied meekly. Brian snorted as he leaned back in his chair and gazed back at her in disbelief.

"You're nuts!" he said sarcastically.

"*Maybe*, but technically we told the truth. You see they didn't have to fake the doctor's death. Not when they had the means to resurrect him...*again*," KC said wryly. Brian sat there thinking for a moment, staring past KC and out at the busy newsroom beyond the glass walls of his office.

"You know what will happen to this place once we print a retraction?" he hissed. KC smoothed out her skirt and re-crossed her legs.

"Who says we have to retract anything?" she asked as a matter fact.

"We knowingly printed a lie, we **HAVE TO** retract it, our credibility is everything!" Brian hollered, much louder than he had intended. He looked around KC to see if he had drawn any attention.

"*Brian, it's only a theory, OK!*"

"But even if it's true, who does it hurt if Katz serves out his sentence secretly until they jab him with a hot dose a few years from now?"

"He'll never get out to harm anyone else, and the world will be free of his memory. Rosa will get a chance to heal mentally and emotionally thanks to the light sentence her self-defense and insanity plea afforded. And she'll be allowed to live peacefully without fretting that the man responsible for so much pain might someday escape justice to hurt someone else. And we can sleep the sleep of the righteous knowing that we did a good thing. All we have to do is play it cool man. Now that I've thought it through, that's what Sheriff Cardwell was trying to tell me. And that's what I guess I'm trying to tell you," KC said, uncrossing her arms. She sat in her seat quietly waiting for

Brian to either cave in or blow up, at this point it was a toss up. He looked across the desk at her, his eyes locking with hers. They sat in silence for a good five minutes and then he leaned forward onto his desktop. Brian rested his chin on his folded hands and bit at his lower lip.

"That was a hell of a story KC," he said from his odd perch.

"Thanks, we aim to please," she answered.

"You really believe all that?" he asked.

"Yeah, I really do," KC replied, scooting her chair forward and leaning onto Brian's desktop from the other side, mimicking his position.

"So what do you want to do now," she asked softly. Brian exhaled and shrugged his shoulders as they sat there awkwardly eyeing each other. Sort of an odd version of pillow talk they had engaged in.

"Let's go and see the man. If this is true I want to hear it from him. *Are you OK with that?*" he said finally. KC winked back at him.

"Let's do it!"

Albany, New York, 18 February 1974
<u>*County General Hospital: 9:15pm*</u>

*"Come on, push you dummy, **push!**"* Carolyn Wong said aloud to the room, puffing out her cheeks and blowing out quick jets of air as she transitioned into the final stages of a long and difficult labor.

Her husband Ken looked up from the Sports Illustrated he was reading to see whom his wife was talking to, and then realized that she was talking to herself. He got up from his chair and tossed the magazine back onto the cushion. He walked up to Carolyn's bed and stopped next to her shoulders, the mattress raised to a forty-five degree angle to help keep her as comfortable as possible given the circumstances. Of course she had been in every position imaginable over the last sixteen hours, from pacing the room, to all curled up in a near fetal position while Kenny rubbed her aching back. But for the last hour or so she had been resting peacefully in a semi conscious state riding out contractions like a real trooper.

Ken was absolutely amazed at how strong she was, and at how focused she could be what with all the violent spasms and painful reshaping of her body as her cervix dilated preparing itself for childbirth. He picked up the washcloth from the container on the table next to the bed and wringed out the cool water. He raised it to her forehead and gently dabbed away the beads of sweat, letting the cool, damp terry cloth rest on her tired eyes for a second.

"Thank you honey," she whispered weakly from under the washcloth. "That feels so good," she sighed.

"It's gotta be soon baby," Kenny whispered back, leaning over and kissing her wet hair. He stroked her hair back out of her face while he let the cool towel do it's magic on her tired brow.

"Oh man Ken, I've gotta to be close to ten centimeters by now," Carolyn moaned, weary of an approaching contraction.

"How many was I the last time she checked me?" she asked. Ken pulled a small spiral notebook out of his shirt pocket and read his notes.

"She said you were three centimeters about an hour and a half ago," he answered.

"THAT'S BULLSHIT!" Carolyn yelled as the next contraction started to ramp up.

"This kid is *soooo* late! Write this down Ken, he's gonna to do some *corner time* for this when he's old enough to sit in a chair!" Kenny stifled a giggle and looked over at the fetal monitor. As soon as he read the numbers he launched right into his coaching routine.

"OK baby, breathe with me now, quick little breaths, *he,he,he,he,he,he,...*" he said encouragingly.

Carolyn reached up and grabbed her husband's tie, yanking him down in a freakishly strong maneuver. Kenny gasped and suddenly found himself eye to eye with a crazy woman, actually startled him uncomfortably. Carolyn looked at him with a face she had never made before in his presence. A really maniacal, scary, Halloween face, like the one they had seen in The Exorcist!

"*I DON'T NEED TO BREATHE LIKE A CHIMPANZEE NUMBNUTS!* I just need someone to check me again. *I"VE GOTTA BE 10 CENTIMETERS BY NOW!*" she bellowed, screaming her way through the contraction. Kenny wiggled his way out of his wife's strangle hold and then immediately removed his tie. No way he was letting her have a chance at that move again, *fool me once*, right!

"The doctor said that she would be back in an hour, that's five minutes from now," Ken said, looking over at the larger clock on the wall, next to the television. Carolyn reached over and grabbed his hand, squeezing his fingers to the point of zero circulation.

"Just go out in the hall and get anyone in green scrubs to come in here and check me out!"

"OK, OK," Kenny replied, wrestling his fingers away from her. He walked out into the hall and motioned for a doctor standing next to the nurses station to come on over. The man pointed at himself, asking *who me*, with his expression. Ken nodded his head vigorously.

"Yeah, yeah, you, we need your help Doc," Kenny said to the guy as he walked over to him.

Ken put his arm around the doctor and pulled him into the room. Carolyn was doing her *he,he* breathing and looked up at the two of them relieved to be getting some attention. She kicked at the sheet covering her, trying to give the doctor some room to maneuver.

"Come on over here Doc, she's sure that she's 10 centimeters by now, can you check her out and then call for Dr. Racher so that we can get this show on the road. I'm afraid she's going to kill me if she has to go much longer!" Kenny pleaded. The man in the green scrubs waved his hand at Kenny and tried to move as far away from the bedside as possible. Kenny looked at him cross-eyed.

"What's your problem man, let's get this over with," he said, reaching over to pull on the man's arm.

"You know, your wife really will kill you Mr. Wong if you let the janitor perform her pelvic exam," said a calm voice from the doorway.

Kenny spun around and saw Carolyn's OB-GYN, Dr. Stephanie Racher standing behind him, leaning against the doorjamb with her arms folded. She pushed away from the doorway and walked into the room shaking her head and giggling.

"Wow, I've seen some noodle-headed father's to be before, but this one's a classic Ken. I may put you in my memoirs with this stunt. Ken looked at her sheepishly, and then turned to glare at the janitor.

"What?" the guy in the green scrubs asked.

"Go on, get outta here Douglas before you see something that will put you off women for at least a month," Dr. Racher teased. The poor man trotted past her and disappeared into the hall as she walked up to Carolyn. Her contraction had subsided by now, but she was weak and tired. This labor had turned out to be much harder than Sophie's, which both puzzled and irritated her. She had been told by every mother that she knew how subsequent births were always much easier.

"Oh Shannon was a piece of cake compared to my Ethan," Maggie Kelly had said at least a dozen times over the past couple of months. Carolyn made a mental note, poison Maggie Kelly's tea at new baby's Christening!

"OK young lady, let's see where we are," Dr. Racher said sweetly to Carolyn, snapping on her latex glove. She pulled up the sheet slightly and reached underneath to check her patient's cervix. She finished the exam in an instant and then pulled the sheet back down over Carolyn's legs.

"It's show time Carolyn, nice work," the doctor said to her.

"You too coach, nice job," she said over her shoulder to Kenny who was standing back by the fetal monitor.

"Uh, thanks," he replied.

"I'll send in the nurse to remove the monitor leads and then we'll wheel you into the delivery room," Dr. Racher said as she scribbled on Carolyn's chart, checking her watch with the clock on the wall.

"Oh thank God," Carolyn sighed.

"I'm going to get ready and call your pediatrician. We'll meet you two at the birthing table in few minutes, it'll be a piece of cake!" Dr. Racher said smiling at the two of them. As she walked out of the room Kenny went over to Carolyn's side and picked up her hand. It was clammy and sweaty, but he put it to his face anyway. He kissed each of her fingers and then let her rake her nails weakly across his scalp.

"My hero," she said softly.

"Are you ready for this Pop?" she asked him with a smile.

"Oh yeah baby, I'm way ready. Let's go meet this kid!" Ken said beaming back at his beautiful wife. Carolyn pulled her hand back and started to fuss with her hair.

"How do I look?" she asked, suddenly worried about her appearance. Kenny started to answer truthfully and then paused.

"You look like an angel sweetheart, *you look like an angel*," he answered, pushing back her sweat soaked hair.

"Alright Carolyn, I need you to be still for just a minute, whatever you do don't push until I ask you to, OK?" Dr. Racher asked from behind the sheets, only her covered head visible from between Carolyn's wide spread legs.

Kenny stood at his wife's side and held her hand, helping her to remain calm and follow the doctor's instructions. He remembered how wonderful he felt when Sophia was born, and he had thought that this time it would just be routine, no big deal. *Boy was he wrong about that!* Kenny found himself tearing up uncontrollably, totally enthralled with the beauty of the moment, of his wife, of his newborn child whom he hadn't even seen yet!

"Just a second longer Carolyn, I'm finishing up with the episiotomy now," the doctor said calmly.

"Hold her hand Kenny and keep her still, you'll be thanking me for this later," Dr. Racher said giggling. Ken grinned and winked at his wife, luckily she wasn't paying attention, or at least she gave no indication that she was.

"OK, are you ready to push now?" she asked rhetorically.

"Help her up Kenny. OK Carolyn, take a breath and give a nice long push, and stop when I say so," the doctor instructed. Ken put his hands under his wife's shoulders and helped her to rise up about a foot or so, making sure to get underneath her to support her effort. Carolyn took in a deep breath and then bore down as hard as she could, first grunting and then screaming as she intensified her effort.

"OK, OK hold it a second," Dr. Racher ordered. "The head has crowned and I want to get ready for the shoulders.

"OK Carolyn, give a little push so I can turn this baby just a tiny bit," she instructed. Kenny looked up at the mirror over the doctor's head and saw their child for the first time.

"Oh man, Oh man," he whispered to the room. The doctor maneuvered the baby's shoulders clockwise just a smidgen.

"OK Carolyn, big push honey," she said. Kenny helped her up again and Carolyn pushed for all she was worth.

"Arrrrggg, come outta there baby!" she yelled at the top of her lungs. Ken watched as Dr. Racher moved around behind the sheet, and then lean back with their child cradled in her waiting hands.

"It's a little girl," she announced loudly.

Carolyn rested her head against Kenny's shoulder and kissed his arm through his surgical gown. She was happy beyond words, tears rolling down her cheeks. She looked up and saw that Kenny had the same tears running down his own cheeks. Dr. Racher finished cutting the umbilical cord and handed the baby to an attending nurse, who carried the child over to be weighed, cleaned and wrapped in a soft receiving blanket on the warming table in the corner. The doctor busied herself with delivering the placenta and then broke the silent confusion in the room.

"Look what we have here," she said, getting everyone's attention with her raised voice. "Carolyn, give me a little push while I deliver the afterbirth," she asked routinely as she continued working. Carolyn leaned back on her elbows and pushed just a little bit.

"Hold it, just a second," the doctor ordered curtly. Kenny peeked over the sheet to get a better look at what was happening.

"What is it doctor?" he asked puzzled, and a little worried.

"Just a minute Dad," she replied.

"One more push Carolyn," the doctor ordered.

Carolyn closed her eyes and pushed, suddenly aware that there was something more than a little afterbirth going on.

"Here we go folks, looks like your daughter had a little company in there," Dr. Racher said as she delivered a second child. "Meet baby boy Wong everybody!" she announced.

"Oh my God!" Carolyn gasped. "How is that possible?" she exclaimed.

"You want the clinical version or the Reader's Digest version?" Dr. Racher asked playfully.

"I'll spare you the details for now. It happens sometimes, the twin is so close, one to the other, that they appear as a shadow in the ultrasounds. Other than that, its still an emerging technology, I'm sure in the future there will be fewer surprises. But if you ask me, that'll take all the fun out of it!" she explained gleefully.

"So, what do you think about that Dad, looks like you hit the jackpot!" Dr. Racher said happily. Kenny looked at Carolyn and then at the two children crammed side by side on the warming table.

"Yeah, what do you know?" Kenny replied weakly.

"*Twins! Oh my gosh Kenny*, Sophie is going to be so excited! And your parents are going to *FREAK OUT!*" Carolyn exclaimed joyfully. She took his hand and kissed it over, and over again.

"Thank you honey, *thank you, thank you, thank you!*" she said through happy tears.

Two nurses walked up to them and handed them each a baby to hold. "Here you go Mom and Dad," the nurses said in unison. Carolyn cradled the little pink bundle while Kenny held the blue one. Neither child made much noise but they both had made quite an impact. Dr. Racher finished working at Carolyn's feet and stood up to get a peek at the newborns.

"That's quite a blessing Mom and Dad," she said, touching the little boy's nose with her finger. Kenny looked at his wife and then at each child.

"You have no idea!" he said softly, silently thanking God for ALL of his children, ALL of his blessings...

Forty

(..."Old man take a look at my life, I'm a lot like you. I need someone to love me the whole night through" Neil Young...)

<u>*Fresno, California, March 1974*</u>

Raymond poured himself a cup of the complimentary coffee from the Farmer Brother's dispenser in the Holiday Inn lobby. He doctored the brew with four sugar packets and a healthy dose of the non-dairy creamer from the condiment table and then helped himself to one of the glazed donuts set out for the guests. This was an unexpected perk, a free breakfast and hot coffee to go with the free stay on the *hot* Master Card. He took the credit card out of his shirt pocket and read the name embossed on the shiny piece of plastic. *"Hector P. Delgado,"* he read softly to himself through a mouthful of half chewed donut. Raymond pushed back the wet crumbs trying to escape his mouth and took a quick sip of coffee to wash them down.

"Aiye, chinga tu madre!" he exclaimed, burning his tongue with the hot drink.

He set the cup down quickly and picked up a handful of napkins to wipe up the little spill from his chin, looking around to make sure that nobody was watching him. Raymond knew better than to call attention to himself. Especially since he and Smiley weren't exactly typical examples of the sort of clientele the hotel was used to serving. The last thing they needed was some

466

nosey desk clerk calling the local Sheriff out to come look things over. He made sure to clean off the counter and the floor where he had spilled a little of the coffee, smiling back at the front desk in case anyone was looking. The desk clerk gave no indication that he had noticed anything; apparently busy helping an elderly couple to check in or out. Raymond tossed the wad of wet napkins into the wastebasket next to the table and then turned to walk out of the lobby.

He stopped suddenly and walked leisurely back to the table and helped himself to a couple more donuts to take back to Smiley. He put one in his mouth and two in his free hand and then exited the lobby without further incident. Raymond squinted as he came out into the bright morning sunlight and turned right to follow the concrete pathway past the pool to room number 122. It was early enough that there weren't too many people scurrying about. Besides which it was Saturday so the place was filled with late sleeping vacationers instead of early rising businessmen. That fit right in with their plans, as he and Smiley wanted to get an early start on running down Miguel. They had traced him to Fresno through a second cousin of Smilely's, and they were pretty sure where he might be holed up. After all, the kid had only one blood relative that he could turn to, so they shouldn't have to look very long for the little bastard. Raymond walked up to the door of their room and kicked at it with the toe of his boot. He could hear Smilely yelling from the other side, he was pretty sure it wasn't welcome back, thanks for the food. The door flew open and Smiley stood there barefoot and shirtless in his half buttoned Levi's.

"What cabrone?" he said, sneering up at Raymond as he held the door open.

"Its 6am Holmes, what's with you man?" Smiley complained as he walked to his bed and flopped back down onto it.

Raymond turned and closed the door with his foot, and then walked over to his own unmade bed and sat on the edge. He set the extra donuts and his coffee on the table separating the two double beds and stuffed the rest of the donut he was gnawing on into his mouth, choking it down in a couple swallows. He gagged a bit and then cleared his airway with a healthy gulp of his drink. Spinning quickly onto the bed, he leaned back against the wall and raised a pillow to place behind his head.

"Early bird gets the worm *ese*," he said to his half-awake partner in crime.

"He ain't goin anywhere homey, twenty more minutes *OK,"* Smiley whined, rolling onto his back and throwing a pillow at Raymond. The soft projectile bounced off the wall over Raymond's head and landed harmlessly on the floor beside the bed.

"Yeah, OK lazy, but I'm going to eat your donuts," he replied, leaning over and spearing the two pastries through the center holes with his finger.

"More for me," he added, taking a bite from each.

"Choke on them vato," Smiley replied, flipping onto his side and burrowing his face into his short stack of soft pillows. Raymond burped back an inaudible reply and turned on the television with the remote as Smiley started to snore softly, already back to sleep.

Fresno, California, March 1974
<u>St. John's Cathedral</u>

Father Willet placed his foot on the upholstered stool at the end of his bed and finished tying his shoes. Pushing himself upright with a grunt, he smoothed out his jacket and ran his hand over his collar before turning to walk out of his room. The priest grabbed the manila folder on the nightstand as he walked past and headed out into the hall of the rectory and started making his way toward his office. He was up much earlier than usual for a Saturday, it was well before dawn, and he had not slept well at all. After a couple of hours tossing and turning he decided that perhaps the issue contained in the folder would be better addressed over a hot cup of tea and some deep thought.

Father Willet held the folder close to his chest as he quick marched the twenty or so yards to his office. He walked through the open door and closed it behind him after flipping the switch for the lights. He walked over to his desk and set the folder down, then rummaged through the right top drawer for his variety box of teabags. Finding it straight away he shuffled through the contents of multi colored choices and selected the blue and silver package, it seemed like an Earl Grey morning to him. Father Willet returned the box and closed the drawer and then walked over to the small table in the corner where his electric teakettle rested and switched it on. It was already filled with water, as it was his habit to do so before he left the office each day. The small red light at the bottom of the kettle came on as he removed the teabag from its wrapping and lay it into the thick white ceramic mug next to it. He turned the mug slightly, admiring the black and orange emblem of the San Francisco Giants, his third favorite passion next to God and Sister Ruth's home cooking, and then walked back to sit at his desk while he waited for the kettle to whistle. Father Willet sat back in his chair; his arms folded in front of him, and yawned deeply, letting out a little sigh as it subsided. He let his eyes survey the room, his inner sanctum, the place in which he had spent thousands of hours over the years, writing sermons, studying scripture, counseling parishioners, laughing, smiling, and crying with them.

He loved this place. It was so full of memories, richly thick with them. And he imagined that if he sat very still he could hear each one of them again, all of the happy and sad conversations, all of his own private thoughts and reflections, each replayed in the stillness of this early morning. Then his eyes fell upon the folder in the center of his desk and the euphoria of the moment faded. His eyes narrowed as he concentrated on the thin, plain manila folder, his expression telegraphing his concern over what it contained. He leaned forward and started to reach for it when the teakettle began to whistle, softly at first, but changing quickly to a shrill scream. Startled, the priest rose quickly and trotted over to the screaming teakettle and switched it off. The loud noise ceased and then ebbed into no sound at all, almost as quickly as it had started.

He detached the plug from the back of the teapot, and then poured the hot water carefully into the big white mug, making sure to keep a finger firmly placed on the lid. That was a mistake you only make once, he thought to himself. Water sizzled and spat as it came out the cooler end of the teakettle and the steam rose and swirled as he filled the thick ceramic mug. He could smell the tea already brewing as he topped off the mug and set the kettle down. And after dunking the teabag several times and adding a little cream, because after all, tea without milk is just uncivilized, he returned to his desk, blowing softly across the top of the mug as he walked slowly and carefully. Taking his seat, Father Willet blew on the hot tea once more and then took a timid sip.

"*Owww, hot, hot, hot*" he said aloud to himself, setting down the mug quickly onto the desktop and wiping a little dribble from his mouth with a handkerchief.

"My word, when will I ever learn," he said, scolding himself.

He reached over and picked up the folder, and opened it. Inside was the single page that had caused so much consternation over the last twenty-four hours. He stared at the paper with the letterhead of the Archdiocese and handwritten words. It was not as if this message was unexpected, on the contrary, he had been anticipating its arrival. But, it was a message that was completely undesired, one that he had been praying they would all be spared. He had known the instant that His Eminence had expressed an interest in the Lopez girl that no good would come of it. Father Villa Cruz was a patient man as adversaries went.

He was the sort of man that should not be easily dismissed, as just another opportunist or meddler where the child and her gift were concerned. A man of grand plans and desires, and more to the point, a man with the means and the wherewithal to accomplish them, no matter whom might suffer in the process. Tina Lopez could prove to be the means to his desired end, and Father Willet knew that Villa Cruz would summon all his power and influence to conscript her support of his goals. Reaching into his jacket he retrieved his spectacles and put them on, drawing the letter closer to him as he read the short note one more time...

William,

I have returned from the Holy City only yesterday, and I wanted to send you a personal note to explain the decision of the Council of Cardinals. Praise to God, I was finally able to convince them of the overwhelming evidence that the power of the Holy Spirit was working through this precious child. The same child that you and your circle of friends have kept hid from the world for so long. I want you to know that the Council and I bear you now ill will. We understand that you and your friends were acting in the child's best interests as you saw them. Trying to protect her from the clamor that would surely befall such occurrences. That being said, and now that the world has been introduced to her, it is the decision of the Council that the Church should control future exhibits of her Holy gift, before your American television turns a divine intervention into a circus.

In addition, the Council believes that the Church would better serve the well being of the child herself as well. It is the thinking of the Council that she would be safest within the walls of the Holy City. And it is also the thinking of the Council that she could be a great instrument of peace with the guidance of the Church and His Holiness, the Pontiff. As you can see William, this matter has expanded well beyond your ability to manage. I have been instructed to take the matter in hand personally. And as a first step, I would like you to approach the parents of the child and explain our intentions. As good Catholics I am certain that you will be able to convince them that we act only in the best interests of the child, on behalf of a just God. Arrange for a meeting between us by month's end, I trust that you will have acquired the necessary cooperation from all concerned by then.

Go with God,
P. Villa Cruz
p.s.
I forgive you you're little vice of gluttony, in your shoes I might have taken the same opportunity to shanghai Sister Demarco...(did you really think such piracy would go un-noticed?)...

Father Willet let the folder fall into his lap as he removed his glasses and rubbed his tired eyes. With his pinky finger he removed a little crust from the corner of his eye and then reached over to pick up his tea mug. Raising it to his mouth, he took a long sip, swallowing a fair amount of the still warm liquid. He stopped for a moment to catch his breath and then he drained the remainder of the mug, setting it back down roughly and pushing it toward the edge of the desk, out of his way. He exhaled deeply, opened the top left desk drawer and pulled out a yellow legal pad. Setting the pad of paper in front of him, he extracted a ballpoint pen from the center drawer, removed the cap and reattached it to the top of the black Bic pen. He let the cap rest against his chin as he gathered his thoughts for a moment.

When he was ready, he picked his glasses up from the desktop and replaced them onto his face, then hunkered down and began writing. Father Willet was determined to keep the Lopez girl from becoming a pawn in the hands of a man whom he was certain meant her more harm than good. And now there was precious little time to think of some way to keep her from landing in the net that Villa Cruz was casting. He tapped the legal pad with the tip of the pen as he wrestled with what to write down first. Presently, in large print he wrote...

This cannot happen...but how?

One: *Gather the team, everyone...but where, we're sure to be watched now?*
Where? Where? Where?...The Donnelly's Anniversary party on Saturday?... perfect!
Two: *Need a decoy to throw off the hounds...Perhaps we can send Father Kelly to grant absolution for the Hernandez girl, maybe send that newswoman, what's her name...KC, she can interview the poor retch or something... they could even take the Lopez girl along with them, that should draw attention away from the meeting... no, wait, that won't do, they're all expected at the Donnelly party as well, Villa Cruz will already know about that...Of course, they could always arrive fashionably late, I'm sure that between Grover and Sheriff Cardwell we could arrange for a small delay.*
Three: *Whatever we come up with, it has to be convincing, Villa Cruz has too many resources to hide her for very long...what, what, what...I'm stumped, this one will have to be a group effort...although something tells me that wily old sinner Gateway will have a trick or two up his sleeve...*
Father Willet smiled as he finished writing and set his pen down. He read over his brief notes and then tore the single page from the legal pad and placed it in the manila folder with the letter from Father Villa Cruz. He leaned

back in his chair and turned his head to look out the window. The darkness was fading as the morning sun slowly rose on the horizon. He rested his head against the back of the large, soft leather chair, suddenly aware of how comfortable that old piece of furniture was. His eyes began to droop and he drifted off to sleep his mind finally at ease. He had a plan now, not a great or sure one yet, but one to dream on never the less. After all, only God knows what tomorrow will bring, and He is always on the side of the righteous, isn't He?

<u>San Francisco, California, March 1974</u>

"SHUT UP JAY," KC shouted from across the table, attracting the attention of the headwaiter and most of the patrons in the busy restaurant.

"Cool it Kathy or you'll get us tossed," Jay hissed back at her through clenched teeth.

"You may not care what people think about you, but this is my town and I have a certain rep around this neighborhood," he whispered harshly to his guest of honor. KC rolled her eyes and drained the last of her wine. She held the empty glass in her hand limply and waited for Jay to take the hint and fill it from the bottle in front of him.

"Oh that's right, where are my manners," Jay said sarcastically.

"Let me just poor a little more gasoline onto the fire," he added, picking up the bottle and pouring the contents into her empty glass. KC stuck her tongue out at him and then took a long sip after he finished pouring.

"Look, I was only teasing, you big baby," Jay said defending himself.

"How was I to know that was a tender issue with anyway? I was joking, OK?" Jay said pleading his case.

There was a long silence between the two of them while KC sipped on her wine and Jay watched her closely for any sign of further retaliation. Finally, he picked up his own glass and reached across the table with it for a truce toast. KC's scowl turned into a smirk and she did likewise, their wineglasses clinking together in the center of the table, right over the serving plate of linguini and clams.

"Forgive me?" Jay asked sincerely as he set his glass down.

"You're forgiven," KC replied softly, setting her glass down as well.

"So what's the big deal? First you blow me off for a month on this celebration dinner for your Pulitzer, and then you jump down my throat for an innocent poke at the wonder geek, Father what's his name!" Jay said, suddenly feeling agitated himself.

"I know, I know, I'm sorry," KC began.

"It's just that after Brian and I confronted Grover about the Katz thing, I went a little nuts. First of all, I was shocked to discover that I had been right, and then was doubly shocked to discover that I was actually OK with what he and his pals had done, does that make sense?" she asked.

"No"

"I suppose not, I guess you had to be there," she added.

"But it's why we're going back to that loony farm to interview the Hernandez chick again, isn't it?" Jay asked tiredly.

"Yeah, sort of. I told old man Gateway that I wanted to see for myself, that it was my right to set things right, ya know what I mean?" KC said, speaking more to herself than to Jay.

"Not really KC. Are you saying that you're going to tell this nutcase that she didn't actually poison that A-hole Katz?" Jay said, answering her question with a question.

"No, of course not. I just want to look into her eyes and see if their plan worked. I want to see if the demon is dead and her heart, mind, and soul are free," KC replied.

"You're nuttier than she is Katherine Littleton, but I still love ya babe," Jay said, raising his glass in a mock toast and draining his own glass.

"Gee, thanks," KC muttered, half smiling.

"So, is that why you want to bring Father bright eyes along with us?" Jay asked, teasing her again. KC glared at him for a second and Jay braced himself for another outburst.

"*No smart ass.* It was Grover's idea that we take him along. He said that Father Willet from St. John's in Fresno thought that it would be good for Rosa to receive absolution. That it might help with her recovery and get her home to her child sooner," KC explained.

"And stop calling him those stupid names, be a grown up OK!" KC snapped.

"Yes boss!" Jay replied, snickering as he poured himself some more wine.

"He has a name you know. It's Ethan, *Father Ethan Kelly*, think you can remember that," KC said flippantly, sipping on her wine while she pushed her food around the plate with her fork.

"Of course it is," Jay replied, pointing at his temple with his index finger.

"*There*, it's in the vault now," he added sarcastically.

KC scrunched up her face at him, making an expression like she just bit into a lemon, and then held out her glass for a refill. Jay poured what was left in the bottle, just a swallow, and then dropped the empty bottle back into the ice bucket.

"See that, time flies when you're having fun," he quipped.

"GARCON!" he called out to the waiter passing nearest them.

"Yes sir?"

"Another bottle of your finest Chianti my good man," Jay requested flamboyantly.

"Very good sir," the waiter replied stiffly.

"Yes, I am very good," Jay said teasing the man, and playing to KC and the room.

"Bravo Jay, always keep them guessing, right," KC said applauding his performance.

"Especially in this town, it guarantees you great service every time!" Jay said, giggling into his wineglass.

"Is that why you never bring any of your girlfriends along with us?" KC queried.

"Honey, when we go out you *are* my girlfriend, don't you know that!" Jay said with mock surprise.

"I swear Jay, no wonder everybody always thinks you're gay when they first meet you," KC said.

"Say what you will, but it keeps me from getting tire chains at secret Santa time every year!" he replied.

"Touché," KC said, raising her glass to toast his flawless logic.

"Merci mademoiselle," he replied.

KC and Jay laughed loudly together as the waiter opened a new bottle of wine, filling each of their glasses in the process. They drank and ate in silence for a few moments, enjoying the latest truce of the evening. Nights out together were never dull, the two of them more like sibling wolf cubs, biting and snapping at one another in mock combat, rough play always followed by long rests. After a while they sat silently, looking around the room as they sipped their wine, and waited for the waiter to bring the desert and coffee.

"So how long have you been in love with this priest?" Jay asked, staring at his friend through the glow of the candlelight. KC sat very still for a moment, careful not to make eye contact with him until she was ready to answer, if she would answer at all, she hadn't made her mind up yet.

"Well?" Jay pressed gently.

KC set her glass down and leaned forward onto her elbows, letting her chin rest on the knuckles of her laced together fingers. She raised her eyes slowly and looked back at her friend sitting across from her. She could see the dancing flames of the candles reflected in his dark brown eyes.

"I don't know really. I just woke up one day and there he was, tucked snuggly away in the center of my heart," KC said softly.

"Just like that?" Jay asked.

"Yeah, just like that," she replied.

"That's not like you," Jay said.

"I know, it's weird, huh. I mean I've always made friends easy enough, but never like this. You know me, I don't trust my heart to many, and I rarely use the '*L*' word, except with my folks, and you of course, but you're the brother I never had," KC said, trying to provide an explanation that made sense to both of them.

"What about Jordan?" Jay asked.

KC had to think about that for a minute. That was the last time she had ever said those three words to anyone other than family, Jay included of course. It was also the last time she had her heart stepped on by someone. She was over it now, the whole thing was more her fault than his. She had set herself up for that little heartache with her anxious heart, looking for something that was never there. Afterward she had subconsciously set out to protect herself from that awful feeling by launching herself into her work and one meaningless dalliance after another. Hey, if it was good enough for guys like Jordan Chen, it was good enough for her, right? KC looked up from the tablecloth and caught Jay's gaze again.

"I thought I was in love with Jordan once. Turns out I was only in love with the idea of being in love," she explained.

"Doesn't mean that it hurt any less though, " she added.

"Does this guy, *I'm sorry, Ethan*, know how you feel?" Jay asked.

"OH GOD NO!" KC exclaimed.

"You think I'm going to steal one of God's fellas, *I don't think so!*" she proclaimed firmly. Jay couldn't help but laugh at the absurdity of her remark, and she was suddenly embarrassed by the attention they were getting from the nearby tables.

"Can you keep it down to a dull roar Jay, you're starting to bother the neighbors," KC pleaded under her breath.

"I'm sorry KC," Jay said catching his breath.

"One of God's *fellas*, that was a good one honey!" he said, wiping a tear from the corner of his eye.

"Well, what would you call them?" she protested.

"I call them priests. But you know what, they're human too Kathy, just like you and me. And they're subject to the same feelings life offers up whenever men and women are brought together by circumstance, fate, or whatever!"

"I think you should tell the guy how you feel. I think that you owe it to the both of you. Let's face it, he has to suspect something KC, you know you can't keep a secret to save your life!" Jay said teasing his friend.

"Ya think?" she asked meekly.

"*Yeah, I think!* Boy howdy KC, for someone so smart you are so dumb sometimes!" Jay said waving his hand at her and draining his wineglass.

"What if he thinks I'm crazy," she worried out loud.

"What if my grandmother had wheels, she'd be a trolley car!" Jay snapped. KC looked at him cross-eyed, "What the hell is that supposed to mean?" she shouted.

"EXACTLY!" Jay shouted back.

KC was about to fire back another syllable salvo when the waiter arrived with their coffee and Tiramisu. They sat patiently in silence while he served the dessert and poured the coffee and then thanked him as he left their table. KC stirred a little cream into her cup along with a packet of sugar and then took a sip of the hot coffee.

"Take a chance Kathy. If he's in your heart like you say, *maybe you're in his?*" Jay said softly.

"Ya think?" KC asked in a soft tone as well.

"Yeah, I think," he replied.

"Thanks Jay, I love you ya know," she said smiling at him.

"Yeah I know, I love you too crazy woman," Jay replied, returning the smile.

"And hey, from now on write Dear Abby for advice of the heart, like everybody else, OK?"

"OK," KC answered with a giggle and a sniffle, "I promise."

"Alright then, my work is done here," Jay said triumphantly. "Now let's finish getting sloshed!

Fresno, California, March 1974

He had seen the car coming from the highway, the long cloud of dust trailing behind it as it made its way toward the small single room trailer where he had been staying since his arrival home. Miguel knew that whoever it was, he had better make himself scarce. It wouldn't take long for anyone to notice that something was amiss, the stench emanating from the ditch where he left his Uncle in a shallow grave of soft dirt and sand could be overpowering when the wind blew in the right direction. Miguel slid open the only window at the far end of the trailer, it faced due north, away from the approaching vehicle. Jumping down onto the hard dry surface he scurried off into the tall weeds that surrounded the trailer. Beyond the weeds were several acres of hay and Sudan grass in which he could hide or make a hasty undetected retreat. He waded in only a few feet and turned back toward the trailer, laying face down on his belly, he cut out a little window in the weeds to peer through.

He had a good line of site and was close enough that he could hear anyone speak in a normal tone of voice, as long as the wind didn't blow too hard.

Miguel watched the dust cloud grow close enough to envelope the trailer. He listened to the wheels slide on the dirt as the car came to an abrupt stop, spraying tiny rocks and clods in his direction. He lowered his head to let the dirt cloud pass over him, keeping his eyes and nose clear of any of the choking debris. Miguel heard the distinct sound of two doors slamming shut and from his vantage point at ground level. He could make out two sets of boots walking around between the car and the trailer.

"HELLO THE HOUSE," a man's voice called out. Miguel listened as someone banged on the aluminum side of the small trailer.

"ANYONE IN THERE?" the man's voice called out again.

Miguel hunkered down and made himself smaller as he watched someone come around the trailer to window that he had just climbed out of. He watched as a small man stood on tiptoe to peek into the open window, his head disappearing into the trailer. Miguel held his breath as the man suddenly jumped down and turned to look his way. The small man took a couple steps toward Miguel's hiding place and then stopped when a loud shout came from the other side of the trailer.

"LET"S GO BILLY, THERE'S NOBODY HERE!" The small man took another step forward before turning back to heed his companion's calling.

"I'M COMING," he hollered back, trotting off toward the trailer. The small man looked back over his shoulder as he jogged.

"HEY RALPH, DO YOU SMELL ANYTHING WEIRD, LIKE OLD GARBAGE?" he yelled as he disappeared around the back of the trailer.

Miguel strained his ears trying to pick up the conversation occurring on just the other side of the trailer, but the wind had shifted and was blowing his way now, drowning out anything that may have been audible otherwise. He heard the engine start and when he was able to look up again he watched the same dust cloud running away from his Uncle's trailer. Miguel put his head down and rested his head on his sleeve for fifteen or twenty minutes, deciding to give his unexpected visitors plenty of time to leave the area. He was weary that they may have stopped up the road to watch the trailer for signs of him after they were out of eyesight.

The boy dozed quietly, taking a little catnap while he waited out his paranoia. He was startled awake by a lizard crawling swiftly over the back of his hands. He rose up and sneezed out the dirt that had accumulated in his nostrils while he slept, then wiped his nose on his shirtsleeve. Miguel got to his knees and started to stand when he saw him. He flattened back out onto his belly and held his breath. The wind had picked up considerably and it must have blocked out the noise of the second car, but there it was, parked behind the trailer on the shady side. And standing three feet to his left was Smiley, cooling taking a leak into the billowing weeds, the splatter of his warm urine spraying onto Miguel's hands and face. Miguel turned his head slowly to reduce his exposure and exhaled quietly, drawing in a slow breath and holding it again. He heard Smiley sigh with relief and then zip up and turn to leave.

"Raymond, let's go man, the little shit ain't here," Smiley called to his friend. Smiley stopped by the car and lit up a cigarette.

"HEY, RAYMOND, come on, it's getting hot out here *ese!*" he hollered into the wind. Miguel turned his head back and took in a deep breath, then scooted over to get a better view of where Smiley was standing. He watched him smoke his cigarette and look around, trying to get an idea of where Raymond had wandered off to.

"YO!" he yelled at the top of his lungs.

"YO SMILELY, OVER HERE MAN, I FOUND SOMETHING YOU AIN'T GONNA BELIEVE HOMEBOY!" came Raymond's excited reply.

Smilely took a long drag on his smoke and then tossed in the dirt, crushing it with his boot as he trotted off in the general direction of Raymond's voice. Raymond appeared out of the tall weeds north of the trailer and motioned for Smiley to follow him. Miguel didn't need to investigate, he knew what they had found, and he knew that his stay here was now over. Suddenly he realized that he had an option, a dangerous one, but an option nonetheless. He reached behind his back and gently felt for the object stuffed into his pants under his shirttail. Miguel let his fingers run over the smooth handle of Smiley's .357 magnum and for a second he actually considered pulling it out. It would be easy to sneak over to the car while the two of them were busy discovering his Uncle's body. He could take care of this worrisome pair right here and right now, instead of spending the next few days dodging them on the streets.

Miguel rolled the idea over and over in his mind, enjoying the thought of giving that big shot Smiley what he had been asking for, what he deserved. He didn't especially want to kill Raymond, he had actually been kind to him from the beginning. But if he did one he would have to do the other, it was a package deal. Miguel's fingers began to encircle the pistol grip and he felt his hand begin to take hold of the weapon. He had nearly convinced himself that this was the only way to deal with this new development, when he was startled out of his deep thinking by the stinging sensation of a bead of sweat dripping into the corner of his eye. He squeezed his eyes shut and rubbed at them vigorously, drying them with his knuckles, removing thick bits of dirt from them at the same time. As he regained his composure he looked up and saw the two men coming out of the weeds. They were holding their noses and laughing hysterically. As they came closer to the car he picked up on their conversation.

"You see, I told you he was here homey," Smiley said as he walked over to the passenger side of the car and opened the door. Raymond opened the door on the driver's side and the two of them stood talking over the roof of the car.

"Yeah you did *ese*, guess we owe your cousin a beer Holmes," Raymond replied.

"Did you see what that little shit **did** to this old dude! That is one sick little bastard *ese!*"

"The sooner we find him and kill him, the better I'm gonna sleep at night," Smiley said shuddering as he climbed back into the car.

Raymond just nodded his head and climbed into the driver's seat after him. Miguel watched as the two of them continued to talk for a moment, unable to hear what they were saying through the rolled up windows. He reached back and felt for the gun again, he still had an opportunity to end it all here. His heart began to race and he felt the beads of sweat appearing on his forehead. Miguel licked his lips and pulled the gun from its hiding place and placed it up by his head. He rose up on his elbows and pulled the hammer back until it locked a second time and flipped the safety into the off position. He heard the engine start and he got up onto his knees, his head just below the tops of the tall weeds.

He was sweating profusely now, and he felt like a lion waiting for the most opportune time to spring on his prey. He heard the car shift into gear and watched as it began to roll forward slowly. He could see the two men laughing inside of the car and he knew that they had no idea that he was just a few feet from them, that they were within seconds of the end of their lives. As the car turned slowly to the right, closing the gap between them, he saw Smiley's profile pass by him. For an instant he started to spring to action, and then in the next instant, he felt himself sit back down on his heels, and he watched as the car pulled away, gaining speed as it disappeared in a cloud of dust.

Miguel exhaled deeply and placed his thumb on the hammer of the weapon. He pulled on the trigger and let the hammer fall softly and safely into place, then set the pistol down in his lap. He raised his arm and wiped the sweat away from his face with his shirtsleeve, then stood to watch the car disappear in the distance. He could have done it, he thought, *he should have done it!* But there were just five bullets left in the gun, and he had plans for each one of them. For now, he would just have to be more careful, stay in the more shadows. He had a job to do after all, a promise to keep, *to himself.*

Forty-one

(..."The Lord protects the simple hearted; when I was
in great need, he saved me" Psalm 116:6...)

Fresno, California, March 1974
St. John's Cathedral

My eyes snapped open wide as my ears and brain were suddenly assaulted by the blood-curdling scream of The Who's Roger Daltry, as he wailed from the clock radio *"we won't get fooled again!"* Flipping myself 90 degrees like a pancake, *my patented Aunt Jemima move*, I reached over and swatted the snooze button on the noisy appliance next to my small twin bed. After I had squeezed my eyes tightly shut and rubbed the gunk out of the corners of them, I checked the time on the digital clock that was setting so innocently on the nightstand. It read 7am in large red characters, formed by a series of neatly arranged bright red dots. I rolled lazily in the opposite direction to face the wall and looked out of the small window in the corner of my little room. Through the sheer curtains I could feel the new morning sun, warm against my face as it advanced across the hardwood floor toward me. If I concentrated hard enough, I could actually see the top of the alfalfa in the field across the street, blowing this way and that in the cool morning breeze.

I've always liked watching the wind blow, the way it made the tree tops dance and sway, silently showing everyone the awesome power of Mother

Nature. Da used to tell Shannon and I when we were small that the wind always came while God was napping, and that he used the Earth as a pillow when he slept. I smiled at that warm memory and then rolled back onto my back and stared up at the bumps and shadows on the acoustic ceiling. Clenching my fists tightly, I slowly extended my extremities in a *big boy stretch*, the usual start of my morning rituals. Sitting up slowly I turned and swung my legs out over the edge of my little bed.

"Rise and shine porcupine," I said aloud to myself, and to whatever fairies happened to be in the room as well.

Another one of Da's wee exaggerations, *"good little fairies look after good little children, you be remembering that sonny…"* With that thought dancing in my head, I jumped up to greet the new day. When my bare feet hit the cold hard wood floor I let out a small yelp and then dashed over to the chair next to the nightstand to hurriedly slip on my soft warm slippers. I reached over and retrieved my bathrobe that was draped across the back of the heavy wooden chair and put it on quickly, shivering as I did so.

The budget at St. John's was modest to say the least, so full time heating was a luxury that we had to sacrifice during the fall and winter months. Actually I had been a bit surprised by how cold it could get here in sunny California. The bright sunshine through the window could be deceiving when compared to the frigid morning air. While I slowly jogged in place, trying to hasten a rise in body temperature, I fumbled with the soft tie of my blue plaid cotton bathrobe. Suddenly the telephone rang, startling me but good, given the hour of the day. I was pretty sure that it was a call from home since the small number of people that I knew in California, were either asleep or in the shower at this time of the morning. Picking up the receiver on the second ring I answered the telephone.

"Hello Mother," I said, assuming that only she would be so totally unconscious of the different time zones. I waited, but there was not an immediate response.

"Hello, Mom, *is that you?*" I asked impatiently, I still had to pee after all. Still no answer just a faint giggle in the distance.

"Come on! Who is this?" I asked again, a little annoyed by now. I sat back down on the bed to help curtail the urge to relieve myself.

"You know me…I'm me, Sophie, Uncle Ethan," answered a familiar little voice.

"Sophia Wong, *you little bug*, what are you doing on this telephone?" I asked, half-expecting Ken or Carolyn to jump on the line before she could answer.

"I miss you," she replied sweetly.

"I miss you too sweetie. Where are mummy and daddy?" I asked in a gentle voice.

I smiled to myself as I said the word *mummy*. Being more of a Mom and Dad kind of guy, *mummy* just sort of tickled me whenever I said it out loud. Actually, terms of endearment always caught my attention. It just never ceased to amaze me, the infinite number of ways people managed to skew a language to suit their own unique personalities. I shuddered and shook off the short mental detour and listened closely for Sophie to answer my question.

"Daddy's at work and Mummy is feeding the babies," she answered.

"OK," I replied.

"And she won't let me help!" Sophie whined. I could just picture her pouting little face in my mind.

"I see," I replied slowly, trying to get a sense of where this conversation was going, and why.

"Sweetheart, you can help mummy with other things, OK?" I said, trying to sound supportive.

"But I have boobies too!" she said emphatically.

I heard the phone drop to the floor and knew instantly that she was probably busy taking off her shirt to prove it. Straining to hear what was going on; I thought that I could make out Carolyn's faint voice in the background. She was yelling something, but I could make out the words. She must have been asking Sophie what she was doing because I heard Sophie shout back, "I showing Uncle Ethan my boobies mommy!"

"OH SWELL!" I said aloud to my room.

Before I could say another word, I heard a bit of commotion as Carolyn's voice came through the receiver and into my ear. I listened as she argued with her four year old daughter, "Let go darn it!" she snapped. Suddenly she was on the line with me, *"Hello?"* she said as if puzzled at who was on the other end.

"Hi Carolyn," I said cheerfully.

"Ethan? I didn't even hear the phone ring," she replied, surprise in her tone of voice.

"'Tis me, the one and only!" I said with a smile.

"Oh, and by the way, you called me," I added.

"What on earth?" Carolyn replied.

"SOPHIA ROSE WONG!" she bellowed loud enough to set my ear ringing. Obviously Sophie had made herself scarce, probably hiding under Ken's robe that usually hung on the wall behind the bathroom door.

"Don't be mad at her Carolyn, it's only a phone call. Heck, I didn't even know she could read!" I said, teasing Carolyn in Sophie's defense.

"What are you talking about Ethan?" Carolyn asked sounding totally flustered.

"When you snapped at her to let go. I heard you on taking the phone from her," I replied.

Carolyn laughed out loud, "I wasn't talking to Sophie you doofus! I was talking to the child with the death suck grip on my poor nipple!" Carolyn said, giggling uncontrollably as she explained the situation. She must have felt me blushing through the telephone line.

"It's OK Ethan, its just a part of life Father Kelly," she said, her giggling turning into a raucous laughing jag at my expense. I waited for her to calm a bit before replying.

"Yeah, well..." I said, starting my response, when Carolyn cut me off to further torment me.

"And why is my child standing in this kitchen stark naked trying to show her Uncle Ethan, *the priest*, her boobies?" Carolyn teased in mock astonishment. It was suddenly very warm in my cold little room.

"Carolyn, honestly, I have no clue what..."

"Relax Ethan, I think I get the picture. Sophie wants to help me do everything with these two. Bath time, diaper time, giggle time, and feeding time. It's really cute, but indulging her just adds hours to all of these chores. Oh, you would just have to be here to understand. I would explain better if I weren't so darn tired!" she said, giving me the short version of what I suspected was a long story.

"I think I get the picture," I said.

"Do you really," she asked sarcastically.

"No," I answered honestly.

"That's what I thought. Shame on you Father Kelly! That'll be five Our Father's and ten Hail Mary's," she replied, giving me the business.

"So, what was it you called about?" she asked. I could hear the baby or babies fussing in the background.

"I told you, I didn't call you, you called me, remember?" I whined.

"I did not either call you!" she snapped.

"Wait, oh yeah...SOPHIA!" Carolyn bellowed on the other end.

"I told you she was smart," I said proudly to the air as I had heard Carolyn set the phone down on the kitchen counter on her end.

"Carolyn...CAROLYN," I shouted into the phone from my end. I could hear her talking to my clever little godchild.

"Sophie, did you call your Uncle Ethan all by yourself?" she asked.

There was a short pause as Sophie answered. I couldn't hear the little girl's side of the conversation. After a moment Carolyn came back on the line, "I'm so sorry Ethan. I had no idea she was capable of a stunt like this," Carolyn said apologetically. I could hear Sophie whining in the background.

"Just a minute baby, mommy's talking to Uncle Ethan. You can have a turn next, OK?" Carolyn said, consoling her daughter.

"Honestly Ethan, this girl has been so hyper, ever since, you know, the incident," she said, turning her attention back to me now.

"Like what?" I asked confused.

"Oh I don't know, lots of little things I guess. But you what the most disturbing one is?" she answered and asked.

"No, what?"

"OK, but if I tell you, you have to swear that you won't say anything to Kenny," she said to me in a very soft voice, like she was afraid of being overheard by someone. But by who, Ken was at work and she was home alone with the kids?

"Why not, what's with all the drama?" I replied, unable to mask the growing concern on my face or in my own voice.

"Come on Ethan, just be on *my* side this once, trust me OK. Kenny already thinks I'm positively paranoid about this, and I don't want to end up back in counseling. I just want to put all the crap of the past year behind us. Sophie is back with us only by the grace of God, and she has a brother and sister now as well. I don't want anything weird happening to change any of that, you know what I mean?" she said pleading with me.

I really didn't understand what she was trying to say, but I truly believed she was sincere in her concern, so I opened my heart to listen to hers.

"Alright, alright, don't get your knickers in a bunch, what's the big mystery?"

Carolyn was silent for a second and then, "Ethan, as God is my witness, I swear I don't think that this child has slept a wink since you brought her home," whispered Carolyn into my ear from three thousand miles away. I pictured her looking down at Sophie as she spoke, making sure that she wasn't listening in. What a strange thought, how would she know that, how could she?

"Did you hear what I said?" she asked, pressing me a little.

"Yeah I heard I just don't know how to respond Carolyn. I mean, what exactly makes you think such a thing anyway? It's not like you've sat up and watched her night after night, have you?" I asked sheepishly.

"Of course not! But let me tell you something, she is up before Kenny each and every morning."

"She's up every time I get up to feed to twins, and when I check on her before I go to bed, she's never asleep. She's just lying there in her bed singing the same song, night after night, it's creeping me out Ethan!" Carolyn said, trying to give me the big picture from her perspective.

"What song?" I asked

"That dumb song you and Paul used to sing to her, what was it now? Oh, I remember, *'little bunny foo foo hoppin through the forest, scoopin up the field mice and boppin em on the head '*...blah, blah, blah..." Carolyn answered.

"And another thing, she has this imaginary friend she talks to all the time now as well, she calls him Jessie I think," she added.

"Oh, that song," I replied snickering.

"There's nothing wrong with that song, every kid learns stuff like that. It's no different than *'one two buckle my shoe'* or *'have you seen the muffin man'*, harmless," I said defending me Paulie.

"And maybe Jessie is just a kid from the playground that you haven't met yet," I added, offering up a plausible explanation.

"Oh Ethan! It's not the song, it's the fact that she's up all night, *every night*, singing to an empty room!" Carolyn snapped.

"And we don't know anyone in the neighborhood named Jessie either!"

"By the way, for the record, smashing the skulls of innocent little field mice IS NOT my idea of harmless child's play bucko!" she added fervently.

"*OWWW!* Will you let go of me you greedy little beggar," Carolyn said sharply to one if not both of her hungry infants.

"Sorry, wait a sec while I button up this blouse and put this one down with her brother," she said, setting the phone down on the counter with a thud. I took the opportunity to sprint to the toilet and take care of business before I had an embarrassing accident. I hit the hallway at a full gallop and nearly made it into the bathroom un-noticed when Father Willet turned the corner.

"Ahh Ethan, you're up, *good!* I need to talk to you about something this morning," he said walking toward me. I turned slowly to face him, placing one foot over the other, crossing my ankles, while trying to not to look too conspicuously panicked.

"*Right!* Hello Father...if you could wait just a sec I REALLY have to go, if you know what I mean?" I said pleading more than asking.

"Yes, yes, of course my boy, go right ahead, I'm sorry," he said apologetically. As I turned and rushed off I could hear him call after me.

"Come see me when you're all together!"

I must have shouted back a reply, but to be honest, I nearly lost consciousness with relief as I stood at the urinal and emptied my bladder. After what seemed like a long time I lowered my gaze from the ceiling and let out a long sigh, *"that was too close,"* I muttered to myself as I got myself together and walked over to the sink to wash up. I lathered up and washed my hands thoroughly and then cupped my hands and filled them with cold water. Stooping over, I raised my hands and sunk my face into the cool liquid, letting it from my fingers, then ran my wet hands through my pillow hair. Standing up straight I opened my eyes and looked at my reflection. As soon as my eyes focused on themselves in the mirror I jumped.

"CAROLYN!" I shouted, turning quickly to race back to my room.

I covered the short distance in about five or six long strides and dove at the telephone handset lying on my pillow. As soon as I picked it up I could hear Carolyn Wong on the other end, "ETHAN, ETHAN..."

"SORRY, Sorry, I just went to pee, *sorry,"* I said, apologizing profusely, slightly out of breath.

"Oh brother, I was just about to give up on you," she answered.

"Are you OK?" she asked with a giggle.

"Yeah, yeah, I'm fine, kid's OK?"

"Yeah they're fine too. The twins are asleep and Sophie is sitting right in front of me eating a pop tart, waiting patiently for her turn," Carolyn replied.

"Well then, where did we leave off? Oh yeah, you were saying that you were worried about Sophie's behavior since the ahhh...incident, right?" I asked.

"I don't know Ethan, maybe it's just me. I mean, I'm looking at her and she seems normal and healthy, just being a kid is all. Maybe it's just the whole miracle thing, you know," she said tiredly. This was the first time I heard her or anyone for that matter use the term out loud, and it made me feel a little awkward, I don't know why. I listened to her talk to Sophie in the background.

"You want some more milk sweetie?" she asked.

"Carolyn, are you sure you're OK?" I asked.

"Maybe it wouldn't hurt to talk with someone?" I added.

"I am talking with someone silly! You're a priest right? And you're my friend aren't you? More importantly, you were there! Who better to sound off to," she explained, her logic making perfect sense. I was glad to hear the smile in her voice, the panic of a few moments ago completely gone.

"Well I am all of those things Carolyn, but I'm no psychologist, and I'm not even a real priest yet for goodness sake!" I replied.

"You're close enough for me Ethan, we all love you Father Kelly!" she said sweetly.

"Listen, Sophie has been dying to talk to you. Oops, let me rephrase that, she really wants to talk to you," Carolyn said.

"OK, she dropped the dime after all," I replied with a chuckle as I waited for my goddaughter to pick up the telephone.

"Hello Uncle Ethan," came Sophie's little voice.

"Hi doodle bug, how's my big girl?" I asked cheerfully.

"I fine, can I talk to Tina Uncle Ethan?" Sophie asked.

"Honey, Tina isn't here with me. She lives at her own house with her mummy and daddy," I answered.

"Oh," she said sounding disappointed.

"What do want to say to her baby?" I asked.

"Say her I love you," Sophie said happily.

"That's sweet little girl. I will tell her you said so next time I see her, OK?"

"OK"

"Uncle Ethan?"

"Yes pumpkin?"

"Say her be careful too," Sophie added.

"OK, but why? Careful of what Sophia?" I asked puzzled.

"I don't know," she replied.

"Sophie, why does Tina need to be careful?" I asked again.

"I don't know."

"*Uncle Ethan, I know a joke,*" she said before I could reply.

"Knock, knock."

"OK, who's there?"

"*Purple*"

"Purple who?"

"Knock, knock."

"Who's there?"

"*Purple*"

"Purple who?"

"Knock, knock.

"Alright, who's there?" I asked playing along.

"*Orange*"

"Orange who?"

"*Orange you glad I didn't say purple!*" she squealed into the telephone receiver.

"That was a good one baby," I said with a courtesy laugh.

"Sophia, why should Tina be careful?" I asked once more.

"*I don't know, bye!*" she answered, the sound of the phone dropping to the tabletop causing me to pull the handset away from ear. Carolyn's voice came back on the line, "What was that all about?" she asked.

"I don't know," I replied stupefied.

"Where did Sophie run off to?" I asked.

487

"She skipped out of here to eat pop tarts and watch cartoons with Jessie, or so she said," Carolyn answered.

"Why? What did she say to you?" she asked. I thought about telling her everything, then thought better of it.

"She just wanted to tell Tina Lopez I love you, that's all," I answered.

"Awww, that's sweet," Carolyn replied.

No good could come from worrying her any further it was probably nothing. And besides which, I would be out their way in June to marry Shannon and Paul anyway. Sophie sounded normal enough, and I felt pretty sure that whatever this might be, it would likely blow over before then. I made a mental note to visit the Lopez later in the day if the car was available and Father Willet was willing to go along. OH MY GOSH, Father Willet, I just remembered that he was waiting for me in his office.

"Carolyn, it was great talking to you this morning, such a pleasant surprise. I guess we found out that our little girl is smarter than the *average* bear!" I said, teasing her, and quoting Yogi Bear.

"We sure did! I'll have to have this phone raised a foot or two, or talk Ken into getting Sophie her own line," she replied with a giggle.

"Yeah, *a princess phone*," I teased along with her.

"Thanks for listening Ethan, I'm sorry for being such a worry wart. It's just that what you and that child did for us is so much more than I can ever understand," Carolyn said softly.

"It wasn't me dear, the miracle stuff is God's department," I replied.

"I understand that, but I believe that he works them through others. This girl Ethan, she's special, she's blessed. And I think you're there with her for a reason, I don't know what it could be, but I feel like it's has to be for something important?" she said.

"OK, that's enough of that stuff," I said, trying to change the subject.

"You take care of our little girl and of those two new babies, what are they're names again?" I asked jokingly.

"ETHAN KELLY, shame on you!" she answered curtly.

"Are you telling me you've already forgotten Kyle and Megan's names?"

"You *are* still planning to be here to christen them after Shannon's wedding, right?" Carolyn asked.

"You know I was, how could I forget, I was only teasing!" I said, praying silently for God to forgive my little white lie.

"Good!"

"OH MY GOD, I can't believe Shannon is marrying Paul Pulchoski!" Carolyn exclaimed.

"*Ahh*, now why would you say that?" I asked, sounding a little hurt for my friend.

"No, no, don't get me wrong, they're perfect for each other, they're *sooo* in love, it's so sweet! I just pictured Maggie chasing him into the next county with a shillelagh when he came to ask for her hand!" Carolyn said laughing out loud.

"Ahh, well you might have been right about that, although Mother would have caught Paulie long before the county line!" I replied, laughing along with her.

"I better go Ethan, I think I hear the twins fussing. It was great to talk to you, and I'll tell Ken you asked after him. Oh yeah, and about Ken, remember, mums the word, OK" she said signing off.

"OK, *mums the word*," I promised. "Bye for now Carolyn, love you girl," I added hanging up.

"Love you too, bye E" she replied, hanging up as well.

I replaced the handset in the cradle and got up to shower and dress before going off to meet with Father Willet. *"Busy morning,"* I thought aloud, *"What's next,"* I muttered as I walked out into the hall, wrestling with Sophie's warning.

Fresno, California, March 1974
St. Francis Senior High School

Tina hurried down the hall, walking as fast as she could without actually running toward the doubled door exit at the end of the long corridor. A small group of girls in front of her reached the exit first and she followed them out into the bright sunlight, and then scooted past them, taking the stairs two at a time to the concrete landing below. She turned sharply to her right and continued her fast walk along the pathway and then left onto the sidewalk in front of the school. There was a small crowd milling about, waiting to board the school bus for home. This was her usual ride, however she wasn't taking this bus home this afternoon.

Tina turned right onto the sidewalk and walked past the waiting bus, blending in with the rest of the student body as they strung out along Fourth Avenue making their respective ways home. The crowd thinned as she continued making her way further away from the school. One by one, and two by two, people peeled off from in front her, taking this street or that. The noise from the giggles and running conversations of the dozens of little cliques grew faint as the number of people sharing the sidewalk dwindled, until finally she was alone in her walk. Tina loved the way the wind felt on her face as she walked. Her hair blowing back slightly in the warm afternoon breeze, it was peaceful.

She held her books in front of her chest with both arms, while her purse rocked in rhythm with her stride along side of her as it hung from over her shoulder. And she took in all the beautiful characteristics of the spring day, the singing birds, the shady lanes, and the spectacular gardens that were beginning to bloom in front of house after house along the way. Her mother had a nice garden at home, and she loved that one as well. But there was just something special about seeing the long row of houses in this quaint neighborhood. Sometimes she wished that she lived closer to town, closer to school and to all her friends. Not that she had many friends, too many people were nervous around her, she could feel it, she always had, ever since she was a small girl.

"They don't know you mija, give them time, you'll see," her mother would always say. But they rarely did, and Tina knew why. It was because she was different, it was because she was a witch, or at least that was what they whispered behind her back.

"Don't look in her eyes, she'll freeze your brain," children would tease.

"Did you feel that? She's cold as a grave that one" older people would say when they passed by, thinking that she could not hear.

But she did hear them, and it often hurt, and she had cried many tears over the years. So many in fact, that sometimes she would go deep into the orange groves around her house and pray for God to take her home to live with Him. And then one day, not so long ago, these things no longer seemed to bother her. Nothing anyone would say or do could make her cry or feel bad anymore. It was if she were wearing a magic suit of armor, one that protected her from anything and everything. Maybe it was only part of growing up, shedding childhood fears and nonsense. Maybe that was it, however, Tina preferred to believe that God heard her prayers after all. And that rather than take her home to heaven, He chose to just leave her be, sending an angel or two down to look after her instead. Anyway, that was her story and she was sticking to it. Tina stopped at the corner of 4th Avenue and Pioneer Street and looked each way before crossing. Seeing the coast was clear, she marched across the street and walked over to the city bus stop on the other side.

Gracefully she sat down on the green wooden bench and lay her books down in her lap, letting her purse settle beside her, still slung over her shoulder. She peeked at her watch and checked the time, it was 3:30pm, and the bus would be there any minute according to the schedule. Tina watched a couple of kids riding Big Wheels across the street. They raced along the sidewalk and the turned sharply to power slide into one another, laughing and giggling as they collided. She smiled, enjoying the peaceful moment, and then looked over as a young mother carrying a sack of groceries and a fussing child walked up to join her on the bench.

"Ola Senora," Tina said politely.

"Ola," the young woman replied.

"Do you need some help?" Tina asked, setting her books aside and standing to take the sack of groceries from the woman.

"Muchas gracias," the woman said as she let go of the sack and concentrated all her effort onto corralling her squirming child and sitting down.

"Aiye, this girl so cranky, its way past her nap time," the woman said to Tina.

"I have brothers and sisters at home, I know what you mean!" Tina replied.

"Did you have to walk far?" Tina asked making small talk.

"No, just over to Javier's Bodega on Western, only a couple of blocks," the woman answered.

"Oh, that's not too far. I'm Tina by the way," she said extending her hand. The young woman reached over and clasped Tina's fingertips.

"I'm Tisha, nice to meet you," she replied. Tina smiled back at her

"You coming home from school?" she asked.

"Yeah, I go to St. Francis," Tina replied.

"*I did too*, at least until this one came along, you know how it is," Tisha said. Tina nodded, "How old is she? What's her name?" she asked, reaching over and letting the child hold her finger.

"This is Elizabeth, and she just turned two last Friday," Tisha answered proudly, looking down and smiling at her daughter.

"*Happy birthday mijita,*" Tina said, cooing at the child. She and Elizabeth sat there playing peek a boo as the bus arrived. The women gathered their things and stood up to board the vehicle. Tisha started to reach for the grocery sack and Tina waved her off.

"I'll get this for you," she said cheerfully.

"Thanks!"

"*De nada,*" Tina replied, turning to pick up her schoolbooks as well.

She reached for the books, and was startled by a young man who had suddenly appeared. He reached down to pick her books up from the bench for her. "Let me help," he said in a small shy voice. Tina looked at him for a moment and her look of surprise softened into a smile.

"Thank you," she said sweetly, as she turned to get on the bus.

The young man followed her up the steps and they each deposited their quarter in the meter box. Tina walked down the aisle to where Tisha had taken a seat and then set her grocery sack on the seat next to her. She turned and took a seat across the aisle and scooted toward the window, politely leaving room for the young man, whom she assumed would sit beside her. He stopped in the aisle next to her and handed her books back to her, smiling but keeping his eyes down toward the floor, too shy to make eye contact. Tina reached across the seat and took the books from his hands.

"Thank you very much," she said.

The young man nodded and looked up slightly to smile back at her, then walked quickly away toward the rear of the bus. She turned to watch him walk away from over her shoulder and then turned back to face forward again, a little puzzled by his actions. Tina looked out the window as she waited for the bus to leave the curb. Watching the traffic flow she suddenly noticed the face of the young man reflected in the glass. She saw that he was looking her way and she smiled, a little flattered at his obvious attention to her. Of course he was way too young, he couldn't be more than twelve or thirteen, but he was a male after all, and a woman always appreciates being noticed!

This little dalliance with pride brought her thoughts to the reason for catching this bus today, instead of going straight home. Closing her eyes, she felt herself blush at her own infatuation with Father Kelly, whom she secretly hoped she would see when she got to St. John's. Tina was a little embarrassed by her schoolgirl crush, but she couldn't help it, he was cute even if he was a priest! But flirting was not the purpose of this trip! She was coming to talk with Father Billy about everything. She needed him to take away the guilt she was feeling about wanting to give back this gift, for just wanting to be normal.

Tina loved the Lord, she loved serving Him, but for goodness sake, couldn't somebody else take a turn, even if for just a little while. Her life had been tough enough up till now, but since the TV interview, the things had begun to escalate. More and more people were recognizing her. Total strangers stopped her on the street, seeking just a minute of her time. Would she sit with them awhile? Would she talk with them awhile? Could she come to their home, they had someone for her to meet? No longer able to hide in plain sight, Tina was worried that pretty soon there would be nowhere she could go to seek sanctuary. She shuddered, shaking the bad thoughts out of her head. Better to take these questions and concerns to God through Father Billy she thought. Her faith had always been rewarded with the truth.

Opening her eyes, she saw that the boy in the glass was still looking her way, and she began to feel just a little uncomfortable. Turning away from the window she looked across the aisle, trying to catch Tisha's attention. The bus lurched forward and drove away from the curb, merging into traffic, causing everyone to pitch forward and then back. The two women finally made eye contact.

"She's finally sleeping," Tisha whispered, nodding at the dozing child in her arms.

"Sorry," Tina said, hoping that she had not disturbed the little girl's nap.

"Oh, she's fine. How far are you going?" Tisha asked as they rocked softly with the motion of the ride.

"To St. John's, about ten blocks or so," she answered.

"Me too!" Tisha replied.

"I mean, we're not going to the church, but we live just around the corner," she added.

"Really," Tina replied.

"You should come by when you finish, I'm making *albondigas* tonight, maybe you could stay for supper!" Tisha inquired excitedly.

"Oh, I don't know, I need to ask my mom. Besides, the buses stop running after 8pm, how would I get home?" Tina replied.

"Oh please, just think about it. You can call your mom from my house. And we can give you a ride home after supper. We've got a pick up truck, Tommy needed it for work, that's why I'm riding the bus today," Tisha said, reaching out.

"I don't know, maybe..."

"*Please, please, please*...I don't have many friends in the neighborhood, all of the women are my mother's age or older. You're the first person I've met near my age since we came back here," she said.

"Come on, it'll be fun, you'll like Tommy, he's a sweetheart!" Tisha pleaded.

Tina sighed, a sure sign that she was giving in, "OK, maybe I can stop by for a little while when I finish with Father Willet," she said, smiling back at Tisha.

"*Great!* You have a pencil or something, I'll give you my address?" Tisha asked. Tina fumbled through her purse finding a ballpoint pen on the second dive, and opened her spiral notebook to a blank page.

"OK, go ahead," she said. Tisha leaned into the aisle and recited her home address while Tina scribbled it down in her neat cursive hand.

"So, maybe I'll see you around five?" Tisha asked, returning to her side of the bus.

"I think so," Tina replied as she closed her notebook and returned the pen to her purse.

They rode along in silence for another couple of stops, listening to the sounds of the traffic and the soft baby snoring of little Elizabeth. Tina watched as people milled about at each stop, exiting and boarding the busy bus. About a mile or so from the church, the bus pulled up to the curb at the corner of 10th Avenue and Riverdale Road. The bell dinged, signaling the stop and the people sitting in front of her rose to exit. As they walked away, Tina felt someone brush past her shoulder. It was the young man that had helped her with her books. He walked past without pausing to acknowledge her, and then stopped a couple rows past. He turned slowly to face back toward her and looked directly at her. He smiled at her, it was a pleasant smile, and she was surprised by the way it made her skin crawl. She smiled back out of reflex and the boy turned and walked to the door, exiting the bus without looking back. Tina turned involuntarily to look out the window next to Tisha and Elizabeth, trying to catch a glimpse of the boy as he walked away. It wasn't important really, but she felt compelled to make sure that he was gone. She was suddenly aware that Tisha was looking at her strangely.

"Are you OK Tina?" she asked.

"You know that kid or something, was he bothering you?"

Tina blinked several times as she disengaged from her visual sweep of the sidewalk and focused on the person staring back at her.

"Oh, uh, sorry! Yeah, I'm OK, um, there's no problem. He helped me with my books when we got on the bus awhile back," Tina said, slightly stammering. Her eyes were no longer looking after the boy, her mind doing the searching now. Tisha studied her new friend's face a moment as Elizabeth began to wake up and fuss.

"You're sure you're OK?" she asked.

"Yeah, I'm fine. It's just that all of the sudden that boy seemed very familiar," Tina replied.

Elizabeth started to whine like all children do when they wake up in a strange place, and Tina leaned across the aisle to help Tisha calm the child. The little girl stopped whimpering and smiled at Tina, a little tear rolling down her cheek. Tina wiped it away with her finger and made a funny face, crossing her eyes and puffing out her cheeks.

"I think our stop is coming up," Tisha said while her daughter giggled at Tina's antics.

"I can see St. John's just ahead," she added, nodding toward the window to her right. The two women started gathering their things, preparing to get off the bus at the next exit.

"*So*, you have my address, its real easy to find, literally right around the corner from the church," Tisha said as the bus slowed to stop at the curb.

"Yep, it's right here," Tina answered, tapping the notebook that she was holding against her chest. "I'm sure I'll find it OK, five o'clock, right?"

"Right, five o'clock," Tisha replied beaming, excited at the prospect of having company.

"I'm so happy Tommy needed the truck today!" she exclaimed, reaching across the aisle to touch Tina on her shoulder.

"Me too," Tina replied, smiling back at her new friend.

The two girls held hands in the aisle until the bus came to a complete stop and then got up to exit together. As they walked away from the bus, Tina couldn't help but look in both directions, up and down the long empty sidewalk. All of her instincts were indicating caution now. And she wasn't quite sure why, but that boy's face, now etched clearly into her mind, was feeling more familiar with each passing moment.

Fresno, California, March 1974

He watched the two women chat for a moment as the bus pulled away from the curb. The baby was squirming in the mother's arms trying to get down. Reaching into his jacket pocket he retrieved a handful of grapes and started popping them in his mouth one at a time, chewing and swallowing quickly. He was famished; it had been almost thirty hours since he last ate. He had swiped this bunch of grapes from the Safeway store in Firebaugh early yesterday morning, after he had drained a couple cartons of chocolate milk while walking the aisles pushing a sparsely loaded basket. He had learned early on that if you were clean and acted normal, it was fairly easy to dine and dash in comfort at most large chain run grocery stores. The small mom and pop places were harder, too easy to be spotted and watched. Besides which, he still had bad dreams of that liquor store and the old man. Miguel watched as the two girls began to walk away, getting smaller and smaller as the distance between them increased. He remained seated at the park bench, enjoying the sweet flavor of the plump ripe grapes. He didn't need to follow them, he knew where she was going, and he knew where she would be going back to as well.

This wasn't the place for their reunion anyway; he had already chosen that location. Today's excursion was just for fun, to see how easy it would be to all of a sudden appear, to see just how invisible he was after all these years. He ate the last grape and then reached into the back pocket of his jeans. He pulled out a folded photograph, deeply creased, and nearly ready to break into sections. The colors had actually begun to fade along the creases where it had been folded and unfolded hundreds of times. Carefully he opened the photo, layer after layer until it lay open before him on the wooded picnic table at which he sat. He stared down at the picture of the man in the dark blue uniform with the red stripes and bright white hat, imagining that he was looking back at him. Then, reaching out, he traced the outline of the man's face, stopping to touch the dark stains on the white cap and the stars of the American flag that hung in the background. He ran his finger back and forth across those textured stains, silently muttering to himself, "*it'll be ok mama, it'll be ok...*"

Forty-two

(..."Don't talk of love, but I've heard the word before. It's sleeping in my memory. I won't disturb the slumber of feelings that have died. If I never loved I never would have cried. I am a rock, I am an island."... Simon & Garfunkle...)

<u>San Francisco, California, March 1974</u>

Jay Namura sat squirming nervously in the passenger seat of the speeding Ford Taurus. Sitting up straight suddenly, he tugged hard on the seatbelt resting loosely in his lap, cinching it tighter by an order of magnitude. Then turning his head slightly and looking out the window, he tried counting the blurry stream of intermittently placed telephone poles and streetlights that lined the roadside as the rust colored sedan hurtled past them. It was a little road trip test he often employed to *'ballpark'* the level of shear panic required to avert pending disaster. SOP actually, *standard operating procedure,* whenever he found himself riding along side of a certain crazy woman, namely one KC Littleton. After a full 10 seconds, when he had counted but one lone pole, he turned back toward the windshield, facing front again. Then, clenching both his fists and his buttocks, he squeezed his eyes tightly shut. *Now,* it was officially panic time!

"*KC!*" he shouted.

There was no reply, but he knew that she had heard him. *Hell,* even the family in the station wagon beside them had heard him. At least that's

497

what he assumed, reading their startled faces and watching them hit the brakes and veer toward the relative safety of the shoulder of the road. It was painfully obvious that KC wasn't paying any more attention to him than she was to the road.

"HEY, SPEED RACER!" he hollered at the top of his lungs, his eyes watering, and the veins at his temples bulging from the extreme pressure of his panic attack.

KC snapped out of her daydream, startled by the volume of Jay's voice.

"What," she asked, whining a response to his outburst, not even bothering to say the word in the form of a question. Jay twisted in the seat to face her as best he could under the restraint of the snug seatbelt.

"HEY LEADFOOT!"

"How about easing up on the gas pedal?"

"Maybe you could try and keep the Speedo in the two digit range, OK?" he answered through clenched teeth, his nostrils flaring slightly. KC pushed her sunglasses down the bridge of her nose and frowned at him. Shrugging her shoulders she replied with mock disgust.

"Waaaaa! Wittle ole me am scared I might cwash, go boom- boom, crunch-crunch! Jeez Louise, what a baby!"

"You should be used to me by now," KC said snorting slightly. She snickered and shook her head slowly at her visibly upset colleague knowing that it would add only to his aggravation.

"Why can't you just let me drive for once, I always offer you know?" Jay asked, opening his eyes slowly as the car slowed to the speed limit.

"Because when I'm stressing driving helps me think. How many times do we need to go over this?"

"Oh! And like I didn't ask you twenty times **BEFORE** we left, *what's the matter Kathy, what's on that evil little mind of yours, you wanna talk, you wanna hug, what's wrong KC, what, what,* **WHAT!***"* KC sat silently and let him rant and rave, she knew better that to interrupt him when he was on a roll.

She was trying her best to keep from laughing out loud at his frantic antics. It was a good thing that she was wearing her big, oversized, movie star sunglasses, because Jay was launching himself into an award-winning tantrum. He was so funny when he lost it like this, she just ate this up with a spoon, thoroughly enjoying his frustrated performance. He actually became cartoon like, creating a uniquely Jay character, complete with the flagrant gestures of *Snagglepuss* the theatrical lion and the whiny voice of *Barney Fife*, it was all she could do to keep from bursting out in a long and painful belly laughing jag!

"*Ohhhhh, but noooooo!* You just answer...*nothing,*" he said flailing his arms about the car as if they were only loosely attached to his body. KC put her hand over her mouth as she curled her lips under her teeth and bit down on them, trying to stifle a meaty snort and chortle.

"*OH,* you think that's funny!" Jay said, folding his arms stiffly, his frustration simmering into anger.

"YEAH, OK, go ahead and step on it, kill us both, I DON"T CARE ANYMORE!"

"Besides, I'm starting to lose my voice," he said, squeaking a little at the end of his sentence. KC released her lips from her defensive bite and sighed audibly. Without looking over at him she reached across the car and touched his bicep through the silky soft material of his Italian polo shirt.

"*Ooooo,* nice fabric Jay man," she said, coughing out a compliment in an effort to get him off his soapbox. Jay twisted away from her and looked out the window, giving her the old silent treatment for the moment.

"*Come on,* you know you can't stay mad at me," she said coyly, trying to coax a smirk out of him.

"Look, I told you everything on the phone before I picked you up this morning. I told you all about my meeting with Brian and old man Gateway. You know all their dirty little secrets now just like I do," she said, stealing a sideways glance at him to see if his ears were on. Jay continued to look out his window, but she could tell that he was listening.

"*Look,* going back and doing follow up with that nut job, Rosa Hernandez, and then chatting with the *presumably* dead Dr. Murray Katz is not the assignment I was hoping for, I hope you know that!" she snapped at Jay, hoping a harsher tact might end this little spat.

"Besides which, I'm going to look like a real patsy when this series goes to print. What if they take back my Pulitzer, I'll be ruined!" KC said, more to herself now than to Jay.

"Wouldn't you be a little preoccupied yourself? I mean under similar circumstances?" she asked rhetorically.

KC averted her attention from their argument for a moment to pass a slow moving eighteen-wheeler, flashing her hi beams as she passed and again after she settled safely in front of the tractor-trailer rig, rules of the road you know. The big green and yellow Mayflower moving rig flashed his lights in response, completing the highway maneuver in textbook fashion.

"Well, did you hear what I said?" she asked her passenger without looking his way.

"Yes I heard you," Jay replied tiredly.

"So?" KC said shrugging her shoulders animatedly, a clear indication that she expected an answer.

"So *no they won't,*" Jay replied.

"*Won't what,* ostracize me, put my mug on the front page of every newspaper and magazine across the country with the caption *liar, liar pants on fire!*" KC shouted.

"They won't take your Pulitzer and they aren't going to barbecue you in the press either," Jay replied calmly.

"*How do you know that?* If it were me covering someone else, it's exactly what I'd do, it's what I'd be expected to do, it's juicy and it's news! People love dirty laundry, they would much rather peek up my skirt than look me in the eye. Its why we don't run *Sally Somebody's* Holy Communion on page one, but we will run over each other to be the first to print the story about her rape or murder! So don't tell me that I've got nothing to worry about Paley, *I've got plenty, with a capital P!*"

"They won't because it's a great story KC, and you're a great journalist. You write like you feel, with all of your heart. When people finish reading what you have to say about all of these recent developments, *at the end of the day,* you'll have them all where you want them. Solidly in Rosa's corner, forgiving of a changed man, and hopeful for the future of a young girl, who has spent her youth as a servant to one and all," Jay replied without turning around.

"KC Littleton will be the last thing on their minds," he added.

They rode along in silence for a couple minutes before Jay twisted back to face her again.

"Now, having said that. Why don't you tell me what is *really* on your mind, cause I'm not going for this *woe is me* bullshit, I know you better than that. What's got your panties in a bunch anyway?"

"And don't give me any more crap about this story or the job, I'm not buying it. I know you better anyone in your world KC, better than you are actually comfortable with. You're struggling with something and it's eating you up, I can feel it. So get it out girl, share with your old pal Jay, and maybe I can help you work it all out pookie, what do you say?" he asked, perking up finally.

KC squirmed in her seat a little while she thought about what he had said, actually stalling as she searched for a lie that he might buy. But she thought better of it, he did know her too well, and lying to him when his antenna was up would be nearly impossible. He was right of course, the story and the job were routine, she would write a great piece, like she always did, this was her thing after all, it was what she did better than anyone! And none of that was what was weighing so heavily on her mind, Jay was right about that as well, damn him! She glanced his way and saw that he was looking right through her, peeling away all of her emotional defenses like the petals of a daisy. Blinking nervously as she did whenever she about to confess, she sighed heavily, puffing out her cheeks as she did so.

"OK, I'll level with you," she started, gripping the steering wheel a little tighter.

"You're right, it's not about Rosa or Katz, or Tina, none of that really."

"Go on, I'm listening," Jay said softly. KC's concentration on the road shielded her from the satisfied smirk on his face.

"Yeah well, I sorta have this problem," she continued, scrunching up her face like she just bit into a lemon.

"And that would be?" Jay asked, loosening the seatbelt a little so he could turn and put his left knee up on the bench seat. KC breathed in deeply a couple of times and chewed on her cheeks, causing her face to appear even thinner than it already was. Finally she just blurted it out.

"I THINK I'M IN LOVE...OK!"

"With the priest, *RIGHT!"* Jay exclaimed.

*"**OH GOD**, you already knew?"* KC said in a panic.

"Of Course!"

"We've been down this road before KC. The restaurant, last week, *remember?"* Jay said, totally exasperated by her memory lapse. He shook his head slowly as he continued.

"Didn't I tell you to dump this on Dear Abby's doorstep the next time you felt yourself drifting into a blue funk?

KC stared ahead at the road, flummoxed momentarily by his remarks. She exhaled deeply through her nose as she recalled the night at The Stinking Rose.

"What a dope KC," she muttered.

"I'm sorry Jay, I don't know why I do stuff like this. I swear I think I'm losing my mind!" she said, apologizing for her absent-mindedness. She shot Jay a sideways glance and batted her eyelashes.

"Forgive me?" she said playfully.

Jay snorted as he puffed out his cheeks and crossed his arms defensively.

"You're a piece of work KC, you know that, a real piece of work!" he snapped.

"I know," KC answered, smiling broadly at the windshield. "And you wouldn't want me any other way, and you know it!" she added gleefully.

"Why me, huh? Why are you always dragging me through your romance minefields?" Jay whined. KC giggled at his antics from the driver's seat.

"I'm sorry sweetie, I am. Is that a bad thing?" she asked, dabbing away a giggle tear from the corner of her eye.

"YES, it really is!" Jay shouted.

"Its not like you couldn't find any number of willing shoulders to cry on ya know. Hell, the way you've been walking around in a fog lately you could have had your pick around the office. The place is lousy with curious bleeding hearts!" Jay added sarcastically.

"*OH MAN*, then everybody knows!" KC exclaimed, squeezing her eyes shut tightly, her cheeks shining bright red in the mother of all blushes.

"Probably," Jay replied smiling devilishly, amused by her reaction.

"Have I really been that transparent?" she asked.

"Yeah"

"*Then he might know as well!*" KC shouted.

"That would be my guess, *isn't this fun!*" he replied, teasing her mercilessly.

KC rocked her head forward then back, and then forward again, as if to surrender to the futility of her over reaction to such a natural phenomenon. She listened to Jay snickering beside her and then reached across the seat to pinch him good and hard through his thin shirt.

"*Owwww,* hey, it's not my fault you're trying to steal one of God's *fellas!*" Jay teased, scooting out of reach of her flesh seeking pinchers.

"Shut up Jay, you goofball! This is serious, I really think I might love this guy. And it's not my fault he's a priest, I didn't put the collar around his neck. Besides, if God really is everywhere and really knows everything, then he knew what he was doing when he introduced us. Maybe he wants us to be together, did you ever think of that, huh?" KC said defensively, thinking quickly if not rationally.

"*No, did you?*" Jay replied, still trying to stay away from her pinching fingers.

"Well sort of...I mean just now I did," she replied weakly.

"Oh man Jay, *I AM* trying to steal God's fella aren't I? Can't I burn for that?" she asked ridiculously.

"How would I know woman? Burning in hell and shit like that is your people's thing. I'm a Buddhist baby, remember, everything is always cool for me. If things don't work out in this life I've always got another one coming, so I don't sweat the small stuff, ya dig!" Jay replied in jest.

"Seriously, take a breath KC you're starting to hyperventilate! Don't make me have to stuff your head in a paper bag girl," Jay said, as his laughter subsided. He watched as she bit at her lip.

"Look, it's probably just infatuation. You know how you girls *love a man in uniform,*" Jay said, unable to resist the opportunity to toss in just one more jibe.

"Very funny, ha, ha, ha"

"*See!* This is why I keep crap like this to myself butthead! *Oh,* you just make me so mad!" KC shouted, raising her right hand and wiping away a tear of frustration with her palm. She looked over at Jay and saw that he was staring at her.

"*I'm not crying you know, I'm just MAD!*" she insisted. Jay knew better, and he reached across and squeezed her shoulder.

"Pull over for a second KC, *please,* just for a sec," he pleaded gently.

KC sniffled and then flicked on the turn signal, angling the car for the shoulder of the highway. She slowed to a stop and put the gearshift on the column into the Park position.

"OK, now what?" she asked, turning toward Jay and crossing her arms, a stern look on her tear-stained face. Jay put his arm across the top of the seat and looked at his friend for a moment, reading her expression.

"I'm sorry Kathy, I was only teasing ya know. Up until now I thought that you were just kidding around," he said defending himself.

"*Well I'm not,*" KC whined.

"I can see that, *peace, peace OK!*" he replied.

"So what are you going to do about it?" Jay asked.

"I don't know," she answered, wiping her nose on her sleeve. There was a long and uncomfortable silence before KC finally spoke up.

"This is supposed to be where you step up the plate and hit one out the park for me doofus, psychologically speaking anyway!" KC exclaimed in frustration.

"Oh, *sorry,*" Jay replied weakly.

"This is kinda new territory for me KC, you just vented and used me as a sounding board. You've never actually asked me for any advice in this area before. Clothes, food, plays, movies, art, or work, I always have answers for you there. But this, well this is totally unexpected. The wrong advice could really hurt, and I never want to hurt you KC, you're a pea in my pod girl," Jay said sincerely, smiling back at her.

"I know," KC answered softly.

"Do you think that maybe he loves you back?" Jay asked meekly.

"I want to say yes, I mean I feel something back from him whenever we spend any time together. But what if I'm wrong, what if I shoot off my big fat mouth and he thinks I'm a nut!" KC whined pathetically.

"*YOU ARE A FREAKING NUT KC, certifiable actually, but then what's not to love!* Seriously baby-doll, I doubt he sees you that way. And if he does, well then I'd say he isn't the guy you think he is! And if he's not then he doesn't deserve your attention or affection. That's what I'd say!" Jay rifled back curtly. They looked at one another for a long minute and then KC asked through her sniffles.

"But you don't *really* think that do you?" Jay rolled his eyes and sighed tiredly.

"*Nah,* I guess not, not really. I've known you for too many years KC, *hell,* I spend more time with you than I do my own family."

"You're my best friend Kathy, I want you to find what you're looking for, don't you know that?"

"I want you to be happy. It makes me happy as well. So, what do I really think? I think that your personal radar is good, *scary good in fact,* far more sensitive than us ordinary people. It's one of the gifts that help you to stand out in this business, doing what you do. Honey, if you really feel like you've felt something back from this guy, then like as not you did, he's only human after all, right?" Jay answered.

KC sniffled and replied.

"Ya think?"

"Yeah, I think," answered Jay. She sniffled again and rubbed under her nose with her forefinger.

"Guess I'll talk to him about it when we see him on this trip. Father Willet mentioned that Ethan and Tina would be joining us at the interview," she said.

"That's sounds doable," Jay replied, drumming his fingers on the back of the seat.

"Or, maybe I'll wait and talk to him at the Donnelly's anniversary party, what do you think?" she asked.

"Whatever seems right to you babe. The party sounds better now that I think about it, you can walk around together less conspicuously, you know?" he answered.

"Yeah, that sounds good, the party then. Thanks Jay man, I love you ya know," she said patting his hand stretched across on the back of the seat. A tender gesture of endearment as well as a ploy to stop his inane drumming that was beginning to drive her nuts!

"I love you too puddin," Jay said jokingly.

"OK, let's get back on the road," KC said happily, suddenly her old self once again. But before she could put the car into gear, Jay opened his door and jumped out. "NO WAY CRAZY LADY," he shouted.

"You slide on over to this side and let me drive! That's the only way we're traveling one more mile together, get it?" he said emphatically. KC smiled and unhooked her seatbelt. She slid across to the passenger side and buckled up.

"*Happy?*" she said, shrugging her shoulders and holding out her hands, palms up.

"Ecstatic!" Jay replied as he walked around the back of the car towards the driver's side.

Sliding in and closing the door, Jay adjusted the mirrors and the seat to fit a *non-dwarf* and then buckled his seatbelt. As they pulled away from the shoulder and merged back onto the road, KC reached across the seat and socked her softhearted friend in the arm.

"Big baby," she said smiling.

"Bitch!" he replied nonchalantly, flicking off the clicking turn signal as they sped away.

Firebaugh, California, March 1974

Tina hopped into the pick up truck on the passenger side and pulled hard on the door to make sure it slammed shut properly. Their old Chevy workhorse had seen better days and recently had acquired a little dent in the passenger door that required some muscle from the passenger to assure a tight seal. Her father climbed in on the other side and started his ignition ritual as he sweet-talked *'lil darlin's'* engine into turning over just one more time for Papa.

"Come sweetheart, you can do it, one time baby, one time," Victor said, pleading, while the engine cranked and cranked. He stomped hard on the gas pedal in a very specific cadence, one he had learned over years of negotiating with *'lil darlin'*, assuring that just right amount of fuel made it into the engine. Tina smiled at him from across the bench seat. She loved to watch her father work, and she especially liked his little routines and superstitions, they gave her glimpses of what he must have been like as a boy. After a few minutes of coughing and sputtering, *lil darlin's* old engine fired up with a backfire, a little puff of black smoke wafting from the tailpipe in back. Victor Lopez smiled broadly and reached out to the dashboard to pet it gently.

"That's my girl!" he said lovingly, looking over at his daughter triumphantly.

"Oh Papa, don't you think it's time you asked Senor Donnelly for a new truck?" Tina asked as she giggled at her father's antics.

"Scrap my *lil darlin?* Oh no *mija*, this old truck still has a lot of life in her. Besides, your schooling is more important than any old truck. If I go to Senor Donnelly for help it will be for something like that," her father replied earnestly. Tina swallowed the rest of her giggles in respect of her father's serious tone and sat up straight in the seat, smoothing out her skirt in the process.

"Si Papa, you're right," she said. Tina leaned forward and stroked the dashboard with her hand gently.

"I love you too *lil darlin*, " she said turning her head slightly to smile at her dad.

The two of them burst out laughing as Victor backed up the truck and turned it around in the big yard. They rolled slowly by the house to keep the dust from spraying the back door. Tina and Victor waved to Maria who was standing at the kitchen window, as they drove toward the road. She waved back cheerfully, her hand covered by a yellow Playtex dish glove. As they past the house Victor sped up a little and reminded Tina to put on her safety belt. She did as she was told and reminded him to do the same.

Victor turned left when they reached the road and the truck spit a little gravel as the tires spun from the dirt to the asphalt. Tina looked out her window at the familiar scenery as they accelerated and started the short trip to Fresno. They were going into town to shop for a gift for the Donnelly's anniversary and for a new dress for Tina to wear to the party. After all, she was a young woman now and her mother wanted her to make a good impression. Maria would have loved to come along, but Gilbert and the new baby were a little too much to handle so far away from home.

"Papa, do you think we can stop at *Young's Five and Dime* while we're in town?" Tina asked her father, holding her hair behind her head to keep it from blowing around with the wind from the open window.

"I guess so *mija*, what do you need?" he replied.

"Nothing special, I just want to get some penny candy for my friend Tisha and her little one," she answered.

"Oh…who's Tisha, I don't remember meeting her?"

"I met her a couple days ago on the bus when I went to see Father Billy. She lives around the block from St. John's. She's a little older than me and has a beautiful little girl named Elizabeth."

"Really, she sounds nice."

"She is Dad, and so is her husband Tommy, I met him as well," Tina added.

"OK then, I guess we can stop at Young's first, it's on the way to the mall anyway," Victor replied.

"Thanks Papa."

"Yeah, OK."

"Hey, you never told us how your meeting with Father Billy went."

"What did you go to see him about anyway?" Victor asked his daughter. Tina did not answer right away and sensing a little tension Victor decided to lighten the mood with a little good-natured teasing.

"You know, your mother and I thought that maybe you had really gone to see that new priest, Father Kelly," he said as he looked over at her, waiting for a reaction. Tina blushed immediately.

"Oh come on Dad, why would you think that," Tina replied defensively.

"I don't know, your young, he's young, you know, nature."

"Dad...I'm *very* young, he's *not so* young, **AND**, he's a *PRIEST* for goodness sake!" she said scolding her father playfully, trying to hide the smirk on her face. It felt good hearing someone else say out loud the things she had been fantasizing about for weeks.

"Yeah, yeah, I know *mija*, but I've seen you smile after him when he wasn't looking. And he is always so nice to you, he seems to really like you too?" Victor replied with a tone of insinuation.

Tina blushed again when she discovered how obvious she had been, and then deeper still at her fathers continued observation.

"He's a priest Papa, he's nice to everyone! Let's just drop this OK, its not why I went to see Father Billy anyway," she said, a little frustrated at the direction their small talk was headed. And a little more than embarrassed by her dad's insightfulness.

"*OK, sorry, I was only just saying...*"

"*Enough Papa!* Let's talk about something else, OK...*por favor?*" Tina pleaded.

"Alright, so what did you and Father Billy talk about the other day?" he asked, changing the subject.

This wasn't a conversation Tina wanted to have either, at least not now, not with just the two of them. She wanted to wait until the party. Father Billy promised that they could all sit down and talk at the party. He had promised to help her explain everything to everyone. She looked out the window a moment and let go of her hair. The buffeting wind blew it all around her head and she watched the countryside pass from behind the thick strands of her long dark locks. She didn't want to lie to her father but at the same time she wasn't ready to get into all of this right now. Tonight would be soon enough, everyone would be there, and she could tell them all at the same time.

"Papa, can we talk about this later, *please?*" she asked softly without looking away from the window.

Victor looked over at her and watched as the wind blew her hair every which way. He was a little un-nerved and concerned by the weak tone of her voice, but he knew her well enough to leave her be when she was in a pensive mood like this. Tina had always brought her problems and confusions to them, eventually, and it wasn't going to hurt anyone to give her the space that she obviously needed at the moment. Victor had learned from years of experience, that within relationships, especially those between the sexes, men and women or boys and girls, or any combination thereof, that pushing and pressing issues usually brought about only terse reactions to the prodding, and rarely any real help at all. In fact, *help* wasn't even what was sought after in the first place. More often than not, the most helpful things a male can offer a female at times like these are his open heart, his open ears, and a pair of kind and understanding eyes. So much can be communicated in a loving gaze. It's like sitting in front of a roaring fire, really warms you up!

"OK *mija*, whenever you're ready," he said gently, reaching over and stroking the back of her head. He couldn't see her smile, but he could feel it, and that seemed like a good way to end the subject.

"How about some *musica*?" he asked cheerfully.

Tina nodded her head, still watching the world go by from her side of the truck. Victor reached over to fiddle with the radio knobs, first switching on the power. The radio dial lit up with a soft green backlight, the station frequency numbers glowing in large black digits. Sounds started to sputter and crackle from the worn speakers in the front door panels and an unknown DJ's voice came on from the airwaves.

"*WOW, that was a great set!* The Beach Boy's with *'I Get Around'* and *'Good Vibrations'* here on Central Valley's own KBAR, 92.2 on your FM dial. What's that Boo Boo, you're ready for a little soul, we'll so are Yogi and me! How about some good advice from Diana Ross and the Supremes, *'You Can't Hurry Love'* ...but you already know that babies, *ya know you do!*" shouted the disk jockey in his hyperactive patter. Tina turned back to sit up straight in the seat and folded her arms in front of her.

"*DAD!*"

"*Lo ciento mija*, I got no control of the radio, really, *I didn't plan that,*" Victor said laughing.

"Well I do," Tina said in a monotone, leaning forward and pushing one of the preset buttons. The radio station changed over to a local country station.

Charlie Pride's voice boomed out of the speakers, "*hey, did you happen to see the most beautiful girl in the world...*" Tina gasped, and started to reach out to change the station again, but Victor gently pushed her hand away.

"No, leave it here *mija*," he pleaded while he sang along. Repeating the chorus, he reached out and touched his daughter's face gently. Tina blushed as her father serenaded her, "*tell her I love her, tell her I'm thinking of her...*"

"*DAD!*"

Fresno, California, March 1974

The young man crossed the street quickly with the light, turning east as he stepped up onto to curb. He slowed his pace once safely up on the sidewalk, and strolled on ahead. Where he was going was a mystery to the two men in the blue sedan. They had been following and watching him since around 7am, when they spotted him getting off a bus on Mayfield Avenue. They had finally found him, and this time they were determined not to let him disappear into the scenery like he had at least twice before. Smiley watched the boy from behind the dark lenses his cheap plastic shades. The boy was carrying a paper sack in one hand and bottle of soda pop in the other. Smiley and Raymond watched as he continued east, never looking back over his shoulder, not even once. The two _cholos_ were convinced that they had not been spotted. And why would they, they had been really, really careful. And besides, for all the kid knew they were still in jail back in LA? It wasn't likely that the kid lost much sleep thinking about them at all. He was rid of them, hadn't he made sure of that when he called the cops to them in the first place. That was Smiley's guess anyway, and it was a good guess he guessed.

"Look at the little shit Raymond. Walking around like he ain't got a care in the world," Smiley said sarcastically without looking over at his friend. Raymond nodded and grunted his reply, taking a sip on the strawberry soda he had bought at a liquor store about an hour earlier.

"_Hey, hey!_ He's turning the corner, _let's go man_," Smiley said excitedly, sitting up and pointing toward the disappearing figure.

"OK, OK, _don't yell at me_, I'm on it homeboy," Raymond replied, putting the car in gear and rolling slowly away from the curb, trying not to draw any undue attention toward them.

The sedan merged smoothly into traffic and accelerated, approaching the intersection where the boy had turned. Raymond signaled a right turn and slowly nosed around the corner, careful not to squeal the tires and risk detection. Smiley got a fast vector on the boy about three quarters of a block ahead. He must have ditched the soda bottle because his right hand was empty now, swinging freely beside him as he walked. He walked at a slow and steady pace into a quiet neighborhood nestled between the main drag in town and the Interstate. It was just what you'd expect to see given its urban location. The doors and windows of each house displayed decorative security bars and screens, making the place look more like a camp than a neighborhood. Not at all run down though. In fact, in pleasant contrast to the harsh realities to the conditions of most neighborhoods in the area, the properties here were well cared for. The lawns were neat and green with colorful flower gardens and smatterings of children's toys in the fenced yards, softening the otherwise grim environment that residents lived with day after day.

Raymond pulled forward and parked in front of a car that was partially blocking the entrance of an alley. They could see the boy still walking up ahead, a block or so in the distance. The boy stopped in front of a freshly painted, white and green home. Its yard was nice and large, and it had a huge front porch, complete with two white wicker rockers visible from the street. The boy turned and knelt in front of the chain-link fence that separated the green grass from the black asphalt. Smiley sank low in his seat in case the boy turned their way. He knew that there was no way that he would be able to see anyone in the car, but better safe than sorry. He watched as the boy reached toward the fence, and put his fingers through the open links. Smiley couldn't see much of the house or yard because of the tall hedges surrounding the house next door. That kind of bothered him, and he thought about getting out of the car for a second. Maybe he would walk across the street and get a clearer view. But he thought better of it, *again*, better safe than sorry.

"What's that little bastard doing anyway?" he said aloud.

"Can you see what he's doing *ese*?" Smiley asked Raymond.

Raymond twisted in his seat and squinted, straining his eyes, trying to make out what the boy was doing.

"No man, I don't see nothing. He's probably just playing with a dog or something, relax *ese*" Raymond replied nonchalantly.

"Yeah, that's probably it," Smiley said agreeing with his buddy's theory, sitting back up in his seat.

"What the fuck is that *baboso* doing," Smiley whined again rhetorically.

Miguel reached back and pulled the hood of his sweatshirt over his head. From that vantage point he could turn his head ever so slightly and get a good look at the car that had been following him for the last hour or so. While he didn't actually recognize the car, he was pretty sure that he knew who was in it. If they were cops they would have been all over him by now. *No*, it had to be those two *chingasos*, Smiley and Raymond. He knelt there, squatting in front of the fence pretending to play with a dog or something while he sized up the situation. He wasn't upset that they had found him, he had wanted them to find him. Miguel had plans for them, they were going to be a big help to him later, they just didn't know it. He narrowed his eyes and imagined that he was making eye contact with Smiley directly, right then.

"You'll be first," he whispered to himself, a wicked little grin spreading across his face.

And with that thought he stood up and continued on down the street, walking deeper and deeper into the well-fortified neighborhood. He made sure to pause now and then to allow the two idiots time to reposition themselves and a safe distance so as NOT to be noticed. Miguel pulled the watch he had taken from the old man in the trailer out of his pocket. It was too big for him to wear, so he kept it tucked in the front pocket of his jeans. He looked at the time; it was still early, around nine in the morning. Returning the watch to his pocket, he wiped at his runny nose with his sleeve. He was starting to get a little hungry now, but he was close to his destination, he would eat well soon. As for Smiley and Raymond, he would keep them guessing until later. They were all going to party together later. If all went as they had planned, a good time would be had by all, *oh yeah!*

Forty-three

(...)"I tell you the truth, unless you change and become like little children, you will never enter the kingdom of heaven"...Matthew 18:3)

Los Angeles, California, 12, March 1974
9:00am

Monsignor, Pablo Villa Cruz finished placing files into his briefcase and closed the heavy leather bag, running the thick strap through the buckle, and latching it in place. He set the case down on the floor beside his desk and then sat down gingerly in the comfortably plush chair behind it. He winced in pain as he settled into the chair, his joints aching severely from the rheumatoid arthritis that plagued his tired old body. Although he had been blessed with good fortune over the years where his career and ministry was concerned, he had been less fortunate with his health. As a child he had suffered from asthma and rubella. And as a young man he had contracted malaria while on a missionary retreat in Central America, a malady that recurred without much warning throughout his life. And now this nagging stiffness ravaged his aging body. Sometimes he questioned the Lord's motives and wondered if he were just being toyed with, wondering if his life were nothing more than amusement for God almighty!

Grunting audibly, he rubbed on aching his knees, but that only seemed to bring more pain than relief these days, given the fact that his hands and

512

fingers were no better off than his knees, ankles and back. The cool spring morning air that gently blew in through the open window wasn't helping matters much either. He had taken to wearing gloves even indoors to keep his hands warm and useful. Silently cursing the housekeeper for her negligence, the priest reached into his jacket and removed the airline tickets from the inside pocket. He set the envelope down on the desktop and leaned back in his chair. He did not remove the tickets from the envelope, he didn't need to, he had already memorized the flight number, gate number, the departure and arrival time, even the seat assignment. Father Villa Cruz was pedantic to a fault, almost anal where his schedules and routines were concerned. He was not one who tolerated miscues and mistakes from anyone, especially from himself. He led an ordered and disciplined life and he expected everyone, especially those nearest him, to do likewise. He placed his hands, palms down, gently on his aching legs and called out to his secretary in the other room.

"Mrs. Hollis!" he bellowed.

A moment later his secretary entered the office through the open door. She was a tall woman, trim and fit. She was in her early fifties, professional in her manner, smartly dressed in a tweed business suit and sensible shoes. She had a small notepad and a pencil at the ready when she stopped in front of the priest's desk.

"Yes Father?" she said.

"Mrs. Hollis, would you please close that window for me? That nincompoop housekeeper of ours has left it open again!" Father Villa Cruz answered, complaining about the help.

"Certainly Father, my pleasure," replied Mrs. Hollis.

"The arthritis is bad this morning, *no*?" she asked from over her shoulder as she walked over to the window.

"Yes, excruciatingly so," the priest replied as he leaned forward and squeezed at his knees.

After closing the window effortlessly, Mrs. Hollis turned to walk back toward the desk. She stopped along the way to retrieve a blanket off the back of a Queen Ann chair which sat across the room near the wall of books stacked impressively floor to ceiling on recessed walnut shelves.

"I'll speak to Doris about that later sir. She only opens the window at night to freshen the room for you sir, *the pipe smoke sir*," she said, pointing toward the rack on the desk on front of him.

"Yes well," he replied sheepishly.

"Please tell her to be mindful to close the window before she leaves then," Father Villa Cruz quickly added.

"I will sir," replied Mrs. Hollis, walking around the desk and dropping the folded wool blanket onto his lap.

"That should help a bit Father," she said as she walked back to resume her stance in front of the desk. "Will there be anything else sir?" she asked politely.

"You've arranged for Carl to drive me to the airport?" the priest asked.

"Of course, he will be here in one hour's time," she answered.

"Have Mr. Hayes and Mr. Solero arrived yet?"

"Yes Father, they are waiting right outside. Shall I send them in now?"

"No, wait ten minutes and then send them in. I need to warm up first so I don't look so blasted feeble!" Father Villa Cruz instructed gruffly.

"Of course Father, ten minutes. Will that be all?"

"Yes, thank you Mrs. Hollis. You do know how much I appreciate your attention to detail?" he replied in a softer tone.

"Yes I do Father, thank you," she said, turning to leave.

"Oh, and shall I send for tea from the kitchen?" she asked, half turning back.

"That will be fine dear, by all means, tea would be nice," he answered politely. Mrs. Hollis nodded and walked out of the room, closing the door behind her.

Father Villa Cruz spread the blanket across his lap and shivered as he waited for the heavy material to work its magic. He leaned back in his chair and contemplated the plans he had made since talking with Father Willet at Saint John's in Fresno. He didn't like Father Willet very much, the man was a peasant as far as he was concerned. But more importantly, he didn't trust him. The Monsignor had known that the minute he left that meeting that Father Willet would be hard at work devising a way to keep him from the girl. Father *'Billy'* and his confederates would do anything they needed to, anything at all, to deny her righteous destiny. Willet and the others actually placed *her* well being above the work of the *Lord God!*

This infuriated the Monsignor, the audacity of their insolence! *How dare they!* The girl was nothing more than an instrument in the hands of God and his Holy Church, to be used in His Holy service. Father Villa Cruz stewed on this thought for a moment and then calmed himself, massaging his legs vigorously, hastening the warming powers of the wool blanket that covered them. He shook his head as if to erase the board in his mind, stopped thinking about whatever Father Willet might be planning, it wasn't important anyway. Everything was already in place, firmly in place. The resources he required had been approved, and they were waiting in the other room for his final instructions.

He took a few minutes longer to recap what he had already planned, in near seamless detail of course. Tomorrow he would be in Rome, and then in two days time he would be at the Vatican for a scheduled audience with the College of Cardinals and His Holiness, the Pontiff himself. He smiled to himself as he imagined their faces, how they would all listen intently to his words. And then, how they would welcome his new *'charge'* in the service of God and the Holy Roman Church. How he would be welcomed into the ranks of the privileged and the powerful, a red robe of his own at last. He imagined how he and this child, this angel on Earth, would travel the globe together, healing the masses, sanctifying his future, his destiny. Father Villa Cruz sat in silence, entranced with his own thoughts, enthralled by the scope of his scheming, convinced of his righteousness. He jumped suddenly in his chair, startled by a loud knock at the opening door.

"Excuse me Father, shall I send in your guests?" asked Mrs. Hollis as she poked her head through the half open door. The Monsignor regained his composure and stood, folding the blanket and walking over to the replace it over the Queen Ann chair.

"*Yes, yes, of course.* Thank you Mrs. Hollis," he replied as he stood near the door to welcome the two men.

They appeared a second later, entering one behind the other in close cadence. The Monsignor greeted each of them as they came into the room, shaking their hands as he did so.

"Thank you Mrs. Hollis," he said to his secretary.

She smiled and walked out, closing the door behind her as she left the room. Father Villa Cruz motioned toward the sofa across from the Queen Ann chair and the two men sat down. The priest settled himself into the comfy wingback chair and crossed his legs neatly, one knee over the other. He was surprised that he was able to do so without crying out in pain. Then again, he was determined to appear strong and in control. As any leader should, as these men would surely expect of him.

"Mr. Hayes, Mr. Solero, I thank you for arriving so quickly," he said to the two men. They nodded in unison without saying a word, looking intently at the priest, studying his face.

"Yes, well I trust your fight was uneventful," Father Villa Cruz added.

"Yes Eminence, the flight went well, *long,* but well," Mr. Solero replied, speaking for the two of them. Father Villa Cruz now knew who the team leader was and he made a mental note to direct most of his attention and instructions to Mr. Solero.

"Good! *Well then,* we have precious little time as I am flying to Rome myself in a few hours. So if you gentlemen will forgive me, I will get right to business," he said to them both.

"Of course Eminence," replied Solero.

Again a knock at the door and Mrs. Hollis entered, carrying a heavy silver tea service.

"Excuse me for interrupting Father, the tea you requested," she said walking carefully toward them. The two visitors who had stood as she entered the room, walked toward her to lend a helping hand.

"*Sit, sit,* gentlemen, I can manage myself thank you," Mrs. Hollis said, waving the two men off.

"There you see, piece of cake," she said as she set the tray on the table between them. The two men sat back down and waited for Father Villa Cruz to respond.

"Shall I pour Father?" asked Mrs. Hollis.

"No dear, that won't be necessary, we'll manage," he replied.

"Very well then, *gentlemen*," she said, turning to leave the room once again. Father Villa Cruz gestured toward the tray, "Help yourself, please," he said to each of them.

"Thank you Eminence," replied Solero, gesturing for Mr. Hayes to do the honors.

Father Villa Cruz studied the two men as they doctored their tea with sugar and cream. Mr. Hayes was young, maybe in his early thirties. He was big, like an American football player, blond hair and blue eyes. That surprised the priest a little given the organization that young man represented. He had expected an all-Italian team, but what did he know of these things. This was the first time he had ever been exposed to this *protective* branch of the Church.

Mr. Solero was more of what the priest had expected. Obviously Italian, he looked Sicilian maybe, perhaps from Palermo. He looked as if he could have been a fisherman once upon a time. He had the tough weathered hands of someone who had labored for a large part of his life. Father Villa Cruz studied their faces; their expressions as they drank their tea, looked back at him.

"Would you care for some tea Eminence?" Solero asked.

"No, no, thank you my son, maybe later," he replied.

"As I was saying, I will be flying to Rome later today. And in a few days I will be meeting with His Holiness himself, in the chamber of the College of Cardinals. Of course these are facts that you already know," Father Villa Cruz proudly, beginning his briefing. The two men nodded as they sipped their tea.

"As you know, you are here to take charge of a young girl and escort her to Rome personally so that she may join me at the Vatican for this audience. I cannot emphasize strongly enough the importance of her presence at this meeting. It is imperative that she be there no later than the fifteenth of this month gentlemen, *do you understand?*" Father Villa Cruz asked carefully.

"Yes Eminence, the fifteenth of March, it will be done," Solero replied calmly.

"And you realize that it may be necessary to bring her against her will, against the will of her parents and others close to her?" the Monsignor added cautiously.

"We have been briefed Eminence," Solero replied in a slow even tone.

"Bouno, moto bouno," Father Villa Cruz replied in Italian.

Solero leaned forward on the sofa, returning his cup to the serving tray, and his associate did likewise.

"I trust there have been no changes then, the girl will be where we were told this evening?" Solero asked, checking his wristwatch.

"I am certain that she will be there as planned. As for any changes, perhaps I should be asking you that question," Father Villa Cruz answered wryly.

"Perhaps you should. She has new friends living near the church, a newlywed couple with a small child. As far as we can see, they will not be any problem. Still, we have people in place to assure that they do not stray far from home tonight," Solero informed the Monsignor.

"I am impressed by your thoroughness, *my compliments*," replied Father Villa Cruz.

"Please look at these photos and tell me if you recognize anyone in them," Solero asked, gesturing to his associate to set several photographs onto the table in front of the priest.

Father Villa Cruz retrieved his spectacles from the lamp table and put them on as the younger man displayed the photos. He held the frames close to his eyes with one hand while he sifted through the half dozen or so pictures. Father Villa Cruz tapped the photo to his far left with his forefinger.

"The young man is Father Kelly, an intern at St. John's. And I believe the woman is a journalist from San Francisco, her name escapes me though. They are standing on either side of Tina Lopez in this picture. I'm certain that you will see them at the party tonight as well. As for the others, I have never seen any of them. Why do you show me these pictures, is there some cause for alarm concerning these people?"

"We're not sure. It is a shame that we were not called upon sooner to investigate these things," said Solero politely scolding the priest.

"Yes well, Father Willet and his friends did a fine job of keeping such a big secret for as long as they did," the Monsignor replied in his own defense.

"Be that as it may Eminence, these others as you call them, are unknowns, random variables potentially. You must understand, that on *your* authority, should they pose a threat to our objective, they may require *special* attention. *Do you understand my meaning Father?"* Solero asked the priest cautiously.

"Perfectly," answered the Monsignor.

"Very well," Solero replied.

He walked over to stand near the priest, and then crouched beside him. With his index finger he pointed at the photo in center of the bunch. "This one, the boy, do you know him?" he asked the priest. Father Villa Cruz leaned forward and picked up the photo. He held it close to his face and studied it intensely for a moment. Shaking his head he set the picture back on the table.

"No, I have never seen this boy," he said finally.

"You're certain that you have never seen him before?" Solero asked again, pressing the issue.

"No, *I have not*. Why do you keep asking?" asked the priest.

"Because I fear this boy is not in these photos by chance. All of my instincts sense this. It's the way he is watching the girl. Not casually, not lustfully, not randomly. He's studying her, *no* he's stalking her. I don't know why, but I'm sure of it," Solero explained.

"What about the other two?" Father Villa Cruz asked, suddenly concerned.

"I don't know, but they shouldn't be too hard to find given their choice of automobiles. We'll have someone keep an eye on them as well. The boy will be harder though, he seems to appear from the shadows and then disappears back into them," Solero added.

"I don't like surprises Mr. Solero, they're never good for business," warned Father Villa Cruz.

"Understood Eminence, I will see to them personally. The girl *will* be airborne in 24 hours," Solero said, confidently reassuring the Monsignor.

"Graci Senori, I have complete confidence in your abilities," Father Villa Cruz replied.

"You're Eminence," answered Solero, bowing respectfully.

The Monsignor stood and accompanied the two men to the door, shaking their hands as they exited the room.

"Mrs. Hollis, please escort these gentlemen out of the building, " he asked politely.

"Of course Father," she replied, getting up from her desk and taking the lead.

"Good luck," said the priest, feebly waving an arthritic hand.

"Bon voyage Eminence," replied Solero as he walked away.

Firebaugh, California, 12, March 1974
10:00am

Maria Lopez hurried across the living room in her bare feet to answer the doorbell, her three year old at her heels in close pursuit, crying hysterically. After wiping her hands dry with a dishcloth, she turned the knob and opened the door. Even though I could barely make out her face through the screen door, I had no trouble at all seeing that she had had a rough start on the day. She ran her hand back across her head, pulling her long hair away from her face. Then squinting slightly and wrinkling her nose, she tried to make out my shadowy face through the dark screen.

"*Father Kelly?*" she asked weakly.

"Good morning Maria," I replied cheerfully.

"Good morning Father, I wasn't expecting you quite so early. Please forgive me, the house is a mess," she said apologizing as she opened the screen to let me in.

"I'm sorry Maria, I tried calling before I left but nobody answered the phone," I explained, walking past her and the toddler at her feet.

"You must have called while I was bathing this one," she replied as she crouched down to pick up her whimpering daughter.

"*Mija*, can you say hello to our guest?" Maria asked her cranky child.

"*NO!*"

"*ANGELA*, you be nice!" Maria said, scolding the little girl.

"It's OK Maria, really. I'm the one intruding on her routine," I interjected guiltily.

"*Hi Angela,*" I said, directing my attention to the teary eyed child, trying to find just the right combination of goofy faces to make her smile. She responded quickly, taking a liking to my impression of Popeye the Sailor, and started giggling. I followed that performance up with a fast round of peek-a-boo and *viola*, order had been restored for the small cost of my dignity.

"Here you go," Maria said, handing Angela over to me.

"As long as you have her attention, I'll go and let Tina know that you're here, and finish dressing myself," she added, pointing down to her bare feet.

"*Uh*, OK, I'll wait for you guys in the kitchen. Got any Cheerios?" I said, walking through the house while Angela busied herself trying to pull off my collar.

"Yeah, the box is on the counter, the milk is in the fridge. You know where everything else is, make yourself at home," Maria shouted from over her shoulder as she disappeared down the hall.

Angela and I walked into the kitchen and set up camp at the table. I set her into her high chair with only a small protest. She quieted down quickly after an encore performance from Popeye. Maria must have been doing the breakfast dishes when I arrived because the sink was still full of soapsuds. I spotted the Cheerios box on the counter and grabbed the box, fishing out a fist full of the toasty oat O's and spilling them onto Angela's high chair tray. She seemed to be enjoying the little break in her routine, specifically the cereal sans bowl and spoon, and gleefully started scooping them up from the tray and into her mouth.

"Atta girl Angie," I said cheerfully to the child while I fixed myself a bowl of Cheerios.

I made sure to add a spoonful of Ovaltine before pouring the milk, a little trick I learned from my sweet-toothed sister. And you know what, it's really good! I think everyone should try it! Then taking a seat beside Angela I settled in to enjoy the quick meal with my sticky little neighbor. Turning slightly to acknowledge her jabbering, I nearly choked to death as I spewed cereal and milk through my nose after catching sight of her ridiculously funny face.

It was totally pockmarked with Cheerios, the jam from her toast proving to be the catalyst in the *toddler's paste* she had concocted from sugar, spit, and strawberry preserves. Of course Maria picked that instant to walk into the kitchen as I was frantically trying to clean the both of us up with a fist full of paper napkins from the holder on the table.

"I guess Home Economics isn't a course at the Seminary, *aye Father?*" she teased through a giggle.

"I wish I had my camera handy, you two look so funny!" she added for good measure.

Angela stopped fussing for a moment to wave to her mother and pose, apparently she was keenly aware of what the word camera. Unfortunately her *pose* consisted of two sticky little hands raised up to her freshly cleaned face! Huffing in frustration, I grabbed another stack of napkins and started working at wiping away the new lot of Cheerios and jam from her face.

"OH ANGIE, not again!" I muttered under my breath.

"Hey Rockefeller, we're not millionaires you know! Take her to the sink and run some warm water!" Maria said, playfully scolding me.

Moving much faster physically than my mind was processing her suggestion, Maria freed Angela from the high chair and whisked her over to the kitchen sink in a single motion. Before I could even turn to follow them with my eyes, the water was running and Maria was rinsing the gooey mess from her child's little round face.

"*There, there, mija*, all better now," she said, cooing at, and tickling Angela.

"I'm really sorry Maria. *I ahh*, I must have choked on a defective Cheerio or something," I said, fibbing defensively. Maria smirked and wagged her index finger in my direction.

"Oh Father, shame on you! That's quite a whopper coming from a man of the cloth!" she said in mock horror.

"*I...I...I...*"

"I was in the doorway the whole time. I know how funny my daughter can be, she's a real comedian this one," Maria said, laughing out loud while I wrestled with my conscience.

She ran a dishtowel under the warm water and wrung it dry. Then she tossed it to me so I could finish cleaning myself up as well, saving a few precious napkins in the process. After dabbing my face clean, I brushed the drying milk from my black cotton shirt, then folded the towel neatly and set in front of me.

"*OK, OK, I'm busted!*" I said capitulating.

"Father Willet is **REALLY** going to enjoy my confession Sunday!" I snapped, feigning frustration.

"God will forgive you Father, He thinks Angela's pretty funny too," Maria said cheerfully.

"*Doesn't He mija, doesn't He!*" she cooed at her daughter.

Angela curled into a little ball in her mother's arms and laughed out loud. It was that universal children's laugh, you know the one I mean. The one that sounds like a cackle wrapped in a snort, wrapped twice again in a belly-tightening guffaw. Caught off guard, I nearly spewed all over myself again.

"That's it, breakfast is OVER!" I said, choking down the only spoonful of cereal destined to nourish me this morning. Maria walked over to swat me solidly on my back while I recovered.

"Maybe you should stick to porridge Father, Cheerios just aren't for you!" she teased.

"*Maybe...*" I replied as the choking spasms subsided.

"*Maybe...*"

Tina entered the kitchen as Maria sat down next to me, Angela in her lap, busying herself with a rolled flour tortilla.

"Hey, what'd I miss?" Tina asked as she pulled up a chair across from her mother.

"Father Kelly was treating your sister to breakfast and a show," Maria said with a smirk.

"Really, sorry I missed that," Tina said while she spread jam on a tortilla and rolled it up.

"It was nothing, *really!*" I replied before Maria could pile on any more quips.

Maria ignored my remark and focused instead on her oldest child.

"*TINA*, is that all you are going to have for breakfast?" she asked rhetorically.

"But Mama, I'm not..." Tina began.

"*Ah, ah, ah...enough!* Here honey, hold Angela while I scramble you some eggs and papas, it won't take but a minute or two!" Maria snapped, moving quickly to hand off the baby and head for the fridge for the eggs and milk. Tina started to reply and then thought better of it, standing instead to put Angela back into her high chair.

"Sit still Angelina, be a good girl, *OK mijia?*" she said softly as she replaced the plastic tray in front of the child. Angela proceeded to tap her half eaten tortilla on the tray, stopping to take nibbles every now and then. Tina sat back down across from me and pushed her own tortilla away from her, a tiny pout on her face.

"*I hear you looking at me LaTina,*" Maria said from the stove without looking over at us.

Tina stamped her foot once under the table, frustrated by her mother's sixth sense, a trait that ALL mothers receive shortly after they give birth I think.

"*Ummm*, Maria, I don't suppose you..." I started to say.

"Don't worry Father, I am making enough for two," she replied before I could finish. I guess that sixth sense could be applied to everyone! Tina's expression softened and she directed her attention to me now.

"So where are you taking me today Father?" she asked.

"*Didn't your parents tell you?*" I said answering a question with a question, immediately scolding myself, I hate when people do that!

"No?" she answered.

"*Sorry Father*, Victor had to stay over in Mendota yesterday and I was just so busy with the kids, I guess I forgot," Maria said, apologizing as she walked over to serve up the scrambled eggs and potato concoction. The aroma was so wonderful, and I was so hungry that I nearly neglected to reply.

"That's alright Maria, its no big deal, really," I said, leaning back so that she could spoon some of the heavenly mixture onto the plate in front of me.

I leaned forward as Maria circled the table to serve Tina and let the steam from the plate rise up and envelope my senses. Nothing like home cooking I thought to myself. I pushed a napkin down into my lap, picked up my fork and shoveled in the first load in a most un-gentleman-like manner.

The heat from the *just made* dish was still steaming in my mouth, causing me to make that goofy face where you suck in as much air as you can to cool off the food that is burning a hole through your tongue. Through watery eyes I managed to choke out a compliment to the chef.

"This...*'gasp'*... is really good Maria...*gasp, gasp!*"

"*Uhhh*, glad you're enjoying it so Father, *thanks, I think?*" she said sarcastically.

I held up my hand with the *okey doke* signal and continued to eat my meal. Looking up, I caught Tina smiling as she watched me eat, embarrassing me just a little for some reason. I must have been an amusing sight as I made a big fat pig of myself. But who could blame me, Maria's food was legendary, rivaled only by Sister Ruth back at St John's. I grinned at back Tina and set down my fork. Retrieving the napkin from my lap, I politely dabbed at the corners of my mouth like any civilized man would.

"How's your breakfast?" I nonchalantly asked.

"Good," she answered smirking.

"*And yours,*" she asked, suddenly appearing older and more mature than myself.

"*Umm*, you know, *its ahhh*, great, its great, you're Mom's a great cook," I answered, suddenly flustered.

"Great!" she replied cheerfully.

"Yeah, *great*," I answered back, feeling a little silly now.

"Do you think either of you can think of any another adjective to describe me? You know like beautiful, glamorous, wonderful, charming, any of those will do," Maria chimed in, teasing us both as she joined us at the table with a cup of coffee. She looked back and forth at Tina and I while she sipped at her drink. Tina resumed picking at her food while I sat there looking unsure of what to do next. I was torn between finishing my breakfast and excusing myself to dash home and start the morning all over again! I could feel Maria's eyes studying me while I sat there mentally twisting in the wind.

"Hey wait a minute...is there something going on here you two want to talk about? *Tina, Father Kelly...?*" Maria said, tossing the question out on the table like a side dish to share.

Tina blushed and lowered her face closer to her plate while I scooted my chair back away from the table as if preparing to make a hasty retreat. Maria started laughing before either of us could say or do anything that could be misconstrued.

"*Take it easy, take it easy!* I was only teasing you," she said, shaking her head slowly and sipping her coffee.

"You guys are too easy," she said, still giggling at our reactions.

"*Maybe too easy, huh*"

"Maybe I ought to be keeping an eye on the two of you after all," she said, her voice suddenly grave with mock concern.

"MAMA!" Tina snapped, stamping her foot under the table again and scooting her own chair away from the table.

"OK, OK, I'm sorry mijia, but I couldn't resist teasing the padre. He blushes just like an apple on the tree whenever I do that," Maria said, trying smooth things over with her daughter. She looked over at me and pleaded for some support.

"Father, *please,* tell her I was only kidding, *por favor,*" she said to me. Relieved that she was only teasing, I started to toss in my two cents, but before I could reply, Angela jumped into the fray after recognizing the only word she understood in our fractured conversation.

"APPLE JUICE, APPLE JUICE!" she chanted, banging her messy little hands on the plastic tray in perfect 2/3 time.

"Déjelo mijia!" Maria snapped sharply, ordering the child to stop pestering her immediately.

Angela quieted down right away, instinctively aware of when her mother meant business. They say that we all have telltale characteristics that tip our hands so to speak. Poker players call it a *'tell',* and it can be a certain look, or a mannerism, or maybe just a nervous tick of some sort. Whatever it might be, it broadcasts our true intentions, no matter how well we think that we're concealing them from the world around us. In Maria's case it was her tone of voice. Not shrill at all, or over the top in any way, but subtle, cool, and subdued. It was just different enough from her normal tone to get one's attention and send a silent and unmistakable message.

"Alright everyone, time out, TRUCE OK!" Maria said over the momentarily silent room.

All eyes darted around the table, person to person, from Tina to Maria, from Maria to me, and from Angela to the refrigerator, still chanting for apple juice under her breath. After a prolonged moment of silence, long enough for everyone to collect their thoughts and catch their breath, everyone in the room over the age of three burst out into laughter, startling poor little Angela into a ferocious crying jag.

"Oh no, bebé pobre, I'm sorry baby," Maria said sympathetically to her child, picking her up from the high chair and walking around the room consoling her.

"Rápidamente Tina, finish your breakfast *mijia.* Father Kelly can fill you in about your trip while you're driving to Fresno," Maria said though a case of the giggles.

"And Father," Maria said, directing her attention to me.

"Yes?"

"Can you set the dishes in the sink for me before you leave? I need to see to this child, it's now officially naptime?" she pleaded rhetorically while she walked out of the kitchen, baby on her hip and a bottle of apple juice in her free hand.

"Yes ma'am," I replied, already on my feet, a dish in each hand, and on my way to the sink. I could hear a fork hitting a plate in rapid succession as Tina wolfed down her cold eggs and potatoes. She finished quickly and I heard her chair skid across the floor as she stood to ferry over the last of the breakfast mess from the chrome and Formica table.

"Here you go Father, that's the last of them," she said, handing over several dirty dishes and utensils for me to rinse and stack.

Shoveling the table scraps into the sink, I reached over and flipped on the garbage disposal. The soggy food disappeared down the drain with a loud gurgling noise followed by a higher pitched whine as the machine finished devouring what was left of breakfast. After switching off the disposal I rinsed my hands under the warm water and then turned off the tap. Tina tossed me the dishtowel that was draped over the handle on the oven door and I dried my hands quickly. We looked at each other then looked around the kitchen, checking for any mess we may have missed. Satisfied that we had passed muster, we turned to exit the room.

"Well that was fun," I said sarcastically.

"Yeah," replied Tina as we walked into the living room.

She picked up a light blue windbreaker from the back of the couch along with a small macramé purse.

"I'm ready," she said cheerfully.

"Me too," I said, fishing the car keys out of my pants pocket.

"Bye-bye Mama, see you tonight at the Donnelly's party," she called out to the house.

I heard Maria reply faintly as I walked out onto the porch and held the door open for Tina. She paused halfway out the door and called back over her shoulder.

"Si Mama, I will," she shouted, waking past me and down the steps toward the car parked in the drive. I reached inside, and closed the heavy front door and then let the screen close on its own while I caught up with Tina at the car.

"You *will* what?" I asked as we got into the car, slamming the doors tightly behind us.

"Keep an eye on you," she teased, buckling her safety belt.

"Oh man! Are we still doing this?" I whined.

"Relax Father Kelly, Mom's just having fun with you," she answered, scolding me gently.

"*Yeah but…I mean…you don't think that I…do you?*" I said stammering slightly.

"Of course not silly! It's just that this is a small town Father, and we have so little to gossip about," she said through a small laugh.

"Besides, everyone knows about you and KC anyway," she announced with a sly grin.

"*WHAT THE…!*"

"*Careful, careful,* Father Kelly, *you know who* is listening," she said sarcastically.

"What's that supposed to mean, *everyone knows about me and KC*? Know what?" I asked totally flummoxed.

"Oh, they've been talking about you two for months!" she added, rocking back and forth and clapping her hands, totally enjoying my reaction to the latest assault on my pious reputation.

"This can't be good," I moaned, gently bashing my forehead on the steering wheel.

"Oh I don't know Father Kelly, I think she's cute!" said Tina, raising her hand to cover her mouth, trying to keep from laughing out loud. I shot her a sideways glance and murmured something inaudible, then started the engine.

"So what are we going to Fresno for?" Tina asked nonchalantly as we drove away from the house. I answered before thinking.

"We're meeting KC and her friend Jay at…"

"*Ohhhhhhh!*" she said feigning accusation with the tone of her voice and the expression on her face before I could even finish my sentence.

"*OH COME ON!*"

Firebaugh, California, 12, March 1974
11:00am

Victor waived at the car as he passed it in the drive. He saw his daughter was driving away with the young priest from St. John's, and who knows where they were going. Nobody ever told him anything around here he thought to himself. He drove through the dust trail that they had left behind and circled the house to park under the elm tree in the back near the tool shed. He set the gearshift on the steering column into the Park position and shut off the engine. Then reaching across the bench seat he slapped the shoulder of his young passenger.

"You hungry hombre?" he asked robustly. The young man nodded affirmatively and smiled weakly.

"GOOD! Cause I could eat a horse," Victor replied enthusiastically.

"You don't talk much, do you?" he asked rhetorically, not really expecting an answer. The boy remained still and silent, waiting politely for Victor to get out of the truck first.

"That's OK, I was pretty shy when I was your age myself. Let's go on inside and see what my Maria has on the table," Victor added, mussing up his guest's hair as he opened the door and stepped out of the pick up truck.

"OK," the boy replied softly, taking a moment to straighten out his hair before he followed.

Victor took off his hat and wiped the sweat from his brow with the sleeve of his shirt as they walked to the open back door of the house. He caught sight of Maria in the kitchen window and he blew a kiss her way with the brim of his Stetson.

"There's my Maria now," he said to the boy, pointing toward the window with the hat in his hand. The two of them walked into the house together after stomping the dirt off of their boots on the small set of concrete steps.

"*Wipe your feet first Panson!*" Maria called from the kitchen.

"We are, we are," Victor answered back, placing his hat on the washing machine as they passed through the utility room. Maria looked over her shoulder and studied the boy standing beside her husband. She nodded toward them.

"And who have we here?" she asked.

"We have Ramon here, *that's who*," Victor said walking over and kissing his wife on the cheek.

"What's for lunch?" he asked as he walked back toward the kitchen table. He gestured for the boy to take a seat, which he did obediently.

"How about a couple sandwiches, and some soup? We've got a lot of ham left over from Sunday in the fridge and some Albondigas from last night right here on the stove, sound good?" Maria asked, already removing the sandwich fixings from the refrigerator.

"Perfect," Victor replied.

"That OK with you Ramon?" he asked the boy.

Miguel hesitated a moment, unaccustomed to the name he had chosen to hide behind. Recovering quickly he nodded vigorously, "*Si Senor, that's OK,*" he said with a smile.

"What's the matter, cat got his tongue?" Maria asked, chiming in from the counter while she prepared their lunch.

"No, he's just shy," replied Victor.

"Must be going around. I just went through a fit of shyness with Father Kelly before you got here," Maria said making small talk.

"I saw him leaving as we drove up, Tina was with him," her husband replied.

"Where were they going?" he asked.

"Over to Fresno, they're meeting up with KC and Jay. Something about an interview with the Hernandez girl, Rosa, *poor thing*," answered Maria, shaking her head slowly while she prepared their meal.

"Oh…so what were you teasing the padre about?" Victor asked.

"*Whaaaat*…why do you say that?" gasped Maria, as if he had hurt her feelings or something.

"*Oh no you don't mamacita*…I know you too well! What did you say to the poor man? Victor insisted.

"Nothing, *really*, I just made a small deal about Tina's school girl crush, that's all," she replied.

"*And?*"

"And maybe I wondered out loud about his intentions…"

"*MARIA!*" Victor gasped playfully.

"Well I was only teasing," she whined in her defense.

Victor laughed loud and hard, as he looked across the table at the boy he had brought home for lunch and taken on for a few days work.

"You see what I have to deal with around here Ramon?" he said to the boy. Miguel smiled back at him and looked over at Maria as she walked to the table to serve the sandwiches. She set the plates in front of the two hungry males and twisted open a jar of mayonnaise and mustard.

"I didn't know what you liked so I'll let you put whatever you want on the sandwich yourself," she said to the boy.

"Gracias senora," he said politely.

"*Ahhh, manners, very nice. De nada mijio,*" Maria answered.

"I'll just finish heating up the soup and bring you each a bowl. Go on now, eat, *eat!*" she said walking away.

"You better do like she says hombre, she has a real temper," Victor said, teasing the boy through a mouthful of food.

"Yes sir," the boy said smiling.

He picked up the knife next to his plate and held it for a moment in his fist, enjoying the feeling of the cold stainless steel. Slowly, he dipped the butter knife into the squat glass jar of mustard, and extracted a healthy dollop of the spicy yellow condiment. Then meticulously he spread the mixture across the top piece of bread, making sure to leave no portion of the slice uncovered.

"Besides, we've got a lot of work over in Mendota to finish today," Victor added, washing down his sandwich with the iced tea Maria had set out for the two of them.

"Don't forget about the party tonight *Panson*, I don't want to be late!" Maria said, pausing with her hands on her hips to make sure that her husband had heard her. Victor finished guzzling his tea before he answered.

"I know, I know, don't worry *chica*," he replied.

"You see what I have to deal with," he directed again at the boy across the table.

Miguel smiled broadly and took a bite of his meal, chewing slowly, methodically. He watched as the two adults playfully exchanged words while he ate. He liked the way they talked to one another, the way they teased one another, the way they obviously loved one another. He suddenly felt lonely for his own parents. The laughter and soft voices that filled the room brought memories to the surface. Good memories, things he had not allowed himself to recall for a very long time. Miguel felt himself softening, the edge he had honed for years starting to dull. He could feel the sentiment in the room enveloping him, making his heart swell, making him weak. He quickly shut his eyes tightly and turned his thoughts inward. He concentrated as hard as he could on anything but the sound of their voices. He focused on whatever he could to distract himself from their conversation. He listened to the sound of his own teeth as they pulverized the food in his mouth. He blocked out everything but the sound of the gnashing, and the feeling of his flexing jaw as he chewed his food in forced silence.

"Hey, Ramon...you OK son?" Victor asked, snapping his fingers from across the table.

"RAMON!" Miguel snapped open his eyes quickly and he was met by Victor's concerned stare.

"Are you OK?" Victor asked again.

Miguel nodded, "Si," he replied weakly.

"Umm, a little too much mustard I think," Miguel added, thinking quickly.

"Oh, well be more careful OK. It's too late in the day to hire anyone else, and we've got lots to do before the day is over," Victor pleaded in earnest.

"Here, drink some iced tea and water down that mustard," he added.

Miguel picked up his glass and gulped down the cold sweet tea, silently scolding himself for bringing too much attention on himself. He drained the glass and Victor reached across and refilled his glass.

"Gracias," Miguel said thanking him.

"Don't worry about it," Victor replied.

"OK boys, soups on!" Maria said cheerfully as she set the steaming bowls down on the table.

"Now if you gentlemen will excuse me, I only have an hour or so before the baby wakes up from her nap. So I'm going into the other room to sit down and do **NOTHING** for a whole sixty minutes!" Maria said with a smile. She kissed her husband on the way out and disappeared into the hall.

"There, you see what I have to deal with Ramon," Victor said, pretending to be annoyed.

Miguel nodded when he finished talking, ignoring everything that had been said, staying focused on the plan. He went over every detail while he ate; his eyes trained on Victor, but his mind far, far away. He paused only to nod at the man across from him whenever the sounds ended, and his lips stopped moving. Miguel let his eyes wander around the kitchen lazily, around the table at which he sat. He imagined the family taking their meals here, right here, at this very table. He wondered which seat was hers, perhaps it the very chair in which he sat. He was close, so very close…

Forty-four

(...)"When I was a child, I used to speak as a child,
think as a child, reason as a child; when I became
a man, I did away with childish things"...1st
Corinthians 13:11)

Fresno, California, 12, March 1974
Heritage House Rehabilitation Center...12:30pm

KC tilted her head slightly, wedging the telephone receiver between her ear and shoulder. She waived over at Jay who was sitting on the lobby's hard sofa, patiently waiting for her to return. She flashed the universal *'just a sec'* signal to the receptionist, which basically amounted to a raised index finger and a quick wink. The girl behind the desk smiled back weakly, more of a sneer than a smile actually, then resumed doing whatever it was she was doing before KC had had the audacity to interrupt her and ask to use the phone. KC mimed a smart-ass remark then turned away and leaned back against the receptionist's desk. *"Deal with this honey,"* she muttered, smirking as she shook back her hair and raised the handset up to her ear. KC was about to send another monotone barb back over her shoulder at the fussy receptionist when she was startled by the voice on the other end of the line.

"Hi, I'm back," Maria Lopez said, slightly out of breath.

"Good, I was getting a little worried," KC replied.

"No need to worry, I was just seeing Victor off after lunch," Maria explained.

"Oh, is that what they're calling it now a days," KC said playfully.

"*Nooo*, nothing like that! You're so bad Katherine, shame on you!" Maria stammered defensively.

"Oh all right, I was only teasing...*sort of*," giggled KC, shifting the handset to her other ear.

"You're too easy, "KC added as she settled down.

"That's so funny! I said the very same thing to Father Kelly earlier this morning," Maria said.

"*Really?* Hey, speaking of the good Father, *he's late!* What time did they leave your place anyway?" KC asked.

"Oh he and Tina left here just about the same time that Victor and Ramon arrived for lunch, maybe two hours ago," Maria answered.

"They should have been here by now?" KC said, checking her wristwatch.

"And who's Ramon? I don't remember any Ramon on your husband's crew?" KC added curiously.

"Don't worry *mishap*, you know what a slow poke the padre is. Give them a little longer, they'll be there soon," Maria said reassuringly.

"Oh, and Ramon is just a stray kid that Victor took in for a few days work, that's all."

"Yeah, O I guess. But I don't think that we'll be able to wait very much longer. They're pretty anal about schedules around here, and I'm pretty sure that my cutesy eyelash batting will go un-noticed," KC said sarcastically, turning her head slightly as she picked up the sound of a muffled giggle from behind her.

"KC I have to go now, Angela is pitching a fit over God knows what? I'll see you all tonight at the party, OK?" Maria said quickly, hanging up before KC could reply.

"OK, *but I*,"*click!*...KC began, cut off by the loud dial tone in her ear.

"How rude," she hissed at the receiver. She turned to replace the receiver and was met by the fluttering eyes and smug look of the receptionist, who was obviously pleased by KC's frustration.

"*Tough call ma'am?*" the girl said sarcastically.

"Oh no, we were just cut off, must have been a bad connection," KC stammered uncomfortably.

"Yeah, don't you just hate when that happens," the girl replied with a smirk, resuming her busy work before KC could answer back.

"*Why I ought a...*" KC murmured as she turned to walk away. Halfway back to rejoin Jay on the sofa, she turned and flashed the same Hawaiian good luck signal that the crew of the Pueblo had flashed the North Koreans a few years earlier.

"Oh that was nice, making new friends are we?" Jay said sarcastically as KC sat beside him in a huff.

"*Can it Jay man*, that little witch needs a good *hiney bruising* if you ask me!"

"You mean ass whipping?"

"Yeah, yeah, whatever you call it, she needs one!"

"Calm down Miss Borden, there are too many witnesses around here," Jay teased.

"Lizzie Borden, I get it, *hardie har har*, that was so funny I almost forgot to laugh! Maybe you can take your act on the road, maybe you could leave like...*oh, I don't know, NOW!*" KC snapped back.

"Did you get hold of momma Lopez?"

"Yes"

"*So*, when is your boyfriend getting here?"

"SHUT IT JAY! Stop teasing me about that, OK?"

"YIKES! Peace sweetness, I'll be good, I swear," Jay replied, startled and pleased by the level of her frustration.

"*Sooooo*, when will he be here?"

"He'll be here soon...*damn it!* I mean Father Kelly and Tina will be here shortly. Stop asking me so many questions will ya!"

Jay pretended to zip his lips and then lock them shut, tossing the pretend key back over his shoulder. He raised his hands palms up and shrugged his shoulders, an 'are you happy now' expression on his face.

"*Huh*, very funny," KC snorted, trying to stifle a smile. She didn't want to give him the satisfaction of knowing that he had cheered her up some. Fortunately she was spared any further pretence as a warm greeting from a smiling middle age woman interrupted their little war.

"Hello there, I'm Celeste Delgado," the woman said cheerfully, extending a pudgy little hand for each of them to shake. The two of them rose from the sofa and politely made her acquaintance.

"Hello, Ms. Delgado, I'm KC Littleton and this is my associate, Jay Namura," KC said as she gently shook the woman's hand.

"*Celeste*, please," she insisted, smiling at each them individually.

"Of course, Celeste, thank you," KC replied, tugging a little harder to retrieve her hand from the woman. Jay pulled his hand back before she Ms. Delgado could get a grip and waved at her instead. "Pleasure I'm sure," he said, quickly thrusting his hands into the relative safety of his own pockets. Ms. Delgado pulled her own hand back slowly and then clasped them both in front of her.

"Well then, why don't we walk over to my office for now. Rosa will be a few minutes longer I afraid, tighter security since, *you know*, the incident," Celeste Delgado said, almost whispering the last part.

KC looked at her for a second, unsure of what or how much the woman knew. Not being a big fan of surprises, KC made a mental note to shake down the woman once they got to where they were going. It was one thing to have to clear the air with Rosa, but it was quite another to have to have an audience as well.

"Actually Ms. Delgado…"

"Celeste, *please!*"

"Forgive me, Celeste. Actually, we are still waiting for a couple more people," KC explained.

"Oh dear, that might be a problem, we have very strict schedules you know. It helps to keep the clients safe and manageable, you understand," Ms. Delgado replied.

"Yes ma'am, but they should be here any minute," KC pleaded.

"Well, if they arrive before we go to meet Rosa in the conference room, I guess that would be alright," Ms. Delgado answered, capitulating just a little.

Jay and KC nodded in agreement and then followed the elder woman through a set of double doors and into the hall, KC right behind Ms. Delgado and Jay bringing up the rear, his equipment bag slung over his shoulder. They walked the short distance to Celeste's office briskly then entered the small room in single file. Ms. Delgado took her seat behind her desk and motioned for the two of them to take a seat in the chairs the faced across from her.

"May I offer you some coffee or tea," she asked.

"No thank you, we're fine," KC replied, answering for both of them.

The three of them looked anxiously at one another in silence for a moment. Then Celeste leaned forward and directed her attention at KC.

"May I ask why your paper is interested in talking with Rosa again? I mean, I thought that you had already run your stories on the Katz murder months ago?" Ms. Delgado asked suspiciously.

"*She's fishing,*" KC thought to herself.

"*Good!* That means she doesn't know about Katz and the boss. One less blabber mouth to deal with!"

"It's sort of a follow up piece. One of the people that we are waiting for is the girl known as the *'Angel of the Valley'* you may have read stories about her as well?" KC replied, stalling for time. The newly appointed hospital director sat up straight in her chair and beamed.

"*Oh my*, she's coming here today? You know, I saw her on TV, such a beautiful child. Do you know her? Is it true what they say about her? Have you seen these things? How does she know the Hernandez woman?" Ms. Delgado stammered, asking her questions in rapid succession.

"*Whoa*, slow down Celeste, one at a time OK," KC replied with a smile. Celeste Delgado blushed and raised her hands to her warm cheeks, somewhat embarrassed by her response.

"Oh my goodness, please forgive me, I'm not usually so star struck. It's just that my whole family, my whole neighborhood was so shocked to learn that such a person actually existed! And so close to home! We were even more surprised that we had never heard a thing about her until now?" Ms Delgado said trying to explain her frustration and curiosity.

"You know, I bet we'd all be surprised to discover what was happening right under our own noses, if we only took the time to pay attention," KC said, trying to sound compassionate. Jay rolled his eyes and put his hand over his mouth to hide the smirk that was spreading across his face. He started to chuckle and then yelped like a puppy when KC covertly pressed the heel of her two inch pumps hard on his big toe. Ms. Delgado looked his way, concerned.

"Are you alright Mr. Namura?" she asked sincerely.

"Yes ma'am, I'm fine," Jay answered in a harsh whisper.

"Maybe a glass of water while we wait?" he asked politely.

"Of course, just a moment," Celeste replied, getting up and walking to the doorway. She peeked outside of her office and called out to the snooty receptionist in the lobby.

"Nicole dear, would you please bring us some water," she bellowed.

KC and Jay snickered under their breath as the woman waited for a distant reply, amused to no end by the manual public address system the State had sprung for at this facility. Jay reached over and pinched KC's leg in retaliation for the foot stomping, and KC pinched him right back just for GP. Just as they were about to launch into a full-scale slap and tickle war, Ms. Delgado turned around and walked back to her desk. Hostilities averted for the moment, the two of them silently agreed to a tentative truce and got back to business.

"Water will be here in just a minute young man," Ms. Delgado said to Jay.

"Thank you," he replied with a short wave and a grin.

"You're quite welcome," she answered quickly, turning her attention back to KC.

"*Now*, while we're waiting, may I ask just what it is that ties this blessed child to Miss Hernandez?"

KC looked over at Jay who had a *'your call'* expression on his face.

Then she turned back to look at Ms. Delgado, the woman was staring at her intensely, like she was about to reveal the secret of life or something. KC felt like telling her to ease up on the doe eyes and to close her mouth, but thought better of it. Filling her in on Tina's role in the birth of Rosa's baby would be a lot safer than spilling the beans about the Katz murder, she had already come to that conclusion.

"You do know that Rosa has a little girl?" KC asked the director.

"Of course, she talks about her all the time."

"You also know who the father is, right?" KC pressed

"Yes, I am well aware of the circumstances that brought her to stay with us," Celeste answered dryly, obviously uncomfortable with any reference to Dr. Katz.

"Did Rosa ever tell you about the day her baby was born?" Ms. Delgado thought for a moment before she answered.

"*No*, I don't believe she ever did." KC nodded slowly.

"That was one of the Lopez girls earliest miracles," she said.

"What happened?" Celeste asked, biting at her lips as she did so.

"Rosa had come to the Lopez home in a panic one day, something was wrong with her baby, she just knew it. Mrs. Lopez had sensed it as well. The baby was dead, Rosa's belly was cold to the touch, and there was no movement, only a sickening stillness. Then suddenly, right there on Maria's kitchen floor, Rosa began to miscarry, it must have been quite a scene, blood everywhere! But before Maria could freak out completely, her six year-old daughter, Tina, walked in calm as you please, and went right over to Rosa and lay beside her. The little girl began to hum a soothing tune and pat the pregnant girl's stomach. Then, much to everyone's surprise, what should have been a miscarriage became instead a live birth. That's Rosa's connection to the angel. Tina wants to reach out again, to talk to Rosa, to tell her that her child is happy and safe. I want to follow up with a story is about this miracle," KC explained, studying Celeste's face as she finished talking.

The woman across from her sighed deeply and then leaned back in her chair. She reached for a tissue from the colorful box on her desk and dabbed at her eyes. She blew her nose noisily and then crumpled the tissue in her hand, holding it tightly in her fist.

"*That's amazing, truly amazing!* The world should know all about this girl, about her gift!" the director blubbered emotionally.

"You know what, a lot of people seem to agree with you, even me sometimes. But think about it, what kind of life would that leave her?"

"Its one thing to be a servant like the Bible suggests, but it's quite another to be a slave if you ask me."

"Not to mention the fact that the human race has a pretty crappy track record when it comes to righteous do-gooders. I mean what do JFK, RFK, Dr. King, Malcolm X, Abe Lincoln, and Joan of Arc, even Christ himself all have in common? KC asked earnestly.

"*They're all dead?*" Ms. Delgado answered sheepishly, blowing her nose into the tissue.

"They were all murdered!"

"And by the very people to whom they had devoted their lives!"

"Laying it on a little thick there, aren't you sport?" Jay muttered softly, leaning her way slightly.

"*WELL ITS TRUE, ISN"T IT!*" KC snapped, startling Jay with the ferocity of her tone.

"*Peace Kathy*, I didn't shoot them!" Jay replied defensively, quickly scooting his chair a few inches away from his passionate friend, no need risking another foot stomping! Suddenly aware of her '*over the top*' tirade, KC shrank back into her seat and lowered her head.

"Sorry you guys, sometimes I get a little crazy when I talk about this stuff," she said meekly. Looking up, she sniffled once and rubbed under her nose with her index finger.

"It's alright dear, I think I see your point where the girl's welfare is concerned. It's just that to my mind, a gift such as hers is meant to be used, not hidden away from those in need," said Ms. Delgado, offering a sympathetic ear as well as her own two cents on the issue.

"I agree with you Celeste, but, *and I can't believe it's me saying these words,* maybe it's better to let God lead her on her path unencumbered, then for any of us to kibbutz and mine that pathway with everything that we might want, you know what I mean?" KC asked sincerely. Ms. Delgado was about to reply when Nicole appeared at the door with a pitcher of water and three glasses filled with ice.

"Excuse me Celeste, here is your water. Oh, and they are ready whenever you are in the conference room," Nicole said, minus the attitude from earlier encounter with KC.

"Thank you dear, please let them know that we will be along shortly."

"Yes ma'am," Nicole replied, turning to exit the room. Ms. Delgado stood and poured them each a glass of water and gestured for KC and Jay to help themselves.

"Why don't we refresh ourselves and wait a few more minutes for your friends. I think that our schedules might be more flexible than I let on," Celeste said, winking at each of them as she sipped at her water.

Firebaugh, California, 12, March 1974
<u>*Donnelly Ranch House...12:30pm*</u>

"*Oh poo Ralph!* Do you really think that we need so blasted many deputies around here tonight? It's party for goodness sake, how are people going to relax with all those uniforms and all that hardware around?" complained Alma Donnelly enthusiastically.

"Now Alma, we're just keeping the lookey-loos away, you know how crazy it's been since Tina went on that television show. And nobody will be in uniform, they'll be in plain clothes and you won't be able to see the weapons they're carrying, I promise," Sheriff Cardwell said, trying to reassure her.

"But why so many, and how plain are they going to dress? I mean can they at least try and blend in, there will be photographers from the Sacramento Bee here tonight you know," Alma whined, accepting the fact that she was going to have to deal with the armed intrusion at her own 35th anniversary party.

"I give you my word, we won't embarrass you," the Sheriff answered bowing overtly, teasing her as if she were royalty.

"*You just stop that Ralph Cardwell!* I'm not kidding around, you guys had better be ghosts around here tonight, *I mean it!*" she said tersely, turning swiftly on her heel, and leaving him standing alone on the back patio.

Sheriff Cardwell sighed and walked over to the steps that led down to the pool area. He spotted Father Willet and Arthur Donnelly sitting at a table in the cabana. They were smoking cigars and sipping Scotch no doubt. He waved their way, raising his arm high over his head and started down the steps to join them. The Sheriff was a little uncomfortable with all the secrecy and security surrounding the evening. And he wanted to quiz Father Billy a little more about why he had arranged for this meeting, why tonight of all nights? What was so all fired important that it couldn't wait a day or two anyway?

"Arthur, Billy, I see you're getting a head start on the party gentlemen," Sheriff Cardwell said, taking a seat next to Father Willet.

"Relax Ralphie boy, have a snort, or are you going to pull that '*I'm on duty*' nonsense?" said Arthur Donnelly through clenched teeth, as he bit down on his half-smoked Havana.

"You know those are illegal don't you Arthur?" the Sheriff replied sarcastically, as he reached into the center of the table, turning a high ball glass from the serving tray right side up, indicating that he was willing to look the other way if they were.

"Touché constable, touché," Arthur answered, pouring the Sheriff a stiff shot of Johnny Walker Gold label.

"Actually, they we're a gift from our publishing friend up north, *you know who I mean,"* Arthur added, returning the heavy glass cap to the decanter on the crystal serving tray.

Ralph Cardwell removed his hat and set it down on the tabletop, then took a long pull of the smooth libation, swirling the warm liquid around his mouth, savoring the rich smoky flavor.

"I've always liked your style Arthur, top cabin all the way, my compliments," said Sheriff Cardwell with a quick wink toward his host.

"Mi casa es su casa amigo," Arthur replied, raising his own glass to toast his friend's kind words.

"Muchas gracias patrone, muchas gracias," Sheriff Cardwell answered back gleefully.

"De nada Ralph, my pleasure buddy boy!"

"Are you two through with all the mutual admiration *bull ore,* I'm beginning to get a little nauseous? Father Willet interjected playfully.

"We're done here I reckon," Arthur said leaning back in his chair, biting and puffing on the thick stogie in his mouth.

"Well that's a relief!" the priest sarcastically, taking a long drag on his own Havana.

"Saw my Mrs. giving you a hard time Ralph. What's put a bee in her bonnet anyway?" Arthur asked.

"Just all the new faces around here. You know how she has to be in control of every little thing around here, especially where the household is concerned. I'm afraid the concept of high level security is beyond her comfort zone patience wise," Sheriff Cardwell replied, draining the last drop Scotch from his glass.

"Refill?" Arthur asked, leaning forward in his chair.

"Nope, ones my limit today. Don't want to push my luck where Alma's concerned!" answered Sheriff Cardwell quickly, waving Arthur off before he poured another round.

"You're a smart man Ralphie boy, I don't care what Billy says about you," teased Arthur Donnelly.

"Gee thanks! Speaking of Father Billy, I'm still waiting to be briefed on this last minute summit."

"What on earth is so important that we couldn't wait and meet when there weren't some many bases to cover? There are going to be over a hundred people here tonight Billy, *and the press to boot!* Wouldn't it have made more sense to get together next week after all the hoopla?" the Sheriff asked, directing his gaze and attention to the man of the cloth beside him.

"Point taken Sheriff, point taken. But like I was telling Arthur here, something has come up," replied Father Willet.

"Don't start with that Villa Cruz paranoia again Billy!"

"Please don't tell me I'm paying twenty deputies overtime to protect Tina from a seventy-year-old arthritic priest that spends more time in Italy than he spends in LA, *please don't tell me that!*" Sheriff Cardwell said emphatically, the vein in his neck thick and pronounced.

Father Willet removed the cigar from his mouth, and while still holding it, expertly laced the fingers of his two hands together, a wriggling trail cigar smoke rising up from his clasped hands. With a calmness that only irritated Sheriff Cardwell all the more, he spoke.

"I can see that you still do not understand the ramifications of a prize like Tina in the hands of a man like Villa Cruz. Let me assure you Sheriff, he is far more dangerous than any ruffian you might encounter from day to day in this small county. Never underestimate the power of a man possessed. That is what you have where he is concerned, a man processed!" Father Willet explained coldly. He watched as the Sheriff winced, and rubbed his temples roughly.

"So what you're telling me is that I'm going to be paying my guys to guzzle champagne on the sly and eat Alma's fancy hors d'oeuvres all night long."

"Well *that's just great Billy*! How am I going to explain that to the County Supervisor at the end of the month? You know that carpet bagging tight ass with the limp wrist, the one from up Frisco way, is just itching to make a name for himself out here in the sticks. And I'd prefer that he didn't use the blood from my ceremonial beheading to color the poster boards for his State Senate campaign, if you know what I mean" complained Sheriff Cardwell.

"Take it easy Ralph," Arthur interjected on Father Willet's behalf.

"The bill for tonight is being covered by our Cuban cigar benefactor, *Grover Gateway himself*! The man has more money than he knows what to do with anyway! So leave the paperwork to me, OK? As far as the swishy Supervisor at the County Seat is concerned, your men are all guests at my 35th wedding anniversary! " Arthur said coolly.

"Let him try and make hay with that! We'll run his bony behind back to Market Street on a rail, Santa Fe style," Arthur added with a wicked chuckle. Sheriff Cardwell snorted as he guffawed an unintelligible reply, looking the whole time at Father Willet.

"OK Billy, for the sake of argument, let's say that I understand your concern. What exactly should I tell my guys to look for? What's he going to do, drive through here in the Pope mobile and kidnap the girl!" the Sheriff said sharply, his words dripping with sarcasm.

"You know what, that's precisely what I want you to watch out for. Well, except for the Pope mobile that is."

"You're serious! You think that a Catholic Bishop is planning a kidnapping? To what end Billy, for what purpose?"

"I *believe* that Villa Cruz has plans for Tina, that she is important to him. I *KNOW* that he has well placed support within the Vatican. And I am worried that he will use our desire for her well-being, our paranoia about outsiders causing her harm, to convince the Pontiff and the Council of Cardinals to seek guardianship, for her personal protection, to protect her service to the Church."

The Sheriff stared back at Father Willet, grinding his teeth as he visibly digested what the priest had said. Breaking off his eye contact with Father Billy, he looked over to Arthur.

"Are you buying into all of this?" he asked Mr. Donnelly.

"I'm inclined to believe him Ralph. I've only met Villa Cruz a couple times, but I have to admit, he's a crafty old devil. I've been a successful man all my life, blessed some might say. And I subscribe to the adage that all successful men have one thing in common, and that's mad dog determination, *persistence man!* People like us will move heaven and earth to finish what we start, be it good or bad. I recognize that quality in Villa Cruz. And if Billy says that he wants Tina, that he needs her to reach a goal he's spent a lifetime planning, then I believe he'll find a way to make it so."

Sheriff Cardwell eyeballed the two men on either side of him intensely, alternating between Father Willet and Arthur Donnelly, holding their gaze for a full minute each. The Sheriff reached for his hat with one hand while he ran the other back through his thick head of hair.

"I still don't see it like you two do. But, I guess you can never be too careful. I'm going to go over the guest list again, are you sure that everyone's name is there, no last minute additions or deletions?" Sheriff Cardwell asked in his most professional tone.

"None that I'm aware of"

"Except maybe Tina's visit to Fresno with Father Kelly and Grover's girl KC. You were informed about that already, right?" Arthur said.

"Yeah, we're on that. I got deputies following both cars as well as people in place at the sanitarium," Sheriff Cardwell said, taking a mental inventory of his personnel assignments.

"If they stop for an unscheduled potty break I'll know about it before the toilet flushes," he added.

"Sounds like you've got everything under control Ralph, I'm satisfied. Father, what about you?" Arthur asked, looking from the Sheriff to the priest. Father Willet cleared his throat and sat up straight.

"I wasn't comfortable arranging for her to be out of the area today, especially with Villa Cruz and his innuendo. But Tina's not a child anymore, and there are other matters to discuss while she is away," Father Billy explained.

"What other matters?" Sheriff Cardwell asked suspiciously.

"Billy?" Arthur chimed in, out of the loop for the first time in the conversation.

"She wanted me to speak to everyone on her behalf. She wanted me to soften you all up a little before she speaks for herself later on this evening. I believe I know what's on her mind, on her heart, but I think its best to let her speak her own mind. She and the others should arrive around 7:30pm tonight, just in time for supper. Afterward, before you and Alma cut your cake, I thought that we could all meet in the library Arthur, and hear the girl out, what do you think?" Father Willet asked. Arthur Donnelly looked over at the Sheriff and then back at the priest.

"I think I'd like to know what you think is on her mind Billy, you know how I detest surprises, they make me nervous," Arthur said gruffly.

"Me too," chimed in Sheriff Cardwell.

"It can wait gentlemen, *trust me*, it's nothing earth shattering. Let's just concentrate on making sure we keep the lid on this little *soirée* tonight. If history is any kind of teacher we should know that we are never more vulnerable than when we are the most comfortable," Father Willet replied, unable to resist a little preaching at the end. Arthur and Sheriff Cardwell looked at one another wryly, then back at Father Willet.

"Really guys, *trust me*, it's nothing bad. But the words should come from her mouth, they're from her heart after all, *trust me…*"

Fresno, California, 12, March 1974
Heritage House Rehabilitation Center…12:55pm

I held the door open for Tina, checking my watch as we walked into the lobby of the rehab center. We weren't too late, only about thirty minutes or so, but it wasn't our fault, there had been a four-car pile up on the Interstate about ten miles outside of the city. A young woman seated at the reception desk, looking rather bored, gave us the once over as we approached. She smiled nicely as we stopped in front of her desk.

"May I help you," she asked.

"Hi, we're here to meet up with a couple of others, Katherine Littleton and Jay Namura. I believe a Mrs. Delgado was expecting us?" I replied cheerfully.

"Sorry, we're a little late, traffic, you know how it is," I added guiltily.

"Yes, well, the others are already with *Ms.* Delgado, but they may have already gone on to the 12:30 meeting *as scheduled*, let me just check for you," she said, laying a not so subtle scolding on me in the process, for my tardiness and my *Ms. Versus Mrs.* faux pas.

"Thank you," I replied, trying to look repentant.

The girl ignored my response and proceeded to dial up somebody with the eraser end of her number two pencil. I looked over at Tina and she made a frowny face and shrugged her shoulders, silently acknowledging her agreement with the puzzled look on my own face. Some people just try your patience naturally. *"Every day is training day as far as God is concerned,"* Father McKenzie used to say to me at least once a week back home.

"Never let anyone steal your joy son. Keep the faith Ethan, and remember that the Lord works in mysterious ways. He doesn't just bring people into your life to inspire and encourage *you*, he also brings people into your life that *need* inspiration and encouragement *from you*. Don't let that devil Satan trick you boy. Don't capitulate and *give what you get* so to speak, rather, give what you need instead."

I must have been smiling broadly while I reminisced about my hometown parish priest's words of wisdom, because the receptionist was looking at me like queerly, like I had a goober hanging from my nose or something.

"Something funny?" she asked dryly.

"What?"

"Am I amusing you or something?" she repeated icily.

"Oh God no, I'm sorry! I was just daydreaming about a friend," I said stammering, suddenly noticing how young the girl was.

"Uh huh," she uttered.

"Bet I know who you were daydreaming about," Tina muttered under her breath.

"Let's not start that again," I snapped weakly. Tina giggled softly and looked up at the ceiling.

"Excuse me?" the receptionist asked.

"Sorry, I was talking to her," I said defensively, pointing over at the snickering teenager on my right.

"Whatever!"

"Listen, I don't know what you're tripping on, but I'm supposed to take you over to the conference room, so if you're through screwing around let's

go!" the girl said bitterly, standing quickly and rounding her desk to lead us down the hall.

"**Hey!** How about a little respect for goodness sake! The man is a priest ya know," Tina said, snapping back at the receptionist's rude remarks. The girl ignored us both and walked briskly away from us toward the hallway. Tina stamped her foot and pointed after her.

"*Did you see that!*" she exclaimed. I took her by the arm and pulled her along with me as I raced to catch up with the angry rehab employee.

"Let it go Tina, don't let her bad attitude *steal your joy* dear," I said to her, smiling to myself as I silently thanked Father McKenzie for imprinting his bit of wisdom onto my heart.

After a short sprint down the hall, we arrived at a small office masquerading as a conference room. The furniture was too large for the room and we had to squeeze along the wall to take a seat at the end of the long table. Fortunately we were the first to arrive, so we didn't have to crawl over anyone in the process. Our slightly miffed escort remained standing in the doorway until we were seated, then left without a word, leaving us to fend for ourselves.

"**HOW RUDE!**" Tina said in a huff.

"*Joy dear*, remember *joy, joy, joy*," I replied cheerfully, twisting an index finger in each of my cheeks, and grinning like a lunatic, showing all my teeth top and bottom.

"Father Kelly! That brat needs a spanking and you know it!" she whined, trying to hide her smile as she noticed how goofy I looked.

"Why don't we let God decide what it is she needs, OK," I said calmly, leaning over and knocking shoulders with her playfully. She snorted a laugh and pushed me away, folding her hands in front of her on the table.

"So why did I need to come and see this woman today? I barely know her, and I really don't remember much about the last time I saw her, I was pretty little," Tina said, changing the subject. I turned to face her way and replied.

"It was Father Willet's idea."

"What for?" she asked.

"He said that KC may upset her today. And that he thought that your presence might provide soft place for Rosa to land if she falls too hard," I answered cryptically. Tina screwed her face into a question mark, "What does *that* mean?" she asked.

"I really don't know Tina, I wish I had a better answer. I'd be guessing, but I think it has something to do with the Katz murder," I answered truthfully.

"Oh, that guy. I do remember him," she said meekly.

"You know, I used to dream about him," she added.

"You did? What about?" I asked, a little stunned by her confession.

"He was always a little boy in my dreams. He would be sitting in a corner, being punished. And I could hear his tiny, squeaky voice praying to God, *help me Jesus, I'll be good, help me Jesus, I'll be good,* over and over and over. That's all," Tina said, looking as if she could hear that voice clearly in the background somewhere.

"When did the dreams stop?"

"A few years ago, maybe four or five years," she answered.

"What do you think they meant?" I asked, gently massaging my chin with my thumb and four fingers.

"I'm not sure, but I think that God was showing me that the poor man was ready to accept salvation with the heart of a child," she answered, her voice distant and faint as if she were speaking to someone else.

I studied her as she sat beside me trancelike, deep in thought somewhere. I watched her eyes fixate on the clock hanging on the wall across from us, her head swaying back in forth, keeping perfect time with the second hand. I snapped my fingers under her nose and startled her back into consciousness.

"Still here sunshine?" I asked playfully.

"Yeah, sorry, guess I sorta drifted away there," she answered shyly, wiping away a bit of saliva from the corner of her mouth.

"Guess you did at that, where'd you go anyway?" I replied cautiously.

"Nowhere, I thought I heard someone calling me," she answered strangely.

"Anyone I know?"

"Yeah, your goddaughter, Sophia."

"What?" I asked, stunned by her answer.

"It *was* her, I'm sure of it!" Tina exclaimed.

"I didn't hear anything?"

"Well I did! She said '*Teeny, Teeny, come back Teeny, I'll play with you, I'll play.*' That's too weird, isn't it?" she asked rhetorically. I started to reply when we were interrupted by a loud knock at the door.

"Well, doesn't this look cozy? Hope we're not interrupting anything important," KC said boisterously as she entered the crowded room, Jay Namura and an older woman who had to be Ms. Delgado in tow.

I stood automatically like the gentleman I raised to be, and waited for the ladies and Jay to seat themselves. Jay nodded a hello my way, and pointed a pistol shaped hand at Tina, acknowledging her as well. Tina waved back at Jay and mouthed a hello to KC as they settled into their chairs. As I sat back down KC made the introductions around the table. When she finished, Ms. Delgado painstakingly explained the ground rules with regard to our interaction with '*client*' Rosa Hernandez, reminding us, *mostly KC*, that this was a privileged visitation. And that at the first sign of confrontation or hostility the interview would be terminated.

"Thank you for being so understanding. We really do have our client's best interests at heart here at Heritage House. Rosa is on her way down as we speak," Ms. Delgado said, never taking her eyes off Tina during her entire dissertation.

I could feel Tina lean back and try to hide behind me and escape the woman's uncomfortable gaze. Ms. Delgado and I shifted forward and back in our chairs as she tried to regain her line of sight Tina's way, and I did my best to subtlety block it.

"Such a pleasure to meet you Miss Lopez," Ms. Delgado said, still dodging my counter moves.

"*I umm...I ahh...*excuse me Father, could we trade seats?" she asked in frustration.

"I'm getting a little dizzy trying to talk around you," she added, smiling politely. Tina grabbed at my sleeve, letting me know that she preferred that I stayed right where I was. She was never very comfortable with her celebrity, and seemed even more skittish than usual now.

"You know what..." I began, prayerfully interrupted by the appearance of Rosa Hernandez and pair of burly orderlies in starched white uniforms. All eyes moved to the doorway as the two men helped Rosa to an open seat, removing her shackles before she sat down.

"Thank you gentlemen, I'll call when we're ready for you," Ms. Delgado said professionally as the orderlies excused themselves and left the room.

"Well, perhaps we'll have a chance to chat before you leave dear," she said sweetly to Tina, finally restoring eye contact in the confusion of Rosa's sudden arrival.

"I guess I only have to introduce Father Kelly here as the rest of you are old friends," Ms. Delgado said smiling at the room.

"Rosa, this is Father Ethan Kelly from St. John's. He works for Father Billy, whom you know well, of course, seeing as he takes your confession here twice a month. Father Kelly is a friend of the Lopez family as well," she said introducing me. I stood and reached across the table, extending my hand.

"*Hello Rosa, pleasure to meet you dear,*" I said, waiting for her to accept my polite gesture. She nodded and took my hand, squeezing my palm weakly, her fingers cold to the touch.

Rosa turned her head and looked over at Tina. They smiled eerily at one another, their eyes locking, a trail of tears meandering down each of their flushed faces. The bond that they had forged so many years ago was suddenly rekindled, strong and fresh, as if no time had passed at all. It seemed as if they were silently reliving those moments during the few seconds that they made eye contact. Then just as suddenly, they broke free from the past with a sniffle and a nod of their heads, rejoining us back in the present. Tina released her hold on my sleeve and sat back in her chair, staring at the clock again. I listened to KC start her interview in the background and studied Tina as she drifted off again. I wondered if Sophie was back in her head, I couldn't help being curious, not after what had happened in Albany. If Tina said she heard Sophie, then I believed her. This was so weird, but it was also *'too cool for school'* to quote Paul Pulchowski.

"What's on your mind baby girl," I muttered to myself, addressing Sophie if she were really here.

"What's on both your minds," I muttered at Tina as well.

"HEY PADRE!" KC shouted. Startled, I looked back in the other direction at KC and the rest of the group, blinking excessively.

"What?"

"You guys are creeping us out," she said, pointing at Tina and I.

"Sorry," I replied sheepishly, gently nudging Tina with my elbow.

"What?" she asked.

"Pay attention you two, things might get a little dicey here," KC said coolly, giving us the stink eye before she turned her attention back to Rosa.

"OK Rosa, this may be a little hard to grasp at first, so I'll go slow..."

Mendota, California, 12, March 1974
TJ's Tacos...2:41pm

Raymond walked up to the car finishing off the last of his four-taco lunch. Stuffing the last bite into his mouth, he crumpled up the wrapper and wiped away a little hot sauce that was escaping while he chewed hurriedly. Smiley sat with his chin resting on his arm, looking out the passenger window watching as his buddy approached the car.

"Aiye Raymond, you are such a pig homey," he said to him as he reached the car. Raymond flipped him off and circled the around the back of the car to climb in the driver's side. He got in clumsily, wiping his hands on his pants before he touched the steering wheel. Raymond reached down and turned the volume up on the radio, using the steering wheel as a drum kit while he listened to the tail end of Led Zeppelin's *'Whole Lotta Love'* playing on the local station.

"Not bad for white boys," he said, nodding his at Smiley who continued to stare out the window.

"Forget them *ese*, what did you find out at TJ's other than how many tacos you can eat at one time?" Smiley asked sarcastically.

"Not much, the chick at the counter says she hasn't seen the little shit all day. She said he usually comes every day around this time, but not today, that figures huh," Raymond replied, picking at his teeth with the cap of a Bic pen.

"SHIT!" Smiley exclaimed, slapping his palm hard against the door.

"How did we loose him this time? We saw him get on that flatbed with all the other *'wetbacks'* from that melon field. We followed them all the way back to their camp in broad daylight, they didn't make any stops along the way. We must have lost them when they all went for their cars, it was like a jailbreak man!" Smiley said, retracing the events of earlier this morning. He reached over and punched Raymond in the arm. "I told you that kid with the yellow headband wasn't him man! Miguel never wears yellow *vato*, he says that color is for women and *maricons*," Smiley lamented.

"I didn't know ese, how was I supposed to know? That kid looked like him from where I was sitting, even you said so," Raymond replied defensively.

"No I didn't," Smiley snapped.

"Yes you did!" Raymond snapped back.

"OK, OK, forget about it *carbron*, let me think a minute!" Smiley barked, surrendering.

Raymond reached down and started pushing the preset buttons on the radio, searching for a familiar tune. Smiley shot him a dirty look and Raymond settled on a country station that was playing an old Hank Williams tune. Raymond hummed along for a minute while Smiley racked his brain, then spoke up suddenly.

"Those two guys are still sitting over there in that orange Dart," he said, nonchalantly glancing at the car across the lot, trying not to appear like he was interested.

Smiley looked over as well, just for an instant, then stretched and rested his head on his arm again, resuming his position, looking out the window. Covering his mouth, he replied to Raymond unasked question.

"Cops?"

"I don't know, but I don't like it."

"What were they wearing, did you see?"

"I didn't notice, *dress shirts I think*, but no ties."

"They got cop haircuts man, maybe we should split, huh?"

"No, I'm gonna go inside and pee. Wait until I get in the door, then you go up to the counter and talk to that chick." Raymond said.

"About what?"

"It doesn't matter *vato*, order a couple tacos and eat them on the bench out front. I'll crawl out the window and see if I can get close enough to have a discussion with the man, gangster style, aye homeboy?"

"You got iron heuvos *ese*, sounds like a plan to me," Smiley replied with a wicked little grin. Raymond opened his door and stepped out. He placed both his hands on the roof of the car and leaned his head back inside.

"Be cool now, follow my lead OK. Make everything look nice and friendly while I introduce Mr. Colt to the driver's fat head. We may have to take these two on a tour of the pucker bushes, you know?" Raymond said coolly as he straightened up and closed the door. Smiley watched him stroll back to the taco stand and disappear inside. He waited exactly two minutes, careful to watch for any movement by the two officers across the way.

He hawked up a thick luggie from his smoker's lung and spit from his perch on the passenger door. Then he opened the door and sauntered out into the bright sunlight and walked up to the counter of the little taco stand. He called out to the girl behind the glass at the counter as he approached, a nice touch of realism he thought.

"Hey *chica*, what's happening momma?" he asked, stepping up onto the curb and up to the counter. He leaned way forward on the counter, forming an '*L*' shape with his body as he waited for the girl to answer him.

"*Ola vato, que pa so?*" she asked, smacking her chewing gum loudly as she smiled back at him.

Smiley shot a sideways glance at the car in the lot, checking on the two men while he ordered a Montezuma Special. The cops hadn't budged yet, and Smiley looked past the girl to see if he could spot the restroom where Raymond had gone. The girl reached out from under the glass and patted Smiley's hand as she called out his order.

"Yo, yo, yo, one '*flaming flatbed*', heavy on the *green weenies*," she shouted, ordering the spicy *taco especial* with extra jalapeno peppers.

"Be ready in a sec. You like everything hot don't you *vato*," she said, flirting shamelessly.

"*Si chica, everything!* What good's a taco without a little hot sauce!" he replied, kicking the flirtation up a notch by darting his in and out tongue between the inverted peace sign formed by two of his fingers.

The sorta young counter girl squealed something unrecognizable in any language and disappeared behind the glass to share Smiley's bombastic humor with her co-workers.

Meanwhile Smiley had straightened up and turned to lean back against the counter. He looked out at the street while keeping an eye on the cops with his peripheral vision, no sign of Raymond yet.

The giggling counter girl reached out from under the glass and pinched his butt. He jumped and turned around as she pushed his order out onto the dirty counter. He started to reach into his pocket for some cash and stopped when she waved him off.

"It's on the house, you're funny," she said, pointing to the sack that he was now holding.

Smiley raised the white paper sack up to eye level and turned it 180 degrees. He caught sight of the phone number scribbled in green ink near the top of the sack and grinned, forgetting about everything but what was stirring in his pants for a few seconds. He lowered the bag and winked at the girl then walked over and sat at the bench, making sure to face the car with the two cops. They were sitting idly, sipping on sodas and pretending to read the newspaper. Some cops were so dumb he thought as he began to munch on the spicy taco. Out of the corner of his eye he saw a shadow pass quickly across the roof of the car next to them. That had to be Raymond he thought.

Smiley quickly stuffed the rest of the taco into his mouth, got up and walked over to the trash can in front of their car. He crumpled the sack into a grapefruit sized ball and threw it violently into the aluminum can. The two cops tensed as they waited for Smiley to make his next move, concentrating intensely on his every movement. *'Just what the doctor'* ordered thought Raymond as he stepped up to the passenger window and leaned in, pressing the barrel of his .357 to the neck of the man nearest him.

"Ola chingasos," he said smugly.

The man froze in his seat, dropping his drink onto the floorboards in front of him. His partner looked away from Smiley just long enough for Raymond's partner to walk up and get the same drop on the driver, only with a very sharp Buck knife instead of a piece.

"Yeah, ola chingasos," said Smiley mimicking his friend.

The driver closed his eyes and exhaled deeply, gripping the steering wheel tight enough to turn his knuckles white. Smiley looked around the car and noticed that there was no radio or shot gun mount.

"Hey, this don't look like any cop car I've ever seen," he said to Raymond, standing on the other side of the car. Raymond took his own inventory of the vehicle and concurred. He jabbed the muzzle of the gun sharply into the neck of the man in the passenger seat.

"You guys cops or what?" he demanded. The two men remained silent, starting a chain reaction that would prove costly in the end.

"Hey! *Baboso*, I'm talking to you!" Raymond hissed into the man's ear from inches away. The man remained calm, stoic even, and said nothing.

"This guy is pissing me off *vato*, I'm gonna shoot him right here!" Raymond said suddenly, cocking the weapon.

"*No, no, no*, not here *estupido!*" Smiley snapped, leaning in the window slightly and drawing blood from the driver. The man breathed in through his nose quickly and tensed, but did not move his hands in retaliation. Raymond looked over at Smiley and frowned.

"Hey, these guys don't want to talk, *fuck em!* Let's kill them now and get on down the road, we're outta here tonight anyway, soon as we do the kid!" Raymond said, pleading a course the action he was currently comfortable with.

"Hold it, just hold on just one second *ese!* Look at these guys, they aren't even sweating here, they're way too cool to be cops man. I don't know what they are, but they ain't cops!" Smiley said, trying to size up the situation.

Neither of the two men moved a muscle, they just continued to look straight ahead out the windshield. Smiley didn't like the way that things were developing. Whoever these guys were, he had the sinking feeling that the longer he hesitated the more likely it was that the tables would be turned on he and Raymond. These guys were professionals, what kind of professionals they were was beginning to bug him. Smiley sighed deeply, finally rationalizing the same conclusion that Raymond had come to moments earlier on instinct. These guys had to die, but not here, too many people, and they still had work to do in this town.

"OK, you two guys scoot to the center, passenger you sit on your buddy's lap and lean forward, hands on the dash. Go ahead driver, you move first and stick your hands into your pants like your scratching your balls. *DO IT NOW MAN!*" Smiley snapped.

The driver did as he was told and the passenger followed. Raymond and Smiley climbed in after them, Smiley getting behind the wheel and starting up the car, and Raymond taking the shotgun seat, pressing the gun into the ribs of the man on the bottom. Raymond put his arm around the two guys in the center and laughed heartily out loud, putting on a show for anyone who might be watching them.

"OK dudes, we're just old buddies now, and we're going for a ride, *ya know*," Raymond whispered wickedly to the two hostages, his taco breath filling the car as he belched loudly.

"Where we going homeboy?" Raymond asked Smiley as they backed out of the parking space.

"We're going to work *ese*, these *maricons* are going to hell!" Smiley replied, sneering as he turned out of the driveway and out into the sparse traffic.

"Ain't small towns cool?" Smiley said coolly.

"Yeah man, this would be pretty hard to pull off LA, ya know?" Raymond answered nonchalantly.

"HORALE!" Smiley shouted over the wind whipping through the open window. *"HORALE!"*

Forty-five

(…"But now abide faith, hope, love, these three; but
the greatest of these is love"…1st Corinthians 13:13)

Mendota, California, 12, March 1974
Donnelly Ranch…3:30pm

Victor Lopez slowed the SWATHER to jerky stop and killed the engine. Then as he twisted on the door handle, he put all of his weight behind his shoulder and hit the door like a linebacker, freeing himself from the stuffy cab. He stepped out from the cab of what basically amounted to a lawn mower on steroids, and stood on the catwalk that surrounded the closed in operator's cabin. Leaning back on his hands, he stretched and flexed his tired muscles, digging his fists into the small of his back and sighing audibly.

"Aye Dios mio," he exclaimed.

"I'm getting way too old for this," he added through a big yawn.

Victor watched as a small flock of doves took flight from over near the irrigation ditch. He took aim with his forefinger as if it were the barrel of a shotgun, and daydreamed about bringing home a catch for Maria to cook up for supper. The noisy swather must have flushed them out as it passed by their hiding place in the overgrown alfalfa. Squinting in the bright sunlight, he pulled the well-worn Stetson off of his head and wiped his sweaty face with a clean towel that hung behind the driver's seat in the giant machine.

He rubbed deep into the corners of his eyes, removing all the grit and grime that had collected there over the last three or four hours. When he finished grooming his eyes he ran the towel over the top of his head and then across his aching neck. He took some extra time to massage that spot deeply with his strong fingers. Then after snapping the towel a couple of times for general purpose, he leaned back into the cab and hung it back onto the plastic hook, affixed to the rear window by a small translucent suction cup.

Pushing himself upright with the hand that rested on the doorjamb, Victor slicked back his damp hair with his fingers and then returned the wide brimmed hat to its perch on the top of his head. He walked around to stand in front of the large windshield and leaned back against it, surveying the freshly cut hay that lay in clumps of yellow and green for as far as the eye could see. He folded his arms in front of him and searched the field for his new helper, Ramon. It didn't take long to spot him. He was over by the irrigation ditch, swinging a sickle like an old pro. Victor was impressed by the kid's no-nonsense attitude. And it was pretty obvious that the boy wasn't afraid of hard work, he liked that. Victor had left him in the ditch to clean the turnouts. It was the least coveted job on the ranch, the one always given to the *new guy* on the crew. Ramon hadn't even flinched when Victor warned him about rattlesnakes in the weeds and under shady rocks. He just gathered up the tools from the bed pick up truck, the hoe, the sickle, the rake, and the spade, and trudged off to the first turnout near the road and started in.

"You gonna be OK?" Victor had asked as the boy had walked away on his own.

"Si senor," Ramon had replied without looking back.

Victor looked back to where the kid had started from and counted the turnouts to where he was currently hacking at weeds and sagebrush. He shook his head in awe of the boy's productivity. In less than four hours he had neatly cleared twelve turnouts, at least twice the number of most new hires. Victor pushed himself away from the windshield with his butt and fixed his eyes back at the first turnout. The water jug was still there, right where he had left it. The boy must have worked the entire time in the heat without so much as a sip.

"Man, I could use a couple more like him," Victor muttered as he climbed down from the big machine and walked over to fetch the water jug.

"HEY... RAMON!" Victor hollered.

The boy didn't acknowledge him right away. He just kept swinging the sickle in a slow rhythm, the sharp blade whistling through the air as it cut down everything in its path, traversing along the wide arc of his swing. Eventually he stopped and turned to face toward Victor, letting the razor sharp hand sickle hang limply at his side. He watched Victor make his way over from the roadside. It was a good hundred and fifty yards from where he now stood.

"GO AHEAD, TAKE A BREAK SON, I'LL BRING THE WATER," Victor shouted.

Ramon nodded and walked around the turnout and up the steep levy, taking a seat on top of the concrete barrier that separated the canal from the fields. The gentle sound of the slow moving water behind him was soothing and cooling. Ramon set the dangerously sharp hand tool in his lap and leaned back to cup a handful of water and splash it onto his face. The cool water felt so good as it washed the grit and grime from his skin. He repeated the refreshing action several times before Victor finally arrived with the water jug and a paper sack containing a couple turkey sandwiches that Maria had packed for them before they left the house.

"*Aye Dios*, this levy seems to get steeper every year," Victor grunted as he walked up to join his young helper on the canal wall. He set the water jug on the concrete between them and the paper sack in his lap.

"*Whew!* It's hot out today, no," he asked Ramon as he fished in the sack for the sandwiches.

Ramon nodded, wiping his face dry with his sleeve. Victor handed him a sandwich wrapped in wax paper and then fished out a cup to fill will cold water from the jug. Ramon quickly gulped down the water and held out his cup for more.

"I knew you had to be thirsty," Victor said with a smile, refilling the boy's cup.

"Gracias Senor Lopez," Ramon replied politely.

He gulped down half of his refill and then tore open the wax paper, pulling out half of a turkey sandwich with all the trimmings munch on. Victor followed suit and then looked over at Ramon while he chewed. He liked this boy, he was a hard worker, and he looked like he could use soft a place to land on this hard earth. Victor took another bite of his sandwich and looked back over the fields that he had just cut. Not a bad afternoon's work for the two of them on their own.

They had cut five acres in four hours and cleared twelve overgrown turnouts as well. Pretty good for one old man and a rookie, Victor thought to himself. He washed down the last of his meal with a full cup of cold water, saving the final swallow to rinse his teeth. Then spat a long stream of water onto the soft rich soil in front of him, wiping his mouth clean with shirtsleeve. Victor set the sack lunch down at his feet and turned around to lean over the wall, lowering his head closer to the canal. He splashed several handfuls of cool water onto his sweaty face and then swiped his hat through the water and put it back on his head, letting the cool liquid run down his sunburned neck.

"I think we've done enough for today Ramon. We'll come back tomorrow and I'll teach you how to rake this hay into windrows, it's easy."

"You'll catch on in no time. Besides, I have to get home soon to get ready for the Donnelly's party. If I'm one minute late Maria will skin me alive," Victor said laughing loudly.

"Who are the Donnelly's?" Ramon asked.

Victor looked over at the boy stunned. This was the most he had said since Victor met him. He reached over and pulled off the boy's baseball cap and then replaced it roughly.

"*So you can talk?* I was beginning to think that you didn't like me or something," Victor teased.

Ramon smiled weakly, taking the last bite of his own sandwich, a few breadcrumbs escaping his mouth as he barred his white teeth.

"Sorry Senor Lopez," he apologized.

"It's OK son, no crime to be quiet and shy," Victor, said supportively.

"The Donnelly's own all this land, as far as you can see in any direction. Senor Donnelly is the *patron* around here. He's a good man, and he has been a blessing to a lot of people in this county, especially to me and my family."

"*Oh...*is it a birthday party or something?" Ramon asked meekly.

"*Naw*, bigger than that."

"It's their anniversary, 35 years I think, or somewhere around there anyway. Imagine that, so many years together and no children. I think that's why Senora Donnelly spends so much time at our house. She's always helping Maria with the kids. Man, she treats those children as if they were her own kin," Victor answered at length.

Ramon smiled as he scooted off his perch on the canal wall, jumping down to the soft dirt below. He handed Victor his empty cup and then policed the area, putting the crumpled wax paper into the sack with the other trash. Ramon trotted back down the embankment toward the turnout to gather up all of the hand tools.

"Just leave them where they are Ramon. I'll drive the pick up over here so you won't have to lug them back up to the road, *OK?*" Victor said, jumping down from the wall, grabbing the jug and the trash as he followed the boy down the steep embankment.

"OK Senor Lopez," Ramon replied.

"*Victor son*, you can call me Victor. You did a man's job for me today, so call me by my Christian name young man," Victor said happily, slapping the boy solidly on the back as he reached him.

"OK, thanks Victor," Ramon said shyly.

"That's better!" Victor started to walk toward the road and then stopped suddenly, turning back Ramon's way.

"You have a place to sleep tonight Ramon?" Ramon hesitated a second, not expecting such a question.

"Si Senor Lopez, *I mean Victor*," he answered nervously. Victor eyeballed the boy for a minute, not really believing him, but not wanting to embarrass him either.

"*Oh...good,*" he replied, turning slowly, continuing on to fetch the pick up truck. He stopped suddenly again, "Hey," he called after Ramon.

"Si Victor?"

"You want to make a little extra money tonight?"

"Sure, *doing what?*"

"I'm not sure yet, but I'm pretty sure that Senora Donnelly could use some help at the party later. You know, in the kitchen or parking cars, stuff like that. Would you be interested?"

Ramon smiled broadly, "Yes sir, I would, thanks Victor," he said, his eyes twinkling, "Thanks a lot!"

"OK, *mui bueno*, I'll see what I can work out. You have any clean clothes at this place you're staying at?"

"*Ummm*, not really Senor Lopez, *sorry*," Ramon said sheepishly.

"*Hmmm*, might be a problem? But you know what, I'm pretty sure we can scare up something suitable from that fancy pants caterer Senora Donnelly always hires," Victor said laughing.

"I'll be right back," he said loudly, waving as he turned to go get the truck.

"OK."

Ramon watched as Victor walked away, comfortable for the moment in the guise he had created. He liked Victor and Maria, he liked the way that they treated him, he liked being needed, being noticed, being appreciated. Before he could get too comfortable, before he could feel the love, Miguel regained control, reminding himself of his purpose. His eyes narrowed as he tracked Victor's progress. He put his hands into his pockets and clenched his fists tightly.

"Don't punk out *ese!*" he said out loud to the freshly mowed the field.

It would all be over soon, he could sense it. The guilt, the loneliness, the heartache, it would all be over soon, it would all be over this very night. He smiled wickedly after Victor and his good fortune.

"Gracias Senor Lopez, *I mean Victor*," he muttered.

"Gracias!"

Fresno, California, 12, March 1974...4:30pm

"*Man*, how long we gotta sit here in this stink homey?" Raymond whined.

"Shut up *maricon*, the sun's going down in about a half an hour, OK," snapped Smiley.

"You want to bury those two *chingasos* in broad daylight, *huh estupido?*"

"There's nobody out here in these fields but us and the rats man. Let's just do it!"

"A few more minutes ain't gonna kill you, be a MAN for Christ's sake!"

"*Aye Dios mio!* Let's leave the Lord out of this man, *seriously*, that's gotta be bad luck or something, ya know!"

"You're an idiot Raymond! You think God don't already know what we done? Give it a rest man, just be cool for a little longer."

"Yeah, but the stink, come on Smiley...I told you we should have stopped and got some coffee for that!"

"*OHHH, RIIIIGHT*, just leave our friends in the trunk back there to rot in the A&P parking lot while we stroll around the market and shop. Give me a break, *baboso*!"

"Five minutes, it would have taken five minutes!"

"*HEY*, let's not argue about it anymore *OK*? I'm getting a headache!"

"OK, OK, I'm over it! How much longer do we have to wait then?" Raymond asked sourly.

"Twenty minutes *cabron*, think you can handle it?" Smiley answered sarcastically.

"Yeah...shut up Smiley before I beat your ass. I'm getting tired of your chicken shit attitude *ese!*"

Smiley snorted an undecipherable reply, folding his arms tightly in front of him, silently signaling that he was no longer interested in participating in further discussion in the matter of Mr. Body 1 & 2. The two of them sat there in silence, impatiently waiting for the sun to set completely, trying not to notice the intensifying stench emanating from the trunk behind them.

"Can I ask a question?" Raymond said as the sun began to disappear below the corn stalks in the large field.

"*One!*" Smiley answered.

"What are we supposed to dig with man?"

A good question actually, Smiley thought, not the stupid one he had been expecting.

"We'll just use the tire iron. The ground is pretty soft here and we don't have to dig very deep, just a couple feet maybe, enough to keep the birds away," Smiley said, making it up as he went along.

"That'll work, good plan *ese*," Raymond replied, nodding his head.

"Thanks, I took a shot!" Smiley said, snapping his fingers for effect.

"Hey, Smiley, did you see some headlights just now?"

"Where?"

Up by the road, *over there*," Raymond said pointing to where they had turned in from the two-lane blacktop earlier. Smiley squinted as he strained to see whatever Raymond was yapping about.

"I don't see anything *vato*, stop spooking me will ya!"

"I coulda swore I saw headlights up there," Raymond said, leaning over the steering wheel, peering intensely through the windshield.

"You didn't see nothing man, cause there ain't nothing to see! Now shut up and let me think!"

"I did too see something man," Raymond muttered sourly, settling back easily into the driver's seat.

"I did too!"

Fresno, California, 12, March 1974
Heritage House Rehabilitation Center ...5:00pm

We watched as Rosa and Tina hugged one another for what for what seemed like hours. Given the emotional meat grinder that KC had just put her through, it was a wonder that Rosa was as calm as she appeared. Tina just seemed to have that effect on her though. Actually, she had that effect on everyone in that way. I guess it was part of her gift, to be able to channel pain through herself and turn it into something positive and wonderful. I continued to run interference for her with regard to Ms. Delgado. The woman was doing her level best to try and scoot past me in that small conference room to get nearer to Tina. Celeste Delgado had a bushel full of questions to ask. She had a powerful need satisfy her intense curiosity about Tina Lopez, like, was she for real or what. I couldn't blame her, it wasn't everyday that one found themselves in the presence of the hand of God. Heck, even with my personal witness, I still didn't totally understand the ramifications of Tina's service to God myself. I was in awe of the girl and her ability to take everything in stride; she just made it all seem so natural. I suppose it must be for her, she had been at this since she was a small child after all.

"Well, that went better than I had expected," KC said, taking my arm.

"What *were* you expecting?" I asked, feeling a little flushed by her unexpected closeness.

"I don't know, I guess I thought that she might turn on the water works and go *Looney Tunes* on us," she replied, frowning as she watched the two of them hold their embrace.

"Hey you two, we need to roll right now if we're going to have any chance of making that Donnelly shindig," Jay Namura interjected.

KC turned and wrinkled her nose at him, some sort of secret code between them. Jay rolled his eyes and slung his soft camera case over his shoulder.

"I'll meet you guys in the lobby. See if you can break up the love-fest over there so we can beat it on down the road," he said as he pushed past us out the door.

"Be right there Jay man," KC called after him, suddenly squished up against me as he passed by.

"Sorry," she said to me with a grin.

"No worries," I replied, making eye contact with Tina while KC remained in her new spot, up close and personal like.

"Excuse me Father, but do you think that I could have just a few minutes with Miss Lopez alone?

"I promise I won't keep her long, I just want to ask her a little about her family, and well, *you know*," Celeste Delgado asked sweet as molasses, peering up at me with those doe-like eyes.

I was half tempted to give in, but then that would leave me alone with KC, who was getting awfully comfy by my side. If she got any closer we would wearing the same shoes!

"I'm so sorry Ms. Delgado, but really need to dash. We're expected at a very important engagement in Mendota, and we should have been on the road an hour ago," I said apologetically.

She looked genuinely disappointed, and I considered capitulating for a second. But when KC pulled my arm closer to her, making me keenly aware of more than just her tight grip on my arm, I stammered out call to my young charge across the room.

"*AHEM!* Excuse me, Tina, we really need to be going dear," I said loudly, stepping toward the door and away from KC's warm form.

Tina nodded in agreement and kissed Rosa's cheek as they broke from their embrace. I walked quickly out into the hall, inadvertently dragging KC along with me as she continued to hold firmly onto my sleeve.

"WHOA! Where's the race? Who do you think you are, *Sea Biscuit?*" KC exclaimed.

"Sorry," I stammered.

"Jay's waiting for us in the lobby," I said pathetically.

"He's a big boy, he'll be alright," KC said sarcastically, still holding onto my sleeve.

"Well, he's right of course, we really do need to get going," I said, my voice squeaking slightly.

"And so we will!"

"Relax Ethan, you act as if you've never stood next to a girl before. I don't have any cooties you know, and I promise not to bite," she said, shaking her head and giggling.

I looked over at Tina who was grinning at my predicament and pleaded with my eyes for her to hurry along. She took pity on me and said her goodbyes to Rosa, then stopped for a second to hug Ms. Delgado, promising to come see her another time. She walked quickly over to where KC and I stood and took my other arm, grinning like a Cheshire cat.

"Ready!" she said cheerfully.

"Careful hon, the padre here is a little squeamish around the fairer sex," KC said, teasing me.

"I know, my mom teases him all the time about that," Tina said, waving her hand limply.

"Can we just go please?" I pleaded.

"Lead the way Columbus," KC said cheerfully, as we finally started to make our way down the hall.

We passed the two attendants along the way, and Tina looked back over her shoulder as we walked by them. I could hear her sigh a moment later and looked back myself in time to see the men strap the restraints back onto Rosa's wrists and ankles.

"Go with God Rosa," I muttered as we walked on.

"Ditto," replied Tina and KC in unison. When we reached the lobby we found Jay stretched out on the sofa reading a magazine.

"It's about time! Do you people have any concept of time what-so-ever?" he asked harshly.

"Give it a rest Jay, we're here now, so let's go," KC snapped back, unimpressed by his crankiness.

"We'll follow you Father Kelly," Jay said, picking up his bag.

"Can I ride with Jay," Tina asked quickly.

"I don't care who rides with who, let's just get going!" Jay exclaimed, walking out the front door.

"It's OK with me," KC said, winking at Tina.

"Great," Tina said, winking back, breaking free from my arm and chasing after Jay before I could protest.

"I don't know…maybe I should…" I said stammering again.

"*Oh come on Father Kelly*, it'll be fun, you'll see. Besides, it'll give us a chance to talk, get to know each other better, what do ya say?" KC said.

I had the distinct feeling that I had just been ambushed. I knew that when we got outside, Tina and Jay would already be in their car with the engine running, making it difficult for me to alter their little conspiracy, *genius!*

"All right," I said finally.

"Good," KC said smiling, still holding onto my arm as we walked up to the car.

I opened her door and she climbed in slowly, gathering her skirt and coat under her legs, very ladylike. I started to close the door and then stopped, opening it up again. She looked up at me puzzled.

"But stay on your side of the car OK, *no funny business*," I said sternly. I must have looked as ridiculous as I sounded because I could see that she was having trouble stifling her laughter.

"Scout's honor," she said, holding up three fingers giving me the Boy Scout salute.

I just rolled my eyes and closed the door. I could hear her laughing out loud while I walked around the car to the driver's side. The laughter ended suddenly, just as soon as I opened the door and climbed in. I looked over at her and saw that she was biting down on her lips, trying to stave off her laughing jag. I shook my head slowly and started the engine. "What have I got myself into," I thought.

"*Oye vey,*" I muttered, putting the car in gear.

That was all it took, KC totally lost control. She burst out laughing hysterically, rocking back and forth in the seat and stamping her feet on the floorboards. An auspicious start to say the least, it was going to be a *long, long, long* ride back to the Donnelly's.

Firebaugh, California, 12, March 1974
Lopez Home ...5:00pm

Maria sat quietly at the vanity table in her bedroom. Half dressed in a black slip and bra, she brushed on her long dark hair. Tilting her head to one side, she gathered it all in one hand, and then pulled it over her shoulder, way out in front of her, so that she could concentrate her strokes on the bottom third of her thick lustrous mane. The Lopez girls all had beautiful hair, soft, full and shiny. They were quite a sight whenever they were out together. Secretly, down deep, Maria really enjoyed all the attention, but outwardly, for Victor's sake she pretended not to notice. She pulled the fist full of hair up to her face and inspected it for split ends, there weren't any, of course!

She shook her head, tossing the long mane back over her shoulder and set the brush down. While she leaned forward to check her pores and complexion before applying her makeup, Victor walked into the room from the hall. He was already dressed in his Sunday best, complete with a new leather bolo with a turquoise pendant, and his party Stetson, a wide brimmed black hat with a smooth leather band. Maria had always liked that hat, she thought it made her man look sexy, and she loved the way the other ladies would check him out whenever they went out together, dressed to the nines. Victor crouched down slightly and tiptoed over to where she sat, concentrating intensely on her look. He slipped his hands delicately beneath her bra straps and started to pull them down over her shoulders. Maria jumped, startled by his presence and slapped his right hand hard with her heavy brush.

"Déjelo!" she snapped.

"Owww, what the hell?" Victor replied, rubbing the back of his hand and looking as if he were genuinely hurt by her response.

"You are such a beast *panson!* Let me finish getting ready, *please*, we're going to be late enough as it is!"

Victor backed away from the table like a wounded animal and sat on the end of their bed. She looked at him in the mirror and smiled to herself as she watched him pout, licking his wounds.

"Don't be such a baby," she said without turning to look back at him.

"I'm not," he replied sourly.

"Yes you are, I can see you right here in this mirror," she said, waving the brush at his reflection.

"Well, why did you have to smack me like that, I was only playing?" he whined.

"Playing my eye! Who do you think you're talking to anyway? You know you can't stop at just a nibble, *no?*" Maria said, teasing her husband playfully.

"But chica, I was only..."

"But nothing! A nibble turns into a taste, a taste turns into a bite, and next thing I know you're cutting yourself a slice!"

"You know I'm right, don't try and deny it!" she said scolding him.

Victor waved his hand at her, surrendering, and got up off of the bed. Standing just out of her reach, he looked around her at his own reflection in the mirror, and adjusted his leather bolo.

"So, do I look alright?" he asked, patting under his chin with the backside of his flat palm.

Maria spun around quickly in her seat and gently let her chin come to rest on her forearms that were now neatly folded over the back of the small chair. She playfully leered at her husband provocatively and smiled a wicked little smile.

"Good enough to eat, *grrrrrrrrrrowlllllllll…*" she said seductively, rolling her *'R's'* in a pronounced and prolonged growl, like a tigress in heat. Victor smiled back at her, "I thought we were running late?" he asked.

"*Late schmate,* let them wait!" she purred, springing from the chair and jumping into her husband's strong arms, her legs wrapping tightly around his waist.

"*Aye gordo!* That belt buckle, it's as big as Texas," she squealed, lacing her fingers together behind his thick neck and leaning back to look up at him from arms length.

"*What belt buckle?*" Victor said slowly, pulling her back close to him. They kissed each other passionately, taking the grand tour all around each other's face, and then fell onto the bed in a heap, giggling like teenagers.

"*Shhhh, Victor, shhhhh,* you'll wake the baby," Maria pleaded as he nuzzled the nape of her neck.

She pushed away from him slightly and she listened for any sound from the other room. Victor paused long enough for her to give him the all clear, and then resumed cutting himself a slice. Taking control for the sake of expediency, Maria pushed her determined husband onto his back, expertly fumbling with buttons, clasps, and zippers, finally working him into the *lazy boy* position. Then curling her lips over her teeth and biting down on them, she rode her personal thoroughbred hard for the finish, slowing slightly at the crucial moment, just in time to grab a bath towel that lay across the pillow, keeping their little detour from spoiling her silks and his coat, mercifully avoiding a lengthy and unplanned wardrobe change. She draped the towel across them, where they remained joined, and leaned back on her hands, resting them on Victor's thighs, letting nature take its course before they separated.

"Are you happy now," she said, smiling and slightly out of breath.

Victor chuckled, his body jiggling, as he began to laugh out loud, spent and satisfied.

"*Stop that panson*, you're just going to start your motor again!" Maria whispered harshly, standing up suddenly on the mattress, leaving the bath towel resting across his lap.

She burst out laughing as she looked down at him sprawled on the bed, his pants around his ankles, and a huge grin on his face. She leaped off of the bed before he could pull her back down, heading for the relative safety of the bathroom. Maria hollered to him from over her shoulder as she ran.

"LET'S GO VICTOR! Get dressed honey, *rapido, rapido!* Now we're really going to be late *Panson!"*

Maria reached the bathroom before he could reply, slammed the door shut and locking it behind her, just in case. She leaned back against the door for a second and caught her breath, then jumped forward a step or two, startled by a soft knocking sound.

"Maria, open up baby, I've got something you're going to need," Victor said playfully.

"Aye Victor, I told you we need to get going," she replied, whining in frustration.

"Just open the door Maria, I promise I'll be good," he said, trying to reassure her.

"Oh, right, I know, you're *always* good, right?" she said sarcastically.

"Seriously chica, just open the door, OK," he said, his tone changing slightly.

Maria exhaled deeply, then turned to unlock the door, opening it only a crack. Victor's hand appeared through the small opening, her evening gown in his grasp. Maria sighed and took the garment from him.

"Thank you," she said sweetly, relieved and surprised that he didn't push through after the dress, looking for another little slice of heaven.

"My pleasure! See, I can behave," Victor said softly through the door. Before she could reply the doorbell rang repeatedly. "That must be the babysitter, I'll go and let her in," Victor announced, turning to walk from the room.

"I'll wait for you on the front porch, OK?" he added, his voice faint as he passed out into the hallway.

"OK, I'll be ready in a minute," Maria called after him. She smiled, then closed *and* locked the door, just in case.

Mendota, California, 12, March 1974
Donnelly Ranch…6:00pm

Diego Sanchez watched his crew as they busied themselves with all of the final preparations for this evening's gala event. He always liked working for Senor and Senora Donnelly. Not just because they paid so well, and treated he and his staff professionally. But because they made him feel appreciated, like he was part of the family, not just another vendor or hired hand. Smiling, he nodded at a server as she brought in a tray of fresh salmon rolls and set them on the long buffet table to his left. She paused next to him so that he could inspect the contents of the tray and then whisked over to the table and set down the heavy silver tray. A rustle of footsteps behind him caused him to turn and see what all the commotion was in the foyer. The ice sculpture had arrived and was being delivered by a handful of burly young men.

"Over here fellas," he called out to the gang of four, pointing to the richly colored mahogany table set up in the center of the large entry way.

The four men walked carefully over to the table and waited while two of Diego's crew covered the fine piece of furniture with some heavy white linen. As soon as the cloth was placed properly the men set the sculpture gently on the table, carefully twisting and turning it in response to Diego's instructions.

"PERFECT!" he said aloud, raising both hands, indicating that the men could back a way now. He signed the delivery invoice then turned back to admire the glistening sculpture.

"It's a beautiful swan Diego, thank you," Alma Donnelly said, walking up beside him, adjusting her earring.

"Yes it is, *isn't it,*" the proud caterer replied happily.

"Everything looks just wonderful! *Wonderful, wonderful, wonderful, wonderful,*" Alma said, doing a 360-degree turn, surveying the foyer and the dining room from where she stood.

"By the way, is that pheasant I smell cooking in the kitchen?" she asked, surprised.

"Of course!" Diego answered proudly. "Only the best for you Senora Donnelly!"

"Oh, thank you, you're sweet," Alma replied.

"It's going to a grand evening, don't you think Diego?" she asked, smiling broadly, positively giddy with anticipation.

"Yes it will be Senora, I have taken great care to attend to all of your wishes tonight," Diego answered sincerely.

"You're a dear man Diego. I don't know what we would do without you!" Alma said, praising him.

"You're too kind Senora, really," Diego replied, embarrassed by all of the attention. Their mutual admiration fest was suddenly interrupted by a loud crash and the sound of breaking glass on the foyer's Italian marble floor, startling them both.

"Good grief! What was that?" Alma exclaimed.

The two of them turned toward the commotion and watched while a young man knelt beside a tray of spilled champagne flutes, frantically picking up the jagged pieces as quickly as he could. Diego raced over to the scene and signaled for a couple helpers to come assist the young man with the clean up. This sort of occurrence was rare on one of his jobs, and Victor was visibly annoyed by the embarrassing mishap. He stooped down and said something inaudible to the young man crouched over the mess.

"*Si Senor Sanchz, lo ciento,*" the boy said apologetically, getting up as instructed and turning to return to the kitchen. Alma Donnelly stopped him as he passed and took his hand.

"You're bleeding child," she said caringly. The boy pulled his hand away and stepped back, sticking his wounded paw into his pants pocket. Alma frowned at him and stepped toward him.

"Don't be afraid, *ahhh?* Diego, what's this boy's name?" she called out to the caterer.

"That is Ramon, he's new. Actually he just started tonight, one of Senor Donnelly's projects. He asked if I could use him part time. So I have him working in the kitchen and bussing tables," Diego answered curtly, staring at Ramon the whole time.

One of the servers, a cute young girl that Alma recognized as Tina's new friend Tisha, had arrived with a damp cloth and a Band-Aid. Alma took the items from her and proceeded to tend to Ramon's wound herself, much to the consternation of Diego Sanchez. He stared at Ramon the whole time, giving him the stink-eye, then smiled disingenuously at Mrs. Donnelly as she turned back to face him.

"All better," she said sweetly, patting the boy's hand as she looked to Diego for approval.

"Yes Senora, very nice, thank you so much," he replied, bowing repeatedly.

"Diego, look at this boy! He's much too small to be carrying these heavy trays around. Can't you find him something less dangerous to do?" Alma asked, pleading on Ramon's behalf.

"Of course Senora. Tisha, take Ramon to the kitchen and tell Javier to put him to work polishing the silver," Diego said to the young woman.

"*Si Senor Sanchez, right away,*" she replied, taking Ramon by the hand and leading him away.

Ramon looked back over his shoulder as they passed by Alma Donnelly and started to say something when Tisha tugged on him harder, pulling him away and out of polite earshot.

"*Forget about it mensa!* Didn't you see the look Senor Sanchez face?" Tisha whispered as they left the room.

Miguel allowed himself to be dragged away, noticing the girl's small round behind for the first time as she pulled him along behind her, toward the kitchen. He watched appreciatively as her cute little bottom swished back and forth in rhythm with the strides of her muscular young legs. She was pretty, really pretty, but he didn't like anyone scolding him. Not her, and not that fat bastard Sanchez either. Miguel didn't care what kind of look Sanchez might have given him back there, or how what icky things this *chica* might say. None of that mattered now. He made a quick mental note, these two had just made his list! Arthur and Father Willet separated, letting the young lady and the young man pass between them as they exited the kitchen.

"*Where's the fire?*" Father Willet called out as the two youngsters disappeared behind the swinging doors leading to the kitchen.

"Let it go Billy, let's find Alma and get this meeting of yours over with," Arthur said curtly as the two men continued on toward the dining room.

"I trust everyone is here?" he asked rhetorically.

"They're all in the library, we just need Alma to complete the quorum," Father Willet replied, nearly jogging trying to keep up with the long strides of the big rancher.

"What about Tina, I didn't notice her?"

"She arrived about ten minutes ago with Father Kelly and Grover's people."

"They're not in this meeting, are they?"

"No, no, it's just six of us, and Tina of course."

"Six, who's missing?"

"Grover couldn't make it. He said he's too old to be attending pity parties." Arthur stopped abruptly, turning to face Father Willet. "*PITY PARTIES?* What in blue blazes is he talking about?"

"I sort of briefed him already on what Tina wanted to chat about."

"Briefed him, why only him? Why did we have to be kept in the dark?"

"What's with all the mystery anyway Billy?" Father Willet raised his hands and placed them on his friend's big shoulders.

"Patience Arthur, I promised the girl that she could have her say."

Arthur puffed out his cheeks and exhaled deeply. "Oh very well," he said, turning to continue on toward where his wife stood, fussing with the last minute details with the caterer. "I still don't understand why all this couldn't have waited until tomorrow?"

"I'll explain that too," Father Willet said, following along closely behind.

The two men walked into the large dining room but saw no sign of Alma Donnelly. They passed into the foyer and by the huge ice sculpture, still no sign. Arthur started to turn back toward the kitchen, when Father Willet tapped his arm and pointed out toward the patio. Through the lace covered French doors they could see Alma chatting with one of Grover's people, Jay Namura.

"There she is," Father Willet said.

"Oh, I see her," replied Arthur, leading the way toward the patio.

He opened the doors and stepped out into the cool evening, a slight breeze dropping the temperature to a comfortable sixty-two degrees according to the outside thermometer hanging on the brick wall to his right.

"Arthur, Billy, I was just talking to Mr. Namura here. Did you know they went to see that poor girl, Rosa Hernandez today?" Alma said, greeting the two men.

"No dear, I had no idea. Mr. Namura, nice to see you again," Arthur said, siding up to his wife and reaching out to shake Jay's hand.

"Sir...pleasure to see you again as well. You have a lovely home, really. Looks like it's going to be quite a party tonight," Jay said enthusiastically.

"Yes, well, Alma's in charge of everything around here, you can thank her for all of this," Arthur said, acknowledging his wife of thirty-five years, kissing her cheek in the process.

"You've done a wonderful job ma'am, really wonderful," Jay said to Alma.

"Why thank you Mr. Namura, that's so sweet," she replied.

"Jay, please call me Jay."

"Alright then, Jay."

"Oh goodness, where *are* my manners!"

"This is our parish priest, Father William Willet, we call him Father Billy around here," she added smiling brightly, introducing the priest to the photographer.

Father Willet extended his hand, "Mr. Namura and I have met before," he said, shaking Jay's hand.

"*That's right*, at Tina's little shindig a few years ago," Jay replied enthusiastically, pumping the priest's hand like a hand crank.

"Nice to see you again Father!"

Father Willet winced and returned Jay's smile, retrieving his hand before any permanent damage could be done. "Likewise Mr. Namura, likewise," he replied, shaking the circulation back into his hand.

"Where is your partner, I don't seem to see her anywhere?" asked the priest.

"She and Father Kelly are out there by that fence over there," Jay replied, pointing over Alma's shoulder to the two figures outlined by the moonlit night sky, standing near the big rail fence surrounding the corral.

"Whatever are they doing way over there?" Alma asked curiously.

"They have a few issues to discuss," Jay said with a wry smile.

"*Really? Maybe I should...*" Alma started, suddenly interrupted by her husband's grip on her arm.

"Not now mother, we have people waiting in the library. Please excuse us Jay, help yourself to whatever you like. As you can see, Diego lays out quite a spread," Arthur Donnelly said, pulling his wife along before Jay could reply. Father Willet cleared his throat and quickly followed after them without so much as a by your leave. Jay just shrugged and trailed after a pretty young server carrying a tray of fluted champagne glasses.

"*Ahhhh*, you're playing my song Artie baby," Jay muttered, catching up to the girl in three quick strides.

Sheriff Cardwell peered out the window, surveying the courtyard below, counting noses and making sure his people were on station. He slid the lace curtain over slightly with his finger, trying to see if he could spot the sentries posted on the drive. Just as he spotted them he flinched, startled by the sudden appearance of Father Willet.

"All's well I trust," Father Willet asked rhetorically.

The Sheriff nodded and released the curtain, letting it fall back into its original state.

"I didn't hear you come in," Sheriff Cardwell said, clearing his throat and regaining his composure.

He looked around the room and saw that the Donnelly's had also arrived. Good he thought, now we can get on with this evening. The sooner it was over the better as far as he was concerned. He had had a sinking feeling in his stomach all day for some reason. Father Willet turned and went to stand beside Tina Lopez, who was seated at the end of one of the two large sofas that faced one another in the center of the huge room. He leaned over and whispered softly into her ear.

"Are you ready child?" Tina nodded and took a sip of her diet soda.

Then set the heavy glass down on the table in front of her, the ice cubes clinking loudly as she did so. She reached up and pulled her long hair back, depositing it all behind her, sitting up nice and straight in the process, her signal to the priest that she was as ready as she was going to be. Picking up on the signal, Father Willet stood and cleared his throat loudly.

"Excuse me everyone, but I think that we're all here now, perhaps we can get started," he announced to the room. The idle chitchat ended abruptly as each person turned toward the priest, and settled themselves into a comfortable listening position.

"*OK Billy*, what's with all the hullabaloo? Why this meeting, why now?" Arthur Donnelly asked.

"There's no hullabaloo Arthur, not really. It's just that while we were weren't looking, busy with life and whatnot, this lovely girl beside me grew up into the beautiful young woman you see before you," Father Willet replied, reaching down and gently stroking Tina's hair.

She looked up at him and smiled, then turned to do likewise at each of the people in the room, holding their gaze individually for a second or two. The room was quiet for a few moments before Father Willet finally broke the silence.

"Hang on Arthur, I can read your mind from here! *Yes*, there is a *point* to all of this," he said, frowning at Mr. Donnelly before continuing.

"I had the opportunity to speak with Tina a little while ago. She came to St. John's to see me a few days ago, seeking advice about a matter of the heart. *And…*" Father Willet began, abruptly interrupted when Tina's mother leapt suddenly to her feet.

"*Aye Dios Mio! You and Father Kelly mija?*" exclaimed Maria Lopez.

"*I'll kill him!*" Victor whispered harshly, standing up quickly beside his wife. Sheriff Cardwell took a step toward Tina's angry father, as did Arthur.

"*MAMA!…POPPI!*" Tina said loudly, throwing herself back onto the sofa and folding her arms in front of her tightly.

"*No, no, no,* nothing like that! *Maria…Victor*, you surprise me, I mean, *really!*" Father Willet said, scolding them both. He pulled his handkerchief from his coat pocket and dabbed at the beads of sweat appearing suddenly at his hairline.

"Calm down everyone, *please!*" Father Willet pleaded.

"We're calm Billy, just get to the point! Don't turn this into one of your sermons for pity sake!" Arthur exclaimed as he encouraged the Lopez's to return to their seats on the sofa next to their daughter.

Victor and Maria did as he asked and reseated themselves beside Tina, while Arthur returned to his place next to Alma on the other sofa.

"*Right… OK*, long story short, Tina just wants to be normal, and lead a dull, plain old, normal life, that's about it!" the priest replied quickly.

"*That's it?*" Alma said softly, looking over at Tina who was still brooding a little after her parent's embarrassing outburst.

Alma got up from her seat and walked across the aisle, sitting down on the table separating the two sofas, directly in front of the Lopez girl. She reached out and took Tina's hands into her own, pulling her gently toward her, and looking directly into her eyes.

"There's more, isn't there dear?" she asked softly. Tina blinked a couple times involuntarily and exhaled deeply. "Yes ma'am, a little," she answered.

"Well tell us dear, we're all family here," Alma said, turning to look back at everyone in the room. Tina looked over at her Mother and Father and smiled weakly at them at first, then broadly as they smiled back at her.

"I went to see Father Billy about a dream. A dream I've been having for quite a while now," Tina said softly.

"*Speak up dear*, what about this dream?" Alma asked.

"*Ahem*, I've been dreaming about when I was a little girl, about the day I first touched that baby," she said, clearing her throat, and raising her voice a little bit.

"What about it?" he mother asked. Tina looked her way, "I just dream about it mommy, I don't know why," she replied.

"What else dear?" Alma Donnelly said calmly, trying to keep Tina on track.

"The little girl in my dream, it's not me."

"What do you mean it's not you?" asked Alma.

"She looks like me, I mean a little bit she does, but it's not me," Tina continued. Alma looked around the room and then back at Tina.

"Honey we're not following you, what is it you're trying to tell us?" she asked, puzzled.

Tina breathed in deeply and then stood up, crossing the room to stand behind the sofa opposite the one she had been sitting on. She leaned forward and placed both her hands on the back of the sofa, positioning herself between Arthur Donnelly and Sheriff Cardwell.

"*The girl in my dream is me and it's not me, does that make sense?*"

"I mean, I'm thinking that maybe God is trying to tell me something."

"Like maybe he doesn't need me anymore, like maybe it's someone else's turn to do these things," she said, searching the faces of the people that she loved for confirmation, and acknowledgement. Maria stood and walked over to her daughter. She put her arm around her lovingly and touched her head to Tina's.

"*Pobre-cita! Mija*, I know this has been hard on you, *you most of all*. And I know this was not something that you asked for or wished for. But surely you know you've been blessed, as have we all to share in your service to our Lord," Maria said, consoling her.

"*No, you don't understand!*"

"It's not that I want to quit or anything like that. Although it's true I have often wondered what my life would have been like without this responsibility."

"*No Mama*, I think that maybe the Lord is trying to let me down easy with these dreams. Preparing me for my return to a normal life without this power, and the responsibility that comes with it," Tina said, answering the unasked questions that hung on the faces of everyone in the room. She looked over at Father Willet, her face suddenly aglow as if she had just answered her own question.

"I think I know what it all means Father," she said running over to him and taking his hands in hers.

"What are you saying girl?" Father Willet asked, unsure of where she heading with her logic.

"What if it's like what it says in the Bible, *that only the children...*or, *ummm, let the child...?*"

"*OH*, Senor Donnelly, is there a Bible somewhere in this room?" she asked in frustration, as she tried to remember a particular verse.

Arthur rose from his seat and walked over to a large table in the corner, picking up an old and thick family Bible. He took it to where Tina was standing and held it open for her in his two strong hands. She began leafing through the pages, not exactly knowing where to turn other than she was sure it was in the New Testament.

"Thanks Mr. Donnelly," she said quickly turning pages and scanning the words. It was something that Jesus said about hiding things from grown-ups and only telling the kids," she rambled, directing her thoughts to Father Willet without looking his way.

"*Oh come on Father Billy*, you've used it in your sermons many times over the years," she added. Father Willet walked over to where she and Arthur were standing and looked over her shoulder.

"Try Luke 10:21 dear, turn there and let's see," he replied, suddenly realizing where she was headed with her explanation.

"*YES!* Here it is. Listen," she said, reading aloud and following the words with her slender finger.

"*I praise you, Father, Lord of heaven and earth, because you have hidden these things from the wise and the learned, and revealed them to little children.*"

"*Oh my gosh*, I think I see where you are going with this," Father Billy exclaimed suddenly.

"You do?" Alma said from across the room.

"*Well...don't just stand there Billy!* Close your pie hole before you catch a fly and then tell us what the hell is so interesting, *the good book here is getting kind of heavy!*" Arthur snapped.

"Let me think a second. Yes, it fits, I don't know why I didn't see this first, some theologian I am!" Father Willet said, scolding himself.

"Billy! Can you speed it up a little?" Arthur protested.

"*Sorry old man!* Here, let me help you set that back down," Father Willet replied, quickly lending a hand as they returned the heavy Bible to the table it came from.

"Who are you calling old, *shorty?*" Arthur muttered as they turned to rejoin the others by the sofas. Father Willet ignored the jibe and went to stand by Tina. He clasped her hands supportively for a second then released them and turned to face Maria and Victor.

"OK, *now*, when was the last occurrence anyone can remember?" he said, asking the room.

"Anyone?"

Alma Donnelly spoke first, "Wasn't it last July, when she ran off with that renegade priest of yours Billy?" Father Willet rolled his eyes, "Ethan is not a renegade Alma! If you recall, I was the one who sent her along with him!"

"Oh yes, I remember now," Alma replied.

"WE ALL REMEMBER BILLY!" Arthur said sternly. "Where are you headed with this anyway?"

"Just a minute...Maria, Victor, have there been any other healings since last summer that you can remember?" the priest asked of Tina's parents. Victor looked at his wife and then back at Father Willet, shrugging, "Not that we can think of," he answered.

"That's what I thought as well. There has not been one single occurrence since last July. Not one, not since shortly after her eighteenth birthday, when she became an adult in the eyes of the State, *and apparently*, in the eyes of God as well," Father Willet said, laying out the foundation for his hypothesis.

The room fell silent while everyone compared notes telepathically. Father Willet waited a couple minutes for all of them to catch up, and then continued laying it all out.

"What if Tina is right? What if these dreams *are* a subtle message?"

"What if through these dreams, God is releasing her from her service, encouraging her to get on with her life, and in doing so, keeping with scripture. By *hiding these things* from the wise and learned, from the adult she has become," he said slowly, watching as every face save Tina's turned into a giant question mark.

"I believe that is exactly what her dreams are saying. And I also believe that God is revealing to Tina's heart, just whom her replacement shall be, *although* I don't think she has figured that part out yet."

"But, I think I might have," Father Willet said with a sly smile. He looked over at Tina who returned his gaze with a shrug of her shoulders.

"Not a clue Father, no idea," she said, answering the question on his face. "By the way, it's true, I haven't helped anyone since Father Kelly's little godchild in New York, she was the last," Tina added.

Father Willet walked over to one of the wingback chairs near the fireplace and fell into it. He swiped at his brow as if he had just finished some arduous task and then leaned forward, placing his hands on his knees.

"Well? Anyone care to challenge my theory?" he asked the room collectively.

"Well I'll be damned," Sheriff Cardwell said, cutting through the silence.

"You got all of that from Tina's ramblings and one Bible verse, did ya?" the Sheriff added.

"*I'm impressed Billy!* Maybe we should trade uniforms! You seem to be a better detective than I am," he said laughing heartily.

"Yeah, I suppose I might at that," Father Willet replied, smiling broadly.

Victor walked over to join his wife and child in a warm embrace, unsure of how he really felt, now that it was all over. Tina buried her face in her father's chest and sighed heavily, relieved and sad at the same time. Alma Donnelly rose and sought out her husband for a similar repose. Father Willet remained in the comfy chair, leaning back, enjoying the love in the room, as well as the satisfaction that his sleuthing had brought unexpectedly. A thought suddenly occurred to him and he smiled. "*So much for all your scheming Villa Cruz,*" he muttered softly to himself.

Fresno, California, 12, March 1974…6:00pm

Smiley stood at the back of the car and waited for Raymond to open the trunk. They had waited an extra hour to satisfy Raymond's paranoia about the lights he swore he saw earlier. Smiley cursed his friend silently and shook his head in disgust while he watched Raymond fumble with the wad of keys on his ridiculously large key ring.

"Come on Holmes, let's get this done *ese!*" Smiley whined loudly.

"Shut up man, someone will here you!" Raymond barked back at him.

"*WHO WILL HEAR US STUPIDO*, there's nobody **HERE!**" Smiley said vehemently.

"It's just you, me, and the stiffs, so come on, *RAPIDO!*"

"Fuck you Smiley. You better shut up yourself or I'm gonna stick you in the same hole as these two *chingasos,*" Raymond shouted, as the trunk sprang open.

"Who *you* calling *chingasos?*" came a low voice from the trunk, startling the two gang bangers.

"*What the f…?*" Raymond started to reply, before a steel-toed boot attached to a thickly muscled leg struck him in the solar plexus, dropping him instantly to the ground in a fetal position.

Smiley let out a little scream and then took off, running for his life. The second man in the trunk jumped out and heaved a lug wrench at the fleeing would-be murderer. The heavy tool struck Smiley point end first, like a short spear, right at the base of his skull, penetrating a good four inches into his head before halting it's forward progress. Smiley fell forward, dead before his face ever touched the hard dirt road. The first man, the one with the steel-toed boot, rose slowly from the trunk, holding a bloody rag to his throat where Smiley had sliced him from ear to ear in a poor attempt at finishing him off. First rule in any assassination, make sure the mark is dead before you move the body! These guys were amateurs, punks, but even so, he and Hayes had underestimated them.

Solero reached over with his boot and pushed Raymond onto his back. The gang-banger's legs remained pulled up to his chest while he struggled to catch his breath. Solero spit on Raymond and stepped on his ankles, drawing his legs down to the ground. Raymond was beyond scared, he had in fact already soiled himself, his pants stained dark at the crotch. But he was defiant to the end, spitting back at Solero weakly, the spittle falling back onto his own face.

"Is that all you got Holmes!" Raymond said, whimpering, his eyes filled with tears like an angry child. Solero looked down at him, almost in pity. Hayes walked up beside Solero, the lug wrench in his hand, retrieved from Smiley's skull. Solero took the heavy object in his hand and spun it once, taking hold of the bent end of the wrench.

"No," he said calmly to Raymond. *"I got this too,"* he added, swinging the wrench in a wide arc down at Raymond, burying the pry bar end deep into his chest and right through his beating heart. Solero watched the light go out in Raymond's eyes, his pupils dilating, and then listened intently as the young man took his last breath.

"Let's go," he said to Hayes without looking over at him.

"The boy?" Hayes asked as he climbed into the driver's seat.

"Yeah, but see if you can find a gas station first, I want to clean up," Solero said closing the passenger door after him.

"I'm on it."

"What about you? You gonna be alright?" Solero asked, glancing over at his partner, noticing the bloody shirt under his sport coat.

"Yeah, I'm OK. Those dorks totally missed the barn. I ended up catching two rounds in the vest, but they only creased me with the headshot at crunch time. I think that the smaller one actually had his eyes closed when he pulled the trigger, Hayes said, snickering.

"What about you?"

"I kept my chin tucked in when he tried cutting my throat. He must have sliced into bone and gave up, totally missed the arteries. These guys weren't killers, just punks. Let's find that kid though, he's something else all together," Solero said, pressing the dirty rag hard against his wounds.

"What about the bodies?" Hayes asked, putting the car in gear.

"Leave them for the scavengers. It'll take the local yokels here days to find them. We'll be long gone by then, with the girl."

Mendota, California, 12, March 1974
<u>*Donnelly Ranch…7:00pm*</u>

Jay waved at KC and I as we walked toward the patio. He had been stealing glances our way for the last hour or so, trying to get a feeling for whatever was going on between us. KC waved back and got a tighter grip on my arm as we walked together, shivering slightly and pulling closer to me for a little extra warmth.

"Thanks Ethan," she said softly.

"For what," I replied.

"*You know*, for not making me feel ridiculous, even though I've acting that way for quite some time."

"It's not ridiculous to fall in love Kathy, really, I'm flattered."

"Don't say that, that's what people always say!"

"Sorry, it's the first thing that came into my head."

"You can't fool me Ethan Kelly, I'm a woman, and a woman knows when a man wants her!"

"Yeah but…"

"*But nothing pardre*, we talked about that on the ride over here, remember. You as much as confessed to noticing how *pretty I am*, *how smart I am*, *what a good person I am*, junk like that! But your words didn't speak near as loud as your body language and your eyes. Admit it, ***you're hot for me!*** I know you're a priest and all, but you're a MALE priest, and my radar's in fine operating condition, I read you loud and clear sailor!"

"*Look KC…*" I started, stopping short of the patio, wanting to stay clear of all the commotion of the arriving guests as well as just out of earshot of Jay Namura. I turned to face her, my back to the party.

"Look KC, let's just say for the sake of argument that you're right. I'm just another sinner like everyone else. And avoiding temptation where you're concerned is right at the top of my list of things to do at this particular moment," I said, holding onto her shoulders and looking directly into her eyes. She was smiling broadly, her eyes twinkling like stars in the night sky above us. Clearly she was receiving a different message than I was trying to send.

"*No, no, you stop that*! Listen closely to what I'm saying here," I pleaded, stifling a smile, trying keep from being swept away myself by her euphoria.

"*Truly Kathy*, I've never met anyone quite like you."

"*NOT* noticing you would be impossible I think, not just for me but for anyone."

"You want a confession? OK I'll give one, a real news flash. You're right, there is a struggle going on in my own heart, and it does concern my commitment to the priesthood versus my desire to be like everybody else, like my father, just another man with a family of my own."

"I have often wondered what my life would be like outside of the Catholic Church. And I have wondered what it might be like to share that life with someone, someone much like you. *But honestly KC, it wasn't you who...*"

The calmness of the night was shattered suddenly by a series of loud pops, *two or three*, sounds that I recognized immediately as small arms fire. They came from inside the house, the gunfire followed quickly by the sound of breaking glass, the shouts and screams of people filling the air. I pushed KC down to the ground instinctively, and covered her body with mine, waiting for a moment to see if any more shots were fired. I pushed up from her a little, looking around to see what I could see. The house seemed quieter, but there was still an uneasiness permeating from the direction of the gunfire. I looked down and saw KC looking back up at me, trying to read my expression.

"What was that? Sounded like a gunshots maybe," she whispered.

"That's exactly what it was, be still," I replied, putting my finger over her lips.

"You're a lot heavier than I thought you'd be. What do you do, lift weights or something," she teased, kissing my finger lightly.

"Stop that!"

"Just finishing what you started," KC said smiling.

"Come on KC, not now, something's not right here."

"You're telling me, get off of me Sasquatch!"

I rolled off of KC and slowly got to my feet, surveying the now quiet house twenty or so yards away. KC whistled softly.

"Hey, how about a hand here," she asked sarcastically. I reached down and helped her up. "Thanks, can you see anything?"

"No, too many people by the French doors. I wonder where Jay went off to?" I asked slightly puzzled by his disappearance.

"That's easy, he's a newshound. He went to get his camera bag silly!"

"You're kidding!"

"Nope! Come on let's go see what we can see," she said, taking my hand and dragging me along.

As we reached the patio I could see that there was a commotion going on inside. We snaked our way into the house and moved cautiously through the crowd of frightened people. I could hear Arthur Donnelly's voice pleading with someone inside to let him call for a doctor.

"*Please son*, let just get some help for him, he's bleeding awfully badly!"

"*SHUT UP, everybody just SHUT UP!*" came the shrill voice of a frightened child.

As I neared the edge of the crowd surrounding the scene, I saw two bodies lying on the floor, face down. The one nearest to me I recognized as Sheriff Cardwell, he wasn't moving. I looked across to the other one, about six feet away, and to my horror, I saw that it was Father Willet. He was shivering as if he was cold and I knew right away that he was in shock. My corpsman training came rushing back to me and before I could think about it I was kneeling beside him, checking the carotid artery for his pulse. The gun-wielding boy turned instantly and shouted at me, *"GET AWAY FROM HIM!"*

I ignored him at first, continuing to take inventory of Father Willet's wounds. I could feel the boy's eyes burning a hole through my back while he waited for a reply, growing more agitated by the second.

"*Look*, if you're going to shoot, **SHOOT!** But you'll have to shoot me in the back, I'm kinda busy over here," I replied, my voice sounding much calmer than I really was.

"I'LL DO IT!"

"*Then do it Miguel,*" I said, suddenly recognizing the voice behind me. The boy rushed up to me and jammed the barrel of his pistol in my ear, splitting my lobe, warm blood oozing down onto my neck.

"I MEAN IT MAN, I'LL DO IT, FOR REALS!"

"LEAVE HIM ALONE!" shouted the shrill voice of a woman.

I turned my head slightly to get a look. It was Tina Lopez. She had stepped out from behind a human shield consisting of her parents and the Donnelly's. I could only assume that Sheriff Cardwell and Father Willet had been standing in the same place only moments before, and had paid the price for doing so. Miguel suddenly swung his weapon down with all of his might onto the base of my skull, knocking me to the floor, seriously impacting my ability to remain conscious. Grabbing my head with both hands, I squeezed both of my eyes shut, trying to will away the pain and stay coherent. Wincing and rolling my head to one side, I watched as Miguel approached the Lopez girl slowly. It was only then that I noticed the knife that he held in his other hand.

Nobody moved, and I panicked just a little when I didn't see KC right away. Where had she gone I wondered, she had been right behind me, I was worried what that crazy woman might do, she was capable of just about anything! I slowly worked my way up to my knees and sat back on my heels. Blood flowed down my neck and over my forehead into my eyes from the gash that Miguel had opened on my scalp. I wiped at it with my hands, but it only made it worse. I looked down at Father Willet and saw that he had stopped shivering, not a good sign, he had probably already bled out. I slowly reached over to check his pulse again, watching Miguel closely. The boy remained fixated on the Lopez girl, twirling the knife at his side and holding everyone back with the .45 automatic. Taking advantage of the opportunity I placed my fingers at his neck and felt for a pulse. It was there, but it was very faint, Father Willet needed attention right now, and there wasn't much I could do about it given the current situation, not without getting someone else shot, like me!

"What do you want here, *huh*? Haven't you done enough, *just leave us alone!*" Tina said, more mad now than scared. Miguel sneered at her, leveling the pistol at her chest.

"That's funny. You know, none of this would have ever happened if you had *just left me alone*. Not any of this, *you hear me bitch!*"

"*What are you talking about **mensa**!* I'm not afraid of you, not one bit!" Tina snapped back at him, her white knuckled fists held stiffly at her side.

"*Stop it mija*, don't push on him!" Maria whispered harshly, afraid for her daughter.

She stood petrified behind her, digging her nails into her husband's shirtsleeve. Victor had had just about enough of all this nonsense, and seemed as if he were looking for just the right opportunity to pounce on the boy. My head ached so much, the pain was beginning to impair my ability to think clearly. I knew that something had to happen soon or Miguel was going to kill again, and his next victim was likely standing right in front of him. I tried to decipher what he had said to Tina.

What was he trying to tell her? What was their connection anyway? It didn't make sense to me, none of this made sense to me. I wiped away another trail of blood from my eyes and then caught site of Victor. He was trying to signal me, nodding ever so slightly in Miguel's direction. I looked over at Miguel and saw what Victor had noticed. The gun that Miguel held was no longer aimed at Tina, the boy had relaxed his arm, and the weapon now hung at his side, pointing down at the floor. Clearly Victor was ready to make a move, and I was pretty sure I knew what he had in mind. All I had to do was dive at Miguel's legs. Victor would jump in front of his daughter and shove Miguel backward over me. And if we were lucky, he'd drop one of his weapons in the fall. Then I could go for whichever one he still held onto. It was risky, I know, but there didn't seem to be too many other options.

I wondered for a second what had happened to all of Sheriff Cardwell's security measures, and then let it go. There would be plenty of time later to sort out what had gone wrong. Slowly, carefully, quietly, I pulled one leg forward and steadied myself on one knee. I could hear Tina and Miguel exchanging words harshly, none of them registering as I concentrated on my next move. I looked directly at Victor. He was inching slowly away from Maria, while he and I maintained constant eye contact. I held my breath suddenly when Maria tried to pull Victor back toward her, whispering something to him excitedly. Victor stopped, first looking at Miguel, and then slowly turning his gaze to his wife. He said nothing and instantly Maria released her hold on his sleeve. Then just as slowly he turned his head back in my direction, stopping briefly to log Miguel's position.

Tina and Miguel's conversation suddenly turned into a shouting match. Everything seemed to slow down in my mind. Miguel's arm began to raise, the gun cocked and ready to fire. He had raised the big hunting knife pointed it in Tina's direction. He was only a couple feet from where she stood defiantly. Victor's chin slowly dipped to his chest and back up again, signaling me to make my move. I put both hands on my raised knee an pushed down hard with my all my strength, springing forward on the ball of my foot, while my legs straightened as I stretched out like a wide receiver making a diving catch. I lost sight of Victor, of everyone, seeing only the legs of my target less than ten feet in front of me. I prayed that Victor was moving as quickly as I and that we had timed everything just right. I prayed that God would be with us. I prayed that Tina would be spared, that no one else would die tonight.

And then all of a sudden everything began to happen in real time. The screams returned, and I felt myself making contact with Miguel's ankles, my arms wrapping around them tightly. All I could see were shoes from where I lay, sprawled on the floor, but I knew that Miguel had fallen over me. I spun quickly to execute part two of the plan, disarm the boy, and came face to face with the business end of the formidable firearm. Stunned, I didn't know what to do next. I couldn't think with all of the screaming. I sensed that something was going on behind me, but I couldn't take my eyes off of the gun six inches from my face. Kneeling, I leaned back onto my heels, my hands raised slightly, palms up, just like you're supposed to do when a gunman gets the drop on you, at least according to every movie I had ever seen. I watched Miguel scramble to his knees as well, holding the gun with both hands now. Dazed and confused for only a second or two, his grip on the weapon steadied. He quickly surveyed the room from his new vantage point, making sure that the weapon did not move a scintilla from where it was currently aimed. He breathed in deeply and exhaled slowly, his face turning from pale to a more normal complexion. I could hear Alma Donnelly in the background, barking out orders excitedly.

"GET SOME TOWELS QUICKLY! WE NEED TO STOP THIS BLEEDING...*HURRY!* Alma shouted frantically at someone.

I started to turn my head to see who had been hurt. I had a sinking feeling that it was either Tina or her father. Suddenly I froze, hearing the familiar sound of a pistol hammer locking once then twice into firing position. I pushed my eyes to their peripheral limit and saw the bare foot of a girl behind me. Sighing, I turned back to face Miguel, silently praying for Tina's immortal soul. The boy looked at me calmly, his eyes wet with tears, but his expression stoic and steady.

"Bless me Father, I have sinned, ya know," he said coldly, the gun aimed directly at my head.

"Is it absolution you want Miguel?" I asked, wincing as sweat and blood dripped into my eye.

"I don't know what that is Father."

"*Forgiveness Miguel*, its forgiveness. Is it God's forgiveness you're wanting boy?"

"No Father, I don't." I looked at him puzzled. "Then why ask to be blessed?"

"*I dunno*, I hear people say that stuff sometimes, it sounds nice. Maybe I just wanted to hear myself say the words too."

"It is nice my son. God's love is good. And, big surprise here, do you know that all can be forgiven with that love."

"*For reals?*" he asked softly, leaning to one side to look past me.

"Yeah, really! The Bible says in the Book of Colossians, to '*put on a heart of compassion, kindness, humility, gentleness and patience; bearing with one another, and forgiving each other*' and guess what, it applies to everyone, no matter what."

"That's good Father," he said in a low tone, his expression almost trance like.

While he watched whatever was happening behind me, I saw several men weaving their way toward us, apparently the cavalry had arrived. They weren't in uniform and I didn't recognize any of them as Sheriff Cardwell's deputies, but what did that matter, they were here and this nightmare would be over soon. I sat very still and made no sound, trying not to give away their advantage of surprise. Miguel leaned back to face me again, smiling. He tilted his chin up slightly and nodded toward the people behind me.

"Senor Lopez," he said slowly. I looked at him trying to read his expression. "What about him?"

"He's a good man, isn't he Father."

"Yes son, I believe that he is." Miguel nodded slowly, "I think so too," he said sincerely.

The men behind Miguel were now in position to pounce. I could see that they were waiting for some kind of signal from me, one that indicated that I acknowledged their intent and that I was ready to get out of the way quickly. I forced myself to ignore them, holding Miguel's steady gaze.

"Tell me Father, do you think your God will forgive this?" he said suddenly.

Before anyone could react, Miguel put the gun under his chin and pulled the trigger, filling the room with a deafening retort, scattering tissue, blood and bone everywhere. Miguel's body was hurled backward, collapsing slightly onto one side, his eyes frozen open in a death stare. I moved my jaw back and forth trying to pop my ears. As soon as my hearing returned my ears were filled with the sounds of hysterical voices, of people fleeing the scene, shouting for help or for loved ones. I focused on the boy who lay before me, feeling a little disgusted by the way one officer kept his boot pressed firmly on Miguel's face, forcing his cheeks into a grotesque fish face, his lifeless eyes seemingly staring back at me. Shuddering, I started to protest when I heard the voice of Victor Lopez voice shouting.

"OVER HERE, OVER HERE!"

My senses returning slowly, I got up and pushed my way to where a small circle of people stood over the body of a girl lying on the floor. A large amount of thick, dark red blood was pooling around her. There were bloody footprints leading every which way, tracking the paths of people who had already fled the scene. I recognized Alma Donnelly kneeling at the girl's feet, timidly holding the girl's shoes in her hands. Moving closer, I wiped away the blood from my own eyes. As I drew near, I took a knee beside Victor. He was firmly pressing a couple of blood soaked towels on the girl's abdomen. The towels were wrapped around the hilt of a very large hunting knife. I reached over and pulled the towels away slightly, my training as a medic propelling me into action. I surveyed the damage; the blade had been plunged about as far as it could be into the belly of the girl. Ironically I had seen this kind of wound before, on the father of the very child that lay silently in death behind us.

I leaned toward Victor and whispered into his ear, *"I'm so sorry Victor,"* touching his head with my own, ever so gently. Suddenly I felt the touch of a small hand on mine and looked up, surprised to see Tina Lopez kneeling opposite me.

"Oh Father, I'm so sorry Ethan," she said through tears of her own.

Confused I quickly looked back at the face of the girl on the floor. My heart rate raced, I felt as if it might explode at any moment. Then, as I realized what had really happened, when I saw who lay on the floor before me, my heart just sank, so deep into my chest that my shoulders seemed to round from the weight. The barefoot girl that we had all been tending to, wasn't Tina Lopez after all, *it was KC!* I looked back at Victor, *"What the hell happened!"* I whispered, my voice cracking slightly.

"She came out of nowhere Father, got right between Tina and me. It all happened so fast, I..."
I didn't wait to hear the rest. I just scooted up to where KC's head
rested, and bent down close to her face. Gently, I pushed back her damp
hair. Her eyes fluttered weakly and then opened wide. It took a minute for her to focus, her eyes were red and wet. She smiled weakly as soon as she saw me, that cute *smart-ass* smile of hers. Then feebly, she
raised her hand and grabbed at my earlobe, pinching it harder than I would thought she were able.

"Well, well, well, it's about time padre, I was getting a little cold down here," she murmured, blinking her eyes slowly.

"Oh man Kathy! Stop clowning around will ya, you need to save your strength," I said sternly, gently pulling her hand from my ear and holding it in my own.

She snickered and squeezed my fingers. "I'm not worried. I got my new fella here with me. By the way, you're gonna have to help me square things with God for stealing one of his collared boys," she said, with an exaggerated wink.

"And then of course the miracle child is right over there," she said weakly, reaching over and touching Tina with her free hand.

"This'll be a piece of cake, *right kid?"* she said, rolling her eyes toward her.

Tina put her face in her hands and sobbed. I looked around at Victor and Alma, they were crying as well. Obviously I was missing something, but I had no idea what it could be. KC wet her lips with her tongue and squinted, wrinkling her face into an curious expression of bewilderment.

"What'd I say?" KC asked, puzzled.

Tina rubbed her eyes and then lowered her hands, leaning down and kissing KC hard on her cheek, her own warm tears dripping onto KC's chin. She cupped KC's face in her slender hands, pausing a second before speaking.

"I'm so sorry Kathy, *it's gone,* I can't do it anymore," she said softly, her voice cracking.

I looked up and shot a glance at Maria Lopez. She nodded her head in silent confirmation, and then looked away, unable to hold my gaze.

KC blinked several times then rolled her eyes away from Tina, and stared straight up at the ceiling.

"*Ah Nuts!* Wouldn't you know it? First time I need a miracle of my own and the cupboards bare! And on the very night my guy confesses his undying love, *go figure*," she said sarcastically, closing her eyes and sighing heavily.

I chewed on my lips, trying to hold my tongue. This wasn't the time for total honesty. I knew all too well how much time was left, she was bleeding out and there was nothing anyone could do about it. The Donnelly's ranch was far enough out in the sticks to assure the outcome of this tragedy, to assure KC's regrettable fate. I touched my hand to her face and waited for her to open her eyes again. Like Paulie would always say, it was time to be a stand up guy now.

"You were right, I do love you Katherine Littleton," I said, loud enough for everyone to hear.

"I'll always love you." Her eyes welled with tears, her expression telling me that she knew her time was short.

"*Psst,*" she whispered weakly, beckoning me closer with her eyes. I bent down, and placed my ear near her mouth.

"You *are* going to at least kiss me goodbye, *aren't you?*" she whispered. I moved my face closer to hers, our cheeks touching. Her tears felt warm on my skin.

"*Just try and stop me!*" I whispered into her ear through her smooth silky hair. I turned slowly toward her, our noses touching gently as I looked down onto her pretty face.

"*Pucker up padre,*" she said weakly, and our lips touched softly.

This would be our one and *only* kiss in this lifetime. I opened my eyes when I no longer feel the warmth of her breath, and pulled away gingerly, my lips peeling away from hers slowly, as if one cell at a time. I reached up and closed her eyes, kissing each of her eyelids before I rose, still holding onto her hand. When I finally looked up I saw the face of Jay Namura looking back at me, kneeling beside KC as well. There was an expression of total confusion frozen onto his face, only his eyes indicating that there was any life left in him. I had no idea what to say to the man, we were barely acquaintances.

But at this very moment, I became keenly aware of just what Jay was feeling in his heart of hearts. Everyone had lost someone or something near and dear tonight. The community had lost a champion of a man in Sheriff Cardwell. The flock had lost a beloved Sheppard in Father Willet. A child had lost everything, his way, his family, and his life. I had lost someone who had given me her heart. A beautiful gift, gift I clearly did not deserve. And Jay Namura, who had the look of someone who suddenly realized that no one is guaranteed a tomorrow, had just lost the love of his life. His eyes betrayed his deep sorrow and regret for lacking the courage to ever tell her so. I reached across KC's body and put her hand in his, telling him silently with my own eyes that now might be as good time as any. In my mind I imagined her hovering above us all, a child once more, holding onto the hand of Father God.

I smiled tenderly at Jay and then looked down at the face of an angel. And at that very moment, this verse from Jeremiah 29:11 came into my head...'*for I know the plans that I have for you, declares the Lord, plans for welfare and not calamity to give you a future and a hope...*'

"Thanks for the nudge Kathy. Thanks for helping me on my way," I whispered, looking up as if to watch her climb the stairway to heaven.

Forty-six

(..."I can do all things through Christ who
strengthens me"... Philippians 4:13)*

Albany, New York, 30, June 1974
Cathedral of the Holy Cross

    I could feel the warm summer sun beating down on my neck through the stained glass behind me. It felt good, but it would have felt a lot better if I weren't wearing all of these heavy robes and such. The place was packed to the rafters with family and friends, all of them waiting for the wedding march to begin, and the appearance of the blushing Bride. Finally the doors opened slowly and I saw my sister at the end of the long aisle standing beside Uncle Liam, one white gloved hand on his arm and the other hidden from view beneath a beautiful bridal bouquet of white roses and heather. I smiled as I watched Uncle Liam pull out his kerchief and nervously swipe across his brow, clearing tiny beads of perspiration. Then he stuffed the neatly folded cloth quickly back into his coat pocket and tugged at his lapel, signaling Shannon that he was ready.

    I could almost swear I saw Shannon roll her eyes in a minor panic. And I know I heard a tiny gasp from my mother in the front pew. Stealing a quick glance over at Paul, I had to stifle a chuckle myself, catching sight of him following my uncle's lead and mopping his own gargantuan noggin with the sleeve of his tuxedo! Kenny Wong, standing in the best man's spot, leaned toward Paulie and whispered something that I couldn't quite make out. Whatever it was, it must have been pretty funny because Paulie snorted out a little giggle, loud enough to attract everyone's attention. It was actually quite a sight to see three hundred heads spin so quickly in unison in our general direction. Paul and all his groomsmen jabbed at one another with their elbows, each of them trying to encourage the others to pipe down and stand up straight. Some things just never change, and thankfully so. I watched the four childhood friends berate and shush one another like we used to, so many years ago in this very same church, under the watchful eye of Father McKenzie. Well we were all grown up now, and I looked from face to face affectionately. There was my big buddy Paulie, who today was joining my family, somehow legitimizing all those poundings he had given me in the old days. And Kenny Wong whom I had grown to admire and respect more and more with each passing year. To my mind, outside of my own father, nobody represented the concept of family better than Ken. In my heart of hearts I hoped to be just like them.

Then there was the most famous member of our little gang, J. Cullen Wainwright Hollenbeck IV, standing there looking rather uncomfortable in his coat and tails. Or, as his mother reminded us every chance she got, *Senator Hollenbeck*, Massachusetts' newest Republican State representative. Who knows, a few years from now he might give ol' Ted Kennedy himself some stiff competition? Finally there was Sparky, the ringleader of our small band of brothers. His real name was Jon, but his grandmother had called him Sparky since his first birthday, born on the 4th of July you see. Of course now he was Dr. Jon Carvalo, a very successful heart surgeon in the greater Albany area. Folks just called him Dr. Jon, not to be confused with *Dr. John*, the beret wearing singer songwriter. Especially if you wanted to avoid a fat lip! Although, at least now he might offer stitch you up afterward. There had been a sixth member of our gang, Michael Alvin Price, a.k.a. Mikey. Sadly, Mikey had not survived the war, killed during a Christmas cease-fire, in a mortar attack on a lonely forward firebase.

I looked into the crowd with that thought wieghing heavily on my heart and sought out a friendly face from that time in my life. I found Carla quickly, seated just behind my family with her husband, my dear friend Sean, God love him. I gave her a little wave and they both waved back to me. Then turning back to the commotion behind me, I considered interceding to help expedite a return to a sense of order to the proceedings. Mercifully, before the *four stooges* could really get into their normal routine, the grand old pipe organ overhead began to blast out the wedding processional. The same three hundred heads now spun back toward the opposite end of the church, no less than a hundred cameras raised to the ready. Shannon turned her head and said something to Uncle Liam, probably something like, *they're playing my song Uncle*, and the two of them began their slow march down the aisle.

My sister was an absolute vision in her dress of satin and lace, her face veiled beautifully in sheer white lace and her head adorned with a wreath of juniper, heather and thistle. Sophie Wong and Gilbert Lopez walked ahead of them, carrying a basket of wildflowers and the small satin pillow bearing two humble rings. The two kids made quite a pair, and the crowd was eating it all up with a spoon. The room suddenly erupted with flashes as dozens of people individually recorded the precious moment for posterity. I looked over at my mother and smiled. She didn't see me of course, as she was pretty busy depositing every single second into her vault of memories through a pair of glistening eyes, her gloved hands covering her trembling lips, and holding back her sobs of joy. I knew that she was wishing Da were here with her now, missing him dearly, as were Shannon and I.

The two children grew nearer and I held out my hand nonchalantly, trying to communicate to them to slow down just a little. Sophie seemed to receive my message, as she reached over to Gilbert and tugged on the sleeve of his coat. I held my breath at her maneuver, expecting either the pillow to drop or Gilbert to sock her. But thankfully, disaster was avoided and Victor and Maria's one and only son got with the program, slowing down to keep pace with his partner in crime. I could see Shannon more clearly now, she was positively radiant, although Uncle Liam was looking a tad woozy. Just as I thought he might teeter a bit, Uncle Richard reached out from the pew with his large paw to steady his older brother. The look of relief on Shannon's face was comical, and the look on my mother's face was priceless. *God love my family*, I thought to myself, there's no other like it in the whole wide world, that's for sure!

Father McKenzie touched my arm, indicating that I was to take my place, a step or two down from the altar, and prepare to greet the Bride and her escort. I looked over at our parish priest and he winked back at me. Then I mouthed a thank you at him, grateful for his willingness to look the other way and allow me to perform the ceremony today, even though technically I was now a minister in the Episcopalian Church.

"I think God will forgive us this *wee technicality* Ethan," he whispered.

"So long as we take each other's confession later, of course," he added, muttering softly as Sophie and Gilbert reached the altar.

I winked back at him and smiled, then stepped down carefully to take my place as we had rehearsed earlier. The children took the places beside the Maid of Honor and Best Man respectively. Carolyn Wong bent down and praised her daughter for her performance, and Kenny placed his hands on Gilbert's shoulders, holding him in place before he could run back up the aisle and escape. In a final crescendo, the organ's deep and voluminous tones subsided and Shannon and Uncle Liam stood before me. Holding my small Bible in my hands in front of me I nodded at the two of them and smiled. My sister beamed back at me and my Uncle winked. Looking up and over them, I addressed Uncle Liam and the church full of well-wishers.

"Who gives this woman in Holy matrimony this fine day?"

Uncle Liam rose up to his full height, all five feet six inches of himself, and announced proudly, *"Her family does sir, her family,"* he said, his thick Gaelic accent resonating to the very ceiling high overhead. I nodded, acknowledging his heartfelt declaration, and then turned to look toward the groom. Paulie didn't appear to be breathing, like a deer caught in the headlights of an oncoming bus.

Clearing his throat, and breaking the uncomfortable pregnant pause before all the whispers began, Kenny saved the day with a little shove and Paul stepped forward to accept Shannon's hand from Uncle Liam. The two of them, my sister and closest friend looked at one another tenderly and then turned to faced me. I stepped toward them, taking the last step down from the altar to the aisle and placed my hands gently over theirs. We three held each other's gaze, sharing a special moment, as if totally alone.

"I'm so happy for the both of you," I whispered softly.

Shannon squeezed my hand and Paul gave me that big goofy smile of his, finally relaxing. Reaching up, I gave his face a little buddy cuff and winked at him.

"You son of a gun you," I muttered, smiling. He winked back and then Shannon gave us *the look.*

"Will you two ejits knock it off and get on with it?" she whispered harshly.

I turned to lead them up the three steps to stand before the altar. We greeted Father McKenzie and then I turned to address the gathering. I placed a hand on the shoulders of the Bride and Groom and encouraged them to kneel. I looked over the two of them at all the guests and witnesses, and then settled my gaze on my Mother.

"Dearly beloved, we are gathered here today..."

Albany, New York, 30, June 1974
The Kelly compound/neighborhood

My mother sat beside me in the limousine, holding onto my hand and gushing on and on about the wonderful ceremony, and the glorious day, and wasn't so and so lovely, and wasn't so and so charming. I listened politely while I watched the familiar sights of my youth pass by me through the tinted windows of the plush automobile. I smiled to myself thinking of Da would have just hated riding in this car. "These things are bobbles of the rich and dandies sonny," he would say. I think if Da were here, he would have driven the happy couple himself, to and from the wedding in his hot rod Camero. And knowing Shannon, she would have loved it as well. She was daddy's little girl after all, first and always. Mother would probably have squawked a bit at first, but in the end, she was Da's best girl as well. Lord how I missed him. I wished he had been here to help me deal with the struggles in my life, small and great. To help me feel certain of my decisions, of the paths that I have followed, am following, and will follow. Surely these are things I take to God in prayer all the time. But every so often I think how nice it would be to hear my father's soothing, familiar voice again. To feel his scratchy five o'clock shadow when he'd peck me on the cheek. Or disappear into his firm and safe embrace. Where he would put his beefy arms around me and squish my face into his chest so I could subtly dry my tears without loosing my dignity.

"*Ethan*, have you heard a word I've said?" my mother asked, pinching my arm good and hard. I blinked several times quickly, breaking free of my little daydream and looked over at my mother.

"Sorry Mom, I was just thinking about Dad," I replied, as I massaged away the sting of her gentle reminder for me to pay attention

"*Awww*, I know sonny, I miss him too, every day I do!" She patted the leather seat firmly with her hand. "Your father would hate this car," she said.

"I know, I was thinking the same thing," I replied grinning.

"You should take the Camero now that your home Ethan, your Da would want you to have it son."

"You really think so?" I said, admittedly excited about the prospect.

"Of course he would silly, and so would I."

"Yeah but Mom, you love driving around in that car. Don't you always say that it feels like Da is riding along beside you?"

"I do and he does, but I'm getting too old for a hot rod sonny. Maybe I could buy myself a nice affordable Datsun or something like that. You can help me pick one out while your home," she said enthusiastically.

"I dunno about that? I mean I'll help you find a car Mom, but Dad will haunt me for sure if I let you buy a Datsun!" I replied. She laughed at that and then continued going on an on about the wedding.

I made sure to look her way while she spoke, not wanting to risk a repeat of the last wake up call. Staring past her while she went about how proud she was of Sophie and Gilbert, I observed several kids, running through sprinklers from yard to yard, just as I used to when I was their age. I knew that I was drifting off into another daydream, but I couldn't help myself, the memories came flooding into my consciousness, filling my mind with thoughts of happy times.

I spied one lone girl of seven or eight sitting on a lawn, playing with a fluffy orange and white cat. She was dragging a twig around the grass in circles and the curious little feline was chasing after it, hopping and pouncing on the small piece of wood, causing the child to laugh out loud. It was all a pantomime to me though, as the only sounds I could hear were those of tire meeting the road and my own mother's voice, droning on and on. The girl on the lawn made me think of Tina Lopez as a child, and the thought of Tina made me remember KC. It had been only a few weeks since that terrible evening, and so much had changed for me personally.

My life was different now, Tina's life was different as well. Everybody and everything seemed to be changing before my very eyes. But my memory of KC remained frozen in time, and for a second I could actually see her face in the reflection of the tinted window in front of me. She was smiling that silly grin of hers, and I thought that I heard her say something to me. It sounded in my mind as if she were shouting at me from a great distance, her voice carrying faintly on the wind saying, *"I'm OK Ethan, I know about…"*

"Know about what?" I said out loud. My mother swatted my arm, blowing a puff of air out briskly.

"ETHAN ANDREW KELLY! Where is your mind boy? It's your sister's wedding day you know, try and stay with it, OK?" she said sternly, scolding me.

"Sorry Mom, look we're here," I said pointing to our house as we pulled up to the curb.

I shot a glance back at the window, but KC's image was gone, and so was the faint voice in my head. Parked cars surrounded the house. And there were people milling about everywhere. I could see them on the lawn, on the porch, through the windows of the house, in the driveway, making their way to and from the backyard. I had no idea how we were going to accommodate three hundred plus guests, but knowing my mother it would come off without a hitch.

"Having the reception here was your idea, wasn't it Mother?" I asked wryly.

"And what if it was! Would you rather be stuffed into some hall or restaurant eating banquet chicken and beans served by strangers, or here at home being catered to by family and friends?"

I just smiled, knowing better than to try her patience with an answer, and stepped out of the big car as the driver opened the door. I helped my Mother out as well and she took my arm. Then together we walked up red brick the pathway to the front porch steps, meeting and greeting people along the way.

"Do you see Shannon anywhere sonny?" Mother asked as we reached the porch steps.

"They'll be along shortly Mom. They were taking more pictures with the wedding party, remember?"

"Oh yes, those scalawags! I'll be giving those boys a bit of my Irish when they get here I will," she said vehemently.

"Did you see how they tried to ruin my Shannon's big day with their shenanigans?"

"Take it easy Mother, remember, *all's well that ends well*," I said trying to keep the peace while running a little interference for the gang.

"Don't you be taking their side Sonny! Not unless you're wanting some of the same poison tongue I'm saving for the likes of them!"

I raised my hands, surrendering, and led her into the house where I could be shielded by the throng or family and friends. I spotted my Dad's favorite chair and was surprised to see that it was unoccupied. I handed my mother off to the first couple that waited to congratulate her and mad a beeline for the chair. I threw myself into the chair just like I did as a child and sank into the warm confines of the soft cushions and the vivid memories. This would be a good place to wait for Shannon and Paul to arrive, I thought, closing my eyes to grab as many winks as possible until they showed up. Maybe if I listened hard enough, KC's voice might return and repeat her message.

Albany, New York, 30, June 1974
Cathedral of the Holy Cross

Paul waved to the boys as they drove off in Cullen's Lincoln Towne car, while Carolyn and the bridesmaids followed closely in their own limo. Shannon tugged hard on Paul's coat tails pulling the big lummox into the car. He conked his head on the door as he fell into the back seat of the long white limousine, and sat beside his new bride clumsily, rubbing where his skull had met the hard metal frame. Shannon pushed his hand away from his face and dabbed at the small bump on his head, kissing it gently as if that were enough to heal the wound. Come to think of it, given the thickness of Paul's head and the euphoria of the day, it probably was!

"Here, let me take a look at that you big baby," Shannon said, teasing her new husband.

Paul gleefully submitted to her fawning and attention, pulling a fistful of her long auburn hair up to his face, breathing in her clean fresh scent. Shannon swatted his hand sharply and wagged a slender finger in his face.

"Lesson one Mr. Pulchowski, there's a time and place for everything!"

"You told my family that I was marrying a gentleman, and a gentleman you'll be! Besides, we're paying the driver enough money aren't we? I don't think he needs a show to go with it now, does he?" Shannon said, scolding him playfully and pointing to the driver's beady little eyes in the rear view mirror.

Paul pushed her hair from his face and peered around him, catching the driver's glance in the mirror. He nodded his head affirmatively and released his wife, leaning back against the seat in frustration.

"You're right, you're right, you're absolutely right, my apologies Shannon girl," he said capitulating. Shannon giggled and kissed the bump on his forehead and returned to her seat beside him. She looked up at the driver and tapped on the window.

"Erh, you there," she said loudly. The driver looked back at her in the mirror, "Yes ma'am," he said politely.

"Let's get going. Oh, and I want to hear those cans behind us dragging, not bouncing, know what I mean?" she ordered cheerfully. The driver smiled back at her and nodded.

"Yes ma'am, reading you loud and clear, the long way around the block, I get ya!"

Shannon slid the darkened window separating the front from the back along its rails slowly, until she heard it lock in place. Then she crawled into her husband's lap and put her arms around his neck. *"Now, where were we Mr. Pulchowski,"* she purred, leaning in and kissing Paul like she never had, at least not before this day.

Albany, New York, 30, June 1974
<u>*The Kelly/Pulchowski Reception*</u>

I woke suddenly to find a familiar face inches from my own. Sophie Wong had crawled into my lap and was attempting to feed me a deviled egg. She must have been at it a while, because there were bits of egg all over my clothes and my face. This delighted my Uncle Glenn to no end, as he sat across from me with the movie camera running. This would be another fine addition to the Ethan Kelly hall of shame do doubt. I would have let fly a few choice words conveying my appreciation for his artistic eye, but my cuss list was already up to volume three and besides, little Sophie was right there as a witness. Actually my little godchild was no shrinking violet when it came to colorful language in her own right. But with my luck Carolyn Wong and or my Mother were likely standing nearby, and both of them could deliver quite a wallop, a fact that I had learned painfully over the years. Picking Sophie up, I deposited her beside the chair while I stood up and brushed the debris from my shirt and pants. Uncle Glenn winked at me and tossed me a dishtowel for my face.

"Thanks Ethan, another good reel for the archives mate," he said gleefully, rushing off before I could retaliate.

Glenn Kelly had come late in my grandparent's marriage, so he closer to my age, more like an older brother than an uncle really. But he was sure to lord it over whenever the need suited him, especially during disagreements and conflicts, knowing that I would be expected to show him the proper respect due him as my elder and as my father's baby brother. It was a maddening situation, but mercifully a rare one, as Glenn had spent most of his life back in Ireland taking care of his parents as they aged. Sophie tugged at my trousers and I looked down at her. She held up what was left of the egg and offered it to me with a wicked little smile.

"Still some left," she said too sweetly.

"So I see," I replied, pinching the wiggly morsel between two fingers and headed for the kitchen.

I could hear Sophie giggling as I walked away, and I decided to count my blessings instead of scold her, since she could just as easily have fed me something from the cat box.

I weaved my way through the crowd and on into the kitchen, where I found my mother carrying through with her promise to give the fellas *what for*. Kenny and Cullen were pinned in the corner between the pantry and the dishwasher, while Sparky stood off to the side, out of striking distance pinch wise, but near enough to share in the nickel lecture. Sparky was street smart, and he knew better than to be the first or the last one into a room.

The second one in always ducks the first attack and usually avoids the follow up if he's cagy, which he was. I could see him snickering at the others as my mother let into Kenny and Cullen. They must have seen me enter the room as both of them looked my way, pleading for help with their expressions. Mother must have noticed their attention drift from her wagging finger, and she spun around quickly, catching sight of Sparky before she saw me.

"AND YOU JON CARVALO, A DOCTOR NO LESS!" she hollered.

"WELL, WHAT HAVE GOT TO SAY FOR YOURSELF MAN? COME ON, OUT WITH IT!"

"Look, Mrs. Kelly, it was an accident, we were just goofing around, we didn't mean no harm" Sparky said, totally blowing his chance at redemption for the moment.

Ken and Cullen quickly took advantage of my mother's sudden shift of attention from them to poor Dr. Jon, and beat it out the back door as fast as they could. I followed hastily, tossing the smushed egg on the kitchen table, catching my two friends at the garage.

"Thanks Ethan, your mom was on a roll, I thought we were gonners," Kenny said, catching his breath.

"Yeah, gonners," chimed in Senator Hollenbeck, suddenly ten years old again instead of the powerful champion of the people, the newest leader in New York State Government.

I snickered at them both, "You're a real piece of work Cullen, you know that," I teased.

"And you," I said turning my attention to Kenny.

"Look what your child's done to my new suit! I hope Carolyn knows how to get egg yolk and mayonnaise out of cotton, because I sure don't!" I said in mock aggravation. The three of us looked at one another and then burst out laughing, long and hard, until our stomachs began to ache.

"Poor...poor Sparky," Kenny choked out through his laughing jag.

He was doubled over with his hand on Cullen's shoulder trying to regain his composure when the loud blast of a horn spilt the air and our eardrums. At last the Bride and Groom had arrived, and my mother came running out from the house through the kitchen door. Sparky followed shortly after her, pulling his tie up over his head and sticking out his tongue as if to hang himself. The three of us burst out into another laughing fit, my eyes tearing so much I could barely make out the faces of the people walking up to me. I steadied myself on Kenny's arm and rose up slowly, my belly still tight and aching from all the laughter. Wiping the tears from my eyes and settling down, I saw that Carla and Sean were the one's who had walked our way.

"Having a good time are you Father Kelly?" Carla asked sarcastically. I sighed heavily and then reached out to shake Sean's hand.

"Sean, Carla, I'm so happy that you could make it, how are you both?" I asked, clearing the wetness from my eyes with the palms of my hand. Sean shook my hand slowly with both of his.

"We're fine Ethan, I mean father, we're both fine, really," replied my old college roommate.

Carla walked up to me and pushed my hand away, not interested in shaking hands. She jumped up into my arms and threw her arms around my neck, hugging the stuffing out of me, just like the old days.

"How are you Ethan," she whispered softly into my ear. Reluctantly, she let me put her down and I looked back at the both of them for a moment, puzzled by their demeanor.

"We heard about what happened in California Ethan, your sister filled us in when she called to invite us to the wedding," Sean said supportively, reading the confusion on my face.

"Oh…yeah well…"

"ETHAN!" called Kenny from where he and Cullen had met up with Sparky.

"What?" I replied, nodding over at them.

"We're gonna go and mess with Paulie's head for a little bit, wanna come?" Kenny announced.

"Be right there!" I answered, turning back to Sean and Carla.

"Sorry about that, my pals, you know," I said, apologizing for the interruption. Carla laughed and waved my apology off.

"*That?* Oh honey, that was nothing. Remember Junior and JoJo, now those guys knew how to interrupt someone!" I grinned at Carla, recalling those two guys. It seemed like ages ago.

"You're right about that Nurse Carla," I said, teasing her like we all used to do.

"By the way, I'm sorry I missed Wesley's funeral and all. I had a little emergency back here at the time, I hope everyone understood," I added, apologizing sincerely.

"Don't worry about it Ethan, we all understood, honestly, we did."

"Hey, but it was a really good gathering though. Everyone that could show up, did, even that devil may care BMOC Aaron Walker. You should see him now Ethan, all dressed up in a suit and tie, and half a head of hair to boot, you'd have cracked up! Oh, and you would be so proud of Junior. He's totally respectable now, still working for Uncle Sam, he's a mailman! And guess what, one of his little conquests followed him home and made a husband and father out of him, a damn good one from what I could see. Maybe you could visit him one day if you ever get back there, he gave me his number to give to you," she said, fishing through her purse for whatever scrap of paper Junior had written on.

"Yeah well about the California stuff, first of all…" I started to say.

"AH HA! Here it is, Carla exclaimed, handing me a folded piece of paper. I should have known she would find it, the woman was a world class pack rat. Sean laughed and shrugged his shoulders at me, "That's my girl!" he said cheerfully.

"Thanks," I said, stuffing the paper into my coat pocket.

"Listen, about that California stuff, I umm…"

"Outta my way Ethan, I gotta cut those idiots off before Maggie kills them all!" shouted Carolyn, as she flew by us, pulling the twins along on a in a red High-Flyer wagon.

Kyle and Megan squealed with delight as Carolyn dragged them over the garden hose, nearly spilling them onto the wet grass in the process. A second later Sophie came tearing after them carrying two half eaten popsicles and wearing another on her brand new party dress.

"Move Uncle Ethan…*LOOK OUT!*" she hollered as she ran between Sean and me, nearly knocking Carla over in her wake.

"This is some party you Kelly's throw mister!" Carla said sarcastically.

"That's my family, what can I say," I replied, sort of proudly.

"About California," I said quickly, hoping to get what I had to say off of my chest before the next interruption, it was only a matter of time after all!

"I know what you're going to say," Carla began, taking my hand in hers and stroking it gently, as if to console me. I took back my hand and then held onto her shoulders firmly to get her attention.

"No, I don't think that you do," I said. I reached over to Sean, pulling him closer to his wife and then took a step back.

"First of all, it's not Father Kelly any longer, it's Reverend Kelly, I left the Seminary and the Catholic Church a couple of months ago."

"Oh, *we umm*, we didn't know," San said awkwardly.

"Not many people do, just my family and a few close friends."

"Look, a lot of things changed after the shootings, at least where I was concerned. I beat myself up for a long time over what happened, feeling as though I let everyone down somehow. A child that I could have helped slipped by me while I wasn't paying attention. A man, who taught me what it really meant to serve God, passed while I struggled selfishly with my own personal issues. And a friend who I truly loved, died teaching me just what its all about."

"Those three people came into my life for a reason. I figured that out after a lot of soul searching and about a thousand bowls of chili at Charley's in Newport Beach. Which by the way is where I put my life back together, one set of waves at a time."

"Early one morning, while I was straddling my board, waiting for new set to roll in, I came to the realization that God puts people in our lives for His purpose. That everyone has a role to play in this ongoing production called LIFE. And in scene after scene, as we come and go in each other's lives, the stage is set and reset. The Lord gives each of us a turn in the spotlight, an opportunity to give a command performance."

"I remember that day, it was 20ᵗʰ of May. I think I'll always remember that day," I said, looking through both Sean and Carla.

Carla blinked repeatedly and then reached out and poked me with her finger.

"How long have you been saving that one up for?" she asked sarcastically.

"Jeesz Ethan, I mean Reverend Kelly, you could have just said, *oh I'm fine, want some punch?*" Carla teased.

"*But noooooo*, you've got to deliver the Gettysburg Address! I swear Ethan you haven't changed one bit! You're still the wide eyed dreamer that you were back in the Nam," she said, giggling like a schoolgirl.

I sighed deeply and looked at Sean, who turned to his wife and pointed her in the direction of the house.

"Leave the poor man alone babe. Why don't you go inside and see if you can find the champagne and bring us some, would you mind?" he asked playfully.

"Yeah OK, but don't go starting any new soliloquies Hamlet," she said pointing at me and laughing as she walked away. I lowered my head and looked at my feet, placing both hands on my hips.

"Guess I went a little over the top, huh?" I asked Sean.

He socked me playfully in the arm, "Nah, I thought what you said was beautiful. It's classic Ethan Kelly, soulful and brooding, the guy I remember best," he said, smiling back at me.

"Listen, I'm glad that you're back, are you here for good or are you just here for the wedding?" he asked.

"Just for the wedding and a short visit with the family, maybe a couple weeks. I'm taking over the ministry at a small Episcopalian church in Merced California."

"*Really?* Sounds like a sweet deal Ethan. Where is Merced anyway, on the coast or what?"

"No, it's inland, about forty miles or so from Yosemite National Park, and a couple hundred miles from San Francisco."

"San Francisco huh? That's interesting. Hey Ethan, this Reverend gig, is that like being a priest?"

"What do you mean?"

"*You know*, the whole married to God thing, *celibacy*, stuff like that." I looked at him queerly, "Why would you ask about that?"

"I dunno, cause I'm Sean I guess."

"You know me, I'm always asking off the wall stuff, messing with people's minds," he answered obtusely, flailing his arms around and acting generally goofy.

"Alright," I said chuckling. "If you really must know, *the answer is no*, I'm no longer bound by that particular sacrifice. You're a real piece of work Sean, you know that!"

"Maybe so, but I just needed to know, I kinda have a surprise for you."

"Oh yeah? What kind of surprise?"

"Well it's sort of like what you said a few minutes ago. Carla may not have got it, but I did."

"What are you talking about?"

"Well, God sort of put someone into my life recently. And lo and behold, we discovered that we had something in common, *sort of."*

I furrowed my brow and stared Sean down. I was suddenly worried that he might be getting ready to confess something that I didn't want to hear. I looked over toward the house to see if Carla were on her way back with the refreshments, then looked back at Sean and whispered harshly.

"You better not be about to tell me you found yourself a playmate!"

Sean laughed out loud at me, *"No, no, nothing like that!* Come on, you know me better than that, besides, you're Mom would kill me!"

"That she would Sean Michael Andrews! That she would!"

"No *Reverend Kelly*, turns out what me and this person have in common is you!"

"ME?"

"Yeah… you!"

"I met her last month while I was visiting our San Francisco offices, after Dad passed away.

I've sort of taken the reigns of his shipping empire, and on some very good advice, decided to venture into the Far East as a trade market. You know, since Tricky Dick opened the doors of opportunity and made nice with Chairman Mao and the People's Republic of China, I thought why not? Quite frankly, that country is the superpower of the future, as far as I can see. So I'm thinking, why not start building bridges now, be one of the first western companies to reach out and follow suit with Nixon's offer of peace and prosperity."

"So what does that have to do with me?"

"Nothing! At least none of the business stuff anyway. It's the woman Ethan, she knows you."

"How do you know that, I mean how does she know me, from where?"

"How do I know that? I'll tell you how I know that! She told me a story one night when Carla and I took her to dinner in Little Italy, over in North

Beach. It was the same story that you told me better than fourteen years ago, back in '68. Remember, when your Uncle Liam drove us back to Albany before you shipped out to the Marines."

I looked at him puzzled, my senses suddenly on high alert.

"The train story, remember?"

"*Oh bolox, wait second, here she is now…over here dear!*" Sean exclaimed, waving to someone behind me.

I started to turn when Carla walked up, struggling with a handful of fluted champagne glasses. I reached out to help her, and she stuck her tongue out.

"Ugh, these things were tough to carry," she said exasperated.

"*Oh hi, I'm so glad you could come,*" she said cheerfully to whoever had joined us.

I handed Sean a glass and held onto one for myself, shaking a little of the spilled liquid from my free hand. I started to turn toward the new arrival as Sean began to introduce us, "Ethan Kelly, may I present my new corporate attorney, Miss…"

"*Brenda*…your name is Brenda, *something. I can't remember your last name, I'm sorry?*" I said, rudely cutting Sean off in mid sentence. Her name had popped into my head the instant I saw her face. She hadn't aged a day!

"I'm impressed, you remembered," she said smiling. "By the way I never did mention my last name on that train ride. It's Li, my name is *Brenda Patience Li*," she added.

"That's so weird," I replied chuckling to myself.

"How so?" she asked.

"Your middle name is *Patience*, get it?"

She looked at me as if the guys from the funny farm would arrive any minute to fit me for a straight jacket.

"*You know*, because I've sort of waited a long time to see you again. I even prayed on it from time to time."

"Really? That's so sweet," she said without blinking her eyes, looking right through me.

I suddenly remembered the look on KC's face the night we had our little talk in the Donnelley's yard. I wondered if my expression was the same as hers now, *neutral*, as if preparing for both good and bad news. I looked right back at her, ignoring everyone else, determined not to blow this chance to get everything off of my chest.

"It might have taken fourteen years to remember your name, but I'll tell you what, I never forgot your face," I blurted out suddenly, gushing like a high school freshman.

"Wow! I'm flattered, truly I am!"

"*So*, hello again Ethan, or is it Father Kelly now? I mean the last time we were together, you were off to Seminary somewhere, Holy Cross I think," she said enthusiastically, extending her gloved hand for me to take.

"Just Ethan, *please*, I never did enter the priesthood," I replied awkwardly, taking her hand in mine and gently shaking it.

"All right, *Ethan then*, I like that," she said cheerfully, nodding her head affirmatively and smiling back at the three of us.

I just continued to stare at her, unable to believe that of all the people that could have possibly shown up here today, she was the last one that I expected to see, and crazy as it might seem, the one I most hoped would. Picking up on my obvious puppy dog state of mind, Carla took pity on me, and graciously intervened on my behalf, picking up the conversation football that I had fumbled.

"*Ummm*, so Brenda, how was your flight anyway, when did you get in?" she asked quickly, stepping forward nonchalantly to dig her heel into my foot.

"*Owwww!*" I squealed immediately, snapping out of my trance. Brenda looked over my way for a second then turned back to answer Carla's inquiry.

"Oh, the flight was fine. It was a redeye, so I slept the whole way."

"I got into Logan around 8:30 this morning and then hopped a shuttle flight to Albany. I'm afraid I missed the ceremony though, sorry, I'm told it was beautiful. But I was able to find a cabbie who was able to read your directions, and here I am!"

"Are you alright Ethan? You look pale," Brenda asked, confusing my infatuation for confusion.

"*He's fine,*" Sean said, coming to my rescue.

"Just a little shy, *I told you*, remember?"

He handed Brenda his champagne glass and pointed over to an empty picnic table by the fence. "Why don't you take our friend here to that table over there and chat awhile. It appears that you two have some catching up to do," he said, winking at Brenda.

"Carla and I are going out front to congratulate the happy couple, we'll check on you later."

Carla gave me a little shove and Brenda took my hand, leading me across the lawn to the table by the fence. It was like walking through a ripple in time. My fate had finally caught up with me. I could hear a small faint voice in my head, whispering *here she is boy, don't screw things up!* We stood beside the table covered with clean white linen and set our drinks down on top of it. Brenda looked up at me, only slightly. I had forgotten how tall she was. She seemed to be waiting for me to say something, and I could hear that small voice again, *"life is too short to die wondering son."*

"Speak now or forever hold your peace," I murmured.

"Excuse me?" she asked.

It was crunch time, now or never, and before I could think better of it, I blurted out, "Why did you come here today anyway?" I held my breath, expecting her to walk away offended by my rudeness, she didn't. She just looked back at me, nonplussed. "I don't know," she answered.

"Why didn't you come after me that day at the train station?" she asked unexpectedly in return.

I thought about that while she pulled her hair away from her face as it flew all about in a sudden gust of wind. I smiled to myself, imagining the sudden breeze as God breathing a sigh of relief, realizing that my awkwardness would not ruin His plans for this day.

"That was such a wonderful day for me, you have no idea," I said finally.

"I think that I do," she replied, tossing her head and gathering her long hair, holding it back while the wind continued to gust.

"Really?" I replied, unable to contain the huge grin breaking across my face.

"Yeah, *really*, and you haven't answered my question," she said, curtly reminding me.

"I guess I was just scared. I mean we had such a good time talking all the way to Albany, I was afraid I'd spoil it all by running after you and saying something stupid," I said, answering her honestly.

"Like what?" she asked coyly. I studied the expression on her face and suddenly felt calmer, more confident.

"I think you already know," I answered. Brenda stared back at me in silence, not blinking even once.

"Do you just want to hear me say it out loud, *is that it?*"

She stuffed her hands into her coat pockets, and let the strong wind blow her hair every which way, then nodded slowly at me.

"*Yeah*, I want to hear you say it," she said softly.

Sighing heavily, I put my hands at my waist and looked down at the ground, then back up quickly.

*"Alright, **whatever!**"*

"Listen, for what its worth, and as ridiculous as this may sound, *I think I might just love you.*"

"More specifically, *Brenda Patience Li*, I think that I might be *in love* with you. And you know what, until this very moment, I had no idea that was a different thing altogether."

I waited for a reply, she said absolutely nothing, *nada*, she just continued to stare back at me in silence. My confidence began to fade rapidly and that same uneasy feeling that had kept me in my seat on that train so long ago, returned with a vengeance.

"*OH MAN, I knew it'd be stupid!* What a dope Ethan, what was I thinking!" I said, vehemently scolding myself.

"Honestly, I meant no offence," I said, fumbling with a weak apology.

"None taken," she finally said.

"*Ethan,* what makes you think that you could be in love with me? You didn't even know my name until ten minutes ago!"

"I know, I know, you're absolutely right! I guess I can't say *exactly why* I feel this way. But I can tell you *exactly how* it feels."

"Really?" she said suspiciously.

"*Yeah, I think so, sure.*"

"I see. *OK,* so tell me then, how *does it* feel?"

Feeling a tad conspicuous all of the sudden, I sat down at the table, and invited her to do the same. Brenda sat down across from me while I drained my champagne glass. Then wiping my mouth dry with my shirtsleeve, I launched right into a lengthy, totally unrehearsed explanation.

"*Well,* I think that falling in love is a lot like falling asleep," I said. The woman looked puzzled and ready to flee the scene. I gulped audibly and then pressed on.

"You know how it feels when you're about to drift off into a really deep sleep, after you've burrowed your way into the perfect position in bed?"

"The covers over your shoulders and your arms tucked away into just the right place. Your head is nestled softly in that sweet spot on your pillow. You feel yourself smiling involuntarily while you rub your cold feet together under the blanket, curling your toes underneath. Then, exhaling deeply, you transition slowly, but surely, from sleep to slumber, from reality to sweet dreams, and for the moment, all is right with the world. That's how it feels."

"That's what it's like to fall in love. And I've done it every night for nearly fifteen years."

We sat there in silence for several minutes, just looking at one another. I began to worry that once again I had stepped over the line. Way too many steps ahead of the other person, *as usual*.

"I really can't explain it any better than that, I can't," I said finally, pushing against the awkward silence.

She looked around the yard for a moment, and I was pretty sure that by now she was convinced I was a complete lunatic. She was probably looking around for Sean and Carla to rescue her, or at the very least, a suitable escape route. I tried to think of something to say to lighten the atmosphere, something smooth like, *KIDDING, I WAS ONLY KIDDING!*

"Look, Brenda, I apologize for..." She reached across the table and put a finger on my lips to silence me.

"I wish I could tell you that I've had similar feelings, *really Ethan I wish I could*," she said softly. I nodded slowly, her finger still pressed firmly against my lips.

"That was a long, long time ago, we were kids. I'd be lying if I said that I thought much about you after that day, if I thought about you at all since then."

I could feel tightness in my chest, and I was aware that I was blinking my eyes way too much, trying not to look directly at her.

"I'd also be lying if I said that I *didn't* feel something back then as well. I don't know, a spark maybe, something I guess, I don't know what to call it, but something."

"If you remember, it was me that spoke to you first. You caught my eye Ethan."

"Sitting here with you now, I'm kind of feeling that same spark," she said, removing her finger from my lips and then gently running her hand across my cheek.

I stopped blinking and looked into her eyes again, enjoying the way her skin felt against my own.

"Do you believe in kismet, Ethan, fate?" she asked, folding her hands in front of her on the table. I involuntarily reached across the table, picked up her champagne glass and drained it quickly.

"Sort of, I call it faith," I replied, wiping my mouth with my fingers and then drying them across my shirt. She smiled at my lame maneuver and then asked, "Where is your faith?"

"In God," I said, answering right away.

"I put my trust and faith in God. *I mean*, I know He watches over me, and I know He keeps His promises. So, like the Psalm says, I have faith that one day he'll *give me my heart's desire.*"

"Me?"

"Yes..."

She exhaled deeply then looked away, ***"This is soooo bizarre!"*** she exclaimed.

"I know," I replied sheepishly. She turned back to face me.

"You know, I have no idea why I'm not running out of here and catching the first flight back to Frisco," she said firmly, tapping her index finger on the tabletop. Before I could stammer out a reply, she stood up suddenly and grabbed my hand.

"Come on, let's take a walk, I feel like walking," she said.

I let her drag me along as we walked briskly out of the yard and down the driveway. Passing through the crowd quickly, we took a sharp right as we passed by the front of the house. Out of the corner of my eye I saw Shannon and Paul, standing with my mother and the Wongs, on the front porch. Shannon waved at me and I waved back from over my shoulder without looking back. Brenda had picked up her pace and we were soon out of earshot of the loud party behind us. We walked hand in hand in silence for about a block or so, and I felt myself begin to grin like an idiot. Brenda was right, this was bizarre, but regardless, for the moment, I was really enjoying whatever it was I was feeling, it was positively consuming me.

I looked over at Brenda and saw that she was smiling broadly as well, her cheeks flushed in a rosy pink hue. Suddenly she broke free from my handclasp, and sprinted a few yards in front of me. She stopped just as suddenly and turned to face me.

"You're a nut Ethan Kelly, you know that, right?" she shouted, slightly out of breath.

"That's Reverend Kelly, and yeah, for the record, I know," I answered.

"Well, then I must have been a squirrel in another life," she said, smiling and jogging back toward me.

Slowing as she drew near, she walked right up and embraced me, wrapping her arms tightly around my middle and rested her head on my shoulder. Slowly, carefully, I let my own arms close around her. My cheek rested against her brow. And we stood there in each other's arms silently, right there in front of old man Kline's house, for a good quarter hour. I could feel her heart beating through my shirt, and her breath, warm and sweet against my neck. My own heart swelled in my chest, feeling as if it would burst at any moment. Now I understood that look on my parent's faces whenever I caught them in a tender moment. It was a look total peace and contentment, of love, true and pure.

"Ethan," she said softly, gently breaking the silence.

"Hmmmm?" I murmured.

"You know what you said before, back in the yard?" she asked, her voice muted against my coat.

"About...?"

"All that stuff about falling in love."

"What about it?" She raised her head and kissed my cheek.

"I can't wait to fall asleep tonight," she whispered into my ear.

I pushed her away slightly and placed both of my hands on her shoulders, then moved them slowly to comb through her silky black hair with my fingers, stopping finally to cup her face in my hands.

"Careful of that first step, it's a long fall," I replied, leaning in to kiss her mouth for the first time.

Her lips were soft and warm and moist, and the kiss lingered, making the seconds seem like minutes. It wasn't the first time I had ever been kissed, but it was the first time I had ever been kissed like this. We pulled away from one another slowly, opening our eyes to read the expression on each other's face. She smiled at me sweetly, and I instinctively looked down at my shoes, shuffling my feet nervously.

"You've been saving that up for a while, haven't you," she said playfully.

"Sorry, *I mean was it awful*? You know, it's been a quite a while since I, *umm*, you know." I said, stammering defensively.

"Relax Ethan, it was wonderful, well worth the wait, believe me," she replied reassuringly.

"For true?"

"Really..."

She stepped closer and laced her fingers together behind my neck, looking me right in the eyes.

"You know, with a little coaching, and lots and lots of practice," she said, leaning in and finishing her thought with another kiss. When she finally pulled away I blinked at her spastically.

"*Whoa*, I'm dizzy," I said happily. She giggled at my goofy response and released her grip on my neck, taking my hand in hers.

"Come on, we better get back before they send out a search party," she said, pulling me after her, backtracking toward my house and my sister's wedding reception.

"I guess we have a lot to talk about," she said as we walked, shifting her grasp on my hand, and lacing our fingers together.

"I guess we do at that," I replied.

"Where do you want to start," I asked.

"Well, how about with your mother? Sean sort of told me some things," she said timidly. I chuckled and put my arm around her shoulders, pulling her close as I picked up the pace.

"Don't worry about her, she'll love you because I do. Besides, we both live in California for goodness sake!" I answered half joking. Brenda pinched me good and hard through my shirt, twisting her firm grip for maximum effect.

"I'm kidding, I'm kidding!" I said, pleading for mercy.

"Seriously, Brenda, she's going to love you dearly because she'll know instantly how happy you make me. You'll see, I swear!"

"That's better," she said cheerfully, as we walked across the front lawn to the porch where Shannon and Paul were holding court. Sean and Carla were sitting in the wicker chairs across from them, enjoying drinks and pleasantries. They caught sight of Brenda and me as we climbed the stairs and stood to greet us.

"There you are, I was beginning to wonder if you had eloped already," Sean teased, drawing a stern look from both Carla and Brenda.

"*Elope,* what's he talking about?" Shannon asked, wrinkling her brow and twitching her nose like Samantha Stevens on that TV show Bewitched.

"You dog!" exclaimed Paulie, getting up to hug us both.

"Don't listen to him, he's high, too many vodka martinis," Carla said, socking Sean in the arm.

"Now you've done it doofus," she snapped, crossing her arms tightly in front of her and turning her back to him.

"Aww, come on Carla, I was just teasing," Sean pleaded.

"*Ethan,* who's your friend," asked my mother, appearing out of nowhere.

Brenda looked from around Paulie's bear hug and waved at my Mom. Well, it was on now, and I silently prayed that Brenda would prove to be as strong a woman as I suspected she was. My Mother pushed past me without waiting for a formal introduction, and taking Brenda by the arm she lead her back into the house for a *little chat.* I blew the poor girl a kiss and mouthed '*I'll be right in*' as she disappeared through the large storm door. Paul gave me a quick '*what gives look*' and then went back to help Shannon mingle with the guests. Turning away from the commotion for a moment, I leaned on the railing around the porch and spotted Sophie Wong sitting alone on the front lawn. She sat very still and pushed at something that lay on the grass with a twig. I focused on whatever she was playing with and recognized it as a butterfly. The insect was fairly large, with beautiful blue green wings and it was obviously very dead. Sophie kept waving the twig over the poor thing, chattering away at it. When she set down the twig and picked up the dead butterfly I started to move away from the rail and walk toward her.

"Sophie, put that thing down right now!" I said, reaching the porch steps. She looked up at me and waved. "It's OK Uncle Ethan, Jessie said I could," she said cheerfully. I looked around, there wasn't anybody near her, and I didn't know anyone named Jessie.

"Put it down honey, the poor thing is dead, let's show a little respect, OK?" Sophie raised her hands to her face and peeked under the top one.

"Wait Uncle Ethan, I'll show you," she said, getting up and walking toward me. She stopped in front of me and then blew softly into her cupped hands.

"That tickles," she said giggling, raising her arms high over head.

Then, spreading her arms wide, she opened her hands, palms up, and twirled round and round. I watched as the butterfly fell from her hand and onto the grass at her feet.

"Sophie, that's not right!" I said scolding her.

She ignored me, squatted down beside the insect and waited for me to come over to where she was. When I did, I knelt beside her and put my hand on her little shoulder, preparing to start my nickel lecture. She reached up, took my hand, and turned it palm side up. Then with her free hand she picked up the butterfly and laid it gently in my palm. I looked down at the creature and shuddered, startled to see it upright, its colorful wings moving slowly, up then down, then up again. And then suddenly, assisted by strong gust of wind, it took flight, fluttering skyward and onto the breeze. I looked down at Sophie, her head was tilted way back as she tracked the flight of the insect gleefully. When she could no longer see the butterfly clearly, she lowered her head and looked at me happily.

"See, I told you Jessie said it as OK," she said, jumping up and running back toward the house. Instantly, I knew who this Jessie character was, and I laughed out loud.

"What a dope Ethan," I muttered.

"Should have seen this one coming," I said to the wind, shaking my head, totally in awe of my lack of foresight.

I got up slowly and turned to look back at the house. I caught site of Tina Lopez peering out of the bay window. She held both hands up to her face, covering her mouth. I didn't need to be inside the house to hear her gasp. The look on her face told me that she had seen everything. Tina nodded at me slowly, and then pointed toward the front door. I nodded back at her and started to make my way back to the house. She was right of course, there was much to talk about. The next child had been chosen. Soon it would all begin again, same story, different cast, *God help us...*

Epilogue

("God is love. Whoever lives in love lives in God, and God in him....
There is no fear in love."...1 John 4:16)

Groveland, California, 2003
Banks of the Tuolumne River

WHEW! I'm tired...That's the most remembering I've done at one sitting since...well, since I can't remember when. Honestly, it's been years since I last thought of everyone and everything that's come to stay and pass through my life. Each one a blessing in their own way stowed away safely in my heart of hearts. I have learned so much about life from the people that God has paraded by me over the years. The kind of lessons that are beyond book smarts, real lessons, about true happiness, real pain, and eternal fellowship. Through these people, the Lord shaped me into the man he always intended for me to be. Because of them, the tapestry that is my life is rich with wonderful memories. Some happy, some sad, all of them fondly remembered.

Shamefully, I am not as near to some as I probably should be, letting life and circumstance inhibit me from nurturing stronger ties. Such is the case with all of us I reckon, sad, but true. Still, I do think of them all from time to time, and when I do, I make an effort to touch base with them somehow, with a card, or a letter, or a telephone call. I still haven't warmed up to these blasted computers and cell phones. They drive me bananas! Brenda is the smart one in the family, thank God for her pointed little head!

Those that have remained close in my life, beyond family of course have remained very close. I'm looking across at Sean, sleeping soundly in the chair beside me, and I have to smile. Poor fella, I guess I talked him into deep sleep will all that remembering. And then there's Carla, his lovely wife, and my dear, dear, friend. She's the only person with whom I can safely remember certain things, events, and people from our past. Our history is closely entangled with bittersweet memories and shared nightmares. I think that God kept the two of us close in order to keep the both of us from sailing away, like so many others had, on a personal trail of tears.

I can hear her in the background right now, she and Brenda giggling while they cook supper. No doubt filling each other in on the intimate details of Sean's and mine shortcomings! We do manage to see the Lopez's from time to time, whenever we go into San Francisco. We make sure to take the long way and pass through the farm country and check in with them. Victor is running everything for Alma since Arthur's passing in 1997. Tina married her childhood friend, Hector, that same year. They live in Cupertino, sort of between here and the city. She has two great kids. A girl named Elena, and a boy named Ethan, I have to laugh! Hector is Rosa Hernandez' younger brother, funny how life works, isn't it? By the way, Alma and Arthur Donnelly adopted Rosa's daughter after her mother died. They said it was a stroke, but I think that it was from a broken heart, after her third denial of parole. She never did find out about Dr. Katz, KC had done a masterful job of layering his story in wheels within wheels. Ironically, he remains on death row, using the system to delay the inevitable. But, to his credit, he has made his peace with God, and truly repented, leading a Christian ministry under an alias in Vacaville.

I miss Father Willet almost as much as I miss my own parents, the man taught me so much about devotion and duty. He also taught me how to live, oh how he did live. I like to think that Sister Demarco found him after going to her glory. She's working directly for Jesus now, feeding the angels, with Father Billy standing first in line! I think most of all I miss KC. There were a lot of things I never had the chance to say. Maybe someday, when I reach eternity, God will explain it all to the both of us. I suspect our paths crossed by Divine design. I believe that perhaps she was an unwitting guide, a teacher if you will. Who, through her unselfish passion for life, her loving affection for me, and her incredible and indestructible spirit, taught me to appreciate just how precious each day is. In the short time that I knew her I became aware of the man that I wanted to be. Her strength inspired me to step out of the shadow of the man built on the dreams of others. Motivated me to finally be who it was I always knew I was meant to be. To seek and to lead the life that would be my true destiny. With that single course correction, I began a journey where every day felt just right, beginning with the day my heart's desire walked back into my life. From that day forward, I would know no boundaries where love was concerned, the bond between us magnetic and deep, for all time. All of these people had a hand in molding me into the man before you today, I am grateful to have known them all. I will carry them in my heart into eternity.

My goodness, how the world has changed since I was a pup. Mother always called me her pup, God rest her soul. She went to join Da, Uncle Liam and Uncle Chuck to walk the glory streets of heaven a while back. Maggie Kelly passed away in her sleep peacefully, on June 17th, summer of 2000, right after Flag Day. It was a full life she had, truly a full life. She even managed to make it to the new millennium, a personal goal of hers.

"I miss you Mom."

"Ta gra agrum duit...I love you"

"What was that?"

"Nothing dear, just blowing a Gaelic kiss up to mother is all. Mostly I'm just sitting here rocking away the day, listening to Sean snooze, and talking to myself like a freaking ejit!"

"Careful there with the French Reverend Kelly! You don't want to be backsliding on such a fine Sunday evening, now do you?"

"Cut me a little slack woman! Hey, is that pot roast I smell cooking for supper?"

"It's your favorite isn't it?"

"That's my girl, you know what? I love you most of all!"

"Save all the sweet talk for the old biddies at church Ethan Kelly. I'm only interested in action! You can show me just how much you love me later on tonight!"

"YIKES! You'll bury me yet Brenda my dove, you'll bury me yet!"

"That's the plan honey, at least you'll go with a smile!"

"You crack me up girl, you know, I really don't deserve you!"

"I know that, for goodness sake, everybody knows that you old fossil."

"By the way Ethan, did I tell you that Tori called today?"

"No, you didn't, how is Victoria anyway?"

"She's doing just fine. Sends her love, and said to be sure and thank her father for the funny birthday card and the 'cee' notes. What's a 'cee' note anyways?"

"It's a hundred dollar bill. Are you telling me a big-shot corporate attorney like you has never heard that term before?"

"No. Maybe that's what they called them in the old days. In modern times we call them 'Benjamin's,' sweetie."

"What are you talking about? I'm a year younger than you!"

"Maybe according to the calendar, but then I'm not the one napping in the rocking chair am I."

"Touché."

"And Ethan, honey, five hundred dollars! I swear, you spoil that child!"

"Well you spoil the twins, so I guess I can spoil my baby girl a little too."

"Speaking of the twins, Tori said that they came into the city and took her out for her birthday."

"Really, where did they go?"

"The Broome Street Bar & Grill, do you know it?"

"No, but I bet it was Sean Andrews who suggested it, he knows every posh bar in New York City."

"Now, now, be nice. We owe that man a lot you know. We would never have found each other without him. Oh, and don't forget, he set Tori up in that nice apartment in Manhattan while she studies at NYU."

"OK, OK, I get it, Sean's a godsend! Shhhh, you might wake him."

"Have you heard from the boys as well?"

"Yes, I talked to Jace on Friday, and Noah called Wednesday last."

"Why is it I'm never around when those two surface?"

"Luck of the Irish babe."

"That was a low blow woman! I'm writing that one down for Saint Peter. You'll need to sweet talk your way past the pearly gates if you're not careful!"

"Oh fiddlesticks, I'll be alright, you'll be right there beside me. Besides, I suspect I'll be a shoe in as a Kelly now, I'll be a legacy!"

"Supper will be ready in half an hour. Try not to doze off, OK?"

"I've never missed a meal in my life!"

"I know…it shows tubby."

"HEY! Who you calling fat, I'm in great shape!"

"I was only kidding dear. Wo ai ni…"

"I Love you too!"

That's an amazing woman my Brenda, smart, loving, and fun. I was so blessed the day she walked back into my life, I thank God every day for His grace. And she's right about Sean as well, without him we may never have met. You know, we've been married nearly thirty years, and I still feel young in her arms. She's given me three beautiful children and a lifetime of wonderful memories already. Truth be told, I still fall in love with her each and every night, just as soon I close my eyes.

It's funny how life twists and turns, each event molding us into who we are, and who we'll be. It's funnier still how desperately and stubbornly we fight for control the wheel, for the responsibility, for the opportunity to steer our own course, to take control of our own destinies. Ironically, if it's destiny we seek, then control is the last thing that we need. Destiny by definition is a predetermined fate, absolutely beyond our ability to control, and to my mind, by Divine design. When I think back on my own life, on the life I just shared with all of you, I thank God for inspiring me to get out of my own way, and let life happen. Left to my own or to some other's will, I truly believe my life would have turned out quite differently.

Not necessarily better or worse, but just different enough to be not quite right, at least for me. I'm getting preachy in my old age, pontificating at the drop of a hat. I think it's time for peace and quite now, listen to the river, and spare you further brain droppings from my aging and wandering mind. Let me leave you with two bits of 'go to' wisdom that I have relied on through the years, to ground me when need be, and propel me when required. Whenever I need a spiritual hug I remember, 'GOD IS LOVE'. Whenever I need a kick in the pants, if I falter, or fear change, I remember the words of a man I grew to respect. Not because of who he may have been in life, but because I saw in him a man humbled by his own privilege, and inspired to change because of it..."some men see things as they are and ask why...I dream of things that never were, and ask why not!"

p.s.
as for little Sophie Wong...that's a story for someone else to tell.

Printed in the United States
213129BV00002B/3/A